# DESPERATE DAUGHTERS

## A BLUESTOCKING BELLES COLLECTION WITH FRIENDS

ALINA K. FIELD   ELLA QUINN   MARY LANCASTER
MEARA PLATT   BLUESTOCKING BELLES:
CAROLINE WARFIELD   ELIZABETH ELLEN CARTER
JUDE KNIGHT   RUE ALLYN   SHERRY EWING

Cover Design by Jude Knight

ePub: ISBN: 979-8-9855874-0-1
Mobi ASIN : B09LTHWR3B
Print ISBN: 979-8-9855874-1-8

# LADY DOROTHEA'S CURATE

CAROLINE WARFIELD

Lady Dorothea's Curate
By Caroline Warfield

Employed at a hotel, Lady Dorothea Bigglesworth has no use for a title. It would only invite scorn, or, worse, pity. Plain Miss Doro Bigglesworth suited her fine.

Ben Clarke dedicated his life to helping the neediest. It gave his life meaning. He tended to forget the younger son of a viscount went by "Honorable."

Neither saw the need to mention it to the other, until they were formally introduced—in a ballroom in York. Shocked.

# CHAPTER 1

*High Harrogate, December 1816*

One look at dear Mr. Clark, the curate's, harried expression, and Doro knew she was right to brave the frightful weather. The Hampton Hotel only permitted her one half-day from work each week. She used the time to assist at Pilgrim's Rest—the rough mission attached to Harrogate's only place of worship, a tiny chapel of ease—so called because it existed to "ease" the burden of travel to St. John's parish in Knaresborough for services. Pilgrim's Rest counted on her. More to the point, its leader depended on her, and she never wanted to disappoint him. She quickly hung her damp cloak and bonnet on a peg by the door and deposited her bundle on the rough table near the hearth.

"Miss Bigglesworth, thank goodness you're here!" Mr. Clarke, the curate responsible for the chapel and the mission attached to it, called from the far corner, where a narrow table and some benches had been set up.

Her stepmother would chastise her for failing to correct him, but no one here knew she should be styled Lady Dorothea or that her late father was the Earl of Seahaven, not that it did her family any good now. Frankly, she would rather the people of Harrogate and of Pilgrim's Rest never found out, not as long as she earned her bread toiling in a hotel. It would only bring down judgement or, worse, pity, and Doro was proud of her work.

She watched the curate help an elderly man in thin coat and shabby trousers to a seat. As always, she was touched by the young man's gentleness with their "guests" as he insisted on calling those who sought his help.

"Shall I set out the mid-day meal?" Doro asked, glancing around the room. She counted eight guests including two children with sad eyes, many fewer guests than they had in warmer weather. She saw no sign of Mrs. Grigg, the vicarage housekeeper, who usually had a warm meal ready before Doro arrived.

The building Mr. Clarke named Pilgrim's Rest had once been a stable, but he insisted that it was being put to better use since he had neither horse nor carriage. It had been cleaned, painted and swept. Doro suspected he did the work himself. Rugs covered the brick floor, and a well-maintained hearth kept the place warm enough.

Mr. Clarke's smile of approval warmed Doro even more. "If you would, please, Miss Bigglesworth. Mrs. Grigg did not feel able to come out in this fierce weather."

Mrs. Grigg regularly complained of pains. She also complained of extra work, the guests whom she insisted were not pilgrims but beggars, and "Mr. Clarke's foolish notions." The curate, for his part, just as regularly reminded her that the poor had maladies the same as the well-off folk who flocked to Harrogate to take the waters. They hoped, he insisted, just as fiercely for relief.

Doro stayed out of the fray. She might have pointed out the truly wealthy preferred the fashionable spas in Bath or Cheltenham, never Harrogate. She knew that, as long as some of the chalybeate and sulphur springs in Harrogate lay out in the open, free for all who could walk or ride to them, both High and Low Harrogate would continue to attract the low and middling classes. Fine families come on hard times, professional folk, and rising gentry kept hotels in business, but the poor had to fend for themselves. Pilgrim's Rest could at least provide a warm meal once a day. Doro suspected the curate provided a bit more when he could.

Doro found two crocks near the hearth. She lifted the lid on one, pleased to see it well filled. If the other held as much, there would be plenty for all, even Mr. Clarke, who was known to do without. A delicious aroma rose from the broth. Mrs. Grigg might disapprove of the mission, but she took pride in her cooking. The soup she sent would be excellent. Assuming donations had been good this week, it would be filling as well. Doro filled the iron cauldron on its hook over the fire and began warming the soup.

She hummed as she laid out bowls and spoons. She opened the bundle she brought, bread still warm from the kitchens of the Hampton, and laid it on a platter. They had no butter, but she doubted the guests would care.

"You bring music as well as bread," Mr. Clarke said, his smile warming Doro down to her toes.

"It gives me joy to be here," she answered and was rewarded with a flicker of heat in his deep brown eyes that sent echoing heat creeping up her neck. She had to shake herself to keep from staring.

*You have no business ogling the man, Doro Bigglesworth. You're well and surely on the shelf, and have nothing to offer a man. Your family needs your earnings in any case, she reminded herself, dragging her eyes away.*

She sliced the bread with care, all too aware that her foolish reaction to Mr. Clarke left her hands shaking. There would be enough to feed their guests and more to wrap in scraps of cloth for them to take with them. The young mother of the two little ones seated across the table watching Doro with solemn eyes would be grateful for it as the day stretched on.

"Have you come far?" she asked them.

"We walked ten mile yesterday," the older one, a boy told her proudly.

"How wonderful!"

"Had to," the boy said, taking a slice of bread and sniffing it with an ecstatic expression.

"Granda had to take the waters. Mam pulled him in th'cart," the boy's little sister added.

Doro prayed the spa waters helped the old man. Glancing back to where he sat, she doubted it would. Most of those who passed through The Hampton Hotel left looking just as they did when they arrived.

"Going on home now Mrs. Hopkins?" Ben Clarke watched the woman tuck a coverlet around the old man in the dog cart, carefully storing a keg of water from the famous spring and the bread Miss Bigglesworth had wrapped for them. He was gratified to see the Hopkins woman's color had improved with a good meal, though it appeared to have done little for her father.

*Thank God for Miss Bigglesworth and the hotel kitchens!*

The handful of other guests had already wandered back to the Stray, Harrogate's common enclosure, where, he suspected, they spent their day sitting under the trees near one of the springs.

The morning's sleet had cleared, and the sun peeked between the clouds. He wafted a prayer of gratitude for that as well, as he ran a hand over the head of the Hopkins boy who had leaned against him.

"Aye, Mr. Clarke," the boy's mother said. "We'll make good time now as you've fed us so well." Her sad smile spoke of courage and strength. *She will need it,* he thought watching them make their way to the road.

"Do you think they can make it home before dark?" Doro Bigglesworth had come up beside him, shutting the door to Pilgrim's Rest.

"Perhaps. Perhaps the Lord will supply them with help along the way. Did you finish tidying up?"

"I rinsed Mrs. Grigg's crocks at the well and left them on the table," she told him.

"Excellent. I'll fetch them for her later." He bowed to her and offered his arm. "May I accompany you home, Miss Bigglesworth?"

As he expected, she dipped into a curtsy as graceful as that of any duchess. The formal ritual had become something of a game with them.

After enjoying her assistance for several months, Ben had begun escorting her back to The Hampton Hotel every week. Five times; today would be six. He knew the precise number because he treasured each one. He had offered to escort her from the beginning, of course, like the gentleman he was, but she demurred. He would look around after seeing to the guests, and she would be gone. He couldn't say precisely what changed, but he looked up one day to meet her intense gaze, and, when he offered, she accepted his escort. Lately, he no sooner left her at her lodging on Wednesday afternoon, than he began looking forward to the following one. The pleasure of her company had become Ben's one indulgence, one he couldn't bring himself to forgo.

Glimpses of sun warmed what had begun as a dreary December day when they reached the road. "Shall we stay to the road or wander through the parkland?" he asked.

"My dear Mr. Clarke, are you asking me to stray through The Stray with you?" An impish grin accompanied the silly pun, though local lore would have it that the name derived from folks doing precisely that from the time the land surrounding the springs was pulled from the Forest of Knaresborough and set aside for the use of all.

He grinned back. "Shall we?" A familiar flicker of guilt fluttered through him as soon as he said it, but he chased it away. Surely, he did penance six days a week. He could enjoy this small pleasure on one of them.

The woman who had become the light of his life sobered. "It will take less time if we keep to the road. I don't want to keep you from your work," she said. Her earnest face and respect meant more to him than he could say. But at her words, his heart sank. He had hoped…

Just then the clouds moved off, sun glistened off the trees in The Stray, and her eyes gleamed. She was teasing! He felt a smile rise from his heart to bloom on his face. "That sun is calling to us, Miss

Bigglesworth. How can we refuse the invitation when such an afternoon will be scarce now that winter approaches?"

"The paths all lead to Low Harrogate eventually, I believe." Her widened grin told him she planned to enjoy their walk as much as he did.

They didn't speak, content, he hoped, with the sounds of nature. In reality, he couldn't find an opening for conversation. In previous weeks they had exhausted one subject after another: a shared weakness for cinnamon buns, novels both loved and abhorred, the sad state of the country's returning soldiers, and always their work. She seemed as eager as he to avoid more personal subjects. The question he longed to ask hung unspoken in the air. He had no right to pay his addresses until he could support a wife.

They passed one of the smaller springs, deserted today. She broke the silence. "Christmas approaches. I presume that will be a busy time for you. I… I wish I could be here to help you."

There. It was as he feared. She planned to leave. "You will go home for the holidays, then?"

"Yes. I have an urgent request from my stepmother. She wants all of us home no later than Twelfth Night. She particularly requested my help in the kitchen for the duration, so I will depart on December 23rd. Mr. Crowley has generously agreed to let me go for two weeks."

Ben snorted. He knew enough about her work to know old Crowley depended on her. She may have been hired as a kitchen helper, but from what she had told him, he could tell she now kept the books and managed the kitchen staff and catering business.

She gave his arm a gentle punch with her free hand. "He is very kind to me! In any case, I won't be paid. The wages will be missed, but Patience writes that it can't be helped."

"Your family depends on your wages, Miss Bigglesworth?" It would explain why he had never seen her in a new gown, not that he believed Crowley paid her well.

"They do indeed, Mr. Clarke. My sisters—particularly the youngest ones—need me." The pride in her voice impressed him.

Kind, generous, hardworking, responsible... Doro Bigglesworth would make a perfect clergyman's wife.

Pointless thought, Ben, as long as you refuse any more lucrative living.

"And you, Mr. Clarke? Will you visit family once the holy days are over?"

"And the pagan feasts begin?" he teased.

"Twelfth Night isn't pagan! At least not much." She grinned. "Family matters."

"You're close to yours." He hadn't answered her question. He wasn't sure how. His brother didn't invite, he commanded; Ben avoided. "Do you have brothers as well?"

An odd expression came across her face. "Goodness no. All girls," she said.

Her reaction intrigued him; there was a mystery about Doro Bigglesworth. The mystery captivated him as much as her laughing eyes, perfect features, and lush form attracted him. Everything about her drew him to her. Clergyman be damned. She was the perfect wife for Ben Clarke. If he had means to offer for one. Until he did, he could not ask her. "Tell me about them. How do you celebrate the winter holidays?"

She did. His Miss Bigglesworth could add storytelling to her gifts. She enchanted him with stories of sisters grown and small, of songs and games and teasing. Of gifts lovingly created. Of pranks and laughter. His own family had never been simple, but there had been joy and affection once, when his mother still lived. He longed to have it again.

Ben would never remember all the names of what seemed like an entire flock of sisters, but the picture Miss Bigglesworth created of simplicity, joy, and an affectionate family would stay with him. He imagined the house, small, neatly kept, decorated with watercolors and knitted cozies, all made by her sisters, with a kitchen garden and flower beds. He pictured simple hard-working folk, respectable and honest.

"When will you be back?" he asked, hope almost choking him.

She looked away; her joy suddenly dimmed. "I plan to come back, but something in Patience's letters worries me."

A desperate fear seized Ben. He couldn't bear the thought of not seeing her again. "Let's both hope so, Miss Bigglesworth." If she did not return, the image of his Miss Bigglesworth in that little house, among her sisters, would be all that kept his lonely heart company that winter.

# CHAPTER 2

Doro downed the last of the apple cake and sighed in pure bliss. It was Boxing Day. Since they had no servants, Bess, her oldest sister, had declared they must be kind to themselves and one another. And so, they had. The younger girls were in their room giggling over the fashion magazines her sister Susana, who was a dressmaker, brought them. The baby sat on the threadbare rug stacking blocks. The older ones had gone off on a ramble. All was right in Doro's world—or would be if Ben Clarke wasn't miles away.

"Patience, you have to give me the recipe for that one. It will make the Hampton famous throughout Harrogate, if not all of East Riding."

"Or course. My secrets are yours."

"All of them?" Doro studied Patience pointedly. Exactly the same age as Doro, Patience was more friend than stepmother, almost another sister. "You've been fit to burst since I got here. And why did you demand that we all come home, for that matter?

"Isn't being together for the holidays enough?" Patience's outrage almost looked genuine.

"If that was the entire reason, it would be enough. But it isn't, is it? Spill it please, dear Stepmama," Doro demanded.

Patience drew herself upright and raised her chin, reminding Doro forcefully that Patience was, after all, the dowager Countess of Seahaven, head of their household. It behooved Doro not to forget it.

The earl's fifth wife, Patience had given Doro's Papa another daughter, the curly-haired moppet on the floor in front of them. For her trouble, she received a pittance from the estate, and struggled to care for them all. Patience and each of the sisters, even the eighteen-year-old twins, did what they could to bring in money, the social stigma attached to wage earning be damned, with Patience's reluctant approval. Doro had enormous respect for Patience.

"Very well, Dorothea. I've had an idea, one that might help all of us, but I'm not ready to share it with everyone just yet. Susana won't be here until Twelfth Night in any case."

Doro leaned forward to listen. "Now I'm frantic with curiosity."

Patience unbent. "You might actually help me refine my thinking—and my budget." She instinctively moved closer and lowered her voice. "I had a letter from my cousin Rose."

"The one who plans to jaunt off to Egypt and the Levante?" Doro rather admired cousin Rose. They all did.

"She left earlier in December. Her town house in York—the most fashionable part of York, I might add—is empty."

Doro blinked at her, trying to make out the point. Patience reached into her pocket, pulled out a key and held it up. Doro gasped. "She's giving you her house?"

"Not giving. Lending. She suggests we all whisk off to York and give you girls a proper Season. Bess had one, but what with mourning and, well, poverty, the rest of you didn't. Now the younger girls face bleak prospects if nothing is done." Patience frowned. "I'm sorry, Doro. It is probably fair to say you all do."

Doro waved that away. "I have made a life for myself, Patience." As to prospects, she had hopes of a certain curate, but didn't dare say it. "What exactly do you propose?"

"Nothing major. Merely time in York. A few parties. The races at the end. Perhaps any or all of you—of us—might meet someone."

Doro shook her head. "I see no point. There are too many of us, and most are past the marriageable age."

"That is absurd, Lady Dorothea Bigglesworth. You are no such thing."

Doro smiled, warmed down to her toes, hoping it was true. "Perhaps, but in that world, the social world? If we dissipate our efforts it won't work."

A sly grin came over Patience's face. "Are you suggesting that we focus our efforts? I had a similar idea. Josefina, Iris, and Ivy are at the most eligible age, and every one of them is a beauty. They would draw the eye of every gentleman in a ballroom. They could take York by storm if we concentrated on them."

"Not without a comfortable portion." Doro tapped a finger on the arm of her chair, biting her lower lip in thought. "The earl made it clear we can split the dowry funds as we see fit," she said at last. "What if, instead of dividing it among all of us, we invest it in the most eligible three. It might just be enough for them each to snag a suitor."

It was obvious from Patience's expression that she had already thought of it. "Their husbands are bound to sponsor the rest of you."

Doro snorted. "Or at least support you and the young ones."

"We will see. If they find wealthy husbands even better for all of us. Can we manage it?"

Doro knew what Patience asked. "First you have to get everyone's agreement to pool the dowry funds. Then there are the expenses. There's no point of doing this if we don't do it right: wardrobes including ball gowns, household expenses, entertainment—a presentation ball at the very least."

"But can we manage it?"

"I'll have to give it some thought. It will depend on what each of us can contribute. Begin making lists, and I'll price things out. If working for Crowley at the Hampton taught me nothing else, it is how to keep books and budget. The others have to agree, though. Don't mention anything to Iris, Ivy, and Josefina until we're ready, but take the others aside one by one. Perhaps we can figure out how to make it work."

Patience waved the key again. "I knew this was lucky the minute it fell out of Rose's letter." She sobered again. "I can't do this without you, Doro. I know you plan to return to Harrogate, but if the sisters agree, there will be detailed planning and arrangements to make."

Doro's heart sank.

Patience reached for her hands. "Whatever—and whoever—waits for you in Harrogate will be there in June, Doro. I know they will.

The plan had value. For the younger three. For Patience and the children. For the others. How could Doro say no? She closed her eyes and considered what she might put in a letter to Crowley begging to have her position back in June. She considered writing to Ben Clarke, but there was nothing formal between them. Nothing at all except hope, and that, she feared, entirely on Doro's part. She would have to cling to that hope alone.

The command, for surely it was no simple invitation, came to Ben on a terrible day.

The number of guests for Pilgrim's Rest had slowed to a trickle by the end of February. That should have been a relief, but Ben was left with nothing to distract him or fill his thoughts—aside from the ever-present ache of wishing to see Doro Bigglesworth. There simply wasn't enough work for a curate at a chapel of ease, and the vicar at Saint John's demanded with increasing adamance that he focus his attention on the larger parish.

Ben rarely got mail, but the first Monday in March, an unusual set of two letters arrived, changing everything. Ben accepted both pieces from Mrs. Grigg along with a cup of tea and a short lecture on his untidy ways.

"Top un's from the vicar. Best brace yourself," she added, before wandering back to the kitchen.

Ben cleared away the sermon he was writing for the handful of dedicated folks that attended the chapel in Harrogate—a smattering of shopkeepers and visitors. He set the teacup down and stared at the mail.

The one on top indeed came from the Vicar of St. John's. Ben sighed. "Best get it over with quickly," he mumbled to the empty room. What he read left him with a sick stomach.

The vicar informed him that, rather than providing funds to replace the leaking roof of Pilgrim's Rest, he ordered Ben to close the place entirely.

"Your little mission is fruitless and unproductive, and I insist that you tend to those who support the parish at large," he wrote. In case Ben didn't understand that "support" meant financial contributions, the vicar specifically ordered Ben to call on Lady Spotsworthy at her home above town. The widow, no longer able to get to services, had complained of the curate's neglect again.

Ben gritted his teeth. *Surely God loves the rich as well as the poor,* he reminded himself, but he still couldn't bear the thought of attending the querulous old woman in her overheated drawing room smelling of camphor in the company of her spoiled pug who found the taste of Ben's boots irresistible. He would be expected to dun the woman for money, and not for Pilgrim's Rest. She vociferously disapproved of his efforts there and may have been the voice that convinced the vicar to close it.

He wondered, not for the first time, if he ought to resign and seek a different position. Manchester, Brighton, and York all had significant populations living in poverty. God knew London did. Perhaps the closing of Pilgrim's Rest was a sign that it was time.

He put the vicar's letter aside and examined the one beneath it. Unlike the vicar's, this one came on high quality, expensive vellum. "The Honorable Eustace Benedict Clarke, Curate, Harrogate" had been scrawled across the front, and it had been franked with the authoritative signature of Viscount Stanbeck. His brother. Harry. It likely contained a lecture. The day kept getting worse. He put it aside, and returned to his sermon.

An hour later, frustrated and unable to concentrate, he set down his pen and put away his writing materials. He rose, determined to clear his head with a brisk walk, but stopped at the door.

*What's the use? A walk won't make the vicar's orders go away. If it is decisions you have to make, you best read Harry's letter too.*

He grabbed up the dreaded missive, positive it contained a lecture if not some demands and a dire threat of consequences, stared at it briefly and stuffed it in a pocket. *Walk first.* He wrapped his scarf around his throat, informed Mrs. Grigg of his departure, and set out.

By the time his wandering led him to Harrogate's small commercial district, one thing had become clear. He couldn't stay in his current position. Without the work at Pilgrim's Rest, he had no desire to do so.

Chilled in spite of his brisk pace, Ben popped into Margaret Wella's tea shop, requested a warm drink, and set the unopened letter from his brother on the table. Glaring at it, one more decision loomed. Should he accept the living at Hornebury—lucrative, prominent, and utterly dependent on the good will of the viscount, his brother? He had refused for three years.

> Ben,
>
> The London Season flourishes this year, and once again you have missed opportunities by refusing to join me.
>
> You must come to York for festivities, provincial though they may be. Two of my horses run there the end of May, and I have decided to take a house in early April. Don't even think of refusing. If you wish your quarterly allowance, you will join me to obtain it. Otherwise, nothing.

Ben leaned his head back in exasperation. He didn't care about his allowance from the estate. Most of it had gone to Pilgrim's Rest as Harry undoubtedly knew. He raised the missive and read on.

> I hope you've finally come to your senses. What good are you doing yourself or anyone else in that miserable little holding? I am quite out of patience with your stubbornness.
>
> Henry Neville Clarke, Viscount Stanbeck.

*What good indeed?* He had no authority, few loyal attendees and no outlet for service to the needy.

But what were his choices? The London Mission Society now sponsored people in China as well as Africa and the South Seas. Helping people appealed; preaching did not. He quickly dismissed that notion. *You would be rubbish at foisting your faith on others,* he told himself.

Since his brother didn't mention the holding at Hornebury, the one next to the family estate, this time, Ben supposed Harry had finally filled it with some worthy fellow.

When Ben was at Oxford an incident occurred that had altered the trajectory of his life. Already bound for the clergy (and likely Hornebury), but not yet ordained, he had been assisting with a ladies' charitable association. One afternoon they distributed baskets in a poor neighborhood and had come upon a tragedy. People on the ground floor of a building made up of multiple miserable apartments directed them to the top floor to the family in greatest need where they encountered catastrophe. A child had died in the night, though whether of starvation, cold, or illness Ben was never certain.

Sitting in the cozy tea shop, he could still vividly recall the mother's utter despair, the tiny body wrapped in a thin coverlet, and the empty eyes of her remaining children. The women who accompanied him reacted in horror. They thrust a basket at the woman, mouthed pious platitudes, and departed swiftly. Ben watched two children tear into the basket, stuffing apples in their pockets and the biscuits in their mouths. They threw the useless religious tracts and linen handkerchiefs onto the floor and began to empty the jam pot with their fingers. All the while the mother stared at the wall. Ben put all his money onto their rickety table and left, shattered by the contrast between real desperation and the smug self-righteousness of the church women, determined to do more, to make the world better.

He glanced back down at the letter. Beneath its formal signature his brother had scribbled, "I miss you," and signed it "Harry."

*What good are you doing yourself or anyone else?* his brother asked, and Ben forced himself to consider the question. Home for term holidays that year, the opulence of Stanbeck Hall had shamed him. He kept seeing the eyes of those starving children. The living at Hornebury, comfortable, familiar, and home, would never be enough for him, he had decided. After ordination, he refused the living. His father harangued him about it, and Harry, not yet Viscount Stanbeck, had told him he was punishing himself needlessly. There were people in need everywhere. When he came into the title, he had given Ben three years to change his mind.

*Is Harry right? Were you merely being stubborn about Hornebury?*

He may have been.

*But what good have you done? Some certainly.* He consoled himself with memories of weary travelers he had assisted. The image of Doro Bigglesworth intruded when he did, bringing joy entwined with sadness. She had never returned.

If he accepted Hornebury, he would have a home to which he could bring a wife. If he married, he would come into a bequest from his grandfather that would enable him to support his Miss Bigglesworth. But he felt certain both doors were closed to him. Harry had surely given the living elsewhere and Doro—if he dared call her that—had left him. He didn't know her location.

*What then, Ben? Will you wallow in tea and self-pity?* That seemed the worst decision of all. He would resign, go to York, and request an appointment with the archbishop. Somewhere in the diocese of York there was a place for him. Meanwhile, he could enjoy his brother's company. He had missed him too.

# CHAPTER 3

The hackney driver put Doro's belongings on the pavement in front of cousin Rose's town house. She paid him and peered up at the imposing facade. She'd grown up in the massive pile that was Seahaven with a sunny bedroom and every comfort, and so the town house didn't intimidate. After four years in cramped quarters at home and work, she quite looked forward to some comfort, even if it meant sharing a room with a sister. These past three weeks sleeping in the kitchens of the Smithson Assembly Rooms left her eager for a good night's rest. She had taken the position in exchange for rental of the rooms for her sisters' presentation ball. She didn't need to stay there nights, now the family had come to town.

She complemented herself on having the good sense to hire a hackney, picked up her valise and bandboxes, and stepped up to the door. A footman would have to collect the chest of cooking tools for her. She grinned at the unopened door. A footman! It had been years since they enjoyed that luxury. *Will Patience manage it here?* She gave the knocker a firm whack.

The door opened on a solemn-faced butler. A very young, very handsome butler. My! They had fallen into a cream pot.

"I am Lady Dorothea, I believe my stepmother has taken up residence here," she said by way of introduction.

His stern face broke into a welcoming—if un-butlerlike—smile. "We've been expecting you." He glanced over her shoulder at the chest on the pavement. "I'll see to your baggage," he said. He left her to carry her own valise and boxes.

*No footman, then*. "You may put that in the kitchen," she told him.

She walked through the deserted entranceway, dropped her boxes in the inner hall and gazed around. She had only a moment to take in the leaded glass window, parquet floors, and polished banister on the staircase when voices from above echoed around her.

"I told you it was Doro, Patience. I saw the hackney."

"I saw it first, Iris!"

The sound of tramping, very unladylike, footsteps followed as Merry, Emma, Iris, and Ivy flew down the stairs followed by Patience, Josefina, and Barbara at a more sedate pace. Doro laughed at the chaos engulfing her in welcome and embraces. Patience took her bonnet and handed it to Ivy who also took her cloak, and disappeared through a door at the foot of the stairs.

"It's a dressing room," Iris told her. "Isn't it clever?"

"Girls, give Doro room. She'll want to tidy up," Patience said.

"But she only came from across town, and we haven't seen her in weeks," Merry complained.

"Have you seen the butler?" Emma, all of twelve and precocious beyond her years, demanded. "But of course, you have. Isn't he delicious?"

"Emma! That is not appropriate." Patience gave her a quelling look. "Barbara, take Doro up to your room so she can get settled. When you're ready join us in the drawing room. It's on the first floor. There will be tea waiting. You can't miss it. Merry, Emma—back up to the nursery please."

Doro didn't have time to think as sisters swept her up the stairs to the second floor and a sunny little room overlooking the street. Smaller than her room at Starbrook and shared with another, but far better accommodations than she had had in over a year. An hour later she found the sisters around a temporary table set up in the drawing room. Papers, neatly arranged, covered the surface of the table, along with a map of York and environs, a city directory, paper and pencils.

"Patience is defining roles and assignments, and we're refining the plan," Josefina explained. Ivy's lovely face lost some of its glow, and an uncharacteristically solemn expression came over her. "We won't fail you, Patience. We are ever so grateful for everyone's efforts. We'll make brilliant marriages and do what we can to help all of you, too. See if we don't."

"Of course, you will. You, Iris, and Josefina are absolute diamonds," Barbara said.

"And you need not worry about us. We're content with our lives. You won't pry Bess out of her work, and I love mine, truly," Doro added. Her words were mostly true. She didn't need a brilliant match. The only man who had ever made her long for marriage, an impoverished curate, lived in Harrogate, a distance away and out of her reach. She put thoughts of Ben Clarke out of her mind. At least, she tried.

Ben left the bookshop on Wellington Street with urgent steps. He had promised Harry that he would meet him at The Race Club, a facility famous for its exclusivity based not on title or class but on the quality of one's horses. Viscount Stanbeck—Harry—was a founding member.

Crossing the street, he spied four young ladies coming from a fashionable millinery shop deep in conversation. All were lovely, two were exquisitely beautiful and very young. They were no doubt here to try their luck in the York marriage mart. What caught his eye however was the attractive one a few years older. Her looks, so like his Miss Bigglesworth, startled him—guinea gold hair, graceful posture, neatly rounded form… This woman, however, had stylishly cropped hair that peeked from under a smart jockey's cap and wore a gown far outside his dear friend's means. None of these young women would ever live in the cozy little house he treasured in his mind and hugged to his heart. It couldn't be her.

When they disappeared around a corner, he followed them, feeling foolish. The woman really did look like Doro Bigglesworth. Perhaps they were relatives. Distant relatives. They walked toward one of the wealthier districts and disappeared into a well-appointed town house, not far from the one Harry rented.

Ben turned on his heels and retraced his steps. *Stop wallowing in foolish dreams! Your obsession with that woman gives you delusions. There is no way she could be here in York. Not in that house and dressed like that.*

He reached the Race Club only minutes late.

"Did you speak with the archbishop?" Harry demanded before they even greeted each other.

"I have an appointment with him in a week," Ben replied.

The major domo who met them at the door kept his eyes fixed on the viscount. Ben had no doubt that he would have been tossed onto the street if he attempted to enter alone, clergyman or not. The man didn't comment on Ben's shabby appearance, but led them to the club's formal dining room, a wonder in dark wood, leather chairs, and paintings of famous horses and their riders. With the racing season approaching, the room hummed with activity. They took a table for two by the windows.

Harry ordered for them with his usual high-handed assumption that he knew best, not that the Race Club menu had many choices. Ben wondered what Miss Bigglesworth would make of it.

"His grace the archbishop must be a busy man," Harry said as the waiter hurried off.

Ben concentrated on his serviette, staring at the table.

"Do you think he's avoiding you?" Harry prompted.

"Not entirely. He's a careful man. I suspect he will send a courier to speak to the vicar in Knaresborough about me," Ben said.

"Is he a stickler for the chain of command?"

"Just careful. He likes to have facts in front of him before he speaks. He'll want to know why I resigned and whether it was voluntary."

"Was it?"

He met his brother's intense gaze directly. "You know it was. I only accepted the post because of Pilgrim's Rest. When he ordered it closed, I resigned. I didn't go to Harrogate to dun contributions from irritable countesses and pompous industrialists."

Their eyes held until both brothers squirmed in the awkward discomfort between them, and Ben expected a lecture on his foolish notions about a clergyman's role.

Harry grunted and looked away, silent for moment while a footman filled their glasses. "Excellent claret," he murmured a moment or so later.

Ben agreed and let himself enjoy another luxury he had missed these past three years. He fiddled with the stem of his wine glass with little to say.

"I made an appointment with a tailor." Harry dropped that gauntlet on the table without warning, and went on before Ben could object. "You can't make morning calls, much less attend a ball in that suit. I thought the major domo was going to swallow his tongue when he saw you."

Ben had no defense. "Thank you."

Harry's stunned expression tickled his brother. "No argument?"

"None. It may help my standing with the archbishop, if I appear in a decent black suit." He waved off Harry's attempt to interrupt. "And I promised to socialize. I will. Perhaps not morning calls but at least a Venetian breakfast and a ball or two. You could have brought the formal clothes I left at Stanbeck Hall."

"They would never fit. I'm guessing you've engaged in physical labor since I saw you last." The viscount gave a dramatic shudder, causing Ben to laugh.

"You know I have. A new suit and evening clothes it is."

"Two suits and formal wear—I won't even take it out of your allowance. I'll never get you married off dressed like that."

*Married.* There it was at last. "You're the viscount in need of an heir. You marry."

"I will. Eventually. I don't have to marry to come into my inheritance. Your bequest from our grandfather requires that you do."

Ben let the challenge go; the words were true enough. He wasn't ready to confide in his brother about the one woman who had caught his eye.

"I heard there's a decent crop of debutantes out in York this year. You might take a look at the Seahaven Diamonds."

Ben snorted. "No, thank you. I found female 'diamonds' to be as hard and cold as the gemstones when you trotted me around London four years ago."

"For heaven's sake, Ben. Don't judge the young women before you even meet them."

"My distaste isn't for young women, Harry. It is for society and the way it forces them to hunt for husbands." Besides, Ben feared he'd already met the only woman he wanted to marry. He doubted he would find another.

"What are your chances at the races this year?" Ben asked. His shoulders relaxed when Harry took the hint and began to describe the three horses he had transported to York.

# CHAPTER 4

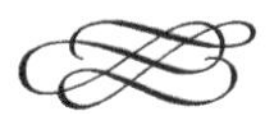

Doro knew how to manage time well. Most days she finished her work at Smithson's Assembly Rooms by noon, leaving her free to make her share of morning calls, which of course were done incongruously in the afternoon. The sisters divided up the calls so as not to overwhelm hostesses and rotated their new day dresses so that no one Bigglesworth wore the same dress twice in a week.

Patience assigned Lady Garner's at home on Tuesday to Barbara and Doro, judging fewer gentleman would be there and needing the eligibles—Iris, Ivy, and Josefina—at more productive households. She directed the older girls to beef up the guest list.

Lady Garner's visitors nattered on as one did during morning calls, bouncing between fashion, the weather, and the social calendar. When the last gentleman took his leave, conversation veered into opinions and description of various gentlemen that skirted ever closer to the edge of improper. Doro caught Barbara's eyes and saw the same reaction there. She prayed her sister didn't succumb to brewing whoops of laughter until they got home.

"Don't you think, Lady Dorothea?"

She paid so little attention she not only didn't know the topic, she failed to recognize the voice of the speaker. *If Barbara bites her lip any harder to keep from laughing, she will draw blood.*

The arrival of a refreshed tea tray saved her, and the conversation moved on. Doro entertained herself by judging the cakes and biscuits. In this case, none were worth noting. On other occasions she had found creative or particularly delicious ideas and scribbled them in her notebook. Once she even slipped into the kitchen to ask the cook for the recipe, using the need to visit the necessary as a ruse.

Ten days in she found the entire exercise tedious. She suspected Iris and Ivy would be astounded to hear she preferred the company in Harrogate. They would laugh at her sudden interest in attending church. She wasn't about to tell them about her curate.

A distraction arrived just when she needed one most. Viscount Tavistock and his sister Chloe arrived for the Season, and Doro greeted them with delight. Merry and Emma's half-sister on their mother's side always added to fun, though Martin, the viscount, tended to be stern. No sooner did they arrive in York than Chloe roped Doro into an adventure.

It wasn't the first contretemps Chloe caused, but this one began innocently enough over tea. Chloe waved a broadside describing a lecture about the suspension of the Habeas Corpus Act. "It is an outrage, you know it is! Parliament overstepped this time!" Chloe bounced in her seat.

"The entire business was an attempt to squelch any effort at much-needed reform," Doro replied, mentally reviewing her calendar. "When is it, again?"

"Tomorrow. Do say you'll come."

"What does Martin think?"

"What my brother doesn't know won't hurt him. Or me."

That ought to be a warning, but Doro ignored it. She agreed to attend, forgetting Chloe's tendency to act before thinking through the possible repercussions of her actions. Doro's first inkling she might have made a mistake came when she arrived at her friends' town house to find Chloe carrying a monkey in a basket. A live one. "You can't take a monkey to a public lecture!"

"Rosario will be ever so good. I won't let her out of this basket," was her friend's response. Doro started to object, but Chloe kept chattering on about the poor dear and Martin's determination to drown it. Doro couldn't make sense of the details, but Chloe clearly saw the monkey as unfairly maligned and in need of her protection. Doro let it go.

She later wished she had looked into the presenters more closely. While Doro tended to agree with the current speaker's position regarding the evils of the suspension, it would have been better if he had actual oratory skills to match his passion. He wandered in senseless circles, and Doro quickly lost interest, studying instead the gratifyingly large crowd in attendance. Most looked as bored as Doro.

Others looked angry, and she suspected she should have asked Mr. Smithson about public sentiment before getting in the middle of so large a crowd. Still, the speaker seemed harmless if incompetent.

Rosario must have been bored too, because the basket shook, and Chloe had to keep a firm hand on the lid. The bouncing worsened. "I warned you about bringing that monkey!" Doro hissed, biting her lip to keep from laughing out loud.

Chloe whispered a response, but Doro didn't hear her, distracted by the sight of a man across the aisle a few rows in front of them. He took her breath away.

*Mr. Clarke! Surely not. Ben Clarke is in Harrogate.* She couldn't shake the thought. The young man wore a shabby black suit. Exactly like Ben. His untidy brown hair curled down over his collar in ways that made her long to run her fingers through it. Exactly like Ben. It was a clergyman's collar. Exactly like...

A second speaker took the podium and people shouted at Chloe—and the monkey—to be quiet. This one, a real firebrand, launched into a tirade on an entire range of issues, ranting about inequities in the upper classes and the plight of the poor. Doro's attention, however, continued to rivet on the man who looked so much like her curate. He dipped his head to the side. Exactly like Ben did when he listened intently, lost in thought, a habit she found endearing.

*It must be him!* Doro ignored the speaker and the monkey's increasingly frantic sounds. She saw only Ben Clarke. She was certain it was he. Had he come to York particularly for this lecture? She clamped down on the impulse to cross the aisle to confront him, determined to wait like a lady until the program ended and greet him properly.

She realized belatedly that something had changed. People shouted their agreement. Others booed. One man loomed over Doro and Chloe from behind, leaning forward to point at the speaker, calling him a traitor to the Crown.

Doro glanced over at Chloe just as the basket's lid popped off and the furry little demon leapt out. It climbed along the backs of the chairs and into the row behind. Doro glowered at the monkey. Someone stormed across the aisle to confront the man behind them, and a fight broke out. People were on their feet, now. "We need to leave, Chloe!" she shouted, but Chloe's attention was on the monkey, now a few rows back.

Doro swung round to search for Ben Clarke, unable to find him in the crowd. Thinking only to get to him, she stepped out into the aisle. Before she could take more than two steps a man's elbow struck the back of her head, and she tumbled forward. Panic seized her when a man's arms came around her. She slapped at him trying to push him away.

"Miss Bigglesworth? What are you doing here?" She stared transfixed into the eyes of an astonished Ben Clarke only moments before she was pushed unceremoniously back into his arms. This time she didn't fight.

Watching his dearest fantasy appear before him, only to transform into a near nightmare shook Ben down to the soles of his boots. The auditorium had exploded in a full-scale riot. He had to get her out of there quickly. He cradled Miss Bigglesworth under his right arm and led her down the nearest row of seats toward an exit, using his left to move chairs, dodging vegetative projectiles, and avoiding agitated lecture goers.

When a crowd of people equally intent on exiting engulfed them in the far aisle, he pulled her closer and felt her hand reach under his coat to grip the back of his shirt. She ducked her head against his chest, which was well because the bonnet she wore would have blocked his vision. The crowd popped through the door and expanded in all directions like champagne released from a bottle.

They ran away from The Philosophical Auditorium, still clutched together until they reached the other side of the square where he set her gently against a tree. He ignored the people still streaming out and away, fixated only on examining her for harm. He found none.

His anxiety eased, he noticed that she wore her familiar blue dress, one he often saw at Pilgrim's Rest. It warmed his heart. A bonnet as hideous as it was familiar covered her tresses. His heart soared with tenderness. The fashionable lady he had seen the week before could never have been his Miss Bigglesworth.

Her trusting expression and glowing smile sent his common-sense scrambling. He seized the opportunity that blessed him. He kissed her, a tender salute to her sweet lips. He couldn't resist.

Her eyes flew wide open. Realizing he had startled her, he opened his mouth to apologize, and couldn't. "Are you well?" he croaked out instead, his voice thick with emotion.

Her smile returned swiftly, and her eyes never left his. One precious lock of her golden hair had escaped. He reached up and tucked it in, sliding his trembling hand down to caress her cheek.

"What are you doing in York?" she asked.

"My brother—" But he didn't want to talk about Harry. "I resigned when they closed Pilgrim's Rest."

Moisture pooled in her compassionate blue eyes. "Oh, Mr. Clarke! What will you do?"

"Ben." He said it firmly. "After that adventure, you ought to use my name."

"I will, if you call me Doro," she replied without hesitation.

He grinned and answered her question. "I have an appointment with the archbishop. We'll see what he has for me. There's an opening for a vicar at Hornebury, I've been told." He didn't mean to blurt that out, but suddenly it mattered very much to him to know what she thought.

She frowned. "Is that what you truly want?"

A pain gripped his chest. "It depends. The interview is tomorrow."

"It's a miracle you were here, though," she said, glancing over at the auditorium.

"I was afraid someone would hurt you," he whispered caressing her cheek. "Did you come alone?"

"No, I— Dear God! Chloe! I have to find my friend." She pulled away and searched frantically around. She began to walk away.

"Wait, I can help." He glanced across the street where things appeared to have cooled.

"No, please. I'll be fine." She paused only briefly.

She obviously didn't want him to accompany her, but honor dictated he not leave her. "I should—"

"I will see you in church," she called breathlessly.

He would have to be satisfied with that. "Which one?"

She stopped, made a half turn, and dipped her head. It appeared his little love had to think for a moment. "Holy Cross," she shouted over her shoulder. She resumed her headlong flight and ran toward the crowd making its way down the main street.

Holy Cross. He knew the place. It was just beyond the Shambles, and Butchers' Row. There was a soup kitchen near it. He smiled. He would see her again. Perhaps they could talk then.

*Doro, you idiot. You should have let him accompany you to find Chloe. You should have told him everything,* she thought, gasping for breath as she ran.

Seeing him there in his overlong hair, his familiar collar, his shabby clergyman's coat in need of a good brush, she had been swept into a world belonging to the two of them alone, the world of Pilgrim's Rest. She wanted to protect that illusion; she didn't want to spoil it with her family's complex problems and explanations.

Running along the cobbles she smiled. She could see her Mr. Clarke—Ben—again. He would be at Holy Cross on Sunday. It had been the first one that popped into her head. She would explain her situation to him then.

She was all the way to Viscount Tavistock's house before she knew for certain that Chloe—and the monkey—were perfectly safe.

# CHAPTER 5

Doro's hopes for a visit to Holy Cross the following Sunday evaporated in Bigglesworth family chaos within days.

"Barbara has the sniffles." Patience stated the obvious. Her insistence about Susana's and Bess's unavailability was more vague but equally firm. "You must accompany the girls and myself to York Minster on Sunday. It is a gathering of the cream of society, and we will not miss it."

Doro couldn't wiggle out. Patience marched her to the great cathedral with Ivy, Iris, and Josefina for services and, what was more to the point, to greet and converse after services with all and sundry—viscounts, an earl, a duke's third son, some handsome young men in uniform, and fashionable ladies of all sorts—showcasing the younger girls, the eligibles as Doro thought of them. More names were added to the invitation list for the ball.

Doro did her bit, but on the way home stood up to Patience. "I won't accompany you next Sunday even if it is a few days before our ball. I have… Plans."

Patience studied her closely, but didn't press for information. Doro loved her like a sister.

Doro's afternoons became a whirlwind of dress repairs, invitation writing, meal planning, and other urgent tasks the following week. Her turns for morning calls came twice. At the first, she found a delightful presentation of lemon cakes with yellow flowers garnishing the tray. At the other, Lady Grincleft served stale biscuits that Doro suspected were left over from a soiree the woman held the week before.

She soldiered on, determined to seek out Ben the following Sunday. When she asked Mr. Smithson where she might find Holy Cross, the old man frowned.

"A lady—no respectable woman— would walk to The Shambles unaccompanied."

"Bad neighborhood?" Doro asked.

"Bordered by worse." Smithson set his mouth in a stubborn line.

"I will be perfectly safe. I'm meeting a, ah, a friend."

Smithson eyed her dubiously. "If I didn't know you, Lady Dorothea, I would suspect you of making an assignation under cover of visiting church." She had regretted telling Smithson her title. He had almost fired her. Instead, he turned into an ally, amused to keep her secret from his socially prominent clients who would withdraw in horror over an earl's daughter working for wages. But in this he would not budge; he insisted one of his footmen accompany her.

She sought the young man privately to talk him out of coming. Terrance, made of sterner stuff, persisted in his mission. "Smithson says he'll have my hide if I leave you before you meet this friend of yours—and not then if he looks dodgy."

She convinced him to meet her around the corner from cousin Rose's town house so he wouldn't bring tales back to the other staff at least, and he didn't fail. By the time they reached the unfamiliar neighborhood, she was glad for his presence. Streets became more sordid as they narrowed, and the stares around her grew more threatening. Squalid little gin shops tucked here and there between empty store fronts and ramshackle businesses. The actual Shambles streets appeared to be more refined, with newer establishments.

She was grateful to step into the relative openness of the church square. Even greater joy! Ben Clarke stood on the church steps hat in hand. He waved when he saw her.

"Never say your friend's a priest, my lady! Smithson will be amused," Terrance laughed. "Best tell him to accompany you next time."

Doro knew a good idea when she heard one, but she had explanations to make first. "Thank you, Terrance. I'll be fine now." She reached in her reticule.

"No need for coin, my lady. Happy to help a fellow employee." The rogue winked and walked away just as Ben reached her.

"A friend?"

"Yes. My friends refused to let me walk to this part of York alone."

"I'm grateful to them. I wanted to escort you myself, but we didn't have time for me to learn your direction." Ben smiled down at her.

That smile and the warmth in his eyes drove coherent thought and good intentions right out of her. *What was it? Oh yes. My direction. Tell him now, Doro.*

The bells of Holy Cross rang out and citizens of all sorts moved in the direction of the church. She needed more time and some quiet to explain her family circumstances, Rose's town house, and The Plan. Leading with her title after keeping it to herself for months seemed unwise. She let him take her into the church.

Doro briefly appeared flustered. One moment she smiled, the next worry—over something Ben didn't understand—marred her expression. He had no time to question it and none to ask why she hadn't met him the previous week. She had come. He decided that was enough and led her into church.

After services, people milled in front gossiping and socializing. Doro, clinging to his arm beamed at him. "People are much the same everywhere. The congregation at the cathedral is more distinguished and dresses more fashionably, but they chatter like magpies just the same."

*What an odd observation.* "Is that where you were last Sunday?"

"Yes, I wanted to explain. I—"

Whatever Doro wanted to explain was lost when Mr. Whitcombe, still in cassock and surplice, strode up, beaming. "Wretched boy, you didn't mention you were speaking with the archbishop when you asked to visit Manna and Bread last week!"

Doro peered up at Ben. "Manna and Bread? What is that?"

"Miss Bigglesworth, may I present Mr. Whitcombe, the curate who assists in this parish," Ben explained. "He also oversees a mission for poor relief—bread, temporary shelter and so on."

"Like Pilgrim's Rest!" Doro's excitement was palpable.

"A much grander scale, I'm afraid, Miss Bigglesworth. The problems and the numbers of the poor in York are much greater," the man replied. "We have a never-ending need for donations and volunteers," he went on hopefully.

"You spoke with the archbishop about this?" Doro asked.

"Among other things." His grace had urged Ben to take his time and pray over it, reminding him that needy people could be found everywhere. Sitting in the opulence of the archepiscopal manor, dressed in silk, with a ruby gleaming in his episcopal cross, Ben wondered how well he understood about the actual conditions in the poorer neighborhoods. Still, Yorkshire had many projects to benefit the poor. Manna and Bread was one, but there was no opening at Holy Cross at the moment.

Whitcombe bestowed a benevolent, condescending clerical smile on Ben. It made him queasy. "Would you like that tour now?" Whitcombe asked.

Soon they were swept along before him to the plain building down a shadowed lane. Only a plain cross on the door identified it as anything special. Hollow-eyed children, weary pale-faced women, and shriveled old men eyed them suspiciously and hugged their soup bowls. A long line snaked toward the serving table.

"Shall we join them in line?" Ben asked.

"Oh, yes!" Doro said.

"Goodness, no," Whitcombe exclaimed at the same time. "We do not sit with the indigent."

Not guests. He managed to make needy people sound like beggars.

Whitcombe ignored Ben's growing scowl. "We do not wish for them to linger. Besides, you certainly can't expect this lady to sit among such creatures."

Ben remembered Doro conversing with an elderly vagabond at Pilgrim's Rest, wiping the face of a filthy child, or commiserating with a frantic mother. *Yes, that is exactly what I would expect*—and she wouldn't call them *'creatures'.* The disappointment in her expression matched his own.

Doro studied three boys sitting alone at the end of one table. All three shoveled soup and bread into hungry mouths. All three wore clothes even a simple household would have long since used for rags. One had a purple bruise covering the side of his face. Ben doubted Doro understood the horrors that faced street children in a city like York or the degradation it caused in boys like this. She looked ready to go to them.

The situation got worse, at least from Ben's point of view. The door swung open and a woman dressed at the height of fashion swept in on the arm of a dandy wearing an elaborately embroidered waistcoat and shirt points so high they scratched his cheek. He hadn't seen them at church. Two footmen carrying baskets came in behind them.

"Lady Bountiful," Ben murmured. *Another one,* he thought bitterly.

"Lady Grincleft," Doro whispered, clinging to his arm more tightly and dipping her head so that he couldn't make out her face.

The intruder—for that's how Ben saw the woman—gazed about the room with distaste, straightened and walked up to the end of the nearest table, donning a smile as false as any mask. "Having the meal these good people generously provided I see. I hope you are all suitably grateful, because we've brought an extra treat." An imperious gesture brought the servants scurrying. They began distributing biscuits to the tables, taking scrupulous care not to touch anyone.

The woman stepped gracefully back, taking her cicisbeo's arm again. Whitcombe rushed forward to greet her with a smile as fawning as his words.

"I need to leave," Doro murmured, dropping Ben's arm.

"I've seen enough as well. I'll escort you home," Ben replied.

She began to say something, but a disturbance broke out. The boys at the end of the table had started a fight with the footman, yanking on the basket and stuffing biscuits into their shirts. Ben instinctively ran to intervene.

"Those vermin are thieves," the grand lady shouted behind him. He didn't turn to look. He managed to separate the combatants, but he made no effort to restrain the boys when they ran for the door, taking the basket with them.

"Did those animals injure you, Mr. Clarke?" Whitcombe asked, arriving after the scuffle was over and Ben had helped the footman to his feet.

Lady Grincleft, as Ben assumed the vision shaking with outrage in front of him to be, was less kind. "Why didn't you retain them? You could have caught one. If you were my employee, I would fire you. Those thieves assaulted my servant and deserve to be brought before the magistrate."

*And be transported over biscuits?*

Whitcombe shifted from sympathy to righteous indignation at her words. "Indeed, Mr. Clarke that was poorly done. They cannot be allowed to get away with this. I assure you Lady Grincleft, we will report this atrocity to the authorities."

*Atrocity?* Ben thought the buffoon overplayed his performance, but he did know his audience—the patronizing lady. He turned to Doro to share the humor of it. She was gone.

Whitcombe went on without noticing Ben's reactions. "I think you'll find Mr. Clarke that you may not be suited to Manna and Bread." If he noticed Doro's absence, he didn't say.

"You will excuse me, Mr. Whitcombe. Thank you for the tour. It was enlightening. My lady, I bid you good day." Ben escaped and almost ran to the door. When he got there, he found no sign of Doro

Bigglesworth. Disappointment crushed him, his shoulders sagged, and he dragged his feet in the direction of Harry's rented house.

You underestimated how upsetting those boys were to her. That must be it.

That didn't feel right, but it was the best he could muster, baffled as he was by her abrupt departure. He still didn't know where to find her. He could only hope she came to church the following Sunday.

Terrance earned Doro's everlasting gratitude. "Thought you might need me," he said, pushing off the wall on the edge of the church square where he had lingered.

Doro glanced back toward the mission and wondered if she should wait for Ben. He had dived into the midst of the scuffle and might be there a while. He no doubt had decisions to make and may need to speak with Mr. Whitcombe as well.

She prayed he didn't choose Manna and Bread. Those people had been horrible. The snobbery had upset her and no doubt Ben, too. She felt certain the biscuits were as stale as the ones Lady Grincleft served her guests, probably more so. The urge to run returned.

*Coward. You're afraid you'll encounter Lady Grincleft, the old bat, and she'll recognize you.* Her sisters couldn't afford the gossip that would cause. She followed Terrance out of the neighborhood with rapid steps and a heavy heart.

If she didn't explain her presence in York to Ben soon, she risked him finding out by accident. She dreaded what he might think. Now she'd left in a hurry again, without knowing where to find him. She would have to wait another week and hope Patience didn't demand her presence elsewhere—and that he could bring himself to Holy Cross after what happened today. She feared she'd never see him again.

# CHAPTER 6

Shortly after dawn on the day of the Seahaven Ball, Doro left home. She would spend the day at Smithson's Assembly Hall overseeing the decorations and the kitchen. It was her major contribution to The Plan as Patience called it. Now that the day of the ball had arrived, she was eager to get it over with. She would have done what she could for her family, and she would be free to face her own life. Her mind ran forward to Sunday and the chance to see Ben, to explain her situation openly. First though, it was vital that this ball be a success.

They had, all of them, put everything they had into this Season and this event for the sake of the twins and Josefina, and much hung on its success. Of the girls themselves she harbored no doubts. They were exquisitely beautiful young women, inside and out. The gowns Susana had created for them showed each one of them off to perfection. Patience had brilliantly executed an understated word-of-mouth campaign to spread the girls' worth—their beauty, their virtues, their skills and talents. She crafted a careful message about their marriage portions—modest but solid—to underpin her messages. It would work. It had to.

Doro had less confidence in York society. Harpies and snakes abounded, ready to spew venom at any sign of weakness. If they caught a whiff of poverty or, worse, trade, they would strike and ruin everything. Her encounter with Lady Grincleft had been a close call.

She entered Smithson's by the staff access door, put on her apron and got on with it. The fruit and vegetable delivery arrived right behind her, and she soon lost herself in examining berries, sniffing cheeses, inspecting pears for ripeness, and delighting in the cluster of pineapples she had ordered to add panache. Plunged into work she loved, she let her anxieties fade away and the day flew by.

Barbara, already wearing the gown they would share, found her in the office going over lists. "Is everything in order?"

"Did you bring the favors for the supper tables?" The sisters had made clever little paper birds in a rainbow of colors, sitting in nests made of strips of gilt paper. Supper tables, tiny rounds designed for intimacy interspaced with tables of four, had no room for centerpieces. The little nests were an added touch designed to reflect grace and light.

"We did indeed. Josefina is putting them out as we speak," Barbara said.

Doro glanced at her list one more time and checked off "nests." She rose and removed her apron, tossing it over one arm. "Shall we take a look at the miracle?" she asked grinning at her sister.

"The ballroom? Yes! And then I need your help with my hair. I brought our kit and the trim for your version of this gown and left them in that private withdrawing room you set up."

The ballroom floor was waxed and ready. It wasn't parquet, but the wood had a golden gleam to it. The tall potted palms from Smithson's stock that lined the floor had been enhanced with camellias. Sparkling chandeliers hung low, ready for servants to light the candles in another hour, just before guests arrived.

"The candles are lovely—very white!" Barbara said.

"You sound surprised. I promised you they would be. Do you smell them?" Doro had been lucky enough to obtain spermaceti candles at half the cost of beeswax, yet far superior to smelly tallow.

"No. Not the least bit, exactly as you said."

Terrance trotted over. "We've set out the planters, arranged the chairs, run dusters over the floor one more time. This room is ready, and your sister and Katy are putting touches on the supper room, Lady Dorothea."

Barbara's eyes flew open in horror. "Does everyone here know who you are?"

Terrance grinned. "Only me, and I don't talk."

"They all know me as Miss Doro Biggs, who will direct things from below stairs. When Lady Dorothea Bigglesworth makes her formal—and hopefully very brief—appearance, no one will realize they are the same person. People, even servants, see what they want to see."

"It will never work!" Barbara said, sighing deeply.

"Patience agreed I could stay away until after supper. Most of my work is done by then, and you get to enjoy the supper dance. It will be dark outside; I can accept a few introductions and avoid some of the more observant of the servers.

Terrance laughed. "There are none, my lady." The cheeky boy winked at Barbara. "And besides, my job is to tell them they are daft fools if they suggest such a thing."

The silence in Viscount Stanbeck's carriage was a blessing. Ben had feared his brother would lecture him on proper behavior all the way to the Seahaven Ball, as if he hadn't been raised to be a gentleman. He was to see the famous Seahaven Diamonds, dance with each, and, in his brother's words, "at least consider them."

"The word is all three have a respectable if modest portion, in spite of the size of the family," Harry mused, shredding Ben's peace. "They will do. Your bequest from grandfather should mirror their portions nicely."

*What does Harry know about what will "do" for you?* Ben grumbled to himself. He swallowed it, determined to do this thing properly. He had agreed to come, he had let himself be trussed in formal evening wear by Harry's valet, and he possessed manners if little else. Dancing with girls reputed to be the most beautiful in York would be no hardship. But they wouldn't be Doro.

"It's a large family?" Ben asked attempting to deflect the conversation from himself.

"Rumor is there are a dozen sisters. Once I heard fifteen, but rumors tend to exaggerate," Harry grinned.

Harry and Ben climbed the steps to the ballroom and a rather unlikely looking butler greeted them, accepted their cards, and announced in a booming voice, "Henry Clarke, Viscount Stanbeck, and the Honorable Eustace Benedict Clarke." Ben cringed, glad at least that his middle name had been included on his calling cards.

The rumors had exaggerated. The Dowager Countess of Seahaven —the very young countess—received them with the three daughters being presented and two others at her side, hardly a dozen. He had to admit the twins and the one called Josefina were breathtakingly beautiful. He recalled Harry droning on about how their mother had once been the stellar debutante of her generation, a renowned beauty.

He had difficulty focusing. By the time he followed Harry into the ballroom, there was a buzzing in his ears. One after another these young women were introduced as Lady something something Bigglesworth. Bigglesworth. Doro never mentioned relatives that were earl's daughters. Sisters, yes. She mentioned sisters. These must be some sort of relatives—probably the ones he saw on the street that day—and if he was right, the whole family certainly ran to female progeny.

He let Harry lead him about the room making introductions, all the while going over what he had just seen. The daughters being presented were indeed lovely, with perfect features and magnificent auburn hair. He preferred the glorious guinea gold of his Doro, but then, he was partial. He'd have to take a closer look at them one by one. He would get his chance. At Harry's urging he was promised to dance with all of them.

Two hours later he was still confused. Each of the Seahaven daughters had been utterly charming. Each elegantly poised. Each would be perfectly at home in an earl's manor or duke's castle. Yet, he kept seeing echoes of his Doro. While they varied in appearance, all seemed to have a determined chin, and each had a competent air and confident demeanor. He couldn't shake the sense of familiarity.

His partner in the supper dance, Susana Bigglesworth, claimed weariness.

"I've danced every dance, Mr. Clarke. Would you be terribly disappointed if we sat?" she said, the good humor lurking in her eyes promising an enjoyable conversation.

"I would not! I have a better idea. Shall we invade the supper room a bit early, get the lay of the land, and commandeer the best table?"

The lady laughed as he intended, accepted his escort, and followed his lead into supper.

He stopped in his tracks just inside the door. Servants busily laid out the feast, hoisting trays and arranging dishes attractively. The woman overseeing the operation with graceful hand gestures and words he could not hear wore a plain gown and a serviceable apron. She also had guinea gold hair and a determined chin, the picture of Doro Bigglesworth.

A gentle tug on his arm brought him back to reality. He escorted his partner to a prime table and held her chair. When he looked back up, the woman had disappeared. Ben questioned his sanity. Had he become so besotted with Doro that he saw her everywhere? Soon he would be afraid to walk the streets for fear every woman had her face.

He forced his erratic thoughts away and concentrated on his partner. *You are a gentleman, and you know how to listen, damn it.* Do so. He vowed to have a conversation with Doro on Sunday.

# CHAPTER 7

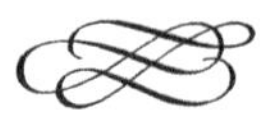

Doro scurried to the private withdrawing room and dropped into a chair. With supper served, she had an hour to change the trim on Barbara's gown and turn it into her own. A gauze overskirt created by Susana would mute the color. No one would notice that it was the same dress. She wafted a prayer of thanks this was the only ball they all needed to attend at the same time. Gown sharing would be easier the rest of the Season.

She chided herself for worrying whether Katy and the other servers could handle supper without her. They were all well trained, but she feared being called to deal with a disaster while in her Lady Dorothea guise. She would be avoiding the supper room. As it was, she had been forced to duck out early. She caught sight of a couple entering out of the corner of her eye. She didn't know who it was, but she didn't wait for them to get a good look. She just left. Katy must have thought she was out of her mind.

Moments later, Barbara shut the door behind her and leaned on it, stars in her eyes. "Oh, Doro..."

"What has happened, Barbara?" Doro gasped. "You look radiant. Is Jack here?"

Barbara nodded, biting her lower lip. "I'll tell you everything later, for I have an assignation! Now help me out of this gown, and don't worry about the dress, I've told him."

Doro stood riveted to the spot, thrilled for her sister.

"Help me with these ties," Barbara said, unhooking the train and turning so Doro could undo the back of the gown. Doro pulled herself together and did as she was bid. In moments, Barbara sat in her shift while the two women began removing the strip of silk embroidered with pink and yellow flowers that Susana had tacked around the hem of the pale blue gown, and the matching, narrower ones around each sleeve. They then added bands of cleverly constructed rosettes and bits of seashells around the sleeves and beneath the bodice and blond lace along the decolletage, overlapping the bodice.

Doro was to forego the train, a blessing for which she was grateful. She let Barbara tie her in back, the opening rethreaded with ribbon in a contrasting color.

"Now the overskirt," Barbara said.

Doro had no way to judge the results. "I wish we had a mirror."

Barbara stared. "It works. She was right; it works. You look a treat and that pale primrose overskirt floats over the blue silk giving it a green cast, almost a saxon green. Not one woman in that ballroom will recognize this gown. Susana is a genius.

Doro went down the servants' stairs from habit and skirted the ballroom. Dancing had resumed. It wouldn't do to make a public entrance. She would be just one more Seahaven daughter. Everyone would assume she had been there the entire time. At least, that was the plan. She slipped quietly in a side door, scanned the ballroom for Patience and made a beeline for her.

She slipped to her stepmother's side, breathless as if from dancing rather than from running down the stairs, and pasted a smile on her face.

"Dorothea, dear, I saw you dancing just now. You are so graceful, I envy you," Patience said, eyes sparkling with laughter. She introduced her to the woman and man with whom she had been conversing, Sir somebody and his wife. The names escaped her as did those of the next five people. One gentleman, introduced as Lord Diomedes Finchley, led her out to dance.

"We meet at last, Lady Dorothea," he said.

"I beg your pardon," Doro said, suddenly wary.

"Lady Chloe Tavistock had me in knots looking for you after the incident at the lecture," he said with an impish grin. "You and the monkey."

Doro grinned back. "You're Chloe's Lord Diomedes!"

"Am I? Chloe's?" he asked, brow raised. He led her into position and the moment passed.

When the dance concluded, he led her back to Patience. Her stepmother now conversed with two well-dressed young gentlemen with dark hair. She smiled up at Doro. "There you are, dear one. Lady Dorothea Bigglesworth, may I make Viscount Stanbeck and his brother, the Honorable Eustace Clarke, known to you?"

Doro's heart froze in her chest. Her hand sagged half way to the gentlemen and she forgot to curtsy. The honorable Eustace looked like he'd swallowed an entire lemon. Whole. Eustace indeed!

*What is Ben Clarke doing here dressed up like a prancing lording? And oh, dear God, what must he think of me?* They stared at one another, incapable of common courtesy.

Patience and the viscount exchanged confused looks, both eyeing Doro and Ben. The viscount cleared his throat. "May we gather you two have met?" he asked.

"Lady Dorothea, may I have this dance," Ben choked out, ignoring the others.

Doro wanted to sink into the floor, but that did not seem possible. She lay two fingers on his arm, and walked to her doom.

Hired assembly rooms have no garden but they do, apparently, have a terrace overlooking the square below. Or so Doro—Lady Dorothea—told him when he demanded to know. She seemed to know the place well. *Can this night get any stranger?* Ben doubted it.

Halfway across the room, she let go of his arm, and he had to skip to catch up with her as she reached the door. He grabbed her hand, half fearing she meant to bolt.

The terrace wasn't large, but neither was it crowded. A few people mingled near the railing. A couple engaged in intimate familiarity in the corner to the far left of the glass doors, shadowed rather less than they obviously hoped by the gloom.

When Doro stopped in the middle, Ben, who still had her by the hand, dragged her to the similarly darkened corner to the right. It provided inadequate privacy, but it would have to do.

One hard yank on her arm swung Doro into the corner, around his front, to a hard stop against his chest. His other arm anchored her fast against his body and his mouth came down on hers. No tender salute this. Passion driven by anger and frustrated desire drove him. He plundered. He invaded. He...

He felt like a cad, but he didn't care. Besides, she kissed him back, clinging to his shoulders like she might drown if she let go. When the need to breathe forced him to pull back a fraction of an inch, Doro closed the distance and kissed him again. That's when he realized she was crying.

"Enough." He held both her arms and set her a bit away. Not so far that she could run off. Just enough to reassemble his scattered wits. "Do you want to explain to me what happened here?"

"You kissed me. Rather thoroughly."

Shame over her tears warred with delight at her passionate response. "Not that! Who are you, and what game are you playing?" he demanded gently wiping the tears from her cheeks.

"Lower your voice." She hissed at him in the gloom. "I'll answer your questions, but keep your voice down." Apparently satisfied that he wasn't going to shout her deception to the rooftops, she went on. "I am Doro Bigglesworth, Lady Dorothea Bigglesworth. In Harrogate the title didn't seem to matter."

"This isn't Harrogate; it is York. Why the deception?"

She snorted. No ladylike cringing for his Doro. "You know what society thinks of those of us who are forced to work for a living. I didn't lie to you about our situation. We needed my wages at the Hampton. My father was indeed the Earl of Seahaven, but when he died, we were left with nothing; Patience struggles to support the children. All of us had to scramble to help. If word got out here, it would ruin everything, destroy my sisters' chances."

"So, you're deceiving all of York instead, so the Seahaven Diamonds can latch on to some wealthy fool and enrich all of you. Are the rumors about their dowries lies, too?"

"No! We pooled all we had, the money meant for the ten of us, and concentrated it on them." She poked him with one very sharp finger. Hard. Several times. "That is precisely what people will think if you spread gossip, and it won't be true. Not true at all."

He grabbed her hand to stop her from jabbing him. "I saw you supervising supper like one of the servants. One minute you're in an apron. The next you float across the dance floor in a gown designed to send a man's imagination where it has no business going. It's dishonest. It's—"

"What about you—the *Honorable* Eustace Clarke. Who precisely is he? You haven't been exactly forthcoming. Sunday, you wandered the Shambles in a shabby coat and clerical collar. Tonight, my stepmother introduces you looking like the answer to a maiden's dreams. Exactly how honorable is that? You never mentioned your brother the viscount in Harrogate either."

She had a point. He started to say Harry's title hadn't mattered in Harrogate, but that was exactly what she said about hers. Ben wasn't ready to concede. He didn't know what to say.

She sagged before his eyes. "Please, Ben. The girls are good and sweet; they deserve a chance, and society can be cruel. We need to talk more. Promise me you won't give out some half-baked story before then. You need to meet Patience."

*Talk. She deserves that much.*

"Not a word. Even to your brother," she said.

"I won't lie to Harry," he protested.

"I'm not asking you to lie. Just… Don't tell him more than you have to," she insisted.

"Deceive him? Let him believe half-truths and falsehood?" He glared at her.

She sighed, dropped her gaze to her feet, and nodded. "Put like that, I can see your reluctance. I'll warn Patience."

"Tomorrow," he said.

Her head bobbed up.

"I will call on you at your home tomorrow." He ran a hand through the back of his neck. "At least now I know where to find you. I may bring Harry."

Her lips trembled. Perhaps she meant to smile. This time when he lowered his head to hers, he went slowly, giving her time to pull away, and touched his lips to hers tenderly. Her mouth moved under his, a tentative exploration and he was lost. He deepened the kiss, pulling her closer.

The door opened on two laughing couples, enough to remind them how little privacy they had. She sighed when he pulled away. He offered his arm. "Tomorrow," he whispered leading her back into the ballroom toward her stepmother and his brother, both watching them come with avid eyes. She disappeared soon after.

# CHAPTER 8

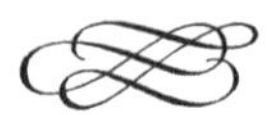

"Are you going to tell me about it?" Harry sat across from Ben in the carriage, his face in shadow.

Ben hoped his was equally obscure. "About what?"

"You danced with the darlings of the hour, three of the most exquisitely beautiful women to make their bows in York in a decade, and they left you unmoved. You are introduced to their older sister and within moments you haul her to the terrace in front of the entire crowd, and come back in with her hair mussed, your cravat askew, and, unless I'm mistaken, her gown slightly off center. Then the lady disappears from the ballroom ten minutes later, and you announce it is time to leave."

"Not correct."

"Which part?"

"I didn't haul her. I merely escorted her as a gentleman would," Ben insisted.

Harry laughed and slammed his head against the back of the seat. "In that case I would hate to see you behave in an ungentlemanly fashion." He sat upright and leaned his elbows on his knees. "What is between you and Lady Dorothea?"

"We met in Harrogate. We became friends."

"You were horrified when the countess introduced you. Both of you. You each looked like you'd seen a ghost. And why did she run off?"

"It isn't mine to tell," Ben said.

"Fair enough. I think. Are you in love with the chit? Because if you are, I—"

"You nothing. My life is my own. And Doro isn't a 'chit.'"

"Doro, is it? I'm right then."

Ben could hear the smirk even if he couldn't see it. "Watch it or I will have to wipe that smug grin off your face."

"What? You seem to have snagged yourself a Seahaven heiress after all."

"She isn't an heiress!" What had Doro told him? They pooled their dowry money for this one Season for the younger girls. Ben didn't care. Harry might, but it wouldn't be his business.

"You still haven't explained her odd behavior. The countess seemed perfectly normal."

"As I said, it isn't mine to tell. I am calling on her tomorrow. Come if you want to get better acquainted."

"God save us. After tonight, half the men in York will be in the Bigglesworth drawing room tomorrow."

Chaos reigned. That is the only way Doro could describe the vases of flowers arriving faster than they could find place for them, or the crowd of avidly curious ladies and, well, avid at least, suitors that occupied every available chair, window sill, and spot on which one may artfully arrange oneself to stand and gape. She feared Ben would call in the middle of this, and he wouldn't be able to see her over the gardenias, much less find space for a quiet talk.

If he hadn't said "tomorrow," she would leave, but then who would maintain the pretense that there was an actual cook in the kitchen? As it was, Mrs. Crewe, their stalwart housekeeper, Maggy, their poor little maid of all work, and the temporary footman, ran their feet off refilling refreshment trays with cakes and biscuits Doro had thought to bake ahead. Thank goodness they had prepared.

In spite of that, Doro had to bake three batches of lemon cakes this morning. Patience normally helped with baking, but she positively glowed with the success of the ball, and it became clear to Doro that her mind was elsewhere this morning.

Another hour passed with no sign of Ben. Doro slipped out of the drawing room to check on the kitchen. A half hour later, she took two sheets from the oven, removed her apron, and walked up the kitchen stairs cautiously, carrying a tray of warm Chelsea buns and hoping things had quieted down. Cousin Rose's house, alas, had no servants' stair.

The kitchen stairs ended in the entranceway behind the main stairs across from the main door. Upstairs, the voices droned on. At the sound of a knock, Doro paused near the top of the kitchen stairs. In her position she would be out of sight. At least she would be if no one looked over the banister of the family stairs on their way up to the drawing room.

She heard the new butler lead yet more gentlemen through the inner hall, hand off their hats to the temporary footman, and direct them upstairs. She took one step down, but stopped when she recognized their voices.

The butler, now at the door to the drawing room, announced the guests. "Viscount Stanbeck and..." He faltered before concluding. "Viscount Stanbeck."

What on earth? Doro took one step up and gazed upward. Ben, half way down on the higher stairs, peering at her over the banister.

"What are you doing?" he asked reasonably. He wore, she noticed, another new suit.

"Baking."

He came down, looking like a man with something on his mind, grinned at her, and grabbed a Chelsea bun.

Before she could react, there was another knock at the door, and the footman went to open it. Doro ran up the remaining steps, plopped the tray on the side table covered with men's hats, grabbed

Ben's hand—the one that wasn't being licked free of the remnants of a sticky bun—and pulled him into the dressing room behind the stairs—not much more than a closet,—and shut the door behind them.

"Doro, what are you doing?" He asked finishing his treat.

"It is madness up there. We would have no chance to talk."

He stood so close their breath melded, and his heat enfolded her. "Are you sure talk is what you want?" he whispered.

Oh, joy of all his dreams! Ben could think of nothing the entire night before but the feel of Doro in his arms. Titles, the Bigglesworths' convoluted plan, Hornebury, the archbishop—none of it mattered. Whatever had to be done, all he cared about is that he and Doro do it together. Now here she was. As close as he might want. Almost. He reached for her.

Doro groaned and tipped her forehead against his shoulder and whispered. "Oh Ben, I am desperately sorry about last night. I came to Holy Cross on Sunday to tell you about the courtesy title, explain our plan, and, and... All of it."

"But Whitcombe waylaid us." He hated the tension in her voice. He pulled her closer with one arm and rubbed circles on her back with the other to comfort, to reassure.

They kept their voices down. What was the point of a good hiding place if you made noise?

Her head popped up. "Those people were so awful, Ben. Please tell me you won't take a position there. Manna and Bread isn't what you want it to be."

"No chance of that. You needn't worry. Dare I hope you have an interest in where I do finally settle?"

"I— Of course I— You—"

He kissed her gently then, moved by her flustered response. Hope soared. "I think you can guess what I'm asking, Doro. I need to know what you think because what matters to me is that you are with me wherever I end up."

This time she kissed him. Thoroughly. Driving everything he planned to tell her right out of his mind. He pulled her closer with one hand and used the other to cup her neck and hold her in place while he deepened their kiss, eliciting gratifying—and arousing—groans from the woman he adored.

When she pulled her head back, he loosened his hold. "Is this a proposal then?" she breathed.

He chuckled. "It isn't the one I planned, nor the one you deserve, but yes."

She kissed him again, a quick salute, but pulled away again when he wanted to explore more thoroughly. "There are some things you should know in that case," she whispered. "We really are poor, especially because there are so many of us. If the girls make good marriages, my wages won't be needed, but there's no dowry for me. I agreed to that."

"I." Kiss. "Don't." Kiss. "Care." He tried to pull her in again, but she put a hand on his chest.

"I know well how to make economies. I don't need servants. But Ben, how will we live?"

He sobered and lowered his hands, taking hold of hers. "I have some choices to make, but I'll always be a clergyman of modest means. I could accept an appointment at Hornebury with a decent stipend and house, and perhaps augmented by an allowance from the Stanbeck estate. Or a less lucrative holding along the coast that serves our unemployed soldiers. Since I will have such a clever wife, I have hopes that we will manage comfortably. Once I marry, I'll receive a bequest from my grandfather as well, one that may enable us to see to our children's future."

She sighed. "Children. We will have children?"

"If you say yes, we will."

"Yes. Oh yes," she breathed and leaned into him, her head on his chest and peace came over him. They would manage. Someday he would tell her about the grieving mother in Oxford and what drove him to Harrogate. But he had done enough penance. Together they would do as much good as they could.

She tipped her head up. and he kissed her again. And again. Her hands came up under his waistcoat, and his began to roam, exploring every curve he could reach.

"Doro, are you in there? Most of the people left and Patience—" Light blinded him momentarily when the door opened revealing a young girl with blond hair and that determined Bigglesworth chin.

"Oh my," she gasped.

Doro straightened but didn't move away. "Mr. Clarke, may I present Miss Emma and Miss Merry Bigglesworth."

He wondered which one was the one running up the stairs shouting, "Mama! Doro is in the coat closet kissing a man."

"It's a good thing we came late," Ben muttered following Doro out of the dressing room.

"You're in the suds now, Doro," Emma said. "You best let me help you straighten before you go up to face the music."

She felt Ben's hands at her back fastening her dress while Emma rearranged the front and pulled it straight.

"Are the guests really gone, Emma?" Doro asked.

"All but some viscount. He said he was waiting for his delinquent brother." Her little sister cast another glance at Ben, now properly dressed. "His words, sir, not mine."

"That sounds like Harry," Ben said.

"Will he be angry?"

"He'll be delighted," Ben said, planting a quick kiss on her nose.

"Mr. Clarke best tuck his shirt all the way in or Mama will take offence," Emma murmured shooting him quick glances.

Doro reached up and straightened Ben's disordered hair. "You're well and truly tied to me now, Ben."

He returned the favor. "I'm thankful for that, the greatest of all possible blessings. Let's go tell them."

They stood in the doorway hand in hand moments later, Emma having skipped in ahead of them, and stared at a room full of people on their feet. Josefina and Barbara kept shooting anxious glances at Patience. Susana looked ready to leap to Doro's defense, and the twins could only be described as hopeful. Doro regretted that Bess wasn't there to hear the news.

Patience, standing next to the viscount who seemed to be struggling to suppress a grin, appeared to anticipate an event. A significant event. They gave her one.

Ben squeezed Doro's hand and gave them what they wanted. "You may congratulate us. Lady Dorothea has made me the happiest of men."

"That means we're going to be married, Merry," Doro said, laughing.

Two hours later, after champagne, excited congratulations, exclamations, and explanations on all sides, Ben and his brother took their leave. Their life in Harrogate, Pilgrim's Rest, the encounter at Holy Cross, had been retold repeatedly, and wedding ideas flowed in and out among the sisters, bouncing back and forth—some discarded, some set aside for later consideration.

Patience kept the sisters upstairs and the viscount waited just outside while Ben kissed her good-bye. Several times.

"Thank you for agreeing to keep our betrothal a secret until the Season is over," she said.

"Of course. We'll be a courting couple and keep Ivy, Iris, and Josefina in the society's focus."

"Only until race week. After the races we'll have our own celebration."

He put his lips next to her ear and whispered, "Oh, we'll have some private celebration well before that." He left her blushing in the entranceway, hesitant to join the others just yet.

# EPILOGUE

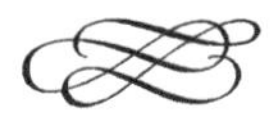

Viscount Stanbeck's prize stallion ran in the third race on the premier day of race week. Doro understood almost nothing of the Sport of Kings, wagers, or horseflesh, but standing at Ben's side in the Viscount's box, and surrounded by those she loved, she knew perfect contentment.

Doro looked fondly over her assembled family. Patience radiated joy. All her efforts and borne fruit well beyond her expectations. The twins bounced with excitement, and the others? Well, it seemed their stay in York had changed all their lives for the better.

As the jockeys nudged their horses into position for the third race, Doro leaned her head against Ben's shoulder, no longer worried what the gossips of York might think. "Was Harry horribly disappointed when you accepted the living at Aberstowe?" she asked.

"He's too happy to see me settled. Aberstowe is a good-sized community, and, they seem eager to have us." The decision made, Ben was at peace. The stipend was better than he had expected, and, lying as it did on the coast above Great Yarmouth, there were former soldiers and seamen among the parishioners. Many of them, unemployed with families to support, needed the services of The Soldier's Benefit Society, which would be Ben's to oversee. Others actively participated in the society's work. "We'll do well there." He smiled down on her.

She glowed up at him. "I am thrilled that we will live by the sea, and the vicarage is lovely—or it will be when I'm finished with it!" Doro became so lost in dreams of the future, she almost missed the race, but shouting brought her back to her surroundings.

The horses pounded to the finish, Harry's horse, coming alas, second. Doro had lost her six shillings. Others seemed less downcast having made more complicated—or wiser—wagers. Harry seemed least downcast of all, which surprised her. In fact, he ordered champagne served in the box. Some of the others trickled in until a sea of Biggleswortbs surrounded them.

The Viscount called for attention and raised his glass. "To Galant Major who had the good sense not to injure himself and spoil my chances of his future progeny."

A hearty laugh greeted that repost.

"And to my brother the Honorable Eustace…"

"Stifle it, Harry," Ben shouted at him.

Harry tried to appear offended, but he spoiled it with a grin, "To the new Vicar of Aberstowe by the Sea. I am pleased to announce—at long last—his betrothal to Lady Dorothea Bigglesworth. To Ben and Doro!"

At that moment Doro believed she was the most abundantly blessed woman in all of Yorkshire. As she met the eye of first one sister and then another, she thought, *Well, one of them anyway.*

THE END

Doro and Ben's life in Harrogate and York is a whole new world for me. This story doesn't connect to any of my other books. If you want to sample my work, try ***A Dangerous Nativity***, which is always free. Or better yet try the first book in one or all of my series:

***The Wayward Son***, book one in my ***Ashmead Heirs***, a series centered on two intertwined families in a small village and on an infamous will left behind by an earl, leaving most of his goods to his illegitimate children. Era: Regency

***The Renegade Wife***, book one in my ***Children of Empire*** series, in which my heroes explore the far reaches of British colonial power in Canada, India, China, and, most recently, Egypt, finding love wherever they go. Characters in this one intertwine with characters in the ***Dangerous*** series. Era: Victorian

***Dangerous Works***, book one in my ***Dangerous*** series, in which four friends, survivors of the Napoleonic wars risk the most dangerous territory of all, the human heart. Era: Regency

# SOCIAL MEDIA FOR CAROLINE WARFIELD

You can learn more about Caroline Warfield at these social media links:

**Website:** http://www.carolinewarfield.com/
**Amazon Author:** http://www.amazon.com/Caroline-Warfield/e/B00N9PZZZS/
**Good Reads:** http://bit.ly/1C5blTm
**Facebook:** https://www.facebook.com/groups/WarfieldFellowTravelers
**Twitter:** https://twitter.com/CaroWarfield
**Email:** warfieldcaro@gmail.com
**Newsletter:** http://www.carolinewarfield.com/newsletter/
**BookBub:** https://www.bookbub.com/authors/caroline-warfield
**You Tube:** https://www.youtube.com/channel/UCycyfKdNnZlueqo8MlgWyWQ

# ABOUT CAROLINE WARFIELD

Award winning author of family centered romance set in the Regency and Victorian eras, Caroline Warfield has been many things: traveler, librarian, poet, raiser of children, bird watcher, Internet and Web services manager, conference speaker, indexer, tech writer, genealogist—even a nun. She reckons she is on at least her third act, happily working in an office surrounded by windows where she lets her characters lead her to adventures in England and the far-flung corners of the British Empire. She nudges them to explore the riskiest territory of all, the human heart, because love is worth the risk.

*Learn more about Caroline at:*
Website: http://www.carolinewarfield.com/
Email: warfieldcaro@gmail.com

# CONCERTO

BY MARY LANCASTER

Concerto

By Mary Lancaster

At the age of twenty seven, Lady Barbara has long accepted her position on the shelf. She is thrilled to put aside her music-teaching in order to help her beautiful young sisters find eligible husbands. But then, a chance encounter with an unconventional and mysterious young piano tuner has her heart in a spin. Can she trust him? And can she save him from the lethal threat hanging over them both?

# CHAPTER 1

There is nothing worse than foul weather for putting one in a foul mood. Having tramped two miles in torrential rain, blown horizontally into her face by the spiteful wind, Barbara hoped grimly that it was worth her while. If the young Hastons had not practiced, they were in for the ear-lashing of their little lifetimes.

Barbara shed her sodden cloak and handed it to the sympathetic maid.

"Oh dear, my lady," the girl said in dismay. "I do hope your bonnet is not ruined by that awful rain."

"That bonnet was born ruined," Barbara admitted, thinking with some longing of the much prettier ones made and secretly sold by her sisters, "but I would appreciate it a little drier when I leave, if you could manage that? And the cloak. Thank you!"

"Of course, my lady!" The maid scurried toward the kitchen with the dripping garments, calling over her shoulder, "The children are waiting for you in t' music room!"

Setting off up the staircase, Barbara eased the damp fabric of her gown off her shoulders and shivered. She hoped there would be a fire in the music room, for the Hastons were subject to bouts of penny-pinching, despite their impressive wealth. If only she could prevail on them to understand they were wasting their money paying for their children's musical education when their pianoforte was so badly out of tune.

At the top of the stairs she paused, her jaw dropping, for she could hear repeated soundings of a distant, perfect E on the pianoforte. Followed by a swift, perfectly in tune octave. She almost smiled, her bad mood clearing like clouds from a summer sky. The Hastons *had* got their instrument tuned!

With lighter steps, she hurried along the gallery to the room beyond the drawing room, and pushed open the door.

There, in front of the piano, she beheld the three Haston children clustered around a strange man in his shirt sleeves. He held a tuning lever in one hand and was shoving out both elbows in an exaggerated kind of way, as if to clear himself a space, while the children laughed up at him in delight.

The man, who seemed amused by the children, sensed Barbara's presence first and lifted his gaze, a smile just dying on his lips and in his sparkling eyes.

He must have been on the wrong side of thirty, and not conventionally handsome, his features being just a little too irregular, as though heedlessly slung together rather than carefully placed. Deep set eyes and dark hollows beneath his cheek bones lent him a slightly shadowed, mysterious look that might have been menacing save for the engaging smile. Even so, as Barbara's sudden jolt of awareness testified, the overall effect was pleasing to the eye.

The children turned to follow his attention and squealed, deserting their new friend to rush upon her in a babble of words so muddled, it was impossible to separate the speakers.

"Lady Babs! Lady Babs! Come and see! Mr. Jack is fixing the piano and it sounds different! Do you like it? Is he doing it right? Is it better?"

Barbara had many younger siblings. And although she was secretly touched by the Haston children's affection and informality, she was also, it seemed, their only source of good manners. So, she looked down her nose and said pleasantly, "Good morning, children."

At once, tugging fingers let go of her gown and her hand. Two hurried curtsies and a bow accompanied a subdued chorus of, "Good morning, Lady Babs."

She then allowed herself to be dragged by the hands toward the piano. She seemed to be magnetically drawn in that direction in any case.

"This is Mr. Jack, the piano tuner," Hetty said, anxious to perform an acceptable introduction.

"He's funny," little Georgiana remarked with a grin.

"And this is Lady Babs who teaches us about music," Hetty finished.

If Mr. Jack found it odd that Lady Anyone was teaching music to a mill owner's children, he gave no sign of it, merely bowing rather than tugging his forelock as she half expected. But then, the tall beaver hat sitting on the piano stool was that of a gentleman, and the coat carelessly discarded beneath of considerably better quality than anything Barbara owned.

"Lady Babs," he said gravely, while his eyes danced, perhaps even seeing the joke that anyone as rigidly polite as herself should allow her wild charges to address her as "Lady Babs".

She inclined her head, murmuring, "Barbara Bigglesworth."

His lips quirked. "What a charming name."

"Is it? I have always considered it rather a mouthful. Is your task likely to be completed within the hour, Mr. Jack?"

"It is. I have only this final octave to finish."

"Then, perhaps the children and I will study the harp for a little while we wait."

"Can't we watch Mr. Jack?" Robert asked, disappointed.

"I suspect he will do better without your supervision."

As she hauled the children off to the harp on the other side of the room, she paused. "Will the harp interfere with your work, Mr. Jack?"

"Not at all," he said cheerfully. "I have become adept at tuning out sounds I don't need."

At that moment, the door opened again, and a footman appeared with a tray. "We thought you'd need it, my lady after your journey in this weather," he said, depositing the tray on the table by the window.

"How very thoughtful," she said gratefully. "Thank you."

In truth, despite the fire burning merrily in the grate, she still felt chilled to the bone, thanks to her damp clothes. Hastily, she set the children to play the scales she had taught them the last time they had looked at the harp some weeks ago, and all but pounced on the tea tray.

"Sugar and cream, Mr. Jack?" she inquired, trying not to hug the tea pot.

"No, just as it comes, if you please."

She managed to pour the tea in a civilized manner and approached him with the cup. He took his head out of the pianoforte to accept it with another of his quick smiles. Attractive laughter lines fanned out around the corners of his eyes.

She was at a loss to place him, for he was nothing like the brisk, respectful tuners who called three times a year at the cottage in Starbrook. His origins eluded her. But then, they were none of her business.

Setting the tea on the little table beside the pianoforte with one hand, he pressed a key with the other and winced. His hands were not those of a working man, but long and slender and sinewy. A musician's hands.

Hastily, she dragged her gaze away and returned to her own teacup, which she cradled in her hands as she made herself listen to the children's scales. At least the harp was more or less in tune, for she had seen to that very recently. While she drank her tea, they each played their scales, and Hetty even remembered the simple tune she had taught them before.

While Barbara listened and taught, she found herself very conscious of the tuner at the other side of the room, deftly and efficiently adjusting the tension on the strings to bring each key back into harmony with its fellows.

He did not interrupt her lesson, but once she happened to glance in his direction and he was watching her while he listened to the final

G. Instead of being embarrassed, he smiled at her and went back to tweaking the string.

A few moments later, he played the keys in the octave in rapid succession, and then ran a finger up the keyboard from bottom to top and back down. A few interesting and dramatic chords sounded, and then he said casually, "Excuse me, ma'am, the pianoforte is all yours."

Barbara rose with relief—the children's fingers were too soft to stand the harp strings for long—and herded her charges up to the piano. There, while Mr. Jack collected his instruments tools into a case, then donned his coat, she began the improvisation game with them. She played a little and let them continue in turn. It was both enjoyable and a useful exercise, and if they had fun, they were more likely to pay attention to the hand corrections and duller theory she also imparted.

Mr. Jack seemed to take an inordinately long time about buttoning his coat. She thought he was listening to the children. His presence disturbed Barbara, but not in an unpleasant way. She had even decided to address him directly, when they were suddenly interrupted by Mrs. Haston darting into the room.

"Ah, sir, you are finished!" she cried in delight. "Lady Barbara, good day, I hope the children are..." She tailed off as she often did, and smiled winningly at the tuner. "I have ordered tea to be sent up. You must partake before you go, while you explain to me simply what I must do to care for this poor instrument."

*Good luck with that,* Barbara thought cynically. She had been trying to persuade Mrs. Haston to have the instrument cleaned, tuned and cared for every three months, or at least twice a year. But she had never remembered until now.

"One of the strings snapped," Hetty whispered to Barbara, since they were on the stool together.

Barbara only nodded, and returned to encouraging a greater lightness of touch on the keys. While she taught and listened to each of her pupils—who had indeed practiced—she was very aware of the low-voiced conversation going on between Mrs. Haston and Mr. Jack. Mrs. Haston was by nature a friendly, fluttery creature, but the third f

—flirty—had never struck Barbara before. She was definitely flirting with the tuner, who said nothing to encourage her. Although he did not nor did he take his leave.

When the lessons had finished, and Barbara had set her pupils their practice for next week, she released them and stood up. But since Mrs. Haston was fishing coins from her purse to pay the tuner, she decided discretion was in order, and sat back down again. Having no intention of leaving herself without payment, she pretended to be blind to his.

While the children joined in the adults' chatter, and coins jingled, Barbara played randomly, moving inevitably into a piece that had been in her head all day. This distracted her entirely, until the silence in the rest of the room finally intruded.

She glanced up and her fingers froze on the keys, for the children, their mother and the tuner were all gazing at her. Neither Mrs. Haston nor the children seemed to know why they were looking, so Barbara could only assume Mr. Jack had begun it. Certainly, there was surprise and unexpected warmth in his eyes.

"Don't stop," he said. "You play it very well."

"Oh no," she muttered, jumping to her feet. "I was only passing time."

"What piece is it?" Mrs. Haston inquired. "I don't believe I have heard it before."

"It's part of a concerto I heard in Harrogate last month," Barbara said. "By a Mr. John Sutton. I was only playing from memory, for I don't have the music."

"Come and have a cup of tea with us before you go," Mrs. Haston begged.

This was part of their ritual. In fact, it was like this with all her pupils. Everyone pretended she was a guest and the money passed so casually across the table or simply dropped into her music case, was never mentioned beyond a brief, "Thank you," from Barbara.

Accordingly, she went through the motions of sitting on the sofa beside her hostess, drinking another cup of tea, and quietly removing the coins in front of her on the table.

"At least the rain has gone off," Robert reported from the window.

"Such a downpour we had earlier," Mrs. Haston remarked, as if Barbara had not walked here through it. "The ground will be so muddy! Shall I send you home in the carriage, Lady Barbara?"

"Oh, no, ma'am, it will be quite pleasant walking now that the rain is off. In fact, I shall be on my way. Thank you for the tea."

"Have you far to go?" Mr. Jack asked.

"No, just to Starbrook," she replied.

"On the Harrogate road?" he said. "I am going that way myself and would be honored to escort you."

She turned her haughtiest gaze upon him. "I do not need an escort."

One eyebrow lifted in apparent surprise. "Neither do I, but I would appreciate the company."

"He is quite the gentleman, I assure you, my lady," Mrs. Haston said seriously. "My husband said so. Though I suppose it would not be quite the thing to shut the pair of you up together in my carriage."

"I prefer to walk, ma'am," Barbara insisted, rising to her feet.

"As do I," Mr. Jack said.

Barbara eyed his coat doubtfully, and then his shiny, mud-free boots. "How did you come from Harrogate, sir?"

"I didn't. I am going there now."

It seemed impolite to inquire further, so she turned back to Mrs. Haston. "I shall come next week if that is agreeable. But if you recall, that will be my last lesson until June."

The children looked flatteringly disappointed.

"Oh dear," Mrs. Haston said anxiously. "I had forgotten. The children miss you so between visits. What am I to do with them for eight whole weeks?"

"You might consider a governess," Barbara suggested. "I would still be happy to supplement their musical education when I return."

"Couldn't you manage to fit us in at all during April and May?" Mrs. Haston wheedled. "Could you really not be spared for an hour or two?"

"No, ma'am, I'm afraid it would be impossible. I shall be too far away. Family commitments." She spoke with finality, for she and her sisters and stepmother had made their decision weeks ago, and all was in hand. She could not walk here from York!

Mrs. Haston, looking disappointed, returned to flirting with Mr. Jack, but her heart no longer seemed to be in it. She was lonely. Her husband had bought this large, country house as a monument to his success and installed his family in it. But he still spent most of his time at his mills, making more money. Barbara doubted that Mr. Jack was the answer to the lady's marital problems, but she had no intention of standing in the way.

Accordingly, she rose and bade them both a civil goodbye. The children trooped downstairs with her, and the maid and the butler himself appeared in the hall, reverently carrying her cloak and bonnet. Both were blessedly dry and warm, and she bestowed a genuinely grateful smile upon the servants, along with her thanks.

With each soaking, the poor old bonnet grew more disreputable, but she could do little about that unless she was prepared to use her best for every day. She looked hastily away from the mirror in the hall, to discover Mr. Jack waiting patiently at the door. She blinked in some surprise, but sailed out of the house in front of him with a curt nod.

As he fell into step beside her, she said abruptly, "Sir, I have no need of your escort. I have walked this way a hundred times. Please use whatever conveyance brought you here."

"I don't think the farmer could oblige me."

"Farmer?" she repeated, distracted.

"He let me ride on his cart from Wetherby. I had missed the stagecoach."

Barbara cast a skeptical eye over his hat, overcoat and polished boots. "You do not have the appearance of a man who journeys by stagecoach, let alone by farmer's cart."

"The people at the inn were very good at looking after my best clothes. The ones in here—" He swung up what looked like a violin case— "have not fared so well. But I would hardly be admitted to the Haston house looking as if I had slept in my clothes."

She eyed the violin case and then met his gaze. She was walking briskly down the drive, he matching his stride to hers with easy, casual grace. "I don't believe you *are* a tuner of pianofortes by trade. Although you appear to be competent."

"Thank you," he said politely. "But you are only half-right. When I was a boy, I worked for a manufacturer of pianofortes by day, and played music by night. I learned enough to get by, and to do favors for friends."

"Mrs. Haston is your friend?"

"If so, a very new one. I met her husband at the inn where I was staying. We appeared to have a mutual acquaintance, and Haston gave me a note of introduction and sent me to his wife."

"But you do not return to Wetherby?"

"I do not. I am amusing myself wandering the countryside of my boyhood, from town to town. Harrogate is next."

"You no longer live in Yorkshire?"

"Not since I was seventeen years old. I ran away from home to become a famous musician, as I imagined."

Barbara felt a tug of empathy. She too had often wished to run away from everything and only play music, not to be famous, but to make her hearers' spirits soar and weep along with her own. But such dreams were not for women, certainly not for earls' daughters. All she had managed was to show off her accomplishment at a few social events during her father's lifetime to largely unappreciative or jealous company.

"Did you succeed?" she asked lightly.

He shrugged. "Up to a point. Eventually. Once I had realized I didn't know as much as I thought I did, that I was not half as good as I imagined. When I had studied, worked and played my way around Europe, dodging the war and various armies as I went, I began to make a modest reputation, especially since the peace. I played in Vienna during the Congress, which helped, earning me invitations all over the world, from Russia to the United States."

"And England? Is that why you are here?"

He was silent. "I don't know."

She regarded him. They had turned out of the drive and struck out over the muddy path that led eventually to Starbrook. He walked like a countryman, loose-limbed and comfortable. Comfortable in his own body, but not, perhaps, in his own mind. There was a brooding look to his brow that seemed at odds with his otherwise sunny nature.

He glanced round and met her gaze. Instantly, his brow smoothed. "What of you, ? Why are you here? Teaching a mill owner's children to play the pianoforte for money?"

"They are not the only children I teach, and it is a respectable position."

"For an earl's daughter?"

She dragged her gaze free but said nothing.

"You said Bigglesworth," he reminded her apologetically. "I think you must be one of Lord Seahaven's daughters."

Her eyes widened. "You knew my father?"

"I would hardly say *knew*. I saw him across a garden once. Does he approve of your independent spirit?"

"He died three years ago," she said flatly. "I don't imagine he cares."

"Then doesn't your brother, or whoever inherited the title?"

"I have no brothers. The title went to a distant cousin who has no intention of wasting his newfound wealth on his predecessor's dependents. We make shift for ourselves."

"We?"

"My stepmother, my sisters and I. We each make use of such talents as God gave us."

"Good for you. I wish I had heard you play more."

Blood seeped into her face. "No, you don't, but I wish I heard you play at all!"

"Why do you like the Sutton concerto?"

She frowned, trying to analyze her feelings about it. "I am not sure. It just seems to make such emotion from such preciseness. I can't explain it. It's clever and yet disdains that about itself… I'm not making any sense, am I?"

"Perfect sense. I'm seeing it in a different light. Which other composers do you admire?"

With this man, there was no casual, shallow small talk. They fell into intense conversation about music, technical, appraising and personal. For Barbara, this was a rare delight, drowning out both her envy and her suspicions of so amiable and itinerant a person. That he was also a dangerously attractive man only added a secret excitement to the joy of talking music to someone who understood. The two and a half miles to Starbrook were eaten up too quickly. She barely noticed the few people who greeted them from the path or the fields.

Mr. Jack helped her over a stile, his grip strong, his manner solicitous without being encroaching. "The land was not so enclosed when I left," he observed, which led down a brief tangent on the evils of enclosure for the majority of country folk and so to reform and revolution, and somehow back to music by the time they came into view of Starbrook.

For Barbara, the parting was too soon, though she would never admit it. She paused at the fork in the path and pointed toward the main road through the village. "That is the road to Harrogate. It's another couple of miles." Wildly, she contemplated inviting him in for yet more tea, until the thought came to her she would appear just like Mrs. Haston. Appalled by that as much as by the prospect of her sisters' questions, she merely held out her hand with resolution. "Goodbye, Mr. Jack."

He took her hand and bowed. "I'd rather say au revoir, for I hope we meet again."

*Harrogate is not so far away...*

She slid her hand free, and turned reluctantly away. She refused to look back until she reached the garden gate, when she risked a glance over her shoulder.

But he was already out of sight.

## CHAPTER 2

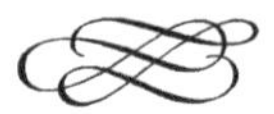

Jack Sutton thought he could probably pass several weeks in York. The bill outside the theatre—an elegant advertisement of his upcoming recital that even bore his likeness—reminded him that he was likely to get more private and lucrative work from that event. At the moment, he was filling in for a violinist in a local orchestra, and on his way to the assembly rooms to fulfill his duty.

Not because he needed to, financially, but because he wanted to keep busy and playing was the best way to distract his brain from the fact that his old home was a bare five miles outside York. And he had been circling ever closer since he had arrived back in England.

If he committed to the series of concerts in London during the Season, he might be able to avoid looking at his old home at all. And yet he had not yet committed to London. Instead, he had come here with the intention of examining the lie of his father's land before he made any decision at all: tie himself to duty and responsibility, or keep his freedom and his dream?

It was a necessary decision, but one he did not want to make. Instead, he swung his violin case high in the air as he strode along the street, and tried to recall each note of the dances he would play this evening. This was dull work and his brain was soon distracted again by the memory of the lady he had met on his way to Harrogate.

Lady Barbara Bigglesworth. She was right. It *was* a mouthful, but one that made him smile. Like the lady herself, it was both haughty and gentle, severe and amusing. And she had the lightest, most sensitive touch on the pianoforte keys. And on the harp strings, but he had noticed her skill most when she had idly played that snippet of his own concerto.

Any praise of his best work still filled him with pride. That she loved it, that it affected her as it did, caused a warmth around his heart that he was at a loss to account for. But he rather liked it, as he liked recalling their conversation, and the unguarded expressions on her beautiful face beneath the execrable old bonnet.

He had hoped he might run into her again in Harrogate. Twice, he had almost set out from there to Starbrook, in the hope of encountering her by accident, or even calling at her cottage. But in truth, he did not need the complication. And so he had circled on to York without seeing her again. In the next couple of days, he really had to go home. Just to look.

The orchestra was already setting up in the minstrel's gallery when he arrived at the assembly rooms. Many of them knew his name. Some were inclined to be stiff, though they had relaxed when he had given himself no airs and simply played, following the leader as he should. As a result, most greeted him this evening with cheerful friendliness as he unpacked his instrument and took his place among them.

Everything was in tune by the time the guests began to arrive, all expensively dressed, and many dripping with jewels. A few gentlemen appeared in military uniform, but most wore formal black silk knee breeches, black coats and snowy white cravats, a few sporting jeweled pins and sleeve buttons, or an outrageously bright waistcoat. The ladies supplied a more welcome wave of color, like butterflies among the bluebottles. Middle aged chaperones in exotic turbans accompanied hopeful young girls, escorted, inevitably by at least one bluebottle.

Except for the ladies entering now. Five beautiful young maidens walked into the room in a group, heads held high, and everyone else turned to gawp with varying degrees of blatancy. Strangers in town then, but very well-dressed strangers, their gowns flowing and tasteful, their jewelry modest. Jack could see no chaperone with them until the master of ceremonies approached them with three eager young bluebottles, and he guessed that two of the women must be young matrons. Then one of the two glanced up toward the orchestra and his heart lurched, for she looked very much like Lady Barbara Bigglesworth, her glossy chestnut hair fashionably but simply dressed, her gown a stunning pale green silk that emphasized her willowy figure to perfection. He could almost imagine she had been dressed with love and knew an urge to undress her in a similar manner.

But this was a far cry from the poverty-stricken lady in the worn cambric gown, rain still trickling down her cheek from her damp hair. No downtrodden, impoverished noblewoman to whom life had been unkind, but a confident lady of the ton, beautiful, even dazzling.

She had not seen him, but he could not take his eyes off her—until he realized the orchestra had begun their introduction to the first dance, and hastened to join in.

While the three youngest girls danced, Lady Barbara and her companion, who looked even younger than she, sat among the dowagers and wallflowers, which seemed utterly ridiculous. Lady Babs was surely no older than five or six and twenty. The younger girls who were dancing must be her sisters. Could the lady beside her be the stepmother she had mentioned?

Intrigued, he watched them circulate around the edges of the dance floor, pausing occasionally to talk to people they knew and then passing on to collect glasses of wine. Lady Barbara moved here with more grace than he recalled from the wet and frozen young woman who had hugged her teacup for warmth at Mrs. Haston's, and trudged home along muddy paths and fields, her face lit by joy and enthusiasm as she talked about music.

He had only ever encountered such obsession before among professional musicians. But none of the female singers or instrumentalists he knew had ever been so desperate to talk. Lady Barbara was deprived of musical company, for which genteel teaching was a poor substitute. The knowledge prevented him from being too much of a coxcomb over her clear fascination with his own conversation.

Barbara and her companion resumed their seats before the younger girls returned from their dancing. The young men to whom they had been introduced during their perambulation quickly closed in to be introduced in their turn to the youngest ladies.

So, this was all for the pretty youngsters. To catch them decent husbands.

*Good luck in York,* he thought cynically. They were more likely to meet merchants and well-off tradesman than landed gentlemen of birth. They would be better off in London for the Season. But perhaps they were en route to London. Had Lady Babs not mentioned something about family commitments to Mrs. Haston? Perhaps York was merely practice.

As they struck up the second country dance, the violin next to Jack grated on his nerves, for it had moved very slightly out of tune. Inevitably, Lady Barbara glanced up frowning, directly at the minstrels' gallery. Somehow, he kept playing without breathing as her gaze skimmed right toward him, then paused on his face.

Her eyes widened, and then, quite without warning, she smiled.

Jack was used to women smiling at him. He encouraged it, in fact, for he thoroughly enjoyed feminine smiles, but he could not recall ever being quite so dazzled as he was now. Perhaps it was the rarity, the way it dissipated the last of her natural severity. Perhaps the openness of her acknowledgment thrilled him. Or perhaps, it was simply she who bestowed the smile who delighted. He had never met anyone like her before.

He felt his lips, his eyes responding instinctively. But she was a lady, an earl's daughter, a guest at the ball who should not even have seen him, let alone acknowledged him, so he snapped his attention back to his bow.

No one would know his idiot heart was singing.

~

Seeing Mr. Jack in the orchestra should not have amazed her—he was a musician after all—and yet it took Barbara completely by surprise. Only when she had betrayed her sheer pleasure in the discovery did the impropriety strike her. At the same time as he looked away, she forced her gaze downward and pretended she was smiling approval at Josefina, who was dancing gracefully down the set.

The last thing she wanted in this desperate attempt to launch her beautiful young sisters into society, was to cause talk on her own account. One did not smile at the orchestra. One did not even applaud them, which always seemed unfair considering there would be no dancing without them.

Keeping the faint smile on her lips, which was surprisingly easy, she turned her attention back to Patience and the gentleman who had approached her. Not for the first time, she acknowledged that, while they had undertaken this enterprise primarily for Josefina and the twins, it was hardly beyond the bounds of possibility for Patience to find happiness in a second marriage. Nor Doro, if only they could extract her from the house.

As for herself, seven-and-twenty was way beyond marriageable age, and she had long resigned herself to being on the shelf. But the pleasure of music and musical conversation was surely not beyond her reach, and with the younger ones suitably established, surely she would finally find the freedom to travel, to learn, to play...

That was in the future. The present was suddenly intensely exciting, because one amiable and talented man was present in the musicians' gallery. Although surely playing in a small provincial orchestra was a bit of a come down for a man who had found fame in Vienna and been invited to play all over Europe? Had he been trying to impress her by exaggerating?

*Why would anyone try to impress me? I am a penniless spinster without influence.*

No, she was the Earl of Seahaven's daughter, chaperone to her lovely young sisters whose interest any respectable gentleman might consider himself fortunate to engage.

Although she did not glance again toward the gallery, her sense of excitement stayed with her as she and Patience made their way to the supper room. Josefina and the twins had partners to escort them, but Barbara had no intention of leaving them there without supervision. Inevitably, in the crush, she and Patience were separated, and she lost sight of the twins—whether by accident or design on their part.

Having little appetite, she ploughed a watchful furrow along the length of the buffet table and was about to scour the rest of the room when she came face to face with Mr. Jack.

He smiled at her with what seemed genuine pleasure and her heart gave a funny little skip.

*Oh, please, no, Barbara Bigglesworth, not at your age!*

"Lady Babs," he said, managing to bow despite the plate piled high in one hand and the bottle of wine in the other. "Well met!" He leaned a fraction nearer, adding in a much lower voice, "Don't give me away, will you? It's something in the way of a wager. And also, no one troubles to feed the orchestra."

Whether or not he was stealing food for the orchestra, he seemed as perfectly at home here as in tuning the Hastons' pianoforte, or tramping through muddy fields to Harrogate. He wore well-fitting evening clothes, too, that made him indistinguishable from the male guests.

"Your secret is safe with me," she assured him, deciding to be amused.

"But you have no plate," he noticed.

"I am not hungry."

"Then you must save it for later. Come, I'll force you a path so you may help yourself."

"No, truly there is no need. I am more concerned with the whereabouts of my sisters."

"Don't you trust them?" he asked in surprise.

"I trust them to get into mischief." Particularly the twins.

"In this place, they would be fortunate," he said wryly. For a second, he seemed to search her face, then he said, "Follow me."

Without further thought, she did, and breathed a massive sigh of relief when they emerged from the supper room into the large, airy, and blessedly empty hallway.

"You don't like crowds," he observed, walking beside her toward the ballroom.

She flushed slightly. "Let us say rather that I have grown unused to them. But don't let me keep you from your supper. Or your wager."

He raised the plate slightly. "You could share, if you like."

"And be responsible for a hungry orchestra? I would never live down the shame."

"We can't have them getting fatter either." He paused before they reached the main ballroom doorway, at a discreet, single door that was slightly ajar. He opened it with his foot to reveal a lit staircase going up, presumably, to the musicians' gallery. "I insist you eat something. One item of your choice."

His tone, like his expression, was half-teasing, and yet there was a trace of concern there, too. The novelty of that made her hesitate when she should have walked away. And then the sound of male voices and guffawing came from the direction of the ballroom, drawing nearer, and without further thought, Barbara stepped inside the door.

As if this was perfectly normal behavior, Mr. Jack followed her, set his burdens down on two different steps, and took from his pocket a large, white handkerchief which he spread on one of the steps and gestured to invitingly, like a king offering a throne to his queen.

Barbara's lips twitched. She climbed the three steps up and sat, while he casually arranged the door to be ajar, but to hide her from view. Then he sat on the step below and offered her the plate.

"I have no cutlery," he said apologetically.

"No matter. I have fingers and a handkerchief of my own," She took a little savory pastry from the edge of the plate and regarded him. "You have joined the orchestra on a permanent basis? I imagined your favored instrument was the pianoforte."

"It is, as a rule, though I've never met an instrument I didn't like. I'm only covering here for a sick violinist. A case of influenza, I understand." He bit into a chicken leg. "What of you? For a teacher so eager to be paid..." He waved the chicken leg in the direction of her finery.

"Why do you think I was so eager to be paid?" she retorted. "All is not what it seems. Suffice it to say that my whole family is doing what it can."

"Yet you do not dance."

She blinked. "Sir, I am seven and twenty. I help my stepmother chaperone my lively sisters. They are the ones here to dance."

"Well, I would rather dance with you. Not that I can in present circumstances, but trust me, I am not the only man who feels that way."

Ignoring the color seeping into her face, she met his gaze. "Are you being kind, Mr. Jack? I assure you, there is no need. How long are you fixed in York?"

"Until the violinist is back on his feet, I suppose." He shifted restlessly. "But perhaps I will go home."

"You still have not been?"

"I still have not even spoken to those I need to."

"Why not?"

He hesitated, then: "Perhaps I am reluctant to give up my freedom."

"Talking does not deprive one of freedom," she pointed out, when she had swallowed the last of her pastry. "You have nothing to lose except peace of mind. Get it over with, and you will still have your freedom at the very least."

"At the very least," he repeated in an odd voice. His gaze was fixed unblinkingly on hers. A smile began to form in his eyes, crinkling the laughter lines, curving his lips, and her heart gave another of its foolish flutters.

Appalled at herself, she stood up. He immediately stood, too, and suddenly he was close enough for her to smell him, all warm, clean citrus and spice and male. Something surged between them, a flash of awareness, perhaps, certainly attraction on her part.

"I must get back to pursuit of my sisters," she said, hoping she did not sound as breathless as she felt. "Thank you for the gallant rescue."

It would have been easy for him to stand in her way. Half of her even wanted him to, but despite the warmth of his eyes, he moved aside at once, even pulled the door open for her and bowed. For an instant, as she brushed past, she thought he would say something more, but he just smiled and then she was out the door.

Only then did she see the gentleman lounging to one side of it, a glass of brandy in his hand. He glanced up from examining his glass, and Barbara felt a twinge of unease. She had been caught emerging from a place she had no business being. And God knew how society loved to talk.

But he merely bowed. She inclined her head distantly and sailed on as though she had every right to have been haunting the steps to the musician's gallery. She went immediately to the ballroom, in the hope of finding her sisters there, but the man with the brandy fell into step beside her.

"Forgive me. We have not been introduced, but I am Lord Allbury. I wish only to be sure that Lord Seahaven's daughter has not been… inconvenienced by some scoundrel?"

She regarded him. He did seem vaguely familiar, a well-dressed gentleman of about her own age, with neat, dark brown hair and elegantly tied cravat. And what appeared to be genuine concern in his expression.

She allowed amusement into her voice. "I assure you, sir, I never allow myself to be inconvenienced! I merely exchanged a few words with an old musical acquaintance. But you appear to know me, sir. Were you acquainted with my father?"

"I remember him calling on my uncle, the late Lord Allbury. I expect we have met in the dim and distant past, so I hope you don't find me presumptuous."

"Not in the least," Barbara assured him, distracted by the sight of the twins tripping past her into the ballroom on the arms of military gentlemen. Iris spared her a challenging grin over her shoulder.

"Perhaps I may fetch you a glass of wine?" Lord Allbury suggested.

She glanced at him once more. Lord Allbury. A baron, if she recalled, with a decent estate not far from York. Perhaps he would be a reasonable match for Josefina. Once she had examined him more closely, of course.

So she chose to smile. "Thank you, that would be kind."

## CHAPTER 3

Jack Sutton found his way to the solicitor's office the following day, so early that he accompanied Mr. Galton himself into the office.

A young clerk leapt to his feet, relieving both the solicitor and the client of their hats and overcoats. The elderly solicitor barked a general good morning and strode off to an inner office, leaving Jack alone with the clerk.

"May I help you, sir?" the clerk inquired.

"Yes, I hope so. I've come to see Mr. Galton. Was that him, by any chance?"

"Indeed yes, sir. Do you have an appointment?"

"No. I came early in the hope I wouldn't need one." He took a card from his pocket. It bore his name, but no address, since he had none. "My name is John Sutton. I would be grateful if you relayed that to Mr. Galton as soon as possible."

The clerk bowed and took the card. "Of course, sir, but Mr. Galton is very busy. I'm not sure he will have the time right now..."

"Ask," Jack suggested, lounging into a chair and smiling.

The clerk closed his mouth and trotted off to the office within.

Mr. Galton himself bolted out only seconds later, and Jack rose lazily to his feet.

"My dear sir!" Mr. Galton exclaimed, thrusting out his hand, although the shrewd old eyes examined him thoroughly from head to toe. "What a delightful surprise! I confess I did not know you as we came in."

"How could you? We have not met in fifteen years, and I did not know you either. You have grown whiskers."

Mr. Galton beamed and stroked the white, hairy sideburns that crossed his cheeks. "Distinguished, don't you think?"

"Utterly," Jack said gravely, and the old lawyer laughed.

"Come in, come in and tell me what you have been doing these dozen years and more. Tea, if you please, Smithers. What a pity it's too early for brandy…"

Mr. Galton might have been getting on in years, but he was as shrewd as ever. Beneath the bonhomie and reminiscing that followed, he was clearly testing Jack, examining his appearance and speech and memory. In the end, Jack took letters from his pocket and silently placed them on the desk between them.

The solicitor drew them nearer, and read them, though Jack had the impression he had already made his determination without them. At last, he raised his eyes to Jack's face.

"John Sutton, eldest surviving son and heir of Lord Allbury. I am thrilled to see you home, sir. Thrilled. I just wish it was not in the sad circumstances of your brother's and your father's deaths."

"I have to thank you for informing me of these events," Jack said, keeping his tone flat. "It can't have been easy to find me."

"You could have come home as easily as written."

"I wrote to my father after Arthur… He did not reply."

"He was a stubborn man. But his quarrel does not prevent you from being heir to the lands and title. He made no effort to exclude you from any of it. You inherit everything, Lord Allbury. I think we may accept that as his late lordship's forgiveness."

"Or his determination not to break up the estate," Jack said cynically. He shifted in his seat. "Look, no one knows I am here. You and I are the only people who realize Allbury's son is still alive. I haven't yet decided that I will stay. If I am presumed dead, who inherits?"

"Joseph Sutton, your cousin."

"Joe? I barely knew him. What happened to Harry?"

"Fever," Galton said succinctly.

"Damn. I liked Harry." He shrugged impatiently, as though to throw off inconvenient memories. "What is Joe like?"

"Ambitious. Cuts a bit of a dash in London, I understand."

"Does he, by God? And the estate?"

"In reasonable condition, though it would benefit from some modernization. Go and look. But what do you mean, you haven't yet decided? It is not up to you. You *are* Lord Allbury and the land, properties, and monies pertaining are yours."

"Meaning…that if I wished it, you would not keep quiet about having seen me? And if I refused my responsibilities, you'd still make poor Joe wait seven years or whatever of my silence to inherit?"

"Which would hardly be fair to the land, tenants, servants, or even Mr. Joseph Sutton. What's more, it would not be fair to you."

"I have a life, Mr. Galton. I have a career in music and even some fame. Enough to be wealthy in my own right. I don't need my father's estate."

"And if your father's estate needs you?"

Jack regarded him with rueful amusement. "A low blow, Mr. Galton."

Galton drained the last of his tea and sat back. "You knew, I think, that I would say more or less what I have. And yet, you came. Why?"

"A good question." And one he had no intention of answering. One he wasn't sure he *could* answer, except the reasoning had something to do with Barbara Bigglesworth. "Tell me, were you acquainted with the old Earl of Seahaven?"

"We ran up against each other occasionally. Why?"

"I understand he did not provide for his daughters."

Galton shrugged. "Spent their portions and their mothers' by all accounts. But I never acted for him, so I could not say. The title has gone to some cousin who has granted the daughters as little as he could get away with. But funnily enough, I understand they are in York for the Season, so perhaps their allowance is not as little as rumor declares."

"Do you know where they are staying?"

"At Lady St. Aubyn's house, I believe. Why?"

"I had something I meant to send. Who is living at Allbury Court?"

"Only stewards and servants. Mr. Joseph offered to move in, but the executors of the estate forbade it until we had heard from you, or gave up the notion of ever hearing from you."

"I haven't made your life easier," Jack observed. "Sorry. I have grown selfish over the years. Perhaps I always was."

"But your music, I understand, gives much pleasure to many."

It had always been his excuse for following his dreams rather than his duty. Now, it rang hollow in his ears.

Barbara returned from the market to a whirlwind of invitations and plans flung at her from all sides. The twins were desperate to attend al fresco parties, concerts, parties of all kinds. Patience wanted to know about the extra costs of decorating the Smithson Assembly Rooms for their ball, and Dorothea was eager to share her ideas for the supper menu which she assured everyone would be both sumptuous and inexpensive. Through it all, the children jumped up and down, trying to tell her about their own outing and something clever that little Jane had said.

Malcolm, the rather handsome butler who had come with the house, cast her a commiserating glance, took her bags from her and nodded to the hall table where a parcel stood.

"It looks like a book," she observed through the chaos. "Is it not for Bess?"

"No, it definitely says Lady *Barbara* Biggleswolth," Josefina confirmed.

"It was delivered by hand, my lady," Malcolm contributed. "Not half an hour ago."

Leaving her bags to the butler, Barbara fought her way upstairs to the drawing room to open her parcel. Not a book of the Bess variety, but a bound set of music.

*Piano Concerto by John Sutton.*

Pleasure seemed to spread inward from her fingertips. She opened the music and found the title page signed by the composer himself.

"Where did you find it?" Dorothea asked.

"I didn't. It appears to be a gift."

"From whom?" Patience demanded.

Barbara looked inside the wrapping, but there was no note or card. She didn't need one. She knew it was from Mr. Jack.

"Well, that will be your afternoon taken care of," Patience said humorously. "I'm sure I can prevail on Doro to accompany us on our calls."

"Have the blue afternoon dress that I wore yesterday," Barbara offered, already on her way to the pianoforte. "It will look better on you, and Susana sewed on a lovely new lace trim last night."

Inevitably time flew as Barbara taught herself to play the concerto —or at least the pianoforte parts. She had to imagine the orchestra for now.

So absorbed was she that she barely noticed when the children went off to play in the garden, and she was actually disoriented when Malcolm the butler interrupted her.

"My lady, Lord Allbury has called. Are you at home?"

Barbara blinked and glanced around her. "Well, no, I think you must deny me for there is no one else here." Besides, his lordship should at least have sent up his card with the butler.

"Lady Bess is in the library. I can ask her to join you."

*Lady Bess* was rather too informal for a butler. Barbara could only suppose it a slip of the tongue since he was used to hearing the entire family call her Bess.

"Um, yes, ask Lady Elizabeth to join us. If she is suitably attired," she added hastily, for when Bess got involved in her studies, she was very likely to forget the standards they had all agreed to keep up while in York.

She was sure the butler's lips twitched as he departed. He really was an odd butler, though it was kind of Cousin Rose to leave him with them.

"And tea, if you please, Malcolm," she called after him.

A few minutes later, Malcolm announced, "Lord Allbury, my lady." His tone was inoffensive, but she could have sworn something close to a glare was aimed at his lordship.

"My lord, how kind of you to call," Barbara said. "You find us quite informal this afternoon, since most of my sisters are out, apart from... Ah, here she is. Bess, is Lord Allbury known to you? Sir, my sister, Lady Elizabeth Bigglesworth."

Bess blinked rapidly, as though adjusting to matters not on the printed page, and greeted Lord Allbury with perfect courtesy. Barbara relaxed slightly, for once Bess chose to take charge, she was the perfect hostess.

And Lord Allbury appeared to be the perfect guest, making pleasant small talk, discussing the history of York with Bess and the Season's social whirl with Barbara.

"Of course, it is nothing like London at this time of year," he said, "but for those wishing for a slightly quieter Season, as I presume you ladies do, it is perfect."

"Then you have been in York for the Season before?" Barbara asked politely.

"Actually, no. I am usually in London."

"What brings you north?" Bess asked pleasantly, passing him a cup of tea. "The races, perhaps?"

"No, actually, though I shall probably attend and have a flutter! No, I recently inherited some property nearby so I've come up to make sure everything is properly in hand."

Barbara was about to make some civil response, when Mr. Jack strolled into the room.

Barbara jumped to her feet, thanks for the concerto about to spill out of her unguarded mouth.

But he took the wind out of her sails, speaking first as he bowed gracefully to the room in general. "Forgive the intrusion, my lady. Your butler seemed harassed, so I said I would announce myself. Ah, perhaps this explains the harassment?"

The younger children came bolting past him into the room. "Babs, Babs, the cat has had kittens and they're like little insects and can't open their eyes. Come and see!"

"Manners, little brutes!" Barbara said severely, causing them to duck into bows and curtsies, except for little Jane, who gazed up in awe at Mr. Jack. Apparently impressed, she grinned. "Bess and I will come and see the kittens in just a little," Barbara said hastily. "Perhaps you should go back and watch them? Take Nurse."

Bess rose to her feet. "No, I'll go now and make sure all is well, if you will excuse me, gentlemen?"

As the children dragged her off, Bess deliberately left the door open.

Barbara glanced from Lord Allbury to Mr. Jack, feeling unaccountably nervous, for they seemed to be eyeing each other with great suspicion. Allbury, especially seemed tense.

"Do you know each other?" Barbara asked. "Lord Allbury—"

"Lord Allbury?" Mr. Jack repeated, apparently amused. "A little premature, surely?"

"Hardly," Allbury snapped. "My cousin is dead."

"How did he die?" Mr. Jack asked with apparent fascination.

"How should I know? But since he spent the entire French wars on the continent, I imagine someone or other blew him to pieces."

"You'll be disappointed. You should speak to Mr. Galton of Galton and Soames in—"

"I have spoken to him and as I told him, anyone pretending to be my cousin is an imposter! I'll bid you good day, Lady Barbara. Please pass on my apologies to Lady Elizabeth for not taking my leave in person."

And Lord Allbury bowed stiffly and stalked out of the room, leaving Barbara to stare after him.

"What on earth just happened? Is he not Lord Allbury? And how do you know?"

He dragged his gaze from Allbury's retreating back to glance at her with a hint of uncertainty. "Didn't you receive the music?"

"Oh, yes, I did!" Distracted, she approached him with her face no doubt wreathed in smiles, Allbury's odd behavior instantly forgotten. "Thank you so much. I have wanted it so badly. I was just at the end of the first movement and was wishing for an orchestra to play it with!"

"I can't supply an orchestra, but if you have any other instrument to hand I can provide some accompaniment, at least."

Delighted, Barbara darted behind the curtain where she had hidden the violin from Patience's eagle eye, opened the case and thrust the instrument at him. Then she sat expectantly at the piano. She sounded an A, and impatiently waited for him to adjust the strings.

There followed one of the most wonderful hours of her life. He played the violin better than anyone else she had ever heard, and yet he complemented her playing rather than stealing the limelight. Until she stumbled over part of the piano solo, and he suggested they swap places. If his violin playing impressed, his performance on the pianoforte filled her with awe. The solo swept her away, more even than at the concert she had heard in Harrogate, and she missed her cue to join in.

He laughed, causing her to, also, and when he repeated the phrase, she came in at the right place. Her whole being sang because she had never played with anyone half so good, or half so understanding of the music, or of her. She wanted to weep, and to shout.

Fortunately, before she was too tempted to do either, her other sisters returned, interrupting to make a fuss of the music and of Mr. Jack, whom she never quite had the chance to properly introduce. He accepted it all in his amiable, elegant style, even when the children and Bess returned somewhat belatedly.

Only when he had left, did all her sisters turn on her with similar expressions.

"He is the best musician I have ever played with," Barbara said with dignity.

"He looks familiar," Ivy said, frowning. "Where have we met him before?"

"I can't imagine."

Jack strode away from the Bigglesworth town house, paying no attention to direction and precious little to traffic. He just knew he could not be still, because he had played music with her, *his* music, and it had felt wonderful. She had not been overawed that he was Sutton. In fact, she had taken it in her stride, never even mentioned it. And his time with her blotted out the sheer impertinence of young cousin Joe using the title.

Joseph Sutton was making a fool of himself. And Jack was beginning to feel his way forward at last. He had always seen his life as a choice: music or home; music or duty; music or his father; music or the title and responsibility of Baron Allbury.

But Barbara, whom he scarcely yet knew, seemed to be widening these narrow choices, where music had always won, even with a certain amount of pain and grief and the resurgence of old resentments. Perhaps it had never been so black and white a choice. But now, just because Barbara played with him—a young lady with little training or experience compared to his—and held her own during even the difficult parts, his mind seemed to be expanding, including all sorts of possibilities. Possibilities that were highly presumptuous, delicious and happy.

Without noticing, he seemed to have walked into a crowd of people on Castlegate. He edged through them, meaning to cross to the other, quieter side. A thundering of hooves and wheels reached him, along with cries of "Runaway!" and "Watch out! Stand back!"

A coach and four horses charged down the road at breakneck

speed, causing everyone to press back closer to the buildings. There seemed no sign of a coachman and Jack had an instant to hope there were no poor souls inside the carriage either, for in their maddened state, the horses seemed doomed to damage themselves and wreck the coach.

And then, giving him no time to react, a hard shove in the small of his back sent Jack stumbling into their path.

# CHAPTER 4

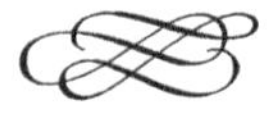

"Lady Babs!"

Despite the over-familiar mode of address—and on a public street where anyone might have heard—pleasure flooded Barbara. She had not seen Mr. Jack for two days and stupidly, it had felt like eternity, even with all the distractions of planning and visits and parties.

She had devoted the morning to her youngest sisters, who had been somewhat neglected in the current rush to see the older girls established. But it didn't take their cries of "Mr. Jack!" for her to realize who hailed her. She would have known his voice anywhere.

Suddenly and foolishly breathless, like a schoolroom miss presented with the reality of her first crush, Barbara turned to greet Mr. Jack, who had just emerged from the stage door of the Theatre Royal.

As elegant as ever, he swept off his hat and bowed, smiling. "Ladies. What a pleasure to run into you! How do you do?"

"We are very well," Barbara managed calmly. "On our way back to the house, since we are at home this afternoon."

His lips parted, drawing her gaze, but if he had meant to ask permission to call during the "at home," he clearly thought better of it.

His lips closed again. Perhaps he thought it presumptuous in a mere musician, and perhaps he was right.

"Do you attend tomorrow's al fresco party by any chance?" he asked.

"Yes, I shall accompany my sisters. I did not know there would be musicians."

He smiled at that, but before he could respond, Emma exclaimed, "Look! It's you, Mr. Jack!"

Barbara turned and followed Emma's pointing finger. A bill outside the main door of the theatre advertised a pianoforte recital next week by none other than John Sutton. A surge of excitement swept through her, but before she could even ask Mr. Jack if he had known about this, her gaze dropped beneath the announcement. To a printed likeness of the composer's face.

Barbara knew her jaw was dropping, her mouth gaping, but it seemed there was nothing she could do about it. And with the knowledge came a sweep of humiliation and hurt and anger.

"You are John Sutton," she uttered flatly. "How could you not have told me? How could you have lied and let me...?" Her breath caught raggedly and she swallowed back the words that only made it worse. "Goodbye." She swung abruptly away from him, seizing Jane by the hand. "Come along."

She could not prevent the children calling startled goodbyes to him as they trotted after her. Nor could she prevent the tears clogging her throat, or the unbearable realization.

*I am a silly, silly old spinster.*

Ruefully, Jack watched Lady Barbara walk away from him. It seemed he should have been more direct. Not that he had given up. In fact, his determination was, if anything, even greater, for he hated to see her hurt. But his life was increasingly complicated.

It had nearly ended the other day when he had stumbled in front of the runaway horses. Fortunately, a complete stranger had hauled him back by the arm, for he could not have stopped his own momentum alone. The speed with which his life could have changed, or even ended, was not lost on him. Nor was the memory of the push that had sent him flying into the road. It could have been someone turning suddenly, catching him by accident, for everyone in the watching crowd had seemed shocked. But it had *felt* deliberate. And a man's back, hurrying away from the scene, had looked oddly familiar to him.

And now Barbara thought he had lied to her. She had taken the Concerto music as a gift, not as a calling card. She was so quick of mind, he had been sure she would grasp his identity from his signed music.

As he reluctantly turned his feet in the direction of his rented rooms, he thought about calling on her during the Bigglesworth ladies "at home". But it would be too public, and she would still be too angry. Tomorrow, he thought, at the al fresco party, he would find a way to be private and explain everything.

If she still wanted to hear.

For now, he should practice. For he did his best thinking while playing the piano. And, besides, there was a surge of music in his head, entirely related to the strength and tragic turbulence of Lady Barbara's eyes, that he needed to write down.

His moment came during the treasure hunt. Whoever had come up with such an idea was blessed, in Jack's book. Despite the chill of the spring day, he and two companions had played elegant chamber music outdoors during the luxurious al fresco repast, and he had found it difficult to take his eyes off Barbara.

Still playing the spinster chaperone, she had sat in the background, watching her younger sisters in a distracted kind of way. He knew she was aware of him only because she never glanced at the trio of musicians, even when Alf blundered.

After the meal, he let the other two drive back to town without him. Leaving his violin with the baskets, while everyone but the servants set off on the treasure hunt, he strolled after them in search of Barbara.

He found one of her sisters, flirting outrageously with a young army officer while they turned over stones and looked behind trees for whatever the blasted treasure was. From instinct, Jack moved off the beaten paths, where the clues were, apparently, hidden, for he had the feeling Barbara would not be playing.

He had hurt her, which was everything. A triumph that he could, a shame that he did, a responsibility that he never should again. He wanted her to be happy. He wanted to *make* her happy, to smooth the worry from her brow and see her bloom in contentment and love of him. There was passion in her he longed to taste.

*Insane. We hardly know each other.* And yet it was an ambition, a challenge, with more riding upon it than anything he had ever considered before.

He came upon her at last by a pond, her back to him. But he recognized the graceful curve of her nape, her straight, no-nonsense posture, even before the elegant little hat and bright shawl he had noticed earlier.

He hesitated, struck by an uncharacteristic nervousness. If she truly did not want to see him, then he would have to leave her be and his dreams would be in ashes.

But he had never been one to give up easily. Or even at all. Nor had he ever been a coward, in any matter save coming home, and that was entirely different. So, he walked toward her, making no effort to hide his presence.

Though she must have heard his approach, she did not turn, which may have been meant as a signal to all to leave her alone. But she was the member of a party and she should not be left alone without her direct command.

"Mr. Sutton," she said when he was still a foot away. Still, she had not turned.

"Lady Barbara." Without invitation, he sat down beside her.

"Not Lady Babs," she observed.

"I would need to know we were still friends for that."

"Were we ever friends, Mr. Sutton?"

"I believe so." He cast a first glance at her. But her face, calmly beautiful, gave nothing away. "I have played with fine musicians all over the world—even the great maestro Beethoven on one memorable occasion—but nothing ever gave me such pleasure as playing with you."

"Is that friendship?" she wondered distantly.

"Oh, I think so. You have talent, sensitivity and passion, but between ourselves, you do not have the skill of Beethoven. Friendship supplied the truest pleasure, a growing closeness, I like to think. Tell me I am wrong, by all means."

She didn't. But then, she didn't tell him anything at all, merely continued to gaze across the pond. Some small creature jumped, glinting in the spring sunshine, and the water plopped.

"I have been blowing in the wind," he said, "trying not to go home. In Wetherby, Haston thought my surname was Jack because that was what our mutual acquaintance called me. I let myself be blown to Mrs. Haston, but I didn't particularly want it to be known that John Sutton was reduced to tuning pianos for a few shillings. In fact, I wasn't sure I wanted anyone to know John Sutton was back in Yorkshire."

"Even friends?" she asked politely.

"By the time I came to York, I was growing more sensible, edging toward what I knew I should do. Names never came up, talking to you. I tried to tell you by sending you the concerto music, newly signed, but I was being too subtle."

"Perhaps my reaction was extreme. Our acquaintance is short, but I had never thought of you as the sort of man who would make fun of an admirer."

"Barbara." From sheer instinct, he reached across and took her hand. "That you admired my music was an honor. I loved that you played with me so naturally."

"I wouldn't have if I had worked out you were John Sutton."

"That would have been my loss."

"And mine," she said so quietly that he almost didn't hear. It brought a quick smile to his lips and hope to his heart. Nor did she draw her hand away. His heart was beating like a schoolboy's when confronted with the object of his obsession.

He stroked his thumb once down the side of her palm and took a deep breath. "There is more. The reason I have been so unwilling to go home is that I am my father's heir and I was reluctant to give up my music, just when my success was growing, in order to take up my inheritance."

At that, she finally turned her head and looked him in the eye. Wary, but listening, and with a trace of sympathy. "I can understand that."

"Will you be more, or less, understanding, when I tell you that my father was Lord Allbury?"

Her brow wrinkled. "Then the Lord Allbury who called on me…?"

"My little cousin Joe. His older brother and mine sadly died, and from what I have found out, he has been living on his expectations in London." *And I'm fairly sure he tried to push me in front of runaway horses.* "I don't like him. I don't believe I want him in charge of my estates."

"He can't be, can he, while you live?" She hesitated, then said, "He is accusing you of being an imposter."

Jack shrugged. "He can accuse all he likes. I have the proof of who I am."

"But you have not yet decided whether or not to use it," she said flatly. Impossible to know what she thought of that.

"I have decided. Seeing you at the Assembly rooms finally gave me the push I needed."

She blinked, clearly startled. "*Me?* Why?"

"I don't know. You were taking responsibility for your sisters with such grace and ease, with no idea of how beautiful, how desirable you yourself might be. I think you have always shouldered responsibility, from when you were little older than your youngest sisters are now. It made me think, made me ashamed of ducking my own duties. I suppose, for me, it has become a habit."

She did not look away. "You do not strike me as an uncaring man. Perhaps you just choose *who* to care for rather than have the choice thrust on you." She flushed. "Not that I would like you to think my own responsibilities were thrust on me. I love my sisters dearly and would gladly do anything for them. Or for my stepmother."

"Your interpretation is kind to me," he said ruefully. "I shall endeavor to live up to it. Would you do something for me, Barbara? As a favor?"

"Probably," she said cautiously, making him smile.

"Do you ride?"

"Yes, but we have no horses now. We had to leave them at Seahaven when my father died."

Jack scowled. "I would like to meet this cousin of yours."

"No, you wouldn't. He is a weasel of a man and wouldn't know a musical note if it struck him in the ear."

Jack laughed. "Well, to the devil with him then. I'll give him the cut direct instead. If I hire you a suitable mount, would you ride with me to Allbury Court tomorrow?"

Barbara forgot to breathe. Without being told, she knew it was not an amatory assignation. He needed to see his old home at last and didn't want to go alone. That he had chosen her made her believe all over again that they were soul mates at heart. And to be friends with the composer John Sutton, Lord Allbury, would never reflect badly on her sisters.

"Unless you have family commitments," he added hastily, giving her an easy way out.

"I am sure there are enough of us to cover for my absence. I would be glad to accompany you."

He gave one of his dazzling smiles, and rose, still holding her hand to help her to her feet. "Then shall we join the treasure hunt? What exactly are we looking for?"

Joseph Sutton had been almost glad to see his cousin in the lowly position of entertaining musician, where no one would pay him any attention. It would all help to make fun of him in public, if and when Cousin Jack was declared Lord Allbury. Old Galton believed him, and the other executors and trustees saw no reason to doubt the evidence Galton had already seen.

No, Jack had to die, and lesser people like drunken entertainers died all the time of their own stupid faults.

Shoving Jack in front of the runaway horses had been sheer opportunism and far too risky. Perhaps it was as well he had survived in case anyone had recognized Joseph at the scene. Certainly, he had been lucky that Jack was too distracted to see him in the crowd. But the impulsive act had certainly given him an idea. At one step removed, it would be as easy as blinking to make sure the disreputable cousin died, and the cousin of ton succeeded to the title and the fortune that went with it.

So, he escorted some merchant's daughter around the treasure hunt with good grace, keeping his eyes open for the Bigglesworth sisters who could add to his consequence, though not as his bride since they didn't have a feather between them to fly with. Although, to be sure, they were making a bit of a splash in York.

When he and Miss Merchant, whatever her name was, returned triumphantly with the treasure, his pleasure was instantly marred by the sight of Jack strolling out of the trees with Lady Barbara on his arm.

*Damn it!* he fumed, sensing some profound intimacy between them. *What is the point of removing Jack from my way if he leaves a wretched son behind?*

No, he could not wait and plan this. Jack had always been impulsive and Joe could allow no quick marriage. Jack's death would have to be soon. Very soon.

## CHAPTER 5

"He was not a bad man, my father," Jack said, as they halted the horses on the edge of Allbury land. "Just a dashed stubborn one."

"I used to try not to think ill of mine," Barbara said, "but it was always a losing battle. The truth is, he treated his wives abominably, and his children no better. He spent their portions, which should have come to us, in pursuit of his own selfish lifestyle, treating them as chattels with the sole purpose of providing male heirs. His one regret when he died, was not that his daughters were cast penniless and friendless upon the world, but that he did not yet know if Patience would bear him a son. He made no push to provide for her or for us. Or for the poor souls who lived on his land or in his household."

Jack regarded her, not with pity but with an empathy that she could bear. "He was a monster."

"Yes, I rather think he was. Many males of the species are brought up, consciously or otherwise, to be selfish monsters. Your land looks cared for, the cottages I can see in no obvious disrepair."

"My father was dutiful. Rough but kind. My older brother was cut from the same cloth. Neither thought music a suitable profession for a baron's son. When, young and rebellious, I ran away and did it anyway, they would not let me come home until I renounced music."

"Which you could not do. *Should* not do."

"Shall we go on to the house?"

He greeted the country people with ease. The older ones seemed to recognize him and grinned, tugging their forelocks and welcoming him back. The steward galloped after them to wring Jack's hand, beaming so widely his face seemed in danger of disintegrating. Jack conversed with him as they rode down to the house, asking after his family and then proceeding to sensible questions about crop rotations and drainage and rents. As they approached the house, the steward doffed his hat to Barbara, grinned again at Jack and went on his way rather more jauntily than he had arrived.

Allbury Court was a rambling old house built around a courtyard. It looked as if it had been built in Tudor times and added to significantly in each century since. It gave Barbara an odd little thrill to see where Jack had grown up. But Jack himself had gone silent, perhaps remembering his childhood, or regretting the years away, years he could have spent at least partly with the family he had clearly loved, and who had, Barbara suspected, loved him too, in their own, stubborn way.

Impulsively she reached out and covered his hand where it rested on his thigh. "Would you rather go on alone?"

Wordlessly, he shook his head, then his fingers turned and curled, raising hers quickly to his lips, before he released her and urged his horse on to a canter.

She went inside with him but gave him distance to greet the housekeeper and other old retainers. She admired the historical parts of the house, and the style of the new, and pretended not to see the tears glistening in his eyes as he stood in his father's study, or in the nursery he had shared with his brother.

Only when they entered the drawing room, and he saw a grand pianoforte in the window, did a sound like an anguished groan escape him. She grasped his hand and for a moment, he clung in silence.

"The old devil told me he had got rid of it," he said shakily at last. "I should have known he never would. I should have—" He broke off, swallowing hard, and she rested her cheek briefly on his arm before walking into the room with him and inspecting the pianoforte.

Because he wanted to, she played a fun little duet with him, improvising as they went, and he was laughing when Mrs. Weeks, the housekeeper, came in with an array of maids behind her carrying tea and sandwiches, scones and cakes.

"A pleasure to meet you, my lady," the housekeeper said unexpectedly. "My cousin served your father as Cook, and if I may say so, was disgusted at your departure from Seahaven."

"Mrs. Jedburgh was your cousin? What a small world! Do send her my regards, and good wishes. From all of my sisters, too. Is she still with the new earl?"

"No, my lady," Mrs. Weeks said with relish. "She had no reason to stay once you had departed. She gave notice and works now for a duke in the south."

"I hope she is happy,"

"She seems content enough. But she will be glad to know I've seen you looking so well. Eat up now, it's a long journey back to York!"

Oddly, Barbara was conscious of a desire *not* to return to York. To let her sisters go on without her, just for a few days. But even if Jack wished it, she could not stay here.

So, after tea they said goodbye to Mrs. Weeks. Jack even hugged the housekeeper, which made her cry, and then they walked around to the stables.

"What did you think?" Jack asked casually on the way.

"I think it is a beautiful house which you can make your own. I think you can make it ring with music and fun, and compose to your heart's content. In between seeing to the land and your tenants. You could have the music *and* Allbury Court."

"That is what I have begun to think." He paused, catching her arm and turning her to face him in the shade of a spreading chestnut tree. A smile played on his lips. With his free hand he tucked a stray strand of hair beneath her bonnet, and brushed his knuckles against her cheek. "Thank you."

"For what? Telling you what you already know?"

"For making me *see* what I already know," he corrected. "Barbara?"

"Yes?"

The smile flared and died again. "Nothing. Just this."

He bent his head and her heart seemed to lurch downward into her suddenly tingling stomach. She could have avoided it, but the truth was, in that moment, she wanted his kiss more than anything in the world.

His lips paused above hers, giving her time to object, perhaps, or maybe just drawing out the anticipation. She parted her lips, raising them to his, and he smiled as he kissed her. A firm, yet tender kiss, slow, exploratory, tasting.

He raised his head, searching her face. "Again?" he whispered.

For answer, she cupped his cheek and took back his mouth and with this longer, deeper kiss, she was lost.

With a soft groan, he loosened his hold of her lips but didn't leave them. "Sadly, we are expected at the stables. If not watched from there."

She gave a shaky breath of laughter and drew herself out of his arms. "You are most improper."

"So are you."

"Not," she said severely, "until I met you."

As they finally walked around the corner to the stables and he exchanged cheerful words with the grooms, she reminded herself that this was an emotional day for him. She was merely his support, his outlet for that emotion.

That was enough for her, though secretly, she would cherish his kisses in her dreams. What she could not bear was for any awkwardness to enter his manner with her, through any sense of obligation or apology.

When she led her waiting horse to the mounting block, he was before her, and boosted her into the saddle himself. He checked the girths and the stirrups, then paused, gazing up at her.

"You are thinking again, aren't you? Over-thinking. Live in the moment, Barbara. It is good to be happy."

How could he know she was happy? Was all but fighting against that happiness with warnings to herself?

His lips quirked. To her amazement, he ducked his head, and actually kissed the toe of her boot. Then he turned away, vaulted into the saddle of his own horse and set off toward the drive.

He talked about the land as they rode the path through the fields, with woodland ahead to the right, pointing out the distant village, and various tenancies and a patch of traditional common land which should, by all conventional wisdom be enclosed.

"Will you enclose it?" she asked.

Before he could answer, a sharp crack rent the air, and with an outraged whinny, his horse bolted.

Barbara's mare, a placid creature until that moment, plunged after him, whether maddened by the sudden noise or picking up the other animal's fear.

It was all Barbara could do to cling on, leaning low over the mare's neck. Ahead, Jack was still in the saddle, trying to regain control. She could hear his voice, soothing and unafraid, over her mare's snorting breath. He kept turning to glance back over his shoulder at her.

At last, the horses calmed. Jack managed to bring his to a full stop, petting the creature's neck and shoulder while he looked back anxiously to Barbara. But the mare calmed too, slowing of her own volition and obediently trotted up to Jack.

"Are you hurt?" he demanded.

"No, I'm fine," she replied breathlessly. "What happened? Is he not used to shooting?"

"He's certainly not used to being shot," Jack said grimly.

That was when Barbara saw the horse's torn ear. There was very little blood, but it looked as if something had taken a tiny bite out of it.

Her stomach lurched and tightened. "That was a ridiculously careless shot!"

"Inaccurate perhaps," he murmured. "But I imagine he took a great deal of care."

"What do you mean?" she demanded. "Why would someone shoot a strange horse?"

Jack shrugged and tried to smile. "No reason, of course. Come, we'll need to hurry if we're to be home before six as I promised."

"Jack, was someone aiming at us? Why would you even think so?"

"Oh, I'm just angry," he said lightly, but she would not be thrown off the scent.

"Has this happened before? Dear God, is someone trying to *kill* you?"

"If so, they are comfortingly inept." He sighed and gave in. "I'm fairly sure someone tried to push me in front of runaway horses the other day. I would have put it down to imagination, or to a one-off act of malice, but *this*, when I am with *you*? No, this is not to be borne."

Barbara had never been a fool. "An old grudge following you from abroad? Or your cousin determined to inherit at all costs?"

He glanced at her, a glimmer of a rueful smile in his eyes before he cast a wary glance around the surrounding country. "I incline to the latter, since no one has ever tried to kill me —apart from a couple of silly duels in my youth—until I came home and proved my identity to old Galton."

She took that in, pursing her lips. "I met your cousin the night of the subscription ball," she said slowly. "Hanging around the door to the gallery where we talked. Could he have been looking for you?"

"Possibly. The bill with my name and face on it was up at the theatre by then, and elsewhere in town, probably."

"Then why didn't he attack you then?"

"Perhaps he thought I would just go away. After all, it's several months since my father's death, and I'd never shown interest in anything other than music since I first left home."

"You must go straight to a magistrate," Barbara commanded, fear clawing at her stomach. Unthinkable that he be taken from the world, from *her* world.

"With what evidence? No, I think I must draw him out."

She stared at him. He was not a soldier, a fighter. He was a musician. "How?"

"I haven't decided, yet, but I'll work something out. Don't let it spoil our day."

Her mouth dropped open. "*Don't let it...?*"

"Exactly." He smiled encouragingly. "A canter through the wood, perhaps?"

He was very good at distraction, and Barbara could not but play along on one level—the same level that wondered and rejoiced at his kisses. With the other part of her brain, she worried, and noted his constant scanning of the countryside while she did likewise.

After such a day, it was impossible to sleep. Even with her evening to herself while Dorothea and Patience managed chaperone duty, Barbara could not stop thinking of Jack, of his danger, and even, occasionally of new possibilities. *Live for the moment,* she told herself severely, and the moment was the happiness of Jack's friendship, and the social success of her sisters.

She was still awake when Dorothea slid into the big bed next to her.

"All well?" Barbara asked.

"I think it is going very well. Josefina and the twins—either or both! —are very much in demand."

"Are you?"

"I don't think of such things," Doro said predictably.

Barbara turned her head in the darkness. "Seriously?"

"Seriously."

"But you have given more than anyone to this venture. More than any of us, you deserve happiness."

"I *am* happy," Dorothea said in a voice that was slightly too determined. "There is no one I could ever think of marrying. Or at least no one who knows I exist. Why? Are you thinking of hopping off your own self-fashioned shelf?"

"No. But...I'm glad we came here."

Dorothea was silent for so long that Barbara imagined she had fallen asleep.

Then her voice came out of the darkness. "Who is he? The musician?"

"Oh, he's not for me," Barbara said, blushing. "But in fact, he isn't just a musician. He is the composer and pianist, John Sutton. And the rightful Baron Allbury."

# CHAPTER 6

Over the next few days, Barbara's sightings of Jack were fleeting. There was no shortage of excitement, since their Tavistock stepsiblings had appeared in York. By the time she encountered Jack outside the glorious Minster on Sunday, the whole of York society knew that he was the true Baron Allbury.

"Is that your way of driving your cousin away?" Barbara asked low when he had bowed to her and her sisters and they had edged a little apart. "Causing the world to accept you?"

"He's still declaring me an imposter. But it means people watch him more closely."

"Yes, but Jack he could *pay* someone to hurt you. Which would distance him from the crime and yet achieve what he wants."

"It would never be distant enough," Jack said. "You couldn't pay a man enough to hang silently while his employer goes free."

That alarmed her even more. "Jack, are you *baiting* him? You could be *killed*!"

He did not look remotely worried. Instead, his eyes grew warm. "Your concern is sweet. It makes me want to kiss you."

"But you won't take it seriously. Do you take *anything* seriously?"

Something changed in his eyes, a spark that deprived her of

breath. "Yes. And one day I will show you. *Seriously,* I have it all in hand and you must not worry. By the by, shall I send you tickets for my concert on Tuesday?"

"You still intend to play? But Jack, you will be alone in front of everyone!"

"In front of a theatre full of people who are constantly watching each other rather than what happens on the stage," he said cynically.

There was time for no more, as others approached them and she had to let the matter drop.

Complimentary tickets for the concert arrived the following day, for which everyone was grateful. Another paying event that cost them nothing.

There was a lot of competition that evening for the best gowns. Barbara, too anxious to care what she wore, let the others choose and wore what was left. It turned out to be her favorite Pomona silk, but this only struck her as she left the house. Had Doro blabbed? Had her sisters conspired to send her to the concert with the most advantage? She didn't know whether to be touched or furious.

Anxious as she was from the moment Jack walked onto the stage and bowed with supreme grace, the music had its inevitable effect on her. He opened with his piano concerto, followed by a Beethoven sonata. And after a short interval, he played pieces by Bach and something wild of his own she had never heard before.

His playing was flawless, uplifting, wonderful, and even she could not worry her way through it. Although, even when she joined in the rapturous applause, she was silently pleading with him to leave the stage.

*Stage...* An idea began to form in her mind, outrageous and impossible.

Or was it?

"Very well," Josefina murmured beside her. "We understand your obsession! Shall we go to the salon to greet the great man?"

This was part of the event, a reception with light supper in a room next to the auditorium. With the crazy idea still turning in her brain, she followed her sisters almost blindly downstairs and along the passage to the salon.

Then, out of the blue, a hand gripped her arm and whisked her behind a velvet curtain. Before she could even object, her mouth was crushed beneath another and protest died unspoken. Instead, she threw her arms around his neck and kissed him back, for she had already absorbed the citrus and spice of his distinctive scent, the very feel of his body and his lips.

"Jack, I was so frightened for you," she whispered against his mouth.

His fingers closed around her nape, gently massaging and she arched into him. "I told you there was no need. But I am sorry for it all the same. Do you love me, Babs Bigglesworth?"

She kissed him again to avoid answering. She was twenty-seven years old and it had been ten years since she had made such an admission, and found it to be both false and unworthy. To a man nothing like Jack Sutton. And yet…

And yet his kisses melted her bones; his fingers caressing her nape made her ache with sheer lust. His mouth moved across her cheek to her ear. "Because I love you," he whispered. "My sweet and only soul mate."

No one called Barbara sweet. Even at seventeen she had been sharp-tongued and down to earth. But with Jack, she actually *felt* sweet. She closed her eyes, leaning into him.

"I do love you," she murmured. "And I want you to live. Will you listen to my idea?"

# CHAPTER 7

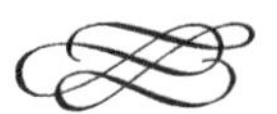

Several hours later, Jack emerged from York's least exclusive but fashionable club, quite clearly the worse for wear. In fact, he felt drunk on love, and had come straight from the theatre reception to here to celebrate success with half the orchestra, and several more noble acquaintances.

The door emptied him into an alley. He stumbled along it, humming through his fatuous smile.

*She loves me,* he kept saying to himself. *She loves me.* He was still repeating the words when someone landed on him from the high wall to his left, and two more shadows emerged from a dark doorway on the right. He went down under the weight of the first, but rolled immediately and kicked out to divert the stabbing blade aiming for his throat. His attacker swore and lunged after the fallen knife.

But the other two closed in for the kill, and suddenly the alley was full of violent shadows, and he wasn't sure if the game had begun, or ended in truth.

Joseph Sutton woke in the bedchamber of his decent inn, with a good feeling about the day. Surely his thrice-damned cousin was already dead. And he, Joseph, would finally be Lord Allbury, without all doubt. He could get his hands on a decent country estate, a house in the best area of London, and enough of a fortune to pay off his creditors and live well. He might even attract an heiress so that he could be even wealthier. The possibilities were endless, if only Jack was dead.

Dressed for the day, he enjoyed breakfast downstairs in the coffee room, and wondered whether he should go out, or wait in his room to receive word. In the end he returned to his bedchamber.

Only a little over half an hour later, he was rewarded by a knock on the door. Hiding his smile, he strolled across the room and opened the door to see, just as he expected, Galton's clerk.

The clerk bowed. "Mr. Sutton, sir, I am afraid there has been a bit of an accident and Mr. Galton has asked that you formally identify the body."

"Body?" Joseph asked with excellently-feigned distaste. "What body?"

"They're saying it's your cousin, sir. John, Lord Allbury."

Joseph curled his lip. "I barely know the man. Galton is perfectly capable of identifying him for legal purposes."

"But you are next of kin, sir," the clerk said, sounding shocked.

In all honesty, identifying the body was something Joseph had not thought of, but if he was to be the next baron, the previous one had to be legally dead. "Where is the damned body?" he demanded ungraciously, reaching for his hat.

"In the parlor downstairs, sir."

Joseph blinked at him. "They brought him to me? It seems a peer of the realm does get greater consideration!" He left the hat and followed the clerk downstairs somewhat jauntily.

However, rounding the landing, he got something of a shock, for the coffee room seemed to be full of people, women as well as gentlemen, and working men holding their caps awkwardly in their hands.

"Ah, is this Mr. Joseph Sutton?" a voice boomed. It belonged to a jovial looking man with a bald pate and an expensive coat.

"Indeed, sir," Galton said from in front of a table.

"Come along then, take a look at the poor soul and then join us. Everyone be seated, if you please."

*What the devil is going on?* Joseph was about to ask when he was distracted by the unmistakable sight of Lady Barbara Bigglesworth, her handkerchief clutched to her face. He shut his mouth, and Galton suddenly moved to reveal that the body was not in fact in the parlor but on a coffee room table.

The clerk whipped down the sheet to reveal the white, but unmistakable face of his cousin Jack. Even in death he looked handsome and caused a stir. *Damn him.*

"Is this your cousin, John Sutton?" Galton asked.

"You know damned well it is."

"Excellent," said the bald gentleman. He had taken a seat at the table slightly apart at the front of the room, so that he faced everyone else. The working men sat to one side in two rows of mismatching stools and chairs. "Then I formally open the inquest into the death of one John Sutton, Baron Allbury."

With shock, Joseph realized he had stumbled into the inquest, complete with coroner and jury.

"Doctor," said the coroner, searching the room for the correct individual, "Have you determined how the poor devil died?"

"Not only that, sir," replied someone Joseph couldn't even see. "But we have in custody the person who inflicted the injuries."

Lady Barbara let out a sob, and someone handed her solicitously into a chair.

Joseph began to have a very bad feeling about unfolding events, until he recalled the inefficiency of the law. Just because they had arrested someone for the crime, didn't mean they had the correct perpetrator. And even if they had...

"Well, that makes our task easier, what?" the coroner said jovially. "Best speak to him, then, as the last person to see our man alive."

Was this really how inquests were conducted?

Two officers of the law hauled up an all-too familiar figure, a shifty, stocky character with an oft-broken nose, a long scar down his face, and bulging muscles in his neck. Christ, how could the fool have let himself be caught?

He glared at the murderer, who grinned reassuringly, thank God.

"And you are?" the coroner demanded.

"George Trunk, your honor."

"And how did you come to attack the deceased?"

"Well, he comes staggering drunk out of t' Gentlemen's Club onto Butcher's Alley. I followed him along t' wall, then jumped on him. With me knife."

"To rob him?" the coroner asked with distaste.

"Lord, love you, no, because someone paid me to do him in."

"Someone paid..." the coroner repeated in disbelief. "Dear me, what is the world coming to? Who paid you to attack the deceased?"

"He did," Trunk said without missing a beat, nodding straight at Joseph.

Joseph's mouth fell open while fury surged up from his boots. "Why, you desperate, filthy liar!"

Everyone was staring at him, including the coroner, who said stiffly, "We are not here to determine guilt or innocence but to determine how the deceased came to die."

"By the hand of that villain!" Joseph declared, pointing at his supposedly tame assassin. He'd see the man hang for this, if it was the last thing he did, the lying, traitorous dog.

"But at your command!" came a deep, cadaverous voice, from a place no voice should ever have come.

Before Joseph's eyes, the body on the bench moved, casting off its sheet with one smooth movement and lowering its feet to the floor. Yet no one but Joseph was paying it any attention.

"So, Doctor," the coroner continued, "you determined the cause of death as stab wounds to the chest? Do we have the blade concerned?"

Joseph's dead cousin pointed straight at him and rapidly crossed the floor to him, and spoke again, in that deep, cavernous voice that seemed to come from beyond the grave. "You! You killed me as surely as if you wielded the knife!"

"No, no!" Joseph cried, scared now beyond witless. "I did not mean him to kill you, just frighten you away! I deserve to be Allbury, you must see that!"

"Liar!" declared the dead-eyed specter. "You paid him to kill me. Confess, or I will never rest and neither will you." The white, ghostly hand reached for his throat.

Truly terrified. Joseph stumbled backward and backward, but the dead Jack kept coming.

*Dear God, this is my fault, I thought I could. I thought I was entitled...*

"You took a life!" Jack intoned.

"I did, I did!" Joseph sobbed. "God forgive me, Jack and my uncle forgive me, I did!"

Abruptly, the whole inn went quiet.

Jack's dead eyes no longer seemed quite so dead. In fact, he smiled. "See? I told you he did it. Mine host, drinks all round, if you please."

As Jack turned away, Lady Barbara all but ran to him, the handkerchief nowhere to be seen. Joseph stared around the room as one of the law officers took him by the arm.

"You tricked me," he said in disbelief. "You bloody tricked me!"

"Guilty conscience, Joe," Jack said with contempt. "It was easy." His lips curved faintly, almost sadly. "I would have paid your debts you know, set you up with an allowance, if you hadn't endangered Lady Barbara or shot my horse's ear. For that, you can damned well hang."

"But...but how did you even escape Trunk and his men?"

"I was ready for them and not nearly as foxed as I looked. Plus, I had more men on my side. As soon as Trunk came at me, my friends poured out of the club. It was quite a fight, but the end was never in doubt. I never even had to damage my hands."

Lady Barbara took Jack's arm, saying, "Is that man really the coroner?"

Jack turned his back on Joseph and walked away. "Actually, he is. Good sport, though, isn't he?"

It was the last thing Joseph ever heard him say.

Barbara, in the midst of people she did not know, none of whom she would consider eligible partners for her sisters, did not want to leave. The inn was full of good humor, triumph and hilarity, and that suited her perfectly.

In return for their help, Jack was buying drinks and breakfast for all who wanted them. The working men who had pretended to be the jury drank ale, grinned, and went about their business several shillings the richer. The orchestra musician who had played the doctor was laughing and toasting Jack in an early brandy. The innkeeper's wife kept bursting into laughter as she recalled the "body" rising from its table to terrorize "the murdering gent".

"So, what's he to you, then?" she asked Barbara, after her third protracted chortle. "Mr. Jack? How come you got to weep over his corpse?"

"Someone had to," Barbara said lightly. "And we are known to be friends. I'm also known to be very proper, so he was less likely to suspect a trick if I was involved."

"That's true," Jack said, appearing beside them. "But I confess I never thought it would go half so well. In Joe's shoes, I'd have laughed."

"Probably not if you'd just ordered the murder of your own kin," Barbara said flatly.

"There is that." He smiled at her. "You are quite a genius, you know."

Her lips twitched in response. "And you are quite an actor. But I'm afraid I have other duties to attend to today." She held out her hand to the innkeeper's wife. "My thanks for the use of your coffee room, Mrs. Martin. It was perfect, and I shall recommend your house without hesitation!"

"Bless you, ma'am, you're welcome." The innkeeper's wife, apparently stunned, took Barbara's hand and curtseyed, though she seemed inclined to stare as they made for the door, cheered on by the remaining occupants of the coffee room.

Jack held the door for Barbara and waved his hat to the room in general.

"Well, my lord, at least you should now be safe."

"Unlike poor Joe. He won't do well in prison."

"You couldn't let him go," she insisted. "He would happily have murdered you, Jack. He tried twice in person that we know of, and once via Trunk and his cronies. And if that is not enough for you, imagine if he had succeeded. Murder would surely have remained his preferred method of getting rid of problems. God knows who else would have died."

Jack threaded her arm through his, squeezing her agitated fingers. "I know. I just can't help remembering the boy I helped climb the old oak tree long ago. But never think me ungrateful for your wonderful idea. Even if he had admitted nothing, that would have been the best laugh of the year."

"There will be a lot of talk," she warned. "Quite the scandal in fact."

He glanced at her with unexpected seriousness. "Will you mind?"

"I have no reason to mind," she said calmly. They were friends, friends who had kissed so passionately her knees went weak at the mere memory, but no more than that. "And the scandal is really his, not yours."

He was silent for a little. She liked his silences as much as his talk and laughter. There was a simple yet wonderful pleasure in just walking beside him, absorbing every movement of his body, every faintest scent of him.

He said, "I'm going to go away for a few days, to take care of business matters and make some arrangements."

"Of course." It felt like a knife through the heart, because he was opening the distance just when she was growing used to the closeness. She had been foolish, assuming…

"I will be back in time for your ball. I hope you will save a waltz for me."

"Don't be silly. I shall not be dancing."

"Yes, you will."

He would not be there to see. She knew that. The silence stretched between them, no longer wonderful at all.

"I'll miss you," he offered.

*Not as I shall miss you. For the rest of my life.* "There is no need to come farther," she said, slipping her arm free. "I am almost home. Goodbye, my lord."

# CHAPTER 8

The Dowager Lady Seahaven's ball was a huge success. Everyone they had invited was here, marveling at the decorations which had turned the familiar rooms they were used to at the Smithson Assembly Hall into a new and fantastic place. The girls, looking exceptionally beautiful and vital, were partnered for every dance. And, almost as good, financial anxieties had been eased by the unexpected but highly welcome alliance with their Tavistock stepsiblings, which also provided a host in the shape of young Tavistock himself.

This boon, plus the early success of the occasion, probably accounted for the bloom she saw in her older sisters' cheeks. Bess looked magnificent and gracious, Susana and Dorothea positively sparkling. Even Patience, eternally worried for her huge, acquired family, seemed to blossom. Barbara's heart ached with pride and love for all of them. They deserved this success.

And if her thoughts occasionally strayed to the absent Jack Sutton—Lord Allbury—she refused to let them remain there. She had known in her heart he would not come, and yet, foolishly, she had hoped.

But that was an ache for another day. This evening had always been the center piece to their plans, long planned and worked for, by Dorothea most of all, and she *would* enjoy the moment. Nothing would be allowed to spoil it.

Since the next dance would be the supper dance, Barbara decided to make sure everything was going smoothly. People were milling between dances, young ladies being escorted back to their chaperones, gentlemen seeking their next partners for the waltz, which was always particularly popular. Keeping the smile pinned to her lips as she moved among them was not difficult in the face of universal pleasure and excitement.

She nodded and murmured greetings to all on her way, and then became aware that attention was turning rapidly toward the ballroom door. An accident of some kind? A late arrival? Praying for the latter, she moved toward the space forming between the door and the dance floor, almost like a corridor.

Across the room, she saw Patience also weaving through the crowd toward the space. But Barbara was first, murmuring an apology as she squeezed between two dowagers and finally saw the cause of the commotion.

One man, who made her heart leap. The new Lord Allbury. No wonder everyone was staring, for since his cousin's arrest, he had been the subject of a great deal of gossip, most of it sympathetic. For even if John Sutton had performed across Europe for money, at least he was a highly regarded composer and the only surviving son of the baron, his father.

Jack strolled through the passage made for him, as though unaware of the degree of interest he was attracting. He nodded and smiled to acquaintances, who, after the first shock, returned his greetings civilly.

Only when his gaze fell on Barbara and he swerved to approach her, did she realize she had stopped dead. Dear God, he was handsome in his evening clothes. *And probably out of them, too.*

*Barbara Biggleswort h, behave!*

How could she when that particular smile lit up his face? When her hand was reaching for his as if for a lifeline? He took it in his sure, comforting fingers, bowing while his gaze never left her face.

"Lady Barbara. Forgive my tardiness. My horse chose this afternoon to go lame, and I have only just arrived back in York."

"Of course, you are welcome, whatever the hour," she managed, looking around a little wildly for Patience who was suddenly nowhere to be seen. "Allow me to offer you champagne? Or the supper waltz is about to begin..."

"The supper waltz sounds wonderful. Might I hope for the honor?"

"Well, no, my lord, I do not—"

"Please."

His voice as much as the glow of his eyes, half understanding, half teasing laughter, left her speechless. Her hand was somehow on his arm and they were walking together onto the dance floor among the other couples, which at least prevented the untoward gawping.

"A five-minute wonder," he murmured, "already over." As the introduction began, he took her in his arms, and her whole body flushed with pleasure, with the excitement she had missed since his departure. "Are you as well as you look?"

"I don't know. I didn't think you would come."

"I promised, Barbara."

And suddenly, the smile forced its way up from her heart. "So you did. I doubted you. I thought you were *escaping* me."

"I know you did. And I almost messed up my cure for that. I have been mostly at Allbury Court, with solicitors and stewards, setting some repairs and alterations in motion with the house and the land and tenancies... I'm babbling. Barbara?"

"Yes?" Waltzing with Jack was bliss and it made her smile all over again. "I am seven and twenty years old, and until this moment I had waltzed only with my sisters to teach them. It is different with a man. With you."

Laughter lit his eyes. "I'm glad, though as a compliment it lacks power."

"It wasn't a compliment. I was stating a fact."

"Then allow me to state another. You waltz divinely. And I have composed a new sonata, for you, about you, which is almost complete, only I need to know what you think. First, though, I want to ask you a very important question, now that I know how things stand at Allbury Court."

Distracted by the wonder of a sonata, *his* sonata written for *her*, it took her a moment to catch up. She was an inspiration to him, however small. "What question?" she asked at last.

"Will you marry me, Lady Babs?"

That swiped the breath from her body, from the whole room, it seemed. "M-marry you? But I can't. The girls…"

"Marrying me need not mean deserting the girls – *any* of the girls. There is plenty of room at Allbury Court. Barbara, live for the moment, for you don't know what will happen next. If you love me, marry me. If you don't, I will take my congé like a gentleman and we will still be friends."

She blinked. "Really?"

"I hope so. But I don't want to be friends. I would rather be married."

"So would I," she whispered, allowing the admission into her heart at last. "Oh, so would I, but Jack, I owe my family this Season. We can do nothing until after May."

"Then we shall be married on the first day of June. If you are agreeable."

Now, she couldn't stop smiling. "I am agreeable."

"Then perhaps there is somewhere we might go to celebrate more privately?"

"And improperly?" she asked breathlessly.

"Most improperly."

"I know the very broom cupboard."

A breath of surprised laughter kissed her cheek. "Broom cupboard?"

"Well, I can't be seen for some time after this dance. My sisters and I have been sharing gowns all month, and it's Doro's turn for this one. You will be astonished by the difference Susana can make with trims and buttons and trains. And it has saved us a fortune."

His eyes danced. Clearly, he was still not sure whether or not she was joking.

But an hour later, he did indeed meet her in the broom cupboard for their private celebration, which was breathless, thrilling, and in every way delightful. And only the first of very, very many such joys.

THE END

# SOCIAL MEDIA FOR MARY LANCASTER

You can learn more about Mary Lancaster at these social medial links:

**Website**: http://www.MaryLancaster.com
**Newsletter sign-up:** https://landing.mailerlite.com/webforms/landing/e2p7c6
**Facebook:** https://www.facebook.com/mary.lancaster.1656
**Facebook Author Page:** https://www.facebook.com/MaryLancasterNovelist/
**Twitter:** @MaryLancNovels https://twitter.com/MaryLancNovels
**Amazon Author Page:** https://www.amazon.com/Mary-Lancaster/e/B00DJ5IACI
**BookBub:** https://www.bookbub.com/authors/mary-lancaster

## ABOUT MARY LANCASTER

Mary Lancaster lives in Scotland with her husband, three mostly grown-up kids and a small, crazy dog. Her first literary love was historical fiction, a genre which she relishes mixing up with romance and adventure in her own writing. Several of her novels feature actual historical characters as diverse as Hungarian revolutionaries, medieval English outlaws, and a family of eternally rebellious royal Scots. To say nothing of Vlad the Impaler.

Her most recent books are light fun Regency romances.

Learn more about Mary at: Website: http://www.MaryLancaster.com

# THE BUTLER AND THE BLUESTOCKING

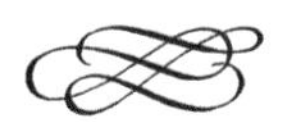

RUE ALLYN

The Butler and the Bluestocking
By Rue Allyn

On arriving in York to visit his godmother, the honorable Malcolm K. Marr did not expect to find her house locked and empty. Nor did he expect to have to break in to the house to find shelter. Least of all did he expect to be awakened at mid-day after the break in to find a woman with the bearing of an Egyptian goddess demanding to know what he was doing in her house.

## CHAPTER 1

"I really need you with us in York." The lamplight flickering over the Dowager Countess of Seahaven's face revealed a determined expression that matched her insistent tone.

"Patience!" More friend than stepdaughter to her fourth and last stepmama, Bess knew she need not explain why she felt embarrassed —in truth, frightened to the point of immobility—at nearly all social events.

"I fail to understand why you believe my attendance in York for the Season is so vital. Aside from my discomfort with even the simple country dances like those held at the Harrogate assembly rooms, such events are filled with nonsense and a waste of valuable time that I could spend on my research into the Rosetta Stone."

She leant toward her work, her delight and wonder spilling in a torrent of words, though she knew Patience had heard it all before. "I promised Mr. Young of the London Royal Society I would transcribe Monsieur Champollion's ideas about the purpose of the stone's hieroglyphs and compare them with Mr. Young's own theories. He hopes my work will verify his theories, or at least explain the differences between his and Champollion's interpretations."

The work was intensive and required close examination. Not only did she have to compare each gentleman's theories with the facsimile she had been given of the stone's inscriptions. She also needed to make an independent and objective analysis of the hieroglyphic, Coptic and Greek scripts.

"I have completed my work on the Greek and am about to begin on the Coptic..." Bess let her words trail off, when her stepmother, younger by seven years, lifted a hand to her forehead.

Patience dropped her hand. "Dearest, you know I admire your devotion to your scholarly pursuits. However, you must also know that my personal understanding of them is small."

Bess placed her pen on the blotter and capped the inkwell. Then she wiped the worst of the most recent ink stains from her hands onto her apron and gave Patience her full attention.

"About this idea of going to York, Patience." Bess gestured at the papers littering her small desk. "I will be much too busy to be of good use with social events. The expense of taking me with you is hardly worth the bother."

"Normally, I might agree with you, if I did not need your help with the girls still in the schoolroom."

"They could stay here with me."

"No." Patience shook her head. "York provides a wealth of opportunity to further their education in history."

Bess tucked her lower lip between her teeth. She'd had a London Season, thirteen years ago when she was seventeen and under the reluctant sponsorship of a distant relation to her father. It had been a disaster.

While her sponsor had been well intentioned, she'd been more focused on the social success of her own daughter. The woman had shown little understanding and almost no patience with Bess's strong love of history and equally strong social ineptitude. With her mother gone, her father, ever self-absorbed, had left Bess to her own devices. Those years between her mother's death and the London debut had been spent devouring nearly every book in the Seahaven library.

She had never learned a proper curtsey nor more than the most rudimentary courtesies. Her conversation was all about Greek philosophers and world history. Her hair had been a coppery red, that only later years later deepened into the burnished auburn she knew was her only claim to beauty.

"Dearest, are you listening to me?" Patience placed a gentle hand on Bess's arm.

"I'm sorry, Patience. Please forgive my wool-gathering, I am listening. In fact, I am certain my sisters can help with the young ones."

Patience pursed her lips. "I suppose that might work. Still, you must agree that giving the three middle girls a Season is a good idea."

"Possibly." Bess plucked at a loose thread at the end of her sleeve. She had removed her cuffs to avoid staining the precious lace with ink. Her opinion of a Season, whether in London or York, could not be of any help to her stepmother or the rest of the family.

Patience straightened in her chair. "Definitely, since Cousin Rose is giving us her house for the months she is gone on expedition to Egypt. Mrs. Crewe has agreed to come with us and help with the cooking as well as supervising all of us with the housework. Once her brother returns home from the Americas, he will come on as butler, but that could be as late as mid-April."

"We've managed without more servants for years. I'm sure you will all still enjoy yourselves." Bess picked up the facsimile she'd been working from and frowned. *I don't recall seeing that sigma earlier. I'd best double-check.*

"Elizabeth, you cannot be listening to me." Patience placed a hand on Bess's arm. "Please stop fussing with that document and pay attention."

Bess sighed and put the facsimile aside. "I am sorry Patience. I do not mean to neglect you, but you know how vital this project is to me. I may actually be able to share credit with Mr. Young when he presents his findings to the Royal Society and the money it brings on completion will pay Mrs. Crewe's salary for the next year."

"For the income, we are all truly grateful, and I am certain you must be thrilled at the prospect of recognition. That has been your hope since before we met. But your sisters have important hopes and needs too, and your help in getting Josefina, Iris and Ivy fired off is essential."

Bess pressed her lips together. "Why?"

"First, we cannot possibly rent this house to help defray expenses, if you are still living here."

"I am certain our vicar and his wife will be happy to house me while you are gone. Especially if I offer to help with the housework."

"Second," continued Patience. "As I have already said, someone must see that the younger girls continue their education."

Bess shook her head. "There are eight of us qualified to see that the three youngest continue with their studies, and five to chaperone the twins and Josefina. Surely you and my sisters can juggle chaperone duties with teaching the young ones?"

A worry line formed between Patience's eyebrows. "Are you certain you don't want to come with us? We'd miss you greatly."

Bess smiled. "As I will miss all of you. However, at least some of you will come back. When you do, I'll be here waiting for you. Besides, if we rent the house, I'll be on hand to assist the tenants with any problems."

Patience's expression smoothed, and she widened her eyes. "Then you'll not mind missing the week-long seminars sponsored by the York Antiquarian Society? I for one am looking forward to Dr. Marr's lecture on medical knowledge in ancient Egypt during the reign of Ptolemy."

"I doubt very much you even know who Ptolemy was." Bess said.

"Which one?" Patience asked. "There were five or six rulers of ancient Egypt by that name, if I remember correctly. I do occasionally recall some of what you tell me."

Bess covered her open mouth then smiled again. "You sly puss. You're teasing me."

All innocence, the Dowager Countess of Seahaven blinked. "I'm afraid not. I saw the notice yesterday when I was in the village to speak with the local apothecary about giving Josefina a fair share of his profits from the sale of her unguents."

"I am certain you were successful, for when you are determined, you always achieve your aims."

Patience inclined her head. "Thank you, Bess. I did succeed."

"However, about the York Antiquarian Society, never say those meetings are being held in April. They are almost always held in November."

"But, dearest Bess." Patience allowed herself a small smile. "I have it from our vicar himself that the York Antiquarian Society has changed the traditional dates to coincide with the York Season in hopes of attracting more attendees and more renowned speakers."

"You know, I am certain, you've said the one thing that could persuade me to change my mind." Bess shed her apron. She stared a moment at her ink-stained hands, wishing she would remember to use the salve Josephina made for removing stains on the skin then shook her head at herself. *A few ink stains are of no import, if I can further the world's knowledge of history.*

Patience's pleased expression would never be called smug. "I thought that might do the trick."

"But you knew it all along; did you not? You simply raised those other issues because you know how much I like a good discussion."

"I also know that sometimes you get so stuck on doing things one way that you occasionally need some motivation to change your mind." Patience sat back in her chair; hands folded in her lap.

Bess smiled again and gave Patience a hug. "That is true. Now I must go and wash before luncheon. We can break the news of my decision to the others when we eat. Don't you dare say a word before then. Barbara has been quite upset with my refusal to go to York thus far. I want to see her happy expression when she learns I've changed my mind."

Together they turned to leave the attic.

"Very well, but after luncheon, you must spend some time with Susana to discuss refurbishing your wardrobe."

"Oh, pish tosh. I'll not be attending any social events, and my other day gown will be perfectly acceptable for the York Antiquarian Society, since women, when permitted to attend, are only allowed in the gallery."

"You will disappoint Barbara again, if you don't at least consider refurbishing a dress or two."

Bess heaved another sigh. "Drat. You are quite correct. I don't wish to see her cast down, but she must understand that I have no interest in social gatherings and will not be dragged into chaperone duties for Josefina, Iris, or Ivy."

"We'll all be very busy. I hope you'll not let your personal preferences deny any of the girls this opportunity."

"I would never be so selfish, Patience. I'm certain we can work out any conflicts in commitments." Knowing her stepmother needed to be able to rely on each of her stepdaughters to do her part, Bess resolved to do all she could to see her younger, and truly beautiful, sisters—Josefina, Iris and Ivy–launched successfully. Nonetheless, she prayed she could help best from behind the social scene instead of in front of it.

# CHAPTER 2

*York, March 28th, 1817*

Just as dawn broke, the Honorable Malcolm Kentigern Marr, younger brother of the current Earl of Strathnaver, stared at the front door of their godmother's York town house. Exhausted and bleary-eyed, he tried to figure out why the knocker was off and the house locked tighter than a medieval chastity belt.

Did he have the dates wrong? He was certain Godmama Rose had said he could visit with her while attending the York Antiquarian Society seminars that would begin on April twenty-third. Most likely it was Godmama who'd forgotten. Travel was her passion, and she could be quite hare-brained when a journey was involved. She would drop everything at a moment's notice, if opportunity arose to voyage to new and exotic locales. On those occasions it was surprising that she remembered to dismiss what servants she did not take with her.

*What do I do now?*

Finding a hotel would be the logical choice. However, the York Season was beginning, and the town was full to overflowing. Besides, arriving at this hour of the morning would not make any reputable innkeeper happy.

The idea of taking a room in a less than reputable hostelry made him shudder. That way was a near certain invitation to damp sheets, fleas, and two-legged vermin. He was much too tired to deal with such nonsense. Damn the hidden pothole that had destroyed a perfectly good curricle, given him and his tiger innumerable bruises, and forced him to pay a needlessly high amount for a ride on the slowest oxcart imaginable. Leaving the curricle in the care of his tiger, Mal and the thick-brogued driver—who drank entirely too much ale as he drove—had arrived at the outskirts of York shortly after midnight. Mal had begged the man to go all the way to the town house, but the oaf refused. "'Tis too lang a way fer me puir beasties. Yer welcome t' sleep in me wagon. I'll be heading t' th' markets first thing in th' morning. After I deliver me onions, happen I'll take ye t' this town house ye talk of, but it'll cost ye another three shillings."

Mal wanted no part of the proffered bed of onions, nor the opportunity to waste more blunt on the most uncomfortable ride in Christendom. The driver had actually charged Mal tuppence for every sip of ale—the water he carried was reserved for his 'puir beasties'—during the long drive. Now Malcolm was cold, thirsty, exhausted, stank of onions and ale, and frustrated at finding his godmother not at home.

No, in his condition a hotel was out of the question. He would stay here, but how to get in?

In the end, he was forced to break a pane in the glass of the door from the herb garden to the house, and cut himself on a shard as he reached to unbolt the latch and open the door. He managed to wash the cut and stanch the bleeding with a clean rag from a barrel in the kitchen. No food could be found save for some bins of flour, sugar and tea. Of course not. If Godmama was traveling, she'd not leave food to spoil. Giving up on the idea of eating, he headed for the study to see if he could discover when Godmama Rose had left and where she had gone.

He found nothing in the study to tell him about his godmother.

However, he did find a decanter of Strathnaver Whisky. From the scent of the brew, it must be a good century old or more. Some of the best whisky available. Aye, that was Godmama, nothing but the best. He poured a tumbler full of the beverage and, taking both glass and decanter, headed for the wingback chairs that flanked the hearth.

Finally, God smiled on him. The woodbox was full of kindling and logs. Soon he had a fire going to warm himself. He settled into the closest chair, put his feet up on an ottoman and sipped his whisky while planning how to tell his godmother that he'd broken into her house. He was in the midst of a complicated story about letters gone astray and misunderstandings when he closed his eyes to ponder the logic and promptly fell asleep.

# CHAPTER 3

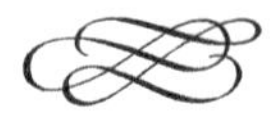

*Noon the same day*

Bess left Mrs. Crewe in the mews to deal with the stableman who cared for the horses and equipages of all the townhomes on the row. She would arrange for the vicar's pony cart to be returned to Starbrook. Meanwhile, Bess would begin the inspection of the premises to ensure that all was in readiness for when her sisters and Patience arrived later that afternoon.

She was delighted to see that the herb garden beds had not run wild. A bit of care from Josefina and all would be well. She approached the door leading into the house and discovered one of the window panes had been broken. She tried the latch, and the portal opened without use of her key. Cousin Rose would never be so careless as to leave doors ajar and broken window glass.

When Bess looked more closely at the glass, she noted small reddish-brown flecks. Blood? One touch confirmed her deduction. But whose blood? And was the intruder still in the house? Impossible to tell, since the blood was dry. Cousin Rose had valuables in her study. Spice lockers from India, illustrated scrolls from Japan, elegant porcelain from China. And most important of all to Bess, a complete map of the locations of the various known Egyptian Monuments—Pyramids, Sphinx, Obelisks, et al—along with a variety of smaller curiosities from the Nile basin. Treasures from Rose's journeys that Bess longed to see. Pray heaven those artifacts had not been stolen.

What to do? Should she call the Watch? And if no one was in the house she would feel most foolish. But she and Mrs. Crewe would be safe. And thinking of Mrs. Crewe decided her. She waited for that worthy woman and sent her in search of the Watch. Then, and only then, when help was already on the way, did Bess prime the pistol—one Patience had insisted she carry in her reticule for protection on the road—and enter the house.

With a plan in action, Bess made a slow search of the first floor. She decided to leave the kitchens for later exploration as she thought it most likely that any thief would have searched first for valuables unlikely to be stored in a kitchen. One room remained on the first floor for her to examine. The study, cousin Rose's treasure room. It would be her refuge once the family arrived and all the social activity began.

Approaching the door, she took a deep breath and prayed she would find nothing. Ready at last, she entered the room but stopped just over the lintel. The room was warm, and... *Is that smoke I smell?* Her heart began to race. She forced herself to make a quick visual survey. She could linger on the fascinating objects later. Right now, she must make certain all was safe. She found the source of the smoke burning in the fireplace at the opposite end of the room. Before she could release a relieved sigh, she froze where she stood. Stretched toward the fire were a pair of booted feet and long limbs encased in fawn-colored pantaloons. The sound of soft snores issued from the same vicinity.

She considered making a rapid silent retreat. Surely Mrs. Crewe and the Watch would be here soon. Thank heaven the family was not here. She could well imagine the noise and kerfuffle that would ensue if her sisters had discovered the stranger. She shook her head. No need to wait for Mrs. Crewe. The pistol gave Bess an advantage. Thus, she decided to confront the intruder on her own. She paced the length of the room until she stood beside the chair where the man slept.

As she approached, she scented something beneath the odor of smoke. She stopped to sniff quietly. Onions? Onions and whisky? That was when she saw the half full tumbler and decanter of amber liquid on the carpet beside the chair. *Is he drunk? Drunken men could be dangerous. Good thing I have a pistol.*

Avoiding the tumbler, she came to stand beside the sleeping intruder. His head lay cocked against the side of the chair. A couple of bruises adorned his high forehead. His night-dark hair lay in mussed contrast against the light-colored upholstery. Save for a small scar that twisted the left corner of his mouth he could have posed for Michelangelo's David. His throat was exposed, his cravat being removed and tossed to the floor on the far side of the chair. He'd removed his coat too and loosened his waistcoat, so his shirt lay open exposing a large V of curl-dusted chest.

A log shifted in the fireplace, stirring Bess from the distracting sight before her. She blinked. *What was I doing?* The weight of the pistol in her hand recalled her instantly to her purpose.

She lifted the weapon, pointed it at the stranger's head, then pulled back the trigger. "Don't move, or I'll shoot." She spoke loudly enough to be heard over the slight snuffling snores he emitted.

"Huh?" The man started, lifted his head, turned to look at the muzzle of the pistol, and stilled. His body's position had not changed. Nonetheless, it was easy to see he was no longer relaxed but alert and wary.

"Who are you and what are you doing in my cousin's house?"

A warm caramel-colored gaze traced upward from the barrel of the pistol past her arm and shoulder to her face. Despite knowing she held the upper hand, Bess's cheeks heated.

*Focus, Bess. Don't stare. Study. What can you deduce?*

Further perusal revealed a handsome form of average size. In the middle of his left arm a rusty red line tinged a torn sleeve. His clothing was finely made and pristine save for the dust on his boots, the damage to his sleeve, and the ink that stained his cuffs. *Does he have other injuries? How much of a threat is he? Can I afford to worry about this?*

Just as she decided she could sort that all out after she had complete control of the situation, he shoved the pistol aside and grabbed for it.

Resisting his pull, she tightened her grip, but the struggle forced her finger to pull the trigger.

BAM!

The pistol went flying.

She leapt backward.

He froze.

Mouths open, they exchanged stares.

Noise creaked from the fireplace, and an avalanche of white plaster crumbled downward to dust the polished hardwood floor.

*Escape*! *Now*!

She spun and ran for the door.

But her feet found only air.

The stranger was faster. The long legs she recalled pressed behind her, and strong arms wrapped around her lifting her back to meet his hard chest and preventing her from using her hands to claw herself free.

A clatter and several shouts sounded from the rear of the house.

*Where is the pistol? He has to have dropped it to catch me so. If I can get it, I could club him with it.* She struggled, attempting to unbalance him and force her release in the process.

"Oh no you don't, my beautiful goddess. No escape for you."

He tossed her in the air, turning her to face him though he held her once more with the same binding clasp. "Now explain why you were holding me at pistol point?"

*He thinks I'm beautiful? What sort of nodcock throws compliments at an attacker*? She blinked up into those fathomless caramel-hued eyes. A dimple showed in his left check, and that odd twist to his mouth kicked upward giving a glimpse of straight white teeth.

*Is he smiling?*

"Unhand her, you cur."

Bess ceased her struggles.

Mrs. Crewe had arrived, and from the clatter of footsteps, she had the Watch with her.

"Of course." He set Bess away from him, but his gaze never left her face.

Bess shifted to take in the entire scene. Yes, there stood Mrs. Crewe, a fire poker in her raised hand. Behind her framed in the doorway, stood two watchmen, one just arriving behind and to the right of the other.

"Cor Bill, who's the toff?" queried the newest arrival. "And who's the lady toff with him?"

"I dunno, Jim. He could be the butler for all I know. When Lady Rose St. Aubyn sent word she was leaving, she said nothing about if her servants would stay or not."

The remarks drew her attention and the stranger's.

Bess managed to stifle into a snicker the irresistible urge to laugh.

The stranger's tawny eyes gleamed, and all his teeth showed.

*No doubt about it. Those strong white teeth prove he is smiling.*

"Who are you, and why are you here?" demanded Mrs. Crewe.

The stranger looked a question at Bess.

Bess turned to her housekeeper and the curious faces of the watchmen behind her. "Mrs. Crewe, I believe we've had a misunderstanding. Would you be so kind as to show the watchmen out?"

"Indeed, Mrs. Crewe. Here are vails for their trouble." The supposed butler stepped forward, coins in hand to give to the housekeeper, who gave the stranger a narrow-eyed look. "Are you certain, my lady?"

Bess nodded. "Quite."

The stranger, his hand still outstretched, looked back over his shoulder at her, that smile doing very odd things to her stomach.

"There is no danger here," Bess assured her housekeeper and the Watch. Why she now believed the stranger represented no hazard to her or her family, she could not have said. The important thing was to get the Watch out of the house before anything else could happen.

"Hmpfh," uttered Mrs. Crewe. In taking the coins, she was forced to lower the poker, but she did not release it. "I'll be back instantly, my lady." With that she turned and ushered the watchmen before her toward the front of the house.

"I think you'd best explain yourself, Mr..." She wondered what concoction of bouncers the man might create to explain his presence here. One thing she knew for certain, he was no butler.

# CHAPTER 4

Now that he had a moment to study his assailant, Mal could not believe his eyes. Her tilted green eyes, ruby lips, and dark auburn tresses held a luster he'd always associated with the ancient Egyptian queens—known as pharoahs in the native literature of the period. Shakespeare had made Cleopatra famous. However, Mal had always preferred the less well known, but more successful, Nefertiti. His dazzling assailant put him forcibly in mind of the few drawings he'd seen of that powerful Egyptian Queen. He could well imagine the statuesque woman with the pistol leading armies and conquering nations in the name of Egypt. Yes, she was a living exemplar of Egypt's ancient female rulers, or perhaps even the most royal of Egyptian goddesses, Hathor, who reigned over sky, sun, sexuality, motherhood, music, dance, foreign lands and goods in addition to the afterlife and was herself one of the many forms of the Eye of Ra.

"Please, sir, I do not have all day. Who are you, and why are you in this house?" Nefertiti had commanded and so it would be.

"Kentigern. Mr. Malcom Kentigern, my lady." He followed the housekeeper's lead in addressing his goddess, but wondered precisely what type of lady this woman was.

"I was about to say that I, uh, I am the butler." Mal kept his gaze locked with that of his Nefertiti. He had no idea if he could imitate a butler or not. He knew only one thing. He had to remain close to the auburn-haired goddess who had woken him at pistol point.

The goddess snorted. "Preposterous. What sort of butler drinks himself into a stupor with his employer's whisky, in that employer's study, and permits himself to stink like onions, and wears ink-stained cuffs? Besides, the owner of this house specifically informed us that all the servants had been let go."

His neck heated. "Yes, ah, uhm, ah-er, I'm—ah—not a very experienced butler and could not find another position. Rose, that is, Lady Rose St. Aubyn is such a kind employer, I knew she would not mind if I sheltered here until I could find work, even as an under-butler or valet. I'm not a proud man." Involuntarily his smile broadened as he uttered that bouncer.

Clan Marr had a reputation as one of the most stiff-rumped, pride-bound families in all of Britain and probably a good part of the rest of the world thanks to his brother—the current Earl of Strathnaver—and their father and grandfather. Whether Mal liked it or not, some of that pride rubbed off on him. Besides he was an expert in his own field of study and knew his pride in that to be justified.

"I doubt my cousin is kind enough to permit a servant—and one several years her junior—to call her by her first name," stated his Nefertiti.

"Nor would she tolerate having anyone, servant or not, break into her house," announced the poker-wielding housekeeper. Her task with the watchmen completed, she took a stance beside his goddess's chair, poker still in hand. Could Nefertiti have had a fiercer body guard? "I came into the house from the back where the glass of the door into the garden has been shattered. There was blood on one of the shards. You'd best check his arms for injuries, my lady."

His bellicose goddess leaned forward. "Roll up the sleeve on your left arm, Mr. Kentigern and hold that arm out where I can see it.

Since the bloodstain on his sleeve made it obvious, he did not bother to resist. Dark red crusted the ragged gash just below his inner elbow making the injury look much worse than it truly was.

"Oh dear," murmured Nefertiti. "Mrs. Crewe, get clean water and the unguents Josefina gave you to bring with us. Then find material and make bandages."

The servant left. The lady rushed forward and practically shoved him into a chair as she issued orders and knelt at his side. Her hand went to his brow. "Thank the good Lord you've no fever. Here, drink this. It will dull the pain."

His half-full glass of whisky appeared before his face held in an elegant hand—long fingers, short nails and dark stains at the wrist, just where cuffs would normally be attached. Fascinating. Did she have scholarly pretentions or was she a follower of that Wollstonecraft woman and penned treatises on the horrors of marriage in her spare time? He longed to know more about her. She busied herself making a pad of his waistcoat and placing it under his wounded forearm.

He took the glass and sipped. "I'm not in any pain."

She snatched the glass back. "You will be," she said as she poured whisky over the wound.

He howled, more outraged at the lack of warning than the fierce stinging of the alcohol on his open flesh. "You've ruined a perfectly good waistcoat and wasted some of Strathnaver's finest whisky. It's well over one hundred years old."

"I sacrificed your waistcoat to preserve Cousin Rose's chair. As for the whisky, Josefina swears by its efficacy in preventing infection. I've personally witnessed the effects and concur unequivocally."

"Who the devil is Josefina, and why would anyone consider her medical opinion worthy of note?"

All the while she'd been speaking, she'd cleaned his wound.

"Here, Lady Bess," said Mrs. Crewe, who had returned with arms full. "Use this salve."

So, Bess was his goddess's name. Was it short for Elizabeth perhaps, or some other more exotic name? He hoped not. Practical and no-nonsense, Bess suited her.

She slathered the unguent over and around his wound, bound the arm with bandages and tied off the cloth then stood. "There. You must present yourself to me tomorrow morning so that I might check the wound and change the dressing."

"That really isn't necessary." He stared up into those deep green eyes. Had she believed his claim to be a butler? Would he be here tomorrow morning to so present himself? He devoutly hoped so. But would staying be wise?

One brow on the goddess's face lifted. "Since I am related to the owner of this property, I stand in place of your employer, and if it is decided you might continue as butler here, you will demonstrate proper respect for and obey the orders of every woman in residence."

So, she'd accepted his claim to be an unemployed butler. He quickly scanned the housekeeper's face. Her disapproval—whether of him or his claim—was patent. *Do I wish to continue this farce?* How difficult could it be to act like a butler for a few days? *Staying will allow me to learn more about my intriguing lady.* He could always leave if the game tired.

"Besides. Even if he is a butler as he claims, we cannot afford to employ him," Mrs. Crewe muttered.

The two women looked him up and down. He'd not felt so examined since his first day at Eton.

"I would be happy to work for room and board," he blurted, having no need of the income but desperate for an excuse to remain. "I doubt you'll find anyone else to perform a butler's duties for so little salary."

"That's true," concurred the housekeeper.

Bess folded her arms across her chest and eyed him suspiciously. "I don't know."

"It would be wise, my lady, to hesitate over employing someone without references," said the housekeeper.

"Oh, I doubt this one will murder us in our beds," remarked the lady who began to gather items scattered about the floor.

Evidently, she deemed him incapable of committing so heinous a crime. He did not know whether to be pleased at her small show of trust or insulted that she completely dismissed him as a threat. *Perhaps celestial Bess pens horrid novels and is inured to the idea of murder and worse?*

His lady drew his attention. "You would be expected to help Mrs. Crewe with her work and any heavy lifting that may be required."

He reduced his grin to what he hoped was a modest smile. "I am happy to serve in any way."

"Mrs. Crewe, please return to preparing the house for the arrival of Patience and the girls. You need not mention this incident to Patience. I will inform her as soon as she arrives," ordered Bess as she gave him a considering glance.

"Yes, my lady. Your stepmama has entirely too much to worry about to be bothered with such as he, but I will remain to observe the proprieties."

"I do not believe that is necessary. He is a servant."

"I beg pardon to disagree. He's a man, and as breaking into this house proves, he is not above perpetrating violent acts when he wishes."

Mal watched the byplay between mistress and servant.

"Nonetheless," Bess said, "We have little time before the rest of the family arrives and much to do. Please start now. Our new butler will join you shortly to assist."

"Now you listen to me, Lady Bess. Someone must maintain the proprieties, and I'll not be telling Lady Seahaven that I left you alone with this stranger." She looked Mal up and down. "I don't trust him, and neither should you." She sat herself in a chair near the doorway.

The goddess sighed. "Very well, Mrs. Crewe. You are most likely correct. I think it best that none of us is ever alone with Mr. ...?"

*I cannot be making much of an impression if she has forgotten my name already*. "Kentigern," he supplied. *It's not a lie, precisely. My name is Malcolm Kentigern. I simply omitted the surname of Marr.*

"Very well, Kentigern." His Bess seated herself in the second hearthside chair. "Sit down, please. You are wounded." She waved him back to his seat.

"I am the eldest stepdaughter of the Dowager Countess of Seahaven," she continued. "You may address me as "Lady Elizabeth. Although, when not in company, I would prefer Lady Bess. My family all know that is my preference. My stepmother will be addressed as

Lady Seahaven. I will inform her of your employment as soon as she arrives. However, she has much to concern her at present, and I will encourage her to leave you and your employment here to me. Not including Mrs. Crewe and Nurse, there are eleven of us who will be residing in this house for the Season, including two children in the schoolroom and an infant."

She nodded, decisively. "I, Lady Seahaven, and the Ladies Barbara, Susana, Dorothea, Josefina, Iris, and Ivy—who are expected to arrive this afternoon—will occupy the bedchambers. The younger ones, Ladies Merrilyn, Emma, and Jane will reside in the nursery. They are traveling with the countess. You will eventually learn which of my sisters is which. If you cannot recall a name, 'my lady', will suffice."

Mal bit back a groan. *What have I got myself into? Eight adult women in a single household and not a man among them?*

Lady Bess had not finished. "Since you have experience of this house, you know it will be very crowded. Your work will be demanding. In addition to greeting visitors, serving meals et cetera, you will be required to fetch and carry as you are needed. You will assist Mrs. Crewe in any way she asks. You may have discerned that our finances do not extend far." She paused, clearly considering how much to tell him.

He waited, hoping she would choose to trust him, despite their unorthodox beginning. He had correctly concluded the scant financial circumstance of Bess and her family and determined then and there to do what he could to help without embarrassing anyone.

"Be careful what you say, Lady Bess," the housekeeper warned.

"He must know some of it, Mrs. Crewe, or he will make unwitting mistakes." She turned back to Mal. "Kentigern, what I tell you now must never be revealed to anyone outside this household."

"I give you my word as a gen... man... of honor never to gossip or share information about you and your family, my lady."

Bess's gaze narrowed. "We accepted our cousin Rose's invitation to live in her town house for the next few months while she is traveling in order to give Ivy, Iris, and Josefina the opportunity to have a Season."

She did not have to say the chance to marry well. That was ever the purpose of women, especially during the Season, even in York.

"This will be our best opportunity to present Ivy, Iris, and Josefina. The other girls are either too young, or like myself, have decided to pursue other opportunities than marriage."

That, Mal decided, was a distinct shame. Yes, the three being presented were probably diamonds of the first water. However, if each woman of the family was as handsome as his Nefertiti, they would all have suitors. If Bess was any example, most likely they were all very intelligent. That the older daughters 'pursued other opportunities' suggested they were industrious and definitely not snobbish. Good, he had a low tolerance for snobs, having met entirely too many of that breed in his life. *What sort of opportunity does my Nefertiti pursue?* He cast another glance at Bess, observing once more the familiar stains where her sleeves ended and her cuffs should have been. Whatever occupied her time, it had something to do with pen and ink.

"So, I shall give you one more chance to change your mind." His goddess's voice called him from his thoughts.

"I could not possibly refuse, when you have been so kind to me and generously offer me your trust. I will do all I can to provide superior service and help you succeed."

*Indeed, I will. I'll begin with a letter to James—I think he's still in London —directing him to bring all of his marriageable friends—especially Sir Vernon Melbarrow and that Du Grace fellow—to York. My brother can use the races as an excuse. However, I'll suggest he and his friends arrive early, or they might lose the opportunity to engage themselves to one of the three sisters being launched.* Still there were at least six to choose from, certainly some would eschew youth in favor of the senior sisters, like Bess. Without knowing precisely why, he frowned at that last thought. Certainly, his Nefertiti deserved a happy marriage as much as any of her sisters. He should be pleased he could provide a few eligible gentlemen for her to choose from.

# CHAPTER 5

Several days gave Mal ample opportunity to observe just how industrious was this family of sisters, for they'd wasted no time establishing themselves in the community and were quite active socially. In addition, all of them sewed with creditable expertise, though Lady Susana was the clear expert with a needle. Lady Seahaven and Lady Dorothea spent hours in the kitchen preparing enough baked goods to feed an army. And there was always a fortifying stew on the kitchen hob. The family did not eat like kings, but they ate well, and no one in the household went hungry. The twins, Ladies Iris and Ivy—when not busy assisting with the sewing—painted delicate flowers on blank, un-fired, bisque forms. Lady Josefina busied herself with preparing unguents and tinctures when not otherwise occupied. Ladies Merrilyn, Emma and Jane kept Bess busy in the schoolroom. However, when her duties as governess were done for the day, she sequestered herself in the study. She remained there during meals and when the other women went shopping or were out making calls. She would prefer, she said, to forgo all events.

One afternoon, Bess was asked to accompany Lady Seahaven and the twins on calls. He'd been prepared to search out a shawl for his goddess as the day was cool, but as he moved past her, he thought he imagined panic in her lidded gaze.

"I know you would prefer not to go," said Patience. "But several women of influence in York have remarked on your absence. Some even wonder if we've made you up out of whole cloth."

Bess hid her terror well, but Mal was close enough to see the small tremors shaking her form.

He reversed direction. "I beg your pardon, Lady Seahaven, I have just recalled that Lady Susana requested I inform Lady Bess that she is needed for a fitting this afternoon."

"Oh, dear. Is it your dress for the ball, Bess?"

Heavenly Bess swallowed visibly. "I believe so, Patience. Please give my regrets to the ladies you visit today. Let them know I look forward to meeting them at the ball, if not before."

"Very well," Lady Seahaven issued a small sigh then turned to the twins. "Come girls, we've a number of calls to make today and had best get to it."

Bess moved toward the stairs as Mal saw Lady Seahaven and her charges out the door. When he returned, she still stood, shoulders now slumped, on the lowest stair.

"Does Susana truly need me for a fitting?"

Now it was his turn to swallow. He wished he could run a finger under the cravat that threatened to choke him. "Not that I know of, Lady Bess. Would you like me to check with her?"

Shaking her head to herself, Bess straightened. "No, thank you, Kentigern, that will not be necessary. Please bring tea and some of the crumpets left from breakfast to me in the study."

"Of course, my lady." Mal watched her go, only moving when the study door closed. He headed for the kitchen. What could have caused so much fear in Bess? Until today, his Nefertiti, who had held him at gunpoint without so much as a quaver, had seemed fearless. He would probably still think so, had he not passed close enough to see her trembling.

He'd seen such fear before in students who were called on in class to recite or respond to a question. Especially in first-year students who had little experience and were filled with horror stories told by teasing upper classmen about canings and humiliation for those whom a professor judged inadequate. But Bess was not a first-year student. Presumably, she had plenty of experience with social events and could not possibly fear society's judgement of her as lacking in anyway. Hadn't she? Hadn't he overheard two of the sisters speaking about Bess and her London Season?

But now that he thought on it, she avoided going out on social calls and attending society events. He'd thought she did so because of her research which so pre-occupied her she often forgot the time.

And that work had him intrigued. His goddess was up late nearly every night, poring over texts and scribbling notes. Every now and then, he would bring her a biscuit and spot of tea. She would nod gratefully and wave him off without even glancing away from the documents scattered across the desk. Occasionally, he dreamt about being a pen or a piece of paper, just so she would touch him. He recognized the scholarly focus because he often experienced it himself. He'd tried to get her to discuss the project, but she'd remained closed mouthed. And she always locked her work away when she retired or left the study for any length of time.

Now he had two mysteries to solve regarding his Nefertiti. The easiest way would be to get her to confide in him. The way a person spoke of him or herself often revealed as much or more than the words that person said. He'd been trying for days to find something that would induce Bess to tell him about her research. Perhaps if he could succeed in that she might be more inclined to confide her other problems. It was worth a try, but first he had to get her to talk to him about more than fetching and carrying for her.

As it happened, a bit of absent-mindedness occurred a day or two later that allowed him to uncover the mystery of her work.

He entered the study with a message. "Lady Bess, forgive my interruption."

Bess put down her quill and lifted her head. "Yes, Kentigern, what is it?"

"Nurse requests your assistance. It seems that Lady Jane has developed an earache, and the Countess and Lady Josefina are not at home. Nurse believes you are best qualified to substitute for the absent ladies."

"Oh dear." She stood wiping her fingers on her apron before removing it. "Is Jane in a great deal of pain? She probably is, since her earaches are usually severe. What about fever?" Bess bustled about the room gathering her shawl and a few books.

"Nurse gave no details but said you would know what was best to be done."

"Very well. Please tell Nurse I will be there shortly. I must go to the keeping room and find the medicaments that Josefina would use."

"As you wish, my lady." He bowed and left to carry her message. She passed him on the stairs as he returned to his duties.

Her hand on his shoulder stopped him and tingling surged down his arm. "Kentigern, I believe I failed to bank the fire in the study. Would you take care of that for me? I've no notion how long I will be with Jane and Nurse."

"I will be pleased to do so, Lady Bess."

"Thank you." She hurried on her way.

Mal returned to the study and banked the fire as requested. He was leaving when he noticed that papers and books still covered the desk. Bess had also forgotten to put away her work. *I'd best do that for her.*

He'd intended only to stack the papers before locking them in a desk drawer then to shelve the books. However, he recognized instantly the first document upon which he laid his hand. It was a very good quality facsimile of the Rosetta Stone engravings.

On the reverse side of the facsimile were scrawled the words, *for B. Biggs*. Did Bess know that noted but reclusive scholar? Or was she perhaps B. Biggs herself? *Biggs could be a shortened form of Bigglesworth.* The possibility intrigued him so greatly, he could not resist exploring further. Seating himself in the desk chair he perused each paper carefully. Then he came to a partially completed letter addressed to Mr. Thomas Young of the London Royal Society.

Dear Mr. Young,

I have made significant progress in my study of your theories regarding the Rosetta Stone. I am nearly certain that you are much closer to a true translation at this time than is Champollion, and the identification of symbols enclosed in cartouches as representing names may well be correct. Further, ...

The missive stopped there. She must have been in the process of writing it when he'd interrupted her.

He was well acquainted with Mr. Young. In fact, though Young was close to fifteen years his senior, they had often collaborated in various studies. The recommendation to the York Antiquarian Society that they invite him to speak had come from Young. What would Bess say when she found out he was Professor Marr? Since that invitation had brought Mal to this house and his encounter with the celestial Bess, he would have much for which to thank his friend.

Thinking of Bess reminded him that she could return at any moment. He carefully stacked the documents together and placed them in the righthand desk drawer, then turned the key in the lock and placed the key on the desktop, so Bess would see it when she came back to her work.

After shelving the books, he left the study whistling, his mind churning with ideas about the ancient Egyptians and the probable translations of the stone found near Rosetta by the French Army in Egypt nearly eighteen years ago. A niggle of worry about concealing his true identity from Bess intruded. He had to tell her the truth, but could not imagine how. She'd boot him from the house the moment she learned of his deception.

# CHAPTER 6

Bess had spent the better part of the day tending to Jane, taking a small meal at the child's bedside. Hours later, when her stepsister finally slept, Bess returned to the study. She found the desk cleared of her work and the key atop the empty surface. Quickly, she ascertained that all of her papers had been stored in the right-hand desk drawer. But how…?

*Kentigern.*

He'd cleaned up for her, knowing she might be detained in the nursery. That had been very thoughtful of him. But had he read any of what she'd been working on? Did he even know how to read? Nonsense, she knew he was an intelligent man, and most butlers read at least a little bit. In addition, he spoke well, the absence of strong accent indicating an educated man.

So, he could have read her work? Would he understand it? He claimed he had no income. If he'd discovered she was the author of all the B. Biggs papers, would he reveal her secret to the gossip columns? Before Josefina, Iris and Ivy truly began their Season, disaster could befall them all.

Bess paced before the fire. *What to do*? Normally she might consult Patience, but her stepmother had far too much to worry about with her daughter ill and getting the girls ready for the York Season. In fact, their first important event would occur this coming Sunday. After Palm Sunday services, the family had been invited to attend an al fresco party at an estate just outside of York. Bess had declined to go in favor of working on the Rosetta Stone project. Patience had been disappointed, but understood Bess's motives involved more than dedication to her work.

Patience had trusted Bess when they'd discussed the decision to keep Kentigern on as butler. Heaven knew Bess wanted to believe the promises he'd given that he would not gossip about their situation. She had trusted Kentigern with the general truth of their circumstances when she accepted him. However, nothing specific had been confided. Now the strong possibility existed that he knew she worked for a living and could easily have surmised the same of her sisters, not to mention their lack of servants. A man without income could gain a large purse from selling gossip about the Dowager Countess of Seahaven and her daughters. Bess needed to be certain that Kentigern could be trusted. She hauled on the bell pull, setting her summons jingling below stairs. Then she moved to sit behind the desk and toyed with the key while she waited.

Minutes passed before the study door opened.

"You rang, Lady Bess?"

"Yes, Kentigern, I need to speak with you." She gestured to the armchair on the other side of the desk.

He sat. "I am happy to assist you in any way."

"Ahem, yes. You've already made life in this house much easier for all of us. However, I must ask you not to touch any papers left on this desk." She studied him closely to see his reactions.

A flush rose above his neckcloth. "I beg your pardon, Lady Bess, but… I noted that you always lock your documents in the desk before leaving. Your concern for Lady Jane caused you to neglect your usual procedure… I simply hoped to assist, by doing as you would do yourself."

The flush and his hesitations gave Bess cause for concern. He could be lying. "Did you read any of the documents?"

"I could not avoid looking at some of them as I straightened them before locking them away."

"Did you read anything of interest?"

That warm caramel gaze locked with hers. "I will not now, nor at any time in the future, lie to you, Lady Bess. I was fascinated to learn that you are involved in translating passages from the Rosetta Stone for Mr. Young of the London Royal Society."

"I see. Did you note anything else?"

"Only that the facsimile of the stone from which you are working is a very good copy. A note on the back of the facsimile suggests it is the property of B. Biggs. I am familiar with that scholar's work on the linking of hieroglyphs found on pottery in the tombs with similar glyphs on the doors at the entrance of those same tombs."

She had to ask. "How interesting, that a butler would be familiar with both B. Biggs and Mr. Young, to say nothing of the various types of work being done with Egyptian hieroglyphs." *Will he tell me how he came by such knowledge?*

"I've not always been a butler. Did you happen to notice that many of the symbols enclosed in cartouches within the hieroglyphic text closely resemble symbols found in both Coptic and Greek texts."

She blinked at him. "Really? I had not progressed as far as the cartouches in my investigations. Please, you must show me." Bess hurried to retrieve her work from the locked desk drawer, spreading the facsimile pages open across the desk and leaving the rest of the papers to one side.

"It is a theory proposed by Jean-François Champollion, several years ago, but has yet to be confirmed with other research." Kentigern rose and sorted through the spread pages of the facsimile, setting the papers to the side until he found a specific text. "Here." He indicated a symbol with his forefinger.

Bess stood, moving to the opposite side of the desk to peer at the several characters Kentigern pointed out. Her shoulder brushed his as she bent to see the exact symbols. She dismissed the touch as insignificant. The shivers coursing through her were naught but excitement at new evidence of the theories she was attempting to prove.

"Yes, yes. I see. Young has written to me to pay particular attention to those." She placed her hand atop his, moving it aside to get a closer look. When had the room become so warm?

"The same pattern of symbols appears here, here, and here." Kentigern took her hand in a gentle clasp guiding her fingers across the document to the images he wished her to study.

Excitement swirled and trembled in her belly. She felt like a child at Christmastide, leaping from one wonder to the next, and all just for her.

"Young believes these might be phonetic representations for p-t-o-l-m-e-s and hypothesizes that all three texts refer to the Egyptian King, Ptolemy V." She tried, without much success, for a serious and sober tone as she leaned so close to the desk that her cheek rubbed against Kentigern's fingers.

"I… uh."

At his stutter, Bess turned her head looking up at him across the span of his hand and arm.

He cleared his throat, "I suspect Young meets resistance to that hypothesis because it would indicate the Rosetta Stone postdates the Pharaonic period, which is regarded by many scholars as the high point of Egyptian knowledge and learning."

"Hmphf." Bess straightened; her fingers still entwined with Kentigern's. "I've never agreed with that opinion. Too many scholars tend to believe that because they cannot understand something it must be of vast importance. Of course, such persons would hardly like to have anyone solve the supposedly important mysteries and debunk their groundless theories. Should I ever attain my dream of publishing and receiving recognition under my own name, I'll not indulge in such nonsense."

Kentigern brought himself to his full height, smiling, and took both her hands. "You sound just like my history professor at Edinburgh."

"You attended university?" She looked up at him, wonder wide in her eyes.

"I did say I had not always been a butler." A dimple peeped out from the twisted side of his mouth.

Staring up at the hypnotic depths in his caramel gaze, Beth knew an unaccountable desire to kiss the small depression. How fantastic to have someone with whom to share her research and her dreams. "Have you always been interested in history?"

Some emotion gleamed in his eyes. He swallowed and nodded. "You?"

Suddenly, unaccountably tongue-tied, she mirrored his nod. "A–always."

"Amazing."

"Yes," she agreed as she rose on her toes.

He bent toward her.

Their lips met in a kiss as delicate as an ancient papyrus scroll. Desire sizzled along her nerves. She'd been kissed before. She knew what lust felt like. But somehow, this was different. Before she could decide how, the kiss ended.

Kentigern stepped back. "I… I'm, uh, I am sorry."

Bess shook her head. "I'm not."

"But…"

"No, I cannot regret such a kiss born of friendship and common interest."

For a brief moment he looked as if he would dispute her point. Then he gave a slow nod. "Aye, but it will not happen again."

*Perhaps*. Short and tender as it was, the kiss had been like no other she'd ever experienced. Most of those had occurred during her one Season. Some had been given with great expertise and left her with inexplicable yearnings. Others had been the bumbling attempts of young men with as little experience of kisses as she. But pleasant or not, she'd never, not once, considered the possibility of kissing the same man twice. Was that what this strange feeling was? Did she want a second kiss from a butler? A butler who knew as much or more than she did about ancient Egypt?

The warmth and hope she'd been feeling fled. "You have not said how you came by your knowledge of the Rosetta Stone and its inscriptions?"

Bess returned to the far side of the desk.

"My interest in history, Egypt especially, has led me to keep abreast of all the published scholarship."

"And you subscribe to the various scholarly journals."

The corners of his mouth—*that dear mouth*—lifted. "I could never afford such on a butler's salary."

"I do understand the frustration of not being able to achieve things simply due to circumstance. That said, how you come by your knowledge is really neither here nor there. I have one last request."

"Anything."

The sincerity in his caramel gaze reassured her. "Promise me, you'll never speak of my work, or the activities you see in this house to anyone."

"I gave you my word when we first met and you agreed to keep me on as butler. But if you need it, I give my word to you again. You may always rely on me."

"Thank you for that assurance. You may go now."

He hesitated at the study door, turning to look at her, but said nothing before leaving.

Bess restacked her papers and locked them back into the desk. Then she fiddled with the key, turning it over and over in her hand, staring at the brasswork as if it held the answers to all questions.

*How could life be so cruel?* She'd finally met a man with whom she shared an abiding interest, and he was totally unsuitable. Would it be so bad, if she abandoned the nobility she'd never wanted for a life of shared scholarship? Of course, Kentigern had given no indication that he wanted to share his life with her. For all she knew, the man kissed every woman who employed him. Good lord, had he played fast and loose with her sisters? Or Patience?

A spurt of fury had her throwing the key at the door. The moment the metal left her hand she felt foolish. If Kentigern were dallying with any of the females in the family, wouldn't they have said something?

*I'm not planning to mention that kiss to anyone. So why would my sisters? Why create a teapot tempest over so small a thing?*

Her fingers touched her mouth. It hadn't felt like a small thing. Kissing Malcolm Kentigern had felt like the most momentous experience of all her thirty years. And at thirty years, she should know better than to make a fool of herself over a kiss. She rose, retrieved the key, and put it in her pocket. No more nonsense, she promised herself as she left to seek her bed.

# CHAPTER 7

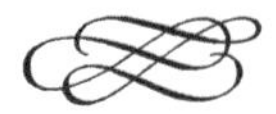

Mal marked time from before and after the day of the kiss; the day his life changed. It had been a simple meeting of lips, not especially passionate, but transcendent. Yes. Definitely transcendent. Although he suspected the change had actually occurred earlier, when he'd first looked into sea green eyes above the barrel of a pistol. He'd known then life would be different, but he hadn't imagined how different.

He spent every waking moment, and many moments asleep, dreaming of holding Bess in his arms of touching her, making her sigh with pleasure, prompting that cat-eyed goddess smile that turned his body harder than the Rosetta Stone. She was perfect for him. But as long as he was a butler, he could do nothing to court her. He could only bask in her presence and hope for crumbs to fall from the table of her courtesy.

But much as he'd enjoyed that kiss, wanted many more kisses from Bess, he cursed that momentous day as well. She'd said she did not think the kiss a mistake as it was given in friendship and common interest. Pah! Common desire, he wished. But she'd also become distant, returning to the far side of that desk, making certain he knew there were barriers—physical and social—that she would not permit him to cross. Nor would she cross them herself.

What if she knew he was an earl's son—second, but nonetheless—and a highly respected scholar in her chosen field? Would those barriers disappear?

As he considered the possibility, he recalled bigger problems. He'd deceived her, and she might not forgive him. She might see him as a competitor rather than a partner. Oh, he wished of all things to be her partner—in scholarship and in life?

And then there was his family. Would James understand and accept into the Marr family a virtually penniless, thirty-year-old woman firmly on the shelf with a strong fear of social events?

As that question arose, the countess informed him they would need the epergne for tonight's dinner party of twenty guests. She also wanted him to insert more leaves into the dining room table to provide enough room for all the place settings. He'd not had another moment to consider how to resolve the many difficulties facing him if he chose to pursue Lady Bess Bigglesworth.

He'd managed the table expansion with little problem. However, the epergne eluded his minimal butler's skills. He'd seen his godmother's huge silver epergne many times, so it should have been in the butler's pantry. But it wasn't. He'd tried to look inconspicuous as he searched the rest of the lower floor only to find it with Mrs. Crewe in the kitchen. Puzzle solved. She must have had it all along. At that moment, she was polishing the silver behemoth with some concoction until it shone like a king's crown.

He waited a moment until she paused in her work before he tapped her on the shoulder.

"Ooh." Startled she leapt around to face him. "You nearly scared the life from me, Mr. Kentigern. You shouldn't sneak up on a body that way."

*Is there another way?* "I'm sorry to have surprised you, Mrs. Crewe. I was looking for that piece. Where did you have it hidden?"

Her gaze sharpened. "Where we always store the silver, in the butler's pantry. How is it you do not know that?" She stuck out her chin daring him to claim he'd known.

He'd told too many lies and half-truths to those in the Seahaven household. It might be a relief to tell someone the truth. "May I trust you, Mrs. Crewe?"

"Depends on your intentions. If you plan to hurt her ladyship or any of my girls, I'll have you before the magistrate this day."

"My intentions are far from harm. I hope to be able to help the dowager countess to launch her daughters successfully. I admit having some assistance with that would be appreciated."

Her eyes narrowed with suspicion. "What kind of help? And why?"

Could he tell her he'd fallen instantly in love, more likely lust, with celestial, bossy, Bess? No, he couldn't do that. "The owner of this house is my godmother. I came to York hoping to visit and not knowing she was traveling or had offered the house to her cousin, the dowager, and her family. Please understand, I would aid the ladies out of sheer kindness, but I also stand in place of my godmother and feel responsible for them."

"That is mighty kind of you, but why pretend to be a butler—especially when you're not very good at it? Why not tell Lady Seahaven the truth?"

*Because I still haven't determined precisely what that truth is.*

He hedged for time. "I'm sure you've noticed that the entire family is proud to a fault and wish to make their own way."

"Aye, it takes little effort to see pride in the Bigglesworths, and they've no fear of working to achieve their aims. They are good folk and don't deserve to be treated with lies and falsehoods."

He nodded. He'd seen every member of the family working at one thing or another in pursuit of launching the three beauties.

Mrs. Crewe was looking at him as if he'd grown three heads.

Had he spoken his thoughts aloud?

"I apologize for my distraction. I agree that the family deserves better than they've received, but how else am I to help? If I told the countess I'm no butler but an ordinary gentleman, she'd send me on my way, and I'd have no excuse to give assistance for which she would surely never ask."

"Hmmm. I see your point. Since I, too, wish this family to have great success, I'll help you be a better butler. If you don't understand how to do something, Ask me."

"Thank you, Mrs. Crewe. You'll not regret this."

"I pray I don't. If you hurt the dowager and her family, the wrath of God will seem nothing to what I'll do to you." They talked for several minutes more while Mrs. Crewe finished polishing the huge decorative centerpiece and muttered something about having to prepare the stew the dowager had requested for luncheon. As they spoke, he asked for her help in finding additional servants beginning with a cook, a maid of all work, and perhaps a lady's maid. He would undertake to pay their salaries, if she could find suitable employees willing to keep their employer's confidence. She could explain to her ladyship that the new hires needed shelter and work more than salary. That way, the countess and her family need never feel beholden to him for his assistance.

Two days later, he had to search out the housekeeper for help once more. Shawls, spencers, wraps, and hats. Lady Bess and the younger girls needed outer wear for an outing on this breezy April day. *Where in the world do butlers find all these things?* Mrs. Crewe showed him where the cupboard was and which items belonged to which family member. He thanked her then hurried to cart two armfuls of clothing up to the foyer. He was busy arranging all in a neat and orderly manner when he heard Bess on the stairs. He'd been in the house little more than a day before he learned to discern her steps from all the others. Now he did not even need to hear her. The very air changed when she came near.

"Oh, Kentigern, thank you. The children will be down presently, but we'll need Lady Susana's pelisse as well. She's put aside her sewing to help with the children."

"I could save her the trouble, Lady Bess."

Her brows went up. "Thank you for the offer, Kentigern, but

herding children on an educational tour of York is not among your duties."

"As you wish, Lady Bess. As for escorting you and the children, your ladyship, I respectfully disagree. My duty is to assist the countess and all her family in every way possible."

"But surely you have other tasks that must be done."

"Nothing that cannot be delayed." *And thank heaven for that. I was not looking forward to polishing my godmother's antique silver table settings.*

She eyed him thoughtfully. "Have you any experience with children, Kentigern?"

He smiled. "I was a child once."

She grinned back. "That's not the sort of experience I meant."

"Ahem, yes, please forgive my attempt at humor. As an adult, I've had little opportunity to encounter children, but I would like to learn. Experience with children could be an asset when I look for my next position."

"Hmm. Very well. Lady Susana really does need to finish the sewing she started. I'll go up to tell her she's not needed and explain that you will accompany the children and me in her place. I'll bring the children when I return."

"Very good, my lady." He gave the correct bow then allowed himself the pleasure of watching her leave. He'd no idea if he would like spending hours with the children, but he was certain he would enjoy any time spent in Lady Bess' company.

# CHAPTER 8

Somehow, Kentigern had found a huge, if rather ancient, carriage with an equally ancient driver. The driver being very aged and—as Kentigern quietly informed her—impeded by lumbago; it was her entirely too well-educated butler who opened the door and let down the steps. Bess entered first, hesitantly placing her gloved hand in his. The memory of her uncovered fingers twined with his was stronger than the kid covering their hands. She let go as quickly as courtesy would allow. Next Kentigern handed in Emma and Merrilyn. He put up the steps and closed the door then climbed up beside the driver.

The girls asked so many questions during the drive to Clifford's Tower—the first stop on their tour—that Bess was challenged to answer them all. In fact, she deferred several about the history of the tower to when they arrived at the building. Kentigern took charge of the girls, as Bess was delayed for a short moment, seeking out a retiring room in which to mend a small tear in her hem. She soon joined Kentigern and her sisters on the second floor of the stone fortress, and stopped to listen to him with her sisters.

"Why is this called Clifford's Tower?" asked Emma, ever the more studious of the two girls.

Kentigern pointed toward the battlements, "Sir Roger de Clifford, one of the rebel leaders who fought against King Henry III, was chained ahm…"

Bess was pleased to note that Kentigern hesitated to describe lurid details of a hanging to a young girl.

"Punished, here. Sir de Clifford was punished for his rebellion." supplied Bess.

"What did the king do to him?" asked Merrilyn.

"The exact details are unimportant. Since he had offended his king, you can be certain the punishment was quite terrible," said Kentigern. "That is why his name has been attached to this tower ever since."

"I don't know," pondered Merrilyn. "I think being sent to bed without supper is a horrible punishment. If the king did even worse to Sir de Clifford, the man must have done something very bad indeed."

"Quite right, sister. Rebellion is a very bad thing. I dare say Sir de Clifford lost a great many suppers."

"Then, in a sense, he is still chained to these stones," whispered Emma.

Kentigern knelt beside her. "That is a very perceptive comment, Lady Emma."

Emma blushed.

Bess enjoyed the easy way Kentigern had of explaining history. It kept her as enthralled as her younger sisters. "How much of the history of the tower have you been able to explain while I was delayed?" she asked.

"He told us about the Hebrew people who died here, and the fire, and the blood on the stones. But, it wasn't really blood, at least that's what Kentigern thinks. He thinks it was iron that leached from the stones of the tower," Merrilyn finished with a disappointed frown.

"Did you want the stones to bleed, sister?" asked Bess.

"It would be ever so much more exciting. I wonder if the ghosts of Sir Clifford or the Hebrews haunt the tower?"

Kentigern stood. "There is no telling, Lady Merrilyn. If you'll come with me," he took each of the girls by the hand. "We'll look at the tower gardens before we go on to York Minster."

"Was anyone killed in the gardens?"

"Not to my knowledge Lady Merrilyn."

"Pooh. Who wants to walk around looking at flowers and trees?"

"Josefina finds gardens fascinating," remarked Bess. Kentigern's knowledge of the tower's history was quite detailed. How did a butler, even one who attended university, learn such things? *If he is a butler.* Bess still had her doubts, but as he'd performed his duties well enough, she kept those doubts to herself. To voice them would only worry Patience, and her stepmama did not need more concerns.

The Minster, like the gardens, proved quite unexciting to Merrilyn. However, Emma enjoyed a long conversation with Kentigern about the various prelates, bishops and archbishops whose primary responsibility had been Yorkshire and therefore the York Minster.

Bess and Kentigern continued daily trips to discover the history of York and entertain the children. Some five days after their trip to York Minster, they returned home from an exploration of the ancient walls of the city. Kentigern had held forth on the various Viking depredations to York. Merrilyn had been thrilled. Emma was full of questions about some of the Viking artifacts that had been on display in one of the small private museums near the walls.

It was well after tea when Bess ushered her sisters through the door Kentigern held open to the foyer of Cousin Rose's house.

A strange voice, a male voice, brought her up sharp. Merrilyn and Emma squeezed forward, pausing at her side.

"I am sorry if Lady Seahaven is indisposed, but as she is in charge here, I must speak with her regarding my brother," the stranger insisted.

At her back Bess felt heat from Kentigern's tall form. In the same moment, his hand settled on her shoulder.

"I will handle this, Lady Bess."

Before she could protest, he'd moved around her and the girls to approach the man arguing with Mrs. Crewe.

"I tell you again, your lordship, Lady Patience does not know a

Professor Marr. You must have mistaken your brother's direction. I'll not disturb her ladyship simply to please someone who doesn't know how to locate a correct address, be he a lord or not." Mrs. Crew shook a large spoon at him. She must have been cooking, for a dollop of something landed smack on the lordship's aristocratic cheek.

"But I insist..." he fished in a pocket for a kerchief.

"Ah, Lord Strathnaver, if you please," Kentigern interrupted.

Uncertain what Kentigern intended, Bess waited. She'd never seen her butler more hesitant. But then this was the Earl of Strathnaver! One of the most highly regarded men in Britain. What could he possibly want here? And why was her butler dancing about from foot to foot as if stepping on hot coals? She noted the earl's dusty cloak. *His lordship has only just arrived.*

He turned toward Kentigern at the butler's voice and actually tilted his head, blinking, as if observing some curiosity.

"P... permit me to take your hat and cloak," Kentigern stammered.

That in itself was odd. Kentigern was the calmest of men, but he was behaving as if meeting an earl were akin to viewing a giraffe or an emu.

"Ma..." the earl began.

"If you will accompany me to the parlor," continued Kentigern without pausing to permit the earl to speak. "I believe I can clear up this misunderstanding. Mrs. Crewe, would you please bring Lord Strathnaver some tea and perhaps some of those delicious crumpets?"

The earl still stared at her butler with an astonished expression.

What in the world was going on? Bess wondered. *Surely the earl has encountered many butlers in his life. Although Kentigern is behaving quite oddly.* He should know better than to interrupt an earl, or indeed any guest.

Lord Strathnaver permitted the removal of his cloak then, his gaze still fixed on Kentigern walked slowly toward the door the butler now held open to the parlor.

Bess looked from the earl to her butler and back again. She saw nothing remarkable about Kentigern. He appeared his usual handsome self. But he fascinated the earl, almost as if Kentigern's appearance in her foyer were completely unexpected. That was impossible. Butlers and other servants were fixtures. It would be more startling if the household did not have one. Bess frowned as she watched the slow ballet occurring between the earl and the servant.

Then, in the moment when the two men stood side by side, she blinked rapidly. *They are nearly identical—lean-framed, the earl slightly taller than Kentigern, black-haired, faces nearly the same shape. Does the earl have eyes the color of warm caramel?* She could not tell at this distance, but she would find out. And she'd know why her normally placid butler was behaving like a cat standing on a hot stove.

It was time she took charge. "Here, Merrilyn, Emma, go on up to the nursery, I must see our visitor welcomed." She was the oldest in the family and would speak with the earl in her stepmother's stead. As for Patience, what was Mrs. Crewe at? *Stepmama is never sick.*

Kentigern was closing the parlor door as Bess approached.

"You need not exert yourself, Lady Elizabeth," he said. "You've had a very long day, and I can easily clear up this small problem."

She beamed at him with what she called her social smile—the expression that had been the only armor permitted her during that horrid London Season—then handed him her cloak. She wasn't about to permit him to clear up what she was certain was no misunderstanding. In the time they'd been in York, she'd come to rely on Kentigern for more than his butler services. Often, when she worked late, they would share a cup of tea and discuss the nuances of translating hieroglyphics. She'd nearly forgotten her early suspicions of him. Though, she'd always believed he was no butler. Unless she was very mistaken, the Earl of Strathnaver could provide answers to questions about Kentigern's true identity.

"Nonsense, I am not in the least tired." She was exhausted. "It would be rude if the family did not greet such an august personage as the Earl of Strathnaver. Please assist Mrs. Crewe with the refreshments."

Forehead wrinkled, he looked from her to where the earl stood frowning back at her butler.

"You may go, Kentigern."

"Yes, my lady." Clearly not happy to be dismissed, he gave a nod and departed.

She walked over to the earl and held out her hand to him. He bowed over it.

"I am Lady Elizabeth Bigglesworth, but I prefer Lady Bess. Please be seated, my lord." She gestured to one of a pair of settees that flanked a low table then settled herself onto its opposite. "What has caused you to honor us with this visit?"

Yes, those tawny, caramel eyes were exactly the same shape as Kentigern's, though perhaps a shade more orange. More like a tiger than a sweet. She knew from news reports and the gossip her sisters brought home from their calls that the Earl was not a man one crossed without serious consequences. It was entirely possible that Kentigern had good reason to be nervous of the man. She grew more certain than ever that Kentigern was no more a butler than she was Empress of Egypt. The Earl studied her with a narrowed gaze as she waited in polite silence for him to reply. The squint he'd acquired indicated he might be wondering how to proceed.

Then his expression cleared. "Several days ago, I was in London, when I received a letter from my brother Malcolm asking me to visit him at this address in York and to bring any available friends with me."

"Interesting. Why this address, and where are your friends?"

"Lord Du Grace and Sir Vernon Melbarrow are obtaining rooms at the Bull and Horn, as I did not wish to impose three strangers on the household without notice. This house is my godmother's. Malcolm had intended to visit with her while attending some sort of antiquarian meeting. But it seems that Lady Rose is not at home. Perhaps Mal forgot to inform me correctly when he wrote."

"Absence of mind is a common problem among scholars. What is your brother's area of expertise?"

"He has always been fascinated by the civilizations that thrived in and around what is now Egypt."

The light dawned, and along with it, ice-cold fury possessed her. "The Strathnaver family name is Marr, is it not?"

"Yes." The earl nodded.

In all her imaginings she'd not considered that Kentigern—no, it was the Honorable Malcolm Marr, respected scholar and noted expert in Egyptology—might be a scion of one of Scotland's oldest and proudest families. *High in the instep* applied to lesser beings outside the rarified stratosphere of the noblesse oblige exemplified by Clan Marr and the Earl, its head. She suppressed a shudder and along with it her ire. That she would save for the man masquerading as her butler. No wonder Kentigern knew so much about the work she did—the lying cur.

"Then your brother must be Professor Marr from Edinburgh University. He is a speaker at the York Antiquarian Society's annual seminars which begin next week."

"That would be my brother."

"Would Professor Marr's middle name be Kentigern?"

The earl studied her a long while before responding with a solitary, "Yes."

"Is it not interesting that Kentigern is the name of the man working in this house as a butler?"

Another pause, shorter this time. "That is, indeed, interesting."

"Even more interesting to me, your lordship, is that our butler resembles you so closely. You could easily be brothers," remarked Bess.

"Ahem. Well as to that. You are an astute woman, Lady Bess. I'll not pretend any longer that I did not recognize my brother Malcolm the moment he entered the corridor. I kept silent because I'd no notion what reason he might have for such a masquerade."

"Neither have I, my lord. You must ask him when he brings the tea."

"Indeed. I think it best if you begin the questioning. You will lose a butler when the truth is revealed. And I would prefer to observe his behavior when he is confronted with his deception."

She stood, unable to sit calmly. If she saw Kentigern once more, she might not succeed in resisting the urge to hit him in the nose. But the lying lout was not in the room, so she must deal with the Marr who was.

"Please accept my apologies, but I would prefer not to be present when you speak with Kenti—ah, Professor Marr. In fact, I would be quite happy never to set eyes on him again."

"Has he offered you insult, Lady Bess?"

"No, no. Nothing more than the deception he practiced on me and my family."

"You deserve an explanation." The earl regarded her with kind eyes.

"Quite possibly, but it is my stepmama, Lady Patience Seahaven, who most deserves the apology. Since she is unavailable right now, perhaps you could persuade your brother to write to her. We are a family of ten women in this household, my lord. Your brother has been the only male living in this house during our time in York. Whatever motive he may have for his behavior cannot excuse the potential damage done to our family's reputations."

"I will endeavor to make certain that no harm is done," the earl assured her.

"I doubt even you could stop every wagging tongue in York. We have had visitors to this house who would easily recognize your brother. On many occasions, he has, in his guise as a servant, escorted me and several of my sisters as well as my stepmother on various expeditions about the city. It is no secret that he has lived in this house."

"Nonetheless, please allow me to do what I can to mitigate any problems Malcolm's charade may have caused."

She shrugged. "Do what you must, but I'll not count on anything. However, removing your brother from this house is my primary wish."

"Agreed. I will take Malcolm with me when I leave. Have you considered what you will tell your family about his disappearance? What will you do for a butler? I would like to help with that if I may."

"I would prefer not to be beholden to anyone. We are not without resources." It wasn't exactly a lie. All of the Bigglesworth ladies were resourceful. What did it matter if the Earl of Strathnaver imagined she meant financial resources? If God were kind, she'd never encounter the man or his brother again.

"As you wish. Please know that my brother and I are in your debt, and if you or any of your family ever need help of any kind, it would be my honor to assist you."

"Thank you," she choked the words out around a lump forming in her throat and blinked back the tears that threatened to spill. "I doubt we will require your assistance. Now, if you will excuse me. I regret that we have no butler to see you and your brother out when you have finished speaking." She turned to leave.

"Seeing ourselves out is no hardship, Lady Bess. I thank you for talking with me and understand your quite justified anger with my brother. However, you should know that this sort of thing is very unlike Malcolm. He has ever been a proponent of truth and holds deceivers in contempt."

Her hand on the doorlatch, she looked back at the Earl of Strathnaver. It was almost like looking at Kentigern, no Professor Marr. *I should be glad to see the last of both men. Why then am I so cast down?* "It seems he is not as strict in his attitude toward deception as you believe." Lifting her head, she swept from the room.

# CHAPTER 9

"Mal, what maggot got into your very educated brain? Breaking into our godmother's house is bad enough but masquerading as butler to a houseful of marriageable women in the middle of York's social Season? Have you lost your mind?"

Mal stared glumly into the fire. "Undoubtedly, I have lost any and all good sense God gave me."

The brothers sat ensconced before the fireplace of the earl's private sitting room at the Bull and Horn. Mal had arrived at the town house parlor with the tea tray to find Bess gone. James had related the conversation he'd had with that lady and her wish to never set eyes on Mal again. James had wanted to leave immediately. Mal had insisted on staying long enough to make arrangements for a new butler. His brother had insisted on accompanying Mal and being included in all arrangements.

Mrs. Crewe had been able to assure Mal that her own brother—who had just returned from the former colonies—would happily come on as butler for the household. The other servants were sworn to secrecy on pain of losing the very generous salaries Mal had been paying them. Receiving assurances of discretion and Mrs. Crewe's promise to contact him if the Bigglesworth ladies encountered the least difficulty, Mal and his brother had taken his leave of them all.

Bess might not wish to see him now, but he would find a way to explain his behavior just as soon as he could figure out why he'd done it. What impulse had led to his charade he was not certain. He did know that he would miss Bess, their conversations about Egypt, and their explorations of York. He'd never met another woman like her: companionable, intelligent, insightful, hard-working, generous and kind. It wasn't right that she and her family had been placed in such straightened circumstances. He wished he knew what he might do to change things.

"Did you hear me, Mal?"

"Huh? Hear you, James? No, I apologize for wool-gathering. What were you saying?"

"I was saying that you are not yet out of the woods. Should word get out that it was you staying with the Bigglesworth ladies, you may well have to marry one of them."

"Preposterous." But was it? He'd been seen frequently in his butler's role and his looks, if one bothered to peer closely at a servant, made him easily identifiable. Wed one of the Bigglesworth sisters? No, not just any sister. Marry Bess. He smiled broadly.

"What's got you grinning like a loon? You can't be happy at the prospect of marriage with that family of females?"

"I might well be happy wedded to Bess."

"Lady Elizabeth Bigglesworth?" James blurted. "She's a blasted bluestocking. Thirty if she's a day. Tongues still wag about her come-out and how she turned down three excellent proposals. Made the distant relative who sponsored her so angry the woman advised Seahaven not to bring her to London ever again."

"Seahaven was a fool," Mal muttered. "From what I've heard of his late lordship, she is better off nowhere near the man. He married five women hoping to get an heir and ran through the fortune of each bride so quickly there was nothing left for the daughters he sired. Apparently, because they were female, he never gave them another thought." Mal glared at the fire.

"And this is the type of person whose daughter you wish to wed?"

"Bess is nothing like him. In fact, none of the Bigglesworth ladies show the least propensity toward selfish, thoughtless behavior. They are all quite industrious and considerate," Mal explained.

"Good for them, but I cannot imagine Lady Elizabeth would look kindly on your suit."

"True, she refused to see me, so she must be quite irritated with me."

"You put it too mildly."

"I'll need to change that. And I'll need to do it quickly, before I speak at the York Antiquarian Society next week. The entire town will be abuzz with speculation once I'm recognized."

"I know of only three things likely to turn a woman's head," James said.

Mal raised a brow in question.

"A title. Something with standing and social power."

"Well, I don't have one; in fact, I hope never to have any such thing. Being an honorable is bad enough."

"True," murmured James. "While I wouldn't wish such a title on my worst enemy, it does have some advantages."

"That says quite a bit, given that you've one of the oldest and most respected titles in Britain. What else?"

"Money, wealth, riches."

"I'm comfortably well off. Bess would never want for anything."

"Since she's spent most of the past ten years on the edge of poverty, comfortably well off might not be enough."

"Probably. And the third?"

"The gift of her heart's desire. Whatever it might be that she wants above all else."

Mal lunged forward and grabbed his brother by the shoulders. "James, I could kiss you."

The earl broke his brother's hold and stepped back. Horror etched his face. "Please do not."

"Right. Most likely neither of us would enjoy it." He turned a circle searching the room. "Where could I have put my hat?"

"Have you taken leave of your senses? First you wish to kiss me. Now you need your hat?"

"Yes, I must have my hat, and my coat for that matter. The evening is chilly this time of year." He rushed to the bedchamber connecting to the far side of the sitting room.

"Brother, what are you about?" James called to Mal through the bedchamber door.

Hat and cloak in hand, Mal reappeared from the bedroom, hurried through the sitting room, and flung wide the door into the corridor beyond.

"Mal?"

He paused on the threshold. "I intend to give Bess her heart's desire." Then he was gone.

"I hope you know what you're doing," James whispered to the air. "Women are mysterious creatures, and I've yet to meet a man who guessed correctly what even one woman wanted."

Mal hurried down the stairs to the lobby. "I need a hackney," he shouted to the room at large.

The person behind the innkeeper's desk waved over one of the porters who approached Mal. Mal told the man what he needed as they rushed outside. Within minutes, he was ensconced in a hackney, heading toward York's neighborhood of neat middle-class homes.

As the driver pulled up. Mal leapt out and tossed a coin to him. "Two more of those if you'll wait for me."

The man tipped his hat. "Aye, sur, I be waitin'."

Mal rushed up the steps of a town house and hammered on the door.

A butler opened up, frowning in displeasure. "Master Nedhelm is at dinner, sir. He asks that you return tomorrow during calling hours."

Mal shoved his hat into the butler's hands and brushed past him. "I'm very sorry, but I need to speak with Mr. Nedhelm now!"

"Corwin, what is all this fuss? I told you to tell..." The white-haired gentleman who stepped from what was probably the dining room, pulled a serviette from where he'd tucked it in his neckcloth. "Is that you, Marr?"

"Yes, indeed, Nedhelm. I regret having to disturb your supper in so unseemly a manner, but I have urgent need of your help."

Nedhelm peered beyond Mal. to his butler. "Close the door. We need not announce our business to the entire street."

The butler closed the door. "Yes, sir. I'm sorry, sir."

Nedhelm waved him off. "Go see if cook has the syllabub ready to serve. Will you join me for dessert, Marr? Cook's syllabub really is quite good. I've an excellent port for afterwards."

Nedhelm was turning back toward the dining room.

"Thank you," replied Malcolm. He could wait through dessert and port to make his request. A couple of glasses of port might make Nedhelm more amenable to what Mal had in mind.

Soon, they were seated at the table with a dish of syllabub each and the maid who had brought it in closed the door as she left.

"What is so urgent that you must interrupt a man at table?" asked Nedhelm.

Mal swallowed his mouthful of the sweet cream laced with white wine and a hint of lemon. All right, he wouldn't wait. "I have a favor to ask."

"Anything, my dear man. I owe you for your help identifying the provenance of those Roman artifacts found last year." He popped a spoonful of the dessert into his mouth.

"I had planned to wait until we were at our port, because once you hear what I ask of you, you may not be quite so amenable." Mal pushed his plate a way. The syllabub was good, but a tad too sweet for his tastes.

"Nonsense, Marr." Nedhelm gobbled another spoonful. "I cannot imagine anything you would ask that I would refuse."

"I need you to send an invitation to a fellow scholar to speak at the antiquarian society meeting next week. Probably the last day, April twenty-fifth, would be best to allow preparation time."

"But our speaker slate is full. The program has already been sent to the printer."

"We could have announcement cards printed then inserted into the program, and the additional speaker could be announced as a surprise benefit for attendees only."

"You want to add a last-minute speaker for a closed session of the meeting? Who is this paragon of scholarship?"

"Ah... um... the speaker is B. Biggs."

Nedhelm's eyes lit up. "We've been trying to persuade Mr. Biggs to attend our little meeting for several years now. Ever since that paper on the relation between pottery and wall hieroglyphs was published. Had I known you were acquainted, I would have sought your help on our behalf."

"My acquaintance is of a very recent nature—" Mal stated.

"Regardless, this is a favor I am delighted to grant. I'm sure when word gets out that Biggs will be speaking, our entire membership will turn out in force. That alone will cover the cost of the extra printing."

Malcolm was glad that his friend was pleased, but his conscience tugged at him. Nedhelm would not be at all pleased to discover Biggs was a woman. *Perhaps I need not tell him.*

"Could you persuade Biggs to accept my invitation to dinner in two days? I'd like to pick his brain on the Rosetta Stone, and discuss the topic of his speech," posed Nedhelm.

Malcolm toyed with his dessert spoon. There was nothing for it, if he wanted to give Bess her heart's desire—recognition of her scholarship by respected members of the scholarly community—he would have to tell Nedhelm now. It would not do for both Nedhelm and Bess to be surprised upon first meeting. Still, he delayed.

"Will Mrs. Nedhelm be present?" he asked.

Nedhelm nodded enthusiastically. "Athena wouldn't miss it. She's not here tonight because she wanted to attend some musicale. Evidently society is all agog over three young ladies known as the Seahaven Diamonds, and she heard they were to be present. Athena loves being au courante nearly as much as she loves an archaeological expedition. Since her interest in Egyptology is nearly as keen as my own, if Biggs accepts, Athena will definitely be present. Why? Is her attendance important?"

"It will make Bigg's acceptance much more likely," Mal admitted.

Nedhelm's gaze narrowed. "He's not a womanizer?"

"No, nothing of the kind."

"Good. Then you will ask?"

Mal nodded agreement. "I will ask on one condition."

"And that is?"

"That you treat your guest with all the respect due a noted scholar of Egyptology."

Nedhelm's brow furrowed. "Why in the world would I not? Biggs's reputation is well deserved."

"I'm glad to hear you say so," Mal said, "Because, without your assurance, I would not consider asking her to accept your invitation."

Nedhelm's eyes widened. "*Her?* Did I hear you correctly?"

Mal straightened in his chair. "You did."

"B. Biggs is a woman?"

"A very talented and knowledgeable woman, who, as we speak, is working to verify a Rosetta Stone translation by Mr. Thomas Young of London's Royal Society."

"The membership will be outraged." Nedhelm narrowed his eyes. "But you say Young respects her enough to ask her to verify his work?"

"He does," Mal confirmed. "If you let that be known—I can't imagine Young would object—and if you, as the association's leader, set the example, I think the outrage will be minimal at worst."

"I might not remain leader very long if I do this. I do have my enemies among the members who would love to see me fail. Inviting a woman to speak to the membership would be just the thing."

"Great reward only comes with great risk. You could cement your leadership of the society for years to come, if you invite Biggs. You might even be noted as one of the most forward-thinking scholars in the country."

Nedhelm preened a bit at that thought then his pride subsided. "Or I could be lambasted for a fool. However, I have an idea how to present this to the membership and gain their support."

"What's your idea?"

"Let it be my surprise, if I succeed. The membership must approve first or I may as well say nothing."

"I understand," Mal said. "Perhaps we could enlist Mr. Young's assistance in issuing the invitation to speak at the seminar. That way the responsibility is shared. Your membership can hardly fault you for following the lead of one of Britain's most respected scholars."

"True, but such a request would take time that we may not have."

"The seminars do not begin for another seven days. My brother, Strathnaver, is in York. I believe I could persuade him to provide a special messenger. With Mr. Young in Coventry at this time of year, we could send our note to him and receive his reply within four days, five at the most."

"That could work, as long as Thomas Young agrees."

"With Strathnaver's backing, I do not believe Young will cavil. Meanwhile, I suggest you extend your dinner invitation to Lady Elizabeth Biggleswort for two days hence. If you are not impressed, I will withdraw my request. However, if you are the least bit impressed by your discussions with her, I insist you grant me the favor of inviting her to speak."

"Hmm. It would be a stimulating dinner. I'll have my wife send the invitation. You'll leave the name and address before you depart tonight?"

"Certainly."

Nedhelm rang for the port and requested a pen, ink and paper along with the wine and glasses.

Malcom settled back to enjoy an excellent port and consider the ramifications of what he was doing. Would Bess approve? If asked to speak, would she accept the invitation? What of that fear he'd noted when she'd been asked to go out on social calls? Did her fears extend to public speaking? Would this action put him back into her good graces or condemn him to eternal banishment? At the very least it could give him the chance to speak with her at the Antiquarian Society seminar, if not before. Then he smiled. All speakers were invited to a closing supper dance on the evening after the seminars closed. Dancing was not his favorite activity, but he could hold his own on the dance floor. More important, he would enjoy having Bess in his arms. He'd make certain she enjoyed it too.

# CHAPTER 10

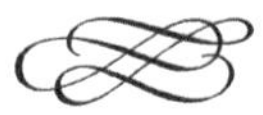

Bess looked up from her work as the door to the study opened. Their new butler, Ethan Crewe entered with the tea tray. He was a much better butler than Kentigern—no she must think of him as Mr. Marr or better yet Professor Marr. But then Crewe was a professional and knew his job in ways Professor Marr never could. He always knew where to find things, and his knowledge of social courtesies was extensive. She could not count the number of times she'd had to correct or apologize for some gaff Professor Marr had committed.

"Put it on the table by the fire, please, Crewe. I need to take a pause from my work."

"An excellent idea, my lady. Shall I leave your mail on the table as well?"

*Mail? I don't expect to hear from the publisher about my latest article for several weeks, and Mr. Thomas Young knows I am working as fast as possible. He is going on expedition to Egypt in June and wants the translation verified before he leaves. As it is only April, I have plenty of time. Who else could possibly have anything to say to me in a letter?*

"Please, Crewe. Then you may go. I'll ring when I've finished my tea." She sanded her pages, placed her quill back in its stand and capped the ink well. Then she stood and hurried to sit in one of the chairs near the fireplace. Nothing would be gained by indulging the inexplicable anxiety she felt. It was nothing more than megrims over the upcoming presentation ball for Josefina, Iris, and Ivy, which, as a loyal and loving sister, she must attend. Her anxiety had nothing to do with missing a certain scholar. She took several deep breaths as she listened to the study door closing. Pouring a cup of the strong dark Egyptian Saiidi style tea that Cousin Rose kept on hand, Bess settled back to enjoy a comfortable pause in her day's exertions. She poured her second cup before opening the one envelope Crewe had left for her.

Dear Lady Elizabeth,

My husband, Nedhelm, and I are great friends of Mr. Thomas Young of the London Royal Society. We have recently learned that you are also acquainted with this gentleman. Hence, we wish to extend an invitation for you to join us for dinner tomorrow night at seven in the evening. Please let us know that you will accept.

With kind regards,

Mrs. Athena Nedhelm

Bess blinked and read the note a second time. The invitation was perfectly proper, except that she had never been introduced to either Mr. or Mrs. Nedhelm. She recognized Nedhelm as the head of the York Antiquarian Society. Indeed, she'd read his papers on the Roman and Viking antiquities of Yorkshire and the insights to be gained there about the area's history. She would enjoy meeting him and his wife as well as spending an evening of food, wine, and scholarly discourse. She missed her conversations with Kenti—Mr. Marr terribly. Since he left, the most advanced discussions she'd had were with Emma about the reasons York's persecuted Hebrews sequestered themselves in Clifford's Tower rather than choosing to leave York for a more hospitable town. Professor Marr had clarified many points, but the child continued to raise questions, evidently brought on by her discussions with Ken—Professor Marr.

Explaining the anti-Hebraic sentiment that still prevailed in much of the country to her very open-minded and thoughtful stepsister had been difficult. Emma was too young to learn of such prejudice and the evil it could breed. However, Bess had never believed in varnishing the truth. Emma had been very quiet for a time after that conversation. Then suddenly she was arguing with Merrilyn and entertaining Jane with her normal good nature. Emma was very intelligent. Bess knew she'd taken time to consider the impact of bias against an entire people and had decided for herself how to proceed if she ever encountered someone of the Hebrew faith.

And how to proceed with this invitation was exactly what Bess needed to do right now. She had to wonder if Mr. Marr were somehow involved. But she could not know for certain. *What to do?*

She stared into her teacup for some time before rising to ring for Crewe. Then she folded the note and slipped it through a slit in the side seam of her dress into one of the pockets she wore beneath her skirt.

"You rang, my lady?"

"Yes. Do you know where the countess is at this moment?"

"I believe the countess and your sisters are in the upper parlor being used as a sewing room. There is a concert tonight that requires much preparation."

"Thank you. You may remove the tea tray."

"Yes, my lady. However, may I say that her ladyship has given orders that, if you are working in this room, you are not to be disturbed. She may be happier if I ask her on your behalf to attend you here."

Bess intensely disliked the idea of interrupting her stepmother when involved in any effort to launch Iris, Ivy, and Josefina. But she would prefer speaking with Patience privately. "If that is her wish, Crewe. Please ask her for me. In which case, you may leave the tea tray."

"As you please, my lady. I will bring a fresh pot and a second cup as soon as I've spoken with the countess."

Bess returned to her chair and sipped at the Saiidi, trying to still her racing heart and understand why she could be so anxious about a mere invitation to supper. *It is not as if I would be spending hours in a crowded ballroom where strangers study me and make me feel like a prize cow on display at a local fair.*

"Crewe said you wanted to speak with me." Patience glided into the room, taking the chair next to Bess. Calm floated in with her, and Bess's heartbeat slowed to a steady thrumming.

"Yes, Patience. I'm sorry to interrupt the sewing, but I need your counsel. May I offer you some tea?"

"Is it that Egyptian concoction that you and Cousin Rose swear by?"

"Yes, I can have Crewe bring something else if you prefer."

"No, no. Every once in a while, trying something different is good for the soul."

Bess touched the side of the pot. "This is still warm." She poured. "Sugar."

"Absolutely."

"The Egyptians like it that way too, so Cousin Rose has told me." Bess added two lumps of sugar to the tea, placed a spoon on the saucer and handed the whole to Patience.

Her stepmother sipped and smiled. "A bittersweet tang, just as I remembered it from when Rose first served me a cup. Now, what is it you wish to discuss?"

Bess retrieved the note from her pocket and handed it to Patience. "Crewe brought me this along with my tea."

Patience perused the short note, sipping on her Saiidi as she read, then put both cup and note aside. "Are you pleased with this invitation?"

"Perhaps. I'm more surprised than anything else. I've never met Nedhelm, though I know of him by reputation. I've certainly had no occasion to encounter his wife, and the invitation comes from her."

"It would hardly be appropriate for a married man to formally invite you. No doubt he asked his wife to send the note."

"But why? I've no reputation to speak of. He cannot possibly know I publish under the name B. Biggs."

"Are you certain? Perhaps Mr. Thomas Young said something."

Bess shook her head. "No, he would never betray my trust in that way. He knows my continued ability to publish rests on the world believing B. Biggs to be a man."

"Does anyone else outside the family know your *nom de plume*?"

"Of course, it must have been Kenti… er, Professor Marr who prompted Nedhelm to issue the invitation. He discovered my pseudonym one evening when he was putting the study to order. I'd been called away to attend to Jane. You remember that evening she had an earache and you were out with the girls."

"Yes, I do recall, and I thank you again for watching over her. So, Mr. Marr's discovery was quite accidental?"

"Indeed," responded Bess. "I swore him to secrecy and was fool enough to believe he would keep his word."

"If he is indeed responsible for this breach, I regret that he did not keep his word. However, I don't believe that is sufficient reason to decline the invitation."

"But I don't know the Nedhelms."

"I do not believe that to be a problem. You don't go out enough to meet anyone. If Nedhelm learned of your presence in town, your connection with Mr. Thomas Young, and your expertise in Egyptology, I suspect he would be very interested in meeting you, regardless of who might have told him of you."

"But…"

Patience raised a hand. "Clearly, I cannot insist you accept the invitation. However, I strongly encourage you to do so. It will do you good to get out and converse for a while with like minds. But you are an adult and more than capable of deciding for yourself."

Bess sat back in her chair. "You make a great deal of sense, Patience. But what could I possibly wear, and how am I to get to the Nedhelm's residence and then home again?"

"I know just the dress. The green one you are planning to wear at the ball. Remember?"

"You don't think that dress is a bit too much for a small dinner party?"

"Not at all. Susana can remove some of the ornamentation in plenty of time for your evening out. If we don't remove too much, adding it back for the ball will take no time at all. As for transportation, we can spare the price of a hackney, if need be, but I think I will write to the Earl of Strathnaver, who very much wants to do us a favor for being so understanding about his brother. Even if the earl does not send his personal coach, I'm certain he would be happy to provide for your transportation to this event."

"If we ask him, Professor Marr is sure to attend. He may even decide I need his escort."

Patience sipped, then cast Bess a sidewise glance. "Would that be so terrible?"

"I've no wish to see the man."

"If he is in attendance, you need be nothing more than cordial to him."

"I'd rather not."

"I see." Patience sipped again. "You would prefer avoiding one man to making new acquaintances in your chosen field who could well ease your way into the scholarly arena."

"When you put it that way, it does sound petty."

Patience smiled. "I've always known you to be an intelligent woman. Do not let one unpleasant incident rule your life and ruin your chances."

*How much does Patience know about my first Season? I've never confided to anyone about the fears I acquired during those events. Perhaps, I've been allowing those fears to ruin other opportunities that might have come my way. Still, the idea of all those eyes on me, judging me. I'm not certain I could do that again. But dinner is not a ballroom crush, or even a crowded concert hall.*

"Very well." Bess put her teacup down on the tray with a decisive thump. "Give me a moment to clear away my work, and we can both return to the sewing room where we can look at that dress and decide what alterations may be best."

*As for The Honorable. Malcolm Marr, Patience is correct, I will treat him with cool cordiality, should I chance to encounter him.* Still, she could not restrain a wistful sigh. She'd never met another person who understood Egyptology or her passion for it so well. Conversation with the man was even easier than with Patience. Bess had always longed for a confidant who shared her interests and understood her feelings. And then there was his kiss. *He's the only man I ever wanted to kiss more than once.*

# CHAPTER 11

Entirely too soon, Bess was dressing for dinner with the Nedhelms.

"Bess, dearest, the earl's coach will be here soon." Patience spoke from the open doorway of the small chamber where Bess slept and stored her few clothing items. She didn't require much, so having the smallest room made sense, especially when her sisters all shared rooms.

"I'm almost ready." She took a last look in the mirror above her dressing table, nearly not recognizing the stranger reflected there.

The dress Patience had shown her just yesterday was a subdued shade of forest green that flattered her skin, gave her eyes a luminous glow, and showed her auburn locks to great advantage. "I don't recognize myself. Wherever did Susana get this material?" The green satin had a small bit of the stiffness that characterized that fabric, but was delicate enough to show every line of her body as she moved.

Iris had insisted on arranging the auburn tresses *a la grecque* and had woven a strand of cream-toned beads among the curls. Susana had hand embroidered the bodice and short sleeves with tiny cream-colored flowers. Josefina had loaned a pair of pale slippers that were only a teensy bit snug. Bess had Ivy's kerchief in the cream and green paisley reticule borrowed from Barbara. Doro had contributed a pair of exquisite long silk gloves.

Patience smiled as she came forward, a small wooden chest held before her. "Your ensemble is lovely but not quite complete. You need these."

Bess recognized the container. "Oh no, Patience. I cannot borrow your mother's things. Those are the only reminders you have of your mother's life and family before her marriage."

"A family which disowned her for that marriage. Mother took these with her when she left to marry my father. Many were used to help them begin their lives together, but a few remain." The younger woman lifted her chin. "They are my things now, and I wish you to wear them, please."

"I'm sorry, Patience. I meant no offense."

"None taken, my good friend and daughter of my heart." She set the chest on the dressing table then opened the box.

"You've given so much to each of us. How could I possibly refuse?"

"Good, because I want you to wear these tonight, and at the ball. They are Jane's inheritance, but you will return them. In years to come, she will be pleased to know that she had a small part in your success. Put out your hands"

Bess formed a shallow bowl with her hands.

Patience lifted a small pouch, opened it and poured out a stream of lustrous, creamy pearls.

Bess placed the jewels on a cleared portion of her dressing table. As she began to unwind the rope of pearls something green sparkled from within. "Is that? Patience this string has an emerald and diamond clasp. And... and earrings that match. This would see our family fed for a full year." She looked up at the woman she respected most in the world. "Why? Why have you not—?"

"We have managed very well with everyone's contributions to the family. There was no need to barter away what little inheritance I could give my daughter."

"But—"

"No." Patience picked up the rope of pearls. "Put those earrings on while I arrange this necklace."

Speechless for once in her life, Bess obeyed.

"I know the late earl, your father, burned through every penny and gem your mother brought to her marriage. Since you have nothing by which to remember her, for tonight, I want you to think of these as hers."

Bess hugged Patience and blinked back unaccustomed tears. "They come from my mother, so of course. I will think of you both when I wear them."

The dowager countess stepped back and blotted her eyes with a kerchief. "I am so very proud of you, Bess."

A knock sounded at the door.

"The carriage is here, Lady Bess." Crewe's voice came from the corridor.

"Coming." At the door Bess looked over her shoulder at Patience. "Thank you."

Patience smiled and waved Bess on her way.

At the bottom of the stairs, Crewe stood ready with a heavy woolen cloak that Susana had trimmed in soft white fur.

"The evening is quite cool my lady."

"Thank you, Crewe. You are most thoughtful."

He opened the door and escorted her along the walk and into the carriage.

The coach door closed behind her as she sat, and the equipage began to move before she realized she was not alone.

"You!"

Malcolm gave a nod. "Good evening, Lady Bess."

Beside him a stern-faced maid dipped her head. "My lady."

"Do not mind Mrs. Toven's presence. My brother insisted she accompany us in the coach to observe the proprieties."

"That was very thoughtful of the earl." Her mind raced, trying to decide what, if anything to do.

She could stop the coach. All she needed to do was rap on the roof.

He watched her closely.

*But then I will never get to meet Nedhelm, and I will miss what I hope will be a lively discussion on antiquarian topics. Why should I spoil my evening just because Professor Marr is so rude as to imagine he can escort me?*

"I gather you remained in the carriage because you knew I would not go with you if I had any choice in the matter," Bess remarked.

His mouth curled in what might be a smile. *That dear mouth*; she recalled their kiss then frowned. *I would do well to recall nothing pleasant of this man. He deceived me and placed my family at risk.*

"I am sorry if my presence displeases you," Malcolm said. "But Nedhelm invited me as well. He is a good friend, and refusing would have been excessively rude. Besides, I wanted to see you to apologize for deceiving you and your family."

"Well, I've no wish to see you and care nothing for your pro forma apologies."

"You have mentioned the first on at least two occasions. As for my apologies, they are most sincere and not at all pro forma. I deeply regret hurting you."

"Did you arrange for this invitation?"

He nodded once. "I won't deceive you ever again, Bess."

"Please do not use my name in so familiar a manner." Her name on his lips reminded her of heaven, so she sternly admonished herself to think of Professor Malcolm Kentigern Marr as the devil personified. A temptation that must be resisted at all costs. "If you must, address me as Lady Elizabeth.

"But you hate being called Elizabeth."

The name was the perfect way to keep in mind that she wished to dislike him just as much as she despised her full name. "Nonetheless, I've no wish to give anyone the impression that I have been at all close to you."

"As you wish, my lady." He settled back against the squabs and turned his head to look out the window.

The journey was short. She preceded him from the coach, preferring the assistance of the coachman.

The door of the house opened before she could lift the knocker.

"Yes?" Said the very superior personage on the other side of the lintel.

"Lady Elizabeth Bigglesworth." She identified herself and handed the man her invitation.

"And Mr. Malcolm Marr." The words came over her shoulder.

She wished the sound did not resonate in her bones. How was she to get through this evening with him always nearby?

"This way, my lady. Mr. Marr. Mr. and Mrs. Nedhelm have asked me to escort you to the parlor."

As she followed the butler down the corridor with Marr at her back, they passed several display cases containing carefully preserved antiquities. Perhaps Mr. Nedhelm would permit her to examine some of them after supper.

The butler opened a door, stepped inside, and motioned her forward. "Lady Elizabeth Bigglesworth and Mr. Malcolm Marr.

Bess assumed the couple coming forward to greet her was the Nedhelms. The woman was as round and tiny as the gentleman was tall and lanky.

Standing between her and the pair, Malcolm faced her and made the introductions.

Mrs. Nedhelm curtsied. "You honor us, Lady Elizabeth. Thank you for accepting our invitation."

"Not at all, Mrs. Nedhelm. I am delighted to be able to accept."

Nedhelm bowed. "You are most gracious to say so, Lady Elizabeth."

"Thank you, sir. I'm looking forward to the evening," said Bess.

With the formalities out of the way, the older man nodded then looked past her to Marr. "Malcolm, I've a recent acquisition that may interest you." He drew Marr to the far side of the room where a tall table stood flanked by a pair of tall candle stands.

"Lady Elizabeth, I must confide that Herbert has been agog since he learned from Mr. Marr that you are the author of the B. Biggs papers.

I am most pleasantly astonished. My father was an Oxford don and, before I married, I had similar ambitions. But Papa would not permit me to submit anything for publication."

*So, Marr has betrayed me.* A part of her heart wept, but a more hidden part—one she deliberately suppressed—rejoiced at finally being able to cast off the deception. *Perhaps Malcolm has done me an unwitting favor.* "Professor Marr should not have told you that. My ability to publish is dependent on the world believing B. Biggs to be a man."

"I'm certain Malcolm intended no offense. And if all goes as my husband plans, you may find you and your work receive more notice simply because you are a woman. You may even see increased demand for your work.

"Exactly what has Mr. Nedhelm planned?" She had visions of soirees and salons where she would be the object of all eyes. *That I will not stand for, no matter how well intentioned.*

"I honestly don't know, Lady Elizabeth. He is being very secretive, even with me. However, I trust him implicitly. He will not do anything to embarrass you. I am certain."

"I appreciate your candor, Mrs. Nedhelm, but do you really think the scholarly community is ready to recognize a woman's contributions?"

Her hostess gave a delicate shrug. "One cannot know until one tries."

Bess decided a change of subject was in order. "I've read several of your husband's papers, Mrs. Nedhelm, and have often wished to ask him a few questions about why he believes the Vikings who invaded York were Danes rather than denizens from farther north."

"Call me Athena, please." Athena smiled as she spoke, and patted Bess's arm. "It's the silliest name for a woman of my stature, but my father was a scholar of Greek and had no idea, when I was born, that I would grow more to the size of an elf than a goddess."

"You show the wisdom of Athena in your attitude toward your name. And I do understand. I was cursed with the name Elizabeth Regina by my father who had pretentions beyond nobility and greatly admired the Tudors. When I finally learned more about Queen Elizabeth, I was happy to accept Bess as she was referred to by those who loved her. So please call me Bess."

"Good Queen Bess," echoed Athena. "She too was quite the scholar."

"She had to be, with men of all countries, including her own, trying to reduce her to the status of mere woman by marrying away her power and authority. She was smart enough never to permit that."

"Please join me on the settee." Athena gestured to a brocaded piece that sat in front of a low table. Two parlor chairs flanked the table at either end. "Herbert and I like to have our wine before supper. We find it aids in digestion. We recently found an excellent sherry and have been saving it for an occasion such as this."

"Then I look forward to sampling the vintage." Bess sat, followed by her new friend.

"Herbert," Athena raised her voice to gain her husband's attention. "Would you please stop fussing with that coin and bring us two glasses of our new sherry?"

"In a moment, dearest."

"Perhaps you would permit me to show the piece to Lady Elizabeth, while you pour the wine," suggested Marr.

"Certainly. May I pour you a glass as well, Malcolm?"

"Yes, please." He put the coin in his pocket.

Two wine goblets in hand, Malcolm followed Nedhelm to where the ladies sat.

He took a seat in the chair nearest Bess and handed her a goblet. "Lady Elizabeth," Malcolm said, "Herbert has just shown me the most amazing piece. He believes this to be the first coin ever discovered that was of Viking manufacture." He held the metal disk out to her in the palm of his hand.

"Truly?" She took the metal from him, too curious about the silver disk to worry about the shiver that passed up her arm as their fingers touched. "Where did this come from, Mr. Nedhelm?"

"Herbert, please."

She looked up briefly. "Call me Bess."

Nedhelm also held two wine goblets. He gave one to his wife and retained the other as he seated himself. "I received the coin from a colleague who had it from a farmer in Lancashire, somewhere near Preston on the banks of the Rabble. My friend believes the coin was minted around the year 700 AD in Scandinavia. I disagree, and believe the most likely source is the English Danelaw and the manufacture of a much later date, perhaps 900 AD."

"It would be difficult to tell from only one piece, and two hundred years is a rather short time difference, relatively speaking," Bess remarked.

"True, true."

"But don't you think these markings on the reverse side might indicate a date." Marr's fingers touched hers as he turned the coin.

A lively discussion ensued that continued throughout supper and well after. The gentlemen decided to have their port in the parlor while the ladies took their tea.

After another hour of convivial conversation, Bess set aside her cup and stood. "I almost hate to leave, Athena, Herbert. However, I have charge of my youngest sister tomorrow and will have to rise early."

Athena rose as well. "We can always continue our discussion another time."

"Absolutely," concurred her husband. "Let me send for your cloak and have notice sent to the mews for your coach to be brought round."

"Thank you both for sharing our supper," Athena said. "Bess, I do hope I will have the chance to meet your stepmother and sisters while you are in York. Do you plan a long stay?"

They began making their way to the front door.

Bess shook her head. "Only until the end of the Season. We'll be returning to our home in Starbrook near Harrogate in mid-May."

"So soon. Then we must plan an event for your family. Perhaps a picnic."

"Oh, there's no need for you to trouble yourself. My stepmother, Patience, Lady Seahaven, is deeply involved in the York social scene.

In fact, we are holding a ball at Smithson's Assembly Rooms on April twenty-second to celebrate the come out of three of my younger sisters. I'll ask Patience to send you an invitation. Do say you'll come?"

"I'll have to consult Herbert, of course. But if we are free that evening, I would love to attend." Athena smiled.

"I'll ask Malcolm to use whatever influence he has with Herbert." The words and his name were out of Bess' mouth before she thought. "I... uh... I mean Mr. Marr."

Athena gave her a speculative look. "We are all on a first name basis here at Nedhelm house."

*Thank heaven she decided not to ask questions. I wouldn't have known what to say. I can't even explain it to myself. But I must admit that, despite knowing better, I've been thinking of him as Malcolm all evening. How could I? I'm furious with the lying oaf—am I not?*

She shook off the disturbing thoughts to bid her hosts a goodnight and assure Athena that a ball invitation would be forthcoming the next day.

# CHAPTER 12

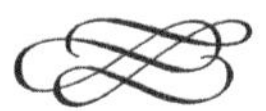

Once settled in the carriage, she ignored Mal and their chaperone to stare unseeing at the nighttime city passing by outside the window.

"You're being very pensive, Lady Elizabeth."

She turned to look at Mal, his face all planes and shadows in the lamplight. She'd let this man kiss her. Shared her dreams and hopes with him—*when I thought him a butler. Is that a problem?* she argued with herself. *Is he a different man simply because he has a different profession from what I originally thought? He lied to me. Did I ever ask him why? Perhaps he had a good reason.*

"Why did you claim to be Cousin Rose's butler?"

He looked a moment at the chaperone who returned the look with a slight nod. Then he studied Bess for a long time. "Would you believe I was afraid for my life? You did hold me at gunpoint."

"And you disarmed me quite handily. No, I would not believe you were afraid, or not so afraid that you could not keep your own identity straight."

His smile gleamed in the lamplight. "I did not think you would believe that bouncer."

"Then why ask me?"

"Because the truth is more difficult to believe. I didn't believe it myself, even as I told you I was a butler."

"What could possibly be so hard to believe?"

"Love at first sight."

"Preposterous." *It is, isn't it? No logical person would believe in such nonsense, and I pride myself on my logic.*

"See. I told you it was incredible."

"Well, of course, it's incredible, because it doesn't exist."

"Bess." He leaned forward and took her hand. "May I call you Bess once more, please?"

She rolled her eyes and attempted to take back her hand.

His grasp was gentle, but he refused to let go. "You and I are both scholars. We theorize all the time, but we don't believe without hard evidence and sound logic."

"So, if you believe you are in love with me, what evidence can you give to prove your theory?"

"I was so stunned by you—not your beauty, which you have in abundance—but by you. A woman who dared to challenge a strange man on her own, with no doubt she could maintain the upper hand."

She'd had plenty of doubts, but not in the moment. Those doubts only occurred to her after the fact when she realized how great a risk she'd taken.

"I was so stunned by you," Malcolm repeated, "that I literally lost my wits. I knew only one thing, I had to find a way to stay with you. Going away at that moment, leaving that house without you was as impossible as the sky falling. I had to find a way to stay close enough to get to know you, a woman like no other in my experience. So, I blurted the first thing that came to mind when you asked who I was."

His thumb traced across her gloved knuckles. Shocks coursed up her arms and through her body as if she'd been completely naked. "I am truly sorry that I ever lied to you, and I beg your forgiveness."

"Let go of me," she whispered.

He released her hand instantly. "May I call on you tomorrow?"

She shook her head. She wanted him, desperately. Too desperately. She needed time to regain her good sense, which seemed to have disappeared along with the wine she'd enjoyed that evening. "Not tomorrow. I will let you know."

"We've arrived." He opened the coach door.

Bess allowed Malcolm to help her from the carriage and escort her to the door.

"Goodnight, Bess." He lifted her hand to his lips.

She felt heat and those shocks again. "Goodnight." Keeping her voice steady was an effort.

He turned and left.

She forced herself not to watch but to go into the house and close the door. To shut out Malcolm Marr as she could not shut him out of her mind.

"Bess?" Patience came down the stairs.

"Yes, it's me." She took her cloak off, placing it on a chair where Crewe would find it, then began to remove her gloves.

"Did you enjoy yourself? Come to my room and tell me all about your evening and the Nedhelms." She moved in the direction of her bedchamber.

"No, not tonight, please Patience. Tomorrow morning, I'll tell you everything. For now, I need to ask you to invite Mr. and Mrs. Nedhelm to Tuesday's ball."

"If you wish it, of course I'll invite them. Are you sure you cannot talk now?"

"It would be better if I sought my bed. I'm to stay with Jane tomorrow. I'll need to be rested."

Patience smiled. "She can be quite the handful."

"A delightful handful to be sure. Goodnight." Bess hurried up the stairs to her chamber. She doubted she would sleep much. She needed to think. Malcolm claimed he loved her. How could that be possible? *How do I feel about him? If he loves me, what does that mean? Does he want me as a mistress? He has to know I would never... But would I never?* The memory surfaced strong and clear of how it felt to be in his arms, of arguing scholarly points with him long into the night, of watching him entrance two young girls by bringing history to life. *I must cease dithering and think about this sensibly.*

*He's a man with a profession. A highly respected scholar. Until his brother weds and has a son, Malcolm Marr is heir to one of the most respected titles in all Britain. He may think he loves me, but I could never be a proper wife for him. If he ever makes such a ridiculous assertion again, I'll just have to tell him in no uncertain terms that we could never be together. There! I've thought logically and sensibly and made the right decision. I should be happy. So why do I feel like weeping?*

# CHAPTER 13

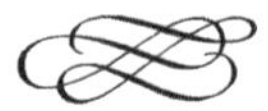

For the next few days, Bess slept poorly and dragged through the hours between breakfast and bedtime, longing to retire to her chamber immediately after breakfast and hide beneath her bedcovers all day. Then one morning, as she perused her correspondence over a light breakfast, she discovered that fate and Malcolm Marr had more surprises in store.

First, there was an invitation from the York Antiquarian Society to present at a members' only seminar on the last day of the next week's seminars. That note was signed by Nedhelm with a postscript to "Please honor the York society with a lecture on the topic of your choice."

*I'll have to write a polite thank you declining his very kind offer. I'll use the excuse that seven days is insufficient time to prepare.* It wasn't strictly true. She could discourse on a large number of subjects with no preparation at all. She shoved away the intruding memory of long evenings talking with Malcolm. Nonetheless, the insufficient preparation time was a reasonable excuse and would avoid other less comfortable explanations.

She reached for the next envelope, surprised to see that it was from Mr. Thomas Young.

My Dear Lady Elizabeth,

"I write on behalf of our mutual friend, Mr. Herbert Nedhelm and beg you to accept his invitation for you to speak to the membership of the York Antiquarian Society. Your help to me over the past few years of examining the Rosetta Stone has been invaluable. I know you to be the equal of any scholar in Europe and far superior to most. For too long, you have lingered in the shadows because of a ridiculous preconception shared by many Englishmen that women are incapable of deep thought. You and I both know that history teaches us otherwise. The queens and empresses of Egypt were among the most intelligent and well-educated rulers of their day. As you well know, England's own Queen Elizabeth is a shining example of the abilities of women. I look forward to reading the account of your seminar in the society's next journal.

With Kind Regards,

Mr. Thomas Young, Foreign Secretary Royal Society, London

"Oh dear," she mused aloud. *With Mr. Young's endorsement, refusing Nedhelm's invitation would be much more difficult. A communicable disease was clearly in order.* "I wonder how easy it is to catch the measles?"

"I beg your pardon, Bess? You cannot seriously wish to catch the measles."

Patience stood in the doorway to the dining room. "It's a horrifying disease," she continued, as she served herself from the sideboard then took her place at the table "Especially in children who do not understand the damage that can be done by scratching the measles pox. And while doctors have more success treating the disease now than in the past, many people who suffer the disease do not survive."

"P… Patience, I did not see you there, and, no, I've no desire to have the measles again. Having it once as a child was more than enough. However, I desperately need an excuse to be unavailable this coming Friday."

"Whatever for?" the countess enquired before sipping her tea.

"I've received an invitation to present a lecture in a closed seminar for the York Antiquarian Society membership."

"Congratulations." Patience lowered her teacup and smiled. "This is thrilling news indeed. You will finally have the recognition you deserve."

"What if I don't want recognition?"

Patience cocked her head. "Do you imagine the members of York's Antiquarian Society will not look kindly on your presentation?"

Count on Patience to cut to the most important issue. "I do not know. I wish life was different, but I've learned that being female is not an asset among scholars." Heavens, it wasn't even much of an asset in society, unless one was beautiful and could engage in witty but empty conversation. *How can I possibly speak before an entire auditorium of men, all judging me, eager to find my work and myself lacking?*

"And, of course, you are willing to let that stand." Patience lifted a forkful of eggs to her mouth.

Bess winced inwardly. "No, but what can I do? I'm just one woman." A woman who, if Malcolm Marr was to be believed, had allowed irrational fear to rule her life for entirely too long.

Patience swallowed and blotted her mouth. "One woman who is uniquely qualified to change men's minds. A woman with a rare opportunity to prove such nay-sayers wrong and show them just how capable women are. I am surprised at you, Bess. Have you learned nothing in all the years we, a family of only women, have been making our own way? I've heard you, seen you long for the kind of recognition received by Mr. Thomas Young and other distinguished scholars. Yet here you sit with the most golden of chances handed to you and bemoan the fact that you are female in a society full of male scholars who, despite their rarified educations, are idiots. Sometimes I wonder why you so greatly wish to be among their number."

"I understand, Patience, and nothing would please me more than to accept this invitation. However, if I do so, every woman in this family will be tarnished when society learns that B. Biggs is a woman. Not just any woman but the daughter of the Earl of Seahaven. What will happen to the suitors that have Ivy, Josefina and Iris so excited? The disapproval won't just be against me, Patience. All of us will suffer."

Her stepmother dropped the toast she was buttering to her plate. "I do so wish you were wrong, but I know you are not. Nonetheless, I implore you to take advantage of the opportunity given to you. If the men courting your sisters are so shallow as to be frightened off by the idea of a brilliant scholarly sister-in-law, then the girls are better off without them. But I've met the men in question, and I do not think they are fools." She resumed buttering her toast. "The seminars do not begin until after the ball, so you have plenty of time. Prepare your presentation, Bess. Allow me and your sisters to stifle any wagging tongues."

"Thank you, Patience, both for your gentle scolding and reminding me that I too often try to get by without help from my sisters." Bess stood. "I will leave you to your breakfast and go to the study to pen my reply to Mr. Nedhelm."

# CHAPTER 14

Malcolm was surprised to receive a summons from the dowager Countess of Seahaven. He was even more surprised to find his brother, his brother's friends, Mr. Nedhelm, and several other gentlemen of high repute had received the same summons.

He took a seat beside James in the Seahaven drawing room. "Do any of you know why we have been called here?"

"No," said James, "But the countess requested my presence, so, of course, I came."

"And the rest of you?" His gaze made a slow sweep of the room moving from man to man as each one confirmed the source of his summons.

As he finished, Lady Seahaven and two of her older stepdaughters entered the room. The butler who had replaced him was carrying a heavily ladened tea tray.

"Gentlemen," said Lady Seahaven. "Before we begin, allow me to make the introductions." When the formalities had been completed, she continued. "My purpose today is to ask for your help in making the final lecture of the York Antiquarian Society Seminars one that will be remembered for years to come. You are all gentlemen of some influence. What I would like you to do is—well there is no better word for it—I want you to gossip. You are all aware that society's current attitude towards female scholars is less than kind. Because my stepdaughter, Lady Elizabeth, has established a stellar reputation with her writings published under the name B. Biggs, we have the perfect opportunity to start to change public opinion. However, we cannot do so without your help."

Murmurs ran like a current through the group of men. Several questions were asked and discussion ensued on the best means of achieving the goal stated by the countess. At the end of the meeting, after bidding their hostess farewell and promising to do all possible to cast Bess's lecture in a positive light, each of the men departed.

Malcolm pulled Kellborn aside.

"Marr?"

"Walk with me. It has been some time since I've encountered a friend of so many years. We can catch each other up on the doings of our families."

Kellborn nodded and exited the town house at Malcolm's side. "It is good to see you too Malcolm. How long has it been? Ten years?"

"I could not say, since I always feel like it was just yesterday we were challenging each other with Latin quotations and trying to avoid the bullying of upperclassmen."

"Ah yes, those were good days at Eton. But you did not really wish to reminisce, did you?

"I wouldn't mind sharing our memories, but I do have a more urgent request."

"Good," Kellborn said. "I've another appointment this afternoon and can only give you a small bit of my time."

"Then I shall be blunt. You are lodging with Sir Westcott Twisden and his stepmother, Lady Twisden, yes?"

"I am, but what of it?

"I've heard from a number of sources that Lady Twisden retains influential connections in York society."

Kellborn nodded. "That is true."

"Could you ask her to praise Herbert Nedhelm's decision to invite

Lady Bess to speak at the York Antiquarian Society Seminars and perhaps encourage the ladies of York to see Lady Bess's appearance at the seminars as a very good thing?"

"Since you are my friend, I will certainly ask her, but I cannot guarantee her reply."

"I would not expect that."

"Do you not think that gentlemen can spread sufficient good gossip? There were some very well-connected fellows at today's meeting."

"I think Lady Seahaven's plan to enlist the good will of York's influential gentlemen is a stroke of genius. Whoever weds that woman will be very lucky indeed. As to why I wish Lady Twisden's assistance, I believe that society's matrons also wield a great deal of influence, and if we don't enlist their aid, we may well find that they take umbrage at Lady Bess presenting a seminar for men. If that happens, the wives, sisters and daughters of York's gentlemen may well seek to undermine whatever good will we gentlemen can generate."

"You make an excellent point. I will do all in my power to gain Lady Twisden's help. However, I think we should go one step further."

Malcolm raised a brow in question.

"Nedhelm should send invitations to York's leading ladies to attend Lady Bess's groundbreaking seminar. From what little I have seen, the mania for all things Egyptian is as strong here in York as it is in London."

"That is an excellent idea. I will speak with Nedhelm this afternoon about changing the seminar from society members only to by invitation only. That way all the society members can be invited, and we can still prevent most of the more biased gentlemen from speaking out when in the presence of the powerful society women in attendance."

"Then I will bid you good day. I will keep you apprised of my success with Lady Twisden or the lack of same."

"I will inform you of my progress as well, Kellborn. Thank you."

"You are welcome, Marr. Let us agree to meet more often in the future."

"Certainly. Good day to you, my friend."

"And to you, Marr."

Malcolm went in search of a hackney, leaving Kellborn hurrying to attend his next appointment. Mal smiled as he gave the driver directions to Nedhelm's residence. Everything that could be done would be done to make Bess's seminar one of the most memorable in York history. If she could never bring herself to love him, he must be satisfied with knowing that he'd seen her greatest wish fulfilled. He refused to believe that she would continue to deny his suit when she learned the lengths to which he would go to please her, simply because he loved her.

# CHAPTER 15

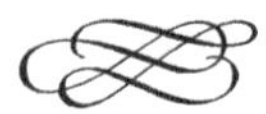

"These discoveries by noted scholars Young, Champollion, Heyne, Akerblad, de Sacy and innumerable assistants are the foundation upon which will be based an accurate translation of Egyptian hieroglyphs. Much remains to be explored about Egyptian history and the arts of this culture. However, before that work can begin, a thorough and accurate understanding of the Egyptian language is essential. That will be the greatest success of those who translate the Rosetta Stone." As she moved into her closing remarks, Bess locked gazes with Mr. Nedhelm.

"My fellow scholars, ladies and gentlemen, I thank you, the York Antiquarian Society, Mr. and Mrs. Nedhelm, and Mr. Thomas Young for making possible this opportunity to share the latest information about the Egyptian language and the work being done to increase our knowledge of that subject."

As she finished speaking a silence reigned. *Good lord, have I embarrassed myself and the society with this speech? What will happen to Patience and the girls if I've ruined our reputations?*

She no sooner formed the thoughts than applause erupted, so loud that she gripped the sides of the lectern to keep herself from dashing off the podium, screaming in fright. Awestruck was a mild word to describe what she felt as every member of the audience stood.

Very soon, Mr. Nedhelm joined her and gave her a large bouquet of yellow roses.

*What in the world?* She pried her hands from the lectern and accepted the flowers, unable to think of any reason to refuse them. *Roses are given to opera singers and actors. I am neither of those.*

Nedhelm nudged her politely to the far side of the lectern then raised his hands for silence.

The audience sat, and the noise subsided to the moderate level of waves on a peaceful seashore.

"Ladies, gentlemen, respected guests and scholars, thank you all for attending this inaugural meeting of the York Antiquarian Society's Lady Scholars Auxiliary. You are all invited to join our speaker and the membership of the York Antiquarian Society at a supper dance to be held tomorrow evening at the Smithson Assembly Rooms. Since the hour grows late, please, hold any questions you have for our distinguished speaker, who I understand has a commitment elsewhere. There will be plenty of opportunity to speak with Lady Elizabeth Bigglesworth at the supper and dance."

He finished speaking with a bow then hurried Bess off the podium and into a small backroom of the Antiquarian Society building.

"Lady Elizabeth..."

"Lady Bess, please."

"Lady Bess, we will wait here for a few minutes and allow the audience to depart." As he spoke, he took the flowers from her. "I'll see that these are put in water for display at the dance, and then later vase and blooms will be delivered to your home."

Bess stared at him scarcely knowing what to say. "Thank you." *There that was perfectly appropriate.*

"The society decided on the vase as a memento for our first lady member. We have had it engraved with the date and occasion of this speech, and most sincerely hope you will return often to speak with us on any topic."

"I... I'm honored. I will treasure both vase and flowers. And yes, as time permits, I will happily join the scholars of the York Antiquarian Society. But surely this decision by the membership was not unanimous? There must be some who would prefer that a woman never darken the society's doors again."

"You are correct, but they are a minority. Most of us could not care less if you are female or otherwise. What interests us, and what you have shown tonight, is the very best of scholarship. I hope you will allow us to print the text of your seminar in the next issue of our journal."

"Of course. Though I would ask that you seek permission from those other scholars whose work I cited in the course of my speech."

"It shall be as you wish."

The door opened. Malcolm Marr entered with Mrs. Nedhelm, Patience, and several of Bess's sisters.

"Let me have those flowers, Herbert." Athena took the blooms from her husband. "You and I must be on our way if we are to arrive home in time to greet our supper guests." She turned to Bess who was staring at Malcolm. "Bess, thank you. Your speech was enthralling. Malcolm has requested the privilege of escorting you to supper, and, since your stepmama and sisters are to join us as well, perhaps he may escort you all."

Athena left, and Patience, eyes sparkling, moved forward. "You were wonderful, Bess. Congratulations. Mr. Marr, will you please escort all of us to the Nedhelms' for supper?"

"It would be my honor, Lady Seahaven." He gave a gracious bow. "However, I would like a private moment with Bess, if you will permit it?"

"Do you promise to be on your best behavior?"

"I do."

Bess had never seen him so solemn.

"In that case, you have my permission. Just for a moment, Mr. Marr. Her sisters and I shall be right outside the door."

On that note, the room emptied, and Bess was alone with Malcolm.

# CHAPTER 16

She'd spent many comfortable hours alone with him during their tours of York's historical sites and their late-night discussions in the town house study. Even the few brief meetings they'd had, including that memorable day when the house was empty with everyone but them at the al fresco party, had been comfortable, almost reassuring. Why did she feel awkward now?

*Because he believes he loves you, you idiot,* scolded her conscience.

"Bess," he took her hand and kissed it. "Several days ago, I begged your forgiveness for deceiving you as to my identity."

"Yes, Mal. I forgive you."

He kissed her hand again. "I want to be certain that you know you can trust and rely on me."

"Dear Malcolm." She leaned forward, stood on her toes, and pressed a kiss to his cheek. His embarrassed flush pleased her greatly. "Does that reassure you?"

He swallowed. "Yes. Yes, indeed." As he spoke, he knelt on the floor in front of her.

*Oh dear, he's not proposing, not now.*

*If not now, when*? queried her very annoying inner voice.

"You know I love you. Please do me the honor of giving me your hand in marriage. I vow to cherish you always."

*Is that what I want? To be cherished?*

*You object to being cherished?* asked her decidedly inconvenient voice. She wished she could banish the thing.

"I've no objection to being cherished."

"Bess, that is wonderful." Malcolm surged to his feet and made as if to embrace her.

She backed up three steps—a good two arms lengths away from him. "I'm sorry. I did not realize I'd spoken my thoughts."

"If you've no objection, then why...?" He gestured at the space she'd put between them.

"Because..."

*This better be good,* said her acerbic inner voice.

*Silence*! She wanted to keep her thoughts to herself, so she kept her lips firmly closed.

"Bess?"

"Because I can't marry you," she blurted.

He straightened and masked his expression. "If that is your wish, I will of course respect it. May I ask why?"

Truth be told, refusing him might just break her heart as well as his. She'd come to rely on his keen insights as she completed her work for Mr. Young. Malcolm had helped her so very much in the few weeks she'd known him. An explanation was the least he deserved.

"Because... I won't be in England."

"Where will you be? I could perhaps join you." His tone was carefully neutral.

"On Mr. Thomas Young's recommendation, I've been invited to be part of an expedition to Egypt being organized by the London Royal Society. We will be leaving June first at the latest. I intend to accept the invitation, so I cannot marry you."

While she spoke, she watched Malcolm's thin-lipped restraint break into a wide grin that spread to include not just his mouth but his cheeks, eyes, his entire face. He positively glowed with joy.

"Oddly enough—or not—I, too, have an invitation to join that same expedition. I'd hoped to persuade you to spend our honeymoon exploring Egyptian ruins."

"You horrid man." She smiled and leapt at him, clasping her arms around his neck and plastering herself against him so he was forced to support her with his arms around her waist. Then she kissed him.

A long while later, she came up for air the third, or it might have been fourth, time. She hadn't bothered to count. "You knew all along about the expedition. Did you know I'd been invited?"

"No, my dear. That was a very pleasant surprise. May I assume you've changed your mind about marrying me?"

"Yes, yes, unequivocally yes. Do you think the expedition organizers will mind having a married pair of scholars on their team?"

"I think they will be quite pleased. If nothing else, we'll be saving the cost of one accommodation. You see, once we are wed, I intend never to spend another night without you."

"Will you travel with me to London?" she asked.

"Only if I can acquire a special license so we may travel as husband and wife."

"Malcolm Marr, you will make me the happiest wife in the world. You do not wish to wait?"

"Not in the least. Now, sweet Bess, we had best hurry to get Lady Seahaven and your sisters to the Nedhelms' supper. I know of at least three men and as many women who long to ask questions of you."

She sighed. "I suppose we must. It is only right that I give back a little of what has been so generously given to me. But we need to discuss our future. We won't be in Egypt forever."

"I look forward to that discussion, but we can delay for a few hours. What do you say we begin our talk on the topic on the way to your home after supper?"

She kissed him. "I think that's perfect. When will we tell my family?"

"So, you don't wish to announce our engagement at tonight's meal?"

"I wish to hug your proposal to myself for at least a little while."

"All shall be as you desire. Have Patience invite Strathnaver and myself to dinner tomorrow. We'll break the news to everyone who matters then."

"Perfect." She smiled and let him help her into her cloak then escort her the few steps from the Antiquarian Society building to the carriage awaiting them.

As they rode through York, Bess pondered the choices she'd made in the past. Had she not listened to Patience, she would never have met Malcolm nor had her greatest wish granted. She'd finally learned not to permit fear to limit her opportunities. For that, and for Malcolm, she would always be thankful.

THE END

The scholars mentioned by Bess at the beginning of chapter fifteen (Young, Champollion, Heyne, Akerblad, de Sacy) and mentioned elsewhere in regards to her translation of the Rosetta Stone texts are the names of real scholars from the period who contributed in one way or another to our understanding of the Rosetta Stone scripts.

# SOCIAL MEDIA FOR RUE ALLYN

You can learn more about Rue Allyn on these social media links:

**Facebook:** https://www.facebook.com/RueAllynAuthor
**Twitter:** https://twitter.com/RueAllyn
**Amazon:** https://www.amazon.com/Rue-Allyn/e/B00AUBF3NI/

# ABOUT RUE ALLYN

Award winning author, Rue Allyn learned story telling at her grandfather's knee and has been weaving her own tales ever since. She and her husband of more than four decades (try living with the same person for more than forty years—that's a true adventure) have retired and moved south. When not writing, enjoying the nearby beach or working jigsaw puzzles, Rue travels the world and surfs the internet in search of background material and inspiration for her next heart melting romance. She loves to hear from readers, and you may contact her at Rue@RueAllyn.com. She can't wait to hear from you.

Learn more about Rue at:
Website: https://RueAllyn.com

# THE FOUR-TO-ONE FANCY

BY ELIZABETH ELLEN CARTER

# The Four-to-One Fancy
by Elizabeth Ellen Carter

*There where the course is,*
*Delight makes all of the one mind,*
*The riders upon the galloping horses,*
*The crowd that closes in behind.*
– William Butler Yeats

The Four-to-One Fancy
By Elizabeth Ellen Carter

Fate has given twins Ivy and Iris Bigglesworth a Season in York. They vow to marry only brothers so the sisters will never be apart. But what are the odds of finding and falling in love with two eligible brothers? Hearts race when they meet two handsome cousins who are betting their future on a risky racing venture. Soon the twins learn there are more than fortunes to be lost and won on a four-to-one fancy.

# CHAPTER 1

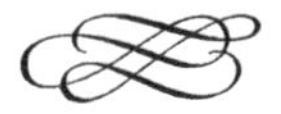

*Starbrook, Yorkshire, January 6th, 1817*

"I think it is the finest work you've done yet."

Iris looked at her sister Ivy with a matching smile—little surprise given they were identical twins, owners of auburn hair, green eyes, and alike in every way.

She examined the small oval biscuit of unfired porcelain with a sense of satisfaction. Indeed, she was pleased with her progress on the delicate miniature portrait.

"Yes, I think that captures her likeness well," replied Iris, "but it should be even more spectacular when it is fired and glazed."

Ivy nodded in agreement.

"I have almost finished painting Tom Parrish's pig," she said. "Do you wish to see?"

Iris leaned across the workbench as Ivy turned the platter to show it in the winter sunlight streaming through the window.

The rim of the serving dish was decorated with depictions of ears of wheat. Dominating the view in the center was a fat pink boar, standing in the foreground of a pastoral scene as it never actually had done in real life.

Iris cocked her head.

"It looks like a loaf a bread with legs, ears and a snout."

Ivy laughed, far from being offended.

"And I tell you, that this is a perfectly true likeness of a Yorkshire champion. I'll have it finished this morning in plenty of time to walk with you to Harrogate and get the pieces in the kiln."

"How much do you think we will make from the cameo pieces? Mrs. Beesworth seemed quite pleased with them," she continued.

"She said they would sell well, so a good amount, I should expect," Iris answered. "I know the money will be welcome."

The twins fell silent and concentrated on finishing their tasks.

Money was always a vexing issue in the Bigglesworth household.

Poor papa.

Henry Reginald Bigglesworth, Earl of Seahaven, had been so desperate for a male heir to continue the name. Sadly, all of his five wives had borne him daughters.

The Earl had been dubbed Henry the Fifth—not only for the frequency with which he remarried but also for the haphazard way he cared for his brood—this is to say with an aristocratic negligence. Not that he was an unkind man—the girls remembered him fondly—he was just rather disorganized.

There had been such high hopes that their own dear mama, the third wife of the Earl, would produce a much-longed for heir. But alas, no luck. First, she gave birth to their older-by-one-year sister, Josefina. Then, maman died in childbirth delivering twins, neither of whom were boys.

With so many offspring, but no males to carry the name, the estate of Seahaven had gone to a distant cousin, leaving the girls in genteel poverty in the picturesque hamlet of Starbrook, just outside of the spa town of Harrogate.

Still, Iris and Ivy were quite content. They shared a dormer room in the cottage. It was a narrow space, when measured rafter to rafter, but it was long. Four sets of windows let in plenty of light for painting.

And, being at the top of the house, it was quiet.

For as much as the twins loved their stepmother and the houseful of half-sisters, they needed an island of calm in a sea of noise and chaos.

There was little else Iris and Ivy knew about their mother, although they were assured by Mrs. Crewe, the housekeeper, that the looks they shared with Josefina made them all the very images of their mother.

"I wonder if Patience will remember to pick up the latest edition of *The Ladies Journal*," Ivy asked quietly.

Iris put down her paintbrush to look out over the rolling dales, dotted here and there with sheep, their white wool glowing in the mid-morning sunshine. They had been spared the snow so far this year, but it wouldn't be long before the dales and moors were covered.

She and Ivy worked since first light, but Patience, their late father's fifth and last wife, had been up long before dawn to make the bread she took to market each day.

It was now closer to noon. Patience would be back soon.

"If she has not, we will not ask," Iris answered.

They were daughters of an Earl, but Patience was the dowager Countess, as well as their stepmother.

At twenty-two years of age, Patience was only four years older than the twins themselves. Yet the young widow took her role as head of the household seriously indeed, particularly since there was her infant daughter to raise, in addition two young stepdaughters—Emma, aged twelve and Merrilyn, aged ten—from marriage number four.

All the sisters loved Patience, who well and truly lived up to her name.

"Agreed," continued Ivy, "but if we get more than we hope, perhaps we can buy the magazine ourselves. It would be nice to see fashion plates of what was au courant in London this Season."

It was a dream, of course. They knew full well there wasn't enough money for a Season in London. Even their dowries were what might kindly be described as modest.

That was another thing that weighed heavily on Patience's shoulders.

"If it is fine tomorrow, we should walk to Knaresborough," said Iris. "In the spring there will be visitors from all over, even from London. They'll come to Harrogate to take the waters and Doro said they all like to take a little souvenir home."

If anyone knew about such things, it would be their half-sister Dorothea, from papa's second marriage. She worked in a hotel in Harrogate favored by the most discerning visitors.

"We could paint some views of the castle ruins," agreed Ivy. "And Mother Shipton's Cave. The side of it looks like a skull. It gives *me* the shivers, but I am sure people will pay money for a watercolor."

"A plaque with Mother Shipton's ancient prophecies?" Iris suggested.

"Do we know what they are?"

"We could make them up in Shakespearean rhyming couplets," she said, warming to the idea. "If we made them entertaining and vague with references to true events of the past and make up future events, would anyone be the wiser?"

"Do you think visitors would pay money for an object turned to stone?" Ivy asked.

Iris inclined her head, thinking about it a moment. Special water dripped from the cave. Every object placed in it became soaked and eventually petrified.

"A hat?" she asked.

"A pair of shoes?" Ivy batted back.

"Gloves?"

"None of which we have to spare. No, best we leave that idea be."

A few moments later there was a knock at their door.

"Ivy, Iris, we need to speak to you downstairs."

The voice was that of that was Barbara, another half-sister, daughter of wife number two, who had joined their household for economy as well as company. At twenty-seven, Barbara was the second eldest of the Bigglesworth girls living in the cottage. She was a pianist and teacher. Unfortunately, not all her students shared her talent.

Also sharing their home was Elizabeth, better known as Bess. At thirty she was the eldest sister, daughter of the first wife, and a scholar of ancient civilizations, particularly Egypt.

The twins looked at one another with the same question in their eyes, but they did not speak it aloud.

Yes, they'd each heard the tension in Barbara's voice.

*Has something happened to the youngsters?*

Yet when Barbara opened the door, peering up at them from the narrow steps which led to their dormer room, there was no fear, only excitement.

Ivy and Iris looked at one another once more. And, in unconsciously mirrored movements, got up from their tables, untied their aprons and followed Barbara downstairs.

# CHAPTER 2

Ivy spared another glance at her sister when they entered the little drawing room. She could tell Iris had no more clue than she did.

Fears for the youngest girls were unfounded. Emma and Merrilyn were on the settee eagerly waiting the announcement with baby Jane sitting on Emma's knee.

What of Josefina?

Their elder sister looked up and gave a brief shake of her head in silent answer to the unasked question.

Where was Bess? She ought to be here, thought Ivy. Perhaps she was too caught up in her translations and research to join them.

Nevertheless, Barbara seemed to know what was going on but said nothing more. She took her place alongside her sisters Doro and Susana who had closed up her dress shop to join them at the cottage this Twelfth Night.

Then her attention turned to Patience who stood with her back to the fire. She held a letter in her hand.

Ivy was struck at how beautiful the dowager Countess was at that moment. For so long Patience had been stepmother to them all, and it was too easy to forget she was a young woman still.

*She is out of mourning. She ought to remarry.*

Ivy hid a half smile, shared by Iris, who no doubt thought the same thing as her.

Regardless of their very modest means, they were happy. They were family, despite the strange circumstances. There was love in this home which made them richer than most.

Envy of those lovely young ladies making their debut in London—begowned in their silks and adorned with jewels—seemed petty. The thought of having a Season like that of her own was as far away as the moon. There would be no dancing with dukes, and earls, and viscounts. No invitations to Almacks, no royal balls.

It was best to put the notion out of her head completely, Ivy decided resolutely.

In truth, it was hard to credit that they had any connection to aristocracy at all, other than the name.

The current earl was a man they had not met, save the once at their father's funeral. In the four years since, the man had never troubled himself to pay a call on the widow and children of his late cousin.

Here, in their cottage, the dowager countess was simply Patience, or occasionally maman. And as for them? Well, she and Iris had become so used to being addressed as "two o' them Bigglesworth misses" wherever they went, it was hard to credit that she and her sister—nay, *all* of the girls here, held the title of Lady.

"I have some news," Patience began. There was an animation in her lovely face that belied the gravity in her tone.

"There *might* be an opportunity to give you a Season."

Ivy and Iris looked at each other and then to Josefina who was the first to speak.

"How?"

The grin Patience had carefully struggled to hide broke out like the sun from behind a cloud.

"Rose St Aubyn, a cousin on my mother's side, owns a town house in York. She is going to Egypt this month and has given us the use of her home."

Emma and Merrilyn squealed. They jumped to their feet and danced in a circle.

"York! We're going to York!"

After giving them a moment to express their excitement, Barbara urged the girls to sit back down.

"Girls, there is more that Patience needs to share with us."

"It will not be easy," Patience continued. "We will have somewhere to live, but we will have to watch every penny. It's not London, but a Season in York will not be cheap. I believe this affords us the very best chance to find husbands for you."

"For us all?" Iris asked, trying hard not to sound incredulous. Ivy knew her sister was mentally calculating the cost. It would be substantial.

Barbara laughed. "You, Ivy and Josefina at the very least."

"But we're all going, aren't we?" Merrilyn asked, eyes wide with hope and yet fearing disappointment.

"Yes, we're all going."

Ivy blinked rapidly, trying to make sense of her jumbled thoughts. Even in a large town house, that would be a great number of people to accommodate. Questions sprang rapidly to mind, but she did not ask them because she knew that not even Patience had the answers.

"You're all very quiet," Barbara observed.

Patience folded the letter and placed it in her apron pocket.

"Well, that is no surprise," she said. "There is a lot to think about and a lot to plan between now and March."

Then she addressed the gathering at large. "Do you feel ready to rise to the challenge? Be as brave as our boys who fought Napoleon at Waterloo? Never forget whose daughters you are. You are the daughters of an earl. You are ladies, deserving of every advantage that affords you. Raise your heads high, my dears. No one will dare look down on the Bigglesworth name."

Iris breathed in deep and squared her shoulders. She reached for Ivy's hand and took it.

There, in the little drawing room, Ivy observed all the sisters present were similarly inspired, including Barbara who prided herself on her very sensible nature.

"I believe I can speak for all of us," she said. "We have made life in Starbrook work for us and there is no reason why we cannot make York an equal success."

# CHAPTER 3

*Tyrell House, outside York, December 1816*

Captain John Bentley, the new Viscount Tyrell, reined his mount to a stop. His cousin Captain James Bentley, did likewise.

"It could be a whole lot worse," said James, shooting his cousin a grin.

From the vantage point on the hill, John turned back to look at a large building which, even at this distance, had seen better days.

Tyrell House had been built in the Jacobean style in the 1620s. Three stories high, made of stone, the building had a pitched roof line and gable ends. It also looked like it had not been remodeled in the nearly two centuries since.

*The family pile.*

He'd joked about it to James on the way up from London, but now he was here, seeing the place for himself. It looked more like a pile than a viscount's estate. Still, with the morning light shining on its mullioned windows, and the remains of the early morning mist hanging low on the lawns, there was something about it which called to him.

"It has potential," John answered, then spurred his horse into a run for the last few hundred yards to his new home with James in pursuit.

*Tyrell House.*

He couldn't remember how long it had been since he and James were last here. Not since they were lads to be sure.

And there were times he believed neither of them would see it again. There had been more than a few close calls on the battlefield during the war with old Boney.

Perhaps it was those brushes with death that pulled the memory of this place out. He'd lain awake in his bivouac, exhausted from the day's fighting and thought about Yorkshire's open fields, the wild moors, the call of the hunting birds high above in the sky on a warm summer's day.

He would close his eyes and imagine himself there, shutting out the sound of the camp around him. Along with the heartrending cries of the injured and dying...

It was nothing short of a miracle that both Captain Bentleys emerged safe from the battles.

Yet, after having such exhilaration and terror course through the veins, a return to civilian life wasn't easy.

It was James who had talked him into pooling some money into a syndicate to purchase a fine-looking colt with bloodlines that branded him a future racing champion.

Would that be excitement enough? John wasn't sure.

Thanks to the death of a distant cousin, he was now a viscount, complete with an estate.

And an idea began to form.

The only person he could trust to say whether he was crazy or not was cousin James.

The two men approached the front of the house and dismounted. It was apparent the gardeners were losing the battle with nature. The gardens were overgrown, but not so far gone as to be unable to distinguish where lawn ended and plantings began.

John knocked loudly on the front door. It was opened by a stern-looking butler. The man was wearing an apron, so clearly they had interrupted his daily work. He was none too happy about it.

"Dint I tell ye go 'round t' back to t' servants' entrance?"

James laughed. "You heard the man, Viscount Tyrell. Around the back of the house it is for us."

The balding butler opened his mouth in horror then moved aside to give them admittance.

"My humblest apologies, my lord," he said, dropping the Yorkshire dialect to something approximating the Home Counties. "We weren't expecting you and Captain Bentley until the New Year."

John hid his amusement. He addressed the man. "I'm sorry to have put you out. We wanted to get to Yorkshire before the winter made travelling from London impossible."

"Quite sensible, my lord," the butler averred, "although I'm afraid you'll have to take us as you find us. The previous viscount spent precious little coin here. Do you have bags with you?"

"Our luggage will arrive on the morrow."

The butler straightened his posture.

"Very good, sir."

James waited until the butler departed, leaving him and his cousin alone in a small drawing room warmed by a newly set fire.

"What do you think? You're not disappointed, are you?"

John shrugged his shoulders. "From what I saw of the accounts before we left London, I knew the place had been neglected. The bones of it are here, but I'd like to do a proper survey of the house and lands.

James cocked his head. He knew his cousin well. They were same age and carried the same Bentley family features—blond hair, and dark blue eyes—which, they had been told, were a throwback to some Viking ancestor.

Not surprising, since they were within ten miles of York which the Vikings called Jorvik.

Together, the cousins had attained the rank of captain. They were as close as brothers.

"You have something in mind. What is it?" John asked.

"Since we're planning to give Crimson Lad his first run in the York Races, it would make sense to stable him here."

"I follow so far."

"What if we set a course for him to practice on?"

James smiled as he watched the penny drop for his cousin.

"A training facility—not just for this horse but others..."

"It would be a lot of hard work, but it could potentially mean a lot of money, especially if Crimson Lad runs as we hope. We could put a percentage of his winnings back into restoring Tyrell House."

The butler, who'd introduced himself as Charlton, entered the room with a tray bearing a tureen of soup and a platter of meats and fruit.

"We will need more than just our hard work alone, we'll need trainers, grooms and jockeys," said John.

"We'll need to become members of The York Racing Club," answered James.

The butler cleared his throat. "Forgive me for saying so, my lord but might I recommend that you and Captain Bentley consider taking part in the social Season of York. You will find it attracts personages of the caliber you might wish to include in your enterprise."

John acknowledged Charlton with a nod, then turned to his cousin.

"So, another partnership?"

James nodded. "How hard can it be? I talked *you* into joining a syndicate."

"Which I haven't had a chance to regret... *yet*," said John.

"And you won't," said James who then made a show of looking about. "The house is certainly big enough for the two of us."

John thrust out his hand. James shook it.

"To the success of the Captains Bentley endeavor!"

# CHAPTER 4

*Tyrell House, Yorkshire, March 1817*

John stood to stretch his back and to mop his brow.

The day was fine and cool, but he still sweated from physical exertion.

The practice track was taking shape. Today they were setting in posts to hold the rails for a regulation one mile, two-furlong circuit.

They had measured out the course with string, allowing for two long straights, then measured the width just so to ensure the safety of horse and rider.

He couldn't believe how much he and James, along with a small army of workers, had accomplished in three short months. They had cleared the trees and bracken on the plot just beyond the stables, which had been in a rundown condition.

The snows came in late January, preventing them from working outside, so they turned their attention to refurbishing the stables.

There had been skepticism when he and James outlined their plans to those who lived on the estate. That changed when the men saw a viscount and a captain of His Majesty's cavalry laboring alongside them.

If the butler and the household staff were disappointed that the new master and his cousin were more interested in outdoor pursuits, it wasn't apparent. On the contrary, the activity outside had spurred on the servants inside. Rooms which had been neglected and closed were now spotlessly cleaned.

Fine china and silverware which had not been used in nearly ten years was now making an appearance at the dinner table.

It was as though Tyrell House had come alive, particularly with news that Crimson Lad was due to arrive with his trainer and groom this week.

Not to mention that, within days, the York Season would begin.

John was surprised how much he was looking forward to it.

Early in the New Year, he had received a letter from the social committee who wished to know if the new viscount would be open to receiving invitations and purchasing a subscription.

If they had not needed the connections, he would have declined. There was too much to do before the horse arrived and preparation for the York Races began.

Everything here needed to be perfect.

Noon came. The cousins were tired, sore and ravenous.

Waiting for them was a salver laden with mail. There were a number of invitations already. More pressing were the bills. Some were for the house; others were for the equestrian facility they'd decided to call Tyrell Park.

These he passed on to James who was in charge of its management.

"The current stables are adequate for the house, but we need them to be four times the capacity," James said. "Another three outbuildings to accommodate staff and equipment should do it."

Then he nodded over at the unopened bills in front of John.

"Repairs for the house?" he asked.

John gave him a lopsided grin. "I'm almost afraid to open them.

We're fortunate the whole roof doesn't need replacing, but it does need repairing before we can consider reopening the upper floors.

"We have a choice—sink everything into getting the training facility up and running, or repair the house. The income will not support both."

"Do we try to raise a syndicate ourselves?" James asked.

"I'd rather we didn't. More investors mean more mouths having a say in how it is run. This will be a winner, but I only trust you to do it."

James raised his glass in a salute. "I appreciate your faith in me."

John returned the gesture. "If only other people could see what we see."

James had no idea why his cousin's words struck a chord, but they did. It was not truly formed in his mind but once there, he couldn't rid himself of it.

"I have an outlandish idea," he said.

John raised an eyebrow "Another one?"

"We hold an event. Instead of attending all these functions in York and trying to sell our vision for Tyrell Park, why don't we show what we have here?"

"The house is in no state to host a ball."

"It will have to be something else. During the day, obviously."

The butler cleared his throat.

"May I be permitted to make an observation, sirs? Lady Clune is chairwoman of the York Social Committee."

"We know that," James said brusquely.

Charlton was not put off.

"It is proper to have a hostess for events where young ladies are in attendance and Lady Clune is a woman of significant influence. I would suggest that she would be flattered to act as the hostess for Viscount Tyrell. And there is something else you should be aware of, sir. Lord Clune happens to be chairman of the York Racing Club."

The butler then went about his tasks, clearing away the plates. He did so with a discreet but satisfied smile. Silence fell across the room, each cousin lost in thought.

James witnessed his cousin's slow grin.

"An al fresco party in the gardens," said John, now thinking aloud. "Music, games..."

"Since it won't be a formal event, small delicacies and pastries can be prepared in advance," Charlton added with an unmistakable note of approval in his voice. "And a pig on a spit can be easily roasted outdoors."

"That would allow us to show the work we've done on the stables and the track," John added.

"Games... A scavenger hunt," said James. "It will ensure people leave the gardens and explore the grounds. It will give them a chance to see the scale of our project."

Now the butler smiled.

"I shall tell the staff, my lord. I believe they will enjoy this as much as the guests."

# CHAPTER 5

*York, March 1817*

Ivy took to heart the admonition to stay close to her sister. They had been to York a couple of times in the past but never before through The Shambles, the city's medieval market street.

Upper stories of timber buildings hung over the thoroughfare, reducing the amount of daylight, giving the place an unsettling feel even when the sun was high in the sky.

It was also market day, and thus more crowded than usual. People surged along the route, and up the ginnels—the tiny alleyways between the buildings, so narrow that two people could not walk abreast.

Eventually they came out onto the main road where stallholders plied wares of every description.

Patience, Susana and Barbara had set them the challenge of purchasing as much suitable fabrics, ribbons, lace, feathers and other adornments with the coin they had with them and no more.

Ivy relished it, and knew her sister felt the same.

They might only have a few day gowns and one evening gown for a Season that lasted two months, but this was not the first time the

Bigglesworth girls had pooled their resources. With a bit of clever sewing and basting, their choices would be nearly endless. A spencer of a different color, a pelisse with a change of trim, the addition of lace decoration at sleeves or an overskirt in an embroidered net, easily changed the look of a simple gown into one of the highest fashion.

The dressing room in their borrowed town house resembled a mantuamaker's shop. At any time, one sister or another could be found with needle and thread at the ready, assisted by a protégé of Mrs. Crewe who worked as both ladies' maid and maid-of-all-work.

Iris slowed down at one stall, eyeing bolts of muslin—plain white, and sprigged, as well as fancy patterns named for the Scottish town of Paisley.

Ivy found some silk thread which caught her eye. It might be used to decorate a sleeveless spencer with some tambour work, which would be much faster to produce than embroidering. She enquired inquired about the cost, then spotted another spool and haggled the best price for them both.

When she had finished, she turned to find her sister had three packages already wrapped in brown paper and tied with string.

They slowly made their way along the stalls looking for other bargains—a simple wooden comb might have feathers added for a headdress. Simple white beads could be strung together and pass as pearls or they could be added to a length of satin and be worn in the hair as a bandeau or on a dress as an under-bust trim.

"We still need to go to the stationers for the colored paper Doro requested," said Iris. "I believe that it's on the high street."

Ivy sighed.

The high street was two blocks away, and her arm carrying the basket was already getting tired.

"Do you know why she's asked for it? She specially requested gilt paper—as much as we can afford."

Iris shrugged. "She's very clever, and I am sure she has seen some wonderful events at the hotel in Harrogate where she works. I cannot think of anyone better to manage the details. Whatever theme she suggests for the ball will be wonderful."

~

Iris watched her sister shift the heavily laden basket onto another arm.

"Here, let me take it for a while," she said.

Ivy shot her a grateful look and relinquished the basket.

After a moment Iris spoke. "Are you nervous?" she asked.

"What about?"

"I feel the weight of expectation—on you, me, Josefina—to find a husband this Season."

Ivy nodded. "Patience has expended an enormous sum to give us this opportunity, that to go back to Starbrook without an offer..."

"It's only because our sisters gave up their portion of the dowry that we have an acceptable sum to offer," Iris added.

"We have our titles, but they mean little," said Ivy.

"We may not be pretty enough to attract the eye of a suitable gentleman." Iris let out a long, dispirited sigh.

Silence fell between them for good long minutes before Ivy asked. "What kind of gentleman would you like to marry?"

Iris considered the question a moment before shrugging a shoulder.

"He must be kind. I'd like him to be handsome. Most of all, he must love family because I would want you to visit me often."

"That worries me as much as not finding husbands," Ivy confessed. "What if we *do*? We would marry and be apart for the first time in our lives."

The notion caused Iris to stop. She turned to her sister.

"I... I can't imagine not seeing you every day," she said.

They remained there on the pavement, each lost in their own thoughts.

"Do you think there may be brothers in attendance?"

"There might," said Iris, tilting her head. "We would need to see an invitation list to be sure. Why do you ask?"

Ivy raised her chin in firm resolve. "It is the only way forward. By marrying brothers, we would be sure to see each other more often than if we married anyone else. We *have* to marry brothers. It is the only way."

The twins found the stationers. They sought out the most colorful paper in stock and tallied it up. It was slightly more than they could afford.

While the clerk looked at them expectantly, Iris and Ivy exchanged a glance. Each knew what the other was thinking—they had a few coppers they'd intended to spend on new paint brushes. If they reused the ones they brought with them, they could afford it.

Ivy pushed the paint brushes aside on the counter and handed over the coins for the paper.

Now the basket was exceedingly heavy. Each twin took the handle, carrying the load between them. It was awkward, but it was the only way it could be done.

Iris returned to her contemplation.

*Brothers.*

*Yes*! That was the only solution. She and Ivy would simply have to find brothers to marry. Surely it stood to reason male siblings of suitable standing would attend this Season. After all, there was a clutch of Bigglesworth sisters in York, should there not be a goodly number of families with an equally large number of sons?

"You never told me what kind of husband you would like," Iris reminded her sister.

Ivy cocked her head. "In truth, I've not given it much thought. Like your dream beau, he must be kind and must love you as much as I love you."

"How do you think you'll know him?"

"I think it will be in his eyes."

"I think it will be in his kiss," whispered Iris.

Ivy's mouth dropped open a moment before she giggled. "A kiss," she said. "Yes, I would certainly think that would do it."

# CHAPTER 6

"Miss!"

There followed another voice, equally insistent.

"Excuse me, miss!"

The twins turned together. Two young men, tall and well dressed, blonde hair shining like newly minted silver, stood a few feet away. One of them held a parcel in his hand—one of *their* parcels.

The two men looked so much alike, they simply *had* to be brothers.

"You appear to have dropped this," said the first, handing it to Ivy.

"Thank you so much, sir," she began.

"We've been shopping, you see," said Iris.

The other gentleman smiled broadly. "Yes, we can see that, and it looks to have been quite the expedition."

Iris glanced at the heavily laden basket they carried. It was a wonder they'd not lost more of their purchases. Patience would be most disappointed if they had.

"Do you have far to go?" said the first. "Your basket must be especially heavy. May we order you a hackney?"

"Oh, we couldn't possibly put you to all that trouble," answered Iris.

"We don't live far away," said Ivy, naming the street.

"That's three blocks away," the second gentleman exclaimed. "Do allow us to carry your shopping."

The twins looked at one another. A silent conversation flowed between them.

*The basket is heavy.*

*We don't know these gentlemen.*

*We have no fare for a hackney.*

*We don't know if they even* are *gentlemen.*

*But they seem nice.*

*They* are *well dressed... but what would Patience say?*

When they turned back to the young men, Ivy and Iris found them in a similarly unspoken conversation.

"Do you know Lady Clune?" the first asked.

The twins shared another quick glance.

"We have been invited to an at-home with her on Wednesday," she said.

The first gentleman nodded. "We have just left her house following an appointment. The good lady *will* vouch for us."

"So, may we be permitted to introduce ourselves?" said the second.

"Captain John Bentley," the first young man snapped to attention and bowed. "At your service, Miss."

"Captain James Bentley," said the second. "A pleasure to make your acquaintance."

Ivy and Iris bobbed a curtsy.

"I am Iris and this is my sister Ivy."

"We are the stepdaughters of the dowager Countess Seahaven," Ivy added.

Ivy allowed John Bentley to take the overstuffed basket while James rescued some of the top-heavy load from toppling before falling into step with Iris for the walk home.

"Do you know Lady Clune well?" Iris asked.

"We are newly acquainted," said John. "My cousin and I have only just returned to Yorkshire, but we do find a lot to commend it."

Ivy wondered whether the two Captain Bentleys might be flirting with them.

*How thrilling!*

James Bentley cleared his throat, a half-grin directed at his cousin. "What *Captain Bentley* is too modest to say, is what *also* brings him to Yorkshire. He has inherited the title of Viscount Tyrell."

Ivy bobbed a curtsy. Her sister did the same.

"Then we are especially honored, my lord, and Captain Bentley," said Iris.

"I think it is we who are doubly honored," said John.

John could have cheerfully throttled his cousin for mentioning his title. It was still new to him and still felt like an honor undeserved. He caught a glance between the two sisters and wondered whether they thought James was being a braggard for the benefit of two pretty young women.

And they *were* uncommonly pretty, with striking green eyes and auburn hair half hidden under straw bonnets—one trimmed in green, the other in violet, to match the sprigs of flowers on their respective dresses—but that wasn't all that intrigued him.

Their mannerisms seemed to mirror each other. They held silent conversations before one answered for the both of them.

"May I presume you are more than sisters? Identical twins?" he said.

"Yes." They answered in unison.

"We have an elder sister," said Ivy, which he made a point of remembering because she wore the green dress. He met her eyes and saw a fleck of brown in the green of her irises which her twin did not have.

"We have another four older half-sisters and three younger half-sisters," said Iris who, he noted, had the lightest smattering of freckles across her nose.

"Did you know you were going to inherit the title, my lord?" asked Ivy.

Iris nodded, as though that was the question she wanted to ask.

"I had no idea, actually," said John. "An elderly cousin on my late father's side passed away when I was on the Continent. I only learned about the title just a few months ago. Apparently, the letter from the solicitors was chasing me around Europe while we were chasing ole Boney."

"The estate itself was a surprise, wasn't it James?" he continued. "Quite a good size, but it has seen better days. I'm sure it's not as grand as Seahaven."

The girls shared a significant glance.

"Were none of your cousin's family still living there?" Ivy asked.

"No, just a handful of servants. I wish there had been," said John. "It's very quiet some evenings with just the two of us—especially after spending so long in crowded soldiers' encampments."

"You'd have let them stay?" Iris sounded incredulous.

John answered without hesitation. "Of course! It would have been as much their home as mine."

But he wondered at the question.

The old Earl of Seahaven had ten daughters. Had the new Earl cast them out?

If so, the man was a cad.

He waited for Ivy—or Iris for that matter—to further explain. But their conversation came to an end when they arrived at their destination.

Ivy's gloved hand accidentally touched his as she took the basket from him. John was delighted to see a light blush brighten her cheeks.

He bowed, but his eyes never left hers.

Beside him, James returned his armful of parcels to Iris.

"Thank you," said Ivy.

"You've both been truly kind," responded Iris.

"May we offer you refreshment?" continued Ivy.

"A cup of tea? A glass of lemonade?" asked Iris.

John glanced to James who couldn't seem to take his eyes off Iris. But keeping an eye on *them* was a woman in the second story window.

"Alas, I wish we could, my ladies, but we've not yet finished our business in town," said John.

It was rather pleasing to see looks of disappointment.

"May we call on you?" said James. "Lady Clune assures us there are plenty of events on the calendar for this Season."

"We would be honored," the twins answered in unison.

He and James lingered until the Ladies Ivy and Iris Bigglesworth were safe indoors before heading back toward the high street.

"Your butler needs a raise," said James.

"How so?"

"It was his idea for us to purchase a subscription for this Season."

John glanced at his cousin who was grinning from ear to ear.

"That was for business."

"Who says it shouldn't be for pleasure as well?"

# CHAPTER 7

As soon as the front door closed, Iris danced about the hallway, hugging the wrapped parcels to her breast as though she embraced a lover, listening to the music in her head, seeing a grand ballroom in her mind's eye.

"Wasn't he handsome?" she said.

"Who?" Ivy grinned, shifting the basket on her arm. "There were two of them, and I cannot decide who was the better looking."

Iris waited until she had her sister's full attention. "I think the viscount *likes* you."

Ivy's face became dreamy for a moment. Iris left her there while she climbed the stairs. No doubt her sister was imagining a grand love affair also. And well might she tease! Did she not just act like a giddy school girl herself just a moment before?

James had said little during their walk, but she appreciated the way he slowed his pace to accommodate her shorter stride while he walked beside her.

She also liked the way he teased his cousin. There was a touch of pride and affection in his expression as he did so. That spoke well of his character.

Iris entered the dressing room, looking for the place to put the bolts of fabric. She glanced at an old wooden table filled with a rainbow of fabric pattern pieces and decided to put parcels on a chair, instead.

"There you are, girls," said Susana. "I thought we were going to have to send out a search party for you!"

Their half-sister was the full blood sister of Barbara and Doro. She glanced out from behind a swathe of fabric where she knelt, sewing the hem on a gown fitted to a wicker work dress form.

"We didn't mean to be so long," Ivy answered.

"We stopped at the stationers to buy colored paper, which Doro asked for especially," said Iris who picked out the thick sheaf of paper and looked around for a place to put it before deciding to set it on top of a tall set of drawers.

"Are you sure that's all that kept you so long?" Susana asked, getting to her feet and stretching her back.

Iris and her sister exchanged glances, each noting the slightly guilty expression mirrored on her twin's face. The look was obvious to all apparently.

"You saw us from the window," Ivy guessed.

"We had bought so much," Iris began.

"The basket became too heavy," continued Ivy.

Iris nodded. "We'd just come out of the stationers..."

As was their custom, the twins took turns in telling each part of the tale.

"And that's how we came to meet Viscount Tyrell and his cousin, Captain Bentley," Ivy concluded.

"Well, from what I saw, you appear to have made a conquest already," said Susana. There was a slight twinkle in her eye belying the small degree of censure in her tone.

Iris and Ivy let out a nervous giggle. Iris feared they might have been cautioned by their older sister.

"I know we weren't properly introduced, but we could hardly refuse when they had been so chivalrous," said Iris.

"Not all men are like that. You know that, don't you? Even ones who appear to be honorable on first blush may have less than savory motives."

"We are not completely naïve," said Ivy. "You did raise us with a degree of common sense, after all."

Susana inclined her head to concede the point. "I know. And I don't want to be a mother hen, but it is so important that we launch you girls well. Patience has spent a lot of money giving you this opportunity. I would hate to have a question placed over your reputations."

"We were in public view all the way, and they were complete gentlemen!" Iris exclaimed. Ivy nodded.

"I don't mean to malign their characters, I'm sure they are who they claim to be, but do *you* know?"

"The viscount said he and the captain had just come from an interview with Lady Clune," said Ivy.

"Then Patience can make discreet enquiries when you go there tomorrow." Susana sighed, kneeling down to return to her sewing.

"You mustn't think I am a bitter old maid," she continued. "A pretty face and pretty manners are not all that go to make a suitable candidate for husband. I want you girls to be happy—married to men who know and appreciate what a jewel they have in their wife."

"And what of love?"

"Love is wonderful if you can find it, but it might not always take the form you expect."

"May we invite the Viscount and the Captain to the ball?" Ivy's voice was soft, polite and cautious, the elation of their shopping afternoon gone.

"That will eventually be Patience's decision," said Susana "Add them to the list for her to vet. If Lady Clune can vouch for them, and your heart is truly set, I'm sure allowances can be made for them.

"But enough of all of that!" Susana said brightly. "Show me what you bought at the markets today while I finish off this hem!"

The twins dutifully showed off their purchases, including the paper.

"I have to admit I have no idea why Doro wanted so much paper, but she did say this morning that she wanted everyone together at dinner to share what she has in mind. All I know is that, between the sewing and the decorations, we're all going to be very busy!"

Patience called up from downstairs. "Susana, I need your opinion on something."

Susana sighed and got to her feet once more.

"You go," said Iris. "I'll finish the hem, and then Ivy and I will start on making the spencers."

Their sister shot them a grateful look.

The girls removed their bonnets and pelisses and settled down to work.

Ivy spread out a bolt of fabric and placed the muslin pattern pieces on it. "Are we being foolish?" she asked.

"In what? Wanting to marry for love?" Iris answered, her attention on placing neat, even stitches to match Susana's. "I had always assumed that I—that *we*—would fall madly in love and said object of our desire would feel the same way."

"Would you marry a man you did not love?"

Silently, they remembered their own mother and the example given by their two stepmothers—the late Emmeline, mother to Emma and Merrilyn, who had been Lady Tavistock before she married their papa, and, of course, Patience.

*They* did not marry for love—not so far as Iris could see. They were very nice women, who might have had their choice of handsome suitors and yet they had chosen to marry the Earl.

Would that be the twins' fate also? To marry simply out of necessity and not love?

It was the reality, after all—she and Ivy *had* to marry, and soonest done.

"Don't worry," said Ivy, though Iris never expressed her concerns aloud, "I'm sure the Viscount and the Captain will pass muster. And if not, I'm sure we will meet more than enough eligibles."

Iris forced brightness into her voice. "I'm sure you're right."

# CHAPTER 8

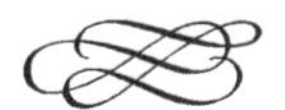

Ivy was glad their town house was close to Lady Clune's city residence. She, along with Iris and Patience, could enjoy the spring sunshine at a stroll, as well as save the cost of a hackney fare.

The light-weight pelisse she wore had only been completed the night before. The color reminded her of the soft green shade of the ferns found on the walk to Mother Shipton's Cave. It also picked up the sprigs of green in her day dress, which had been embellished with a length of cream lace basted into the bodice that matched the trim on the pelisse.

With the work they had done, she could wear a different style for a week and only the most eagle-eye would spot it was the same dress.

Iris' dress was similarly adorned, except her pelisse was the color of violet. Green and purple. They were the colors they had always gravitated too as children—no doubt encouraged by the older Bigglesworth girls to ensure the twins could be told apart.

Today, Patience was dressed as befitting a dowager countess—a simple but fashionable gown beneath a blue pelisse, the color of sapphire. The only piece of jewelry she wore was an elegant cameo brooch set in a blue jasper ground.

"Patience, my dear! How grand to see you in York!"

Newly emerged from a carriage was a woman aged in her forties, dressed in the height of fashion. Beside her was a younger woman who regarded them with friendly curiosity. A daughter, it appeared, as she was the very image of her mother, Ivy observed.

"Virginia!" Patience exclaimed. "It is good to see you too. May I present my two stepdaughters, Lady Ivy and Lady Iris Bigglesworth?"

The twins bobbed in unison.

"Girls, this is Lady Virginia Fernshawe, and this must be Matilda." The girl acknowledged the greeting with a curtsy. "My, you are very much a young lady," Patience continued. "I remember you when you were a very little girl, only going into the school room."

"Matilda has just turned sixteen," her mother stated proudly.

Patience and Lady Fernshawe continued their conversation up the stairs, leaving the three younger girls to follow in their wake.

"Is this your first Season?" Matilda asked shyly.

"It is," Iris answered.

"I like the idea of parties and a new wardrobe, but I don't know if I'm ready for a husband. However, papa says I shall not have to choose immediately."

Ivy's heart went out to the young girl, and she knew Iris felt the same. She took Matilda's hand in hers.

"I promise we shall be friends and navigate the Season together," she said.

"Let's make a pact," Iris added. "We shall all marry for love and for no other reason."

Matilda squeezed Ivy's hand, and her smile brightened as the three of them entered Lady Clune's drawing room to be introduced.

The woman was seventy if she was a day. Only the lines about her eyes and mouth, and the rich vein of silver that ran though her hair, gave her away. She was as spritely as a woman half her age, and thus the day was an extremely pleasant one, not at all like Ivy had imagined.

She hadn't confessed as much to her sister, but had wondered whether or not Lady Clune would be a dragon and be condescending to them because of their straitened circumstances and lack of a meaningful dowry.

Instead, the good Lady seemed to consider a pleasant disposition and the ability to hold an engaging conversation to be the measure of a young lady's suitability. Judging by the approving looks they received, Ivy was confident that she and Iris had passed her little test.

"There is a new activity which is a late addition to our calendar," Lady Clune announced.

Ivy noticed Patience take a breath and hold it. Their resources would not stretch to an expensive event.

"It is an al fresco party with fun and informality being the watchwords. I am to be hostess on behalf of the new Viscount Tyrell and his cousin."

Whether Lady Clune had not seen, or had chosen to ignore Patience's discomfiture, she did *not* miss the fact Ivy and her sister sat to attention and exchanged a glance at the name.

Patience smiled and nodded towards them. "A couple of days ago the viscount and the captain came to the assistance of two damsels in distress weighed down with too many parcels."

"How very like them to be so gallant," said Lady Clune approvingly. "They each served with distinction in the cavalry, you know. But they have their work cut out for them at Tyrell House. I'm sorry to say that the late viscount's lingering ill-health made him somewhat of a recluse in his later years, but the viscount has assured me the gardens will soon be back to looking their best."

Lady Clune continued. "Countess, I understand all of your stepdaughters have elected to spend spring in York with you."

"Indeed, that is the case." Patience set down her cup of tea.

"Then the al fresco party is an invitation extended to you all—after all, there is no limit as to how many people can gather together out of doors!"

But that was not the end to the invitations. Lady Clune handed Patience a sheaf of tickets to every conceivable entertainment suitable for young ladies—dances, recitals, art exhibitions, museum tours, boating jaunts on the River Ouse...

"Unfortunately, I cannot secure enough tickets for all of your daughters, Countess, but I'm sure there is enough variety to share."

Lady Fernshawe was also handed a suite of tickets on Matilda's behalf.

"It's been my pleasure and privilege to meet every young lady who has had her coming out in York for the better part of thirty years," said Lady Clune. "I wish you much happiness, joy—and most of all, success!"

Later that evening, Iris fanned out the invitations like playing cards, keeping the print at the front face down.

"Choose one."

Ivy walked her fingers across the tops of the cards in one direction and then another until she settled for the card in the center. She pulled it out from her sister's hand and turned the card over.

It was a recital followed by supper.

"This is the recital where Barbara has been invited to play!" Ivy exclaimed.

Iris nodded excitedly.

"You promise you will tell me all about it, won't you?" she asked. "I'll wait up for you. I want to know what everyone is wearing, who is doing anything interesting. I want to know how Barbara played. *Everything!*"

Ivy giggled and took her sister's hands. "I promise. By the time I finish recounting, you will feel like you were there with me."

# CHAPTER 9

The Merchant Adventurers Hall didn't look like much from the street. The door, flung wide this evening, was located between two shops.

The passage led out into a courtyard where the hall itself stood proudly, as it had done for more than four hundred years. Little square panes of glass threw uneven light along the stairs that led up to heavy coffered oak doors.

"If I did not know better, I would expect to hear the sound of dulcimers and psaltery," said Ivy.

"I agree," Patience nodded.

Dating back to the medieval period, the Merchant Adventurers Hall was originally a guild hall, and indeed was still used for regular meetings for the venerable organization.

Inside the Great Hall itself, large timber posts ran down the center of the room from which beams rose like branches of a great oak tree to carry the weight of the great arched ceiling above.

In one corner, musicians were tuning up their instruments. They spotted Barbara, who was in deep conversation with some gentlemen.

Ivy owned to feeling more than a little knot in her stomach. This was the first function she had ever attended without her sister.

It was strange not to have Iris at her side, but she was glad to have Patience for company.

Tonight, Ivy decided against wearing a plain green gown, choosing instead one in lavender. Lilac fabric left over from making the pelisse had been fashioned into a spencer with puffed sleeves and decorated with cream lace on the bodice and at the wrists.

Iris had dressed her hair this evening, winding a ribbon in a matching color through her auburn curls. She had even made her a necklace of white, even beads that looked like a strand of pearls. Indeed, one would not even know the difference until examined up close.

Patience looked no less beautiful. She wore a silk gown which, until a few weeks ago, had been out of fashion, but with a few artful alterations here and there, it looked most *au courant*.

The attendance of the dowager Countess of Seahaven attracted the attention of some of the guests—some who had been acquainted with the late earl, and others who remembered Patience from years ago.

After having been introduced to so many people, Ivy wasn't sure how she could possibly remember names and faces, but she soon found a familiar and welcome one.

"Thank goodness, I found you," said Matilda. "I don't know anyone else here. Oh, I feel so overwhelmed that I cannot tell if you are Lady Ivy or Lady Iris!"

Ivy offered the girl a pat on the arm. "I am Lady Ivy. Let us take a walk around the room together and I will tell you all the names I can remember, then you won't be so nervous when you are introduced properly. What do you say to that?"

They had completed a lap of the room and even managed a few words to Barbara before spotting Patience and Lady Fernshawe in conversation.

Then Ivy saw a man entering the hall. She came to a sudden halt. Matilda looked at her, askance.

"It's him!" Ivy turned her back, snapped open her fan and waved it briskly.

"Who?"

"The Earl of Seahaven."

Matilda frowned. "The Earl? But I thought Lady Seahaven was a widow... *ohhhh.*"

"We haven't seen that man and his odious wife since papa's funeral. He sent his man of business with the demand to vacate Seahaven," Ivy whispered harshly.

"Then we must tell your stepmother."

Ivy glanced over to Patience, who was now in conversation with another group of people.

The last thing she wanted to do was to ruin her stepmother's evening. With any luck the concert would soon begin, and they'd all be seated. There might even be a chance that she would not have to see the earl and countess at all.

The earl's tall, thin, pinch-faced wife swept into the assembly like a duchess.

Ivy was forced to step back lest her feet be trampled. That caused her to collide into the back of another guest.

She turned to apologize only to find a familiar face casting a baleful expression in the direction of the Earl and Countess of Seahaven. The man muttered a word of contempt for them under his breath.

Then he looked down to her. A momentary look of surprise became a smile which was returned.

Viscount Tyrell's blue eyes twinkled with merriment. "We must stop meeting like this, Lady Ivy."

In his day clothes, John Bentley cut a virile figure, but in evening dress he was more than handsome. He was *sublime.*

Ivy dropped a curtsy.

"I should not mind if you wish to come to my rescue again, my Lord."

Her answer seemed to please him because he seemed disinclined to look anywhere else but into her eyes. He only came to himself when Matilda discreetly cleared her throat.

Ivy made the introduction.

"May I escort you ladies to your seats?" he asked.

Matilda giggled and readily accepted. Ivy gave John a serene smile and took his arm. He cleared a path through the milling crowd to where Patience and Lady Fernshawe waited.

Once again, Ivy performed the introductions, mindful of the very specific look Patience cast her way.

"Do you have a seat reserved, Lord Tyrell?" Patience asked.

"Alas, I do not, my lady. I attend alone," he said. "My cousin James has had to beg off this evening."

"Then you must join us now and for supper afterwards."

"I'd be honored."

Ivy had always been aware of her twin's presence, even when they were out of sight of one another.

She never felt this way with any of her sisters, even Josefina. As a girl, she quickly realized that being a twin was something special—two but also one.

So, what could account for the fact that her whole body was aware of the man seated beside her?

She felt the heat of his body even though there was an appropriate space between them.

When he opened the program, she was aware of the length of his fingers in his satin gloves. When he applauded the performance, she breathed in his scent of cedar and orange.

As though he knew her eyes were on him, Viscount Tyrell turned to her. Her heart tumbled a few beats, leaving her just a little breathless.

*What might it be like to kiss him?*

Ivy lowered her lashes but not before seeing John's eyes fall to her lips.

Did he sense something between them as she did?

# CHAPTER 10

John had hoped to go the entire evening without having the dubious pleasure of being introduced to the current Earl of Seahaven. Alas, Lady Clune had other ideas.

He gritted his teeth and trailed behind the good lady.

He'd heard the earl and his wife being announced when they arrived at the recital. He recalled the questions Ivy had asked him about whether family members lived at Tyrell House when he had inherited his title.

*Was that what had happened to Ivy and her sisters? Did the current Earl of Seahaven cast them out?*

If so, it was a damned caddish thing to do.

Not surprising that he was not kindly disposed to the man on first sight.

And then, when the earl's scarecrow of a wife pushed her way through the crowd to secure the best seats, John wondered whether the bump that pushed Ivy into him was not somehow deliberate.

Nevertheless, he fixed a pleasant expression as Lady Clune made introductions. John nodded as expected, given the man's superior rank. Yet he determined to be no more friendly than required.

The Earl of Seahaven was about a decade-and-a-half older than himself, John estimated, which would put him in his late thirties. Already there were signs that the man was not as healthy as he ought to be.

A redness in the nose indicated a fondness of a little too much drink. A bit of softness around the middle indicated an equal love of food.

He was also introduced to the countess who, no doubt, was a diamond of the first water in her day. At a distance, she could still claim the title of handsome, but her beauty now was brittle.

After bowing to the woman, John found himself wishing more than anything else to be back in the convivial company of Ivy and her stepmother.

"Did I hear right, Tyrell? You have an interest in the old gee-gees?"

John gritted his teeth at the use of such a juvenile term for horses. He answered: "Indeed, we do, sir. A very promising colt we hope will do well at the York races."

"Well, I've been known to back a few winners in my time," the earl boasted. "A bit of success with the fillies, if you know what I mean."

John *did* know, and his contempt for the man grew.

"Oh, there's more to Lord Tyrell's interest than just the horse," said Lady Clune, cheerfully oblivious to the rising tension between the two men. "The viscount and his cousin are looking to build a training facility for racing horses."

The earl burst out laughing. "I'd say you're a damned fool. It's one thing to have a flutter, quite another to sink your life savings into it."

John's jaw ached from gritting his teeth to prevent himself from setting the man on his arse—peer or not.

"Would you care to wager on it, my lord?" he found himself saying.

He watched the earl's changing expression closely—humor, smug satisfaction, surprise, then curiosity.

"A wager, you say?"

"A hundred pounds on a winner. You pick the race."

John heard Lady Clune gasp.

If his rational self had been in charge of his brain, he'd have simply ignored the earl, but insult had been given, not just the one to himself, but the greater one to the Bigglesworth girls. The idea of becoming their champion greatly appealed.

"You're not seriously considering taking up this pup's ludicrous bet, are you, Charles?" said the countess with disgust. "Don't be such an idiot."

"There, there, my dear," her husband replied, condescendingly patting his wife's hand, all the while keeping his attention on John. "I know what I'm doing."

The earl thrust out his hand.

"I accept your wager."

John glanced down at the man's hand, then back up to his face. He did not accept the hand.

Then he gave a curt nod, saying only, "I'll see you on race day," before pivoting on his heel and walking off.

And he kept walking until he was outside in the fresh air. He breathed in a great lungful of it.

The rain-scented air served to help cool his temper.

*One hundred pounds. It was an obscene amount of money and it wasn't as though he was Midas.*

Still, he could not bring himself to regret the wager—despite the fact there would be a hell of a lot of explaining he'd have to do to James to account for risking such a sum.

"Your bet with Charles is the talk of the night."

John looked up and found Ivy standing a few feet away, silhouetted in the doorway.

"Forgive me for ruining your evening," he said.

Ivy shook her head and stepped forward. A lamp illuminated her face. To his relief, she was not angry with him.

"You haven't. Not at all. Charles has that effect on a lot of people."

"I would hate to think that my rush of temper would serve to make trouble for Lady Seahaven. I shall apologize for putting her, and indeed you all, in a difficult situation."

Ivy shook her head once more and touched a hand to his arm, before withdrawing it, no doubt concerned that she'd been too familiar.

The effects of the brief touch lingered.

"There is nothing that man can do that he hasn't already done to us," she said. "We live simply and frugally, but there is nothing we lack. Truly. We do what we can to make our own living. Most of all, we love each other—so that makes us wealthier than Charles and his wife."

Once more, John's head did war with his body. Now it was because he wanted to sweep Ivy into his arms and kiss her.

He did the next best thing. He took Ivy's hand and brought it to his lips. Her own lips parted and the little sigh of pleasure warmed him.

"How did you become so wise?" John hadn't meant the question to sound seductive, but that was the apparent affect. Ivy swayed toward him, a blush heating her cheeks.

"Ivy? Are you out here?"

They started and took half a step away from each other.

"May I call on you?" he whispered.

Ivy nodded and turned away.

"Here I am, Matilda," she called back.

John watched the two young women go back into the hall with the strange, unsettled feeling that his life had changed for good.

# CHAPTER 11

"Lady Iris Bigglesworth, Lady Fernshawe, and the Honorable Miss Matilda Fernshawe."

James heard the names clearly, despite being in conversation with a couple of gentlemen about plans for Tyrell Park.

He watched Iris, along with the Fernshawes, chat with the hosts of this dance. Then Iris and Matilda linked arms and made their way around the room in an anticlockwise fashion. That meant, as soon as they reached three-quarters of the way around, James would be close enough to make himself known.

What must the Bigglesworths think of himself and his cousin?

Frankly, he didn't know what to think either.

John was a viscount. He was supposed to be the responsible one, so when he returned from the recital last night with the tale of a hundred-pound bet, James didn't know whether to throttle his cousin or cheer him on for the way he dealt with the Earl of Seahaven.

James bowed before the two ladies.

"Lady Iris, Miss Fernshawe."

He was delighted to see Iris' lovely face brighten with recognition.

Her friend dropped a curtsy. "It is good to see you again, my lord."

At his frown, Iris smiled.

"Matilda, I'd like you to introduce you to Captain *James* Bentley," she said. "Captain, may I present Miss Matilda Fernshawe."

"Oh my," said Matilda. "Forgive my mistake, Captain. You look so much like the viscount!"

James bowed and sought to smooth over the younger woman's embarrassment.

"Worry not, dear lady. It is a mistake that happens frequently. It was even more common when my cousin and I were in uniform. Imagine the confusion when a messenger was sent out with orders to 'Captain Bentley'. In the end it saved a lot of angst to put us in the same regiment and have us do the same thing."

Matilda's uncertainty disappeared, but not her blush, so she excused herself to go and greet some mutual acquaintances.

"And speaking of confusion, I do have a question to ask, Captain."

James loved the way merriment manifested itself in Iris' green eyes and her smile. Not even a fine layer of face powder could hide the faint smattering of freckles across her bridge of her nose, which he found endearing.

The tease in her voice was not exactly flirtatious—no, she was too well brought up for that—but there *was* the promise of it.

James liked it a lot.

"Anything in my power to grant, my lady," he said.

"How did you recognize *me*, since I also bear a striking resemblance to someone else."

"I could say it was because of your outstanding loveliness," he said.

To his delight, Iris understood him to be teasing her and her smile became a grin.

"Ah, but I have an equally lovely sister who looks like me in almost every way," she responded.

"Then I will confess to hearing your name announced."

"Honesty at last, Captain!" Iris laughed. "I must commend you for it. Speaking of lookalikes, where is your cousin?"

"I sent him to bed last night without his supper, and he is to remain there until he learns to behave himself in company."

James was delighted with his grave delivery. It fooled Iris for a moment. Her smile became a perfect 'O' of surprise before she caught him in a grin.

Iris lightly tapped his arm with her fan in gentle admonishment. He offered her his arm.

"Would you take a turn with me about the room? I really do need to speak to you about what happened between John and the Earl of Seahaven. I trust your sister made you aware of what happened?"

Iris nodded in answer to the question. Ivy had told her the whole thing from beginning to end.

As for herself, she had dismissed the significance of it as men being braggards, as was their wont, but Ivy insisted it was different, and that the bet was made under gross provocation.

During the recounting, Iris felt something shift inside her, and it was difficult to explain. There was something different about her sister, her twin, her closest companion, and she could guess its cause.

*Ivy was developing tender feelings for Viscount Tyrell.*

And here, walking alongside arguably the most handsome man in this assembly, Iris could easily understand how one might develop a preference for a Bentley man.

"My cousin is not a reckless individual, I want to assure you of that," said James who then paused for a moment as though searching for the right words to say. "He wished me, in the most sincere terms, to convey that if I were to meet with any of your family today."

Iris gave his arm a little squeeze of reassurance.

"Then, on behalf of my family, I must request you to tell your cousin that he has caused no discomfort. I beg him, and you, to give it no more thought. In truth, the current Earl and Countess of Seahaven are strangers to us. They have paid us no call and neither have we been invited to attend them."

James let out an audible sigh of relief and came to a stop.

"It does set my mind at ease, and for John as well," he said. "He holds your sister in high regard."

Iris looked up at him.

How strange that she should be so certain of what he *really* wanted to know without actually saying the words. That only ever happened with Ivy.

She gave him the answer. "You have my assurance that my sister's regard matches his."

His face had a touch of color from the sun which set off the blue of his eyes. It would be too easy to fall into them and lose herself there.

Next, she was drawn to James' lips. They had compressed a moment before tilting up at the edges, as though he was fighting the emotion behind it. She glanced up to his eyes, then down to his mouth which had now opened into a wide smile.

"You cannot know how pleased I am," he said. "Do you know what it is like to live with a man who is already half in love and doesn't even know it?"

Iris, too, felt full to bursting. She giggled. "No, I cannot say I can answer directly to that experience, but I do know what it is like to have a sister with a similar complaint."

Soon she became aware of a young man who hovered near with an earnest look on his face and a gold pencil case open, ready to beg a dance.

James raised her gloved hand to his lips and pressed a kiss there.

"Please save me a dance," he said, more of a plea than a request.

Ivy looked down at the dance card which dangled from her wrist. "The quadrille?"

James bowed formally. "I wait with eager anticipation, Lady Iris."

# CHAPTER 12

James could understand how his cousin could become besotted by a Bigglesworth girl. Lady Iris was not only lovely to look at, she was also charming. Did he also mention gracious? He was grateful that, between dances, she had been at pains to include him in her circle of acquaintances. It didn't take long to find himself enjoying not only her company, but also that of the other guests.

Lord McDonnell was from Edinburgh. He and his friend Lord Swinburn were both attending York University studying architecture and were interested in visiting Tyrell House. They talked of John's plans to restore the manor and his plans to make the finest equestrian park in the north.

He danced with Matilda and also her mother, Lady Fernshawe, and found them both to be exceedingly pleasant ladies.

But ultimately, there was only one dance he was looking forward to—the quadrille.

He enjoyed dancing and had been told by many a partner that he was very good at it. Now, as he offered his hand to Iris, James knew he would be dancing as well as he had ever done in his life.

James closed his hand around hers and led Iris to their place where they joined another three couples. They waited for their turn to hop-skip, their fingertips brushing as they passed from one end of the square to the other.

He was peripherally aware of the other dancers about them, but he only had eyes for Iris until the dance took her away from him a moment.

Then both her hands were in his once more.

The contradanse continued for another six movements until their hearts were pounding from the exertion of it.

"Do you have another partner who awaits you?" he asked, hoping the answer would be no.

He got his wish.

She shook her head and opened her fan. "I should like to sit the next dance out, if you please."

He did please, and escorted her to a seat before returning with refreshments. He took the seat beside her.

"I'm afraid you still have us at a disadvantage, Captain," she said.

"How so?"

"You know all about the 'unfortunate' Bigglesworth women—"

James interrupted. "I should hardly call you that."

Iris acknowledged the compliment with a tilt of her head and continued, "yet we hardly know a thing about the Bentley men, other than just the barest account. You must tell me more so I can feel justified in encouraging my sister's interest in the viscount."

Over the years he'd seen other men become calf-eyed over a pretty woman, dancing attendance to them like bees to a flower. He mocked them once, but now no longer. He couldn't help himself. He was drawn to Iris in a way he'd never felt before.

"I see! You wish me to proclaim my cousin's virtues," he said. "Very well. Next to me, John Bentley is the finest man I know."

There was a pause. James once again feared that his attempt at humor had fallen flat.

Iris' speculative raise of the eyebrow and quirk at her lip assured him that she was more than happy to play along.

"A paragon of all the virtues, I'm sure," she replied.

Nevertheless, James took her enquiry seriously. He *wanted* her to know him, and John, too, of course.

He told her about their family. His father and John's father were brothers and very close. Given their eldest sons were the same age, they were raised together, coming and going to each other's households regularly since they resided only a few miles apart.

Then the war came.

James spoke of it only in the most general terms. A delightful evening with a beautiful woman was no place to talk about the ugliness of war, so instead he spoke about how the hardships were easier to endure knowing that a man closer than a brother fought at his side.

There had been no thought of titles other than it being a piece of family lore. They were aware of the connection, of course, but the family tree was large and the branch they were on remote.

News of their distant cousin's passing had followed them all over the Continent, and it was only after the war that John had learned of his inheritance. By then, they were considering a new venture.

James watched for signs of boredom from Iris, but there was none. She seemed to enjoy his recounting, even laughing at stories of boyhood misadventure. He started on a tale of a frog and the headmaster when a man approached claiming her for the next dance.

Disappointment speared him.

*I know how John became besotted with Ivy.*

James wasn't sure where the thought had come from, but once there, it wouldn't leave.

If there was any consolation to be had, it was that Iris seemed reluctant to end their conversation too.

They stood at the same time. Iris offered a smile that he hoped was just for him, before she turned to greet her dance partner.

The idea of watching Iris dance with another man held no appeal. James left the main assembly to take a walk through the gardens.

In order to distract himself, James turned his attention back to the work he and John had been doing over the past few weeks. The practice course was completed. The trainer and groom arrived yesterday and both were impressed with what had been accomplished.

Now they could put Crimson Lad through his paces and get his condition to top form.

Work on extending the stables and rebuilding a couple of abandoned cottages into accommodation was far from complete. But if they could do enough to show the York Race stewards that they were serious, word would quickly spread throughout the county—perhaps even across England itself if they did a good enough job at it.

James recalled John's impetuous bet with the Earl of Seahaven once more. He shook his head. When the time came, he hoped John chose his horse well—a one-hundred-pound stake on a four-to-one fancy would be a very handy windfall.

# CHAPTER 13

It rained.

Unrelenting rain for two whole days, going into a third. Thoughts of boating excursions on the River Ouse or walking along the ramparts of the wall that marked the ancient boundary of the city of York, were put aside.

The Bigglesworth girls had plenty to occupy their time. Under Doro's keen eye, all the girls, including Emma and Merrilyn, made decorations and centerpieces for the ball. It was weeks away, but in reality, it would be upon them before they knew it.

Ivy and Iris were painting a cameo for Patience and each of their half-sisters. Their little project was a secret. Each piece would be unique and feature something that represented each one.

For Josefina, it was lavenders—pretty and sweet but there was more to her than what one could see with one's eyes. Lavender had health properties and Josefina knew all medicinal herbs.

Susana's cameo would be a pair of scissors and a spool of thread for her dressmaking.

Barbara was a virtuoso on the pianoforte; her cameo would feature a ribbon of musical notations. Bess was very fond of the mysterious treasures of Egypt so they had copied out a line of hieroglyphics from one of her books.

Doro was more difficult to define. She attended social reform meetings when she was not occupied with her work at the hotel. In the end the twins decided to represent her as a glass epergne spilling over with flowers to represent the many aspects of her life.

They also did one for their stepsister, Chloe Tavistock, who was in York with her brother. Chloe was an absolute dear with a heart as big as the world. She loved to rescue things and had a pet monkey which sat on her shoulder, so a keepsake of mischievous Rosario would be their gift to her.

The one Iris worked on now was one for Patience, a table full of books because she loved to read, and if some of her stepdaughters married, she might actually have some time for herself.

Ivy raised her head up and looked out at the gloom and sighed.

"You're thinking of the Viscount." Iris said. A statement, not a question.

"And whether he is anxious about the rain. The al fresco party is at the end of this week."

"I believe the rain is starting to ease."

"Do you think so? I hope it is."

Iris set down one brush and picked up another that was finer still.

Her dance with James had lived in her dreams for days now. There was no mistaking the flutter in her stomach when he looked her way, the lingering touch of his hand as they passed in the quadrille.

"How do you know what love feels like?" she asked.

"I don't know exactly," Ivy answered. "I do know that I think of John often. I imagine what he's doing, I imagine what we might do together. Is that the way you feel about James?"

Iris nodded her head and set aside the cameo, satisfied with her work for the day.

"So, are we certain it *is* love?"

"I don't think we can be too sure. Everything we know about them, from our conversations, and from Lady Clune, indicates that they would make very suitable husbands. But the trouble is, we do not know exactly how the gentlemen feel about us. Do men fall in love the same way as women?"

~

John watched the easing rain from the study window. He didn't mind confessing to being distracted.

There was a pile of correspondence on his desk which obliged him to remain cooped up, yet he'd hardly made a dent in it.

He *could* say that it was concern about getting the track up to standard, or hoping the lawns dried out in time for the al fresco party, but that would not be completely true.

Reddish-brown hair and cat-like green eyes figured in his dreams more and more. Lady Ivy Bigglesworth was more than just a pretty face. He liked her poise and her practical good sense. He could see himself married to a girl like that.

*Married? Where on earth had that thought come from?*

It had startled him at first, but almost immediately it took shape in his mind.

On his desk were plans for renovating certain rooms in the house. Just a few weeks ago, he would have gone with the decorator's recommendation. Now he wanted another opinion, a woman's opinion. *A wife's opinion.*

And when he imagined a wife, she looked exactly like Ivy.

*Whack!*

John felt a wad of balled-up paper strike his head and roll to a stop at his feet. He turned to face his assailant. His cousin lounged in the doorway with a grin on his face that identified him as the culprit.

"You've been wool-gathering for ages," said James. "I even called your name twice."

John picked up the wad and threw it back with all the force he could muster. James stepped back and caught it with the skill of a wicket keeper.

"There are days I wonder whether we've bitten off more than we can chew," John confessed.

"We've been in tougher spots on the battlefield," James shrugged. "What's particularly bothering you?"

It was John's turn to shrug. James was right. He just needed to gird his loins and commit. He would attend to whatever was in his control, and leave to Providence what was not.

"Nothing, I suppose," he answered at length.

James tossed the paper ball from hand to hand as though it were indeed a cricket ball.

"Lady Ivy would make a lovely viscountess, you know," he said.

John regarded his cousin, wondering whether there was any tease in his voice, but there wasn't.

"You're not just saying that because you've developed a fondness for her sister Iris, are you?"

His arrow hit the mark. James looked away, sheepish a moment.

"Perhaps," he shrugged, "but that's not the important thing, right now. Neither of us can consider marrying until we have a home we can offer and a living to sustain us."

"The al fresco party," John sighed.

"And the York Races," James nodded.

"And Tyrell House."

"And Tyrell Park."

John turned away from the window completely to return to his desk. "Then we have a lot to do.

James hurled the balled-up paper into the fire and took his seat at the desk, opposite his cousin.

"Here, pass me the accounts for the stables," he said.

John obliged, before making one last look out the window. The rain had eased and in the hills in the distance, he spotted the beginnings of a rainbow.

Now that was a good sign indeed.

# CHAPTER 14

James Bentley had been up at first light walking around the staging enclosure that had only been completed the day before. The white painted railings that encircled the racing track took on a pinkish glow as the sun rose a little higher in the sky.

On his way back to the house, he'd stood to admire the three large marquees on the garden. Empty now, but soon to be festooned with bunting and filled with tables groaning with food. He stopped to talk to a couple of the kitchen hands who had set one of the roasting pigs over hot coals to begin the long, hot, and arduous task of turning the spit.

*This was it.*

Today they needed to impress the stewards at the York Races and members of the York Racing Club. While they didn't need financial backing to complete the project, they did need customers. And the men who took an interest in horseracing were *very* exacting in their standards.

Now washed and dressed, James cast his reflection a final glance in the looking glass, making a final adjustment to his cravat. There was that low thrum of tension through his veins which was akin to the awareness he felt just before he rode into battle.

He met John on the top of the stairs. He looked every inch the viscount. James felt a surge of pride for his cousin. He was a good man. He took his role of master of Tyrell House seriously and even in the short time they'd lived here, he had noticed improvements for the better.

James didn't underestimate the importance this day held for Viscount Tyrell, either.

John acknowledged his presence with a nod. They didn't need to say more. This would be one more battle they rode into together.

They approached the landing. Waiting below in the Great Hall were two rows of servants, dressed in their liveries and pressed uniforms. In the center were the senior of them—the butler, the housekeeper and the cook.

On sight of the viscount, the assembly burst into applause.

James could see by the set of John's shoulders that he had not been expecting this.

The butler raised his hand. The clapping ebbed.

"My lord, on behalf of the servants of Tyrell House, may I say how proud we are to be attached to this great house," he said. "You and Captain Bentley have given life to this place that we feared was long gone. We want to do you proud today."

James couldn't resist a grin at seeing his cousin lost for words.

"On behalf of myself and the viscount, who is still to find his tongue,"—this elicited laughter—"I want to thank all of you for the outstanding effort not only with this major event, but also with the building of Tyrell Park, which we hope will bring more jobs and more prosperity to this village."

John nodded his agreement, then stepped forward. "I could not wish for a better household. You have far exceeded my expectations. I only have this to say, I hope you enjoy yourself as much as the guests today."

~

The carriage was not a large one, and with five women in it, was quite confined, but no one seemed to much mind.

The Bigglesworth girls did not have access to a carriage of their own, and it was Lady Fernshawe who generously offered Patience, Iris and Ivy a place with herself and Matilda.

"I should say that after the rain we've had, the roads are in surprisingly good condition," said Lady Fernshawe.

"We are much obliged to you," said Patience, then she directed a nod to her stepdaughters with a twinkle in her eye. "I know Iris and Ivy looked forward to this outing."

Iris reached for her sister's hand and squeezed it.

Given the outdoor nature of the al fresco party, they elected to wear walking dresses, the same ones they wore when they first met the Viscount and his cousin. Iris wore her customary lavender sprigged dress, while Ivy's dress featured sprays of lily of the valley.

"Look I see the house!" Matilda called. "Oh, it looks so pretty against the hills."

Neither Iris nor Ivy were close enough to the window to see the view for themselves until they rounded another bend which put them on a rise not far from Tyrell House.

The golden stone of the gothic house glowed in the mid-morning sun, and red and white striped marquees covered the front lawn.

Ivy squeezed her hand. Iris nodded. She could guess what her sister was thinking because she had the same thought herself—soon they would see James and John. Although it had only been five days, it might well have been five weeks.

By the time they had arrived and stepped out of their carriage, they could hear the sound of music.

"There's Barbara!" said Ivy.

Iris spotted Doro with Emma and Merrilyn.

"Come see," said Merrilyn, excitedly, "There's croquet to play and tennis too!"

"I hope to see the horses," said Emma, trying to sound more grown up than her younger sister. "Do you think the viscount might let me?"

She made the appeal to Patience.

"I think you should ask Ivy, as she appears to have the ear of our host," she said.

Ivy nodded. "If I can possibly entreat his lordship to do so, then I shall."

Emma clapped her hands with glee.

"You won't have long to wait," Lady Fernshawe observed. "There, I do believe, are our hosts. Oh my, don't they look especially dashing?"

"Mama," gasped Matilda in mock horror. "You are a married woman! You are not supposed to notice particularly handsome men."

Her mother's response was a gay laugh. "I am allowed to say so, because *I am* a happily married woman."

The banter back and forth might have gone on longer, but Iris ceased to notice. All she had eyes for was the man on the right who walked in long, matching strides alongside Viscount Tyrell.

She knew he and his cousin would personally greet all the guests today, but why was it that her heart made a little leap when James bowed low over her hand in greeting?

Oh, how she wished she could speak to him alone and find out where his heart lay.

# CHAPTER 15

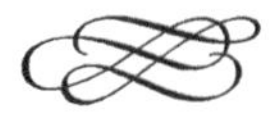

Ivy watched John greet his guests, spending a moment or two in conversation before continuing on his way. He spent time with everyone like this, including sparing a word or two for the servants who worked diligently to ensure the guests lacked for nothing.

It said a lot about a man's character to see how he treated others when not observed. She ventured out from under the marquee to enjoy the spring sunshine and to admire the grounds.

There Merrilyn and Matilda, along with Iris, were playing croquet with James Bentley, Lord McDonnell and Lord Swinburn.

Her eyes followed the line of the hills and dales, the paddocks and pastures surrounding the grounds and spotted a sun-dappled patch of lawn that would make a fine rose garden.

Ivy looked back to the house itself, examining its lines and proportions. She would love to come back and sketch it one day.

"Ah, Lady Ivy!"

She turned to see John walking toward her.

"I was admiring the house," she said. "It is magnificent."

"I have to make a confession; what you see is largely for show," he said. "The servants have done an excellent job giving the outside a true spit and polish, but the inside still needs a lot of work."

"May I see?" she asked.

"I hoped you would ask," he said, giving her a grin that made her heart beat in triple time. "I have had some plans drawn up. I've let the architect suggest whatever he wishes, but I want to have other eyes look at it. And I daren't risk James for his view on matters of taste."

Ivy inclined her head.

"So, you are asking for a woman's opinion?"

John bowed.

"My lady, you have found me out."

Ivy laughed and accepted his proffered arm.

She entered the hall. The oak paneling that dated to the time of the Tudors was largely intact. A large staircase rose impressively to the floors above. She noticed that all the doors that led off the hall were open. Light spilled from them, so she imagined the curtains were open to let as much sunlight in as possible.

She glanced into one of the rooms. That would make a lovely morning room, a place to have breakfast or for a lady to claim as her study. The furniture was comfortable but out of proportion to the room and the walls were much too dark.

Ivy ventured her opinion and found John looking thoughtful.

"Then what about this room?" he said, taking her across the hall to another. "It is not wide, but it is long. Would it work as a music room?"

They climbed the stairs to the living quarters and here Ivy could see decades of neglect that could not be covered by diligent cleaning. Only two bedrooms were in use in a wing that boasted eight bedrooms and anterooms.

"And what of the floor above?"

"It's too dangerous to go up there just yet. The roof has leaked for decades, apparently, and my distant cousin simply closed off the upper floors and didn't address the issue," said John. "I've ordered that the first thing repaired, but there's not much money left to do anything else to the house."

"I still haven't changed my mind," said Ivy. "Tyrell House is lovely. I think it can be made to be a jewel once again."

She wondered whether John heard her. He had a faraway expression on his face. Was something amiss? She frowned. He reached out and brushed her cheek with his fingertips.

Ivy was enraptured, unable to do more than just look deep into his eyes as he leaned forward and kissed her.

The reality was as wonderful as her dreams.

She stepped forward into his arms. His kiss deepened, her lips opening to his.

*This is the way a first kiss should be.*

If it went on forever, she would be the happiest of women. Alas, John pulled away.

"Could you be happy here, Ivy?"

For a moment she lost her voice and couldn't answer him. Was he proposing marriage?

"Would you be happy with me?" he continued.

This time she had her voice.

"Yes, oh John, most definitely yes."

His expression, which had turned grave, now brightened. John pulled her into his arms once more and swung her about. She squealed in surprise, then laughed as he laughed.

"I will ask your stepmother for permission to court you properly. If she agrees, would you be pleased with an autumn wedding? Even if the house still requires work?"

"We will make this a home together," she told him.

His lips found hers once more, his body hard against hers. Ivy began a tentative exploration of the firm muscles beneath his jacket, the hard planes of his back. His lips traced a line to her ear. Warm sensual eddies ran down the full length of her body.

*She loved him. And she knew it with every fiber of her being.*

"I've fallen in love with you, Ivy," he whispered.

"John, darling," Ivy sighed. "I love you, too."

He threaded his fingers through hers as he led her downstairs and back out into the garden. To her surprise, he did not let go of them as they approached the assembly and the gesture didn't go unnoticed, and certainly not by Patience who watched them both carefully.

"I promise to have a word with the countess," said John.

Another guest approached wishing to speak to him. John excused himself.

*Iris.*

She needed to know before anyone else. Ivy hoped her sister would be happy that she had found someone she could love fully. And yet, there was something unsettling about beginning a life on her own without her sister by her side.

Ivy searched the crowd, just as the band struck up a flourish to announce Lady Clune.

"Ladies and gentlemen," the hostess called out. "We have a special entertainment for you this afternoon. A treasure hunt! You will soon be given, at random, a red ticket, a blue ticket or a green ticket by one of the servants. We want no one cheating! As soon as you have your ticket, head out to my left and you will find three servants under a different colored banner. Find the color that matches your ticket and the footman will give you a piece of paper with your clues!"

Ivy refused a ticket, much preferring to wait until John returned. She approached Barbara, who was pointedly ignoring the attentions of a handsome gentleman to whom she had been introduced as piano virtuoso and composer, Mr. John Sutton.

"Well?" Barbara asked. "Does that mean what I think it means?"

Mr. Sutton offered her a kind smile over Barbara's shoulder before stepping away to give the sisters privacy.

Ivy nodded in answer to Barbara's question. She received a warm embrace in return.

"I am so happy for you, dearest."

# CHAPTER 16

James pretended to keep an eye on Crimson Lad as Peter Tiny, the groom, put the colt through his paces.

His attention—out of the corner of his eye at least—was on Lord Clune, chairman of the York Racing Club.

The man was in his early seventies but carried himself with a great deal of vigor. Only the steel grey of his hair and the deep lines down each side of his mouth gave his age away. What he didn't give away was his opinion—not a sigh, not a blink, not a blessed clue! And it was his opinion which mattered most.

James wondered how much he could gnaw the inside of his cheek before drawing blood.

As for the club steward? Well, he had already won the man over with a tour of Tyrell Park's facilities—those in existence, anyway. For those that weren't, James used his imagination to describe what he and his cousin intended to build.

After two turns around the circuit, Tiny slowed Crimson Lad from a gallop to a trot, giving James a nod, which told him he was pleased with the horse's performance. The colt had earned a cooling rub down and an extra measure of oats for his good work.

And *still*, Lord Clune said nothing.

James deliberately looked everywhere except at Lord Clune. He'd be damned if he was the first to break.

Crimson Lad, now relieved of his saddle, headed toward the stable with a high-stepping gait that indicated the young horse was pleased with his run too.

Down a path, past a wooden gate and perimeter fence, about fifty yards from where they now stood were the marquees. The wind brought with it the sound of a lively reel being played.

"Not bad, Captain."

*Not bad?* James considered the blood, sweat and tears that had gone into the track and its buildings. He needed far more assurance than just 'not bad'.

Lord Clune turned, rested his hip against the rail, pulled out a fat cigar and took his sweet time lighting it.

"You are entering Crimson Lad in with the colts this year, aren't you? He looks ready for it."

James nodded. "That's the intent, sir."

"Humph."

*That's it?*

"How much are you looking to charge owners to train here?"

James named a not unreasonable figure. Lord Clune nodded while taking another puff on his cigar.

"You have my recommendation."

James took a deep breath. The aroma of fresh burning tobacco and the redolent smell of horses filled his nostrils. When he breathed out, he grinned and thrust out his hand.

Lord Clune, with a twinkle in his eye, returned a firm handshake. "With facilities of this quality, we can rival Newmarket. Won't that be grand, lad?"

"Indeed, we will. Thank you, my lord. I also speak on behalf of the viscount to say that we are very pleased to have your endorsement."

"Speaking of which, where is your cousin?" said Lord Clune. "I want to invite you both to my club tomorrow night. I will introduce you to a few men who might be very interested in what you have here."

They made their way back toward the marquee but not before James caught Tiny's questioning eye. He gave the man a thumbs up. The groom grinned and ran back into the stable to share the good news.

James did his best to master his own expression but he could not quell the excitement running through him.

He and John were one step closer to all their hard work paying off.

Iris made her way over to Barbara.

"Have you seen Ivy?" she asked.

Barbara nodded. "I thought I caught a glimpse of her walking with Viscount Tyrell about ten minutes ago," she answered. "What do you think? Do you think our host is serious?"

"I am sure that he is serious—his cousin told me so."

"Ah, the handsome Captain Bentley," Barbara teased. "And what about you, ma petite soeur? Could there be a double engagement before the end of the summer?"

Iris blushed. "I don't know. He… well… I…"

Barbara nodded behind her. "I see him. He looks as though he's searching for someone. Oh, he's coming this way."

Iris turned away, just as James approached. He looked agitated.

"Lady Iris, may I entreat you to walk with me?"

She frowned. "Why, of course. Is anything amiss?"

"No, no, nothing like that. But let's go to the garden, where it is quiet."

Iris allowed James to take her arm, casting a glance back at Barbara who acknowledged her with a knowing look and a nod.

To her surprise, James led her down one of the lesser paths that had been allowed to grow a little wild. Here and there she spotted little paper Chinese lanterns in red, blue and green, each with a little tag beneath it. For the treasure hunt, she assumed.

"I went looking for John but I couldn't find him. But I just had to tell someone."

There was such excitement in James' voice that she wondered at its cause. Iris' heart went flip-flop.

"We have the endorsement of Lord Clune," he said. "And his personal invitation to race Crimson Lad at the York Races."

Iris clapped her hands together. "Oh, Captain! I am so thrilled for you and the viscount, too."

James took her hands in both of his and brought them to his chest.

"Please, call me James," he said softly.

"Only if you call me Iris."

He gave her a heart stopping smile before leading her further through the copse of trees that opened out to the edge of a lake. To the right was the ramshackle remains of a boathouse covered in moss. Ferns grew out between the planking.

"Now you have seen all we have to offer here at Tyrell House. What do you think?"

"I believe you have the beginnings of something truly grand. What you and your cousin have managed to achieve in such a short amount of time is wonderful. But what of your equestrian facilities? Did Lord Clune approve of those also?"

James grinned, and his eyes lit up. Iris could see how he must have looked as a youth. It endeared him to her all the more. It would be so easy to fall in love with James Bentley.

"He did. I had to tell someone before I burst with it."

"I'm glad you chose me," she said shyly.

There was a shift in his expression. The unalloyed joy became burnished with something else Desire? Tenderness? Iris didn't have the vocabulary to describe what she saw in his eyes.

But her heart knew.

Her lips parted, anticipating the kiss moments before his mouth found hers. She savored the experience, drawn into James' embrace, twining her arms around his neck to draw him closer.

"I think I should like Ivy as a sister-in-law."

Iris stepped out of his embrace and frowned before the import of his words sank in.

"If Ivy is your sister-in-law that would mean…"

James chuckled.

"I would like to marry you, if you'll have me. I am not the richest of men. Creating Tyrell Park is not without risk. There is much hard work to do before we are self-sufficient. But when I toil out here, I find myself wondering what you would think of it, if whether what we are building would please you also."

Iris brought her hands to her mouth afraid of bursting into tears. That would give him the wrong impression. She giggled instead.

His expression was both hopeful and cautious.

"Yes, James. I will marry you!"

James pulled her into his arms once more. The promise was sealed by another passionate kiss which left her weak at the knees.

# CHAPTER 17

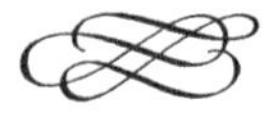

*The St Aubyn town house, York*

The town house reminded John of a field headquarters. Everyone, both servant and young lady alike, moved with such purpose that it was tempting to snap to attention and salute when the butler escorted them to the front parlor where Countess Seahaven sat at a small writing desk.

"Thank you, please serve tea here," she said.

The servant closed the door behind him, markedly reducing the noise from the rest of the house. This room was now an oasis of calm.

Patience rose from her seat. John and, beside him, James bowed and waited for her to direct them to sit. She took a chair opposite.

He and James sat and exchanged a glance. James raised his eyebrows, telling him silently that he should speak first, given that he was a viscount.

*Coward.* John hoped his cousin understood the message he silently conveyed.

"My lady, thank you for agreeing to see us," he began, "especially given how occupied you are with the upcoming ball."

The dowager countess gave a nod but could not quite hide a slight smile.

James spoke. "My cousin and I wish to express our sincere admiration and affection for Lady Ivy and Lady Iris."

John nodded. "It is our fervent desire that we find favor with you and that you grant us permission to court Ivy and Iris with a view to marriage."

At that moment, the butler returned with tea, forcing John to wait patiently while the cups and the sugar were set on the low table, followed by the teapot and a small plate of little delicacies.

The servant withdrew. Patience took her time to pour tea—just the right amount in each cup.

"Sugar?"

"Yes, two lumps please," the cousins spoke in unison.

Patience smiled a moment, took up her tea cup, sipped, then returned it to the saucer.

"I do know Ivy and Iris are delighted by your interest and consider themselves in love with you, too, Lord Tyrell; Captain Bentley."

John felt tension ebb from his body.

"However, I have to say I have some reservations in giving my endorsement to this match."

Tension increased once more.

"May I reassure you, my lady," said John. "We can provide bona fides of our characters from our colonel.

"There is our endorsement by Lord and Lady Clue," James added.

"Ah yes," said the countess. "Lord Clune is chairman of the York Racing Club is he not?"

"Indeed! In addition to the income from Tyrell House, which I have to admit is modest, we do have a great deal of hope in Tyrell Park—"

"—yes, I did see that at your al fresco party," Lady Patience interrupted. "It is a credit to you. But I cannot help wonder whether you risk too much. It is one thing for bachelors to gamble on a new venture, but it is another thing entirely to risk the financial security of a wife in such a manner."

John cast a glance his cousin's way.

"I... *we...*," James inclined a head towards John to include him, "are both mindful of what is at stake—personally and professionally—should we not be successful. I am confident that any trust in us regarding the welfare of your stepdaughters will not be misplaced, regardless of what happens at the York Races in a fortnight's time."

The young dowager countess picked up her tea cup once more, and gave them both a meaningful look. "Then let us review your circumstances in a fortnight's time, gentlemen."

John never felt more dispirited in his life.

It wasn't often that he had been found wanting and what he had hoped would be a joyous occasion, where he could publicly declare his intention, had to be, at best, postponed.

Yet Lady Seahaven was right.

He and James *were* taking a risk, but it was a calculated one.

The Tyrell House estate did have an income. And if Crimson Lad won, there would be the prize purse, along with the recognition and prestige that went with it.

There would be potential clients at the race. If a quarter of those who promised to stable and train their horses at Tyrell Park made good, they would be close to half subscribed.

Patience cast a commiserating expression their way. How sad that he hungrily accepted the morsel of kindness thrown his way.

"As you probably well know, Ivy and Iris are not extravagant creatures," she said. "They have been raised without many of the things girls of their class would be expected to have, but still, they are daughters of an Earl and ought to have a life that befits their status. In matters of love, it shouldn't matter if you were paupers or kings, but I know from the bitter reality of my own circumstance, that a man must be able to provide for his wife and children. I only wish the very best for my girls," she said.

Out of the corner of his eye John saw James nod.

"Rest assured, my lady, that we three are of one accord. I love Iris, I would give my life for her. I know John feels the same about Ivy. And we love who they love. Ivy is a cherished sister to me."

"As Iris is to me," said John. "And we respect you, my lady, and agree to hold off on any further talk of marriage until after the York Races."

With their interview at an end, they took their leave of the countess.

"Wait."

Both men watched Lady Seahaven rise from her seat.

"I have had many a sleepless night over what to do about securing my stepdaughters' futures," she said. "I love them as though they were my own flesh and blood. I have hopes, as well as trepidation, about their future security. On meeting you both, my mind has been very much reassured. I can see you are men of fine character and you sincerely love my twins. Please don't take my interview today as a refusal, but rather a postponement."

# CHAPTER 18

*Smithson's Assembly Rooms, York, April 22nd*

It was noon, and the Seahaven ball was hours away, but the Assembly Rooms were a-buzz with activity.

Barbara was in earnest discussion with the band leader about the positioning of the orchestra.

Bess was conducting workmen on the placement of a veritable botanical garden's worth of potted plants and shrubs—some actually in flower. Already the plants filled the air with a heavenly scent.

Under Doro's supervision, Emma and Merrilyn assembled the table centerpieces of gilt paper nests and colored paper birds and then artfully arranged the remaining birds in and around the shrubs. Chloe Tavistock kept a careful hold on Rosario's lead. The light-fingered little monkey had a penchant for things that glittered and already had a little paper bird in her hand.

The twins had learned that Chloe's brother, Lord Tavistock, had pooled funds with their family in thanks for taking Chloe under their wing this Season.

Ivy and Iris stood back as Mrs. Crewe's brother and a hired porter hung a large bolt of fabric across the back wall. How Susanna had managed to piece together something of this size, they had no idea.

Each sister sought the hand of the other as the sheet dropped, revealing a naïve, but charmingly painted trompe l'oeil of an Italianate garden with a fountain at its center. After spending so much time painting miniatures Ivy and Iris were exceedingly nervous about their contribution to the hall's decoration.

It was the largest piece they had ever painted, and they had worried about the scale and perspective of such a huge piece.

The hubbub in the room fell to silence. The twins turned, watching the expressions of those there. Patience beamed with pride. Merrilyn was agog. Susana offered a nod of approval.

One pair of hands clapping turned to two and then more. Even Rosario brightly chattered her approval.

"Well, I never in all my born days seen such a sight," announced Mrs. Crewe. "It's like the outdoors have come inside!"

Indeed, the plain interior of the assembly rooms had been transformed into a magical garden.

"But it's time for you to leave," the housekeeper continued. "Countess, my ladies, you have a ball to ready yourself for. You leave the rest of the arrangements to us."

And to show she meant business, Mrs. Crewe waved her hands, shooing them toward the door.

As they milled together at the entrance, Emma looked about. "What about Doro?" she asked.

"She is in the kitchen supervising the staff," Patience answered.

"But she won't have time to get ready!" Merrilyn protested. "She'll miss out."

Barbara bobbed down and gave the girl a hug. "She won't. I'll make sure of that."

Once home, Merrilyn resisted the idea of a nap and only relented when Patience assured her that they would *all* rest before getting ready.

~

The hall clock chimed five o'clock. The St Aubyn town house was a hive of activity that rivalled that at the Assembly Rooms that morning.

Josefina knocked and entered the twins' bedroom.

"Patience gave me this," she said, showing them a Morocco leather box. "It belonged to our mother."

She opened it to reveal a suite of jewelry in a fitted case. A strand of pearls, a matched bracelet and earrings.

Ivy was overcome with emotion and hugged her eldest sister. Iris blinked back tears.

"I thought since there are three pieces, it would only be right for each of us to wear one," Josefina continued.

"You're the eldest," Iris replied. "These are yours and they will look so lovely with your gown."

"Maman would have wanted us to share," Josefina insisted.

Iris joined in the embrace. They stood together like that for long moments.

"Josefina, you should wear the necklace," said Ivy who then turned to look at Iris.

"The earrings?"

Iris nodded.

"I will wear the bracelet," said Ivy.

The girls hastened into their dresses. Ivy and Iris opted for simplicity. Their gowns were of cream silk with overskirts of crepe de chine which Susana promised would glimmer in the lamplight—soft mint green for Ivy, and for Iris, the color of hyacinth.

Josefina's gown featured rich hues of amber that brought out the sunset flame of her hair.

Ribbons of a slightly darker shade had been added to their gowns, along with decorations of white beads painted to resemble pearls. More of the white beads had been strung and woven through their hair.

All three sisters descended the staircase together mindful of the impression they needed to make—over the past weeks, they had been fêted as the beauties of the Season.

There had been no shortage of interest and invitations, but many would-be suitors had recognized Ivy's and Iris's hearts had already been captured. Now their attention had turned to Josefina who had so far shown no partiality.

Nevertheless, all eyes would be on the Bigglesworth ladies tonight. To launch well would help pave the way for Emma's and Merrilyn's own eventual coming out and ease their stepmother's burden no end.

Iris sought her twin's hand and gave it a squeeze.

They would not let Patience down.

# CHAPTER 19

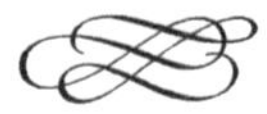

*Smithson's Assembly Rooms, York*

James stepped out of the carriage and glanced at John, wondering whether his cousin was as nervous as he was.

He didn't mind admitting that their interview with Patience had rattled his confidence a little.

Both men would have had to have been blind not to see the attention the twins had received this Season. Men who were wealthier, more established, and of higher status made no secret of their interest.

Iris and Ivy could match exceedingly well with any number of men.

Had Patience spoken to the girls? Counselled them against an uncertain future?

He hoped not, for his sake and his cousin's too.

John's face did not give him away. The title of viscount seemed to rest more easily on his shoulders now.

They entered the Assembly Rooms and encountered a world of delight—a veritable Garden of Eden. He nudged John and nodded to the elaborate backdrop. John looked at it and returned a grin. They knew it was the work of Iris and Ivy.

"Do you see them?" John asked.

"No, but I do see Lord Cuckoo with one of Iris' relatives," James answered.

"For God's sake, don't let Dom Finchley hear you call him that," John hissed. "He may be shorter than us by several inches, but he could still land us on our arses."

James simply gave him a grin. They both knew Captain Finchley and his reputation for valor. James liked the man. His use of the nickname was meant with affection, although others used it with malice.

He was about to point out some other faces they knew—Lord McDonnell and Lord Swinburn, Lady Fernshawe and her daughter Matilda—when his attention was captured.

"I…uh… I," he stuttered.

"I see them too," said John.

Seeing the delight in Iris' face set his mind at peace. He watched her nudge her sister who blushed prettily at seeing them.

James was aware of the sensation of falling in love all over again. Not just with Iris's beauty, which she had in abundance, but with every aspect—her grace, her charm, her talent.

He looked at John once more. One didn't need to have the preternatural affinity of a twin to recognize that his cousin felt the same way about Ivy.

Ivy's dance card was nearly filled but she was more than pleased to add Captain James Bentley to her list. If this was the man her sister had her heart set on, then she wanted to know him better.

"When did you know you were in love with my sister?" she asked.

James smiled at her direct question.

"When I realized I could trust her with what was dear to me."

That was not the answer she expected. Waxing lyrical about her loveliness? Absolutely. Being poetic about her grace? Certainly.

"When Lord Clune gave his endorsement to Tyrell Park the first person I wanted to tell was John, but I couldn't find him."

*That's because at the time, he was kissing me.*

Ivy blushed.

James lightly squeezed her hand, and smiled as though he could read her mind.

"I saw Iris and knew in that instant, there was no one else I would rather share this moment with. And not just that one—*every* moment. I want her to be at my side always. I cannot imagine a future without her."

The sincerity in his eyes impressed her more than the words themselves. His whole being seemed to radiate with it.

"I know how much you love your sister," he continued. "I want you to be assured that her heart is safe in my hands. It is my goal to earn your trust so I will be a brother to you as you are a sister to me."

"You seem a little distracted tonight, my lord."

John glanced away from watching Ivy dance with his cousin to look at his own dance partner. Iris looked up at him with a mischievous smile. It was a little disconcerting to dance with a woman who looked so much like the woman he loved, and yet was not her.

There were subtle differences. Ivy had a fleck of brown in her green eyes, and Iris did not. Iris was given to being more direct, more ready to tease, whereas Ivy had a calm presence about her that he couldn't quite explain.

"I hope I can be forgiven for my lack of attention to you, Lady Iris," he answered with a smile of his own.

"Perhaps you can," she said. "Your cousin and I are very keen to see you settled."

"As I am for my cousin, dear lady."

Iris inclined her head with a dreamy smile on her face. They made their way around the dance floor.

John caught sight of other Bigglesworth sisters, including Dorothea, whom he had not seen earlier in the night. He recalled his earliest conversations with Ivy and how the Earl of Seahaven had cast them out of their home.

Suddenly it became important to him to let Iris know that she would never have to worry about such a fate ever again.

"My cousin and I share much, but not everything. So, I hope you forgive any presumption of my part," John began.

"On what account?"

"On where you shall live once you and John marry."

Iris's step faltered ever so slightly.

"You will never have to worry about home. It is at Tyrell House with Ivy and me," he said.

"Thank you." Iris blinked away tears. "Being parted from my sister was one of the things I feared from this Season.

John squeezed her hand. "It will be *our* home, not only for my new wife, but also her sister and my cousin whom I love as a brother."

The midnight hour drew near. John and Ivy, James and Iris took a stroll out onto the terrace to breathe in the cool jasmine-scented air. There each couple parted to find a dark, discreet corner. Kisses and loving caresses were exchanged in the moonlight, a tender promise for a time to come.

# CHAPTER 20

*The York Races, Early morning*
*Red sky in the morning, shepherd's warning...*

James noted the flame-colored sky on this late spring morning. But despite the aphorism, there appeared to be no foul weather looming.

Tendrils of mist hung low on the track, where trainers and their horses took one last practice run before the day's races.

James hadn't slept last night. He was awake at first light to accompany the trainer, and Peter Tiny, the groom, to the racecourse to get Crimson Lad settled.

Fortunately, the Lad was not put off by the arrival of lots of strange horses. On the contrary, the colt was filled with energy, ready to rise to the challenge—but did he have the discipline to last the distance?

There he was, with steam rising off his flanks, just leaving the track. James approached.

"How'd he go, Tiny?"

"Like a right champ, guv. He's going to have a grand race today."

The sky lightened. Pink, then gold, as the morning sun rose higher in the sky. Now he could see the racecourse clearly, as though a curtain had been raised and a play about to begin.

Two feminine figures approached. James recognized them immediately. He jogged over to meet them.

"Iris! Ivy! What are you doing here?"

The young women looked at each other and smiled.

"No one knows we're here," said Ivy.

"We've brought you a gift." said Iris.

"It's actually a gift for Peter Tiny," Ivy said, pulling out of a basket a silk shirt in a patchwork of white, purple and green diamonds.

"Tyrell Park should have racing silks that stand out," said Iris.

"We made it from material left over from our ball gowns," added Ivy.

He was touched beyond words. Iris took pity on him and reached out and took his hand.

"I believe in you," she said and then looked to her sister who nodded. "*We* believe in you."

Ivy smiled and gestured toward the stables. "I shall see if this fits Tiny."

She left them to head in that direction. James was grateful for his future sister-in-law's discretion.

James took Iris' hand and kissed it, taking only the smallest of liberties, given they were in public.

"We cannot stay long. We didn't tell anyone where we were going, but Ivy and I will be back with the others later today."

"Captain! Captain Bentley!"

James turned. Peter Tiny hurried towards him. A few yards behind, walking hand-in-hand, were Ivy and John.

"I've never 'ad a racin' silk fashioned by real ladies before! Init grand, Captain?"

"It suits you very well, Mr. Tiny," said Iris.

James prayed to the Good Lord above that everything went their way today because there was only one thing he knew for certain—neither he nor John would be happy until they married Iris and Ivy.

~

There was a great deal of benefit to be had in having a title, John decided.

Although there were titles grander than viscount, that alone seemed sufficient to open a few doors.

He and James earlier agreed on how they would divide the work for today.

James would stay close to the track and the stables to get to know the men who trained and rode other horses. Some would be useful contacts, others would be rivals, and it was important to know who was who in this industry.

John would parlay his title in the more refined company of the gentry who enjoyed the sport of kings, but left the mechanics of such enterprise to hirelings. Today, he would entertain the great and the good who had a curiosity about the upstart cousins and their plans for horse racing in Yorkshire.

The bookies were already gathering outside the main pavilion. The most organized of them had chalkboard A-frames that listed the upcoming race, the horses and the odds.

John stopped to put a private wager on Crimson Lad who was still showing ten-to-one odds over the much-fancied Random Oath, who showed four-to-one.

John noted the coincidence. There was another four-to-one odds game they were playing today. He and Ivy, James and Iris—the four of them with one goal in mind.

He spotted Lord McDonnell's party and went over to greet them. He and James had promised a chance to meet Crimson Lad so the men could decide for themselves whether the colt was a good bet for today.

He was banking on their enthusiasm to do the advertising for him. The more people who talked about the horse that might beat the four-to-one fancy, the more interest there would be in what he and James were doing at Tyrell Park.

With young McDonnell suitably enthused about Crimson Lad, he invited them to enjoy his hospitality.

One of the marquees, which had been employed to great effect for the al fresco party, was now erected on a little hillock overlooking the main straight. The servants from Tyrell House had done him, and themselves, proud once again.

The marquee had been turned into a cozy retreat from the sun with carpets and chairs. There was an ice chest with chilled refreshments and hampers with delicacies. He'd also made it a holiday for the servants, most of whom would be here today.

This was a campaign, meticulously thought out with as many contingencies covered as possible. Like the battles he and James fought in Europe, everything was guaranteed except the outcome.

Seeing Ivy this morning served to remind him what was truly important. Their success today would mean nothing if she was not at his side to share it.

He smiled, recalling Tiny's delight with the hand-made racing silks. The gesture reminded him of tales of yore when a medieval knight would receive from his lady a favor in the form of a ribbon.

With such good luck, how could they lose?

# CHAPTER 21

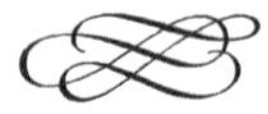

"Isn't it exciting!" exclaimed Ivy who watched the race through Lord Tyrell's telescope. "I can understand why so many people attend these events."

Iris smiled at her sister, but without the use of a spyglass to see the horses in detail, she soon turned her attention to observing the crowds.

Never before had she seen so many people in one place. It was exhilarating. She spotted James making his way past the crowds on the stands.

Her heart swelled with pride at the sight of him. He and his cousin had worked so hard, and they deserved their success. However, this venture still required a great deal of luck.

Perhaps it would come today.

She carried half a crown in her purse, saved from her pin money. She would ask James to place a bet on Crimson Lad on her behalf.

Patience wouldn't necessarily approve, but surely there was no harm in wagering such a little sum?

Iris left the marquee to meet him. James spotted her and gifted her a smile that warmed her heart which made her fall in love with him just a little bit more—more than she ever thought possible.

"I fancy placing a bet," she said to him, loud enough for others to overhear. James knew her game and was most willing to play along.

"Most certainly, my dear," he said, handing her a race booklet. "Who do you favor?"

"I like the name of this one. Yes, Crimson Lad," she said.

"Crimson Lad," she repeated a little louder.

The name attracted the attention of a man in a stovepipe hat. He turned. To Iris's surprise it was the Earl of Seahaven.

"Is it any wonder my late cousin's family are in penury, if this is how they fritter away their dowry?"

Iris dropped a curtsy out of habit. James did not bow, and the slight was noticed.

The earl glared at James contemptuously.

"Oh, it's you, Tyrell."

Iris was about to correct him, when James put a hand on her shoulder.

"I look forward to taking your money today, Seahaven. What was the wager again? *One hundred* pounds?"

Iris heard a gasp from the crowd, which now sensed the business off track was more exciting than the activity on it.

Seahaven looked back smugly at his friends. "This is the pup I mentioned to you. Fancies himself in the top drawer. I've seen your nag, Tyrell. At ten-to-one, he doesn't stand a chance against Random Oath—fit only for the knacker's yard, but as they say, a fool and his money are soon parted..."

Seahaven's party sniggered.

"Better to have earned wealth than inherit it," said James, his voice betraying his contempt.

"You forget how you come by your own title," Seahaven responded.

"At least women and children weren't cast out into the street for it."

Unease rippled through the throng.

Seahaven's face reddened with anger. He glowered at Iris. She did not wait for him to make a remark. She squared her shoulders, lifted her chin and said: "Shame on you cousin, for treating our family so poorly."

"Since your pockets are flush, perhaps we should double the bet," said James.

Iris gasped. It was an audacious move. The Seahaven estate was reasonably prosperous and two hundred pounds was an incredible sum to wager.

"Enough's enough, Charles," said one of Seahaven's friends. "You've had your sport, let's move on before we miss the start of the next race."

Seahaven said nothing, and James appeared to want to press the advantage.

"Billy!" he called over to one of the bookmakers. "Would you hold a private wager for us?"

The bewhiskered man gave a gap-toothed grin.

"Right ye be, sir."

Iris wanted to ask James if he was certain, but part of her was still so angry at Seahaven's insult to her family that she silently cheered him on.

"My friend here fancies Random Oath at four-to-one," said James. "I plan to wager against him. If the earl's horse wins, I will pay eight hundred pounds. If my horse wins, he pays me two *thousand* pounds."

Billy scribbled down the particulars of the bet and the amount the losing party would pay the winner, less his own commission, of course.

James added his signature. Billy offered the betting book to the earl, who gave them a most evil glare before he added his scrawl.

"Lady Iris, shall we move on?"

"I still wish to place my wager on Crimson Lad, my lord," she said.

James gave a curt nod.

"Make a note of that Billy. My lady wishes to place five pounds on Crimson Lad."

*Five pounds?* She only had half a crown on her.

Iris accepted James' stiffly proffered arm. She gave Seahaven the haughtiest glare that she owned before walking back toward the marquee.

As soon as they were cleared of the crowds and less chance of being overheard, James spoke.

"The five pounds is a gift from me," he said.

"That's very generous considering you've bet another one hundred pounds and put at stake eight hundred should you lose. And you, pretending to be your cousin!"

James flashed her a grin. "It won't have been the first time you know. John and I would swap identities at least once during a school term."

Iris giggled, part in amusement, part in nervousness. She glanced behind her where a crowd milled around the bookmakers. Reports of that juicy little tête-à-tête between James and the earl would be across the racecourse in moments.

James squeezed her hand in silent reassurance.

"It will be all right. I promise."

Iris squeezed his in return. "I know it will be."

Even so, she worried. The stakes were high enough already; now they were even higher.

# CHAPTER 22

Ivy knew something was wrong as soon as she saw her twin. No one else would know anything was amiss, not even Josefina. But Ivy knew. She hurried out of the marquee to meet her.

Then she noticed James was not himself. The kind and affable man she had grown to like over these past weeks was subdued. She watched him find a small smile as he excused himself to talk to his cousin.

"What's happened?"

She listened quietly as Iris recounted the experience of seeing the Earl of Seahaven, and the insulting things he said about their family that resulted in the extraordinary bet.

"This is not going to endear our intendeds to Patience," said Iris. "What are we to do?"

"There is nothing we can do except hope and pray that Crimson Lad beats Random Oath."

Ivy drew her sister into the cool shade of the marquee and watched James speak in low tones to John. She knew the moment James told him of the bet. Her beloved's back stiffened. John gave several curt nods before resting a heavy arm on his cousin's shoulder. There was even a hint of a smile.

Ivy took Iris by the hand and approached.

John smiled at them both.

"I can't be angry with him for doing what I did... so, in for a penny in for a pound."

"Eight *hundred* pounds," said James.

"Only if we lose and two thousand pounds if we win."

The hushed conversation attracted the attention of Susana.

"Well, I can't say this will be kept a secret for long," she said.

"Do you think we could use this to our advantage?" Ivy asked.

Iris nodded. "It will certainly draw more interest into the race."

John looked at James who shrugged and then responded. "No publicity is bad publicity, I suppose."

He pulled out a pocket watch and looked at the time.

"Our race starts in about half an hour. Let's see what the reception has been to our wager before we take our seats in the grandstand."

Ivy spotted Matilda Fernshawe on the arm of Lord McDonnell but she left his side as soon as Iris waved to her. John and James excused themselves to speak to Lord Clune.

"Is it true that Viscount Tyrell made a fantastic bet with the Earl of Seahaven?"

The twins nodded in unison.

Matilda danced on the spot and clapped her hands. "I couldn't be more thrilled! I was forced to attend an at-home with the countess. She was such a horrible creature, not a patch on your stepmother. I'll be cheering as loudly as I can—you'll hear me from the other side of the stands. I've already asked McDonnell to place a pound on Crimson Lad. I wouldn't have before, but when I heard what that monster did to your family, I want to rub his nose in it too."

More people they encountered on the way to the stables expressed their best wishes for the upcoming race—it seemed that the Earl of Seahaven was not terribly well-liked. John received cards from various gentlemen who wished to make appointments to inspect

Tyrell Park for themselves, while others affirmed their intention to train their horses there.

Ivy looked up at John, proud to see he was receiving the recognition that was his due. She loved him utterly and completely.

Their progress down to the stables was halted by a parade of horses being led out into the paddock.

"There's Crimson Lad," said Iris. "Tiny does look good in his silks."

James called over to the trainer. "How is the Lad doing?"

"He's getting a little agitated now," he said. "He knows his race is about to come up. Are you going to be joining us in the ring, Captain?"

"We'll be in the stands to get a better view of the back straight; that's where I think he'll make his run."

"Right ye are then!" He called before following the procession down to where the horses were being assembled.

A man stepped up to a podium on the edge of the track and waited while stewards and jockeys marshalled their horses to more-or-less line up behind a wide chalk mark on the turf.

"How soon before they start racing?" Ivy asked.

"Some of the horses are a bit skittish and refuse to stay in their place," James answered. "As soon as the marshal on the podium raises his hand with his kerchief in it, we'll be ready to race.

"I'm having trouble seeing Crimson Lad," said Iris.

"Tiny's trying to keep him in the middle of the pack," said John. "He'll get a better start than being at the barrier."

"And Random Oath?" Ivy asked. "What colors are his?"

John pointed. "Yellow with a black star."

The marshal raised his arm and waved his kerchief.

The colts were off and running.

Ivy thought her heart would hammer right out of her chest.

Crimson Lad was not the first to cross the starting line, but neither was he the last. In fact, two of the horses failed to cross altogether and could not be persuaded to take up the chase. Trainers came and led the recalcitrant beasts off the track.

She searched for the green and purple diamonds on Tiny's back.

She spotted him approaching the back straight, but at that angle and distance, she couldn't tell where he placed in the pack.

John and James kept their eyes fixed on the race through their telescopes.

Iris sought out her hand and gripped it tightly.

"Crimson Lad's in third place," John announced.

"Random Oath is closing," said James.

The horses approached the inside straight. The crowd rose to their feet.

"Crimson Lad won't make it," Ivy cried.

"No, there's another lap to go," Iris answered before the thunderous sound of hooves drowned out all but the heartiest calls of encouragement. Ivy squeezed her sister's hand even tighter as the horses approached the back straight for a second time.

The field had spread out and a group of four horses led them. Crimson Lad was one of them. So was Random Oath.

Random Oath was half a length behind the horse out in front. Crimson Lad trailed him, but by only half a head. The horses left the back turn and approached the front straight for the final time.

"Come on Tiny, come on Tiny, make your move," James muttered.

The crowd in the stands surged to their feet yelling for their favorites.

Ivy gasped as Crimson Lad appeared to fall behind the lead horse and Random Oath.

On the stand below, the Earl of Seahaven glanced back at them and sneered.

Tears welled in her eyes. She spared a glance at her sister who also looked ready to burst into tears.

"Now Tiny! Now Crimson Lad," John yelled.

As though horse and rider could hear him, Crimson Lad picked up speed. Just two furlongs out, the Lad headed towards the outside rail to avoid Random Oath and the leading horse.

The three horses were neck-and-neck at the last furlong but Crimson Lad managed to pull ahead—by a nose... by a head...by a half-length...

By the time he passed the finishing post Crimson Lad was a full length in front.

The crowd erupted into deafening cheers. Ivy and Iris let out twin squeals of delight. Ivy was pulled away from Iris. She fell into John's hearty embrace.

"We did it!" he yelled above the noise of the crowd before swooping in for a quick but devastating kiss.

Next to them, Iris and James also embraced. Each cousin reached out a hand for a long handshake.

Ivy caught a glimpse at the Earl of Seahaven, his face pale. Random Oath had placed third. The man looked ready to cast up accounts. He shuffled away along the stand but not before John called out his name.

"Seahaven, it will be my pleasure to call on you tomorrow for your two thousand pounds!"

The man's head slumped to his chest for a moment before snapping back to attention.

Ivy looked around to see what caused it. There was his wife, the present Countess Seahaven, her face filled with thunder.

"Which has the most sting, do you think?" James asked. "The loss of two thousand pounds or a tongue lashing from that harridan?"

# EPILOGUE

For decades, Tyrell House was a byword for rustication. It held that title no longer.

It had been said that the al fresco party could not be bettered. But its reputation might have been rivalled by the country dance to celebrate Crimson Lad's outstanding race and the official opening of Tyrell Park that went on for a day and a night.

Now, just a few weeks later came the grandest celebration of all—an engagement party, *a double celebration* paid for, in part, by the Earl of Seahaven, although he was not a guest.

Friends and neighbors came from three counties to celebrate the engagement of Lady Ivy Bigglesworth to Lord John Bentley, Viscount Tyrell, and Lady Iris Bigglesworth to Captain James Bentley.

Lady Clune returned from the dance floor fanning herself vigorously. She turned to Lady Hampstead-Wycke.

"Well, I've never known a Season like it, have you?"

The woman opened her mouth to speak but Lady Clune continued. "No fewer than fifteen betrothals and *seven* from the Bigglesworth family alone! I would call that a great success, wouldn't you?"

Lady Hampstead-Wycke attempted an agreement, but Lady Clune was not done yet.

"Of course, it wouldn't have happened without my involvement, of course. Fine matches all, every single one of them. It is rare that so many well suited find true love as well, wouldn't you agree?"

Lady Hampstead-Wycke learned her lesson and simply nodded this time.

"It truly makes you believe in love, does it not?" Lady Clune sighed. "Perhaps it is time for me to retire as chairwoman of the York Society, for I cannot believe that there will be a year better than this one."

At this Lady Hampstead-Wycke made sure she jumped in first.

"*Retire?* You?"

Lady Clune let out a laugh.

"You're right, of course. It *is* my burden to bear. Perhaps I could manage another year after all."

Iris dutifully closed her eyes and allowed James to lead her by the hand.

"No peeking now," he said.

"I promise! My eyes are closed, I cannot see a thing."

"Good."

"Will you at least give me a hint?"

James stopped suddenly. Iris bumped into his embrace and felt his lips on hers. The kiss was unexpected as it was delicious for its spontaneity.

"You didn't need to bring me all the way into the garden for a kiss," she said.

"That's not the surprise," said James. "Are your eyes still closed?"

"They are."

Iris tried to guess the location. Grass under feet became gravel. James opened a gate and aided her through.

Soon there were the sound of horses and the redolent odor of the stables.

"Now you can open your eyes."

Iris did and came face to face with the largest pair of brown eyes she had ever seen. They belonged to a pretty bay mare. She stroked the horse's nose

"This is Primrose Lass, and she is yours."

Iris turned to James who searched her eyes closely to see how his gift would be received.

"It's been so long since I've ridden. In fact, not since we had to leave Seahaven."

"Ivy told me how much you enjoyed riding."

Iris threw herself into his arms. James kissed her, heedless of the watching eyes of horses in their stalls.

"Beloved Iris, you gave me something to fight for, something to believe in. My world is brighter with you in it," he whispered.

Iris was nearly overcome by emotion. She whispered.

"I love you, James, with all my heart."

Then there was no need for words when their lips met and their kisses grew even more passionate.

Ivy giggled, as John led her down a path toward the lake, the setting sun turning everything around them to gold.

"You are host, surely we'll be missed!" she said.

"Let them," he said. "It seems like we haven't had a moment together since the York Races."

"We've attended every party, soiree, and celebrated our engagement together."

John pulled Ivy into his arms.

"A moment *alone* together," he said.

"Ahh..." Ivy's reply was cut short by his mouth descending on hers for a deeply passionate kiss.

Her knees went weak, and she clung to him returning his kiss with equal fervor.

The kiss ended with hammering hearts.

"My love, how do you feel about a wedding at York Minster Cathedral? A double wedding?"

Ivy's eyes widened.

"Truly?"

"One of the privileges of being a viscount, I've learned."

John kissed her once more.

"My darling, I cannot wait for our life together to begin."

Ivy caressed his cheek.

"As far as I'm concerned, it already has."

*Four hearts, one lifetime of love.*
*And they lived happily ever after.*

THE END

# SOCIAL MEDIA FOR ELIZABETH ELLEN CARTER

You can learn more about Elizabeth Ellen Carter at these social media links:

**Website:** http://eecarter.com
**Facebook:** https://www.facebook.com/ElizabethEllenCarter
**Pinterest:** https://www.pinterest.com/eecarterauthor/
**Instagram:** https://www.instagram.com/elizabeth_ellen_carter/
**BookBub:** https://www.bookbub.com/authors/elizabeth-ellen-carter
**YouTube:** https://www.youtube.com/c/ElizabethEllenCarter

# ABOUT ELIZABETH ELLEN CARTER

Elizabeth Ellen Carter is an USA Today bestselling author and award-winning historical romance writer who pens richly detailed historical romantic adventures. A former newspaper journalist, Carter ran an award-winning PR agency for 12 years. She lives in Australia with her husband and two cats.

Learn more about Elizabeth Ellen at:
Website: https://www.eecarter.com

# LORD CUCKOO COMES HOME

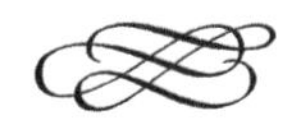

JUDE KNIGHT

Lord Cuckoo Comes Home
By Jude Knight

Dom Finchley only came to York as a favor to his half-brother, who asked him to attend a meeting there. After a devastating break with the Finchley family followed by ten years at war, he is keen to get the favor done and then leave to build the home he's never had. A place to call his own.

Then he meets Chloe.

Chloe Tavistock is past the age for the marriage market, and unfashionable in her shape, her opinions, and her enthusiasms. She is not going to find a husband in York, whatever her fond brother might think.

And then she meets Dom.

Two people who never found a place to fit just might be a perfect fit.

# CHAPTER 1

The monkey did not want to stay in the basket. Chloe had to hold down the lid while pretending nothing untoward was happening. It was a struggle to maintain a half smile of polite interest to convince those around her that she was listening to the speaker.

She didn't dare look at Doro. Her friend had her gaze focused forward with a determination belied by a certain twinkle in her eye and the occasional tremble of her lips. If they met one another's eyes, they would collapse into giggles as if they were twelve or thirteen again and sharing a schoolroom.

Chloe needed to not think about Rosario the monkey or Doro's amusement. Which meant, of course, that was all she could think about. The lecture might have helped, but the man currently droning on about the iniquities of the Habeas Corpus Act was too boring to actually make any sense.

The lid kicked under her hand. She bent over to rap it with her knuckles, just as the audience started clapping. The sudden roar of sound, of course, made Rosario even more desperate to get out of the basket.

Doro leaned closer and hissed out of the side of her mouth, "I did suggest the reform meeting might not be the best place for a monkey."

"I couldn't leave her behind," Chloe protested. "Martin threatened to wring her neck when he caught her."

Doro's amusement bubbled out in a gurgle. "Rosario did steal Lord Tavistock's cravat pin," she pointed out.

It was true, but not the whole truth. In the two weeks since Chloe rescued Rosario from a mob of villagers, she had stolen several things a day, bringing them all to Chloe with every expectation of approval.

The villagers had told Martin, Chloe's brother, the Viscount Tavistock, that the original owner was in prison awaiting trial for theft. A cravat pin, two pair of sleeve links, a cross belonging to cook, a pair of Chloe's earrings, one jeweled buckle from a shoe, and a handful of other small objects witnessed to the thief's small hairy accomplice.

"Martin will calm down by the time I am home," Chloe assured Doro, hoping it was true.

The next speaker had risen, and someone behind demanded the ladies be silent. Chloe looked around and winced an apology at the large man glaring from the next row of seats.

Two rows behind him, a fair-haired gentleman caught her gaze and winked one twinkling hazel eye.

The speaker, a little man with a bristling beard and burning eyes, began his oration. Boredom was not going to be an issue this time. A voice that was surely too large for the man's body boomed through the room, calling for them to protest the iniquities under which the workers suffered. "I love the King as much as anyone," he claimed, at full shout, "but his son plays at building pleasure palaces while his government oppresses his people and drives us into the workhouse."

At the man's rant, Rosario threw herself against the lid with renewed determination, rocking the basket despite Chloe's attempt to keep it still.

Behind them, someone booed. The speaker shouted him down, but a jeer came from another corner. Then the first missile flew, straight past Chloe's head.

Chloe ducked and lost hold of the lid of the basket. Rosario shot out, into the crowd, jabbering her distress. "Rosario!" Chloe shouted.

Doro edged up beside Chloe, avoiding the fight that had broken out in the aisle and threatened to impinge on her seat. "We need to get out of here," she said.

She was right. All around them was chaos. Some people were still hurling projectiles at the stage, though the speaker had disappeared. The chairman of the meeting had given up calling for calm and was wringing his hands while dodging pieces of rotten fruit and vegetables.

Others were wrangling in couples or groups, a few verbally but most with fists, elbows and feet. Chloe began edging along the row towards the nearest wall. She would just have to hope Rosario found her. Chloe and Doro had to get out of here.

When Dom Finchley saw the first turnip sail towards the stage, he had the fleeting thought that the thrower should have used it earlier, to cut short the drone of the previous speaker. And then two more turnips flew, followed by an apple. Several men descended on the perpetrator. Someone threw a punch. In less time than it took to take in a deep breath, the room was in chaos.

Dom recognized the thrower. An agitator—one of the army of less-than-honorable spies employed by the government. Dom supposed he was himself working, at one remove, for the government, but to observe, not to interfere, and certainly not to cause a riot where innocent people might be hurt.

His report back to his sponsor would be scathing, and not about the behavior of the reformists, either.

For the moment though, he was trying to keep out of the way of flying fists while working his way through to where he last saw the two ladies.

He'd noticed them as soon as he took his seat. Their clothes did not look out of place, and their hair—what he could see of it under plain bonnets—was simply dressed. But only those schooled in the art since early girlhood had the carriage of a lady. They sat as if chairs never had backs and their spines consisted of an iron rod each.

At first, he'd thought them a woman and child, and had wondered at the idiocy of bringing a young girl into a potentially dangerous crowd. The girl had something in a basket. A kitten perhaps. Or a puppy.

Then she turned. He saw her chest in profile, and his mouth went dry. No child this. He ripped his gaze from lush curves and upwards to a determined chin, a pert nose, and chocolate brown eyes fringed with dark lashes. The eyes met his with open curiosity. He smiled and winked. Her eyes widened before she turned her back on him. The next speaker began.

A few minutes into the speech, the rumpus started, and Dom started working his way toward the ladies. He had to get them out of here. Both of them. Not just the little elf who so fascinated him.

He stopped in his tracks at the sight of a monkey shooting up out of the crowd, leaping from head to head and clambering up the drapes. Not a kitten or a puppy, then.

A bit of ducking and weaving, a judicious punch when necessary. At times like this, he was grateful that he was slighter in stature than any of his brothers, the other two official sons of the marquess who was married to his mother and the two legitimate sons of his actual progenitor. He could wriggle through gaps in the brawling crowd that would compel a burlier man to stop and fight.

Six years at a public school had taught him how to give a good account of himself if forced to violence. Nearly a decade at war had cemented the lesson. But the priority was to reach the ladies. Ah. There was the elf, on her own, backed into a corner, clinging to her basket.

Ten feet further down the wall was a door. Dom had no idea where it went, but out of the fight, he hoped. He shouldered past the men who were blocking her in, and stopped in front of her. "There's a door this way, Miss."

The elf's curves were even more mouth-watering close up, but Dom couldn't afford to think about them. Someone thumped into his body, and someone else tried to barge past his arm. He made himself a wall to protect the elf, who was standing on the tips of her toes and peering around at the crowd. "I have lost my monkey," she explained. Then, as an afterthought, her brow creased, "and my friend."

"Let me get you out to safety," Dom begged, "And I'll come back and look for your friends. Both of them."

He was moving toward the door as he spoke, herding her along without touching her. She came willingly enough, though she continued to throw those anxious glances.

Then came a shout from the main door to the hall. "Troops!"

The call was taken up by a score of voices, and a hundred people stampeded at once. Someone caromed into Dom's back, pushing him against the elf. He slid his arms around her to shelter her. The blows and pokes from behind would leave bruises, but not on the lady if he could prevent it.

Even in the stress of holding back the crowd, a small and primitive part of his mind was assessing the lush softness against which he pressed, and enthusiastically suggesting that love was more fun than war.

It was only for a moment, and then he was able to step back, take a breath for control, and reassess their escape path. The door he was aiming for was blocked with men struggling to get through. At that moment, a few feet away, a fabric hanging on the wall shifted, and the monkey's face poked out, followed by the monkey, who launched itself into the elf's arms.

"Quick," Dom said, looking back over his shoulder to the main door, where those who had been trying to get out that way had reversed and were scattering across the floor to other exits. Two steps brought him to the hanging. He twitched it aside and disclosed an open doorway with stairs leading upwards. "Go up. I'll try to find your friend. If the troops catch up with you, tell them you're with Captain Finchley."

She nodded her agreement.

He caught her arm as she passed. "May I know the name of the lady I am honored to be assisting?"

Her smile transmuted the strong planes of her face into beauty. "Chloe Tavistock, Captain Finchley. And my friend is Dorothea

Bigglesworth. A straw bonnet and dark blue pelisse. Guinea-gold hair and blue eyes." Dom nodded his thanks, impressed. She'd maintained her calm and thought clearly enough to describe Miss Bigglesworth, while he was still assuming that any other lady he found must be the missing friend.

He closed the door behind her and dropped the fabric hanging back into place. Now where...? Ah! The brim of a bonnet poked up just beyond the short flight of steps that led to the stage. The hall was emptying, and Dom found it easy to dart across the room, avoiding those who were, by now, more interested in escaping the oncoming troops than in continuing the fracas.

He reached the woman by the stage just as she turned, and knew straight away that it was not Miss Tavistock's friend. This lady had a blue pelisse, but the hair under the straw bonnet was decidedly auburn. She eyed him warily.

"May I see you to safety, Miss?" Dom asked, offering an arm. She looked beyond him, her eyes widening in alarm. Dom turned to see a militia sergeant and two troopers approaching, the sergeant with a pistol and the troopers swords drawn. Idiots. Did he and the lady look dangerous? If nobody was killed today, it would be a miracle.

"Stand down, sergeant," he ordered, his voice crisp. "I am reaching for my identification papers," he added, and suited action to word.

The sergeant approached cautiously, his gun steady, and took the papers with his other hand. His eyes widened as he read the letter that introduced Dom. It was signed by the Duke of Haverford and bore that noble gentleman's seal.

The sergeant nodded and passed the letter back. "I beg your pardon, my lord. Can't be too careful."

*Being careful,* Dom thought, but didn't say, *would preclude carrying loaded guns and naked swords into a volatile crowd of unarmed civilians.*

"Can you make sure that this lady is escorted safely to wherever she wishes to go?" he said instead.

The sergeant narrowed his eyes. "She's not a revolutionary, sir, is she?"

"She is an English gentlewoman, Sergeant, and innocent of any involvement in today's events." Or not. But Dom really didn't care. "As is Miss Tavistock, who came here with me to observe, and her friend Miss Bigglesworth. I need to look for Miss Bigglesworth. Miss Tavistock is worried about her. The lady is wearing a straw bonnet and dark blue pelisse. She has fair hair and blue eyes."

The lady with the auburn hair was regarding him as if he was some sort of alien. He winked at her and she turned away.

The sergeant lifted his eyebrows in a pleased widening of the eyes and smiled. "Yellow hair? I saw a lady who meets that description, Captain, my lord, sir. A clerical gentleman was escorting her away from here."

Dom nodded. "I will inform Miss Tavistock."

# CHAPTER 2

Upstairs in a little gallery, Chloe watched from behind a balustrade as Captain Finchley approached a woman by the stage. She thought she recognized Doro's bonnet and pelisse, but when the woman turned so Chloe could see her face, it was a stranger.

The soldiers came, and three of them accosted Captain Finchley and the woman. Chloe's arms tightened around Rosario until the monkey squeaked. But Captain Finchley gave the leader some papers to read, and then the soldiers drew themselves up straight and saluted.

Chloe apologized to Rosario, patting her down until she realized that the monkey's jacket was lumpy. With a sinking heart, she investigated the monkey's pockets, pulling out a cravat pin, a hair pin, a utilitarian brass shoe buckle, an ornate snuff box, and a shiny acorn shape that looked as if it might have come from a watch fob.

Rosario chattered: her 'I'm a clever monkey' sound. Chloe wanted to cry.

"What do you have there?" Captain Finchley was looking over her shoulder at the little haul. He whistled. "An enterprising fellow, your monkey."

"I cannot seem to break her of the habit," Chloe said. "I have only had her for two weeks, and her former owner trained her to… well, you see."

"That sounds like a story worth the telling," Captain Finchley observed, his eyes twinkling.

A clatter on the stairs warned them, and Captain Finchley, without hesitation, swooped up the little haul and deposited it in his coat pocket while turning to face the door.

A burly militia man, two others on his heels, burst into the little space. "Now who have we here?" growled the first man, looming over poor Captain Finchley while Chloe shrank back against the balustrade, cradling Rosario against her chest.

Captain Finchley, who was at least twelve inches shorter than man who glared at him, didn't budge an inch. He sighed, for all the world as if he was bored beyond belief, flicked an imaginary speck of dust off his sleeve, and handed the man a document. "My credentials, corporal." His voice changed to the bark of command. "And you two troopers, sheathe those swords before you pink someone."

The corporal was reading the document, which appeared to be a letter finished with a large seal. When he spoke, it was with a mix of suspicion, resentment, and reluctant respect. "You would be this Captain Lord Diomedes Finchley, then, would you?"

"I have that honor," the gentleman answered.

"And this Duke of Haverford sent you?"

Captain Finchley tipped his head to one side and raised his eyebrows. "Now that you have read the letter, corporal, I will have it back, thank you." He held out his hand. The corporal hesitated then handed over the letter.

"You'll have to leave now, sir," he grumbled. "We are clearing the building." He turned his attention to Chloe. "You'll come along with me, Miss. You and that wild beast."

He took a step forward but no further. Captain Finchley had put out an arm to stop him. "Miss Tavistock is with me, corporal. Get about your business, now."

They glared at one another, but the corporal's eyes fell first. He growled a wordless complaint and led the other two militia men away.

"Oh!" Chloe exclaimed. "I have to find my sister!"

Captain Finchley's eyes widened. "Your sister is here, too?"

Had he forgotten already? "Doro. Miss Bigglesworth."

"Ah! Miss Bigglesworth. I am told a lady meeting that description was escorted away by a clerical gentleman. I expect she will be relieved when you arrive home safely."

"Oh, we don't live together. I live with my brother, and Doro is staying with her stepmother. Our stepmother, I suppose, except Patience married my stepfather after I had already gone to live with my great-uncle."

"Another interesting story, I perceive. But perhaps we could save it to beguile the walk back to wherever it is your brother resides?" He held out his hand to help her up. "Do you have a leash for your little furry friend?"

"No. She chewed through it. That's why I had her in the basket, but she has chewed through the ribbon keeping it shut."

"Perhaps my handkerchief might do service at least until we are safely out of here."

He threaded the handkerchief through the slot in the basket, then helped Chloe tuck a protesting Rosario inside before inserting a corner of the handkerchief through the slot in the lid and tying a firm knot.

"I'll just leave the monkey's little hoard at the bottom of the stairs." Captain Finchley put the items down one by one, artistically scattering them as if they had been dropped in a hurry. "I daresay someone will think it his lucky day when he comes across them, but at least you and I shall not be arrested for being accessories to a monkey, which would be exceedingly embarrassing, do you not think?"

He offered Chloe his arm. He escorted her straight past the groups of militiamen who were roaming the hall and out into the street.

"I was so afraid when those men threatened you," said Chloe. "They were so large!"

"Yes, but that made it easier," Captain Finchley assured her. "I was at the right height to bite their..." his eyes slid sideways to meet hers and he grinned before finishing, "knees."

Chloe wasn't entirely certain, but she thought he was being naughty. Still, she chuckled even as she blushed.

"I was never in danger," he added, sounding serious again, though his eyes still danced. "I am their superior officer. Or, at least, I was. Haverford said he'd put my rank in his letter in case I needed to throw my weight around. The extra gilt on the shoulders makes me a little heavier, you see, and when you're my size, you need all the help you can get. It's not really my rank any longer, though. I've sold out."

"What should I call you, then? Lord Finchley?"

"Good heavens, no. I'm a younger son—and not really even that, except by grace and favor. Except I am, but... That's another story, but hardly one fit for a lady's ears. I don't suppose you could call me Dom?"

"I could not. I barely know you, Lord Diomedes."

"If you must lord me, could it not be Lord Dom? Please? Diomedes sounds like a very stern fellow." He flattened his mouth into a sour line and furrowed his brow. "Monkey? A monkey is not a pet for a lady. Humph."

"You sound just like my Uncle Swithin," Chloe observed.

"One of those is he? A joy leech?"

Chloe had to chuckle. "That is just the word! He was a joy leech!"

"He is dead, then, your Uncle Swithin?"

"A year ago. More. It must be sixteen months, now." She and Aunt Swithin had been out of their blacks for Christmas.

"I am sure propriety demands that I now express my sympathy for your sorrow," Lord Dom observed, "but I have known too many joy leeches in my life to do any such thing."

Chloe couldn't agree more. "It is a terrible thing to say, and I am sure it makes me a very bad person, but after the first shock, I felt so much lighter! Martin—he is my brother—Martin is not very good at fun, and he worries a lot, but he does at least like me to be happy. Uncle Swithin thought we should all be miserable, for life is a vale of tears, and it would be irreligious of us to enjoy ourselves."

"I am quite certain Uncle Swithin was wrong," Lord Dom. "I may not always have been attentive during regimental services, but I am sure I can remember the chaplain exhorting us to rejoice, like good Christians. Perhaps Uncle Swithin didn't read the Bible?"

"Oh, he did, all the time. He had favorite passages."

Lord Dom pulled a face and nodded. "Which he read over and over, and used to justify puffing himself up in his own consequence." He nodded again. "I know the sort."

Chloe giggled, for Lord Dom was exactly right.

"And was Aunt Swithin another joy leech? Was there an Aunt Swithin?"

"There still is," Chloe assured him. "She is my chaperone." She paused doubtfully. "Only she has digestive troubles. She also sleeps all the time, and she forgets things."

"The best kind of chaperone," Lord Dom assured her, and added, "I dare say after being married to Uncle Swithin she has had all the joy leeched out of her."

"I used to think so," Chloe told him, "but I think she was just hiding it." She and Aunt Swithin had celebrated last Christmas with all the traditional activities, food and trimmings, none of which Uncle Swithin had permitted. Martin had made no objection, had commented the house looked nice, and had even purchased a Twelfth Night gift each for her and Aunt Swithin.

"She can be rather startling in her opinions," Chloe added.

"Opinions are new to her, I imagine, so she is trying as many as she can." Lord Dom sounded as if he knew all about the Uncle Swithins of the world.

"You are rather wise, Lord Dom," Chloe said.

Lord Dom's eyes twinkled, and he winked one eye. "I do apologize. I didn't mean to be wise."

They turned into the street where Martin had taken a house. Chloe was still laughing at Lord Dom's apology when she heard her name shouted.

"Chloe Tavistock!"

~

This, Dom suspected, was the stern brother. Several years younger and at least half a foot taller than Dom, he was bearing down on them at speed, his face drawn into such lines of fury that Dom half expected him to be blowing steam out of his nose.

"Oh dear. Martin is not pleased," Chloe commented. She looked concerned but not alarmed, and Dom informed his battle-ready body it could stand down. Clearly, she did not expect physical retribution from her brother. Still, Dom would stay until he was sure that Tavistock would not harm her.

Tavistock didn't seem to see Dom, all his ire focused on his sister. The monkey in its basket reacted to Tavistock's baritone rant, its nervous chitter providing a falsetto counterpoint.

"Chloe! I was just coming to look for you. Lady Dorothea was so worried. How could you go to that infernal meeting when I expressly forbade it? Are you hurt? Did anyone offer you insult? Aunt Swithin is beside herself! I could throttle you. I really could. When I think what could have happened..."

Dom relaxed when Tavistock asked about his sister's well-being before the extravagant threat that was clearly nothing more than relief for his feelings. Chloe apparently thought so, too, for she ignored the risk to her pretty neck, saying. "Doro and I were separated, but Lord Dom found out she had been escorted safely away. Has she sent a message, Martin? I should let her know that I am safe. Martin, this is Lord Dom. He rescued me, and insisted on escorting me home. Lord Tavistock, Lord Dom Finchley." She turned to Dom, her brow furrowed, and her upper teeth worrying her plump lower lip. "Should I have said 'Lord Diomedes'?"

"Please don't," Dom told her, offering Tavistock his hand to shake and bowing slightly. "Pleased to meet you."

Tavistock looked nothing like his sister. He was tall, slender, and dark-haired with grey eyes, whereas she was short and curvaceous with light brown hair and eyes that were deep pools of chocolate. But something about the expression as he frowned at Dom gave them a family resemblance.

"I am grateful to you, my lord. She should not have been there." His frown deepened. "Did she go with you?"

"Martin! I went with Doro. I only met Lord Dom when he put himself between me and some men who were fighting, and not paying attention to bystanders. And then he stopped the soldiers from taking me away for questioning."

The starch went out of Tavistock as he and Dom exchanged a glance full of knowledge about the worse things that might have happened to an unprotected lady in such a crowd. "I *am* grateful to you," Tavistock said, sounding sincere this time.

"She was easy to rescue," Dom assured him. "She kept her head, which is more than many ladies would have done."

"She's got bottom," Tavistock grumbled. "Too much, sometimes. Come on home, Chloe. Doro is waiting to make sure that you are well."

"I'll leave you to your brother, Miss Tavistock," Dom said. "May I have the honor of knowing which house is yours? With Lord Tavistock's permission, I would like to call tomorrow to see how you and your hairy friend have recovered from your adventure."

Tavistock raised his eyebrows at the 'hairy friend' crack, then saw that Dom's eyes were focused on the basket. "Infernal monkey," he muttered. "We are at number nine, Lord Diomedes. Thank you, again. Come on, Chloe."

## CHAPTER 3

Martin kept the rest of his scold till Doro had exclaimed her relief and left in their carriage, which Martin insisted on having prepared for her. Then Chloe had to listen to a long lecture on irresponsible behavior, putting herself in danger, disobeying the head of her family whose responsibility it was to protect her, and (for good measure) keeping inappropriate pets.

She found it easy to promise to attend no more reform meetings. The one speaker she'd heard had been disappointing, and while the riot had been an adventure, she did not need Martin to point out that she was lucky Lord Dom had been at hand to protect her. Indeed, his general and vague description of the harms that may have befallen her were nothing to the gruesome horrors she had imagined on her own.

Martin was still seething when they met for dinner. He barely said a word until Aunt Swithin distracted his attention by lamenting that she had missed the meeting. "I was so looking forward to it, dear Martin," she told him, blissfully oblivious to his shocked horror, "but I suffered an upset to my digestion, so I told the girls to go ahead without me. Did you have an interesting time, Chloe?"

After one glance at Martin's face, Chloe had to keep her eyes on her plate, though she managed not to laugh. "I only heard the one speaker, Aunt Swithin: Mr. Thomas, whose articles you liked so much when I read them to you. I'm afraid he writes much better than he speaks. After that, the meeting broke up, and Doro and I came home."

Another swift glance at Martin's pained expression almost overcame her gravity.

"Aunt Swithin?" he demanded. "Are you telling me you approve of these revolutionaries? I cannot believe it. What would Uncle say?"

"Not revolutionaries, dear," Aunt Swithin insisted. "I would never support revolution. Those poor dear children in France! But reform, yes. The government is trying to bully the people instead of listening, and it is not nice, dear. Nobody likes a bully."

Martin opened his mouth and then closed it again. Chloe waited for him to scold Aunt Swithin as he had her, but instead, he changed the subject. "Chloe is expecting a gentleman caller tomorrow, Aunt Swithin. Lord Diomedes Finchley escorted Chloe home from the meeting, and asked to call again."

"Finchley," Aunt Swithin said, and then repeated it. "Finchley. Ah, yes. The Marquess of Pevenwood's third son." Aunt Swithin had taken her responsibilities as the female educator of a young viscount to include a devotion to memorizing Debretts. She was also, even under the harsh rule of her husband, addicted to the gossip news sheets, entering into a conspiracy with Cook to read them in the kitchen when Uncle Swithin was out spreading virtue and gloom around the neighborhood.

She showed the fruits of that research in her next remark. "The one they call Lord Cuckoo, because everyone knows the Duke of Haverford laid him in Pevenwood's nest. The old Duke of Haverford, who died two years ago, not the young one, who was a dreadful rake but is now devoted to his wife, or so they say. Very admirable, but much less interesting." She sighed.

"Now where was I? Around fifteen years ago, Pevenwood sued Haverford for criminal conversation, but Haverford's affair with the boy's mother was ancient history. The boy was nine or ten, I believe, before Pevenwood found out that the boy was not his own get and took the case. The Duke refused to give evidence, the Marchioness denied everything, the evidence was all gossip or circumstantial, and the case was dismissed."

She sighed. "I always felt sorry for the little boy. A soldier, is he not? Does he wear a uniform? A man looks so delightful in a uniform. Does Lord Cuckoo have money, though, Chloe? One cannot imagine that Pevenwood left him any, under the circumstances."

Poor Lord Dom. Chloe could do nothing about his tragic origins, but she could speak up for him to some degree. "Lord Dom—he prefers to be called Lord Dom, not Lord Diomedes," and definitely not Lord Cuckoo, which sounded like a cruel schoolboy joke. "Lord Dom has left the army. I do not know what he plans for his future, nor do I know how much money he has. It is surely none of my business, Aunt Swithin."

"Only if you wish to marry him, my dove. Money does not buy happiness, it is true. But one is able to be miserable in some degree of comfort. I always wished that Swithin had more money."

"Aunt Swithin," Martin protested. "Uncle Swithin was a very—" his pause for thought was telling. "Upright man," he concluded.

"He never wore a uniform though," Aunt Swithin complained. "I do love a man in a uniform."

Martin's reply was a gurgling noise, as if he had choked on what he wanted to say. Chloe took pity and changed the subject. "I am visiting Lady Seahaven and the sisters tomorrow morning. Aunt Swithin, will you come with me? I can go with my maid, if you prefer."

Martin surprised her. "I will escort you, Chloe. I wish to pay my respects to Lady Seahaven, and I should visit our sisters."

"They will be thrilled, Martin." Mama had given her second husband, the Earl of Seahaven, two daughters, Emma and Merry. They had remained with the Earl of Seahaven when Mama died and Uncle Swithin insisted on Chloe being returned to her brother's household.

Chloe had kept in touch in the intervening years, but Martin had only met his half-sisters after Uncle Swithin's death.

Martin twirled his wine glass between his fingers. That was

another innovation. They never had wine or any other alcohol while Uncle Swithin was alive. "Lady Dorothea was telling me about their ball, Chloe, and I had an idea," he said. "What do you think of us asking Lady Seahaven to make you one of her protégées?"

"She has been very kind about including me when she and her step-daughters go calling," Chloe observed. Lady Seahaven and the Bigglesworth sisters had started with some personal connections and a few recommendations from relatives, and had brokered them into introductions to most of York Society.

"Precisely," Martin agreed. "They know many more people than we do, and their ball will be much better attended than any entertainment I could put on for you. But I would not wish you to be neglected in such a big crowd of sisters."

Aunt Swithin cackled. "Only three sisters that count, Martin. Lady Seahaven is giving the ball for the Seahaven Diamonds, and quite right, too. Next to them, no one will notice our Chloe, nor any other female."

"Aunt Swithin," Martin protested, "Chloe would make a fine match for any gentleman of discernment."

"Josefina and the twins can only marry one man apiece," Chloe pointed out, though privately she agreed with Aunt Swithin's assessment. Short and dumpy as she was, she suffered by comparison to the Bigglesworth sisters who were her age and older, let alone the three younger girls who would have been reigning beauties even in a London Season.

The three had been dubbed the Seahaven Diamonds after their first public appearance in York, and the sooner they selected from among their swarming suitors, the better all the other marriageable ladies in York would like it.

"Besides, Aunt Swithin, it isn't just about the ball. If Lady Seahaven agrees to sponsor me, hostesses who are inviting the Seahavens will include me in their invitations. I will have many more opportunities to meet eligible gentlemen." *And much good it might do me, for I shall still be unfashionably plump, two years past twenty, and far too opinionated for most gentlemen.*

Martin nodded. "That is what I thought. I shall ask Lady Seahaven, then, shall I? I will, of course, offer her the money I planned to spend on a party of some kind. Do you think that would be the right thing to do?"

Chloe nodded. "Absolutely."

After dinner, he showed Chloe some books and trinkets he had brought for the little girls, including for Lady Seahaven's little Jane, who was only three. "If I am giving gifts to our sisters, I can't leave the baby out," he said.

Sometimes, Chloe was quite hopeful that, out from under Uncle Swithin's control, Martin was becoming almost human.

When they saw her the next day, Lady Seahaven was delighted to take Chloe under her wing, "Though it seems silly for me to be your sponsor, Miss Tavistock, when you and I are the same age. At the very least, you must call me Patience, as your stepsisters do. When they are not calling me 'Mama' to tease me."

She objected when Martin offered to help finance the ball, "and any other expenses you incur by allowing Chloe to join you."

"But, Lord Tavistock, your sister is part of the family. I cannot think it proper to charge you a fee."

"The fact is, Lady Seahaven, that I am at a standstill," Martin explained. "Chloe and I were tutored at home, as you know, and our guardian was not a warm man. Nor were those few social connections he maintained at the right social level for a viscount's sister. Aunt Swithin is as much out of her depth as I am, and besides, grows more peculiar by the day." As Patience could see for herself, since Aunt Swithin had barely said good morning to her hostess before announcing that she would go and find Bess, the eldest Seahaven daughter, because Bess did not have cotton wool between her ears.

Martin leaned forward in his seat, gifting Patience with a winning smile. "If you will treat Chloe as one of your own flock, I am persuaded she will fare much better than my aunt and I could manage without your help. I would not think of putting a monetary value on the advantage to Chloe of your sponsorship. You are doing me an enormous favor, and all I can say is thank you. But I have budgeted for a season for Chloe, and it is only fair that the money I was going to spend doing a poor job should go to helping you do a far better one."

Chloe was impressed by the speech, and so was Doro, who commented, "That is reasonable, Patience. Lord Tavistock's money added to ours will allow us to make more of an impression than either of us could manage on our own."

That settled, Martin was carried off to the schoolroom by an ecstatic pair of schoolgirls. At twelve and ten, and used to a house full of women, Emma and Merry were awed and fascinated by their adult brother.

Chloe was drawn into a wide-ranging discussion of budgets, suppers, invitation lists, and musicians, with Doro and her older full sisters, Barbara and Susana, as well as Josefina and the twins, Ivy and Iris. Twice, one of the sisters slipped out to fetch tea and cakes. At one point, Martin strolled in to say he had an engagement at the club he'd joined and would walk Chloe and Aunt Swithin home if they were ready to leave. Chloe said, "You go, Martin. Aunt Swithin and I can walk five hundred yards through the quietest part of town in broad daylight."

An hour later, when Patience called a halt so she and those who were accompanying her could change for afternoon calls, Aunt Swithin was nowhere to be found. The impossibly handsome butler said she'd spent some time with Bess but left long before Martin.

Chloe thought about asking Patience for the loan of a servant to walk home with her. But it was, after all, broad daylight, and Patience had retreated to her chamber to get changed, as had the sisters.

Martin was right. Aunt Swithin really was growing more peculiar by the day. Chloe only hoped she had gone home. At least Rosario could be locked in a cage when not directly supervised, but one could hardly do that to one's aunt.

She reached the corner and hesitated. A left turn was the quickest way home, but straight ahead would take her to the bookshop that ran the circulating library she had joined during her first week in York. It was not much out of her way. She could ask if the book she was waiting for had been returned, and then take a shortcut by the narrow way that ran along the back of houses to join up with the street where she lived.

# CHAPTER 4

Dom left Thursday Market with a spring in his step and his coat pockets bulging. He'd wandered the stalls and the crafters shops that lined the nearby medieval streets, and found people who could make exactly what he wanted—an unusual courting gift, to be sure, but he thought the lady would like it.

Was he courting? After one meeting? Granted, he had returned from war with the vague notion of finding a bride and starting his family. He had not intended to look about him yet. He was in the north to inspect the estate he had unexpectedly inherited from his mother's uncle, and in York as the last place on a round of reform meetings to fulfill Haverford's errand.

That said, though, choosing a wife here in the north was not a bad notion. A bride with family here was more likely to accept his desire to live in Yorkshire most of the year round. More likely, too, to give their hand to the younger son of a peer who had been repudiated by his supposed father.

Dom didn't have wealth to make him more eligible. The estate was large enough, but needed work to be made profitable again. Haverford had given him a loan to do the necessary work, and he was confident he and his potential family had a bright future. He could offer a wife a comfortable home and some elegancies, but certainly not every luxury.

He'd like to smother Miss Tavistock in luxuries. It sounded as if she hadn't had many under the rule of the dire Uncle Swithin.

This was all too fast, though. He'd only met her yesterday, two days after he'd arrived in York. She was at the top of his bride list, but to be fair she was so far the only one on it.

On the other hand, she interested him more than any other lady he'd ever met. It wasn't just the physical response, though he didn't discount the importancc of that. She intrigued, challenged, and amused him. She went to reform meetings. She rescued monkeys from thieves. She laughed at his jokes.

He wanted to know her better, that was certain. Yes. That was the way. Get to know her. Not courting, then. Not quite yet. But definitely a step in that direction.

Absorbing as his thoughts were, his soldier's instincts continued to scan his surroundings. The song he was humming died on his breath as two tall gentlemen rounded a corner towards him, talking so intently that they didn't notice him at all.

Though he hadn't seen them in a decade, he recognized them instantly. Totters—Pevenwood now, since his father's death—hadn't changed a bit, except that his hair had receded a little from his forehead. Gary had just turned twenty on the night Dom left. He had broadened into adulthood in the last ten years and showed early signs of thickening into middle age.

What on earth were his Pevenwood brothers doing in York?

Dom didn't want to meet them. He turned into the alley he'd found yesterday—a shortcut to the Tavistock residence—and hurried his steps when he saw a group of men clustered around a female who was attempting to back away.

He broke into a run. He would intervene to help any woman, but he'd seen that redingote before. Some primitive part of him had no doubt of the identification. *Mine*! it growled, and when one of the insolent tormenters dared to put a hand on Miss Tavistock's arm, grinning at his companions, Dom had to fight back a red fog of rage.

Fighting eight men might feed the possessive beast, and he was confident they'd all walk away bleeding. But he couldn't guarantee they wouldn't overwhelm him in the end, and then what would happen to Miss Tavistock?

He nudged one of the men out of his way and stepped into the circle, already talking, waving the pin he'd just pulled from his cravat. "I beg your pardon, my lady. I did not think it would take me so long. I found it, though." He wafted the pin with one hand and knocked the offensive hand from Miss Tavistock's arm with the other, making it look purely incidental to tucking her hand inside his elbow.

"When I suggested you stroll ahead, my dear lady, I did not intend you to take the shortcut to your brother's home. Though I suppose we must hurry. Lord Tavistock will be sending out the servants to find you, and he may never let me escort you again if he finds I allowed you to step ahead of me."

Several of the men stepped backward when he called Miss Tavistock 'lady', which is why he had done it. They fell further back when he mentioned Lord Tavistock. Dom could deal with the rest. Grooms, by the look of them. He raised a single brow as he pretended to notice them for the first time.

"Do you know these persons, my lady?" he asked, allowing his voice to drip doubt as thick as treacle.

"No, Lord Finchley, I do not," Chloe replied. "I was just declaring my disinterest in any acquaintance." Clever girl. Omitting his first name to give him a spurious rank had several more of the grooms slinking back into their mews.

Dom allowed the other eyebrow to drift upwards as he fixed the ringleader with a glare. "You made a mistake," he told the man. "Don't compound it."

*There's always at least one idiot.* The man took a swing at him, just as one of the other grooms exclaimed, "Here, that's Cap'n Cuckoo. Leave 'im be, Ted. That's Do-or-Die Cuckoo, that is!"

The warning came too late for the idiot, whose blow had missed its target when Dom swayed to one side. Dom used the idiot's own fist to tug him away from a collision with Miss Tavistock, which would have been a piece of impertinence too far.

Idiot stumbled a few feet away, propelled by the force of his missed swing, and then roared as he caught himself and turned back toward his tormentor. Oh dear. A bull-brain. The man who had recognized Dom was shouting further warnings at Idiot, who ignored him.

"Would you be kind enough to step to the side of the lane?" Dom murmured to Miss Tavistock, who further showed her intelligence by immediate compliance. She was out of the way just in time. Bull Idiot charged, both fists swinging. Again, Dom swerved out of the way, but this time, he stuck out a booted foot, so Bull Idiot hurtled into the dust of the alley.

He rose again, still roaring. In Dom's peripheral vision, a few of the remaining bystanders clenched their fists and hunched forward. Those on one side halted when Miss Tavistock invoked her brother's title and their own sense of fair play. On the other, the groom who'd called Dom by his old army nickname interposed himself between the would-be assailants and the conflict.

Dom was, for a few moments, too busy to pay any more attention to those who were watching, as he allowed Bull Idiot a glancing blow as the price of getting close enough to finish the fight. A kick to the family jewels, a fist to the chin as Bull Idiot bent in half, the side of the hand to the back of the neck as he went down.

Dom stepped over the groaning man and offered his arm to Miss Tavistock. "Shall we continue our walk?"

She took her place beside him with admirable composure. "Shall we repair to my brother's house, my lord? I find myself in need of a cup of tea."

"An excellent idea," Dom replied, only half his mind on the nonsensically calm conversation. His ears were doing service for his eyes, listening for movement behind him. Apart from some muttered conversation and a few groans, the alley was calm. His swift sideways glance as they turned the corner confirmed that his erstwhile opponent was still curled in a ball in the middle of the alley, and that the spectator numbers had swollen as more grooms emerged from their separate stable-yards.

They were ignoring Bull Idiot. From the enthusiastic arm waving, Dom guessed they were refighting the battle.

Dom let his own readiness for battle seep from his muscles and nerves. The street was a fashionable one, and busy enough that even Bull Idiot would think twice about accosting a lady on it. Besides, Miss Tavistock's house was only a hundred paces away.

Miss Tavistock was trotting to keep up with him. What a wretch he was. She must be overset by such a display of violence, and now he was dragging her down the street. He slowed his pace. "I am sorry you had to witness that, Miss Tavistock."

She surprised him, looking up into his eyes with her own wide and shining. "I am sorry you had to fight that horrid person, Lord Dom, but I am not sorry I witnessed you bringing him low." She blushed and ducked her head. "Oh dear. Now you will think me dreadful. A proper lady would be swooning."

"Please don't," Dom begged. "A swooning lady would be dreadfully inconvenient." He slowed still further, pleased to draw out their time together. "I was very impressed with how you kept calm during the situation."

She blushed still deeper, the rosy hue spreading from ear to ear and down to disappear beneath her redingote. "It was all my fault. I have taken that shortcut before, my lord, but never on my own. I did not realize..."

*Yes, and why is she on her own?* It was not his place to ask, but he did not need to, for the explanation was tumbling out of her, along with her proposed assault on York Society under the umbrella of the Seahaven family, her concern about her Aunt Swithin's increasing eccentricity, and her pleasure in the two new books that were the cause of her detour from the straight, much safer, way home.

"May I come in?" Dom asked, when their slow dawdle fetched them up on the pavement outside the Tavistock town house. "I know it is early for a call, but since I am here..."

At that point, the front door opened and a man—a butler by the look of him—erupted onto the doorstep. "Miss Tavistock, come quickly. Your monkey..."

He disappeared back inside.

Miss Tavistock muttered, "Oh dear. Someone must have let her out."

Dom followed her into the house. They stepped in on a tableau. Several women servants gathered around one of their number who sat on the parquet floor of the entry hall, her apron over her head, waving a bloodied hand in the air and wailing. On the stairs that rose from the hall, an elderly lady was cackling with laughter. Two footmen were poking at the chandelier with brooms. No. Not at the chandelier. At the monkey who had taken refuge there.

"That beast has bitten Peggy, Miss Tavistock," complained a woman dressed all in black, right down to the apron. A housekeeper, if Dom had ever seen one.

"How did she get out of her cage?" Miss Tavistock wondered.

Peggy wailed louder, and the housekeeper glared at her. "I can't get any sense out of the girl, Miss." She drew her dignity around her and returned to her complaint. "But I can't be having a beast in the house that bites the maids. You must see, Miss Tavistock, that the monkey is not fit to live with civilized people."

"We shall discuss this later," Miss Tavistock decided. "For now, please take Peggy to the kitchen and see to her wounds. You may call the doctor if you think it appropriate. I want everyone cleared out of the entrance hall immediately. We shall not get Rosario to calm down enough to descend by poking at her."

What a soldier's wife, Miss Tavistock would have made! One wild situation after another, and all met with calm competence. Dom backed her up by removing the brooms from the hands of the footmen and sending them after their fellows.

~

It was too much to hope that Aunt Swithin would take her dismissal with the servants. She sank onto a stair near the upper landing, settling her skirts around her. "Well, Chloe? Are you going to introduce your handsome friend?"

"In a minute, Aunt Swithin. Hush, now." She changed her voice to a sing-song croon. "Rosario. Come down, Rosario. It's safe now, darling. I've sent all the noisy people away."

Dom edged around her to make his way up the staircase and sit on the step below Aunt Swithin's. "I'm Dom, and I take it you are Mrs. Swithin. Or should I say Lady Swithin?"

"Heavens no, dear. Swithin never had a title. Except for Vicar, until he told the bishop and the rector that the established church had too little regard for God and too much for the established order of society. If he had remained Vicar Swithin, might I have been called Vixen Swithin?" She cackled, startling Rosario, who leapt two layers higher in the chandelier.

"Hush!" Chloe whispered. "Please," she added.

Mrs. Swithin mimed clamping her lips shut and turning a lock on them, then winked at Dom. He grinned back and turned to watch Chloe crooning soothing nonsense to the monkey. Rosario, indeed! The villainous monk called Rosario in the gothic novel *The Monk* had in truth been a conniving female by the name of Matilda, who had disguised herself in order to pursue the man with whom she was infatuated into the very monastery.

Dom wondered which member of the little household had named the capuchin. She did not look like a villainess at the moment, to be sure. She had consented to lower herself by one hand from a sconce, setting the chandelier swinging. As he watched, she dropped into Chloe's arms, wrapped her own around Chloe's neck, and laid her head on the lady's breast with a little sigh.

"Butter would not melt in her mouth," Mrs. Swithin commented, in a loud stage whisper. "Who would have thought that such an innocent scrap of a creature has set the house at sixes and sevens?"

Chloe climbed the stairs towards them, still murmuring to Rosario. Dom stood as she approached, moving to one side to let her pass. Without changing her tone or looking away from the monkey, she said, "Aunt Swithin, would you take Lord Dom to the parlor and order tea? I shall just put Rosario back in my room. I will be with you shortly, my lord."

"Come along then, lad," Mrs. Swithin instructed, after Chloe had continued on up the stairs. "Help me up." She thrust out a gaunt hand, and he helped her to her feet. "When I sat down, I forgot my old bones. Aging is a terrible thing, my boy." She cackled again. "Better than the alternative. I am not looking forward to meeting Swithin again."

She directed him to the parlor by way of tucking her hand into his elbow and dragging him in the correct direction. "Have I shocked you, Lord Diomedes?"

Dom suspected she intended to, and refused the conversational sally, saying instead, "Perhaps he won't be in heaven?"

Mrs. Swithin shook her head at that. "I have no hope of it. He was tediously virtuous. Now, tea. Do not expect much. I daresay the whole household is still in the housekeeper's room, advising on the treatment of a bite that did not even break the skin, and which the silly girl deserved for opening the cage when she has been told over and over to leave it alone."

She tugged on the bell as she spoke, then noticed he was still standing. "Sit down. Sit down. Tell me about yourself, Lord Diomedes. Or is it Captain Lord?"

"Just Dom, if you will, Mrs. Swithin. I have sold out of the army."

She fixed him with a suspicious glare. "You have? How do you plan to support yourself, then? Do you have a position? An inheritance?"

*Inquisitive old besom*! On the chance that she was concerned for her niece, and not just rudely obvious about satisfying her curiosity, he answered politely, if vaguely, "I am not in danger of starving, thank you for asking." Thanks to his long-dead mother's brother. He was taken by surprise when the solicitor's letter arrived. It said his uncle had died and Dom was his principal heir.

Dom had seen the man once in twenty years. On his eighteenth birthday, when he had approached the Marquess of Pevenwood about his future, the marquess had informed Dom that he'd supported his unfaithful wife's brat for long enough. He would allow Dom to live under his roof until he was twenty-one, but nothing more. No allowance. No university. And certainly, no boost into a career.

Dom did the round of his relatives, hoping that someone would buy him the commission he longed for, or at least loan him the money. His mother's brother refused him, and Dom never heard from him again until the unexpected bequest. Perhaps the man regretted turning his nephew away. Or, possibly, given the condition of the estate, he would have helped at the time, if he'd had the money.

Mrs. Swithin's next question recalled Dom from his memories. "Ready to settle down, are you?"

"One can grow tired of constant travel," Dom replied, "particularly when people insist on shooting at you." As a description of the past decade, it worked, though on the whole, the army had suited Dom, and Dom had suited the army.

Mrs. Swithin's ruthless interrogation covered his history, his prospects and his intentions. He managed to put her off with vague answers, quips and anecdotes, but expected her to demand at any moment that he open his mouth so she could examine his teeth.

He was rather dazed by the time Chloe arrived, leading a procession of servants bearing the tea makings and plates of food—a cake, little pastry cases with meat filling, some slices of bread cut into small triangles and spread with a savory conserve.

Chloe was still carrying the monkey. "I could not leave her," she explained. "She is too upset. I am sorry I deserted you for so long. I went down to see Peggy. She has a bruise but is mostly upset because she feared I would dismiss her. She opened the cage, though she has been told not to do so. She said she just wanted to pat Rosario, but of course Rosario tried to get out of the cage. Peggy panicked and tried to slam it shut. Then Rosario panicked and..." she trailed off and shrugged helplessly.

"Perhaps these might help?" Dom pulled his packages from the pockets of the coat he'd draped over the arm of the chair, since the servants had been too occupied when he arrived to offer to take it.

One handed, since the other hand was occupied in stroking Rosario, Chloe undid the bow of string on the first package and unwrapped the brown paper to disclose the harness.

The harness maker and smith had collaborated to produce something as pretty as it was practical—rose-colored leather patterned with punched stars and circles that disclosed the metal forming the foundation of the harness. Rosario would have no chance of chewing through that! But the metal was wrapped in the softest of calf leather to protect the monkey's skin.

The second package was the leash, which could be clipped to a loop in the middle of the back. It was made of a light but strong chain, with the same rose leather forming a hand grasp at the other end of the chain.

Chloe lifted it this way and that, her eyes shining. "Why, it is marvelous, Dom. Lord Dom, I mean. Wherever did you find it?"

"I had it made," he explained. "I wasn't sure of the size, so I had them drill a couple of holes for the buckles. It buckles at the back, since that part had to be leather only, and I didn't want her to be able to get her teeth to it. If it doesn't fit properly, I'm to take it back, and they'll make another hole or two."

Chloe had to try it, of course. She managed to persuade Rosario to don the harness, clipped the chain to the back, and set Rosario on her lap, where the monkey proceeded to pick at the harness, sniff at it, and generally examine it as best she could.

Chloe turned her delighted gaze from her pet to Dom. "Lord Dom, how can I ever thank you. You could not have thought of anything to please me more."

"Cream, milk or lemon?" Mrs. Swithin asked. "Sugar?"

On campaign, Dom had learned to drink his tea strong and without additives. "Just tea, thank you, Mrs. Swithin. I am glad you are pleased with it, Miss Tavistock. I thought also of a warm coat for

Rosario, one without pockets. But I guessed you could probably handle that yourself.

"Without pockets," Chloe repeated. She beamed at him. "Why did I not think of that?"

"It won't stop the little fiend," Mrs. Swithin warned as she handed Dom his cup.

"It will limit her to stealing only what she can carry in her hands," Chloe retorted.

~

Lord Dom stayed a little over his half hour. When he stood to go, he asked if he could call again the next day, but Chloe explained she had promised to make calls with her stepmother and stepsisters.

"I could come at one of the clock, if that suits, and we could perhaps take a stroll along the New Walk? I could be sure to have you back in plenty of time for your afternoon calls."

He appeared anxious for her to agree, which had to be ridiculous, for what would a successful, personable man like him want with a woman like her? "Yes, I would like that," she said. She might as well enjoy his interest while it lasted.

He took his leave then, and Aunt Swithin showed every sign of wishing to dissect the visit, so Chloe declared the need to feed the monkey and to mend the hem that had been slightly torn in the scuffle in the alley. She escaped to her bedroom.

Nonetheless, it was only a temporary escape. She had to endure a dinner in which Aunt Swithin regaled Martin with a description of the call, including Aunt Swithin's opinion of Lord Dom's intentions and his eligibility.

Chloe did her best to divert the discussion to plans for the ball, and Martin talked about his trip with a man he'd met at the club he'd joined—a Captain James Bentley. Bentley and his cousin, who was a viscount, were debuting a colt in the race meeting that ended the York Season, and Martin had been out to see the horse and the cousins' training facility. Aunt Swithin kept returning to Lord Dom. She was convinced he was courting Chloe.

As always, Martin retreated to his study after dinner. Chloe followed. "Martin, I hope you will not take Aunt Swithin seriously."

"Do you like the man?" Martin asked.

Far too much. "He cannot possibly be interested in me, Martin," Chloe protested. "Not romantically. I mean, look at me!"

Martin did as asked, studying her with a puzzled look. "What do you mean, Chloe? Why should he not be interested in you? Any man would be lucky to win you for a wife."

"You have to say that because you are my brother. But I am too short, and too..." she waved her hands helplessly in the general vicinity of her bust, feeling the heat rise to her cheeks at the thought of discussing the curves that had so offended Uncle Swithin. "My shape is not ladylike, Martin." She lowered her voice, though there was no one to hear her but Martin. "Uncle Swithin said I looked like a barmaid, and that no gentleman would ever make me an honorable offer."

Martin muttered something under his breath that he would not repeat when Chloe said she hadn't heard it.

"Not something I should have said in front of a lady. Look, Chloe, Uncle Swithin was a bit peculiar. You know that, don't you? Ignore anything he said about your..." He flushed red. "He was odd about women. He blamed the women, but he was the problem." He picked up the papers in front of him, rifling them and dropping them edge first on the table to straighten the pile, keeping his eyes from meeting hers. "He liked curvy women, Chloe. Most men do. He had impure thoughts, and they made him feel guilty. Do you understand what I am saying?"

Chloe thought she did. It was a nauseating thought. To distract herself and Martin, she returned to the main point. "Do you seriously think Lord Dom might really be interested in me? To court, I mean?"

"It seems so," Martin said. "Has he asked to meet you again?"

"To take me walking," Chloe admitted.

"Do you want to go?" Martin asked. "Or do you want me to warn him off?"

"Warn him off?"

Martin sighed. "I am your brother. If you have a suitor who is objectionable to you, it is my job to warn him off."

Chloe blushed. Lord Dom was not objectionable. Not in the slightest. "No. I do not want you to warn him off."

"Well, then." Martin shrugged. "Go walking and see what happens."

# CHAPTER 5

The bustle of York had been startling to Chloe, whose entire life had been lived in the country. Since she'd left the Seahaven household eight years ago, her social circle had comprised her aunt and uncle, Martin, and the servants and tenants on Martin's estate, Uncle Swithin having alienated all of the neighbors by sermonizing against them.

In the past three years, she had been able to make several brief visits to the Seahaven ladies in their household in the village of Starbrook. But their lives were as constrained by their money woes as hers had been by her uncle's peculiarities.

York's size, its variety, the number of activities available to a gently born lady—all of these were a revelation. She had thought her life one of giddy pleasure before Lady Seahaven took over her social calendar. Now, it had become a whirlwind of calls, walks, rides and entertainments.

Even the work for their ball and a couple of formal dinners—one at the Seahaven residence and one at her own—was sociable. So many women were involved that it couldn't help but be a time for talking and laughter, and for cementing friendships.

Lord Dom added to the excitement. Every day, he managed to

sequester a little of her time. One day a walk. The next day a visit to an art gallery she had mentioned. The day after ices with her half-sisters, who were delirious with joy at the attention their sisters' suitors saw fit to bestow upon them.

Every day, he had a treat for Rosario, who—with a strong leash and a coat with no pockets—was frequently included in Chloe's outings. Most days, he also had something for her. A flower. A book of poetry. An article about The Habeas Corpus Act.

Lord Dom was courting her. She was almost sure of it. Not that he spent his time in flowery flirtation, and a good thing, too. She much preferred his mix of sensible conversation and cheerful jests. Instead, he indicated his intentions by his diligent presence.

Every day, he asked about Lady Seahaven's plans for her afternoon and evening, and he managed, somehow, to obtain invitations to most of them. If there was to be dancing, he asked for two of her sets. If the entertainment required them to be seated, he was so frequently to be found in the chair beside her that the Seahaven ladies took to saving it for him.

Other gentlemen showed an interest, too. She did not have enough hours in the day for the walks and rides to which she was invited. She only ever sat out a dance when her feet were sore, and then some gentleman usually begged the favor of sitting with her.

They were not just overflow admirers from the Seahaven daughters, and she could acquit them of being after her fortune, since she did not have one, only a modest dowry. Though many of their compliments struck her as insincere or just plain ridiculous, and flirtation made her uncomfortable, she was forced to conclude that at least some of the gentlemen who pursued her did so because they found something about her attractive, especially when two of them proposed marriage.

And Martin proved to be right. The way that men's eyes gravitated to her décolletage and then heated suggested that many men did like curvy women. Lord Dom never stared at her chest. While she did not want him to be so offensive as to examine her figure in public, she could not help but wonder whether he found her curves attractive.

Of all the men who sought her attention, Lord Dom was the only one who had captured hers, but the Seahaven ball came and went, and he still said nothing to confirm that he wanted her for his bride.

Dom wasn't sure of his next step. He had met Chloe just before she had burst forth on the York scene, where she was an immediate success. Of course, she was. Quite apart from her luscious figure, she was pretty, intelligent, charming, unassuming, and altogether delightful.

Dom was not the only one to be enchanted. Chloe had at least three or four other serious suitors, all taller, more handsome, and wealthier than Dom, and without a question-mark over their birth. So far, Dom seemed to be the favorite, but he lived in fear of being supplanted by a rival.

The bold courage that had won him his army nickname urged him to beg for her hand, to secure her as his bride before someone else could do so. He had known her for only a short time, but something in him had screamed 'this one' from the very first, and every meeting since had confirmed the instinct.

His rational self urged caution. It had, after all, been only sixteen days. Even if she did seem to prefer him as escort and dance partner, that didn't mean she thought of marriage. Though she had come for the Season, which argued for a willingness to choose a husband. But she had told him herself she was only in York to spend time with her sisters, and because her brother had insisted.

He tossed the options back and forth as he walked to the livery stable to pick up the curricle and pair he had hired for an excursion a couple of days after the ball. Propose and risk rejection. Carry on as he was and allow someone else to gain the lady's attention. He had to find a middle way.

As always, he was alert to his surroundings; a habit from a decade at war. He ducked his head to hide his face in the shadow of his hat brim as his brother Pevenwood came down the steps of a building on the other side of the street, and stopped on the pavement to address his companion, the man Dom was convinced was Gary.

Dom hadn't seen them since avoiding them the day he had rescued Chloe in the alley. What were they doing in York? What would they say if he crossed the road and introduced himself? Would they deny the acquaintance? Embrace him as a long-lost brother? He snorted his disbelief. Not the latter, he was sure.

The pair of them strolled off together down the street in the opposite direction to Dom's. Let them go. At least they were not participating in the York Season, for if they were, he would have seen them.

A man passed his brothers and walked towards him. Lord Tavistock, Chloe's brother. Dom did want to see Tavistock. He might have some insight into his sister's feelings, though whether he would share that insight with Dom remained to be seen.

Tavistock crossed the street, and Dom moved to intercept him. "Tavistock! Good afternoon! May I walk with you?"

Tavistock returned the greeting. "Good day, Finchley." He moved obligingly to one side of the path to give Dom room to walk beside him. "I'm told you are escorting my sister to some sort of a garden party this afternoon."

"Yes. We are meeting Lady Seahaven's party, so Mrs. Swithin thought she might be excused."

Tavistock sighed. "Aunt Swithin is... I'll tell you, Finchley. I'm more grateful than I can say for Lady Seahaven. Do you have sisters?"

That was an awkward question to answer. "My mother had no daughters," Dom replied, cautiously. How much did Tavistock know about Dom's family history?

The young lord proved that he'd heard the rumors with his next remark. "Of course. I had forgotten the claim that you are Haverford's get. I hope I don't offend by mentioning it?"

Tavistock obviously shared a family tendency to blurt socially questionable truths. Since Dom found it amusing in Mrs. Swithin and endearing in Chloe, he might as well accept it in Tavistock, too.

Better that than the usual nattering behind his back. Dom had walked in on many a conversation that turned mute then started up on another topic, and he was familiar with sly innuendos accompanied by smug glances. But few people referred matter-of-factly to his dubious parentage as if it was no more significant a detail than his eye color or his taste in cravat knots.

Tavistock continued, oblivious to Dom's reaction. "Haverford acknowledges three half-sisters, does he not? But they would be his responsibility rather than yours. Sisters are a worry, Finchley."

"So says Haverford," Dom agreed. "Being concerned about a sister's wellbeing and her future happiness seems to go with being a brother."

"Precisely. And now all these men want my permission to marry her, and most of them older and better connected than I am. How am I to know what is best for her? I have never understood Chloe."

Dom took the news like a punch in the gut. "All these men?" he managed to choke out.

"Two," Tavistock amended. "And you, I have to suppose, since you are the most persistent of them all. You are courting my sister, are you not, Finchley?"

Dom nodded. "I am," he admitted. "I came to York to run an errand for Haverford while I was in the area, but I am staying because I met Chl— Miss Tavistock. I have no idea how she feels about me, however."

Tavistock shrugged. "No point in asking me," he said. "She refused the other two, and both seemed eligible enough to me. I think she enjoys your company, but she has always been adamant she will not marry. She hasn't told me she has changed her mind."

"Then you have no objection to my suit?" Dom persisted. They were nearly at the livery. Though he had not intended to have this conversation yet, it was good to know where he stood with Chloe's brother.

"I will tell you what I've told the other two. I will investigate anyone who is serious about her, and I will tell Chloe what I find out. But Chloe is an adult. She will make the decision. Not me."

That was fair. Dom spread his hands in a do as you please gesture. "Investigate anything you like about me. I can give you the names of my military commanders, and can instruct my solicitor and agents to provide you with information about my finances."

Tavistock stopped to face him, regarding Dom with his head tipped thoughtfully to one side. "Once you know whether my sister is interested, we shall discuss the settlements," he suggested. "Talk to her, Finchley. Tell her you want to court her. Aunt Swithin and I have both told her that you and others have marriage on your minds, but I don't think she believes it. She hasn't much confidence in her powers of attraction."

Dom nodded. It was good advice. "Thank you," he said. "I will tell her." The corner that led to the livery was a few yards down the street. "I am picking up a curricle for our outing. May I give you a lift?"

Tavistock refused, citing another engagement, and they parted at the corner. It had been a fortuitous encounter. Dom now had his middle option, and how simple it was. Talk to Chloe about his hopes and intentions, and they had half an hour's drive before them in which to begin.

# CHAPTER 6

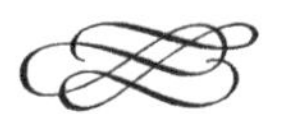

Lord Dom arrived several minutes early. Chloe saw him out of the parlor window as he talked to the urchin who was usually to be found hanging around outside the Tavistock door. The lad went to the horses' heads, and they bent to examine him, and to facilitate his caress of their necks. He was obviously fond of animals, and they returned his regard. Rosario always greeted him with enthusiasm, whenever she saw him.

Lord Dom checked his pocket watch to see how close he was to his time. Chloe was already wearing her gloves and bonnet. She picked up Rosario, making sure that the monkey's leash was firmly attached. "Lord Dom is here, Aunt Swithin. Are you sure you do not wish to come?"

"Run along with you, child. I plan to read the latest *Teatime Tattler*, and perhaps have a nap. You have a good time with your stepsisters and your young man."

Was Lord Dom her young man? He was about to knock on the door as she opened it. "Miss Tavistock! It is a lovely day for a drive. I see you have brought your hairy chaperone?"

Chloe took his hand and allowed him to aid her balance as she climbed up to the seat. "I hope you don't mind, Lord Dom. I had to leave Rosario at home this morning while I was at Lady Seahaven's writing thank-you letters, since the schoolroom party were not home to entertain her. Aunt Swithin promised to take her out and let her play in the garden, but she forgot, so the poor beast was shut in her cage from the time I left until I got home."

Lord Dom went around to his side of the curricle, took his own seat, and held out his hand for Rosario to shake, distracting the monkey from her focus on the boy with the horses. "You are very welcome, Sister Rosario." He grinned at Chloe. "She adds a certain air of adventure to our outings, do you not think?"

Chloe blushed at the sly reference to Rosario's escapades. Earlier in the week, she had climbed a tree in Tower Gardens and refused to come down until Lord Dom had borrowed a ladder from the gardeners' shed, whereupon she had climbed down the other side of the tree. If Emma and Merry had not cornered her, she would have been up another before Chloe could have reached her.

Two days ago, she had stolen an ice from a passing waiter, tasted it, then thrown it with unerring accuracy at the back of the waiter's retreating head. Lord Dom had soothed the man's irritation with a large gratuity.

Then there was the concert, where Rosario conceived a passion for the brooch on the hat of the dowager in the next row, and reached out to snatch it when Chloe became lost in the music. Had it not been for Lord Dom's quick action—the monkey's hand was within an inch of the target when he jerked her back by her leash—the ensuing apologies for Rosario's complaints would have been for a much worse offence.

"I will keep tight hold of her today," Chloe promised.

"Or I will," Lord Dom agreed. His smile warmed away her embarrassment. "She does not mean to cause mischief, I know. We will endeavor to keep her out of trouble, you and I."

He called out to the urchin who stood at the head of the horses. "Thank you, Sam." He tossed a coin to the lad, who caught it one handed without taking his eyes off the monkey. "You can let them go, now."

"I could get up behind and look after the 'orses where you and the liddy are going," Sam offered.

"Not this time, thank you," Lord Dom replied, and moved his hands in a signal to the horses, saying, "Walk on, boys."

Soon, they were clopping swiftly through the streets and out through the city gates. The estate where they were meeting Lady Seahaven was thirty minutes away. Lord Dom broke the silence. "I met with your brother today."

Chloe stiffened. Not Lord Dom, too. Two men had asked Martin for her hand in marriage, without first consulting her wishes. Martin, bless him, told them both to apply to her. One she knew as an interminable bore. She asked him why he wished to marry her, and he replied that she was a good listener. She refused him politely.

The other was charming enough, but even before he went behind her back to try to make an arrangement with Martin, she could not warm to him. His proposal was done in proper form, but with an overtone of smugness that would have argued against accepting even if she had been inclined.

She asked him the same question. He told her she was the loveliest creature he had ever seen. "Lovelier than the Seahaven Diamonds?" she asked. He colored. "In a different way," he hastened to add. "Truly, Miss Tavistock, I am convinced you will make me a good wife, and my father says I must marry."

Chloe was certain he would not make her a good husband. Her refusal appeared to take him by surprise. He tried to convince her that Martin had already agreed and her acceptance was not required. Caught out on that, he assured her that she need not have hopes of Lord Cuckoo, since everyone knew Pevenwood had cast him out when he was eighteen, so he was penniless and hanging out for a rich wife.

He, himself, did not mind that Miss Tavistock was not wealthy, he explained, since he had a large allowance from his father, which his father had promised to increase when he took a wife. She wished him luck and told him that wife would not be her.

And now Lord Dom had taken the same path, speaking to Martin as if she were property with no wishes or opinions of her own. "I did not know you had called," she told Lord Dom.

Lord Dom shook his head. "I did not call. I saw him in the street while I was on my way here and walked with him for a bit." He slowed to pass a group of girls who were half on and half off the road as they foraged in the hedgerows, filling their baskets with snippets of green. He chirruped at the horses to set them trotting again. Looking straight ahead, he added, "He assumed I was going to ask for your hand in marriage. Which I wasn't."

He wasn't? How embarrassing. How… how disappointing.

"Not from him," Lord Dom added. "Not before I'd talked to you first. I am courting you, Miss Tavistock, not your brother."

That was better. Chloe turned her head to examine his face. His eyes were firmly fixed on the road ahead, but he must have felt the weight of her regard, for he shot her a look and an anxious smile. "Did you know I was courting you? Lord Tavistock said you did not, and that I should tell you."

"I was not sure," Chloe admitted. *I hoped so*. The words occurred, but she kept them in.

Lord Dom grimaced. "I am not very good at it, it seems. I have never done this before. And then I met you."

He turned his face to her, and must have checked the horses, for they slowed to a walk. "You probably think this is all too fast. I am afraid I am rushing my fences and will take a fall. But I am more afraid that—if I hold back and say nothing—someone else will win your regard in my place." His laugh was a nervous expulsion of air. "Do you think… Could you tell me if I have a chance, Miss Tavistock? Maybe give me a hint about how to get better at this courting business?"

"I don't know," Chloe replied. When his face fell, she hastened to add, "I have never been courted before, Lord Dom. I never thought anyone would wish to marry me, but Martin insisted on this Season in York." She wanted to bounce in her seat and repeat the word 'Yes' over and over in fast succession. She resisted, and tested him with the question that had stymied the other two. "Can you perhaps tell me why you wish to marry me?"

"I think I can," Lord Dom said slowly. He looked along the road ahead as he spoke. "I was attracted before we met, when I saw you across the room at the meeting. That was to be my last engagement in Yorkshire. Then you impressed me with your courage, your sense of humor, and your quick thinking, and I wanted to stay to get to know you better."

He shot her another of those anxious glances. "But the moment of attraction came first. I don't know if I can explain it better than to say it felt like recognition. Something in me saw you and said 'that's her'." Another of those short barks of laughter. "It sounds mad, does it not? I am glad I listened, though, for every meeting has confirmed my first impression. You are the woman I can picture spending the rest of my life with."

He looked so apprehensive that Chloe blurted what she was thinking. "It was the same with me, Dom."

He dropped the reins to turn to her and take both of her hands. "Chloe! May I call you Chloe?" The horses, his soft control suddenly absent, tossed their heads and quickened their pace. Dom had to grab for the reins again to exert his will on them.

His soft laugh was exultant. "I lose all my senses when I am with you."

Chloe, coming to her own senses just in time to grab at Rosario's harness as the monkey started a flying leap for a passing tree, knew exactly what he meant.

"We turn here," Dom told her, suiting action to word and setting the horses between two ornate gateposts. "We can talk more on the way home, Chloe. My darling."

Pevenwood and Gary were at the garden party. Dom saw them almost as soon as he and Chloe arrived, as they looked around for Lady

Seahaven's party. He steered Chloe down another path. "I do not particularly wish to meet those two people," he told her.

Chloe visibly restrained herself from peering around him. "Who are they?" she asked, then corrected herself. "Never mind. You do not have to explain yourself to me."

"Do I not?" Dom smiled down into her lovely eyes. "If I am planning to ask you to share your life with me, I think you do have a right to an explanation."

He took a deep breath, wondering where to start. Chloe, that wonderful woman, said nothing, giving him the time to compose himself.

He had better start with the cause of the breach between himself and the family he was raised in. "Your brother knows about my family scandal. Has he told you?"

"Aunt Swithin told us both. She reads the scandal columns in the news sheets, and she remembers your... the marquess's divorce case."

"Attempted divorce case." It had changed his life. Or, rather, the fight between Pevenwood and his wife had changed Dom's life, but the public application for divorce and ensuing trial had let the whole world in on the secret.

"I was ten years old. My brother Totters, the heir, must have been eighteen, for he is six years older than Gary, my next brother. Gary and I were born only eighteen months apart, and were the firmest of friends. We never saw much of the marquess and our mother, or of Totters. But we had each other."

Rosario, who had been sitting on Chloe's shoulder, leapt across to his and embraced his face with one long cold hand.

Dom swallowed the lump in his throat and continued. "The marquess and our mother were seldom in the same place at the same time, and when they were together, they fought. Usually about the marquess's affairs. In one of those fights, Mother told the marquess that I was the son of the Duke of Haverford, and not his son at all." Dom had heard them yelling at one another.

Chloe did not need to hear the detail—that she'd found herself with child after a brief dalliance with Haverford, undertaken in revenge for one of Pevenwood's periodic infatuations. That she'd coaxed Pevenwood back into her bed and then convinced him that the ensuing child was premature.

"Pevenwood and Haverford had never liked one another. I think he could have ignored anyone else. When my mother confronted him with the affair, he threw her out and me with her. And he began divorce proceedings. After they failed, he had to take us back, but by then, he'd turned Gary against me. They called me Cuckoo. Gary started it, and even the servants took it up."

Gary's defection still hurt, all these years later. More, even, than his mother's. "Mother didn't stay. She moved to another of Pevenwood's houses, and I never saw her again. She died three years later." He fell silent, remembering those days.

"Dom," Chloe said, squeezing his arm in a warm gesture of support, "I am so sorry. No one deserves to be treated like that. From the sounds, the marquess and his wife were both guilty of disloyalty to one another and cruelty to you. And your brother, who lost his best friend too, just because he wanted to please his father."

Dom had not thought about the position in which Gary found himself. "I suppose you are right, my darling. Trust you to see it from both sides." He took a deep breath. "Anyway, the people I was avoiding are Totters and Gary. My brothers the Marquess of Pevenwood and Lord Pythagoras Finchley. I haven't seen them or heard from them since I turned eighteen."

Chloe dimpled when she smiled. "Gary is Pythagoras? I take it Totters is Aristotle, then. Who was the enthusiast for Greek philosophers?"

"Pevenwood," Dom admitted. "He insisted on the names, or so I am told, and my mother on the nicknames. "Look. There is Lady Seahaven."

Chloe turned obediently in the direction he indicated as Rosario clearly decided the emotional crisis was over and clambered back to Chloe's shoulder. "You should talk to them, you know. Perhaps you may never again be friends with your brothers, but the marquess is dead and so is the old Duke of Haverford. You brothers are all adults now, and you deserve a chance to see if you can put the old hurts behind you."

"More wisdom," Dom commented. "I will hope our children take after their mother, Chloe."

"You haven't proposed to me, yet," Chloe pointed out.

"We are about to be surrounded by your stepsisters," Dom said. "This might not be the best time."

# CHAPTER 7

Rosario was edgy today. It wasn't the people who insisted on cooing at her, and offering her fingers to hold and twigs or ribbons or bits of food to grasp. Chloe had taken Rosario to several events where the monkey's admirers had thronged even thicker, and she seemed to bask in the attention.

But today, between preening and showing off, she tried to edge away from Chloe, tugging at her leash as if hoping to find it detached from the person at the other end. Her eyes kept scanning the landscape. She chittered to herself from time to time, a plaintive worried sound.

In the end, when even taking her for a run across the lawn did not rid Rosario of the jitters, Dom suggested a row on the lake.

Several little pleasure boats were tethered to the low dock that edged the expanse of water. Dom led Chloe past the punts, a couple of canoes, and the larger row boats. The one he chose was just big enough for the three of them.

He handed Chloe down into the boat while Rosario clung to her, staring wide-eyed at the water and commenting bitterly in a shrill gabble. "It will be fun," Chloe assured the monkey, who was not convinced, and sent up a loud screech when Dom made the boat rock as he dropped into it.

He fumbled briefly with the oars, then pulled them strongly away from the dock. "Gary and I used to spend most summers on the lake at Bethancourt," he commented. "I had forgotten the trick of it, but it comes back."

"Did you always want to be a soldier?" Chloe asked.

"Yes, for as long as I can remember. Gary and I had complex battles with battalions of soldiers back in nursery days. We planned to join up together and win glory for King and country." His wistful smile faded, and his face hardened. "After Pevenwood threw me out, I thought I was going to have to take the King's shilling."

Chloe gasped. "He threw you out?"

Dom's shrug belied the hurt that lingered in his hazel eyes. "Perhaps an exaggeration. It was my eighteenth birthday. He said I could continue to live in one of his houses until I reached my majority, but I could choose one he didn't visit. He said I was no son of his, and that he'd more than fulfilled any obligation he might have had to his wife's brat by paying for my education until I could stand on my own two feet. I asked if I might have the money to purchase a commission, and he turned me down flat. So, I walked out."

"The old fiend!" Chloe wished he was here. She would—she would push him in the lake, that is what she would do. "What a nasty old man! Well done you for becoming such a good person despite him!"

"I am not a saint," Dom warned. "But I will try to be a good man for you, Chloe. I can promise, if nothing else, that I want a true marriage, where both parties are faithful. Where they respect one another, and look after one another's interests." The wistful smile returned. "And I would like to be an involved father."

It sounded appealing. Chloe barely remembered her own father. Her step-father Lord Seahaven was more absent than cruel. He ignored all the females in the nursery, and it was well known that his only interest in children was in siring an heir. As for Uncle Swithin, he readily explained to anyone who would listen that a family was a yoke around the neck of a godly man, and his cross in life was to be burdened with a wife and his nephew's children.

She returned Dom's smile. "Did you, then? Take the King's shilling and win a commission in the field?"

"I went to all the relations I could think of. As a last throw of the dice, I even went to the Duke of Haverford, and was being refused an audience when the Marquis of Aldridge arrived and invited me to talk to him, instead. He purchased my commission and paid for my kit. He said it was the least he could do for a brother."

"That was good of him. And you have stayed in touch. He is the duke, now, isn't he? His seal was on your letter." Aunt Swithin had often read bits from the gossip columns about the duke when he was the Marquis of Aldridge. He had married two years ago and disappointed many avid readers by becoming a devoted husband.

Whatever his past, Chloe was predisposed to like him for his kindness to Dom.

"That's right. Haverford asked me to go to a few reform meetings while I was up in Yorkshire to see my estate."

He had continued rowing throughout their conversation, and as he made that remark, he gave a strong stroke with the oars that propelled the boat into the cool shade of trees that hung over the water from a small ornamental island, one of several that dotted the lake.

Chloe felt a tug as the leash slipped through her hand and Rosario took a flying leap from her shoulder up into a tree. The monkey was gone in a fraction of a second, leaving behind madly swishing branches and the rustle of leaves.

"I let her go!" Chloe cried. "Oh, Dom, I am so sorry, but we must land and look for her."

Dom made another powerful sweep with the oars. "Of course. I'll circle the island and see where we can land. Don't worry, darling. She won't be able to go far, and we'll soon have her back safe."

Finding a place where they could get ashore proved to be harder than Dom expected. The island had no handy little jetty; not even a flat area of dry bank at a suitable height to step safely out of the boat.

Most of it was heavily wooded, with twisty willows that hung over the water's edge so that they could not get close enough to the bank to clamber onto land, and the few clear patches were on banks higher than Dom's head. One of those had the remnants of a landing place. Random piles stuck forlornly out of the water, a couple with scraps of beam and bits of decking still clinging. A stair must have led up the near vertical bank, for the top of it hung crazily in midair, a good eight feet above the water.

Dom rowed on, until they had circumnavigated the island.

Chloe was anxiously peering into the trees. "This is where we started, yes?"

"It is," Dom confirmed. "I'm going back to where the wharf used to be. I can tie the boat to the posts that are in the water and climb the bank."

She nodded. "I am so sorry to be so much trouble."

*Uncle Swithin strikes again.* Dom figured the old man was responsible for Chloe's habit of apologizing. "You are no trouble, Chloe. Rosario is just a tiny bit of trouble, I'll concede. On the other hand, she has given me an excuse to spend a bit longer alone with you."

Her smile was a perfect reward. Though it occurred to him that a kiss would be even more perfect, even if more perfect than perfect was grammatically impossible, as one of his teachers used to insist. He was thinking nonsense, but her smile turned his brain to mush, so he might as well get used to being nonsensical, for he hoped to make her smile often.

Just ahead, they would turn and reach another face of the island, the one with the high banks. Dom began to ease up on his left stroke and deepen the right, looking over his shoulder to confirm his direction.

"Wait!" Chloe commanded.

He looked back towards her, and past her in the direction she was peering.

"Do you see?" she asked.

Yes. Movement in the willows behind them; a slender shape that ran out along a branch on all four legs, tail held high.

"Rosario!"

The monkey checked and gazed towards them, then dropped into a thicker patch of young willow withies and out of sight. Even as Dom turned the boat, the foliage began a violent shaking and Rosario's screech rang across the water towards them, angry with an edge of panic.

"Something is wrong," Chloe diagnosed.

Dom focused on his rowing. "Tell me when I'm around ten yards out," he said.

Somewhere in the distance, he was aware of a high voice shouting "Pepper", and idly wondered what was going on.

"Ten yards to go," Chloe warned.

Dom backed oars, feathering them slightly so that the boat glided into the clump of willows that still shook with Rosario's struggles.

And they were struggles. When they managed to clear enough foliage out of the way to disclose the monkey, they found that she had caught her harness. Somehow, two branches at an angle to one another had slid up between the monkey and the leather then sprung apart, so she hung in the air, head down. All of her twists and turns were making things worse, not better.

She bared her teeth at them as they approached, and screeched again.

"That is no language for a young lady," Dom told her, sternly.

Chloe cooed soothing nonsense until the monkey calmed enough to allow Chloe to stroke her. That gave Dom the opportunity to examine the offending branches. They were too thick to bend and too green to break. And the knife he had with him was not big enough to cut through.

"I will have to undo the buckles, Chloe," he said. "Will you hold her still?"

That wasn't easy, either. At some point since she left them, Rosario had been in water, and the leather was swollen and stiff. She wouldn't keep still, either, constantly twisting to see what he was doing.

At last, the second tongue slipped free of the second buckle, and Chloe was able to lift the monkey out of the harness. One armhole held the harness to the tree, but a lazy stroke with an oar took the boat the length of the branch, harness and all.

"Back to shore?" Dom asked Chloe, who was occupied taking off the monkey's wet jacket, drying her with a handkerchief, and soothing her with a constant stream of words, both endearments and scolds.

"Yes, please. I need to get Rosario warm. I am sorry..."

"No apologies needed, Chloe. When we left home with her, I expected an adventure, and this has been a relatively scatheless one." Though he was coward enough to hope that the monkey would calm as she grew older, since the constant disruption to social occasions could grow wearisome if repeated. Perhaps he should look around for a companion for the beast, a kind of a personal groom, a monkey keeper. That way, Chloe could keep her pet, and he could keep his wits.

"Your brothers are waiting on the deck," Chloe told him. "And that's odd. The urchin who lurks near our house, the one who held the horses, he is there, too."

Dom glanced over his shoulder. The boy Sam, with whom Dom had struck up an acquaintance while waiting for Chloe, was peering fiercely at Chloe. No. At Rosario.

Dom's battle instincts stirred.

At that moment, Rosario screeched again, and took a flying leap into the water. Chloe lurched after her, flinging herself against the side of the little boat. Dom leaned the other way to balance the boat, just as Chloe realized she was tipping it and threw herself backwards.

Too far. She went straight over the side, and the boat rocked back the other way. Dom stood up and dived into the water after Chloe.

It would have been a spectacular and brave rescue, if the water had been more than three and a half feet deep. As it was, by the time he reached her, she had found her feet.

"Oh, Dom," she said, her face moving with strong emotion. "This time, you have to let me apologize!" she insisted.

He grinned. "A somewhat wetter end to our boat excursion than I intended," he admitted. "Come on. We had better go and find your monkey."

He held up his hand, as if he was about to lead her into a stately dance, and she raised a dripping arm and placed her hand in his. Gallant lady. From the dock, a few yards away, Pevenwood commented, "Well played, miss."

Beyond him, Rosario was hugging and being hugged by the boy Sam, the monkey's chittering and the boy's murmurs mingling in an ecstatic greeting.

Gary knelt at the edge of the walk, reaching out a hand, and Pevenwood came up beside him to offer another. Lady Seahaven hurried towards them with several of her stepdaughters in her wake.

Dom released Chloe's hand into Pevenwood's, and she lifted her other hand to Gary.

"Chloe, allow me to present the Marquess of Pevenwood and Lord Pythogaras Finchley," Dom said, as he cupped his hands above the water where Chloe could see and then sunk them for her to put her foot into. "Gentlemen, Miss Tavistock, my intended." A little presumptuous of him, but she did plan to accept when he proposed, did she not?

Pevenwood and Gary pulled and Dom lifted. Chloe, little elf that she was, rose like Venus from the water, and Lady Seahaven was there to wrap the glories displayed by wet cotton in a shawl and hurry her away to the house.

"Lord Dom," she said, over her shoulder, "will you deal with the monkey and then get yourself up to the house to be dried?"

Dom regarded his brothers with wary interest. Up close, they seemed well. Pevenwood looked much like a younger version of his sire, though the previous Pevenwood had never worn such a benevolent smile. "You are a hard man to track down, Dom. Gary and I thought we might see you when you arrived in London. Then we heard you'd gone away to Yorkshire. We went out to your estate, but they said you were in York."

"I thought..." Dom swallowed. "The marquess said the whole family wanted me gone, and that I need never bother speaking to any of you again."

Pevenwood shrugged. "That marquess is dead."

"Stupid selfish old man," Gary added. "We are your brothers. He had no right to speak for us." He flushed. It looked like anger, rather than embarrassment. "He told us that you'd walked out, saying you never wanted to see any of us again. That you'd refused an allowance from him and gone to Haverford's family."

"Lies," Dom told him.

"We know," said Pevenwood. "We found correspondence after he died. Dom, we know we didn't stand up for you when you were a boy, but we would like the chance to make amends."

"Me especially," Gary said. "We were friends once, and I always regretted being mean to you. Even while I was doing it."

Dom shivered, and Pevenwood whipped off his elegant coat. "Take off your coat and put this on. We'll have to get you up to the house before you take cold."

Unlikely. Dom had been much wetter and much colder more times than he could count while on campaign. "Just a moment," he said, turning to look for Sam and Rosario.

The boy was legging it across the lawn, the monkey clutched in his arms. Dom took off in pursuit, and a moment later Gary passed him. He easily outdistanced Dom and soon overtook the boy. "Here he is, Dom. Is he stealing your monkey?"

The boy let loose with a string of imprecations, within which was the claim that the monkey belonged to him, and not to Dom or the lady. "She's mine," the boy insisted. "My dad took her, and now he's gone, so Pepper is mine, again."

Pevenwood strolled up, still carrying Dom's coat. "Bring the boy and the monkey up to the house, and we'll get it sorted while Dom changes into dry clothes."

~

"Sam is the son of the thief who was arrested," Dom explained to Chloe and her twin step-sisters, who had come along for propriety as they rode back to York in Pevenwood's carriage. Gary, with Pevenwood for company, was driving the hired curricle back to the stable, and they were going to have dinner with Dom after he had escorted the ladies home and changed into clothes that fitted better than the ones borrowed from their host.

"Sam was working as a groom—he says his mother made him promise not to turn out like his father. When he found out that his father was in prison and the monkey was missing, he left his job to come and find her. He has been watching your house for a chance to steal her back."

Chloe looked up towards the roof. "I suppose if she is his, he has a right to keep her."

"As to that," Dom said, "I had an idea. He needs a job, and we've already seen that he is good with animals. And Rosario—Sam calls her Pepper—needs a full-time keeper to take care of her when you can't. So, I've hired him. He'll be coming home with you, Chloe, if that is acceptable."

Ivy clapped her hands. "Chloe said that you give the best tokens of appreciation, Lord Dom, and that is the finest yet. How clever!"

Chloe looked worried. "Is it proper?" she asked.

Dom smiled at her concern. "There is a way to make it proper, my love. A certain question. Are you ready to hear it from me yet?"

Chloe blushed, and looked up at him from under her lashes. "You mean right now this minute?"

"We could sing loudly, put our fingers in our ears and look out the window," offered Iris.

"Thank you for the kind offer," Dom told her, "but it might take an edge off the romance." To Chloe he suggested, "Tomorrow morning?"

"Noon," she said, firmly. "Come at noon and ask your question, and I shall give you your answer."

From the curve of her lips and the sparkle of her eye, it would be the one he longed for.

# EPILOGUE

Chloe was being dressed for her wedding. She was to be married in the Minster, by the Archbishop of York in person. It was all very grand, but—as Haverford's duchess pointed out—she and Dom were all that mattered, not the surroundings or the illustrious marriage celebrant and congregation.

The duchess was helping her prepare this morning. She and the duke had set off for York as soon as they had received Dom's letter announcing his betrothal, and the couple's intention to wed in the week after the York races.

They had picked the date and location to make it easy for the Seahaven ladies to attend the wedding, though Martin suggested marrying in the parish church near the Tavistock estate, and Pevenwood offered to host the wedding at his own home, where Dom had spent most of his childhood. Gary put in a bid for London, where Dom would be able to present his wife to the *ton*, and both Pevenwood and Martin liked that idea.

Dom was only half-joking when he suggested they run off in the night to his own estate and wed there, just the two of them.

Chloe told him it had to be York. She wanted Susana present to see Chloe in the dress Susana had designed and made for her. She wanted Doro to stand up with her. She wanted Patience and all her stepdaughters, especially Emma and Merry, to be there to share her day.

And now they were here, in her bedchamber, as many as could squeeze into the room. Susana stood by with the gown. It was a confection of peach with an overdress of silver net, embroidered with pearls and trimmed with Brussels lace.

Emma and Merry perched side-by-side on the bed, in their best clothes, watching everything that was happening. Doro and Barbara stood over Chloe, dressing her hair while Patience and the duchess hovered close by to offer suggestions and comments.

When Pevenwood accepted that Chloe and Dom were adamant, he announced that he would hold a grand wedding breakfast for them after the ceremony. Then the Haverfords sailed up the coast from London in the duke's private yacht, landing at Hull. The duke also wanted to host his half-brother's wedding breakfast, and assured Chloe and Dom that his estate outside of York would be a much better venue than Pevenwood's hotel.

Pevenwood pointed out that Haddow Hall was at least an hour from York, whereas his hotel was just around the corner from the little church of Holy Trinity, where the couple planned to be married.

The marquess and the duke descended into a wrangle, all the more intense for being conducted in polite gentlemanly drawls, until Her Grace informed them both that Lord Tavistock would host the wedding breakfast for his own sister, and they could find something else to do to show that they respected and esteemed the half-brother they shared.

Whereupon, Pevenwood and Haverford offered to go together to the Archbishop to acquire the necessary common license, and before anyone else knew what they were about, they had arranged for York Minster and the Archbishop.

Susana and Doro settled the gown over Chloe's head, being careful not to disturb her coronet of flowers or a single curl or pin in her coiffure. Chloe smiled at the memory of Pevenwood's and Haverford's smug faces when they returned with the news. Dom didn't like having his own arrangements superseded, but admitted to Chloe that he was actually delighted.

"It will be something to tell our children, when we bring them into York to show them the sights." He grinned. "And I must admit that it's nice that my brothers wanted to do this for us."

Dom waited in a pew at the front of the quire before the main altar in York Minster. He had arrived fifteen minutes before the time appointed for the ceremony, and he was sure at least an hour had passed. "What if something has happened to her," he muttered to Gary, who was standing up with him as his best man.

Gary repeated the assurance he had given three times already. "Nothing has happened." He once again checked his pocket watch. "She actually is late this time," he acknowledged. "By two minutes. You're very anxious to get leg shackled, brother."

"You'll see when it is your turn," Dom told him.

Gary clapped a dramatic hand to his heart and fell back a step. "Cursed! My long-lost brother has cursed me!"

Dom glared, but his lips twitched. Like most bachelors, Gary had no idea that a prediction of marriage was a blessing, not a curse. Dom couldn't wait to make Chloe his and begin his life with her at his side.

A stir around him had him turning in his seat. The Duchess of Haverford was taking her place beside her husband. The Dowager Countess of Seahaven, Lady Susana Bigglesworth and Lady Barbara Bigglesworth were joining the others of their party in their pew.

"She's here." The whisper was from the footman who had been posted in the porch to watch for the bride's arrival. The Archbishop appeared from somewhere and crossed to stand facing the congregation.

Dom took his place in front of the cleric, with Gary beside him, and watched as Emma and Merry walked towards him, one after the other, their faces solemn. Doro followed. Dom saw none of them. His gaze was drawn to the beloved figure behind, being conducted up the aisle by her brother Martin.

Her lovely eyes met his and clung, and an endless moment later she was before him, placing her hand in his as the Archbishop and Martin exchanged the prescribed words. At least, Dom assumed they followed the format. His senses were filled with his bride.

"You are beautiful," he murmured to her.

The Archbishop was explaining the purpose of marriage. Dom allowed the sonorous voice to drone on while he basked in the presence of his beloved. He collected himself in time to make the responses required of him, to speak the vows that bound him to her; to thrill to her voice speaking her vows in return.

To think it had been barely six weeks since they met. He had arrived in York to carry out a task for his illustrious half-brother, determined to leave immediately after for his new estate, to see if it could become the place of his own for which he yearned.

So much had happened since then. He met Chloe and fell in love. In winning her, he had also gained a whole family—not just her brother and her aunt, but her Seahaven connections. He had been reconciled with Pevenwood and Gary.

Dom had found his place. Not his estate. Not even his new status as the acknowledged brother of both the Marquess of Pevenwood and the Duke of Haverford, an acknowledgement refused by the fathers of both those gentlemen, and all the more precious for the love with which it was tendered.

His place was at Chloe's side. As the Archbishop proclaimed them husband and wife, he smiled down into her loving eyes. After ten years of roaming, Lord Dom had come home.

THE END

In my books, the dukes of Haverford and their legitimate sons have been scattering children on the other side of the blanket since time immemorial. Dom is one who had the good fortune to be raised in wealth. In others of my books, you can meet the two legitimate sons of the previous duke, less fortunate offspring without his acknowledgement, and his wife, the Duchess of Haverford, who has made it her mission to find and help those connected by blood to her husband and sons.

The Duke of Haverford we meet briefly in this book is Dom's half-brother, formerly the Marquis of Aldridge. He appears in many of my books, most notably *A Baron for Becky,* where his career as a rakehell begins to deviate from the trajectory taken by his wicked father. In *Melting Matilda,* we see him as loving older brother of the heroine, and in *To Tame the Wild Rake,* the fourth in the series *The Return of the Mountain King,* he finally gets to be the hero, winning his forever lady.

Dom's and Chloe's story may become part of a new series about the unacknowledged children of the old duke.

# SOCIAL MEDIA FOR JUDE KNIGHT

You can learn more about Jude Knight at these social media links:

**Website and blog:** http://judeknightauthor.com/
**Subscribe to newsletter:** http://judeknightauthor.com/newsletter/
**Bookshop:** https://judeknight.selz.com/
**Facebook:** https://www.facebook.com/JudeKnightAuthor/
**Twitter:** https://twitter.com/JudeKnightBooks
**Pinterest:** https://nz.pinterest.com/jknight1033/
**BookBub:** https://www.bookbub.com/profile/jude-knight
**Books + Main Bites:** https://bookandmainbites.com/JudeKnightAuthor
**Amazon author page:** https://www.amazon.com/Jude-Knight/e/B00RG3SG7I
**Goodreads:** https://www.goodreads.com/author/show/8603586.Jude_Knight
**LinkedIn:** https://linkedin.com/in/jude-knight-465557166/

# ABOUT JUDE KNIGHT

Jude Knight always wanted to be a novelist, but life got in the way for decades and she nearly lost the dream. She wrote a thousand beginnings, but it took a huge life event to shove her into writing an ending. That was in 2014. Eight novels and counting later, plus short stories and novellas galore, she's living her dream: writing historical fiction with a large helping of romance, more than a dash of suspense, and a sprinkling of humor.

Learn more about Jude at:
Website and blog: http://judeknightauthor.com/

# I'LL ALWAYS BE YOURS

ELLA QUINN

I'll Always Be Yours
By Ella Quinn

All her life Miss Harriett Staunton believed she was the natural daughter of an earl. In the merchant society in which she was raised, that only garnered improper proposals. Knowing she would never wed, she moved to York, far away from her London family.
Lord Sextus Trevor needs to wed. Unbeknownst to him, his father has arranged a marriage. But before he is even told about the betrothal, he's whisked off to York, where he meets Harriett Staunton and must find a way to defy his father.

# PROLOGUE

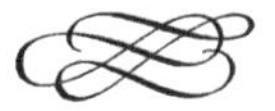

*March, Somerset Castle, Gloucestershire.*

"Belling!" The Duke of Somerset drummed his fingers impatiently on his desk. "Where are you, man?"

"Here, your grace." His secretary entered his study carrying a sheaf of papers. "I have found the owner of the land you want and..." Belling took a breath and let it out... "he has a marriageable daughter."

Somerset narrowed his eyes at his secretary. "Who is it?"

The other man's face lost some of its ruddy color. "Minor gentry, your grace. But I am convinced he will give up the land as the dowry for his eldest daughter."

That would have to do. The piece of land in question would be a fine addition to the dukedom's holdings in Lincolnshire. "What do you know about the chit?"

Belling juggled the papers, pulling one out from the middle. "She is twenty-five. Very popular in the local market town and area for her charitable work. She has kept house for her father since her mother died." He glanced up. "I'm afraid that she has never been out and has very few of the accomplishments needed for the wife of a foreign officer. She also shows no indication that she wishes to change her circumstances."

"I care nothing about her desires. Sextus will wed her. She will agree. I have received word he'll be back in England to look for a wife. This girl will do as well as anyone else."

"Yes, your grace." Belling straightened his papers. "I shall begin the negotiations immediately."

# CHAPTER 1

*April, London docks.*

"What the deuce?" Lord Sextus Trevor had no sooner left the ship upon which he'd arrived than he was bundled into a large traveling coach with a young matron he thought he remembered and a gentleman he didn't know at all. Apart from her most unusual turquoise eyes, the lady looked a great deal like Sextus's mother, Catherine, Duchess of Somerset.

Convinced he wasn't being abducted he settled onto the comfortably padded bench. "I take it we are related?"

Her eyes began to twinkle as a wide smile graced her face. "I am your sister Thalia. This…" she motioned with her hand to the gentleman "…is my husband Giles."

"Ah, yes. I received letters about your marriage." Sextus looked at the baby sleeping on her lap. It couldn't be more than a few months, if that. "But where are Hawksworth and Meg?" Sextus's eldest brother and his wife, the Marquis and Marchioness of Hawksworth. "I understood I would be staying with them."

Giles, the Duke of Kendal, placed a protective arm around Thalia. "You were until Meg received a letter informing her that the duke had arranged a marriage for you. We are ensuring that you never receive the letter he sent to you informing you of your pending betrothal."

Thalia closed her eyes and shuddered. "Be thankful you are of age, and he must have your agreement to any marriage."

Considering the truly horrifying marriages the duke, their father, had arranged for two of his sisters, one to a peer who had killed three of his wives, and the other to a pox-ridden duke in Scotland, merely so that he could have property he wanted, Sextus had to agree. "I am indeed fortunate. But if I am not to remain in Town, where are we going?"

His sister smiled again. "You will be attending the Season in York. Giles and I are taking you to Marcella and Octavius. Friends of Meg's, Viscount and Viscountess Beaumont, who live just north of York, and have leased a town house large enough to accommodate all of you. Lady Beaumont is very familiar with the local gentry and peers in the area. Granted, anyone who has a daughter to launch or who can afford it will be in Town, but she is convinced you will be able to find someone suitable."

Sextus regarded Kendal's amused mien. "Do you not have an estate somewhere in the area?"

"We do." Kendal stretched out his legs. "But having a duke and duchess attending the York Season is bound to cause more comment than an earl and countess who are known to live in the area. Neither Marcella nor Octavius have gone about much. It will be their introduction to York's Polite Society as well as yours. I have met Beaumont and his lady. Meg was right in asking them to sponsor all of you. I will add this required them to leave Town and return north."

That seemed to be above and beyond what one should be able to expect even of friends. Sextus quickly sifted through all that had been said and unsaid. "I take it that the lady the duke selected is not suitable. And not only does he not read the York newssheets, but unless there was something interesting that would be picked up by the London papers, he will likely not discover I am there."

Kendal inclined his head. "Correct. From what we were able to discover, the lady is the eldest child of a country squire and is content to remain with her father. The property is not entailed, and she stands to inherit."

"In addition to that," Talia said, "she is not particularly well educated beyond the basics." She raised a brow. "No foreign languages."

What the devil had the old man been thinking? "What does he expect me to do with a wife like that?"

"I'm not sure he cares," Kendal drawled. "I am positive there is property that he wants involved."

Of course, there was. Sextus had heard all the stories. He glanced at the infant. "How old is the baby?"

"He is three months." Thalia stroked the infant's head. "We brought him to Town so that everyone could see him. His sister is with Nurse in one of the other carriages."

"A boy." He grinned. "Congratulations."

"He is no more nor less loved than our daughter." There was a warning note in Kendal's voice.

Apparently, Sextus's newest brother-in-law was as liberal as the rest of the family, excepting the duke of course. "As it should be. What is his name?"

"Alexander Julian Ciprianus, Marquis of Breadalbane," Thalia pronounced proudly. "We call him Alex."

"Not Breadalbane?" The heir was usually called by his title.

"Not by me." There was a militant look in her eyes. "Enough people will call him that. He is my son, and I will call him by his first name."

Definitely on the liberal side. "If you do not mind, I will take the opportunity to sleep."

"Not at all," Kendal said. "I will as well."

Miss Harriett Staunton poured tea for her guest, Lady Beaumont. Since Harriett had moved to York several months ago, her ladyship had been a Godsend. They had met at a fabric shop where Harriett had been selecting material for hangings in her house. Lady Beaumont struck up a conversation about the benefits of changing out curtain and bed hanging fabrics with the seasons. After that, Lady Beaumont had invited Harriett to tea. She had been surprised to have been so welcomed by her ladyship and Lord Beaumont, who was completely devoted to his wife and family. The merchant community in London had not been nearly as kind to her. Not kind at all. In fact, during her one short Season, the only offers she had received had been ones she would never accept.

"Now." Lady Beaumont accepted the cup of tea from Harriett. "I believe I have some possible matches for you. I am determined you shall have the come out you never had."

And that scared Harriett to death. She had become very used to remaining in the background and devoting herself to charities. "I know you said that the gentry do not care much about..." she could not bear to say the word illegitimate out loud "...people like me. I simply find it hard to believe."

"My dear..." her ladyship set down her cup and leveled her kind gaze on Harriett, "you are still an earl's daughter. It is a shame he did not recognize you, but he has provided for your support and education. You have all the accomplishments a lady must have."

That had never helped her before. She even knew all the dances, yet her Season had been so short she had never been to a ball or even a local assembly. Still, her ladyship was offering Harriett the only opportunity she would probably ever have to find a husband and have a family. "I shall trust you."

Her ladyship smiled. "You will do well. I have every confidence we will soon be celebrating your marriage." Lady Beaumont picked up her cup and took a sip of tea. "Now, I must tell you my husband has taken a house not very far away on Blossom Street for the Season. I am also sponsoring, so to speak, the brother and sister-in-law of a good friend. They have not gone about much, but you might have heard of them, the Earl and Countess of Somers. Also staying with us will be his brother Lord Sextus Trevor."

Harriett had heard of the earl and countess. The son of the Duke of Somerset, the earl was a retired navy captain. The countess had been born and raised in Tortola and was the half-sister of the Duchess of Wharton. In a strange twist of fate, the earl had been awarded his maternal great-uncle's earldom. "Are you sure they will want to meet me?"

"Quite sure." Lady Beaumont sounded extremely confident. "You will see how different the gentry are from the middling set." Lady Beaumont set down her cup again and rose. Harriett quickly stood as well. "I must be going. I expect my guests to arrive at any time. I will send around a note inviting you to join us for a stroll on the New Walk and then to tea."

"Thank you." A walk would be a much easier place to get to know new people than having everyone sitting around—in her case nervously—at tea. Harriett said a brief prayer that all would be as her ladyship planned. She accompanied her mentor to the door. "I look forward to hearing from you and meeting your friends."

Lady Beaumont took Harriett's hands and gave a reassuring smile. "All will be well. I promise you." Neathercote, Harriett's butler, opened the door. "I will see you soon."

"Thank you, again, my lady." She made her way to the morning room in the back of the house.

When she entered, she found her former governess now companion, Miss Ellen Gobeley, in a comfortable coze with Harriett's old nurse, Honeybourne. They both glanced up.

"How was your visit with Lady Beaumont?" Ellen asked.

Harriett bit the inside of her lip. "She is going to sponsor me for a Season."

"There, I knew she'd do what was right." Honey's Scottish burr was even more noticeable than usual. "She might have married an English lord, but she's a Scottish lady to the bone."

"She also has some gentlemen in mind she thinks might prove to be good matches." Harriett blinked back the pricking of tears. "I have been content, but to be a wife and mother... Well, that has always been my dream."

"Dear Harriett." Ellen patted the space next to her on the sofa.

"Come sit with us and tell us everything. I shall ring for tea and some of Cook's biscuits."

The tea, accompanied by ginger biscuits, arrived in short order, and Harriett proceeded to tell Ellen and Honey everything her ladyship had said.

"A duke's son." Honey breathed.

"Two duke's sons." Ellen laughed. "And the sister of a duchess. Your company is becoming quite grand."

"I have not met them yet." Counting one's chickens before they hatched was never a good idea. "Her ladyship says they will want to meet me, but after my previous experiences I dare not get my hopes up."

"Rubbish," Honey said. "You are as genteel as any other lady."

But was Harriett really a lady? They had had this argument many times in the past, and she was not going to have it now. "We shall know soon enough."

"Indeed, we will," Ellen agreed.

Harriett prayed that this time would be different.

## CHAPTER 2

Five days later, Sextus, his sister, Kendal, and their entourage arrived at a sprawling Elizabethan style manor house. His brother, Octavius, stood on the steps next to a lovely young lady. She must be Marcella. He covertly studied her features. Yes, one could see she was a mulatta, but she was really not that different from their late queen. Yet the duke had been in a rage over the marriage and not only because Octavius had thwarted him.

"Here we are," Thalia said rather unnecessarily.

Sextus chastised himself. He must be weary to think so unkindly. "We are. How long will we remain?"

Before she could answer, footmen opened the coach door and Octavius and Marcella approached.

"As you have probably surmised, I am Marcella." She took his arm and began walking him to the door. "You look fagged to death of traveling. A hot bath and a cup of tea will be just the thing. Unfortunately, we are going to York immediately after luncheon. When we arrive, you will be able to remain in one place for a bit."

A hot bath and tea sounded very English and truly delightful. "I understand it's not far."

"About an hour." She gave him a rueful look. "However, I do not know what Serena Beaumont has planned."

Sextus couldn't think of a response to that. Lady Beaumont would have planned activities that promoted the goal of finding him a wife. He was shown into a bathing room where a large tub was already being filled under the watchful eye of Lovel, his valet.

"I shall send a footman when luncheon is ready." Marcella smiled. "You should know we are all here to help you."

Sextus returned her smile. "And I greatly appreciate your efforts."

Two hours later, he had said farewell to Thalia and Kendal. An hour after that, he had arrived at a commodious town house in York where they were greeted by Lord and Lady Beaumont. Lady Beaumont was a striking woman with auburn hair and amber eyes. Beaumont was a tall, well-set up gentleman with golden-blond hair and blue eyes. He had his hand rather possessively on his wife's waist.

"I hear he used to be a terrible rake before he met Serena and married," Marcella whispered. She picked up her skirts and climbed the two stairs. "Serena, allow me to present my brother-in-law Lord Sextus Trevor. Sextus, Lady Beaumont."

When he bowed over her hand, he could have sworn he heard Beaumont growl. "Thank you for your assistance in my search for a wife."

"Robert, stop."

Sextus kept his grin to himself. So, the man had growled. How amusing.

"You are most welcome. Once I heard of your dilemma, I knew we could be of help. Your family and ours have been friends for many years."

Marcella took Sextus's arm again as they were shown into a sunny room looking out onto a garden. "What do you have arranged for us?"

Tea trays followed them into the room and were put on a low table between two sofas. He took a large stuffed chair at one end of the sofa where Marcella and Octavius sat. Lady Beaumont sank onto the other sofa, and her husband took his place next to her. As she poured, he handed out the tea, biscuits and small tarts.

Once she took a sip of tea, she glanced at Marcella. "I have some ideas of ladies who might be good prospects. I am quite fond of one lady in particular." Her ladyship looked at Sextus. "She is fluent in German, French, and Italian, paints a bit, and plays both the piano and the harp. She is twenty-two and living with a companion."

"My dear," Lord Beaumont said. "You should tell Lord Sextus about her appearance. Listing her accomplishments first will give him the opinion she is not much to look at."

She gave her husband a look of long suffering, but her lips twitched. "I suppose you are correct." She glanced at Sextus. "She is quite pretty. She has thc most glorious chestnut hair and bright green eyes." Raising her chin, she looked at her husband again. "And she is neither too shy nor too forward."

Marcella started to laugh. "She has you there, Robert."

"She usually does," he replied ruefully.

"Oh, dear." Lady Beaumont glanced at Sextus. "You must call me Serena and Robert either by his first name or Beaumont. We will be living together for the nonce."

"Thank you. Please call me Sextus."

Lady Beaumont drew a sheet of paper from her reticule. "Now that that has been settled, I have a list of things I have planned. Tomorrow, I have invited Miss Harriett Staunton to go for a stroll with us on the New Walk." She lowered the paper and looked at him. "She is the lady I told you about. She will also join us for tea. She is the natural daughter of the Earl of Seahaven. It is almost obligatory to attend the functions during Race Week. And I shall give a small ball. I have also received invitations to other events. We will go through them together and decide which ones to attend."

It suddenly struck him how important it was for him to find the right lady to be his wife, and how little time he had. How long could Damon and Meg put off the duke? It appeared Miss Staunton might be the perfect lady for him. At least she seemed to possess the qualities he required in a wife. Unlike the lady his father had chosen for him. Sextus looked forward to meeting her.

"Have you heard when the tailor will be ready for Sextus to be fitted?" Octavius asked.

That got Sextus's attention. What tailor? "Fitted for what?"

"New clothing." His brother directed a rather pointed look at him. "Your style of dress is decidedly European. It will be noticed."

"And commented upon," Beaumont said. "The very thing we do not wish to happen." He glanced at Octavius. "I expect him here shortly. My valet sent word when you arrived."

Something wasn't making sense. "How is he going to make anything in time?"

Octavius rolled his eyes. "We had your valet write down your measurements, and Kendal sent an express letter to the tailor here. I would have preferred to use Weston, but there wasn't time."

"Nielson is excellent," Beaumont said. "I have used him in the past."

"I hadn't even thought of my clothing. But looking at the two of you I can see the differences." The fabrics were different as well as the buttons and trim. Although subtle, it would mark him as not from England. "Thank you."

Beaumont inclined his head. "I wish I could take credit. It was Hawksworth who thought of it."

That didn't surprise Sextus. His eldest brother had lived on the continent as well as in England. "He does seem to have a knack of thinking of everything."

A knock sounded on the door and a dapper little man appeared. "My lord, Mr. Nielson has arrived."

Sextus rose. "Take me to him. I hope he has something I can wear tomorrow." When he'd meet Miss Staunton.

The next afternoon, Harriett stared at the three walking gowns her maid had laid out. "The emerald green."

"That's what I thought, Miss." Wyborn picked up the other two garments and took them into the dressing room.

Lady Beaumont had sent a note around late yesterday afternoon that the outing in the New Walk would be today. She planned to bring her two children, Elizabeth, who was four years old, and William, who was two. Harriett wondered if their nursemaids would accompany them as well.

She raised her arms as her maid placed the gown carefully over her head, then sat on the chair in front of the toilet table for her hair to be dressed. Several minutes later, Harriett left her room. She reached the top of the stairs when the door opened to the Beaumonts. With them were a couple who must be the Earl and Countess of Somers, and a gentleman who looked very like the earl and could only be Lord Sextus Trevor. Both Lord Sextus and his brother were tall with silvery blond hair and warm blue eyes. However, from there the details of their features were different. The earl's face was more weathered from being at sea, whereas Lord Sextus's complexion was pale. Lady Beaumont had said he had been in Russia. Although both were broad shouldered, the earl had clearly done more physical work. Not that Lord Sextus appeared in any way soft, but he had obviously lived a different life. At that moment, his eyes met hers, and she knew he had been studying her as she had been studying him.

Harriett walked down the rest of the steps and curtseyed. "Good afternoon."

"Harriett, my dear." Lady Beaumont drew Harriett forward. "Marcella, please let me introduce you to my friend, Miss Harriett Staunton. Harriett this is the Countess of Somers." They greeted each other. "Harriett, allow me to present Lord Sextus Trevor, and his brother, the Earl of Somers."

The earl remained by his wife and bowed, but Lord Sextus stepped forward and took Miss Staunton's hand before bowing. "Miss Staunton, it is a pleasure to meet you." He tucked her hand in the crook of his arm and proceeded out the door. Glancing back, he said, "Are the rest of you coming?"

Harriett was so shocked at the way he immediately took possession of her, she barely noticed everyone else following them out the door. No man had ever treated her thus. What was worse was she did not know what to think about it. Although his arm felt strong and somehow comforting, they had only just met.

On the pavement, one young nursemaid held Miss Elizabeth's hand, and another had Master William's. Lord Beaumont put William on his shoulders and took Elizabeth's hand. Harriett could not help but slide a look at Lord Sextus to see what he thought of his lordship's parenting, but again, he was already gazing at her.

"I see Beaumont is affectionate with his children. My brothers and sisters are the same. However, it is not what we experienced growing up."

"My mother was very affectionate." Harriett had always known she was loved. Mama had said she and Papa had loved each other very much, but Harriett had never met her father. He had never visited them. "I will be loving with my children."

Lord Sextus's gaze switched to Lord Beaumont. "I hope to be as well."

Although she was pleased with his comments, this conversation was extremely personal for two people who had met only mere minutes ago. "I was told you are stationed in Russia."

He looked at her like he knew what she was doing. "Yes, for several years. My next assignment is to the Hapsburg Court."

She had found some information about the Russian court in the books that came with the house. It seemed both opulent and dangerous at the same time. For some silly reason she was glad he would not be returning. "Is that a promotion of sorts?"

"It is. The Hapsburgs have greater power than the Russians." He stopped and tilted his head. "Despite its wealth, the Russian court is not as sophisticated. There is an element of brutality that does not exist in the European courts." He began strolling again. "I am looking forward to the change. Have you ever traveled?"

Harriett wished she could look inside his mind. Did he want to know if she was an experienced traveler or if she would like to travel? "Only if you call going from Harrogate to London and from London to here traveling. I would love to visit other places."

"Lady Beaumont tells me you are fluent in some languages."

How much had her ladyship told him? Did he know about Harriett's parentage? "Yes. I had tutors in French, Italian, and German. Unfortunately, I no longer have an opportunity to practice with native speakers."

"But you would like to do so?" There was a tone in his voice she could not place. Inquisitive, yet, at the same time urgent.

"I would." She smiled at the image she had of speaking one language with a person and another with the next person.

"Sometimes one has to hide that one speaks a language."

That was a tantalizing thing to say. "Why?"

A smile hovered around his well-defined lips. "To get them to say something to another in their language they would not say if they knew you spoke it."

How interesting! "I must say, that sounds like fun."

"It can be." His eyes warmed as he smiled. "It can also be quite gratifying when you discover something you otherwise would not."

Harriett could not help but to join in his pleasure. "I can imagine."

"If you wish to practice, I am happy to speak with you in one of your languages."

Naturally, he would know those and others. "I would like that, but it would be rude to speak a language the others might not know."

"I wouldn't worry about them. I know for a fact they all speak French. Or we could speak it between the two of us," he said in French.

His whole being seemed focused on her. Harriett's chest felt as if butterflies had taken over. This was the most exciting thing to have happened in her entire life. And was that not a sad state of affairs. She replied in the same language, "French it is."

"*Bon.*"

If she was not careful, she was going to lose her heart.

*Somerset Hall, Northhamptonshire.*

Somerset scowled at the missive in his hand. How dare that man tell him he and his daughter were leaving Town if Sextus didn't visit them soon.

"*Belling*!"

"Yes, your grace." The secretary rushed into the duke's study.

"Has the letter to Lord Sextus been delivered?" The damn thing had gone out ten days ago, and there had been no response.

"The messenger took it to Hawksworth House, but he was told Lord Sextus had not yet arrived. To the best of my knowledge, he is still not in England."

"Contact the Foreign Office and find out which ship he took."

"I already did, your grace, but they could only tell me the ship he took from St. Petersburg to Helsinki. After that he would have changed ships."

Somerset broke the pencil he'd been tapping on the desk and threw the pieces across the room. The damned boy could be anywhere between Helsinki and London. "In other words, we have no idea how long he is planning to take to get here."

"No, your grace." Belling wrung his hands. "The only way to find out is to send men to all the possible ports along the way."

Somerset could not believe his plans were falling apart before his son even arrived. "Did he write to anyone when he expected to arrive?"

"The duchess said she had not received a date."

Naturally, if any of his children knew, they wouldn't tell him. "Have someone ask around at the London docks. Look for ships arriving from Norway, Holland, or Denmark."

"As you wish, your grace. The queries will go out today."

One way or another, he'd keep that damn squire and his daughter in Town. "And Belling, find out what will keep Waggleston in Town."

"Yes, your grace."

Somerset took out a sheet of pressed paper. It was time to have his old friend Thornfield put his nose to the ground as it were. If there was any talk of Sextus arriving, Thornfield would hear about it.

# CHAPTER 3

Sextus resisted the urge to draw Miss Staunton closer as they strolled The Walk. Thus far, it appeared Serena Beaumont could not have chosen a better lady for him. Miss Staunton had all the qualifications of a diplomat's wife. What he needed to know now is if they had or could develop the type of passion and meeting of the minds that would make a happy marriage. They had to want the same things out of life in order for their future to succeed.

"I believe Lady Beaumont mentioned you enjoy charity work. In what types of charities are you involved?"

Miss Staunton focused her bright green eyes on him. "Helping children. I have only been in York for a few months, but I have learned what the most basic needs are. Yet, I believe there needs to be a better plan when it comes to the future of children who do not have families or have families who cannot provide for their futures."

That sounded like what his married sisters were doing. "What do you see as the failings?"

"Putting them in the lowest forms of employment or apprenticeships and not ensuring the children are treated properly. We had one boy of only six years return with serious burns from being forced to clean chimneys that had not been sufficiently cooled. That is unacceptable."

It sounded like the master should be arrested or taken to court. But he knew how hard that would be and the funds it would take. "I agree. What will you do?"

Her brows furrowed, and she stared ahead of her. Sextus missed having her looking at him. "I have asked my solicitor to look into it."

If only he could help. Then it occurred to him he might be able to. "If you would like, I can write to my brother who is a barrister. He might be able to be of assistance."

In a flash her expressive gaze was his again, and she was smiling. "Oh, would you? That would be wonderful!"

He didn't want her to think he had solved all her problems. Nonus might not be able to help at all. Still… "All I can do is ask. It is his decision to make."

The joy in her face dimmed. Sextus's letter would have to be persuasive. "Yes, of course. I understand. Thank you for offering to contact him."

"That, Miss Staunton, would be my pleasure." He smiled down at her.

Thankfully her lovely lips tilted up again. "Thank you again.

Now, how to approach his next query? "What do you dream about for your future?"

She glanced away toward the ducks in the river then back to him. "I have not allowed myself to consider it overmuch. I do not expect to wed." Pain of some sort clouded her eyes and the sparkle faded. "My aunt attempted to bring me out among the merchant society in London. I was not accepted."

There was no surprise there. The French term bourgeois had come to represent the narrow-minded attitudes of merchants to natural children and the women who birthed them. Their loss was possibly his gain. "They are not the only society in England or even the world."

Miss Staunton heaved a sigh. "I know, but they are the people I was brought up around."

She was as lady-like as any female he'd known in the *ton*. "But not educated as."

"No." She shook her head. "It is a conundrum I have never understood. Why educate me as a lady?"

Why, indeed. There was a mystery here Sextus would enjoy delving into if he had the time. And time was a problem. Despite all the actions his family had taken, the duke was bound to find out he was in the country. "May I say that I am very glad you are a lady?"

She flashed him a quick glance from beneath her lush dark lashes. It was an innocent look, but more than enough for his body to respond to her allure. A beautiful pink painted her cheeks. "Thank you."

Sextus had never lacked for female company. Nevertheless, he was always extremely discreet. But none of his paramours had infused him with an immediate desire to take her somewhere and discover if she would respond to him the way he was responding to her. He wished he had time for a longer courtship, but needs must. "What if you had an opportunity to marry and have children, a family?"

Her white teeth bit down on her plump bottom lip. "I have not allowed myself to wish. It would be too painful."

Her tone was sad and full of longing. Was it too soon to raise her expectations? He gave himself an inner shake. They had only just met today. He had at least a week or two to change her mind. "After your experience, I understand."

"Look. There is a girl selling bread. Shall we feed the ducks?"

Miss Staunton was very good at changing the subject. Another talent that a diplomat's wife required. "That sounds like a lovely idea."

When they stopped, the others caught up to them. Beaumont bought a bag to give to his daughter. She laughed and giggled as the ducks came around to be fed while her father hovered protectively over her. Sextus had an image of a chestnut-headed child feeding ducks, but he was the one with her. He glanced at Harriett, who was speaking with his sister-in-law. She would fit in any ball room on the continent or in England. When the next image he had of her was in his bed, he was almost positive she'd fit into his life even better.

"I had no idea York was so beautiful." Lady Somers said.

Harriett had been trying not to stare at Lord Sextus as she and her ladyship spoke. "It is lovely in spring. I found the end of winter a bit dreary."

Lady Somers laughed. "I found it tedious in the country. All it did was switch from snow to rain and back again."

"Welcome to England." Harriett grinned. It was a bit daunting speaking with her ladyship, although less so than before she had met Lady Beaumont. "It must be quite different from the West Indies."

"It is a different world." Lady Somers's voice sounded as if she was thinking fondly of her home. "We will go back to visit, but this is home now." She glanced at her husband who was talking with Sextus. "Aside from the duke, the family could not have been more welcoming. I thought, perhaps, it was because my sister is a member..." she gave Harriett a significant look... "but I have come to realize they will embrace anyone who is a good person." Her ladyship linked her arm with Harriett's. "Did I tell you it took less than two weeks for Octavius and me to fall in love? It was only a day for Thalia and Giles."

"One day!" Harriett was what? Shocked? Astounded? And why was Lady Somers telling her this? Did she think Harriett and Lord Sextus were falling in love? Her heart began to beat more quickly. She glanced at him and caught him looking at her. His eyes warmed as a small smile formed on his lips. What would it be like to feel those lips on her own? Only one man had attempted to kiss her, and she had put a quick stop to his advances. But something deep inside of her told her she would not stop Sextus. Thus far, their conversation had nudged her to begin thinking about another type of life. One filled with love and adventure. If he asked, could she do it? She had not had much luck trusting men.

"Did I frighten you?" Lady Somers patted Harriett's arm. "I did not mean to. Forget what I said. What happens will happen. It is clear *I* would not make a good diplomat's wife." A rueful look formed on her ladyship's face. "I did it again. Perhaps I had better stop talking."

Her ladyship appeared disgusted with herself, and Harriett laughed. "It is no matter."

"It will be if I scare you off," Lady Somers muttered darkly under her breath.

If it had not been clear Harriett was not meant to hear the remarks, she would have laughed again. Indeed, rather than frighten her, she felt better about how quickly she had formed a liking for Sextus. Drat! Lord Sextus. She must remember to keep that mental distance until a decision had been made.

They joined the others. This time, when he took her hand and tucked it into the crook of his arm, it seemed the most natural thing in the world. Still, despite how quickly some of his family had decided to wed, she could not allow her hopes to get too high.

He bent his head, and his breath brushed her ear, sending a pleasurable shiver down her neck. "Did you enjoy your chat with Marcella?"

"It was illuminating." Did he know how quickly his family decided to wed?

"From what little I have seen, she is very forthright."

"She is indeed." Harriett chuckled to herself. "How long have you known her?"

"Little more than a day. One of my sisters and her husband fetched me from the London docks and whisked me up here. I was handed over to Marcella and Octavius. After luncheon, we came to York. That was yesterday."

And he had already been introduced to her! "Your family does act quickly."

He arched a light brown brow. "As do the Beaumonts."

Very true. Lady Beaumont had had this in mind all along. "It does seem that way."

He grinned at Harriett. "The ducks have moved on. Shall we be on our way?"

She matched her grin to his. "Yes. I have not been on this walk before."

By the time they returned to the house the Beaumonts had leased, she and Sextus, *Lord* Sextus, were chatting as if they had known each other for years. Then again, other than Lady Beaumont, Harriett had never really talked to another person about herself so much. And he told her about himself. At several points, his brother and sister-in-law joined in the conversation, broadening her knowledge of his family. To a person, they all appeared to have the ability to make decisions quickly and with admirable determination. From what she could tell, they were like the duke in that respect. Unlike him, they wanted what was best for their brothers and sisters.

"I am ready for sustenance," Sextus said as they entered the house.

"I, as well." She had been a bit concerned when Lady Beaumont insisted Harriett join them for tea after their walk. Then again, she had had no idea how well she and Sextus would go on together.

"It is really not my place to ask, but will you join us for dinner as well?" He handed his hat to the butler. "If you wish her ladyship to invite you, I will ask her to do so."

Harriett almost rolled her eyes. "I have no doubt you would. Common courtesy requires you to, at the very least, gain her permission."

"As you like." He turned to Lady Beaumont who was divesting herself of her bonnet. "My lady, may Miss Staunton join us for dinner?"

Covering her eyes, she shook her head.

Her ladyship did roll her eyes as she chuckled. "Miss Staunton, we would greatly like it if you would dine with us this evening."

Sextus seemed to be holding his breath as he stared at her. Inclining her head graciously, she accepted, "Thank you for asking me, my lady. It would be my pleasure."

Little Elizabeth had apparently been watching, for she gave her mother a narrow look. "Mama, you rolled your eyes. That is not allowed."

The gentlemen suddenly found something else to look at in the hall, as their shoulders shook in laughter. Marcella covered her mouth, and Harriett was hard pressed not to burst out laughing.

Her ladyship took her daughter's hand. "No, it is not allowed, and even under great provocation, Mama should not have done it."

The little girl screwed up her face. "What does prvication mean?"

Just then, Nurse made herself known. "I will explain it while you have your tea."

Elizabeth nodded her curly head and took Nurse's hand. "It is important."

"Yes, it is." The older woman and child went up the stairs followed by a nursemaid carrying the baby.

Once they could no longer be seen, Lady Beaumont sighed. "That will teach me to remember who is around when I break the rules." She led them into the morning room and tea followed as they were taking their seats.

Harriett chose one of the small sofas. Sextus sat next to her. "What shall we do tomorrow?"

"As you can imagine, not much will occur until after Easter," Lady Beaumont said. "We have been invited to a garden party in the afternoon the day after tomorrow. In four days' time, there is to be a meeting of the Ladies Reform Association with speakers that I would like to attend."

Harriett had heard about the meeting. "I would like to go as well."

"I should attend as well," Lady Somers said.

"I will accompany you," Lord Beaumont drawled. "I like to keep abreast of what is going on."

"As will I," Sextus quickly agreed.

"Whither goes my wife, I go too," Lord Somers said.

Lady Beaumont glanced at all of them. "Then it is settled. The garden party the day after tomorrow and the meeting in a few days. I am sure we can come up with other places to visit in between."

"Excellent." Sextus accepted the cup of tea Harriett handed him. "Who has a guidebook? Do we require one?"

"I do," his sister-in-law replied. "I even remembered to bring it with me. I shall peruse it before dinner."

About an hour later, Sextus escorted Harriett to her town house. "I shall call for you at half past five if you can be ready that soon."

That was only an hour and a half from now! Harriett refused to let him see her panic and schooled her countenance. "I will be waiting."

He raised her hand and instead of kissing air above the back of it, turned it around and kissed her palm before folding her fingers as if to hold the kiss. Her aunt and uncle would be scandalized. "I look forward to seeing you then."

The door opened, and her butler bowed.

"I should go."

For a moment, Sextus searched her eyes. "Soon."

"Soon." Oh dear. How was she to resist him? She was half in love with him already.

"Miss Gobeley and Mrs. Honeybourne are in the morning room."

"I shall go to them. I will not be dining at home this evening. Tell Wyborn I need to dress immediately. His lordship is coming to fetch me in just over an hour."

"Yes, miss." Neathercote bowed again. "I will let her know straightaway."

Harriett knew her companion and old nurse would be waiting to see how the day went. Ever since she had told them about her ladyship's scheme, they had been both excited and afraid for her.

Both of them looked up with anxious eyes when Harriett entered the room. "I have been invited to dine with Lady Beaumont and her guests." There was no reason she needed to tell them Sextus had insisted until something more substantial happened. "I was introduced to Lord Sextus Trevor and his brother and sister-in-law, Lord and Lady Somers. We had a very pleasant walk and tea."

Honey's eyes had brightened when Harriett had mentioned Lord Sextus. "Do you like him?"

"I do." She was not going to admit more. "However, it is much too soon to know if we are right for each other."

"Have you made other plans?" Honey asked.

"I am attending a garden party with them the day after tomorrow in the afternoon." That should keep them distracted for at least another day.

"I am very glad you had a good time." Ellen appeared calm, but she always did. "We will see you later this evening or tomorrow morning."

Harriett chose a silk evening gown of Pomona green with gold trim and the pearl necklaces that had belonged to her mother and the matching drop earrings. The walk to Blossom Street was not far, but it was too long for evening slippers. "Which shoes?"

Her maid stood tapping her chin with one finger. "You have a pair of low leather shoes that will not be harmed by the pavement."

"What a good idea, and I rarely have an opportunity to wear them." In fact, Harriett had forgotten she had them.

She thought she looked well, but was more than pleased when Sextus gazed up at her as she descended the stairs.

He extended his hand. "I should not comment, but I cannot keep my thoughts to myself. You are even more beautiful than I thought you this afternoon."

Heat rushed into her cheeks as she reached the bottom tread. "I am not used to such flattery."

He kissed her hand and, again, tucked it into the crook of his arm. "It is the truth, not flattery, and you will have to get used to it."

Oh dear. Smug looks appeared on the faces of her butler and a footman. This would be all around the house the moment she left. Well, she would simply have to deal with that later.

"Shall we go?"

"I suppose we should." He sounded disappointed. "However, I intend to proceed at a mere amble."

# CHAPTER 4

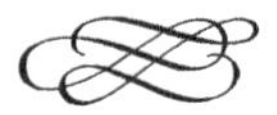

Later that evening, they decided the next day's activities would include a visit to the local cathedral called the Minster. Afterward, they would take a drive out to the St. Mary's ruins where they would have luncheon.

By the time they returned from their jaunt, Sextus was determined Harriett would remain in his life. The only real question was how much time she'd need to see they were meant to spend their lives together.

What had been nagging him was why the Earl of Seahaven had never visited her or her mother, but had paid generously for her education and maintenance. And was apparently still paying. At least, that was Sextus's supposition. Harriett had told him her uncle would never divulge from whom the funds came. That was a mystery that must be solved. That said, he was glad he had a family to give her. Letters had been flying to and from London as if they had wings. Everyone, it seemed, was exceedingly happy with Lady Beaumont's matchmaking efforts.

The following day was the garden party. It would be the first time he and Harriett were seen in public. An immediate sense of pride filled him that he'd escort her. At the same time, there was the ever-present fear the duke would find out about her. Sextus realized he was clenching his fists. If the old goat or one of his tools laid a hand on Harriett, he wouldn't be responsible for his actions.

"Concerned about Miss Staunton?" Octavius asked.

Sextus's jaw dropped, and he shut it with a click. "How the devil did you know that?"

"Simple, really. Tomorrow is a public event, you will be there with Harriett." His brother raised a brow. "I can't imagine you intend to allow some other gentleman to walk off with her." Sextus's body prepared for battle at the mere thought. "And if the duke finds out, she'd be in danger." Octavius shook his head. "You've already fallen in love and decided to wed her. If it makes you feel any better, none of us has taken much time at all in recognizing the person we wish to marry."

Everything his brother said was correct. Sextus had no idea he was so transparent. He'd never been so before. "So much for me being inscrutable."

"I'm quite sure you are with everyone else." Octavius smiled. "As many years as we have been apart, we all seem to have many of the same traits. I doubt anyone outside of us knows what you're thinking." He narrowed his eyes slightly and stared at Sextus. "That, by the way, includes Harriett."

"Good Lord." Sextus dragged a hand down his face. "You're right. I had better tell her how I feel and soon."

"Excellent idea," his brother said in a voice as dry as an old riverbed.

The question was still when.

The next day, when Harriett floated down the stairs in a gown of yellow muslin, Sextus thought he'd died and gone to heaven.

She smiled as she placed her elegant fingers in his hand. "Good afternoon, my lord."

"Good afternoon to you." He tucked her hand in the crook of his arm. "My carriage awaits."

Her eyes flew open in shock. "You have a carriage here?"

"No, I'm borrowing one of Beaumont's. He had it brought down from his estate." Because Sextus had wanted more time alone with Harriett. He lifted her easily into the vehicle, reveling in the feel of the curve of her waist. Knowing there was only muslin and a bit of linen between his flesh and hers. "I would like it if you called me Sextus."

She blushed prettily. "Only if you call me Harriett."

"Harriett." This was progress. He was mesmerized by the warmth in her beautiful green eyes.

Her gaze flicked away for a second. "Sextus, we should go. My neighbor across the street is staring at us."

"Yes, of course." It was then he discovered he still had one hand on her waist. He must be more careful with her reputation.

Climbing into the other side of the curricle, he mentally reviewed the directions he'd been given before starting the horses. "Have you discovered anything more about the reform meeting?"

"Not really." Her brows drew together, and she tilted her head to one side. "There are to be at least two speakers. Unfortunately, there are so many problems that need to be addressed, I do not know on which subjects they will speak."

That was what both Serena and Marcella had heard as well. The whole thing made him nervous. Lately the government had been taking a hard stand against any type of reform. "I hope you do not mind, but Beaumont, my brother, and I have decided not to accompany you ladies. While you attend the meeting, we will be at the pub across the street."

"Not at all." The feather on her hat waved as she shook her head. "If it were not for the fact that this is now my home, I might not go either." She gave him a knowing look. "I do read the newssheets, and I know what has happened elsewhere."

Sextus decided to ignore her comment about living in York and give her a contrite smile. "I am aware you are well read. I am merely wary."

"I as well." She folded her hands into her lap, but rubbed the silk of her reticule between her thumb and forefinger. "I—I am glad you will be close by."

That soothed his inner warrior. "I'd never let any harm come to you."

Harriett flashed him a look he couldn't read. His brother was right. He had to declare himself soon. They rode in companionable silence for a few minutes before pulling up at the end of a line in front of a town house.

She seemed to be focused on the carriages in front of them, when she said, "Other than my outings with you, this is the first entertainment I have attended."

"Are you nervous?"

"A bit. As you know, the few events I attended in London did not go well."

He covered her fingers with his own. "You need have no fear here. I'll be with you the whole time."

Harriett gazed down at his strong hands and knew she had fallen in love. She wanted to believe he felt the same about her but was still too afraid to trust in herself. "Thank you." She forced herself not to stare at him. "It is a lovely day. Sunny but not too warm."

She knew he was focusing his considerable gaze on her. When she met it, he said, "Do we have to discuss the weather? I thought we were past that."

"Nerves." She forced herself to laugh lightly.

Sextus frowned. "This is more serious than I'd thought." He rubbed his thumb slowly along her wrist causing not only little fires to light and race through her veins, but a sense of confidence as well. "Trust me. We will get through this."

One way or the other. She tensed, preparing herself for being looked down upon. "I shall."

"My lord." One of the Beaumont footmen had come up to the carriage. "If you wish, I will take care of the horses so ye can join the party."

Sextus glanced at her. "Would you like to walk the rest of the way?"

"Yes, please." Their destination was only three houses away, and she was wearing half-boots.

He threw the reins to the footman, and jumped gracefully down from the vehicle, then came around to her side and lifted her slowly down to the ground. His hands slid over her waist and up slightly to her ribcage. What would it be like if they had gone to her breasts? Something, some sensation like a spark, speared though her body. When her feet reached the pavement, she did not know if her legs would hold her, but Sextus made sure she was standing before he took her arm in his. She wished she had had someone to tell her what went on between a man and a woman and if this was normal.

"Are you all right?" His voice was soft against her ear.

"Yes. I just was a little wobbly at first." And he was not helping.

A smug expression appeared on his face. "I have you."

But did he mean that the way she wanted him to?

Ahead of them, a lady was announced as Lady Barbara Bigglesworth, and Harriett froze. The lady must be one of her half-sisters.

"Harriett?" Sextus whispered.

She bit her bottom lip. "Did you hear the name?"

"Yes. She needn't concern you. Unless you wish to meet her?" He searched her eyes and waited.

"I will not go out of my way to be introduced to her." To the best of her knowledge, they did not even know she existed.

"Very well." He guided her through the door where he gave their names to the butler, and they were announced before being shown through a door to the garden.

Lady Somers waved and Harriett and Sextus strolled to their party. "The gods must be smiling upon them," her ladyship said. "Even though we have not been here very long, I have learned the weather in the north is chancy."

"It appears that everyone who is anyone and not in Town is here," Octavius opined. "However, I've not recognized any of the names as being ones I have heard before."

Harriett interpreted that piece of information to mean no one present was a good friend of the duke's. She glanced at Sextus. "Shall we stroll? There are some paths that must lead somewhere."

Lady Beaumont laughed. "Unless this is a rare, larger garden they will not lead far."

"That doesn't mean we can't explore." Sextus had his hand on Harriett's waist, but now moved it to take her arm. "Shall we?"

"Yes." They ambled along the path for a short way until they came upon a fountain with cherubs cavorting around a young couple. Cupid was holding a bow and arrow pointed at the man. "I wonder if he shoots more at women or at men."

"That is an interesting question. I have no idea." Sextus turned her to face him. "Harriett..." Giggles from behind a bush stopped him from speaking and he glared at whoever was behind the shrubbery. "Obviously, this is not the proper place for the discussion I wanted to have with you."

Her heart began to flutter as if it would fly off on its own. Had he been about to propose? Drat whoever that was for stopping him. "No, I suppose not."

They walked back to the main garden where long tables of food had been set up and servants were present to serve the guests. "Are you hungry?"

"A little." If they were not going to be able to speak alone, the least she could do was sample some of the dishes.

"I see the others. Will you trust me to select for you while you sit with the ladies, and I fetch and carry?"

"That would be nice." She could only suppose that was how this sort of thing was done.

Several minutes later, Lady Somers announced, "Our gentlemen are returning. I cannot wait to see what they have for us."

Harriett followed her ladyship's gaze to see Sextus and the others followed by two footmen. "Goodness, it looks as if they have brought a bit of everything."

"If we like something particularly," Lady Somers said, "we should take a piece of it with us. Meg told me her sister and her sister's friends do that. It sounded like an interesting idea."

"Hmm," Lady Beaumont mused. "My cook is always looking for new receipts."

Harriett smiled at the calculating look on her friend's face. "I have no idea what my cook would say, but I think it is an excellent idea."

Sextus placed two plates on the table and slid into the seat next to hers. "What is an excellent idea?"

"Something Lady Somers heard about taking a sample of something home and asking our cook to copy it."

"Interesting." He placed a lobster patty and some asparagus on her plate. "Did I guess correctly?"

Harriett loved lobster patties and asparagus. "Very well done."

Lady Somers leaned toward Harriett. "I would like you to call me Marcella. I feel as if we are already friends."

"Yes, indeed," Lady Beaumont commented. "I have been thinking we should have been on a first name basis long before now. We have been friends for a few months." She laughed. "And I am not that much older than you."

How wonderful. Harriett felt a broad smile growing on her lips. "I would love that, and please call me Harriett."

"Yes, do call me Octavius," he grinned as if he knew something she did not. "However, I believe the only one who calls Beaumont by his first name is his wife."

Beaumont inclined his head. "And my housekeeper when she is angry at me and addresses me as *Master Robert*."

They all laughed as he assumed an offended look. Serena patted his arm. "That does not happen very much at all these days."

"You must taste this lemon tart." Marcella held up the object of note. "It is wonderful. Try one and tell me if you can taste what makes it so good."

Harriett took a bite of the one Sextus handed her. "I believe it has a hint of lavender in it."

Serena tasted hers as well. "Yes. I think you have it."

A settled feeling, a feeling she was finally home came over Harriett. She had never been more accepted or included before. If this was to be her future, she would gladly accept it. She just prayed she was not reading too much into Sextus's behavior.

# CHAPTER 5

The day of the meeting had arrived. Sextus, Octavius, and Beaumont had made arrangements for their ladies to be as protected as well as possible. Both Octavius and Beaumont had received news the Home Office was taking a grim look at any type of dissent. What the Home Secretary apparently did not appreciate was that members of the gentry and the peerage might also attend these meetings.

They had assembled in the parlor Beaumont was using as his study. Sextus glanced at the other two. "It is agreed then; one footman standing next to the ladies, one stationed at each exit, and two grooms outside watching the crowd."

Beaumont nodded. "At the first sign of trouble, a signal will be given to whichever footman can most safely get our ladies out."

"Will they agree, I wonder," Octavius said.

"It is Serena's plan," Beaumont replied. "She is telling them about it now."

The thought of Harriett in danger made Sextus's blood run cold. "They are all intelligent. I cannot believe they would willingly put their lives in danger for a meeting."

His brother's lips had been tightly shut, then he let out a breath. "No. You're right. I just don't like it."

"None of us do," Sextus agreed. "But I have learned one must deal with the circumstances one has been given. Marcella and Serena live in the area and should know what is going on. I plan to take Harriett away as soon as I get her to agree to marry me." The last two days had been a farce of him trying to find enough time alone with her to propose. He'd been thwarted by everyone from children to servants. The next time, he was going to actually make a plan not to be interrupted.

The door opened, and Serena looked in. "We are ready to depart."

The crowd outside the building was already large and growing when they arrived. He took Harriett's hand. "Are you certain?"

She nodded decisively. "I am. If it goes wrong, Serena explained the plan to leave."

"Very well." He kissed Harriett's hand. "I will be waiting."

The pub across the street had tables set up outside, and he, Octavius, and Beaumont took seats there and ordered ale. Once a half hour had passed, they began to relax. "Perhaps this will simply be a long wait." Then a contingent of troops arrived as well as what looked to be a group of plainly dressed men slipping into the building. "On the other hand, I might be mistaken."

"Agitators." His brother's tone was hard. "That's it. We're getting them out." He signaled to the groom closest just as a shout came from inside.

The coachmen had been walking the horses up and down the street, but now moved the coaches in position to depart. From the back of the building, Harriett and the others appeared around the corner. Striding forward, he reached her before she got to the carriage. "What happened?"

"Produce began being thrown. That is when we decided to leave." She glanced at the footmen around them. "They were able to get us through the crowd."

He helped her up the steps and followed. "If the government isn't careful, they're going to have their own revolution on their hands."

"I agree. It was clear regular citizens did not start the melee."

Heedless of Octavius and Marcella who entered the coach, Sextus hugged Harriett to him. "I'm glad you're safe."

"Everything happened so quickly. It was touch and go for a while." She grinned. "I hit one of the men with my parasol."

He looked at the broken piece of fluff. "I'll buy you a much sturdier one."

Suddenly the air stilled and only the two of them seemed to be present. The pulse of her neck increased its tempo. "Will you?"

"Yes. Harriett, when we get to the house, I need to speak with you alone."

She gave an imperceptible nod. "Very well."

He pulled her closer when the carriage turned sharply around a corner.

Harriett sighed softly. This was where she wanted to be for the rest of her life. In his arms.

As soon as they entered the house, he took her hand and addressed Serena, "I do not want to be disturbed for at least twenty minutes."

She grinned. "Robert's parlor. I'll keep everyone away."

He pulled Harriett into the room and locked the door. "Now…" he glanced around, shook his head, and dropped to one knee. "Harriett, I love you, and I want to live the rest of my life with you. I want you to bear my name and be the mother of my children. I want to travel through life by your side. Will you marry me?"

Her throat closed and tears sprang into her eyes. "Yes. I want the same things. Yes, I will marry you."

Before she could blink, he was on his feet and pulling her into his arms. "Thank God. Thank you."

His lips lowered to hers, and she closed her eyes, puckering her lips. Lightly, he feathered his mouth over hers, and the tingles she had almost become used to when he touched her felt more like lightning pulsing through her. When she opened her mouth to gasp, he entered.

The feeling when he caressed her tongue with his was something she had never imagined, never could have imagined. He tilted his head, deepening the kiss, and his fingers lightly stroked her cheek, then dropped to her breasts. Suddenly, her nipples ached to be touched, and she pushed into his hand. She let out a moan and for a moment had not realized where the sound came from.

Sextus broke the kiss. "We have to stop, or I will make love to you here." He pressed his forehead gently against hers. "It will most likely kill me, but we will wait until our wedding night."

Harriett's heart was pounding so hard she could hear it. Was this what her parents had experienced? How could her father have left Mama after that? "Yes."

He kissed her softly and placed his arm around her waist. "Let's go tell the others."

"Wait. I want you to hear everything about my heritage that I know." Her heart dropped to her feet. Once he found out who her mother was, he might not want to marry her.

His brow furrowed. "I know you are the daughter of an earl."

"But you do not know who my mother was."

Harriett had sent for Honey and Ellen. Once they arrived, Harriett and Sextus gathered everyone in the morning room to tell them about their decision to wed and about her heritage.

"Your mother was the daughter of a merchant?" Lord Beaumont's tone reflected his shock.

Serena had been right. No one in the *ton* cared about Harriett's legitimacy. What had not been said was that blood was more important.

Sextus squeezed her hand. "I give not a whit who Harriett's mother was."

"I am not saying *you* should." Beaumont raised a brow. "However, I would be very surprised if your superiors did not. It would be better if her parents had been married. Not by much, but more acceptable."

Now she understood why everyone here changed the subject whenever anyone asked about her family. They had not known, and therefore, did not wish anything said. But this conversation was so opposite of any she had ever had before about her parentage. If she was not careful, she was going to explode. "Do you mean to tell me it is perfectly acceptable to be a natural child of a lady and the earl, but not of a merchant's daughter and the earl?"

Lord Beaumont shrugged. "I don't make the rules."

"There is no point in this discussion." Sextus tightened his grip on her hand. "We will be wed."

Lord, how she loved him. But Lord Beaumont was right. If he married her, it could hurt his chances of advancement. "Sextus, no. I cannot ruin your career."

He turned to her and searched her face. "My love, I would rather give up the Foreign Office than not live the rest of my life with you."

Tears filled her eyes. He might think that now, but what about later?

"That's it." Honey rose from where she had been sitting next to a window. "I watched your mother and father have their hearts broken. I won't stand by while it happens again." She took a breath and let it out. "The earl is not your father, and your parents were lawfully married in Scotland."

At first there was dead silence, then pandemonium broke out as everyone started asking questions at the same time.

"Quiet." Octavius's tone caused everyone to stop speaking. Some had their mouths still open. "Now. Obviously, this is good news, and we all want to know why such a secret was kept. However, we need to hear the rest of the story." He focused on Honey. "Mrs. Honeybourne, please tell us exactly what happened." Then he gave a stern look to the rest of them. "You will have the opportunity to ask questions when she has finished."

Honey had taken her seat while everyone had been talking. "Harriett, your father's name was Aldwin Bigglesworth. He was supposed to have joined a walking tour of Scotland when he met your mother. She was visiting an aunt on your maternal grandmother's side of the family who lived there. Her governess was unable to come, so I went. Your great-aunt lived in a manor house at the edge of the same village I'm from. I took it as an opportunity to see my family." Honey took a sip of what must now be cold tea. "Your parents met while we were doing some shopping. He was looking for a ride to where he was going to meet his friends. He never went. Instead, he got a room and started spending time with your mother. I've rarely seen two people look happier. Of course, they wanted to wed right away. I tried to get them to wait the year until Aldwin turned twenty-one, but he was so sure everything would be fine. He had an allowance meaning he could support your mother. But they decided to keep it a secret from their families. The vicar wouldn't marry them without their families knowing, so they went to the blacksmith to wed."

When Honey paused to finish her tea, Harriett squeezed Sextus's hand. This was almost unbelievable.

Honey focused on Harriett again. "When Aldwin didn't meet his friends, they sent word to the earl and the hunt was on. It didn't take long to track them down. The earl was furious. I believe your great-aunt knew because your grandfather arrived a day later and he was just as angry as the earl."

A footman arrived with more tea for everyone and Honey refilled her cup. "You see, your grandfather hated the aristocracy. Them not paying their bills caused him to almost go bankrupt. When he built his business back, he made sure it didn't depend on them. The only thing he had in common with the earl was they both wanted the marriage ended." She glanced around the room. "The earl said he was going to get the marriage annulled, but your parents wouldn't agree. You see, the marriage had been consummated. That day, the earl sent your father to the army. Of course, we didn't know that at the time. Your grandfather took your mother back to London. He trusted the earl to end the marriage. Then we found out about you, and we had no idea where the earl had sent your father." Honey's eyes misted over. "The long and short of it was that your father had died a short time after arriving in Spain. The earl promised to support your mother and provide for you as long as she agreed to the story that you were his natural child. She never agreed, but she didn't tell anyone. It was more important for you to be taken care of." She shook her head. "The earl threatened everyone he thought knew about the wedding if they said anything. Your grandfather told me I'd be let go if I talked. What neither of them knew was that I was there to witness the marriage."

Sextus looked like he'd eaten a lemon. "Sounds like something the duke would have done."

"Duke?" Honey asked. "What duke?"

He narrowed his eyes. "Somerset. Why?"

"I heard that name," she said. "I think it's how they found poor Aldwin."

"That makes sense." Sextus nodded. "He goes to his estate in Scotland every year. It's not far from Carlisle."

"That'd be it then." She looked at Harriett and waited.

Harriett was in shock. Her whole life had been a lie. "I am having a bit of trouble taking all this in. My parents were *married*?"

Honey nodded.

"And I am not the earl's daughter. How I wish Mama had told me."

"In a way she did," Honey said. "She wrote almost every day in her journal over the years. There are several of them. Before she died, she told me to get the journals and keep her brother from finding them. I have them all with me."

Mama kept journals? To think all this, the story of Mama's life and Harriett's beginnings had been kept from her. "When we go back to the town house, will you please get the journals? I would like to read them."

Honey nodded.

"You do realize this makes you Miss Harriett Bigglesworth." Sextus grinned. "Soon to be Lady Sextus Trevor."

His brother rolled his eyes.

Marcella glanced at Harriett frowning. "What business did your grandfather have?"

"The same one my uncle has continued. S and S Industries." She did not know much about it except for the fact it had made her uncle extremely wealthy. "Do you know it?"

"Know it?" Octavius grinned. "I'm invested in their rail venture."

"I am as well," Lord Beaumont said. "And that is only one of the many things S and S has their hand in."

Serena looked as if she was trying to remember something, then suddenly her face cleared. "I have it. Do you have a cousin named Pamela who is eighteen?"

Harriett nodded. "I do. She is my uncle's eldest daughter."

"She is about to marry the Marquis of Yardley's heir. When we were in Town, I heard the agreements had been signed and a date set."

Lord Beaumont's brows shot up. "You're right. I was there when Yardley was being congratulated. It appears he was at *point non plus*. His son suggested the match."

"Ah. Another scion of a noble family finding love," Serena beamed. "There will come a day in the not-too-distant future when marriages between the peerage and the merchant class will not be unusual."

Harriett looked at her friends and then at Sextus. "This changes everything."

"Not for me." He released her hand and slid his arm around her shoulders. "I was going to marry you no matter how much you meant to sacrifice yourself."

"The one thing that will not change is the duke's reaction to having his plans thwarted yet again," Octavius said in a dry tone. "We have two options. Sextus can either purchase a regular license here and wait for five days and hope word does not get back to the duke, or we can decamp to Town, get a special license, and you can marry with the rest of the family in attendance."

"I have no doubt that by now he will be searching for you." Marcella matched her husband's tone.

Harriett wanted this to be Sextus's choice. The only family she really had was Honey and Ellen. She would take both of them with her. "It is your decision, my love."

He was still for several long moments seemingly at nothing. "London. I'll write to Meg and tell her I am on the last leg of my journey and will arrive in about ten days. She will write Mama giving her the information. She, in turn, will let the duke know what Meg has been told. Then I will write Hawksworth and ask him to book passage for me, my wife and our retainers and servants to France as well as the onward journey to Vienna." He turned to Harriett. "We will wed the day after I procure a special license. Does that suit you?"

It did, but she needed to ask if it suited her staff. "Honey, Ellen, will you come with us?"

Ellen frowned. "If you think I can be useful."

"Harriett will not be the only lady who has a companion," Sextus said.

Ellen smiled. "Very well, then. I would love to visit Europe."

"I wouldn't miss it," Honey said. "I'm sure there will be at least one babe for me to take care of and nursemaids to supervise."

"Excellent." Sextus grinned at Harriett. "I have been living in rooms, but now we will require a staff."

Harriett didn't know if all her servants would wish to leave England. "I will ask if they will accompany us as well."

"Perfect." He glanced at his brother. "When do we depart York?"

Octavius raised a brow. "As soon as we have settled the servant question and pack. Tomorrow?"

"No." Marcella shook her head. "I think we are probably looking at the day after. We might be used to traveling quickly. That does not mean Harriett is."

Beaumont rubbed his hands together. "This means we can go home."

His wife blew out a breath. "This means we shall return to Town." Serena patted the hand he had on her shoulder. "I will not miss this wedding."

Harriett was thankful it was still fairly early in the day. "I must return to my house and speak with my servants."

"Would you like me to accompany you?" Sextus asked.

That might be for the best. Her servants did not know him well at all and soon they would be working for him. "Yes, please."

"In that case." Marcella rose. "I will go with you. He cannot be seen entering a single lady's house alone."

Her words almost knocked Harriett off her mental balance. She had never had to follow the rules a lady must adhere to before. Thankfully, Ellen had taught her what they were. "I am a lady."

"My dear, Harriett," Serena said softly. "You have always behaved like a lady. If we could tell the world the two of you are betrothed, it would not be that much of a problem. But Marcella is correct. Even with Ellen, it would be better if she accompanies you. It will not appear so singular if several people arrive at the same time."

Harriett would be happy when the duke was no longer a concern.

# CHAPTER 6

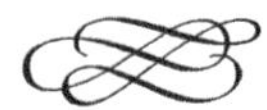

Sextus would be glad when he and Harriett were wed. As it was, he agreed with Serena's assessment. He was going to do his best to chivy the ladies along. And he knew just the person to do it.

"We..." Ellen glanced at Honey... "had better go with you as well. There is much to do."

They all rose and went to the hall. Sextus took his hat from the Beaumont butler. "Tell Lovel I want him at Miss Staunton's house immediately."

"Yes, my lord."

Harriett tucked her hand in the crook of Sextus's arm. "Who is Lovel?"

"My valet. He has been with me since Oxford. If anyone can assess how long and what it will take to get you and your household ready to travel it is he."

She seemed to consider that for a moment. "You said you were in Russia for several years."

"I was, but the Russian court moved around the country. Often with little notice to those of us following." Sextus repressed a shudder at the mad scramble it had many times been. "It was keep up, or be left behind."

The corners of her lips lifted. "I look forward to hearing what he has to say."

The walk was made in less than five minutes. This was the first time he had been past the elegant hall. "Is all the furniture yours?"

She looked at it thoughtfully. "I bought the house fully furnished, thinking to change it over time. If it is at all possible, I would like to keep it."

He hadn't considered her property at all until now. Sextus had an inheritance from one of his mother's many family members, but what would happen if he were to die? He would provide for her and their children. Harriett must have a home in which to live. His father certainly wouldn't do anything for her. "I think you should keep all of your property, real and otherwise, to do with what you please. It shall be detailed in the settlement agreement."

"Thank you." Her tone was soft and thoughtful. "I should like to invest the funds."

"Speak with my brother, Hawksworth, when we arrive in Town. He handles my investments for me and some of my other brothers. Due to his prowess, Octavius has become quite wealthy."

They stopped just before the entrance to her town house. "Your family appears to be very close and made of good people. Is the duke really that horrible?"

Sextus wished he didn't have to tell her all the terrible things his father had done, but she deserved to know that she could never trust him or any of his tools. "You will have plenty of time to hear the stories on the way to Town. First, we must prepare to depart as quickly as possible."

Lovel caught up to them as the door opened. "My lord, I was told to come straightaway."

"I am in need of your expert advice." He glanced at Harriett. "My dear, allow me to present Lovel. The most capable valet a gentleman could ever have."

Lovel performed a formal bow. "Miss Staunton, it is my pleasure to meet you and to serve you in whatever capacity I may."

When she slid a look at Sextus her eyes twinkled. "Thank you, Lovel. I look forward to hearing what you have to say. You should also make the acquaintance of my dresser."

"Yes, indeed. We will need to work closely together." There was an energy coming from the servant Sextus had never noticed before. Was he glad he'd now be part of a larger household?

With Harriett's hand still tucked in his arm, they entered the hall.

She handed the butler her bonnet. "Neathercote, please gather the staff in the drawing room. I have an announcement to make."

He glanced at Sextus. "Yes, miss. Shall I bring tea?"

"Perhaps later." She looked behind her and drew Marcella forward. "I am glad you came."

He had forgotten she was with them. "Lovel, join us."

Harriett led them to an elegantly appointed parlor.

Sextus stopped at the door. "I can see why you kept the furniture."

"The previous owner had excellent taste." She drew him to one of two small sofas in front of a fireplace. "There was little for me to do."

The butler entered the drawing room, and the rest of the servants followed quietly, clearly expecting something but not knowing what.

Harriett rose and he stood with her. "First I would like to tell you that I have accepted Lord Sextus's proposal of marriage."

Broad smiles broke out around the room, and Neathercote said, "On behalf of the staff, we wish you much happiness."

"Thank you all." She returned their smiles. "Naturally, such a change necessitates further change. Lord Sextus is in the Foreign Service, and his next position is in Vienna. I would like to take as many of you who want to go." Some of the servants glanced warily at each other. "If you do not wish to join us, I will give you three month's pay and a reference." She looked at Lovel. "Mr. Lovel is his lordship's valet. You may ask him any questions you need answered before you make your decision."

Sextus felt the tension running through her. She truly did want to keep her staff. He decided to assist them by saying, "If you come with us and decide the new place is not to your liking, we will pay for your travel back to England."

Relief showed on a few faces. Hopefully, that would do it.

Harriett's hand brushed against his. "Those of you who desire to consider our offer may do so now. Mr. Lovel will join you shortly. Those of you who have decided to come, please remain."

Neathercote, the housekeeper, Mrs. Mollison—whom their children would no doubt call Molly—a woman Sextus supposed to be Harriett's maid as well as two footmen and two housemaids remained.

"When do you wish to depart?" Neathercote asked.

Harriett nodded to herself as if making a decision. "As soon as humanly possible. We will travel to London for the wedding. Most of his lordship's family is in Town. From there we will board a ship to France. Lovel…" she motioned him to step forward… "has a great deal of experience in packing for travel."

The servant Sextus thought must be her dresser pursed her lips. "I can have everything packed and ready to go by the end of the day. Fortunately, we all have traveling trunks."

"You had best start now," Harriett said.

The dresser left the drawing room taking one of the maids with her.

"Do you know what you will wish to take from the house?" Mrs. Mollison asked.

Harriett glanced at Lovel and shrugged one shoulder.

He inclined his head. "Miss, if I might suggest an arrangement that will suit those coming and those remaining?"

Sextus didn't understand. "Remaining?"

"My lord, I overheard Miss Staunton say she would like to keep the town house. It would not be wise to leave it empty. I suggest that those who do not want to accompany us remain here."

Harriett clapped her hands together and grinned. "Lovel, you are a genius. I do not know why I had not considered such an option."

The man actually flushed. "You have had a great deal about which to think."

"Miss," Mollison prodded, "What are we taking?"

"If I may," Lovel said. "Linens are most important. Silver, crystal, china, small pieces of furniture that are important, books that you wish to bring, and anything else you cannot live without." He glanced at the butler. "We will need to hire a carter for most of it. Do you know one in town?"

"Yes. I'll send Simmons over straightway."

One of the footmen whispered something to the remaining maid and left.

"Mrs. Mollison, come with me." Harriett squeezed Sextus's hand as she turned to address him. "Will you go with Lovel downstairs and speak to the remaining servants?"

"Of course." Raising her hand, he kissed it. "This went better than I thought it would."

The butler led him and Lovel to the servants' hall below. "There has been a change," Neathercote announced. "Miss Staunton is keeping the house and will require a staff to care for it." One of the maids broke into tears, and the cook wiped her eyes with her apron. "However, if any of you wish to speak with Mr. Lovel, here he is."

Lovel turned to Sextus. Keeping his voice low, he said. "I know Miss wanted to bring everyone, but it's better this way. We will need local servants to help us adjust."

Sextus remembered something of the sort being mentioned in Russia. "I'd forgotten that. Naturally, our staff will need to rely on their knowledge and language skills."

"Just so, my lord." His valet addressed the small number of servants remaining. "What would you like me to tell you?"

Deciding he was no longer needed here, Sextus made his way back to the hall and the now empty drawing room. Where would his betrothed have got to? He ambled down one corridor to the back of the house, then back to the hall to the other corridor. Not finding her there, he mounted the stairs to the next floor and was almost knocked down by Mrs. Mollison. He grasped her arm as she wobbled.

"I'm sorry, my lord. I didn't see you there."

"I don't expect you would have. Can you tell me where Miss Staunton is?"

"Yes, sir. Down the corridor to the last door on the left. She's with Lady Somers."

Before he could say anything else, the housekeeper was gone. He found Harriett and Marcella armed with notebooks. "Where are you off to?"

"The library." Harriett gave him a brief smile. "I want to make a list of the books I want to take."

"Don't stint. It is hard to find books in English, although French and German should be readily available." Every room they passed on the way to the library was a hive of activity. "When do you think you will be ready to depart for the Metropolis?"

"*I* will be ready by tomorrow morning. But you had better ask Neathercote when the household will be ready."

What Sextus had better do was to speak with the carter and his valet. He had no idea if his furniture and such was in London waiting for him or already on the way to Vienna. If his possessions were in Town, Harriett's property could be added to his. If not, he'd have to arrange separate passage. He wished it were simply a matter of being able to send the household ahead, but he dared not leave them to attempt foreign travel by themselves. "I'll do that now."

An hour later, he collected Harriett and Marcella who had just finished in the library. "I'm famished. Things are proceeding apace here, and, as far as I can see, there is no more for us to do. Let's have luncheon then we can return."

Harriett pushed a curl that had escaped behind her small shell-like ear. An ear that Sextus would dearly like to trace with his tongue. Unfortunately, nothing like that was likely to occur until they were wed. "That is an excellent idea."

Harriett was glad she did not have to bother her servants with preparing luncheon or dinner for that matter. They would need all the time they had to get everything ready. She did wonder when Lovel would have time to pack his and Sextus's belongings. They returned to the house the Beaumonts had leased and joined them and Octavius in the family dining room.

"How is it going?" Serena asked.

"Well." Harriett was pleased she could say it and mean it. "Some of my servants will travel with us and others will remain to look after the house."

"Neathercote, our butler..." Sextus slid her a look as if to ask for her confirmation, and she gave him an imperceptible nod... "believes all will be ready for a morning departure."

"We will follow shortly thereafter," Beaumont said. "I have something to which I must attend before we can depart."

A small smile hovered around Serena's lips as she gazed at her husband, causing Harriett to wonder what the business was.

"Octavius, I told Harriett that we will send our steward over on a quarterly basis to look over the accounts," Marcella said.

He lifted a brow. "This will do for the nonce. But I'll ask him if he can recommend someone who can be trusted under the circumstance."

"Yes, of course." Harriett did not think any of her staff would steal from her, but while the cat is away... "A permanent solution must be found."

"Perhaps we can help as well," Serena said. "Our steward has an assistant who might be worth considering."

Moving from London had not been nearly as much work. The tension that had been knotting Harriett's shoulders began to seep away. It might be better to rely upon the Beaumonts. They had been in the area for generations. Marcella and Octavius were newly arrived. "I will accept your very kind offer." She thought she heard a small sigh of relief from her soon-to-be brother-in-law. They had finished eating, and she needed to go back home. "Thank you for luncheon. I must get back in case anything requires my attention."

Sextus rose as she did. "I'll accompany you to your door."

"Thank you." As they passed a door, he opened it and pulled her in with him. "What are you doing?"

"Kissing you. It occurred to me that we will have very little, if any, time alone until we are wed." His hands framed her face, and his thumbs caressed her cheeks, as he gazed into her eyes. "I can't believe how much I need you."

His lips touched hers and after a few seconds his tongue pressed against the seam of her mouth, and she opened for him. It was truly amazing how good it felt when his tongue caressed hers. Slowly, she returned the caress. She wrapped her arms around his neck, and he slid his hand down her back and over her bottom. Something flared inside her, urging her to press closer to him.

Then he broke the kiss. "We had better stop."

Sextus's breathing was as ragged as hers.

"I suppose we must. How quickly can we get to Town? I seem to remember it taking days when I traveled here."

"This, my love, will not be a leisurely trip. When I return, I'll write my letters and send them by express. All should be prepared when we arrive." He kissed her lightly. "Come, we both have work to do."

That was a fact. "How will we send everything to Vienna?"

"If all my possessions are in London, then your property will join mine to be shipped. If not, they will go separately. I'll ask Hawksworth to coordinate with the Foreign Office."

"That will make it much simpler." And it was a relief not to have to worry about her possessions.

"Yes. They have great deal of experience moving people and their households around."

When they reached her house, the carter's wagon was standing in front of it and boxes were being carried out. The first floor had trunks stacked against the railing and footmen in Beaumont livery were carrying them down and toward the back of the town house.

For a moment, Harriett could only watch the activity in amazement. "I never expected so much to be accomplished so quickly."

"One must merely put one's mind to it." Sextus kissed her hand. "And have willing workers."

Wyborn, her maid appeared at the railing. "I left out an evening gown for dinner and a carriage gown for the morning. This small trunk has everything you will need during the journey. The rest is being loaded onto one of Lord Somers's coaches."

It was all happening so quickly, but Harriett had none of the nervousness she had experienced when she had had to move to her uncle's home or when she came to York. Rather, a sense of calm bloomed within her. This was the right decision. "Thank you."

"Oh, miss, I'm excited to be traveling." Wyborn grinned. "I never expected to be able to."

Neither had Harriett. Then Sextus had come into her life, and everything had changed. "No." She smiled. "Neither had I."

# CHAPTER 7

By the time the sun began to rise the next morning, their assemblage had passed through the city wall headed toward Doncaster. Sextus and his brother sat on the backward facing bench, and Harriett sat with his sister-in-law across from them. He looked forward to the day when they could sit together in a carriage alone. The previous evening, they had eaten a quick dinner before Sextus, Octavius, and Harriett had gone to manage the final packing arrangements. In the end, they had three carriages carrying the items deemed necessary as well as their servants.

Sextus lounged back against the plush leather cushions, and stretched out his legs, just nudging Harriett's foot. Glancing at him, she flashed him a smile before turning back to what Marcella was saying.

The sun was low in the sky when they arrived in Newark-on-Trent and drove into the yard of the While Hart Inn. "I need to stretch my legs." Sextus held his arm out to Harriett. "Will you join me?"

"I will." She put her hand in the crook of his arm. "Twelve hours in even a well-appointed coach with good company becomes tedious."

He gave her a rueful grin. "Be thankful you're not traveling in Russia."

"Oh dear." Her green gaze flew to his. "I had not thought of that. Was it very dreadful? How do you think the journey to Vienna will go?"

"There are parts of Russia where there is nothing for miles, and parts that are very dangerous. Our travel to Austria will be much slower." He drew her closer to him, so that her skirts brushed the top of his boots. "I plan to make frequent stops so that we are able to visit the cities along the way."

"My lord," Lovel hurried up to them. "Dinner will be in an hour."

"We won't be long." Sextus glanced at Harriett. "A short walk."

Towing him along, she started strolling away from the inn. "At this point, anything is better than nothing. Although, I suspect I shall be so tired after dinner I will fall straight asleep."

"Tomorrow will not be much better." If they kept the pace his brother had planned, they'd arrive exhausted.

"I know. Marcella told me." Harriett sighed. "Perhaps tomorrow we can play a game of some sort."

That gave him an idea. "I do have some traveling games. I'll have Lovel find them."

"Wonderful! I'll look forward to it." She yawned. "Perhaps we should go back. I do not understand how I could be so tired when I did nothing but sit all day."

"I agree." Yet it always seemed to be that way. "It would be better to avoid falling asleep over one's soup." He guided them along the road back to the inn. By the time they'd arrived, the coaches and horses had been stabled, and candles burned brightly in the inn's windows. "Let us find our chambers."

He should have expected to see his valet and her dresser waiting for them to take them to their respective rooms. Less than a half-hour later, they joined Marcella and Octavius in a private parlor. Miss Gobeley and Honeybourne had opted to dine in their rooms. Dinner consisted of a vegetable potage, roasted lamb, buttered haricot vert, potatoes, and a strawberry tart. A very good claret was served with the meal. "I didn't know strawberries were in season here."

"They are not," Marcella said. "They must have been grown in a green house."

"They taste wonderful," Octavius said after swallowing a bite. "The food is the main reason I stop here."

"The rooms are comfortable as well," Marcella added. She wrinkled her nose. "Unfortunately, we must get an early start again tomorrow. It will be another long day."

Harriett gave a weary nod. "I expected as much."

Sextus wished he could save her from this rapid mode of travel. If only the duke would leave them all alone, they could court and wed in a normal manner.

She finished her glass of wine and when Marcella rose Harriett did as well. "I am for my couch."

She did look as if she would fall asleep on her feet. "I'll escort you."

"Thank you." Harriett smiled gratefully and took his arm. In just a few more days, this would all be over, and they would be married.

He kept pace with her up a set of stairs wide enough for two. "Just remember. It is for a good cause."

"I shall not forget." She gazed up at him, and he dropped a light kiss on her lips. That would have to hold him for now.

The next day started the same as the first. Wyborn woke Harriett when it was still dark. She washed and dressed, then joined the others in the private parlor for breakfast. She was still tired. Perhaps that would help her sleep in the coach, something she was normally unable to do.

They stopped in Stilton, where they partook of an excellent luncheon that included the famous cheese of the area. Harriett had been able to doze in the carriage and was feeling much better when Lovel followed by her dresser surreptitiously slipped into the parlor.

Sextus glanced up quickly. "What is it?"

"The duke," Lovel said. "His coach arrived. It appears he plans to dine here."

"Of all the rotten luck." Marcella scowled.

"What the deuced is he doing here?" Octavius said. "He's supposed to be in Scotland."

Under the table, Sextus's hand found Harriett's. "One can only surmise that he has decided to take an active role in my marriage."

Ellen's brow furrowed as she looked at Harriett. "My dear, what will you do?"

Marcella pulled a sheet of cut foolscap from her reticule. "Meg made contingency plans."

Octavius's eyes widened. "Why was I not told of the plans?"

Marcella shrugged one shoulder. "You were busy with other things." She opened the paper and ran a finger down it. "We are not very far from Huntingdon where the Marquis of Huntingdon has his main estate. You…" she glanced at Sextus and Harriett… "are to go there. Even if the Huntingdon's are not in residence, the servants will get you to Town."

Harriett knew they couldn't all go there without being discovered. "But how will we travel to their estate?"

"Coach, miss," Wyborn said with a decisive nod. "You will ride to the next town in the coach Mr. Lovel and I have been travelling in. When we get there, we will find a stage coach that services the area."

"The only other problem is getting out of this inn." Sextus looked at his valet. "From what I have heard, the duke travels with several outriders and other servants."

"Yes, my lord. Some of them were carrying pistols. His lordship's valet went to inform the head coachman to expect some changes."

"If I may make a suggestion," Honey said. She waited until they all signaled their assent. "Harriett, you go with Wyborn to the servants' coach. My lord, you go out the back, skirt around the building, and meet the coach on the road."

"I beg your pardon, ma'am, but there is no back way," Lovel said apologetically. "There is a side door in this wing."

"Thank you, Mr. Lovel. That will work even better."

"I am sorry to bring this up," Ellen said, "but Harriett, my dear, you cannot travel with Lord Sextus by yourself. Even in a stagecoach."

"I will take Wyborn. We can make it seem as if we are traveling together."

The dresser nodded. "I've plenty of experience on a stagecoach, and I'll take good care of her."

Footsteps sounded in the corridor.

Octavius glanced at Sextus. "You two had better go. Marcella will remain here with Miss Gobeley and Mrs. Honeybourne."

Marcella handed Harriett the paper. "Just in the event you need it."

She stuck it into her reticule. "Thank you." She hugged her soon-to-be-sister-in-law. "I trust I will see you again soon."

Lovel opened the door and looked both ways before waving to them to follow. He took Sextus to the right while Wyborn took Harriett the opposite way.

When they reached the yard, a footman was speaking with one of the coachmen. "Ye can ask all ye want. I don't discuss his lordship's business. Now be on yer way. Here comes his lordship's valet which means I've got to get goin'."

The earl's valet arrived, carrying Harriett's traveling trunk. "That should do it. We cannot waste time. You know how his lordship is."

Harriett got in the coach followed by her maid, the earl's valet, then Lovel. As soon as the door closed, the coach moved forward.

"Mr. Lovel, your bag and his lordship's are in the trunk," the valet said. "I thought something like this might occur."

She had known none of the duke's children liked or trusted the man, but apparently their servants held the same opinions. She glanced down the road but could not see Sextus. She would not leave without him.

"What's the plan?" the coachman asked.

"We will find Lord Sextus on the road and pick him up." Harriett prayed he did not have any trouble leaving the inn. "After that, you will take us to the next good-sized town where we will take a stage-coach to Huntingdon."

"Very good, miss." The coach rolled forward.

They had reached the end of the building when the carriage slowed, the door opened, and Sextus jumped in, slamming the door behind him. He settled next to her. From the corner of her eye, she saw a man lying on the ground. "Who is on the ground?

"One of the duke's tools. The duke's secretary saw me and sent one of his outriders after me. The man insisted I come with him, and I insisted I had no interest in doing so." Sextus shrugged. "I was more insistent."

Expecting to be followed, the coachman gave the horses their heads and kept a good pace until they arrived at Alconbury Hill where they were lucky enough to be able to buy inside fares for the four of them. Fortunately, the journey was not far, and when the stagecoach stopped outside of the city of Huntingdon, the driver directed them to an inn where they could hire a coach to take them to Lord Huntingdon's estate. They arrived to find his lordship away from home, but his steward had been told they might be visiting.

"I will arrange a carriage to take you the rest of the way to Town," the steward said. "You will be staying with Lady Bellamny."

Sextus had heard of her ladyship. She had helped facilitate Meg and Hawksworth's wedding. "Thank you. This must seem like a great farce."

"I will only say that the Duke of Somerset is not well liked by his lordship, and when he heard of the possible difficulty, he immediately offered his assistance. He would have invited you to stay with him in Town, but the ladies decided Lady Bellamny would be better suited."

He spent a second wondering who the ladies were, before realizing it was his sisters, sisters-in-law, and Meg's friends. "I suppose all we can do is be guided by them."

"That would be for the best, my lord." He indicated a stout older woman in a mobcap who had arrived. "Mrs. Jones will show you to your rooms."

"I feel as if I am living in a novel," Harriett whispered as they climbed the stairs.

Sextus had been having the same feelings. "I do not understand why we have to endure this madness." Except for the fact that Somerset never let anything go as long as there was a chance he might have his way. "I wonder if Octavius and Marcella were able to get away without encountering him."

"I suppose we will hear about it when we arrive in Town." Harriett sounded distracted, and he wanted to soothe her.

When they reached the first floor a footman stood waiting.

"Quarles," Mrs. Jones said, "Please take his lordship to the room we prepared for him."

Typical. Sextus thought sourly. He was put in one wing of the house and Harriett was in another. That had to have been the doing of Lady Huntingdon. Not that he would have gone to Harriett's room, Sextus assured himself. He'd take no chance that she would be left without a husband and with a babe. As much as he wanted her, wanted to spend the night with her, and hold her in his arms and make love to her, it would have to wait until they were wed.

The next morning as Sextus and Harriett were breaking their fast with the steward, he said, "You will travel by easy stages the rest of the way. Tomorrow evening you will stay at one of his lordship's houses near Bishop's Stordfort. The next day you will finish the journey to Town."

Sextus didn't understand. Haste had been the key to all of this. "Why not do it all in one day?"

"Because you have been forced to make a detour, other plans have been put in place." The steward poured a cup of tea. "I am not privy to the details, but suffice it to say everything will be set by the time you arrive."

That left Sextus with a great deal to ponder. An hour later, after they settled into a comfortable traveling coach, Harriett apparently had the same thoughts. "I wish I knew what was going on."

"As do I." Not only did Sextus not like the lack of control, but having to spend yet another night in the same house as Harriett without being able to make love to her was going to kill him. He'd been walking around with at least a partial erection since they'd left

York. Now there would be an extra day added on to his pain. He hadn't even dared to touch her. If she melted into his arms like she did the last time he'd really kissed her, he wasn't sure he could hold back. And he had the feeling she wouldn't want him to. No, this was up to him. Perhaps he'd ride up with the coachman. Not that he could do anything with both their personal servants in the coach. Still, it was going to be another day of suffering. He just hoped that they'd be able to wed soon after arriving in Town.

# CHAPTER 8

"How the devil did he get away from you?" Somerset was disgusted by how easily his diplomatic son had defeated one of his best bully-boys. One of the man's eyes was swollen and there was a bruise rising on his jaw.

"Didn't think ye'd want me to 'urt 'im, your grace. When I went to grab 'im, he got two 'its in. Knocked me out 'e did."

Somerset wondered briefly what Sextus had been doing in Russia that he was so quick to react. "Get out of my sight." He turned to Belling. "I don't suppose you had any luck at all in detaining Lord Octavius?"

"No, your grace." The secretary pressed his lips together disapprovingly. "When I told him you wanted to speak with him, he told me he had no time. I had his coach followed but there was no sign of Lord Sextus. That was when we found Billy."

If it wasn't for the fact yet another child was defying him, Somerset thought he might be proud of the boy. As it was, he was holding onto his temper by a fine thread. "They had to have been traveling together. Send some men out and see what you can discover. Tell them to meet us at Somerset House."

"Yes, your grace."

"And make sure the people we have watching my children's houses and those of their families are keeping a sharp eye out. I'm not letting Sextus slip through my fingers."

"Yes, your grace."

~

On the afternoon of the fourth day, Harriett and Sextus arrived in London. The coach turned into a mews behind a series of town houses. The journey from Huntingdon had passed without any difficulties, but she was unable to believe there would not be more problems ahead of them.

The carriage door opened, and a footman stood ready to assist. Sextus jumped out and offered Harriett his hand.

The servant bowed. "Miss Bigglesworth, my lord, Lady Bellamny said to take you to your chambers before meeting her in the dining room for luncheon."

Harriett did not think she would ever get used to being addressed as Miss Bigglesworth. "Do you happen to know where my household servants are?"

"No, miss." The footman shook his head. "But I'll warrant her ladyship will be able to tell you."

She glanced around to see her dresser already being ushered through the side gate to the house. "Well, then." She tucked her hand in the crook of Sextus's arm and smiled at him. "It is high time for us to find out how our marriage is being arranged."

The tips of his lips tilted up. "Indeed, it is." He bent his head until his lips hovered over her ear sending delightful shivers down her neck. "I cannot wait to make you mine."

For days, she had been fighting the urge to go to him. If it had not been for her fear of getting with child before she was married, she would have. "And I to make you mine."

They were shown rooms in the same side of the house, which was an improvement over the last two nights. Harriett hoped that meant they would soon be wed. After she washed her face and hands, Wyborn helped her change into a walking gown.

"A footman is waiting to take you to her ladyship."

"Thank you." Soon they would know everything. Or, at least Harriett hoped they would.

When she stepped into the corridor, Sextus, waiting with the footman, held out his arm. "Ready?"

"Yes." Ready to begin the rest of her life.

The footman opened the door, and Harriett's jaw dropped at the number of people in the room.

"What the deuce are all of you doing here?" Sextus sounded none too pleased.

A tall gentleman with dark hair rose. "Is that anyway to greet your family?"

"The duke—"

"The duke has no idea we are here." He bowed to Harriett. "Allow me to make the introductions. I am Hawksworth, and this is my wife, Meg."

Harriett curtseyed, and Marcella gave Harriett a sympathetic smile. She had heard the names and stories of Sextus's brothers and sisters, but now she had to put the names with the faces. She gave herself an inner shake. This was good practice for being a diplomat's wife. "It is lovely to meet you."

Meg Hawksworth smiled. "You as well."

Hawksworth continued, "Our mother, the Duchess of Somerset."

The duchess was a bit taller than medium height with the same blond hair and warm blue eyes Sextus had, and, it seemed, some of her other children had the same eyes. Harriett curtseyed. "Your grace."

"I am so pleased to finally meet you." She turned to Sextus. "And to see you again. I only wish it could be for a longer period of time."

Hawksworth continued, "Anna, the Duchess of Wharton and Quartus, our brother."

*Marcella's half-sister and her husband.*

Harriett started to curtsey again, but the duchess stayed her. "If you curtsey every time you are introduced to one of us your knees are going to give out."

"I have heard so much about you. It is lovely to be able to put a face with the name."

After Anna came Aglaia and Guy, the Duke and Duchess of Bolton, Thalia and Giles, Duke and Duchess of Kendal. The couple who brought Sextus to York. Harriett never knew a family to have so many dukes in it. Then there was Euphrosyne and Charles, Marquis and Marchioness of Markville, and Lord Septimius Trevor who worked at the Home Office.

Hawksworth turned to an older, stout lady dressed in purple. "And our hostess, Lady Bellamny."

Harriett curtseyed. "My lady, thank you for the use of your home."

Sextus bowed. "My lady, I add my thanks to those of my future wife."

"I am exceedingly happy to be able to assist you." She turned her dark eyes on Meg. "While we dine, tell our new arrivals the plans for their wedding."

It was not until then that Harriett noticed the table was laden with platters of fruit and sandwiches.

She and Sextus took the empty chairs as one of the plates of sandwiches was passed to them.

"This is our proposal," Meg said. "Lady Bellamny is having a very exclusive *al fresco* party this afternoon for family and a few close friends." Harriett hoped the Huntingdons would be present. She would like to thank them. "Septimius arranged the special license through a friend who works in Doctor's Common. Quartus will conduct the ceremony. We were spoiled for choice when it came to ships. The one we decided upon is not as elegant as some of the others, but it is fast and will get you to France in good time." Meg took a sip of lemonade. "You will leave directly after the ceremony in order to catch the wind in the right quarter. I imagine you, Octavius and Marcella are exhausted by your travel from York. Fortunately, the rest of us were already here for the Season."

Harriett nodded. No rest for the weary then, and she would not be wearing a special gown for the ceremony. She shrugged inwardly. That was fine. It was more important to be wed.

"The duke will be watching the docks," Sextus said.

Hawksworth raised a brow. "We know. That is the reason you are not leaving from the London docks. The schooner is anchored in the Thames near Greenwich. You will sail to Antwerp. It will take a bit longer, but that is one port the duke will not be watching."

It sounded like a good plan. As long as the weather held.

"Your staff is already there along with the baggage you are taking with you," Meg said. "Now let us finish eating and prepare for the wedding."

Sextus reviewed the scheme and found nothing of which to disapprove. "How did you get here without being seen?"

"Another friend who lives on Green Street," Bolton said. "We all met at Brooks and walked from there. We will leave through his house as well."

Sextus glanced at Meg who added, "We were invited to luncheon and stayed for the party."

He was impressed by the scheme. "It appears as if everything is in place."

"Believe me brother," Thalia said in a dry as dust tone, "We have a great deal of experience dealing with the duke."

Sextus glanced at his mother, but she was in close conversation with her ladyship. He wondered what she thought about all these rushed marriages.

They finished eating, and his sisters and mother retired with Harriett upstairs.

Harriett should be able to have a normal wedding. His jaw tightened. "You do know having to take these measures is ridiculous."

Markville raised his brow. "It is. But no more ludicrous than me camping out before Somerset castle trying to find a way to get Euphrosyne out or convince the duke to allow me to marry her."

Sextus had heard about that in the letters his family wrote to him. He huffed a sigh. "You have me there. All I had to do was punch one of his bully-boys."

"So that was the man on the ground," Octavius said. "The duke attempted to speak with me, but I told his secretary that I had nothing to say to him."

Of all of them, Octavius had been away from the duke's orbit for the longest time. "Harriett and I wondered if he would attempt to get information from you." Sextus nodded. "When does he finally give up?"

"After the wedding," Hawksworth said. "In England that is. In Scotland, it's a rush to consummate the marriage."

"Good Lord." Sextus would be glad when they got on the ship. He glanced at his brothers. "I need someone to stand up with me."

Octavius grinned. "We discussed it and decided it should be Hawksworth for you because he did most of the planning, and Marcella for Harriett since she is closest to her."

"Thank you." Sextus rose. "I suppose I should bathe and dress for my wedding."

The butler opened the door and announced Lord Beaumont. He entered and looked at Sextus. "I have some interesting news for Harriett and you."

"She has gone to prepare for the wedding."

"In that case, I'm sure my wife will tell her. There is an inheritance from her father's mother's side of the family. Have the settlement agreements been signed yet?"

"No," Hawksworth said. "They have been prepared. I was going to review them with Sextus and Harriett before the wedding."

Beaumont handed him a sheaf of papers. "Even though he knew about Harriett, the current Earl of Seahaven had been attempting to work out a way to keep the inheritance for himself. He was persuaded to give it to Harriett once he discovered that he was not the only one who knew who her father was."

Hawksworth handed him the papers just before Sextus was about to grab them out of his hands. His jaw almost dropped as he read the provisions. "Fifty thousand pounds?"

"And jewels from her father's maternal grandmother," his brother said.

Sextus glanced at Hawksworth. "She shall keep it in trust for her use."

"I agree that is the best decision. None of us wanted to take the chance that our wives would be dependent on the duke."

"How did you even know to ask about her inheritance?" Sextus asked Beaumont.

He shrugged. "I had a feeling, and I knew the current earl is suffering financially."

Harriett was glad she had been sitting when Serena Beaumont announced that Harriett had an inheritance in addition to the provisions that had been made for her. In fact, she felt a little light-headed.

Meg pressed a glass of chilled white wine into Harriett's hand, and she took a sip. "Even after discovering my parentage, I never dreamed I would receive an inheritance."

"My husband had an inkling there might be something that went to your father," Serena said. "He was, after all, a younger son, but he had a different mother. Once we found out about your father, it was easy to discover who his mother was. Robert had his solicitor look through the probate records. And after you left, he went straight to the new earl and demanded he give it to you."

"From what I've heard of the earl, I doubt he wanted to give it up."

A slow smile grew on Serena's face. "Robert can be very persuasive. He had also taken Mrs. Honeybourne to the solicitor to attest to the marriage.

Harriett remembered Honey saying she had an errand to run. "That is where she went."

Serena went to the door, opened it and returned with a small chest, placing it on the toilet table. "These are from your father's maternal family."

Harriett opened the chest. Inside were several velvet bags. She picked one and opened it, taking out a long strand of pearls interspersed with emeralds. "I will wear this today."

"If you are going to wed anytime soon," Lady Bellamny said as she strolled into the room "you must bathe."

Fortunately, Harriett's hair had been washed last night. She made quick work of taking her bath that Wyborn had perfumed with lavender oil. Harriett donned an emerald-green silk-twill gown. Once her hair was up, her soon-to-be-sisters and mother-in-law, who had been in a group discussing something, turned as one.

The Duchess of Somerset smiled gently. "We are so very happy to welcome you to our family." She held out a pair of emerald and gold earrings. "I hope you will wear these today for your wedding. It is something old."

"They are beautiful." Tears pricked Harriett's eyes as the duchess embraced her.

"You must call me Catherine. All my daughters-in-law do."

"Thank you, Catherine."

Harriett put on the earrings, and Anna grinned as Meg held out a pearl bracelet. "This is something new."

Blinking back more tears, Harriett had trouble speaking for a moment. "Thank you."

Marcella hugged her before opening her hand to reveal three pearl-tipped hair-pins. "These are borrowed."

"I will be sure to give them back to you right after the ceremony." Harriett handed the pins to her dresser who fixed them in her hair.

Then Aglaia, Euphrosyne, and Thalia were next. Aglaia handed Harriett a blue box. This is something blue." She wrinkled her nose. "We hope you like it. When Marcella described how you looked, we knew we would have to be careful because of your coloring."

Harriett took the box and opened it. Nestled in it was a turquoise stone set in gold with small diamonds. "It is beautiful! Thank you."

Harriett pinned the brooch to her gown.

A knock came on the door. Wyborn opened it then turned back to the chamber. "His lordship wants to know if you are ready."

"Yes." Harriett nodded. "I am. Oh, who is standing up with me?"

Marcella glanced at Serena who nodded. "Serena. Although, I

would be honored to attend you, you have known her much longer. That is what you want?"

"Yes." Serena had been with Harriett from the beginning of her time in York, and if it had not been for her friend, she never would have met Sextus. "Yes. It is what I want."

Marcella smiled. "Now that is resolved, let us go so you can be off."

Harriett was not looking forward to more rushed travel, but she was looking forward to being married to Sextus.

# CHAPTER 9

Sextus stood in Lady Bellamny's garden. Hot house flowers added to spring bulbs that had just come up. He'd been told there would be a wedding breakfast not long after the ceremony. The guests were trusted friends, and the number of coaches would disguise Harriett and Sextus leaving in the event any of the duke's bully-boys were watching.

His eldest brother nudged him. "She has arrived."

He turned, and his breath left him. My God, she was beautiful. How she managed to look so elegant and collected after everything she had been put through during the past days was a miracle. He took in the emeralds she wore and was glad he had selected an emerald wedding ring from the ones Hawksworth had shown him. "She is exquisite."

Hawksworth chuckled lightly. "I thought you might say something like that."

Instead of Marcella, Serena Beaumont attended Harriett, and Robert Beaumont stood next to her to give her away. That was as it should be. The Beaumonts had done more for Harriett than her family ever had.

Quartus took his place in front of him and opened a small prayer book. "Dearly beloved..."

After Robert placed Harriett's hand in his, Sextus vowed to himself to never let it go. They said their vows with strong, firm voices, although she blushed rosily when he looked into her eyes and promised to worship her body. For some reason, his brother left out the part about her obeying him. Then again, knowing the ladies, that was probably a good decision.

They were gazing into each other's eyes when Quartus said, "I now pronounce you husband and wife. Please step over here and sign the register."

Sextus stared at his brother and Octavius grinned. "Everyone forgets that they must sign the register before they are legally married. I've just started adding the instructions to the end of the ceremony."

His brother, sisters, and their spouses nodded smiling.

"Let's get it done."

The guests arrived shortly thereafter. They were able to meet and thank the Marquis and Marchioness of Huntingdon and their son and daughter-in-law, the Earl and Countess of Huntley. It had been the countess's idea for Sextus and Harriett to go to her in-laws.

"It would not be a place the duke would look for you," Caro Huntley explained.

They also met Marcus and Phoebe, the Earl and Countess of Evesham. Phoebe said, "We put our heads together and decided my husband's ship would be the fastest."

He smiled at them. "I sailed her from the West Indies to England."

"We thank you," Harriett said.

The atmosphere was relaxed, but Sextus wouldn't be happy until he was on that boat and sailing down the Thames. It wasn't until then that it occurred to him Harriett might suffer from *mal de mer*. He took her aside. "Do you know if you become ill on boats?"

She grinned. "As a matter of fact, I do not."

*Thank God*!

They had each consumed two glasses of champagne when Hawksworth came over. "It's time for you to go."

Harriett gave a tight nod. "Thank you for everything."

He hugged her. "We take care of our own. You will be well guarded on your journey to Austria."

Sextus held out his hand, but found himself embraced by his brother. "We all contributed to your guards. They are former military and offered to remain with you once you reach your destination. They have also been trained as either footmen or grooms and speak at least one other language."

"Thank you." He'd been planning to hire outriders when they reached the continent.

"Coaches and horses have been sent ahead," Hawksworth said. "You taking your time getting to England gave us an opportunity to plan."

Sextus's throat closed, and for the first time in years, he was close to tears. "Reading letters, as good as they are, is not the same as being on the receiving end of your generosity and that of the others. We could not have done this without you."

His brother patted his back. "Say farewell to the others."

Although he managed to keep his tears in check, the same could not be said for Harriett and the other ladies. It took a good half-hour before they walked out the back gate and into the same coach in which they had arrived. And they were still not alone! Her maid and his valet were with them. He couldn't get to the ship fast enough.

Harriett pulled the shade on her side of the coach more than half-way then slipped her much smaller hand into his. "Meg said we should take care not to be seen until we are out of London proper."

There was no sense in courting discovery. He pulled his shade down as well and tightened his grip on her hand. "From what I remember, Greenwich is just over an hour from Town."

Harriett nodded, but didn't answer. The afternoon traffic slowed their progress, and it seemed as if everyone was holding their breath. Finally, from the lower portion of the window, Sextus could see the buildings thinning as pastures took their place. "We're out of London."

Sighs of relief filled the coach, and they raised the shades.

Harriett squeezed his fingers. "Thank God. That was worse than the mad dash to Alconbury Hill."

"It was." He smiled at her. "I knew Octavius would be able to delay the duke at least until we had a good head start. This time, we didn't know in which direction to look for trouble."

About forty minutes later, they turned into a tree-lined drive and pulled up before a large manor house, and Harriett mused, "I wonder whose house this is."

Sextus wondered as well. "I don't think it matters. We'll be met by a dory that will ferry us out to the ship."

An older man dressed as a groom opened the door. "Good day, my lord, my lady. I'm the stable master. If you will follow me, I'll take you to the boat."

Two other servants went to the back of the coach.

"Thank you." Sextus jumped down and held his hand out for his bride. "Not long now."

Harriett smiled at him. "It will be a relief to be away."

The stable master showed them around the house to a dock built on the shore of the Thames. Beyond it lay a large schooner at anchor. Several people stood at the rail watching. Two sailors helped Harriett and her maid into the boat. As soon as they were settled, Sextus and his valet joined them.

"Have you been waiting long?" he asked one of the men.

"No, mi'lord. The captain had a schedule."

*Why does that not surprise me?*

The rest of their servants were already on the ship, and before the greetings were done the anchor had been weighed and the sails unfurled. A tall man with sandy brown hair joined them. "Allow me to introduce myself. I'm Captain Winsome. My steward will show you to your cabin. I have instructions to keep you below until we reach the mouth of the river."

This escape had been well planned indeed. "How long will that be?"

"Just over five hours," Captain Winsome said. "We'll have to be towed in some parts. You'll find food and drink in your cabin. I will see you for dinner in about three hours."

Wyborn and Lovel were leaving the cabin as Sextus and Harriet arrived. "Everything has been prepared, my lord," Lovel said.

"Thank you." Sextus had been on enough ships to know cabin space was at a premium. Still, he and Harriett were finally alone, and he didn't intend to waste this time. He held out his arm to her. "Shall we, my love?"

"Indeed." She placed her fingers on his arm. "Do you have any idea how long the journey will take?"

"At least a full day. I expect we'll arrive by this time tomorrow."

"A full day." A slow smile grew on her lips. "Alone."

"At least for the next three hours." Sextus led her into the cabin and removed her cloak.

She was amazed at how comfortable it appeared. "Look at the size of the bed. I expected something much smaller."

"From what Evesham said, he renovated it for his wife's utmost comfort when they sailed to France. I had no idea it would be this luxurious."

Turning around, she took in the room. A table was bolted to the floor opposite the bed, bookshelves with pieces of wood to keep the books from falling lined one wall, and a wardrobe was attached at the end of the bed. A small, cushioned bench had been built under a large window, and Turkey rugs covered the floor. "This is amazing. I could almost live here."

Sextus chuckled as he drew her into his arms. "If only we could sail to Austria."

She started to answer, but his lips captured hers and the fires she had been keeping well banked flared to life. She was finally a wife. Marcella had taken Harriett aside during the wedding breakfast and told her what to expect. That had been very helpful. Her ignorance had been causing her a great deal of worry. Sextus deepened the kiss, and Harriett lost her ability to think. If it had not been for a slight cooling of her back, she would not have known her bodice had been undone.

Next, her hair tumbled down. He threaded his fingers in her tresses. "Beautiful. I love the way it curls." He shrugged out of his jacket without removing his lips from hers. "I want to see all of you."

There must be something she could do for him. Reaching up she removed his cravat-pin and untied his neckcloth. "I want to see you too."

"Soon, my love." As his lips traveled down her neck, her stays fell to her hips and her chemise followed.

He licked one nipple, and she thought she would die of pleasure. Her body was quickly becoming an inferno with the heat coalescing between her legs. Her breath grew ragged as he pushed down the garments bunched around her waist. "Now. I want you now."

"Not yet." He grinned against her breasts.

Harriett unbuttoned his waistcoat. "This must go." Obediently, he took it off, and she reached for his shirt. "Now this."

"Your wish is my command." The shirt went next, flying across the room.

A wide expanse of naked male chest confronted her. His skin was stretched over muscles she did not know a gentleman could possess. Pale, blond hair covered the upper half, and thinned as it reached below his chest, over his stomach, and into his breeches. Tentatively, she touched it. The hair was as soft as a babe's. She ran her fingers through it, then bent her head to lick his nipple.

"Ah, Lord, Harriett that feels good."

"I was told it might." She smiled as she undid his breeches. "I was also told you might like this." She reached down and rubbed the already hard length of him.

Sextus lifted her out of her clothing and placed her gently on the bed. "I am glad you received instruction, but this is not going to last long at all if you try to use all you learned."

He took off his shoes and her half-boots then his breeches slid to the floor. Goodness, it seemed large. Yet, she trusted that he would fit. At least that is what she had been told. "What should I do?"

He settled into bed next to her. "Allow me to worship your body." Moving her further onto the bed, he began kissing her again. At the sight of him, she had fretted a bit, but soon the flames were licking her veins again. He moved his hand to her mons and her hips rose to meet it as he prepared her to accept him. "Almost ready."

"I am ready now." But he did not listen to her protest.

The next thing she knew pressure between her legs increased and suddenly she was riding wave upon wave of pleasure. Before she finished, he pushed into her and pain shot through her.

"Are you all right? Do you want me to stop?"

"No." She rose up to meet him. "I want to make you mine."

He chuckled as he slid slowly forward. Soon the pain gave way to pleasure as the welcome tension built again. Sextus claimed her lips as she came again, and he came with her. After a moment, he rolled off her, drawing her to his side as he did. "I was yours before, but even more so now."

Harriett turned his head and kissed him. "And I am yours even more so."

The corners of his beautiful eyes crinkled as he gazed at her. "We are each other's, and I am very glad of it." He raised his head. "Do you want some wine and food?"

She had not expected to be hungry but she was. "Yes, please. What time do you think it is?"

Sextus threw his legs over the bed. "I'll be able to tell you as soon as I find my waistcoat. My pocket watch is in it."

Glancing around the room she noticed clothes flung everywhere, including his cravat-pin. "The pin for your neckcloth is on the floor."

"As are your hairpins." He was busy picking up their things.

She felt guilty for not helping, but she was not nearly as comfortable with nudity as he was. "Perhaps if you find my robe."

He tossed his shirt to her. "Use this."

She held it to her nose. It carried his scent, clean with a hint of ambergris. After donning the shirt, she began to hang their garments while he poured the wine.

He gave her a glass. "To us and our family."

Even now, a babe could be forming inside of her. "To us."

~

*Two weeks later, Somerset House, London*

*Belling*!" Somerset shook the newssheet in his hand. "Have you seen this outrage?"

His secretary hurried into his study. "No, my lord. What happened?"

"What happened? What happened is that Lord Sextus wed two weeks ago, and we had no idea it had occurred."

Belling's mouth opened and closed like that of a fish. "But we had men everywhere. Even at that party Lady Bellamny held."

"Never mention that old besom's name to me again. That's where the damned wedding took place! Get me a glass of wine." He drank a large swallow. "I want that land. If I can't get Sextus, Septimius will have to do. At least I know where he is."

~

*One month later, Vienna*

"Have you finished the letter yet?" Sextus asked as he strolled into Harriett's parlor.

"I am just doing it now." She attached the seal and sanded the missive. "After receiving the note from my uncle Staunton explaining that he knew nothing more than he had previously told me about my parentage, I decided I would write to him about the baby as well." She rubbed her stomach. They were both excited about the prospect of a child. "I hope your family will be as happy as we are."

"You know they will be." He strode over and wrapped his arms around her. "Everyone will be ecstatic."

And this child would be raised with two parents and a lot of aunts, uncles, and cousins.

THE END

Despite what many people think, the British aristocracy was very accepting of any illegitimate child who had been acknowledged by his or her father and raised accordingly. It was the middle-class who took a dim view of children born out of wedlock. We know this from writings and diaries that date from the Georgian into the Victorian eras. This attitude shocked Americans who came over to England looking for husbands for their daughters.

If you'd like to know more about Meg and Hawksworth, their story is in *Miss Featherton's Christmas Prince*. Caro's and Huntley's adventures are in *Desiring Lady Caro*. Septimius was introduced in *Lady Beresford's Lover*. Those books are all part of my series, The Marriage Game. Lady Bellamny is an old friend who shows up in The Marriage Game, The Worthingtons, The Trevors, and Lords of London.

I hope you enjoyed this latest Trevor book. If you haven't already done so, please keep up with me on Facebook, Instagram, and on my mailing list. All the links can be easily found at www.ellaquinnauthor.com. All my books are there as well. I look forward to hearing from you.

# SOCIAL MEDIA FOR ELLA QUINN

You can learn more about Ella Quinn at these social media links:

**Bookbub**: https://www.bookbub.com/authors/ella-quinn
**Facebook:** https://www.facebook.com/EllaQuinnAuthor
**Instagram**: https://www.instagram.com/ellaquinnauthor
**Twitter**: https://www.twitter.com/ellaquinnauthor
**Website**: http://www.ellaquinnauthor.com

# ABOUT ELLA QUINN

USA Today bestselling author Ella Quinn's studies and other jobs have always been on the serious side (political science professor and lawyer). Reading historical romances, especially Regencies, were her escape. Eventually her love of historical novels led her to start writing them.

She is married to her wonderful husband of almost forty years.

Learn more about Ella at: Website: http://www.ellaquinnauthor.com

# LADY TWISDEN'S PICTURE PERFECT MATCH

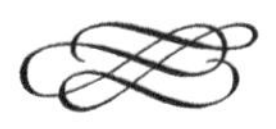

ALINA K. FIELD

Lady Twisden's Picture Perfect Match
By Alina K. Field

After years of putting up with her late husband's rowdy friends, Honoria, Lady Twisden has escaped to York where she can paint, investigate antiquities, and enjoy freedom. Then her stepson appears with a long-lost relation in tow. Promised York's marriage mart and the hospitality of his cousin's doddering stepmother, Major August Kellborn is shocked to find that his fetching hostess is the one woman who stirs his heart.

# CHAPTER 1

*St. Hedwig's Place, York*

Honoria, Lady Twisden, accepted the stack of late mail from her housekeeper and reached for the teapot. After hours spent planning menus, writing letters, and posting her accounts, she'd finally sat down for a midday cup of tea.

"Thank you, Mrs. Dunscombe." She cleared her throat, wondering whether she ought to remark on the changing colors of the bruise the woman sported. The housekeeper had begged an afternoon off the week before to attend a meeting of like-minded reformers. The newssheets had filled columns reporting on the melee disrupting the gathering. Mrs. Dunscombe had fortunately not been taken up by the soldiers, nor, she claimed, had she participated in brawling. She'd merely run afoul of a forceful elbow in the terrible crush of the fleeing crowd.

Honoria had let the matter rest then, and she didn't wish to bring it up now. She'd had a difficult enough time convincing the hard-working woman to take this post. No sense in chiding Mrs. Dunscombe about her off-duty excursion when she herself had approved the half-holiday.

"Ye might as well hear it from me, my lady. Cook is fit to be tied. Found two more in a fresh sack of flour. Had to throw out the lot."

Honoria fought the urge to shudder. The mice of Twisden Manor had been her companions for fifteen years, but she *would not* share a home with their brethren in York.

"We need a cat. Find us a good mouser, Mrs. Dunscombe."

Here, at least, there were no useless hounds to bedevil the cats. Ignoring the housekeeper's harrumph, Honoria picked up the stack of letters and studied them.

Perhaps *stack* was too lavish a term for this clutch of letters. There'd been more in the days before when her effort to embrace York society had paid off with a few invitations.

She shuffled through the current batch as she sipped her tea. Her mother-in-law's fat letter would be bulging with gossip about Harrogate, along with complaints about the taste of the medicinal waters there and her continuing lumbago. The Twisden steward had written as well—she prayed that Wes was not plaguing the man again about changes for the home farm.

If so, she was determined to not interfere. As the new lord of the manor, Wes must find his own way. She'd raised him to manhood, and trained him to be sensible, and though he had all the rosy-eyed exuberance of youth, she knew he would not overtax the estate budget by restocking his late father's kennels with a new, useless pack of hounds.

The third letter was addressed in a feminine hand she didn't recognize. Perhaps it was another invitation, one she'd be grateful for. Upon her arrival in York, she'd discovered that her main acquaintance here, her cousin, Rose, had taken herself off to Egypt—the lucky woman. How she envied Rose her ability to travel at will.

Still, she was happy to begin this adventure. She'd been delighted to encounter her niece, Patience, two Sundays in a row attending services at York Minster: the two high holy days, Palm Sunday and Easter. Patience had recognized her old Aunt Honoria, even though their last meeting had been at Honoria's wedding, when Patience was no more than a child. As it happened, Patience had moved into

Rose's vacant home for the Season, along with her flock of step-daughters.

Honoria took a long drink of tea and set down the cup. "Please have Meg clear my dish here before our wee friends come up from the kitchen for a repast of crumbs. I'll read these in my study."

The housekeeper grunted and picked up a tray. "I've set Meg to dusting upstairs, so I'll take your plate and your tea things. As to the cat business, milady, they bring their own sort of mess, Cook says, and she's not wrong. I'd liefer set out more traps." With a small head bob, the housekeeper departed.

Honoria rubbed the spot between her eyebrows where a headache threatened. Having her own home didn't mean she could have everything her own way, not if she wanted to have servants. Why on earth had Wes arranged such a large house for her? It was within her budget, but just barely. She needed enough help to keep dust and vermin at bay, and she couldn't afford to pay the sort of wages servants would demand of an autocrat. She'd try it Mrs. Dunscombe's way.

After all, Honoria only had the lease until Midsummer, and then, fingers crossed, she and her maid, Olive Bixby, would leave England for more exploring.

She passed through into the drawing room and paused to survey her work, ready now for callers. The curtains had been shaken clean, the carpets beaten, and every scratched and faded surface of the Queen Anne pieces coated with beeswax. She'd labored alongside Mrs. Duncombe, Meg, and Bixby, along with two young girls who came in as needed and went home at night to their families.

Lady of the manor she might have been, but she was no stranger to work. While Cook scoured the kitchen environs, Honoria and her crew had gone through the dining room and the two stately suites on the first floor, and the three smaller bedchambers on the second floor, and the small attic servants' rooms. Not that she was especially egalitarian—she simply wanted the task done, and as quickly as possible so she could get on with the true purpose of this repairing lease.

The faintest of rustles stirred the curtains and made her pause.

*No*. That had been merely the cool breeze. They'd cleaned away all temptation and closed up all the holes. They'd not seen any active vermin in this room, but the open window might tempt some in. She drew down the sash and stepped back.

It was as pleasant as a house could be for the five single women living there, four servants and their widowed mistress, all living without benefit of a *Male* presence to give them the sort of countenance her late husband would have mandated. The thought made her smile, savoring her independence, and she passed through to the hall.

Wes hadn't known about it, but the house had one room that called to her daily, the second-floor bedchamber that looked out on York Minster. She called it her study; it was really her studio. And her easel and paints beckoned her right now. Tomorrow was soon enough to begin seeing the sights of York.

As she crossed the battered black and white tiles of the hall, the knocker resounded.

Her blood spiked with a mix of apprehension and anticipation, and just a tad of annoyance. *She had callers.* Her painting must wait—and thank heavens they'd made the house presentable.

Meg was upstairs dusting. Mrs. Dunscombe was below stairs. Honoria smoothed her hair, ran her hands down the sides of her old day gown, and heaved the heavy door open.

*"Mother?"*

Wes was here, on her doorstep. Unexpected.

"Good heavens." She mustered a welcoming tone. "What a surprise."

"A pleasant one, I hope." A grin split his handsome face.

He had his father's blue eyes and dark blond hair, and none of his corpulence. She shoved the uncharitable thought aside and extended her hands.

He reached her first and lifted her, planting a kiss on her forehead, with all the exuberance of the six-year-old she'd taken into her heart.

Laughing, she told him to put her down.

"Why ever are you answering your own door?"

*Here comes the scold.* Having reached his majority and taken over the responsibility of the estate, the dear lad had begun trying to manage *her*. That was but one of the reasons she'd left Twisden Manor.

"Where is the footman? We need him to fetch in our trunks."

*We?*

Looking past the broad shoulder she saw another figure approaching and…

*Good God.* Heat swamped her and flamed in her cheeks. Dark eyes shot darts at her over a grimly set, thin-lipped mouth. The palpable sternness of Wes's companion sent a shiver of awareness through her. It was a familiar shiver, one she'd indulged during her tedious days at Twisden Manor when she'd found herself fighting off mad imaginings.

Wes's laughter shook her tongue loose. "My goodness, sir," she said. "You bear an uncanny resemblance to—"

"Old Ebenezer Twisden," Wes said. "Yes, it is as if the old Warden has come back to life, Mother. As soon as I laid eyes on him in Brampton, I knew he must be a relation. And do you know who he is, Mother?" He laughed again. "I've written to Granny to tell her. She'll be in alt when she reads the news."

A man of perhaps forty, he was about the same age as Wes's ancestor, the Warden in the painting at Twisden Manor who'd been in the King's service for many years when that portrait was done. This new incarnation of Ebenezer wasn't a particularly tall man, not as tall as Wes, but he still towered over her.

Old Ebenezer cleared his throat.

"But of course," Wes said. "Where are my manners? Mother, may I present my cousin, Major Augustus Kellborn. Gus, this is my dear stepmother, Lady Twisden."

While she curtsied, managing not to wobble, he dipped his head, never taking his gaze away.

*Good holy heavens.*

"We had a good meal at the last inn stop," Wes said, "but a cup of tea and a few biscuits wouldn't go amiss while the servants ready our rooms."

"Your rooms." She blinked. Wes expected her to take in him and this handsome cousin who made her skin tingle but... *There is no way.* This was her home. It was true that Wes had stepped in and helped her with the estate agent when he fussed about leasing the house to a widow living alone, but she'd made it clear to Wes that she paid the rent. He knew, too, that she wanted… needed some time away. She'd explained all that when she concocted this plan to spend the Season in York.

Sighing, she led them into the drawing room. "I fear I have no spirits to offer you, but I can bring up some of my elderberry wine, or if you have a flask, you must feel free to imbibe. Make yourself comfortable, and I shall return directly."

Fleeing the parlor, she paused on the backstairs, pressing a hand to her pounding heart. Augustus Kellborn was the stuff of every naughty dream she'd entertained about Ebenezer Twisden. Attired in his flowing dark wig, long coat, breeches and high boots, Ebenezer Twisden had pinned his gaze on her through countless dinners with Sir Melton and his endless stream of tiresome, rowdy guests. Long ago, Ebenezer had served as one of the Border Wardens, rounding up rievers and imposing the Crown's law. Family legend said he was a fierce and brutal warrior. One could see it in his eyes.

She had, at first, been intimidated by Ebenezer's image, and then intrigued, and then she'd begun imagining the virile fighter stepping out of the painting and shoving his sword into Jeremiah Ripton's belly. Repeatedly.

One could see a similar strength of will in Major Kellborn, and she knew of his heroism from tales told by her mother-in-law.

What a ninny she'd been, and what a ninny she was being now. She'd give the men tea and the names of the best inns in York. Cousin to her late husband though he may be, Major Ebenezer could not give her household of women countenance, and she'd rather he took his skin-tingling, heart-hammering, cheek-heating virile male presence elsewhere. It would be harder to turn Wes away, but she must at least try.

## CHAPTER 2

Major August Kellborn, late of his Majesty's army, beat back an impulse to seize young Sir Westcott Twisden by the neckcloth and shake him.

He'd had long experience beating back that sort of urge with the young nodcocks he'd shaped into officers. He could do so now as well.

Gus paced to the window and looked out a sparkling clean pane onto the narrow street. Their traveling chaise wasn't visible, but Sir Sancho stood unaccompanied, busily watering a lamppost.

Gus had been in his cups the day he'd met Twisden at a horse market in Brampton, else he wouldn't have allowed the young pup the informality of his first name, respectable though Wes was. The malaise of his first long winter's sojourn at Whitlaw Grange, his new estate near what was once the Debatable Land, had made him more sociable than was his wont.

Still, he'd found the friendly lad more sensible than most his age, and the family connection had intrigued him. His late mother had written frequently about the Twisdens, the jovial late baronet and his amiable wife. He knew of their mutual ancestor, Sir Ebenezer Twisden as well, and so, he'd jumped at the chance to visit Twisden

Manor. His very resemblance to the old warrior was astonishing, and Gus had been impressed with the well-run estate. Much of it the late baronet's sensible widow's doing, Gus's valet had learned.

And so, when Wes proposed visiting his stepmother and attending the York races and then sweetened the deal with the notion of a marriage mart—it had been a very long, lonely winter—Gus agreed to this sojourn in York.

He turned back to his young erstwhile host. "*Practically doddering*, you said."

Wes looked up from pouring spirits from a flask into a tumbler. "What?" His blue-eyed innocence was genuine. Wes saw his step-mother as an ancient, when she could scarcely be much beyond thirty. He ought to have paid more attention to his mother's descriptions of the Twisdens.

"I cannot stay under your stepmother's roof, Wes."

"Whyever not?"

"She is not by any means doddering. She's a widow, and one young enough that even with you here some of the time..." Wes had planned to depart for several days to visit his Grandmother in Harrogate. "The presence of a single man in her household might stir gossip."

"She's three and thirty and is known to be very proper. Plus..." He glanced back at the closed door and lowered his voice. "Though she's clever and good, she's plain."

Gus gazed back at the now empty street. Perhaps plain was the right word to describe each of Lady Twisden's entirely unremarkable features. But taken as a whole, he would call her appearance amiable, moving, and in fact... pretty. The spark in her eyes when she spotted him, the color rising in her cheeks, those had stirred him as well.

Behind him the door opened, and nails pattered across the plank flooring and then hushed when they hit the carpet. Sir Sancho plopped at his feet.

"Took the liberty of letting himself in." Rompole, Gus's former batman and now valet stood in the doorway. "Tired of waiting on the footman. Ye did say yer ma wouldn't mind the mutt, Sir Wes."

Gus bent and patted the head of the brindled terrier. "Old boy, you and I will be finding an inn. Let us hope they'll allow us to share a room there."

"Nonsense," Wes said. "Why, at home, we had dogs in every room."

The door rattled and Lady Twisden poked in carrying a tray. A sturdily built woman of middling age sporting an apron and a bruised eye appeared behind her, equally laden.

To his credit, Wes jumped up, took the tray from his mother, and carried it to the large table near the other window. Rompole offered his assistance to the puckered-up servant who scowled through her fading bruise and ignored him.

Lady Twisden turned from directing the trays and her gaze settled on Gus's boots. Or rather, on Sir Sancho, who sat squirming and attempting to wag the tail he was sitting on.

"A dog." The words floated out on a low breath that might have been a sigh of relief but was more likely a squelched growl.

"Meet Sir Sancho, Mother." Wes made introductions, blissfully unaware of the lady's reaction. "Gus's Spanish terrier. He's learned English now though, haven't you Sir Sancho. Attached himself to my cousin and came all the way from Spain. I say, Mother, do you plan to pour?"

She ignored him, piercing the dog with a look that was anything but amiable. Lady Twisden had depths.

For his part, Sancho appeared smitten. He faced the lady, dancing from one forefoot to the other, his rump bouncing on his wriggling tail.

Gus swallowed a chuckle. The loyal dog had never displayed such ardent discomposure before, not even when tempted by food. And *now* he would play the faithless cur. "He wishes to greet you, my lady."

She blinked and leveled a prim look at both master and beast. "After which he may go out to the garden. Come, Sancho."

When she extended her hand, the dog—*his* dog—trotted over to her, sat, and lifted a paw. She took it and shook, and Sancho licked her hand.

Rompole let out a breath through his teeth and muttered, "Well I'll be."

"Oh-ho," Wes said. "Well-mannered, isn't he, Mother? Go ahead and get to know him while I pour. You won't want to send him to the stable after you've made his proper acquaintance."

"I don't have a stable," the lady said.

Wes froze with the teapot in hand and frowned. "Dash it all, no you don't. We'll have to find a place for our horses, Gus." He turned on the other woman. "You, ma'am, could you send one of the footmen—"

"This is my housekeeper, Mrs. Dunscombe," Lady Twisden said, releasing Sancho's paw. "And I don't employ a footman, Wes."

Gus signaled his valet. "My man, Rompole, here, will accompany Sancho to the garden. And then I will take both horses along and see to their stabling. We'll find an inn to accommodate all of us."

Honoria let out a sigh of relief. Major Ebenezer was an insightful gentleman. As was his dog, so far, though the animal was making no effort to leave with the servant.

"*What?* No, Cousin," Wes cried. "You don't mean to go to an inn when you could reside here in comfort with family. We've come for the races, Mother, and for a bit of society. You wrote, did you not, that your niece is here with a houseful of marriageable daughters." He winked at her. "Gus is an eligible bachelor, you know."

"As are you, dear one." She winked back at him. "I fear, though, that you both might find an inn more comfortable than the home of a widow with only a few servants."

"Hire more." Wes waved his hand and then handed the Major a sloshing cup.

She intercepted the cup and returned it. "Sit down, Wes. I will take over the pouring. Major?"

"Milk only, my lady, and thank you." With the slightest of smiles he accepted the fresh cup and a plate with a slice of seedy cake—still warm from the oven as it was the dessert for the evening's meal, hastily coopted for these unexpected guests.

His lips had quirked like that when the dog sought her out, a flash of humor that made her wonder if he'd trained his terrier to beguile reluctant ladies. Sir Melton would have loved such a trick if he'd bothered to train his slobbery hounds to do anything else but track scent.

When she took her seat, the dog settled down at her feet, remarkably well-behaved and seemingly not at all interested in her plate. Sir Melton's hounds would have been atop the table by now, lapping up everything except the hot tea. Perhaps Spanish terriers were better bred than their English cousins, or else the vicissitudes of war had taught the dog manners.

"I'll go to the agency myself and find you some footmen," Wes said.

She carefully sipped, holding back her first instinct to scold. Wes was a man, and she must treat him as such, especially in front of an older cousin he admired.

Before she could form a response, the major stood. "Please excuse me, but I can't keep the postilion waiting. Rompole will fetch your trunk into the house, Wes, and we'll be on our way."

The servant, who like Dunscombe was somehow still in the parlor with them, shuffled his feet like the dog had done earlier. "Er, Major, I already carried in both trunks. Untied the horses and found a boy to watch them. Chaise has gone off to the posting inn. The lad said he couldn't wait."

"There. You see, Mother? Rompole has settled everything for us." Wes flung out a hand and the crumble of cake he was holding flew toward the window.

The terrier alerted and shot after it.

So, Spanish terriers were not so decorous. Only a bit better behaved than Sir Melton's—

A loud squeak from the corner preceded a vigorous shaking. Sancho returned, dropped a bundle of fur near her toes and ran off again.

Her blood surged and drained, and she heard a squeal—her own—and a startled huff and found Mrs. Dunscombe peering over her shoulder. Sancho shook violently and returned twice more. Three fat mice lay at her feet, not even twitching.

"Better'n a cat," Mrs. Dunscombe whispered. "I'll get the shovel."

"Rompole will see to the, er, removal," the major said. "Apologies, my lady. Sancho is a fierce ratter. I fear I haven't been able to train him to restrain his natural instincts."

Honoria looked at the pile of dead rodents then nodded to Dunscombe. "Ask Meg to ready the first-floor bedchamber for Sir Westcott and the front bedchamber on the second floor for Major Kellborn." She broke off a piece of biscuit and let Sancho nibble it from her hand. "Well done, Sir Sancho. Well done, indeed."

"You won't regret the company, Mother."

Wes had joined her in the parlor for a much-needed talk before Major Kellborn came down for dinner. Outside, the sounds of horses clopping and wheels clattering signaled a busy time of day in this neighborhood of tradesmen and professional men.

All at his leisure, Wes leaned back in his chair and crossed one leg over the other. "And we have Sir Sancho to thank for convincing Gus to stay."

The thought of the dog had her shaking her head and chuckling. That wee bit of fur had been resolute, sitting like a statue at her feet and refusing to heed his master's call. To his credit, Major Kellborn had taken the betrayal in stride. Accepting the dog's fickleness with good grace, he'd turned his back on Sir Sancho and followed Wes and his valet upstairs. Once the major left, Sir Sancho rose immediately at Honoria's command and allowed her to escort him to the kitchen. Upon his arrival there, he'd headed straight for the larder and gone to work at once, forestalling any objections by Cook. In fact, he'd won her over so completely that she barely fussed at the necessary menu changes and extra mouths to feed.

After, Honoria had retired to her own bedchamber to change for dinner and bend Bixby's patient ear fretting over stretching the budget. There'd been room in her budget—just barely—to help Patience with funds for the fête she was hosting at Smithfield's Assembly Rooms on the twenty-second of the month. The proposed ball was, after all, a noble endeavor, meant to help each of the young Bigglesworth ladies find a worthy husband. Why, even Patience, who was lovely and such a young widow, only two and twenty, might marry again.

The Bigglesworth stepdaughters ranged in age from thirty to Patience's only daughter by Seahaven, her three-year-old. There were five—or perhaps six—of an age to marry. Patience's greatest hopes were for a stepdaughter, aged nineteen, and a set of eighteen-year-old twins who all had been deemed diamonds of the first water.

Poor Patience! What a responsibility. The arrangement of Honoria's marriage to Sir Melton had been a near thing, given the puny size of her dowry. At eighteen, she hadn't been quite desperate to marry, but with her parents' health failing and her sister's disgrace, a practical marriage had seemed prudent. She would have wished for love, though.

It was too late for Honoria, but the Bigglesworth girls ought to have a chance at more than practicality. Perhaps one of the young ladies would be a good match for Major Kellborn or even Wes. Though Honoria couldn't imagine her stepson being ready just yet to settle down into matrimony.

Right now, she and Wes needed to discuss money, a topic both vulgar and necessary. In the old days, before he'd reached his majority, she would have spoken quite forthrightly, and he would have paid respectful heed to her concerns. But since needing to seek his help with the leasing agent, she was finding this new Wes a bit too high-handed.

"I wonder if we may dragoon the Major's man for some of the duties we might otherwise bestow on a footman?" she mused. "You know, it may be a challenge to find a man for a position that will end in a matter of weeks. In fact, I had difficulty engaging a housekeeper and Cook. And, well, to be perfectly honest, Wes, as I have always tried to be, not wishing to be a burden to you..." She took in a breath and framed her words. "I've carefully budgeted for my future travels."

He slapped his leg. "Is that it, old dear?"

The condescending endearment had her bristling, and she clamped her right hand firmly with the left, else it might fly out and slap him. "*Old dear?*" she asked, managing to keep her tone even.

He laughed. "Dear Mother. You have only to ask. I'll foot the wages for a couple of men." He straightened and snapped his fingers. "And the wine bill shall be mine, and anything extra your cook will need, as we certainly want to make our illustrious war hero comfortable."

Major Kellborn did not seem to be a peacock, and she rather doubted he thought of himself as either illustrious or a war hero. In fact, it seemed possible such accolades would make him uncomfortable.

Though Major Kellborn's name had rarely been mentioned in the dispatches published in the Yorkshire Post, her mother-in-law, a prodigious letter-writer, had followed his military career through her many correspondents, and with a great deal of pride. After all, Major Kellborn's late mother had a been a cousin of Wes's grandfather, and a dear friend to the dowager Lady Twisden.

"You may as well pay a visit to your grandmama at Harrogate," Honoria said. *And take Major Kellborn with you.*

"I plan to."

"And when he does, Lady Twisden, I shall remove myself to an inn." Major Kellborn had appeared in the doorway, quite earlier than expected. He'd changed out of his tight-fitting dusty buckskins and coats and attired himself in dark coat and trousers and a brocaded but tasteful waistcoat. He looked every bit the gentleman, and not a provincial one, but one who'd traveled in the best society.

She was glad she'd worn her best gown, a blue sarsenet she'd had made when she came out of mourning.

"Sancho may of course, stay in service to you, my lady." Major Kellborn's lips didn't curve up, but his eyes twinkled.

Wes sprang out of his seat. "You must come with me to Harrogate, Gus. You must meet my grandmother. She's followed your military career as avidly as if you were her own son. The young ladies can wait a few days to fawn over a war hero."

The major dipped his head, almost hiding the grimace. She'd been right—he was uncomfortable with the attention.

And perhaps it had to do with the age of this elderly admirer. He might not grimace over accolades from the younger ladies. She must see if any of Patience's girls had a yen for a military man.

A distant knock sounded—the door knocker.

# CHAPTER 3

What now? "It's an odd time to call," she said, rising. Mrs. Duncombe was busy with dinner preparations. Meg and Bixby were below stairs helping as well, and the major's man had gone out to tend to some business involving the men's horses.

"Be seated, Mother." Wes strode to the door, looked back over his shoulder, and grinned. "I'll play footman."

The major watched him leave and then turned back to her. "I truly don't wish to impose on you."

"You are not," she lied. "And the dog *is* very helpful."

He did smile then, eyes crinkling, lips turning up in a way that made her almost feel giddy. "I've grown very attached to the little cur, but I fear we must part ways. Sancho has chosen you."

"Oh, no, of course I cannot—"

"He'll give you no option. He chose me the same way, just walked away from his last master and never looked back."

"No." She shook her head. "You must take him with you when you return home. I'm only in York for the quarter. And after that, I plan to… to travel."

He smiled again. "Sancho is a good traveler, as long as there are no boats involved. Will there be boats?"

Before she could answer, the door opened, and Wes waved an arm with a flourish. "Look who is here, Mother." A wizened lady with twinkling blue eyes entered.

*It just needed this.* Her mother-in-law had arrived.

The lady went right up to the major and reached for him. "Augustus Kellborn. When Westcott wrote, I knew I must come and join you. What a pleasure to see you again."

Honoria may as well turn the house over to all of them and go to an inn herself. Oh, but then she wouldn't have her glorious view of the Minster and she wouldn't be able to *finally* finish a painting.

Gus rested his spoon and patiently answered the dowager's umpteenth question about his new estate in Cumberland. He'd inherited Whitlaw Grange from a childless relation, and after his first winter there, he understood why the man never married. It was a fine house for a man who liked hunting, fishing, and Roman history, but where a lady was concerned, not even the well-maintained manor house with its modern conveniences could compensate for the remoteness of the location.

They talked about mutual family members as well, Wes's grandmother providing more details than he could. He'd been both gone for many years *and* a poor correspondent. But when she ventured into his military career, he parsed his words, and carefully avoided wincing at memories he'd sooner not discuss.

"Was Talavera as frightful as the papers reported?" The dowager Lady Twisden paused her spoon over the custard. "No, do not say a word. I know it must have been, and you don't want to speak of it. And besides, Honoria is sending me that *look*."

Honoria. Gus gazed down the table at the other Lady Twisden, Gus's stepmother. *Honoria*—what a pretentious name for such a down-to-earth lady. She ought to have a pet name—Nora, or perhaps Honey, like the color of her hair. Yes, Honey would be better, as she was smiling, a sweet and genuine smile, directed at her mother-in-law.

She'd taken her mother-in-law's arrival with amazing grace—after barely a flutter of her eyelids and a momentary rise in her color, she'd embraced the older lady and ushered her upstairs to change out of her dusty carriage gown.

Following that, she must have gone below stairs and cast whatever spell had been needed upon the meager group of underpaid—if he was to believe Wes—servants so that they were able to sit down to dinner only a quarter hour later than planned.

Now, Gus sent her a grateful nod and turned to the dowager. "My mother always spoke fondly of you, my lady. Perhaps tomorrow when we are both rested from our travels, I may answer all those questions about Spain."

"Oh, dear boy, you must not *my lady* me. You may call me Cousin Genny, as your mother did."

He dipped his head. "And you may call me Gus, Cousin Genny, as Wes does." He held his breath, wondering if Wes's stepmother would allow him the intimacy of using her Christian name—the formal one, Honoria. He would save pet names for a closer acquaintance.

And a closer acquaintance there would be. She was just the sort of lady for him. On the practical level, she knew how to thrive in the country, but wasn't averse to getting away and traveling.

But when she smiled at him and her color rose, practicalities weren't foremost on his mind.

"What are your plans for your stay in York?" the dowager asked.

"Why, we're here for the races, Grandmama," Wes said. "They're not for a few weeks, but we shall find ways to keep occupied until then. I should like to visit some of the stud farms in the area. Find a spare for my stable." He lifted a hand. "Nothing extravagant, Mother."

"And you, Honoria? Have you called on your niece?"

"Yes, I have, and we've met at a few social events. It's been a whirlwind getting the house sorted, but I intend to call on her often now that we are both more settled."

"Whatever will you do with the rest of your time, Mother?"

The lady sat up straighter, hiding what was certainly an urge to bristle at her impudent stepson's tone.

"There's a great deal of society in York," Honoria said, her cheeks tinging a lovely shade of pink. "I've made the acquaintance of Lady Clune, and through her I've received invitations. For the inquiring mind, there's much to see in York, a great deal of Roman history."

Her eyes brightened at the mention of Roman history, and he was delighted to see they had a common interest to pursue while he pursued her.

She tipped her head and went on. "The York Antiquarian Society is quite active. I've been introduced to the director, Mr. Herbert Nedhelm, and his wife. And there's to be a guest lecture by a visiting scholar, Dr. Malcolm Marr, who will speak on ancient Egyptian medicine."

The mention of Marr drew him out of his romantic strategizing.

"Would that be Malcolm Marr, Strathnaver's younger brother?" he asked.

"Yes." Cousin Genny nodded. "I believe so. Is he not a particular friend of yours, Gus?"

"Since Eton," he said. "I'll look forward to attending his lecture."

Wes laughed. "Roman history and Egyptian medicine. What else do you plan to do here, Mother?"

"Now that she's turned you loose to run Twisden Manor, Wes, she'll be painting, will you not, Honoria?" the dowager asked.

Color rose higher in the younger lady's cheeks.

"Honoria was run ragged by that son of mine, Gus. She had little time to pursue her own interests. Not that Melton thought ladies should have their own interests."

"Drawing pictures of old buildings," Wes muttered.

"I am sure," Cousin Genny said, "that we might find you a better drawing instructor in a city as big as York. Wes had a drawing instructor for a time, Gus, but I believe Honoria learned more from the lessons. You will see, Honoria, with help and practice, how much your work improves."

"Oh yes." Honoria picked up her glass, her cheeks now the same rosy hue as the wine. "What think you of this claret, gentlemen?"

Cousin Genny waved a hand. "I can see they've both had their glasses refilled, Honoria. Now, you must tell me more about your visit to Farnley Hall. Was Turner there?"

"Turner?" Wes said. "You visited Turner, Mother? By yourself?"

The flush in Honoria's cheeks poured down into her modest decolletage. A yearning to see how far the pink flowed warred with an urge to send Wes's chair flying.

Had Gus stayed at an inn, he wouldn't have stumbled across this sort of family tableau. Though Honoria was no blood relative of either of the Twisdens, the family was close. Only one's beloved relations could inflict such embarrassment.

Aside from the color in her cheeks, Honoria held her composure. Gus stayed all his yearning and urges, curious to hear how she answered.

"I stopped with Bixby at Farnley Hall when I was passing through Otley. The housekeeper was most kind, and no, Mr. Turner was not visiting, nor was Mr. Fawkes in residence, else I wouldn't have imposed."

The mention of Fawkes jiggled Gus's memory. "Would that be J.M.W. Turner?" he asked. How would a lady residing in rural Westmoreland be knowledgeable of *that* Turner? "I saw some of his watercolors in London."

Her eyes lit. "I have never visited London, but the art tutor had. I've read of his work, and I was able to see some of his sketches and paintings at Farnley Hall. I admire his technique. What did *you* think of the paintings you saw, sir?"

Gus heard a note of challenge and groped for words. The man's landscapes and seascapes were certainly dramatic.

She shook her head. "I suppose they're not to everyone's taste. My late husband was not fond of art either, unless the subject was hunting or dogs." She turned a strained smile on Wes. "To answer your earlier question, I do intend to paint, but as I said, there is much history to explore in York, and I intend to see it all. This is, after all, an ancient city. Constantine was proclaimed emperor of Rome by his men here. In fact, I plan to begin my exploring tomorrow."

Wes sighed. "It would be indiscreet for you to go exploring on your own. You must wait until the day after when I am free." He signaled for more wine, and the rail-thin woman serving them strolled over. "Thank you, Bixby," Wes said. "Tomorrow, you shall not have to perform footman duty. I'll be visiting the agencies in the morning to bring in more help."

"Bixby will accompany me tomorrow, Wes. Major Kellborn, this is my maid, Olive Bixby, who has been kind enough to serve us tonight. Do not worry, Wes. I'll leave my jewels and my piles of gold at home. We two older ladies shall be perfectly safe walking the city walls and exploring the Shambles."

Bixby looked unconvinced and kept her mouth closed as Rompole would not have done. Wes, an equally imprudent male, opened his mouth. "Mother..." He cleared his throat, preparing a pompous objection. More sensible than many young men who'd just inherited Wes was, but he hadn't yet learned how to wield his new power tactfully, especially where this kind lady was concerned.

"I should like to accompany you, Lady Twisden," Gus said. "If you'll allow it."

"You'll find yourself stopping at every shop," Wes said, "and no footman to carry the packages."

Honoria sent her stepson a bland look before bestowing a polite smile on Gus. "Of course, you may join us, Major Kellborn. I daresay you'll find us tiresome, and then you may make your excuses with a clear conscience and search out a pint of ale."

Her hair shimmered in the candlelight, and though she held his gaze, her lower lip quivered just enough to tell him she was either nervous or amused. He would never find this lady tiresome.

She turned that bright smile on Wes. "As for you, dear boy, since you'll be free the day after tomorrow, you and I shall pay a call on my niece, Patience, Lady Seahaven, and her young ladies."

Wes sighed. "Of course. Are they pretty, these young ladies? I hope they are at least pretty."

"What a question," Honoria exclaimed. "I can safely say that I've seen all the girls, and Patience and her stepdaughters are all very comely. But remember, beauty is in the eye—or perhaps the heart—of the beholder, as I have always told you."

Cousin Genny clapped her hands. "Well said, Honoria."

"Indeed," Gus said, sending the lady a long look. "I have always found that to be true."

Cousin Genny grasped her grandson's hand. "It's what I ought to have told your father when he was your age, Wes. Your mother, God rest her soul, was too pretty for her own good. But the poor lass had not an ounce of sense."

"Are the Bigglesworth girls spirited, Mother?" Wes asked. "I cannot abide a melancholy girl, no matter how much beauty. That was my own mother's problem, wasn't it, Grandmama? She wasn't lacking in sense; she was just too gloomy. Father always told me it was my stepmother's spirit that convinced him to marry her."

"Your stepmother isn't spirited, you goose. She's sensible and stubborn, as she had to be living with my son in the middle of nowhere."

Gus cleared his throat, sensing Honoria's discomfort. She was studying her dish of half-finished custard. "And sensible stubbornness is a mark in any lady's favor," he said.

When she looked up, he couldn't read her expression. "I shall not require you to join us in calling on my niece, Major. However, Patience is hosting a ball several days from now at the Smithfield Assembly Rooms, and I shall impose on both of you to attend the ball. In fact, I'm one of the sponsors for this event, and I intend for it to be a great success. Patience is a very young widow, only two-and-twenty, with several marriageable stepdaughters. I'm not asking either of you to choose a bride, though how wonderful if… Well in any case, I require you to dance with each of the young ladies, and Patience, as well."

Cousin Genny chuckled. "Westcott, I'll join with Honoria pushing you onto the dance floor. Cousin Gus, will you be so gallant as to dance with the young ladies?"

Gus tapped the table and furrowed his brow, pretending to think about the question. He sent his hostess his most imperious look, the one that set all the raw recruits shaking.

She blinked, and then held his gaze steady. There was a world of patience in the woman.

"I shall do it," he said. "On one condition. Lady Twisden, Honoria, you must allow me two dances with *you*."

Wes laughed. "Mother don't dance."

She blinked again, shuttering a flash of irritation. "I may be a bit rusty, but if you will risk some embarrassment and your toes, I agree to your terms, Major."

"Never saw you stand up at a party," Wes said. "Always pushing the young girls out onto the floor. Why, only last month, Ripton was complaining that you'd always…" He sat up straighter. "Why, Mother, Ripton is coming to York. He must have arrived by now, and I know he'll call on you soon." He turned back to Gus. "Jeremiah Ripton is local gentry, a good friend of my father."

"I am sure, Wes, that it's you he wishes to see," Honoria said. "Best meet him over a pint somewhere."

"Of course, he'll call on you, Mother, especially now that both of you are widowed."

She grimaced and signaled the maid. "Mother Twisden, shall we leave the two gentlemen to their spirits and withdraw to the parlor?"

"Yes," Cousin Genny said. "But I'll retire to my room. I have letters to write. Bixby, ring for Jones, please. She must be finished moving Honoria's things by now."

"I'll help you up," Honoria said. "In fact, I believe I'll retire as well. Gentlemen, why not have your sherry in the parlor and turn in whenever you wish?"

Both ladies and the maid departed, leaving him with Wes.

This was certainly not the respite from Cumberland he'd expected. He'd thought to come to York to attend the races, take part in society, and perhaps... perhaps meet a lady he might want to marry, all from the sedate comfort of the doddering widow's guest bedchamber.

And he found it was the widow he wanted.

Wes clapped him on the shoulder. "I hear that the taproom at the Golden Fleece is favored by some of the sporting men. What say you we have our nightcap there?"

A maid—a younger girl than the other—entered and curtsied. Wes sent her to fetch their hats, and within minutes, they set off walking.

# CHAPTER 4

A mixture of gentlemen and tradesmen glanced up at the new arrivals entering the Golden Fleece's busy taproom. Gus and Wes had barely found seats at one of the tables crowding a back corner when Wes lifted a hand and signaled a man across the room.

The fellow rose and came to join them. Of an age with Gus, he was what the ladies would call handsome: fit and with a full head of curls, a square jaw, and gleaming teeth. He also wore a smug certainty about him that Gus instantly distrusted.

"Twisden," he exclaimed, "well-met."

Wes made introductions. The new arrival was Jeremiah Ripton.

Ripton waggled his eyebrows. "How is your lovely stepmother?"

"Fit as a fiddle and all settled in."

Gus's blood heated. The waggling eyebrows, the leer… the oaf's intentions toward Honoria were clear. Her nodcock of a stepson didn't see it.

Now he understood her reaction to the man's name at dinner. She was too sensible and intelligent not to see through this lout. The urge to grab Ripton by the neckcloth was almost overpowering. But he restrained himself; he'd learned self-control in hard schools.

Wes called an order to the barmaid. "Where are you staying,

Ripton? I daresay Mother might have a spare chamber for an old friend of my father's."

Gus raised an eyebrow at him.

"No." Wes laughed. "You're right, Gus. I had best ask her first. Gus, here, may have taken the last free bedchamber, but of course, you understand, Ripton, Gus is family."

And he would never remove himself to an inn if there was any danger of Ripton taking his vacated bed.

He held his tongue on that subject and joined the discussion about hunting and dogs—Ripton had bought out most of the late baronet's kennels.

"What of you, Kellborn?" Ripton asked. "Do you hunt?"

"Gus's only dog is a ratter," Wes said. "A damn fine one. He's won over Mother."

Ripton's gaze narrowed. "You've won the lady over with a dog?"

Gus smiled benignly, aware that he was stirring the man's jealousy. Ripton clearly thought he himself had a claim on Honoria.

Wes slapped the table. "The dog has won her over, Ripton. Took to her right off and plopped three fat mice at her feet." He laughed. "Dead of course."

Ripton's answering chuckle was false. "One more round," Gus said, signaling the maid and then changing the subject to the favorites for the upcoming races. Ripton was a man who crowed about his wins and never mentioned a loss. He was the smartest judge of horse flesh in Westmoreland.

Whoever Ripton claimed to be going for, Gus would bet against.

"This is the best you could do for your stepmother?" Ripton asked.

They'd paused in front of Honoria's town house. The ass had joined Gus and Wes for the walk home, no doubt angling to see where Honoria lived so he could prey on her another day.

"Best I could do?" Wes said. "Why, Mother would have taken two rooms in a boarding house if I'd let her have her way. *No fuss*, she said. But I couldn't allow that. She's plump enough for better quarters."

Rompole yanked the door open before Ripton could open his damned mouth again.

"Good of your man to play porter," Wes said.

Ripton sized up the burly valet, slid a glance Gus's way, and then wished them a good night.

Gus watched him leave, wondering when he'd have the opportunity to plant him a facer. When he turned back to his valet, Rompole was frowning at the back of Ripton's coat.

"Thank you, Rompole," Gus said, handing over his hat. His man was the sort to know where he was needed. It was why Gus tolerated his less than refined qualities. Well, that and the way he could shine up the foulest boots.

Gus followed his host up the stairs.

At the landing, Wes paused at a door, frowning. "I unpacked a tolerable bottle of brandy. Join me?"

The door led to a sitting room, and beyond that the bedchamber.

"Spacious, isn't it?" Wes asked, pouring a glass. "Mother's is equally large, or so the estate agent said." He handed over a glass. "Or was. She's given over the room to Grandmama. I don't know where she's moved."

"At least *I* haven't displaced her."

Wes waved a hand. "Oh, Mother don't mind. She has plenty of money if she don't follow through on her harebrained plan to go off to Scarborough and paint the sea. She ought to come home to Twisden Manor and paint the brook if that's how she wants to fritter away her time. What think you of Ripton? He's been after her for years—I shouldn't know that, but I do. Mother would never have anything to do with him, even after Father died. Of course, Ripton's wife was still living then. Honorable of Mother, but now that Ripton's lady has passed, I believe we could bring him up to scratch with my mother and have a guarantee of keeping her close to home. Will you help me?"

His hand had tightened around the squat glass, his throat going dry. Ripton and Honoria? The notion was appalling.

Gus eased his grip, drained his glass, and said, "No."

"She's lonely." Wes went on as if he hadn't heard. "It would set her up fine, and our man would make sure she had a respectable dower. I thought to ask for a pair of the hounds back as part of the settlement."

He reached for the bottle and topped off his glass. Poor Honoria.

Not even a forty-two pounder could dislodge Gus now. He'd well and truly remain here between this young ass and the old one he'd met at the Golden Fleece. If Honoria wanted to travel and paint and had the funds to do so, why shouldn't she?

Maybe he should go with her.

"Ripton is not interested in *marrying* your stepmother, Wes," he said. "You said yourself, he's been after her since before either your father's death or his wife's. I've known many men like him. Let me say this plainly: he wants to bed her."

*As do I.*

Wes's head jerked up, and his color rose, and for a moment he wondered if he'd expressed his own interest out loud.

Never mind. "Your friend, Ripton is a sporting man who likes to win. He's taken your mother's refusal as a challenge, that is all. I know you care for her. It would be unkind of you to have her think he's planning marriage."

He left the lad sitting speechless and took the flight of stairs up to the next floor. A dim lamp illuminated four doors in the corridor. Light seeped under two of them, his own and the one across from his.

A soft scrabbling and a woman's chuckle made him pause with his hand on the latch. The sound came from the room across from his.

"*Now* you need to go out?"

The door opened and Sancho bounded out, pouncing on him. He bent to rub the dog's ears and when he straightened, his breath caught. Honoria stood in the doorway, her robe open over a filmy night gown, her unbound hair cascading about her shoulders.

~

Honoria froze in place, as speechless as the man trailing his gaze over her deshabille with the same haughty arrogance as Sir Ebenezer.

Well, perhaps there was more heat in the Major's eyes, and it was stirring an answering sensation in the pit of her belly. Or, at least in that vicinity.

How odd. She shook off her paralysis. "He's decided to go back to you, I think." She stepped back and pushed the door.

Before she could close it, Sancho darted back into the room and disappeared under the tester bed, his collar medallion rattling on the plank floor.

She scoffed. "Brazen fellow."

"He was just greeting me." The deep baritone sent ripples along her skin. "He knows I'm just, er, here."

Yes, he was. Still there, standing stock-straight, gaze locked on her eyes, perhaps fighting whatever was pulling his attention to her bosom.

Another flutter of heat traveled through her.

He pointed at his door. "Rompole is with me. If Sancho needs to go out, just knock and one of us will see to him."

She reached for her belt and cinched it, and his gaze wandered all the way down to her bare toes and then skittered back up again, lighting an urge to throw herself at him. Thank heavens, he was chaperoned.

"I'm sorry I couldn't offer your man a room tonight. I don't know where Wes thinks he can put two footmen." She pointed down the corridor hoping for a respite from that molten gaze. "That door is a lumber room, and the other is Bixby's. We'll move Meg in with her and give Rompole Meg's attic room."

"There's no need. He's found a cot. Rompole and I have often shared quarters as needed." He smiled and another shiver went through her. "Sancho as well. If you wish to be rid of him, take him by the collar and bring him over to me."

He had Rompole, and she had Sancho, who would be a terrible chaperone. He'd probably welcome the Major into her bed.

And where had that thought come from? Perhaps she should move

Bixby into her room to protect her from this madness. She might squeeze the maid in between her easel and the writing table.

He was looking at her again, and it made her flutter all over.

She never fluttered, except perhaps during those dinners under the relentless gaze of Sir Ebenezer. Steeling herself, she found her tongue and began babbling again.

"Yes, well, perhaps if the footmen are sturdy, they can shift things around and sleep in the lumber room. Bixby will not let them misbehave."

He stepped closer. "I *am* imposing, my lady."

# CHAPTER 5

So close, he was. Close enough for her to catch a whiff of the starch that stiffened his neck cloth, and the hint of brandy on his breath. A white hair stood out on his sleeve—a gift from Sancho—and her fingers itched to reach for him and brush it away. She gripped the ends of her belt and noticed the spot of dried lapis lazuli on the tip of one finger. "No." She shook her head. "Your bedchamber was completely available, as was Wes's. And my mother-in-law… well, I couldn't require her to climb an extra flight of stairs. I'd set this bedchamber aside as my, er, study, but my stay is intended to be so short, I never had the bed removed. So, you see, all is well."

His gaze slid over her shoulder into the well-lit room. "Is it also your studio?"

"I do paint in here."

He gave her a long look. "I hope you will one day let me see your work."

Her work. In her bedchamber. Oh, she might invite him in right now, but she wasn't the sort to welcome men into her bedchamber, in fact, she'd had a time of it keeping Melton's friends away.

And having him view her painting? He'd laugh, just like Melton and Wes always did.

His steady gaze had her hands itching again. She tugged her belt tighter, holding in the strange heat rippling through her. He wasn't so much interested in her amateurish rendering of York Minster as he was in her bosom because he couldn't seem to keep his gaze from moving there. She'd seen that sort of look before, though she'd never come close to this sort of inner turmoil before.

And blast it, this was her home. She wouldn't have male guests trying her on, be they distant cousins, or war heroes, or Sir Ebenezer look-alikes. Besides, she would have to face the morrow with him escorting her and Bixby.

"Well," she said, injecting a note of cheer. "I shall see you at breakfast and we may discuss what sights to see tomorrow. Do you have a particular interest?"

He bit his lip and smiled. "Yes, I find I do." He bowed. "Until morning then, my lady. Sweet dreams."

She closed the door and leaned her forehead against the cool wood. And then laughed. She'd been pursued before by the drunken sots Melton called friends. Jeremiah Ripton had been the most determined, but she'd always known she was no more than the fox or the hare they were chasing, and she'd never considered allowing herself to be caught.

Until now.

~

"Is all well?" Gus asked as he met Honoria in the front hall of her town house.

"I fear it is just the two of us today. Bixby feels it's imperative to stay here arranging Rompole's room and preparing for the arriving footmen. She has chores for your man as well."

"I see. Yes, put Rompole to work." Rompole didn't need his own room. In fact, the presence of a chaperone helped Gus curb his own baser urges toward the lady across the hall. But Gus sensed his servant might have an interest in the lady's maid, so he let the matter stand. "Did she wait until Wes departed to tell you this?"

Honoria gave an elegant little shrug that she might have learned in a French drawing room. He wanted to slip his arm over her shoulder and let his hand linger there.

"It's just as well," she said. "Bixby has no enthusiasm for historical sites."

"What does she like?" Rompole might like to know.

"She loves fashion, especially the French fashion plates. But only that. She's a country woman, and she has no interest in seeing Paris fashions on Parisians."

"Well at least she's not sporting a black eye." He raised an eyebrow. "Rompole asked your housekeeper about her injury."

She chuckled and led him out the front door. "Dunscombe attended a reform meeting last week. Matters got out of hand. She swears she didn't engage in fisticuffs but was injured making her escape."

"It's a very egalitarian household you run, my lady."

She halted and looked up at him. "As to that, Major, if we're to spend the day together, just the two of us, in an *indiscreet* perusal of ruins, you may as well call me Honoria."

"Is it still indiscreet if I'm along?"

She shrugged again, and he almost chucked her under her chin.

"Well then, you may call me Gus."

"On a day when I'm chasing Roman history, I rather prefer Augustus."

He bowed and offered his arm, and they proceeded down the street to the Shambles.

Hours later, after touring the Minster with the help of a guide, and resting a while on the benches inside, they proceeded to visit the city wall. As they turned a corner, the minster bells began pealing.

"Do you hear that?" Honoria paused in front of Bootham Bar and cocked her head. "Oh, they are glorious, are they not?"

*She* was glorious, but she wasn't ready to hear that from him yet.

They'd ambled through the Shambles, where the lady ordered groceries and visited Orsini's apothecary, fetching powders for Cousin Genny. And then they'd visited the bookshops on Stonegate street and in Bookbinder's Alley, where he learned that, though she shared his interest in history, she also enjoyed the occasional romantic novel. He counted that as a good sign.

"They're certainly loud," Gus said. "But you're right, the sound is magnificent." He glanced at his fob watch. "It's an odd time for bells. In Spain, when the cannon balls weren't knocking over belltowers, the Papists rang the Angelus three times a day. Not at this hour, however."

"What adventures you've had. I suppose you've seen magnificent city walls like this one."

He gritted his teeth. He'd help knock a hole in a wall like this at Burgos.

The press of her hand on his arm brought him back to the present.

"Forgive me, Augustus. Your adventure wasn't a Grand Tour."

He set his hand atop hers. Watching her color rise did something to his heart and made him smile. "No forgiveness needed. Shall we walk on through the garden?"

"I'd rather walk along that wall and peer over it like a Roman soldier. Or..." she smiled up at him. Over the course of the morning, they'd settled into an easy companionship, and she'd beamed up at him like that frequently. "I know you will say the Romans didn't build those walls. But my guidebook says there were Roman-built walls there first. Probably not as sturdy as these."

"Oh, I don't know. The Romans built quite an ambitious wall to the north, and some of it stands today."

"Hadrian's Wall."

"Yes."

"I would *so* love to see that. The Romans had a fort at Brough, a short ride from Twisden Manor, but there is nothing Roman remaining, though there is a grand Norman-built castle on the site, or what remains of it. How I would love to explore something so ancient as Hadrian's Wall."

"Then you must come home with me to Whitlaw Grange and

explore. I've discovered a little-known section of the wall running across my acreage."

"*Really?* How can you know?"

"I suppose I can't know for certain, oh ye of little faith. Perhaps it was part of a holding pen for the local cattle reivers. However, I've found a Roman coin or two in the area and, having visited a very sturdy portion of Hadrian's Wall north of Haltwhistle, I can say with some certainty that my stacked stones look just like theirs."

"And you found coins. I should *love* to see your bit of antiquity and sketch it."

"It's not as grand a subject as York Minster. Is that what you're painting?"

She'd brought out her pencil and a small pad during their tour of the Minster.

She nodded. "I have a very good view of it from my study."

"Your studio—bedchamber—study?"

She laughed and more color tinged her cheeks. "Yes."

He squeezed her hand. "Will you allow me to see it? The painting I mean. I draw a little, you know."

"As a gentleman ought to be able to do. I tried to tell Melton—my late husband—that Wes should have lessons. In fact, I enlisted one of his visitors to stay longer during one of Wes's school breaks and give both of us lessons. Melton said that was too much of a girlish thing." Her gaze shifted to the floor. "He said when our daughter was a little older, she and I could take lessons t-together." She eased in a breath and swallowed. "One miserably cold winter several years ago, before Melton deemed her old enough to paint, she was struck by a fever and… and I lost her."

An old grief swept over him. There was no greater pain for a parent, his mother said, after each of his siblings had died, and he knew that must be true, because he'd suffered as well. "She was your only child of the marriage?"

"The only one born to me. But of course, I have Wes."

She had Wes, and cared deeply for him, which explained why she tolerated so much from the lad.

"He's been mine since he was six, and I love him dearly. What of you, Major? You've told us much about your life, and yet so little. I might apply to my mother-in-law for more information, but I fear she doesn't know all your history. Did you ever marry?"

"No. And I have no children." As far as he knew. He'd always been careful. "I did, however, have a fiancée for all of two weeks, until some lordship's son and heir arrived at camp and the lady saw a chance for a coronet."

"Oh dear. You were crushed."

"As one is in those circumstances." The girl had done him a great favor, though, leaving him free to travel hither and yon in his soldiering, unattached and available for the lady before him. The thought of a future with her filled him with hope. "I did, however, recover."

"Aunt Honoria? Is that you?"

Honoria turned away from Augustus's heated gaze and saw Patience advance with two of her stepdaughters—the twins. She groped for the names… Ivy and… Iris.

Glancing back, she saw a flare of interest in Augustus' eyes. Well, why not? Patience was young and beautiful, and so were the twins with their sparkling green eyes, auburn hair, and appealing sweetness.

Swallowing an unaccountable surge of envy, she hastened to make introductions—the girls had thankfully dressed in colors to match their names—and watched as the twins latched onto each of the Major's arms, peppering him with questions about his army service.

Patience linked arms with her. "Look at those two magpies. I'm so happy I was able to give them a chance to put away their paints and have a Season."

"The girls paint?" There were so many Bigglesworth girls, she hadn't had a chance for a deeper acquaintance.

"Yes. Such lovely miniatures." She leaned in and whispered. "Their work is always in demand."

"I paint as well. A little. I should love to talk to them about their painting."

"You'll surely have a chance, though perhaps after we get through this ball. The plans are well underway, and the girls are busy sorting out gowns. We've sent the invitations and are starting to receive replies."

"I shall be there with Major Kellborn and my stepson, and they've both promised to dance with each of the girls."

Patience squeezed her hand. "Thank you, Aunt. I so wish my mother was alive to join us. She spoke fondly of you when I was growing up."

Honoria blinked back a surge of moisture. Her sister Emily had been shunned by the St. Aubyn's after her marriage to a man in trade. "Oh yes. Oh, how I missed her after she married. You must tell me all about—"

*"Mother. Gus. We've found you."* Wes's voice boomed out, turning the feminine heads.

And Wes wasn't alone. Jeremiah Ripton had joined him in this ambush. The dastard was attired like a peacock from an earlier generation in a Pomona green coat and gold and red striped waistcoat.

# CHAPTER 6

Jeremiah Ripton sent her an oily smile and bowed over each lady's hand as Honoria made introductions.

"What a jolly group of young ladies you must have," Wes told Patience. "Mother and I were planning to call on you tomorrow."

Patience smiled. "I shall make sure all the young ladies are there to meet you. Aunt Honoria tells me you've promised to dance with each of them."

"Indeed, I shall. As will my cousin here. Ripton, you must come as well and stand up with some of the ladies."

Patience sent Honoria an inquiring glance and said "Of course we will welcome another dancing gentleman. And now, we must run, as we are meeting Doro at one of the shops. Girls?"

"Must we?" Ivy said. "Oh, I suppose we must. But you must come along tomorrow, Major and answer all of our questions."

Iris giggled, and both girls went off with Patience.

"Handsome girls," Ripton said. "Lady Seahaven looks very young to have twins as old as Lady Ivy and Lady Iris."

"They're stepdaughters," Wes said. "Lady Seahaven's just a much younger stepmother than my dear mother here."

"The *ancient* one," Honoria murmured.

Wes nodded and went on, "And I daresay, Gus, Lady Ivy showed a marked interest in you."

She sighed. They were spirited and beautiful young ladies, and, for all that Augustus was much older, he was a fine-looking and virile man.

"They are merely curious girls," Augustus said, taking her hand and tucking it over his arm. "Wes, we ancient ones would like to continue our tour of York's ancient history. Shall we wish them good day, Honoria, and visit the ruins?"

Ripton laughed, too loudly. "We've been dismissed, sprout. Lady Twisden, I shall call on you tomorrow.

"No, that won't do," Wes cried. "Tomorrow we'll be out paying calls. You must come to dinner tomorrow night."

A shudder went through her. Ripton, at dinner—she'd hoped to never look across a table at him with a fork in her hand; the temptation to spear him might be too overpowering.

"We shall have Miss Jones even us up," she said.

Wes grimaced at that, as she knew he would, and Ripton smiled too broadly. "I should like to join you, but I have a previous engagement tomorrow night."

"The day after, then," Wes said. "What time, Mother?"

"The day after is Sunday," she said. "We'll have naught but a cold collation in the early afternoon, as the servants don't work on the Sabbath."

"Not one of them?" Wes frowned. "And I had no luck at the agency today. Well, you must come anyway, Ripton."

They sauntered off together, Wes wondering aloud about the nearest watering hole. Augustus watched them go, his thoughts indecipherable.

"Who is Miss Jones?" he asked. "Another candidate for the marriage mart?"

"Miss Jones? Hardly… but, oh, that is unkind. Why should she not seek marriage? Except, of course, that she's older than me, and I daresay older than you."

"I'm fast approaching the ancient age of forty," he said. "Eight-and-thirty to be precise."

"Ah, well, then I am just a green girl at three and thirty. But Miss Jones is perhaps of an age with Ripton. She's a gentlewoman fallen on hard times and my mother-in-law's companion. She didn't join us for dinner last night because she was moving my things and unpacking."

"A match for Ripton, then?"

Jones? The thought of the outspoken but dignified lady matched with Ripton made her shudder. "When Melton died, I persuaded Wes and his guardian to sell the hounds to Ripton. It was more important to repair the tenants' roofs than the kennel's dry rotted walls. Now *that*—a pack of prime hounds—was a good match for Ripton. I convinced Wes to keep back two bitches and a male and start his own pack." In the kennels, instead of the parlor, thank you very much. "Miss Jones tends to say what she thinks and offer unwelcome correction. Upon occasion to Wes."

He threw back his head and laughed. "Just what any young buck deserves. I look forward to meeting her."

The laugh changed him completely, driving out the dour, frightening warrior. She had a feeling he didn't laugh much, and she wanted to see him do it again.

*Two days later*

"You must come with us, Mother." Wes batted his hat against his leg. "Tell her, Gus. It's a fine day, and Granny will like your company. The fresh air will drive away your headache."

Outside, Rompole was helping Cousin Genny and Miss Jones into the borrowed open barouche. With the three men accompanying them as outriders and Rompole playing coachman, there was plenty of room for Honoria and her maid. But of course, her maid had gone off to enjoy her free day, just like the other female servants.

Gus supposed it was such a fine day Honoria would rather work on her painting than journey out to Knavesmire to see the racetrack and grandstand. Plus, there was the matter of the unctuous Mr. Ripton, who'd taken a seat next to her at table that day, nudging her with his elbow. He'd continued to hover over her as she'd passed around cups of tea. It was especially annoying to hear him gush about what a particular friend Honoria was to him.

"I will stay here," Honoria said. "Enjoy your afternoon."

"I should like your company," Gus said, "but you need not come with us. You and Sancho must enjoy your peaceful afternoon. I'll scout for Roman ruins and drive you out to Knavesmire on another day."

"Let us at least bring Sir Sancho," Wes said.

She glanced back toward the dining room, where dishes were still sitting out. Sancho would be needed here, and the loyal dog knew it.

"Come, Sir Sancho." Wes beckoned. Sancho remained seated and sent him a baleful look.

Gus clamped on his hat and took Wes by the shoulder. "Until later, Honoria."

Wes grumbled his way down the steps. "She'll go back and clear that table."

"Most likely."

"We could have had Rompole do it."

"He's playing coachman."

"There would have been a good chance for Ripton to walk with her and woo her."

The urge to smack the lad was overpowering. "On that issue, she's made her feelings clear. If you open your eyes, you'll see it."

Honoria tidied up, let Sancho run wild through the garden while she deadheaded flowers, and then went up to her studio.

She smiled. Her studio-bedchamber-study, as Augustus had called it. The smell of paint and turpentine greeted her. Sancho padded in behind her and sniffed.

"You did well today, Sir Sancho." The only rat that had caught his attention today was Ripton. He'd growled, actually growled, at the oily man. And then Sancho had intervened in almost every attempt by Ripton to sit close to her. She'd have given the dog a seat at the table if it wouldn't have been too shocking.

From across the table, Augustus had watched Ripton like Sir Ebenezer used to do in her fanciful imaginings at Twisden Manor. If Ripton had tried anything more than elbow-poking, Augustus might have drawn a fireplace poker.

She liked him. Well, perhaps more than liked him. He was intelligent and thoughtful, dignified, but no pompous ass. If she could believe her ears, they had a common interest in antiquities. Not art, perhaps; or at least not Turner's sort of painting. But at least he hadn't openly scoffed about Turner. She would have to broach the subject again and learn his true feelings.

And she would dearly love to hear about his travels—not the battles, not unless he wanted to talk about them.

He was just the sort of man she might once have dreamed of meeting, before she'd been shackled to Melton, before widowhood had granted her this liberty.

Sancho stopped at his water bowl and then scooted to his favorite spot under the bed clanking his collar along the floorboards, while she tossed aside her shawl, changed into an old gown and drew on her paint-stained smock. The complaint of a headache had not entirely been a lie, but bedrest wasn't called for. She needed to paint.

Drawing open the window, she let the spring breeze cool her cheeks while she studied the twin west towers with their gothic crowns and compared the image on her canvas. Close up, the detail was astounding; from a distance it was hard to render the magnificence. Was that line straight enough? Was the shading right?

She prepared her paints, one eye on the sky.

The view troubled her. It was true that the day was fine, but there was a miasma to the floating clouds, a yellowish-brownish haze that had nothing to do with sunlight filtering through. Coal smoke, perhaps? Though few people kept fires going once true winter had passed. She reached for her brush and palette and in a matter of minutes, lost herself in her work.

The sound of the kitchen door opening pulled her out of her reverie. One of the servants was back early, and a good thing because she was parched. She'd ring for a cup of tea in a few moments.

Pausing to freshen her palette, she daubed on a bit too much tint. But never mind, she was no Turner after all.

Immersed in her murky sky, she didn't notice the minutes passing until the floor outside creaked and the door opened.

A low growl came from under the bed. Sancho had not entirely taken to Bixby, and he might not like the maid disturbing him, but at least Honoria would have her tea soon. "Shush Sancho," she said. "Greetings, Bixby. How was your afternoon?"

Sancho's nails tapped as he clattered out. She felt the swish of his tail and glanced down. He'd stationed himself before her, head lowered facing the door, growl deepening, poised to strike.

Air whooshed from her, and her breath tightened. This wasn't Bixby. Jeremiah Ripton had crossed her threshold.

She looked past him to the empty doorway and took in a slow breath.

"You've returned early," she said, keeping her voice steady. "Is Lady Twisden with you?"

"No, but I left her in good hands, probably enjoying her picnic by now. Kellborn went to fetch food from an inn." His gaze skittered to the floor. "Kindly call off his ill-trained cur."

"You mean to say, the others aren't with you?"

In reply, he smiled and licked his plump lips.

She heard her own breathlessness and tried to swallow the rising panic. Ripton had tried this sort of tactic before during a house party. Two of the hounds had saved her, and after that, during his visits, she'd slept in the nursery, or Bixby's room, or wherever he wouldn't find her. The man fancied himself handsome and irresistible. She'd never thought he'd follow her to York, or that Wes would be knuckle-headed enough to encourage it. Though, in fairness, her frankness with Wes hadn't stretched to bedroom matters.

She mustn't show fear or temper, which would only whet Ripton's desire. Yet, he would be made to leave, and soon. She'd find a way.

"With no horses running," she said blandly, "I knew Knavesmire would be a bore. Go down to the drawing room and wait for me. I'll come down directly as soon as I put away my paints and shed this smock."

His gaze trailed over the bulky smock. The stains were old; he might not recognize that most of the paint was dry.

His boot moved an inch and Sancho's growl erupted into a sharp bark.

She eased in a breath. "Come now, Ripton. You're an old friend of Sir Melton. Do take yourself downstairs and wait for me there. Wes will have some spirits somewhere, and I'll fetch them for you. Your presence here is inappropriate."

"Come now, Honoria."

The unctuous tone raised her hackles.

Unfortunately, he went on. "What could be more appropriate than Melton's old friend comforting his widow. You've allowed Kellborn to… why his bed is right across the corridor from yours."

"How would you know that unless… You've poked into the other bedchambers?"

"Looking for you, my dear. I wonder, hmm, have you discarded all that prim propriety, or was that all a ruse? If you're welcoming Kellborn to your bed, well, why not comfort an old friend who's just lost his wife?"

# CHAPTER 7

Bile rose in her. She quelled a momentary urge to spew out her luncheon and glared back at him. The answering heat in his eyes made her skin crawl, and she'd daresay, Sancho's as well. The dear boy was only a few vicious growls from clamping his jaws on Ripton's leg, and then who knew what retribution Ripton would attempt to wreak on the loyal dog?

Her fingers tightened around her palette and brush. She still had a thumb hooked in the hole in the palette and the fresh bubbles of color drew her attention.

For a man who'd just returned from a long ride to the country, Ripton was, aside from his boots, surprisingly dust free. His white neckcloth sparkled. His brown coat and blue and yellow brocaded waistcoat were unspotted. No mud colored his buckskins.

"This is outside of enough," she muttered. He'd always been a peacock; let him look like one. She scooped a quick brushful of Rose Madder, added a generous bubble of Naples Yellow and held the brush before her like a wand. "Augustus Kellborn…" She jabbed at him and watched pigment fly… "is an officer and a gentleman. He would never enter my bedchamber…" She waved the brush and an orangey splat drove him a step back… "Uninvited." With a quick flick of her wrist, speckles of paint stained his chin and neckcloth.

"Damn you, you vixen." He roared, snatched the brush, tossed it aside, and grabbed for her.

Before his pursed lips could clamp down on hers, he jumped back and roared again.

Sancho had a grip on the meaty buckskin. Ripton's hand flew out. The dog squealed, but the valiant lad had locked his jaws and didn't let go.

"How dare you." She slapped her palette against his face. Startled, he tugged at the board, but his hand slid away covered in paint and he looked at it in horror. She whipped the palette again and the business side struck the side of his head.

Genuine Ultramarine streaked from his temple down to his jaw, and a nicely blended orange dripped from his prominent nose. He looked so like an image she'd seen of an ancient Celtic warrior that she wanted to laugh, except that his burning eyes told her he'd be fetching his claymore soon.

"*It's your own fault*," she shouted.

"You want to play?" he growled. "We'll play. First get this cur…" He shook his leg, trying to dislodge the dog, who was making his own attempt to shake the life out of Ripton's leg.

"I don't want to play. I want you out. Sancho, let him go."

Nothing happened.

"Sancho, suéltalo."

The commanding baritone came from the open door. Sancho froze, rolled his eyes that way, and let go of his prize with a deep growl.

"*Augustus*. Thank God you are here."

Ripton shook out his injured leg and glanced at the door. "Go away, Kellborn, and take your cur. Honoria asked me to find a way to return, and she and I are not finished." He brushed at his neckcloth, left a smear, and then, looking around, reached for her shawl.

"Stop right there." A fireplace poker came down on Ripton's arm with a sharp crack.

"Damn you," Ripton shouted.

Augustus had, in fact, armed himself with a poker. "Bless you, Augustus." She sent him a grateful smile and tossed Ripton her painting rag and watched him smear paint into his cheek.

Fresh paint stained her smock and her skirts; even Sir Sancho had not been spared. It was well worth it.

"Were you having a painting party, Lady Twisden?" There was humor in Augustus's voice.

"One must improvise," she said. "Creativity is at the heart of art."

Ripton wiped at his face, rubbing the paint around and removing very little of it. "Laugh if you will, Honoria. I can make things difficult for Wes. He thought to get those hounds back but—"

"Hounds? Wes doesn't want those hounds badly enough to…" She eased in a breath, steadying herself.

Dratted Wes. He probably did want the hounds, but surely he wouldn't have wanted *this*.

"I didn't want you in my bed at Twisden Manor, and I don't want you in it here. And Wes? Why on earth would you threaten him? He's done nothing to harm you. In fact, he's made you the owner of the most prestigious kennel in all of Westmoreland. I wish you much joy of those hounds. Have them sleep in the bed with you every night. Melton did."

"As I recall they slept in your bed as well while you were visiting other bedchambers."

She grimaced, quelling the urge to slap him again. "You're absurd, Ripton. Augustus, if you'll show him out, I'll tend to Sir Sancho and then go back to my painting."

Augustus saluted and turned his icy gaze on her erstwhile ravisher. A shiver went through her along with a thrilling awareness as Ripton surrendered to a superior will.

When the door closed, she set aside her palette and brush, dropped to her knees, and pulled Sancho into a tight embrace, blinking back a rush of moisture.

"What a marvelous little warrior you are," she said, turning her cheek for his enthusiastic tongue. With the skirt of her smock, she cleaned the worst of the paint from his sleek hair, examining him for injuries. "Cook's hambone will be yours, Sancho."

He licked away all her tears and left her laughing, and then took himself back under the bed.

Outside, the late afternoon sky was darkening, disrupting the view she'd been painting. The Minster was static, unmoving, a solid thing that had stood for centuries. But above, the clouds had shifted, like the state of her heart.

Her plans and her dreams weren't impossible. There might be idiots along the way, like Ripton, and annoyances like her meddling son, but a defender might come at just the right moment in the form of a valiant dog from under her bed or like a warrior stepping out of a centuries' old painting. She wasn't alone.

She glanced at her easel. Augustus hadn't had time to notice her painting. Thank goodness. The sky wasn't quite right. She found her palette and brush and went back to the canvas.

Gus said not a word as he escorted Ripton downstairs and opened the door, performing the duty with a decorum and civility the dastard didn't deserve.

Inside, he was seething. When he returned to the carriage with the basket of food from the inn and learned Ripton had left, he'd made his own excuses and departed, riding like the devil to get back in time. Honoria was alone in the house, and Ripton knew it.

For his part, Ripton, grumbled all the way down the stairs, cursing the paint that clung to his skin and clothing. He hadn't cursed Honoria yet. Just let him try.

Ripton paused at the door and glared. "I was provoked," he said. "Deceived. Honoria is—"

"A lady."

Ripton spluttered and then his gaze narrowed. "If you knew... why the hunting parties at Twisden Manor were absolute debauches."

"With the two Lady Twisdens in residence? I rather doubt that." He still gripped the fire poker he'd armed himself with. He might have to use it.

The fool went on, as if he hadn't spoken. "My wife wouldn't attend. But Honoria was there hosting all of them. And never in her bedchamber at night."

"But you were?"

Ripton blinked.

"In her bed?" Gus prodded.

Ripton's mouth firmed.

"Perhaps she was in her husband's bed," Gus said.

"Sir Melton? Hah. The man was impotent for the last ten years of his life. Blubbered about it to everyone when he was in his cups."

Gus sighed and opened the door wider. "On your way, sir, before Twisden and his grandmother return and start asking uncomfortable questions."

*And before I have to beat you to a pulp.*

The only horse on the street was his own. He wondered where Ripton had left his. He hoped it was a long walk to a very public place so everyone could enjoy Honoria's brush technique.

Ripton took the few steps to the street, straightened his shoulders, and sneered back at him.

"And one more thing," Gus called before the other man could speak. "If I hear any more disparaging gossip, you and I will meet."

He closed the door and set the poker aside.

Honoria had been magnificent, wielding her paintbrush like a bayonet-tipped rifle, shooting splotches of color instead of lead. He needed to speak to her, privately, before the others arrived.

Upstairs, he paused at her door, wondering if she'd view his knock as another interruption worthy of more paint flinging. Chuckling, he decided he must take the risk to his neckcloth and coat.

# CHAPTER 8

Before he could knock the door opened.

"I wanted..." They both spoke at the same time.

He dipped his head and signaled that she should speak first.

"I wanted to thank you." She chewed on her lip and heaved in a breath. "And to disabuse you of the notion that I invited that... that imbecile to my bedchamber."

His opinion mattered to her. "Oh, my dear." Heart lifting, he started to reach for her and thought better of it. She'd just been assaulted by one suitor. Better to not rush his fences. "You're very welcome. And do not fear. I sized Ripton up the first night I met him." *And you.* "Only a loutish fool barges into a lady's bedchamber without permission."

"Quite." She paused, hands clutched at her waist. "And what was it you wanted?"

"I wanted to ask if I may enter and see your work."

Another long pause ensued. He held his breath, waiting.

"I see," she said finally. "Without barging in, you mean." Though no smile appeared, her lips quivered. "Will Sir Sancho bite you if you misbehave?"

"He won't because I won't misbehave. I find I very much value your good opinion and your friendship, Honoria."

"And thus, you will give me false compliments on my skills with the brush?"

"The brushwork I've observed so far today has been impressively creative."

She laughed then, a from-the-heart release of pent-up emotion, if he was any judge, and he couldn't help but join in.

"The blue on his cheek..." she said, choking. "Oh my. I suppose he'll go crying to Wes who thinks he's a capital fellow, but... Oh, Augustus, it's so nice to laugh with a friend."

"Then may I come in?'

Sancho poked his nose out, thumped his tale, and then slid back under the bed. Should Augustus turn out to be a lecher like Ripton, Sancho would be no help to her.

But... she didn't think he'd try to importune her, and even if he did...

She swallowed, remembering Sir Ebenezer's intense gaze from the canvas, so like Augustus's. Both men were so... dashing. To have all that heated warrior focus turned on her by a living man was almost irresistible.

If Augustus hated the painting, worse, if he made fun, would she be able to finish it? It was almost complete now, except for the sky. And of course, except for any touchups to the wobbly lines of the structure.

Who was she fooling? Even if he liked it, she'd go back and dab paint here or there until Midsummer arrived and her lease expired. Then she would have to stop, package it up and send it back to Twisden Manor for storage until she landed on her feet for good in some country cottage or city lodging. Perhaps by then there would be more paintings to share a wall with York Minster.

Augustus put up his hands. "Forgive me. I'll leave you in peace." He turned away.

"Wait." She reached for him, stopping just short of touching him with her paint-stained hands. Biting her lip, she nodded, and said "I was merely deciding. Please come in. If you hate it, you must feel free to tell me."

She could withstand the critique, somehow. *But please, God don't let him laugh at it.*

He went straight to the window first and looked out. The Minster rose behind the crowded buildings of the surrounding neighborhood, the twin towers touching the streaky sky.

"What a magnificent view," he said.

Then he stepped back and turned toward the easel. He paused for long moments, turning that intense gaze on her work. He didn't rub his chin, or shake his head, or nod. Only his eyes moved, up and down, side to side.

Then he looked at her and his lips turned up.

Her heart fell. He was going to make some joke about it as Melton or Wes would do. It was too blurry, the lines too indistinct, the colors all wrong.

"Yes," he said, nodding.

"Yes, what?"

He reached into his coat. "My sketchbook. I carry it with me often. An old habit from my Peninsular days when it was useful for, er, landscapes, and as a pastime to fill the quiet hours." He flipped open a page to a pencil sketch. "This is my work."

It was a picture of Sancho pouncing on prey. With just a few incisive strokes of the pencil the dog's vivacity leapt off the page.

"It's so very good, Augustus. His personality shines through. You must find my work dread—"

"No, that's not why I'm showing you this picture of Sancho."

At the mention of his name, Sancho crawled out from his under-the-bed lair.

"And here you are." Augustus's large hand settled atop the dog's head, his thumb sweeping over an ear.

Envy stirred in her. Or perhaps it was madness, to be envious of a dog.

As if he'd read her mind, he turned his smile on her and went on. "When I viewed Turner's work in London, I didn't... well, I'm a literalist, I suppose. When one is outlining a plan of assault, precision is helpful. I've always been drawn to portraits, or paintings of horses." He laughed. "Or dogs. Yes, forgive me. I enjoy George Stubbs's work. And I like restful landscapes."

"Restful landscapes before battle."

He took her hand and his gaze slid to the canvas. "Yes. I've seen enough scarred, tumultuous landscapes after the fighting."

"Oh. Augustus, I'm sorry. It was thoughtless of me—"

"No." He set a finger to her lips. "What I'm trying to say is that Turner's work with his play on light and shade, and yours, are steeped in, well, *feelings*. Your Minster is marvelous, gothic, and haunting. Are you working on the sky?"

*Marvelous*. Did he truly mean that?

"The sky?" he prompted.

"The sky. Yes. One would like a beautiful blue, but this is closer to the true one as it is now."

"They say the strange skies and cold weather might be due to a volcanic eruption in Java two years ago."

"Yes," she said. "I read of that. It's such a big world." She would never see Java, but she'd like to go as far as France, and in her wildest dreams, Italy.

He nodded and pointed to the narrow settee at the foot of the bed. "May I sit while you work?"

The only person she'd ever allowed in the room when she was painting was Bixby, who had no interest in art and who ignored her completely while she tended to Honoria's wardrobe.

"I won't comment or give advice," he said. "I have no skill with paints."

The mere notion of being watched made her hand tremble, but why not be brave? "Certainly. And here." She handed him back his sketchbook and pointed to the dog, who'd stretched out at her feet. "Sir Sancho is posing for you."

He smiled, drew out a pencil and opened to a blank page.

Nerves rattling, she picked up her palette, dipped her brush and turned back to the sky. A touch of yellow here. A hint of white there. Were her Minster towers too blurry? She stepped back and decided to leave them, and then returned to the sky until finally she had it right. Almost right. For now.

"We're losing the light." She tidied up and found her tinderbox, walking about the room and lighting lamps and candles while his pencil flew.

A thump and voices below stairs told her the others had returned.

"I suppose I must send you away before you're discovered here," she said.

He grunted, made one last flourish, and patted the empty space next to him. "Have a look. If you hate it, you must feel free to tell me."

She took off the smock and tossed it aside, deciding whether to take another risk. Like the bed, the settee could accommodate two people, but only if they squashed in close.

Heart racing, she squeezed in next to him, and accepted the sketch pad.

Her breath caught. The subject was a lady, shown in three-quarter view, her attention directed away, Tendrils of hair dangled at her neck and over her cheek. "It's meant to be me."

"Yes."

"She's too… That is how you see me? Well, the work is very precise, but to say that this is me…" She stood and he rose with her. "This lady is pretty."

"Yes. That is how I see you. You're pretty, Honoria." He tucked a lock of hair behind her ear and the heat rising in her cheeks rolled downward. "Shall I list your attributes? You have a straight little nose, full lips, hair the color of dark honey with the sun streaming through it, and rosy cheeks that seem to grow pinker when I'm around. A man notices a thing like that. And your eyes shine with intelligence and good humor. Yes. You are very pretty."

Speechless, she forced her mouth closed. Pinned under Augustus's dark gaze, she grew even warmer.

His big hand cradled her cheek, surprisingly gentle. "And I like your painting of the Minster. In fact, I should like to take it home with me to Whitlaw Grange and hang it over the mantel in my study. I should very much like to have you at Whitlaw Grange as well."

"My painting?" Over his mantel? She wasn't sure she wanted to part with it.

"Yes. And you must come as well. You can make sure it's correctly displayed."

"You want me to visit you? If you have ruins, perhaps I could paint… What? What are you doing?"

Augustus had dropped to one knee, sliding his hand down her arm to grasp her hand. Sancho bestirred himself and stretched.

"I don't want you to come for a visit, Honoria. I want you to come as my bride. Will you marry me? Will you make me the happiest of men?"

*Marry? Marry Augustus Kellborn?*

His dark gaze pulled at her like a magnet, the desire in his eyes matching the heat rising in her. Her head dipped. Just a few inches more and…

She straightened and tried to get hold of herself. "We've had but one outing together."

"And one dinner and luncheon. And don't forget we attended church together."

"You rescued me, and now you are being chivalrous. You're acting in haste, and there is no need."

His eyes twinkled. "I'm chivalrous? I rather like that."

"You're smiling now. That is better. Now, please, get up."

He complied, still holding her hand. "You haven't answered my question, Honoria. Will you marry me?"

Heart hammering, she stared up into his dark, intent gaze. "Augustus, you must agree this is precipitate. You cannot mean… you'll meet a bevy of young women looking to marry."

"It's you I want."

"But... but." He'd shown no interest beyond what was polite and appropriate for a house guest. "Until now, I had no notion... no hint of any interest on your part."

"I escorted you on your outing. I sat next to you at church. I would have snared your hand for a private stroll away from the picnickers today if you'd gone along with us. When I saw that Ripton had disappeared, I had a suspicion he'd be coming back here, so I returned in all haste only to find you rescuing yourself. And now, I want to make my intentions clear."

"Clear?"

He nodded. "Yes."

Did he feel the same wicked heat rising as she did? There was humor in his dark eyes, not lust.

She shook her head. "I don't think you can be serious, Major Kellborn. Offering marriage when you haven't so much as tried to kiss—"

"Kiss you? Why so I haven't." He leaned close and brought his lips a hair's breadth from hers. "May I, my lady?"

Her heart threatened to melt into a puddle. He was letting her decide.

A spurt of madness lifted her heels, tipping her forward.

Her lips touched his in a featherlight connection. He angled his head and brushed a kiss over the corner of her mouth, over her cheek, and jaw, and down to her neck where his touch sent a ripple of need through her. Such softness, such tenderness, from such a hard man—it was a marvel, one that sent her hand sliding around his waist, and her other groping for his shoulder. She raked through the dark curls of hair at his collar and when he brought his lips back to hers, she sighed and gave herself up entirely.

While he was gentle, she grew demanding, and he accommodated her, touching her, letting her sighs and moans guide his skilled fingers. In the dark recesses of her mind, the thought flashed that Melton had never kissed her like this.

She ran a hand down his chest and while his lips found the spot on her neck again, she glanced at the bed.

Augustus lifted his head and stepped back, his hands at her shoulders steadying her. A moment later the door opened.

She heard a startled gasp, and then the sound of the door snicking shut.

Heat burning her cheeks, she laughed. She was a wanton who'd just been eying up the bed and plotting to lead Augustus there. Who would have known? She'd certainly shocked Bixby—that had been her maid's wheezy gasp.

When she lifted her chin, she found Augustus watching her. The look was… almost smug, and that thought made her smile again. He had a right to his little victory. If he was aiming at seduction, he didn't require much more persuasion than that kiss, which was so much more than any kiss she'd ever shared with her husband or had stolen from her by one of his brash drunken friends.

She was a widow. She could do what she'd never done as a married lady—she could take a lover, one who was, if she wasn't mistaken, highly skilled. Well, at least more skilled than Melton, because how would she know beyond that?

"I am very glad you asked for that kiss," he said. "I am certain now that we will suit."

She had asked for the kiss? Well, she supposed she had. It didn't mean she would marry him. They would suit in that way for a while, but she knew they would eventually have to leave the bedchamber and then what? Then she'd find herself in a moldering manor house far on the outside of nowhere, running a household while he hunted and fished and went to horse auctions with her stepson. She'd have little time to search out Roman ruins, and she'd never visit Paris, or any other grand foreign city.

She wanted to see something of the world before she retired to kick up her feet in the country. Augustus would want to marry and be home by Michaelmas. And he'd want to start filling his nursery.

At the thought of babies, her throat thickened with longing. She'd loved and lost her child, and there'd been no others. Many children didn't survive, so the more babies a man fathered, the greater his chance for an heir. Augustus needed a young wife for that, not a widow of three and thirty.

She wouldn't marry him, but perhaps she could pay him a visit, as soon even as next summer. After all, she *would* like to see those Roman ruins on his estate. Perhaps there'd be a christening, and all of his new-found Twisden relations could attend.

And for that reason, she wouldn't take him as a lover. Imagine greeting his young wife a year from now, especially if he married one of Patience's girls? She was, perhaps, putting too fine a point on it, but making love to Augustus would feel like betraying his future wife.

# CHAPTER 9

Honoria's body was saying yes, but Gus could see that her mind was working through a series of arguments about his proposal, and taking her to a decided no.

Well at least she knew where he stood; and he knew she wanted him. And he certainly wanted her. More negotiations would have to follow. More wooing. How he was supposed to go about that, he wasn't sure.

He'd complimented her painting—sincerely, as it turned out. And he'd kissed her, and she'd kissed him back quite ardently, instead of slapping him with her paint brush.

He still had a chance with her, he just needed to puzzle out the right tactic.

"We've shocked your maid," he said. "I take it she's never seen you in the arms of a man other than your husband?"

"She's never seen me in any man's arms." She shook her head. "That kiss was… a revelation. But I must say—"

He set his finger to her lips. "Say nothing." A revelation, was it? Well, then, he definitely had a chance. He just needed to forestall any more buts and learn what else she was looking for in a husband. "My offer stands on firmer ground than ever." If only she knew how firm he was feeling. "But be assured, I won't invade your bedchamber. I'll wait for an invitation."

He tucked an escaping curl behind the feminine shell of her ear, dropped a kiss on her forehead and crossed the hall to his own room.

Rompole was there applying a shoe brush to a boot with some violence. "Annoying woman," he said.

"I beg your pardon?"

"Not Lady Twisden." Rompole looked away, biting back a smile. "I mean her scrawny maid, Bixby."

"And when did you encounter her? She wasn't along for the picnic. Where are the others?"

"Which question do ye want me to answer first?" Rompole raised an eyebrow, and when Gus crossed his arms, he laughed. "The young sir spotted a gaggle of red-haired young ladies he knew and had me haul all of them to a fine house and return the carriage. I ran into *that woman* on the street, and she buttonholed me again with questions, fretting and complaining all the way home."

"Again?"

"Aye. Pain in my arse, she's been."

Gus shrugged out of his coat. "What is Lady Twisden's maid asking about?"

"France. Her lady is fixing to travel there come July and is taking her along. She don't want to go. Don't want to get on a packet boat. Don't want to deal with foreigners especially since she don't speak the language and her lady only knows a smattering."

He crossed to the small chest of drawers where a bottle of brandy stood three-quarters full and poured himself a dram.

*Honoria had plans.* What an idiot he was. He hadn't thought ahead to what she would do after York. He'd supposed she'd return to Twisden Manor—in fact, Wes had implied that she'd return there, at least when he wasn't plotting her marriage to Ripton. And he himself, being another male dunderhead, though not so great a one as Wes, had fixed on preventing the abomination of a marriage to Ripton and never questioned the notion of Honoria returning to Twisden Manor.

"Where in France are they going?"

"Bixby ain't going there. Looking for another position and wringing her hands over it. Can't be responsible for her lady when it's just two ladies traveling alone, an' she's not to tell the young sir else he'll hop on the boat and go with them. She had a mind to do just that, 'ceptin' then they'd have him along and he's a thorn in her side and everyone else's."

Wes would want to follow Honoria to France just like he'd followed her to York. Perhaps he'd think to bring Ripton along as well for the trip.

But two women alone traveling through France—Bixby was right. Honoria was smart, and solid, but not sophisticated. And if she didn't have friends there to guide her...

Rompole frowned and shook his head. "Can't say as I disagree with her about the lad."

He raised an eyebrow at his valet. Further chastisement wasn't needed because he couldn't disagree either. Wes was young, and lively. Gus had enjoyed Wes's company in Brampton and at Twisden Manor, and, finding himself a bit bored at the time, had jumped at the offer of hospitality in York. Where Wes's mother—stepmother actually—was concerned, the *young sir*'s exuberance led to a tendency to be overbearing.

The lady wanted to travel. He'd like to see France again himself, and not with a saber in hand. It would make for a lovely honeymoon destination. Bixby could travel on to Whitlaw Grange, if she wanted to stay in her lady's employ, and they'd hire a temporary French maid for the new Mrs. Kellborn.

Would she trust him? Would she believe his good intentions? Would she say yes?

He needed to know exactly where she wanted to go.

"Rompole," he said. "I have an assignment for you."

"You take up too much room." Honoria nudged the backside wedged up next to her in the bed. When her bedmate lifted his head and yawned, she pulled her hand from under the covers and ruffled his ears.

In the days since his master's marriage proposal, Sir Sancho had moved from his safe hidy-hole under the bed to the soft coverlet on top. He'd performed his extermination duties admirably; it had been days since he'd dropped a prize at her feet, so she'd allowed him the comfortable respite.

Since her elder sister, Emily went off to be married, Honoria had always slept alone, even during her marriage. When Sir Melton's hounds found their way into her bedchamber instead of his, she swiftly chucked them out. Surprisingly, she didn't mind the little terrier's presence. In fact, even in this smallish bed, he took up little room. Besides, he was always a gentleman, rather like his master.

Reminded of the master in question, she reached for the book on the bedside table. Morning had broken with enough light for her to peruse *Galignani's Paris Guide*. It was the last in a series of travel guides delivered from the shop in Bookbinder's Alley, all for Augustus. Gargiolli's guide to Florence had been the first, followed by Nibby's Roman guidebook, and Miss Starke's highly detailed travel memoirs, *Adapted for the Use of Travelers and Including a Guide to Sicily*.

Sicily! Having read the historical account included, she'd added the island as a desired destination.

She'd intercepted the books and burnt her candles to nubs reading them before having Meg deliver them to Augustus's room. Odd that, despite spending almost every day in his company, he hadn't mentioned a desire to travel. And she didn't bring it up. They'd attended a party, a picnic, a musical night, and visited a gallery, always in company, never alone.

What was he up to? Perhaps she should just walk across the hall and knock on his bedchamber door, hand him the book and ask.

No doubt though, it would be Rompole answering. Augustus would be out on an early morning ride.

She pushed back the covers and stood. Patience's ball was tonight, and it seemed possible that there would be a betrothal announced—perhaps more than one. She'd promised to pay a call on her niece and help with last minute preparations, but nevertheless, she must find a moment in this busy day to speak with Augustus.

Chuckling, she shrugged into her robe and went to the washstand. Perhaps she'd confess that she'd waylaid his books, and he could help her plan her itinerary. In fact, she'd bring the Paris guide to the breakfast table, and give it to him in person.

~

Gus was the first to arrive at the breakfast table.

The surly housekeeper entered after him with the coffee urn, a plate of toast, and a question about his eggs.

He was comfortable with her directness; she reminded him of Rompole. His own housekeeper was just as efficient, but far more deferential. In the many long months since he took up residence at Whitlaw Grange, he'd kept a close eye on the servants, and gone over all the estate books himself. His housekeeper, his butler, and his steward, all local people, happy for the work, ran a tight and honest ship. He was content to leave them to it.

He hadn't realized how much wanderlust he was feeling until Wes invited him to visit York. And if Honoria wanted to travel to the Continent—well, he'd be happy to show her every old church between Calais and Palermo.

"What, ho? Up already? And you went riding. Why didn't you wake me?"

Wes had arrived.

Gus slid the plate of toast his way, wished him good morning, and teased him about sleeping late.

"You'll wish you slept in when you're yawning through the steps of a quadrille, Gus. And don't forget, you've promised to dance with all the young ladies. Isn't that right, Mother?"

Honoria stood in the doorway carrying a book. When he smiled at her, her color rose in that enticing way he wanted to explore more.

Gus pulled out the chair next to his and waved her over. "You promised me two dances, Honoria, my love. They must be waltzes."

"I say." Wes looked up from his cup. "Are you flirting with my step-mama, Gus?"

The young buck had finally noticed.

"What have you there?" Gus ignored him and nodded at the book.

"This was delivered for you yesterday, Augustus."

"A book?" Wes asked. "What book?"

Gus reached for the tome, sliding his hand around her much smaller one, feeling the jump in her pulse. "It's the latest travel guide to Paris, Wes. Did you have a chance to look at it, Honoria?"

She smiled, and then laughed and took her seat. "I couldn't help myself. It's so filled with fascinating details."

"You must feel free to borrow it. I have others for Florence, Rome, and Sicily. Those are at your disposal as well."

Wes's knife paused above the marmalade dish, and he looked up. "You're making a Grand Tour, Gus? Why, what with the war, I never had one myself. Father always talked about what fun he had on his. When are you leaving? After the races, surely. We'll dash home then, and I'll prepare to go with you. Mother, you can keep Twisden Manor in hand while I'm gone, can't you?" He gazed toward the window. "Paris," he said, dreamily.

Honoria's gaze had dropped to her empty plate. Gus reached for her hand and squeezed it.

"Actually," he said, "I've lost interest in the races. And, much as I enjoy your company, Wes, I have a different traveling companion in mind for a visit to Paris."

She turned an astonished gaze on him, her face flooding with delicious color.

"Yes." He smiled. "Paris. Then Lucerne, Venice, Florence, and the ruins in Rome. A packet to Sicily. Then, perhaps a stop in Malta. I have a friend there who would welcome our visit."

"See here." Wes had stood. "What—"

"Oh, sit down, Westcott," Honoria said.

He felt her small hand rotate within his and squeeze him back.

"I'm not returning to run Twisden Manor," she said. "That is *your* responsibility, and if you need a hostess, your grandmama will relish the duty until you find your own Lady Twisden."

Wes remained standing, his color rising, his glower deepening.

"My intentions are entirely honorable," Gus said.

"Are they? And you, Stepmama. Father's been dead little more than a year."

"Yet you were anxious to hand me over to Ripton," Honoria said calmly. "Who, by the way, Wes, is most assuredly not interested in marriage."

The red flames in his cheeks deepened to purple.

"You didn't know," Honoria said. "But of course. You thought he was a gentleman like your father, or you."

"I'll speak with him," Wes spluttered. "With father dead, I'm the head of this family and—"

"Don't be a goose," Honoria said. "He's no different than many of your father's other friends. Probably like many of the young gentlemen you know. And he's your near neighbor. You'll want to keep on good terms with him."

"He's different than *me*," Gus said. "I repeat, my intentions are entirely honorable."

Whatever thoughts flew through Wes's young brain contorted his lips and brows until he finally resumed his frown. "You must speak to me first, Gus."

"Westcott," Honoria said. "You are the child of my heart. I love you, and I would never shame you, and though you are the head of the family now, this house in York is mine until Midsummer. Mrs. Dunscombe," she signaled the housekeeper who was lurking, eyes bright with interest. "Sir Westcott will take his breakfast in the drawing room. Please see that he's comfortable there."

"*Mother!*"

"Augustus and I need a private moment. Close the door on your way out, Wes."

"You may issue your challenge later," Gus said, unable to resist the urge to tease the lad.

"There'll be no need for that," she said. "We will come in and speak with you in a moment."

~

When the door closed, Augustus took her other hand in his, sending her heart pounding, as if it wasn't already slamming her ribs like a blacksmith's hammer.

"Which of the guidebooks was your favorite, Honoria?"

She let out a breath. "You knew? How—"

"Bixby told Rompole."

That news wasn't surprising. Her maid had been fretting since they left Westmoreland. She was a countrywoman with no spirit of adventure. "The traitor."

"She fell into my plan readily. According to Rompole, she really doesn't want to travel."

His thumb swept over the back of her hand, and her breath tightened around the familiar scent of shaving soap, and leather, and horse, addling her brain further.

"We may have just met," he said, "but I've known of you through my mother's letters. *How lucky Twisden is,* she used to say. *He's found such a clever and good lady*. She wanted me to find someone like you to take as my bride. And then, when I met Wes, he said the same thing, that you were *clever and good*."

"And old," she whispered.

Gus threw back his head and laughed. "You can imagine my surprise when his stepmama turned out to be a pretty young widow not at all in her dotage. I wanted to yank him up by his neckcloth and shake him."

"I should like to have seen that. Though… he is rather taller than you."

"But not as experienced with yanking neckcloths."

"Very true." Wes was a pudding head sometimes. Taking up his father's baronetcy had puffed him up too much. "Imagine him trying to fight a duel with you Augustus. I worry about him."

"He'll be all right, Honoria. I don't think he'd ask to meet over just any small slight. He adores you, you know."

Tears sprang to her eyes, and she squeezed them back.

"I've a great deal of experience I could apply to advising Wes as his stepfather."

Moisture flooded her throat and she couldn't speak.

"That is, advising by letter. Otherwise, in-person talks will come after the honeymoon. And only when we are in the neighborhood of Westmoreland and not traveling."

He had more traveling in mind than the Grand Tour he'd outlined today? "But what about your estate?"

"We'll spend time there, as well. You must paint those ruins for me. After our honeymoon."

Dizziness threatened, and the squeeze of his hands steadied her.

"I have good people in place at Whitlaw Grange, and I'll take you there first when we return. Perhaps by next spring or next summer. We'll invite the rest of my newly discovered Twisden relations."

Hadn't she thought of visiting for a christening then? A child to hold and to love. It wasn't impossible.

She blinked back tears and shook off the thrill of that hope. "I thought that you had an interest in Ivy or Iris. A younger woman would—"

"No," he said. "Never. It's been only you, Honoria, from the moment I crossed your threshold. This inheritance was a surprise from a childless relation on my mother's side. If you and I don't have a child, I suppose we shall just have to leave Whitlaw Grange to Wes."

His dark eyes glowed with intensity, reminding her of Sir Ebenezer, who'd simultaneously frightened and intrigued her. Augustus didn't frighten her.

What sort of man was he? He'd served the Crown honorably for decades. He'd been a good son to the mother who'd shared stories in letters to Wes's grandmother. He'd been patient with Wes. He had a regard for family. He wasn't a weasel like Ripton, or an oaf like Sir Melton.

And he hadn't laughed at her painting.

*And his kiss...*

She freed her hands and tugged him close. "When do you plan for this journey to begin?"

He reached under his coats and produced two documents. "This," he said, "is a letter from an agent in London."

She perused the lines. He'd booked passage three weeks hence to Calais on the King George for himself and his wife.

Three weeks. She couldn't become his lady in three weeks' time. They'd first need to call the banns and then marry, and then still have time to travel to catch the packet...

She was falling into his plan just as Bixby had.

A firm finger lifted her chin. "Honoria, my love, I have more than ample funds to pay for the trip. This other document is a license from the bishop here. We have five days to fashion a proper settlement—you may keep all your dower, and I will provide for our children out of my funds—and then we'll be married at the Minster."

"You obtained a license. That was very... very confident of you."

"Yes. What say you? Will you be my bride?"

She glanced at the agent's letter again. Travel to France. As the bride of this man... who she wanted.

She wouldn't go as his mistress. She'd meant what she said about not disgracing Wes. And he meant what he said about his honorable intentions.

And... children. He was thinking of that too, and why not? She wasn't too old for children.

When his fingers brushed her cheek, she had a good look into his eyes and saw a hint of uncertainty, a touch of vulnerability, a dogged determination. And admiration. For her, a plain widow of three-and-thirty.

Their lips met, drawn together by matching desire, and need, and true regard. Hearts pounding in time, their tongues dueled and long moments later Honoria found herself on his lap, her hair spilling around her shoulders.

And then suddenly, he'd set her back, one hand cupping her breast, the other her cheek. "An answer, my lady."

"Yes," she said. "Yes, yes, yes."

It was Sir Sancho who finally interrupted them. Gus heard the door to the breakfast room open and paused with his hand down the front of Honoria's gown. He saw a flash of white fur and heard the dog scamper past and went back to his ministrations.

Moments later, Sancho pounced on Gus's boots.

"Stop it," Gus said. "You're scratching the leather. Rompole will skin you alive."

With a defiant bark, Sancho pounced again.

Honoria drew in a sharp breath and he followed the line of her gaze.

A dead mouse lay at their feet—a gift from Sir Sancho. She squirmed, breathlessly sucking air and then jumped off his lap and pointed.

On the table, a mouse munched on the corner of toast he'd abandoned for sweeter things.

"To arms," he said, and tossed the terrier onto the table.

Her hands flew first to her cheeks, and then over her eyes. "Not on my breakfast table," she wheezed.

Locks of hair fell over her cheeks and shoulders. She looked ridiculously tumbled and lovely, her lips pink and puffy, her bodice loose.

In moments, Sancho had conquered, and by the time Honoria opened her eyes he'd arrived at her feet with his offering, leaving a battlefield of splashed coffee, toppled over salt cellars, and forks strewn about like the sabers of the fallen.

Her eyes squinted hotly. "Sir Melton's hounds—"

"Were ill-behaved. I know. Wes told me." He'd been just as appalled at the stories as Honoria.

"I won't have—"

"No, Honoria. I wouldn't have had to send him into the fray if we'd been paying attention. It was our fault, you see. In the future, we must pay better heed. And your rules, my love, will apply. We'll even prevent him from sleeping under our bed if that is your wish."

A fresh wash of color rose in her cheeks.

"Or on our bed." He laughed. "Yes. I heard he'd weaseled his way into a more comfortable spot. Bixby told Rompole." He went to the door and found, as he suspected, both her maid and his valet lurking. He beckoned them in, crossed the room and took Honoria in his arms.

"Rompole, Bixby, you may be the first to wish us happy. And then, Rompole, dispose of these bodies. Bixby, your mistress needs your assistance." He dropped a kiss on her forehead. "Honoria, my love, I'll just go speak with the *head* of the family. Why don't you join us in a few minutes?"

She smiled, and then laughed. "Oh, I will. Melton wasn't much of a disciplinarian with the lad. Don't thrash him too badly when you take him in hand."

# EPILOGUE

*Rue de la Paix, Paris, Late July, 1817*

Honoria's brush paused over her palette, and she studied the small canvas before her. The painting was, perhaps, finished.

"Lovely." Strong arms came around her waist causing her hand—and in truth, her insides—to tremble. Not her stomach though. That had finally settled for this day.

"I thank you for waiting until I lifted the brush." She'd sensed more than heard her husband's stealthy approach, detecting a waft of his citrusy shaving soap and the currents of air in the still room.

"Yes, I remembered to be cautious of your brushwork," he murmured.

She leaned back and savored his embrace. "What think you, Augustus? Shall I add more color? The sky is rather bluer today. Perhaps less yellow, more blue?"

Fingers brushed at her hair. A kiss to her neck stirred a shiver.

"It's whatever you see, my love. You're the artist."

"I don't want future visitors of Whitlaw Grange to comment that all of my skies were murky-muddled."

"Mmm-hmmm." He pushed the neckline of her robe away and uncovered the strap of her nightgown. "I'm glad you're feeling better this morning."

She squashed a laugh. Almost three months married, and Augustus's interest hadn't waned. Nor her own. In fact, she'd discovered an untapped enthusiasm for marital relations.

Because of Augustus, because of his regard, and caring, and love.

As it turned out, they'd stayed for the York races, returning from a brief honeymoon—and privacy—in Harrogate to the house on St. Hedwig's Place. They'd attended the Antiquarian Society lectures and been witness to more than one happy engagement. Honoria wasn't the only one well settled. Patience's girls had done well during their Season in York. And Patience herself... well, her dear sister's daughter had found her own second chance at happiness.

Unencumbered by their servants and dog—Rompole, Bixby, and Sir Sancho had retired to Whitlaw Grange—Honoria and Augustus had made a leisurely trip first to London and then on to France. In Paris, they'd spent mornings in bed, afternoons touring, and evenings strolling along the Seine. Here and there, she'd sketched, and finally settled on the simplest view—from this window of their hotel bedchamber where the Palais Brongniart, the Paris stock exchange stood. Though the building was still under construction, her painting was complete. Probably.

"What think you, Honey? If you are finished with Paris, shall we move on. Where would you like to go next?"

She laughed, quickly set aside the brush and palette, and turned into her husband's arms. "You decide."

He cradled her jaw in his hand. "Chartres, I think," he said. "But first..."

He slipped a hand under her knees, and she found herself floating, and laughing, and landing softly atop the big bed.

Opening her arms, she welcomed him, and brushed back a lock of dark hair from his eyes. "I see you are letting your hair grow," she teased. "Very soon you'll look even more like Sir Ebenezer."

His lips quirked. "My ancestor? The fellow whose portrait hangs in Twisden's dining room?"

"Yes." She'd never told Augustus about her Sir Ebenezer imaginings. But that could wait. She had other news to share. "I think we ought to ask Wes for that painting, or at least have it copied."

"What is that dreamy-eyed look, wife? I'm feeling a prick of jealousy." His smile, and the light touch of his finger tracing her jaw told her he was teasing her back.

"Sir Ebenezer used to keep watch during Sir Melton's dinner parties. It was a great comfort to me, having a fierce warrior staring daggers at some of the guests."

"You have me for that task now."

"Too true, and I absolutely love you for it. But I was thinking, we might hang your portrait next to Sir Ebenezer's. And then, on cold winter's nights, we can tell the children the story of their ancestor's battles with reivers."

He lifted his head, and then propped himself up on an elbow, his gaze searching her face, a smile slowly breaking. "It wasn't the escargot making you queasy."

She tapped his nose. "I wondered how long it would take you to notice. And it's far too early to be sure of anything." She raised her head for a quick kiss. "Is your heart set on Rome? I'm willing to forgo the Colosseum and travel straight to Sicily."

"The Romans were there as well. But can you—"

"Yes. There are excellent midwives in France. I shall consult with one and then we may set out. I'll sketch but leave off painting at each stop. We'll take our time, and even traveling by easy stages, we can be home by Christmas."

"You've thought this through." He frowned and opened his mouth, and she set his finger to her lips before he could speak.

"No one can predict the future, Augustus. Tell me, were there not women with child following the drum? I know that I'll have an easier time than they did."

"Very well. But we must keep you well fed, and well rested, and, as you said, travel by easy stages." He fell back and stared up at the canopy. "And perhaps I'd better not make demands—"

"Oh no you don't." She rolled atop him, nipped at his neck, heard his soft chuckle, and felt his surrender.

THE END

# SOCIAL MEDIA FOR ALINA K. FIELD

You can learn more about Alina K. Field at these social media links:

**Amazon Author Page:** https://www.amazon.com/Alina-K.-Field/e/B00DZHWOKY
**Facebook:** https://www.facebook.com/alinakfield
**Twitter:** https://twitter.com/AlinaKField
**BookBub:** https://www.bookbub.com/authors/alina-k-field
**Instagram:** https://www.instagram.com/alinak.field/
**Goodreads:**
https://www.goodreads.com/author/show/7173518.Alina_K_Field
**Pinterest:** https://www.pinterest.com/alinakf/
**Newsletter signup**: https://landing.mailerlite.com/webforms/landing/z6q6e3

# ABOUT ALINA K. FIELD

USA Today bestselling author Alina K. Field earned a Bachelor of Arts Degree in English and German literature but prefers the happier world of romance fiction. Her roots are in the Midwestern U.S., but after six very, very, very cold years in Chicago, she moved to Southern California where she only occasionally misses snow.

Learn more about Alina at: Website https://alinakfield.com/

# A DUKE FOR JOSEFINA

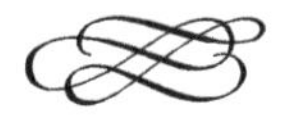

BY MEARA PLATT

A Duke for Josefina
by Meara Platt

Lady Josefina would much rather spend her time studying plants and their healing properties, but her father, the Earl of Seahaven, has died and left the family impoverished. Marriage seems her only alternative until she meets the handsome Duke of Bourne in an apothecary in York's ancient Shambles. He offers her an intriguing proposition, a fake betrothal and a king's ransom as reward, if she returns with him to his estate and finds a cure for his sister's illness. But will the true reward be his heart?

# CHAPTER 1

*York, England, April 1817*

The chapel bells of York Minster rang with their unmistakable *bong, bong* to sound the midday hour as Lady Josefina Bigglesworth excitedly made her way through the busy streets toward the Shambles and Mr. Orsini's apothecary. She tugged her serviceable brown wool cloak more securely about her shoulders to fend off the wintery chill to the April air, unable to contain her smile as she burst into the little shop filled with antiquarian herbal remedies and declared, "Mr. Orsini, I have found it!"

The old man laughed affectionately as she rushed toward his cluttered counter. He stood behind it, his head barely visible, for he was a small man with thin, white hair and spectacles almost as large as his face. "Josefina, you are jumping like a little kitten. Calm down and tell me what you have found."

She glanced about the small shop, noting only one other occupant, a big man with broad shoulders whose back was turned as he studied the wares on display in one of the musty corners. "The perfect location for my medicinal herbs and flowers, but it is on private property and I will require the owner's approval to plant anything on his grounds."

"That is wonderful, my little Josefina," he said in his thick Italian accent. "Have you spoken to the owner? Will he grant it?"

She shook her head. "He hasn't yet, but I am sure he will now that he is back in town for the York races. You do know about horse racing, don't you Mr. Orsini? Our courses are as popular as Newmarket's or Ascot's. But that is beside the point. What I meant to tell you is that his magnificent conservatory is just standing there untouched, the soil beds fallow, so why should he not allow me to grow my healing remedies there, especially when it is for a good cause?"

"Yes, financing your debut Season is an excellent cause."

She coughed. "Oh, no. I don't mean the earnings it will bring in for that, although we are quite desperately scraping along at the moment. And then there's the matter of convincing our benefactress, Rose St. Aubyn, that I must stay here long enough to attend to the blooms. Well, I am confident that problem will take care of itself since she is off in Egypt or on her way to India and will not be returning anytime soon. I meant the good it will do for the ill and infirm. Between you and me, Mr. Orsini, I dread going to these glamorous balls and assemblies. I detest being paraded about like a racehorse up for auction. That is what the marriage mart is all about, even here in York's quieter society."

"Nonsense, I am certain the men are falling at your feet. You are a lovely girl, Josefina."

"I am a boring girl, apparently. Most have found me exceptionally dull company because my mind is on my plant medicines. I offend them because I do not give a horse's backside about the new cravat they may be sporting or who the Newmarket favorites will be this year. I do feel badly though because these York races are important to the happiness of the twins, Iris and Ivy."

"Ah, yes. You've spoken to me of their young men. It is time you found one for yourself."

"I dread it, Mr. Orsini. I surely do. My family sponsored an assembly ball just this week and I ought to have tried a little harder to pretend I admired Lord Buckley's cravat and the splendid way his valet knotted it. But I did dance with a viscount and a Right Honorable, and did pretend to be interested in their horses. But about the conservatory..."

She took a breath, glanced at the big man who still had his back turned to her, and returned to the topic at hand. "I would offer to split the profits with the owner. Fifty-fifty I should think is more than fair since he will be supplying the land and I will be supplying my considerable knowledge of healing lore."

"That does seem fair."

"I thought so, too. Or do you think I should propose a sixty-forty split first, me taking the sixty? Then I could pretend to give in and settle for fifty-fifty."

"Josefina, I think you ought to bat your beautiful lashes at him and toss him that engaging smile of yours. He will give you all of it for free."

She laughed merrily. "Dukes do not get rich by giving anything away for free."

Mr. Orsini suddenly pinched his lips. "Duke, you say?"

"Yes, and I expect he is insufferably arrogant. Aren't they all? Although, I have not met any as far as I am aware. Anyway, I would not know how to play the coquette. Nor am I very good at hiding my feelings. How am I to giggle adoringly at every stupid comment he makes? He would see right through my falsehood. Although, he might not if he is truly an idiot. Do you think the Duke of Bourne is an idiot?"

One of the book displays the other patron had been standing near suddenly toppled with a resounding crash.

Mr. Orsini's face seemed to have drained of color, his complexion now as white as his hair.

The patron appeared to be having difficulty as well, in turns coughing and seeming to choke on his laughter, no doubt a response to his embarrassment, as he righted the now empty display shelf.

"Let me help you!" She darted to the man's side and bent along with him to gather the books that had spilled on the floor. "Be careful, sir. Most of these are old and quite dusty. They will stain your fine cloak. It is a terrible shame, do you not think? There does not seem to be any demand for these wonderfully informative antiquarian books."

"I cannot imagine why," he wryly intoned and began to read their titles. "The Healing Properties of Mold. Marshmallow and Mucus. Peppermint, Hiccups, and Your Bowels."

"That one is particularly interesting," Josefina managed to respond as the breath squeezed out of her.

*Blessed Mother.*

Was there ever a handsomer man created?

Dark hair that was thick and wavy.

Dark eyes as fathomless as the ocean depths, and just as dangerous in their ability to draw you in and drown you.

Muscles. Lots of them.

She began to stack the books back on the now righted display shelves.

The man gathered the last of them and turned to her. "Thank you… Josefina… forgive me, I did not catch your entire name."

"Lady Josefina Bigglesworth. Oh, please do not laugh. It is awful, isn't it? One would think my father or any of his ancestors would have changed the name over time. I do not see why it could not have been shortened to Worth at the very least. Josefina Worth would have been far more elegant. My father was the Earl of Seahaven. Gone now and having inconveniently left a trail of female offspring, myself included, with little means of support."

Gad! What was she doing?

He had asked for her name, and she had gone on in excruciatingly irrelevant detail about her family history and the sorry state of their financial affairs.

He must be appalled.

"I see," he said with surprising kindness, for even she had cringed at her dim-witted response. "Hence your need for the conservatory, to provide you with the much-needed income."

She nodded. "Yes, but it is not really about the income. Although I cannot deny it would be much appreciated. There is so much good I can do with my knowledge of healing lore. But I cannot apply any of it without the medicinal plants themselves."

He placed the last of the fallen books back on the display.

She studied his hands, for he had removed his gloves when bending to assist her. Fine strong hands. He sported an impressive ring on one finger. "Sir, may I be so bold as to ask your name?"

"Gareth Hollings, at your service."

"A pleasure to meet you, Mr. Hollings." She blushed, unable to look at him without her cheeks turning hot, probably as red as strawberries, because there was something in his manner she found overwhelming. "You seem quite an elegant fellow. The sort to go about in the finer circles. Would you happen to know the Duke of Bourne?"

"Indeed, I do."

She gasped and smiled at him, barely able to contain her delight. "Would you... that is... could you... would it be unpardonably forward of me to impose on you? Of course, it would be. But it is of vital importance. How well do you know the duke?"

"I can say in all candor that he and I are very well acquainted. I doubt anyone knows him better than I do."

Josefina glanced up and silently thanked the angels who were obviously looking over her today. Well, it was about time. Where were they when her father had keeled over and thoughtlessly left ten daughters unprotected, give or take a few daughters because how could one know for sure who was his and who was not, and who else would come out of the woodwork to claim him as their father?

She regarded him in all seriousness. "You may respond honestly to my next question. I will not be hurt if you refuse my request. Well, obviously I would be terribly disappointed. Devastated, actually. But I would completely understand if you considered me impertinent and—"

"Lady Josefina, just ask your question."

She nodded. "Would you introduce me to the Duke of Bourne?"

"Done."

Mr. Orsini groaned. "Josefina..."

She turned to him, having forgotten about the sweet, old man while her heart was in palpitations over the possibility of meeting the duke. "Mr. Orsini, isn't it wonderful? Once I take the full measurement of the fallow beds, I shall return here to discuss which plants ought to be grown. Comfrey, lavender, yarrow, sweetmeadow, are musts, of course. Start making lists right now, if you wish. Write down what medicinals are in short supply and what basics you must have. Digestives, relaxants, bone-healing, and the like."

She returned her attention to the handsome gentleman beside her. "But I am getting ahead of myself. He may refuse me even after we are introduced. Mr. Hollings, would he be that heartless?"

He arched an eyebrow, his eyes glittering magnificently as he studied her. "He can be difficult at times."

"But you are his bosom friend and could persuade him, could you not? Or is he really very difficult? As immovable as a block of stone?" She began to nibble her lip. "I can deal with stupid. I can deal with stubborn. But I do not know how I shall deal with stubborn and stupid all wrapped up in one. And what about the profit share, Mr. Hollings? Should I offer fifty-fifty or start at sixty-forty?"

Mr. Orsini started to say something, but Mr. Hollings tossed him a warning glance so he snapped his mouth shut.

"I think you should propose an eighty-twenty share. You being the eighty."

Her eyes rounded in surprise. "I could never do that. I am amenable to a partnership. I don't wish to cheat him. Then again… I would be doing all the work, wouldn't I?"

He grinned.

Goodness, he had a nice smile.

"What would he be contributing other than an insignificant piece of property that he did nothing to earn other than being born on the right side of the blanket?"

"And first in line," he added.

"Yes, the luck of being the eldest." She nodded. "And by allowing me to work my fingers to the bone nurturing these plants that will save lives and prevent devastation to impoverished families, he will gain a reputation as a visionary and doer of good deeds."

"I take it back," he said with a chuckle. "I think you must offer him ninety-ten. You being the ninety."

"Mr. Hollings!" She shook her head furiously. "How can you suggest such a thing? Is he not your good friend? Even I think it is unfair, and I would be doing all the work."

"No, Lady Josefina. It must be ninety-ten."

She cast him a stricken look. "But he would have to be an idiot to accept such a bad bargain. Please, Mr. Hollings. Will you not reconsider and support me in offering him a greater share?"

"No." He put his gloves back on, covering that extremely fine ring of his. "The deal is done. He has accepted ninety-ten."

"*Has* accepted? But I have not even spoken to him yet." Tears welled in her eyes as she realized this man had been having her on the entire time. "Goodbye, Mr. Hollings. I suppose you will share a hearty laugh at my expense at your elegant club tonight. Well, go ahead and report your amusing encounter with the most gullible girl in York and possibly all of England. Your well-heeled friends will find it hilarious, I am sure."

"Josefina–"

"I am so sorry I confided in you. Not your fault, of course. All mine."

She turned to dear Mr. Orsini who had been standing quietly behind the counter and wringing his hands all the while. "My sincerest apologies to you as well. I thought we had a patch of land, but I see that I have been made the butt of a jolly jest and must keep looking. I won't give up. I promise you."

Both men stood in silence as she started for the door.

However, she had not taken two steps before Mr. Hollings took hold of her hand to prevent her from walking out. "Josefina… may I call you that? I am the one who owes you the apology. At the very least, an explanation."

She ought to have jerked out of his grasp, but he held her with surprising gentleness, so she gave a curt nod and allowed him to proceed.

"The deal is done. I am not jesting. You have your ninety percent.

You may start your planting whenever you like."

"Mr. Hollings, enough. I can take no more of your distorted humor. Let me go on my way."

"Not yet, Josefina." He would not release her hand. "Obviously, you have not been studying your *Debretts Peerage* or you would know the significance of the Hollings name. Nor did you seem to appreciate the significance of my ring."

"It did look impressive," she acknowledged.

"Because it is the signet ring worn by the reigning Duke of Bourne since the days of Magna Carta. Sound familiar yet? I am Gareth, eighteenth Duke of Bourne. I am your idiot duke."

# CHAPTER 2

"You are my duke?" Josefina muttered numbly.

Gareth nodded, unable to take his eyes off this beautiful girl with big, green eyes that sparkled like starlight and auburn hair that magnificently framed her heart-shaped face. The wind had blown a few wisps out of their pins and those wisps now curled about her ears and forehead in soft ringlets.

"To be precise, I am referred to as Gareth Bourne because I am the duke and this is how these rules of address work. My family's name is Hollings. I should have revealed my identity from the first, but I am a cautious man and needed to get a better sense of you first." Also, intrigued by her enthusiasm and surprisingly charming manner, he had no wish to bring their conversation to an abrupt end, which would have happened the moment he identified himself.

The way she contemplated how to approach him and how much to offer had fascinated him. And how was he to know the mention of his family name would not set off greedy little bells in her head?

Every young woman entering society had to be familiar with him and his title. After all, how many eligible dukes were there in York?

No matter, he and Josefina were now making progress.

She had called him 'my duke' and not 'my *idiot* duke', an appellation he probably deserved for giving her a hard time.

"Join me for tea at the Castlegate Hotel tearoom. We shall discuss the supplies you will need to start your work. How many gardeners should I place at your disposal?"

Josefina began to nibble her lip.

Was she fretting? What had he said to overset her now?

And why was he suddenly aching to taste her rosebud lips? To feel the touch of her mouth against his? "What is the problem?"

"I cannot afford gardeners. I planned on doing the work myself."

"Yourself?" He was surprised this lovely girl had not received any offers of marriage yet. She was thoughtful, enterprising, perhaps a little on the chatterbox side, but he attributed it to her passion for her project. "No, you shall not do any heavy lifting on your own nor shall you pay for anything. All of it shall come out of my ten percent of the profits. And if the profit is not enough to cover my expenses, so be it. I can easily afford the loss."

He bid good day to Mr. Orsini and led her out of the shop before she insisted on offering him a higher percentage. "Have you ever been to the Castlegate's tearoom, Josefina? They serve an excellent afternoon tea throughout the day. You needn't worry about returning home after sundown. I shall have my coachman drive you to your door."

She hesitated a moment. "Thank you, Your Grace. I should like to join you. But I cannot ride with you in your carriage because I have no chaperone. I think tongues will wag if I am even seen having tea with you. May we walk to the hotel instead of ride? It is not very far. And I shall walk home on my own afterward. You needn't concern yourself."

He wanted to scoff and tell her not to be absurd, but he understood how precarious her situation was. A young woman should not have to pay her own way to afford her first season or dig around in the soil all day to earn her pay. Nor should she be walking on her own through the streets, especially after nightfall.

Was anyone chaperoning her? It did not appear so, for she seemed quite comfortable running about town on her own. She might get away with traipsing about the streets of York in daylight, but if she was attending the society balls and soirees, who was providing escort? And who was sponsoring her?

One thing was for certain, Josefina badly needed supervision.

He agreed to walk her over to the hotel, but he was not going to allow her to walk home on her own. He would stick her in his carriage even if she howled in anger the entire way.

But another thought crossed his mind as they strolled to the hotel. She would be seen taking tea with him. Speculation would be rampant they were courting.

Well, that would not be so bad for her.

It might give her a bit of cachet to be seen with England's most eligible bachelor. She might even attract a better quality of suitor. A girl as beautiful as Josefina had to be much sought-after.

She did not appear at all impressed by the men laying themselves at her feet.

He stifled a grin, quite liking this about her.

They entered the hotel's tearoom and were immediately noticed by one and all.

"It is beautiful," Josefina murmured, looking around and commenting with approval on the frescoed walls and gilded, domed ceiling.

The major domo took their cloaks and handed them to one of the stewards, then led them to their table. "It is good to see you again, Your Grace."

"Thank you, Franklin." He glanced at Josefina who did not have a haughty bone in her body and seemed eager for introductions to be made. "This is Lady Josefina... um, daughter of the Earl of Seahaven."

"A pleasure to make your acquaintance, Franklin."

She cast him an irrepressible smile that the man obviously found captivating, for he bowed obsequiously and could not contain his admiration as he said, "The pleasure is all mine, m'lady."

Franklin never admired anyone.

As major domo in this vaunted establishment, he had finely honed his 'I am bored and I know everyone who is anyone so you cannot impress me' look. But Josefina did have an entrancing way about her. He could not blame Franklin for doting on her as though she were his own granddaughter.

After all, she had even managed to charm him, and he was a jaded duke.

Josefina cast him an impish smirk once they were seated and alone for the moment. "You forgot my family name when introducing me to Franklin, didn't you?"

He arched an eyebrow.

"I am only teasing, Your Grace. Even I wish to forget it. But it is Bigglesworth, if you need to reference it again."

He chuckled. "I shall make every effort to keep it in mind. Are you hungry?"

"A little," she admitted. "I dashed out of the house early this morning without taking so much as a cup of tea. I wanted to walk about town and scout potential garden plots. It is hungry work, I must say. There is so little to be found within the city walls, certainly no suitable home with a conservatory attached that would allow me to grow plants all year round. I did find one belonging to the royal family, but the guards threatened to shoot me if I dared step foot on the grounds."

She sighed and shook her head. "I only wished to speak to their head gardener, but they would not allow me even that. Then I noticed your elegant house and its beautiful conservatory in the back garden as I was dejectedly walking back home."

He frowned. "My garden is surrounded by a stone wall. How could you see my conservatory?"

She cleared her throat. "What?"

He leaned closer and frowned. "Answer my question, Josefina."

She sighed. "I may have scaled the wall."

He wanted to grab her by the shoulders and shake her soundly. He wasn't angry so much as worried she might have been hurt. "You scaled the wall?"

"Yes."

He made a choking sound, barely able to remain calm. "Did you not see my dogs patrolling the grounds? You are fortunate they did not rip out your throat."

She winced. "Well, you see. They did approach me, but I happened to have some treats in my pocket that dogs particularly like."

"What treats?"

"Shortbread and lemon biscuits."

"This is what won them over? How could you be sure it would work? And you just happened to have..." His heart was now pounding, for carrying a few stale biscuits was no protection whatsoever.

"I have faced this situation before." She cleared her throat again. "Your dogs are lovely, by the way. Quite affectionate once they became accustomed to me."

"And what of my staff? I have gardeners, and morning deliveries from local merchants. Their entrance is in the back."

"Your lovely dogs warned me whenever anyone was approaching, so I was able to hide in... never mind. You won't punish them, will you? I am sure they would have sensed if I meant any harm and growled ferociously to alert you to the presence of an intruder in your midst."

He simply stared at her, astounded.

She stared back at him.

He heard the whispers at the table behind him. "He cannot take his eyes off her, nor can she take her eyes off him. Who is she, I wonder?"

"The Earl of Seahaven's daughter, Lady Josefina," said the major domo in a hushed tone when the occupants of that nearby table called him over to question him. "She is charming. He is quite smitten."

"She does have an elegant look about her," whispered someone from yet another table. "I wonder if he is in love with her?"

*Blessed saints.*

He wanted to throttle the girl, not kiss her.

Well, all right. Kissing her had crossed his mind, but that was before he learned she had scaled his wall and made bosom friends of his attack dogs.

She rested her hands on her lap. "You are angry with me."

"That does not begin to describe my feelings."

She looked as though she was going to cry. Worse, she looked as though her heart was tearing to shreds. "I ought to go. I suppose our agreement is off. I am so sorry. What I did was inexcusable. I do not blame you if you never want to see me again." She took a deep breath and released it in a ragged exhale. "I am truly sorry. Just give me a moment to compose myself and I will leave quietly."

"No, you have not had your tea yet."

Her eyes of darkest emerald—gad, they were glorious—rounded in surprise. "What does it matter whether I have had my tea? Do you not think it is best for me to disappear from your life forever?"

"I think it is best if you stay and allow Franklin to bring us enough cakes to feed the entire royal French court. As for our agreement, it is still on. The fact that I wish to wring your pretty neck changes nothing. You shall still have your ninety percent share, and I shall have my ten."

She cast him a vulnerable smile. "I do not know what to say other than to apologize again. You are kinder than I deserve. But I promise you, I shall never again violate the sanctity of your home… well, I did not enter your home, only your garden. But it is a part of your grand property, and I was utterly thoughtless and in the wrong."

"Are you trying to talk me out of forgiving you, Josefina?"

"No. However, you do deserve an apology. I give it to you yet again, a heartfelt one. I will close my mouth now and not utter another word."

He laughed softly. "Then I shall have a very dull conversation with myself."

"Why are you being so nice to me?" But she managed a charming smile, even though she obviously still felt contrite. "I do not think you could possibly be dull, even if only talking to yourself. There is something quite… substantial about you. So many of these lords are mere jackanapes. Not you, though."

"Thank you."

"You have intelligent eyes. And an appealingly wry manner."

"I thank you again."

"But I think being a duke has trained you to hold yourself apart from others, refrain from allowing anyone too close. The few friends you do allow into your confidence ought to feel honored."

He made no response, merely motioned to the major domo to bring on the feast.

She enjoyed her chamomile tea and the strawberries buried under clotted cream. The strawberries were served over Devonshire splits which she devoured. Her eyes grew wide as more delicacies were brought out. Apricot flambé. A pineapple. Florentines, curd tarts, gingerbread. Maids of Honor, which were a particular favorite of his. Bath buns. Marzipan birds.

"Your Grace, please. This is too much. How on earth did they obtain these fruits at this time of the year? Do they grow them in their own private conservatory? I never thought of doing such a thing, planting fruit trees, that is. But this would be an excellent way to provide additional income. We could—"

"Discuss it another time, perhaps?" He signaled to the major domo to clear the food away.

Josefina reminded him of a hungry, little kitten, looking quite forlorn as the trays of fruit and cake were whisked off the table and crumbs scraped away. She had mentioned having sisters, quite a few of them. Since she was working to afford gowns for her season, he expected her sisters were doing the same.

They probably scrimped on everything, including their food.

How thoughtless of him!

He was hoping to impress her and instead he was grinding her face in the dirt, showing her all she could not have. He needed to make things right, do something nice for her family. Although why he should feel any responsibility was beyond him. He'd only met the girl a few hours ago. "Josefina, let's talk business."

Her eyes immediately took on that ensorcelling sparkle. "Yes, please."

He had ordered a glass of port for himself and more tea for her. He waited for their steward to leave them before proceeding. "You obviously know of my ancestral home in York since you saw fit to invade it."

She blushed. "I did apologize for that."

"I know. I am not mentioning it for that reason. I also have an estate near Scarborough overlooking the sea."

"I am sure it is quite lovely."

He nodded. "It is. I have been riding back and forth between here and there because…" He took a deep breath. "My sister is not well."

"I am so sorry." Josefina seemed genuinely saddened. "What is her ailment? Has she been treated by physicians? Of course, you would have spared no expense to have the best. Have they helped?"

"No, they have done nothing but poke and prod her to no effect."

"Are you asking for my help? Because I would be willing to assist in any way I can. This is entirely the point of my mission, to provide plant medicines that might ease an ailing person's pain." She leaned toward him, seeming to forget that the tearoom patrons were still watching them.

This was one of the odd but loveable things about her. She did not seek attention or ever consider that people might actually want to watch her.

"Your Grace, can you describe her illness to me?"

Another odd thing was the trust he was ready to place in her, this young woman who could not be more than twenty years old. But he had faith in her ability to attack a problem with a fresh outlook, to think for herself, and not rely on established medical dogma.

He was so tired of these medical experts offering the same failed treatments for Clarissa. "I think it is several ailments wrapped up in one fragile body. She is about your age, although I am not certain how old you are."

"Nineteen," she volunteered. "Very nearly twenty."

"She is seventeen… a hotheaded seventeen. I had opened our estate, Cumbe Grange, at Christmastide because she was enrolled in a private girls' school near there, and I thought it would be nice for us to spend the holiday together. In any event, this is where I keep my horses. I had planned to remain here through the York races since I have several entered."

Her attention was riveted to him.

"I test them here at York before sending them down to the big Newmarket races. But my point is about Clarissa." He realized he was clutching his glass so tightly by the stem, it threatened to crack.

He drank his port and set the glass aside before continuing. "Clarissa is an excellent horsewoman, but not even she was good enough to ride one of my new purchases, a devil of a horse that had yet to be properly broken. We had saddled him, intending to leave him alone to get used to the weight of it on his back and then afterward walk him around the corral for a bit."

He shook his head and groaned. "I do not know what possessed her. She took him while our backs were turned. We had returned to the stalls to trot out another of the horses when we heard her scream. I thought she had fallen off that beast. Now, I wish she had. But she held on as he took off, leaping the fence and heading into the open meadow."

"Around Christmas? There would have been snow on the ground, certainly patches of ice."

"Yes, Devil's Spawn, that is what we named him, slipped on an icy patch and threw her. He recovered and galloped off. She was thrown into a tree and cracked several ribs. Broke her leg. She was in too much pain to move, so she lay in that icy puddle until we finally found her."

Josefina appeared genuinely stricken by his sister's situation. "The poor thing. I assume she now suffers from a lung infection. I can prepare infusions of lavender and thyme that will ease her breathing. A little in steaming water ought to help. What about her bones? Have they properly set?"

"Yes, her ribs are healed and her leg should have done the same, only... she refuses to walk. I have not pushed her because she is often times weak and running a fever due to her lungs. But I think it is her spirit that has suffered worst. I cannot talk to her. She will not listen to me. And she detests the parade of physicians who come to attend her."

He motioned for the steward to bring him another port before getting to the point of this conversation. "Josefina, I would like to amend our agreement."

She eyed him warily but waited to hear him out.

"Come to Cumbe Grange with me. I have a conservatory there twice as large as the one in York. You shall be my guest. Mine and Clarissa's. Our aunt, Lady Philidia Dawson, lives there with us. She is well respected among the ton and no one will question your presence with her serving as your chaperone."

"Your Grace, I cannot possibly—"

"Stay until October. That will give you time to plant your herbs and flowers, and reap the rewards. Hopefully, you will also develop a friendship with my sister. Please, accept to be my guest. Whatever you need, you have only to ask. That includes gowns and any accessories for yourself. Excursions to York to see your family since I expect you will miss them."

"We shall not be here much beyond the end of the races. I believe that is sometime in May. Then we return to our home in the village of Starbrook."

"Wherever you desire to go, I shall take you. Do not be angry with me, Josefina. All my wealth and power is meaningless if I am to stand by helplessly and watch my sister die."

She gasped. "No, she won't die. I won't let her."

He raked a hand through his hair. "Does this mean you have accepted? What she needs is a friend like you. As for our agreement, if you come with me and grow your plants in my conservatory at Cumbe Grange, I will give you one hundred percent of the profits. Of course, the expenses will all be mine. Your seeds, garden implements, fertilizers, pots, everything you require. You have only to ask."

"Your Grace, stop." She shook her head in obvious dismay. "Do not bribe me. We shall keep to our original agreement. You do not need to offer me anything more. Well, two or three serviceable gowns because my sisters and I share clothes, as you've probably surmised. But I do not want anything fancy. People will talk as it is. For you to take me to your estate near Scarborough…" She eased back in her chair. "I don't know. Perhaps I had better give it more thought. You must understand, I cannot afford to be ruined."

She shook her head as her dismay mounted. "Truly, my family cannot afford it. This is my greatest concern. One misstep on my part, and all my sisters will be irreparably damaged."

"The damage would be minimal if my aunt and I were to sponsor their come-outs."

She nibbled her luscious lower lip, the one he ached to nip and lick and tease. "That is ridiculous. We have gone from my planting some herbs and flowers in your York conservatory to your absorbing the cost of a Season for me and my sisters? I think we have gone too far afield. But is it possible to bring her here? Do you not think she might like York? I would be happy to visit her every day. I could work in the conservatory garden each morning and then visit her each afternoon. It is only once the flowers bloom and herbs mature that I will need to spend time preparing the tinctures, powders, and poultices."

"No, Josefina. She refuses to budge. But I know how to bring you to Cumbe Grange without ruining your reputation."

She cast him a hopeful look, because it was obvious she wanted to help his sister and felt as frustrated as he did in not being able to do it. "Do not suggest my stepmother join us because Patience is not old enough to be deemed suitable. Oh, I know she is a married woman and a widow, so that would pass as proper if people were inclined to be kind. But many would make something of her youth. Besides, she has the little ones at home and cannot leave them."

"I will not impose on your family at all. No, I was thinking that I could marry you and that would solve all our problems."

She regarded him as though he were demented. "Marry you? *Marry you?* You are asking me to marry you?"

She did not realize their steward had just come up behind her and had heard her repeat his proposal. The man rushed to the major domo to report the news, and was overheard by several other stewards who were now reporting it to the patrons they were charged to serve.

It took no more than a minute for the whispers to swell to an excited buzz around the tearoom, as though a thousand bees were now buzzing around their hive.

Josefina was now laughing at the preposterous notion, a response the other patrons mistook for joyful acceptance. After all, who would not be overjoyed to marry the Duke of Bourne?

Was he not the catch of the season?

The catch of a lifetime?

Well, he had truly gotten himself into a fix.

He had meant to say, a *pretend* marriage... or rather, a *pretend* engagement. Then he could scoop her away to meet his sister and aunt, all proper since everyone would believe she was his betrothed. After she had reaped her plants and turned them into medicinal powders and tinctures, he would have dumped an enormous monetary settlement on her and allowed her to quietly end their betrothal.

But he had said 'marry'.

Forgotten that crucial word... *pretend*.

There was no help for it now.

He took Josefina's hand in his and raised it to his lips. "Smile, Josefina. Everyone is looking. And yes, I am going to marry you."

# CHAPTER 3

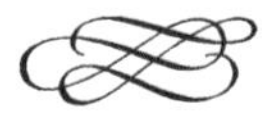

"You and I? To be married?"

The Duke of Bourne cast her an appealing, and yet slightly tense, smile. "That is usually how it works when a gentleman proposes to a young lady."

How had this happened?

Josefina had known the duke little more than an hour or two, and now she was to be his duchess?

The smile froze on her face as every patron and server in the elegant tearoom now stared at her while the duke put his warm lips to her hand again and kissed it.

Time suddenly froze, for not a soul in the room moved. All gazes were fixed on them, some joyful, some in shock, and some in abject horror, for how dare she—this upstart—steal England's most eligible bachelor from under their very noses?

She wanted to stand up and assure everyone this was all in jest. But the duke still had hold of her hand, and there was something sincere and a little desperate in his regard. She could not find it in her heart to utter a refusal or give away the absurdity of their situation.

In truth, she could not speak at all.

The touch of his lips to her hand now had her in distinct danger of swooning. Were he ever to kiss her on the lips, she might faint. She had never understood those silly, young ladies who flushed hot and fluttered their fans over one man or another, but she did now.

If he did not release her hand soon, she would make an utter nodcock of herself.

She realized he was not releasing her hand because he was awaiting her response, which had to be an acceptance or she would humiliate both of them. But how to say it? A simple yes seemed not enough. A gushing cry and tearful nod seemed too much.

Finally, she said, "Your Grace, I would be honored to be your wife."

He released the breath he must have been holding. "Thank you, Josefina."

If he said something more, she did not hear it over the applause and cheers of those in the room. It was not thunderous applause, for there had to be several hearts broken now that the duke was betrothed to her.

The damage having been done, they rose to leave. He took her arm, locking it in his by placing his hand over hers in what may have appeared to be an affectionate gesture, but she suspected it was meant to keep her from running away.

She had no intention of running.

She wanted use of his conservatory, whether in York or his Scarborough estate, it did not matter, although York would have been so much simpler. He wanted her help in restoring his beloved sister's spirit and was ready to give her everything for it.

He was offering too much.

She really had to lecture this duke on the art of negotiation, or he would bankrupt his holdings within a matter of months. To offer her ninety-ten when he knew she was ready to accept fifty-fifty in their business arrangement was folly. Then to follow it up with a proposal of marriage when she had been willing to help his sister for no compensation?

Utterly absurd.

He must have read her thoughts, for he suddenly broke into hearty laughter.

"It is not funny, Your Grace. I have no desire to attach myself to a man who does not know how to manage his investments, or worse, is a spendthrift."

He led her out of the hotel and into his waiting carriage. There was no mistaking it was his, for there was none finer in the queue of elegant conveyances, and who could overlook the magnificent lion and rose crest embossed on the door?

"I assure you, Josefina," he said, taking it upon himself to place his hands about her waist and lift her in, "I could not run through my money even if I dropped a thousand pounds a day on bad investments or frivolous entertainments, which I assure you, I do not."

She stared at him as he settled in the bench across from her. Her seat was of softest leather, nicely padded, and the leather tanned to a rich and beautiful maroon color. "Are you jesting?"

"No."

The carriage rolled away without so much as a jounce. Or was she merely too distracted to notice anything but him?

"You are that wealthy?" It was beyond crass of her to ask, but this all seemed like a mad dream to her. She wanted to pinch herself to make certain she was awake. Perhaps his dogs had attacked her, and she now lay bleeding in his garden, the blood spilling from her torn throat.

"Yes, I am that wealthy."

She groaned.

"What is the matter, Josefina?"

They had so much to say to each other, and she was afraid they would not have enough time to talk before they reached her home, which was not even her home, but a town house graciously loaned to her family by a kindly relative.

"Wait! Where are we going?" She peered out the carriage window as they slowly made their way through the crowded streets approaching York Minster. "You do not know where I live."

He took her hand to calm her. "I am not abducting you. We are merely driving around York so that you and I may speak in private. We shall not go beyond the old walls. I promise you."

Her head was spinning.

How could she be so stupid as to get into a carriage with this duke? Everyone in the tearoom knew this is what she had done. "I am ruined."

He gave her hand a light squeeze. "You are betrothed."

"For how long, Your Grace? Is this what you wished to discuss with me? The terms? A shilling for every smile coaxed from your sister. A pound for every time she leaves her bed. Two pounds if she leaves her bedchamber. Ten pounds if she sits outdoors? And once she is healed, how do we break it off? You do mean to break off our betrothal, do you not?"

She took a deep breath and continued before he had the chance to respond. "It is only a question of who is to do it. If you were a gentleman, you would allow me to be the one. But I would be ruined anyway. Did you ever think of that?"

"Josefina–"

"Who would ever believe us when we told the world I did not wish to marry you? I do not care for myself, for I shall always have my plants and can hopefully scrape a living out of them. But my sisters will suffer worst, for who will have them after I've made a scandalous fool of myself over you?"

He cast her an indignant frown. "Do you think I would ever treat you so badly?"

She had angered him, but she did not care. After all, he was the one who had opened his big mouth and got her into this fix. "I do not know. Isn't this entirely the point? We do not know each other. But you have maneuvered yourself into gaining exactly what you want, have you not? Now I am the one completely reliant on your good will to preserve my reputation. And do not worry, I am not so deluded as to believe you really wish to marry me."

He said nothing, merely regarded her thoughtfully.

What was he thinking?

She did not care.

She had to worry about herself now.

Her lungs felt squeezed so that she could hardly catch her breath.

"I would have helped you for nothing. All I needed was a proper chaperone to preserve my good name. There was no need for this ridiculous subterfuge. I ought to have refused your proposal in front of all your elegant peers."

"Why didn't you?"

"Because of the look in your eyes. You needed me. In that moment, I could not hurt you."

"I have treated you very badly, and you deserved none of it," he admitted. "Join me at Cumbe Grange. Help me with Clarissa. Plant your herbs and flowers. No matter what happens come October, I shall settle the sum of five thousand pounds in an account for you at your bank."

She gave a snorting laugh. "Five thousand?"

"Not enough? Very well, ten thousand."

She wanted to hit him for his arrogance. "First of all, I have no bank. To have a bank, one requires funds to put into an account. I have no bank, and I have no account because I have no funds."

"Very well, twenty-five thousand pounds."

She frowned at him, and next she really would hit him if he did not shut up. "Stop tossing these absurd numbers at me. I am not a fortune hunter. Your offers make me feel dirty, if you must know. Taking your money for a kindness to your sister? It is insulting. But I must also be practical because as I've said, I have no money. I would be a fool not to take any. Will you let me give it some thought? I must speak to my sisters and stepmother. Whatever I ask would be for them."

He frowned back. "I am sorry my offer makes you angry. It is not at all intended, I assure you. Nor will I be asking anything more of you than to be a friend to my sister, if you understand my meaning. Do what you can to heal her. It is not an easy task, and I am too cynical to expect a miracle."

She blushed, indeed understanding what he meant. "Will you be around at all? Not that I ask for myself, Your Grace. But you are an important part of your sister's healing process."

He nodded. "For as long as you need me and to do whatever you wish. I assumed we would remain at the Grange through the summer and into autumn's harvest. I will only leave when business requires, no more than a week or two at a time. Most of my properties are in northern England. I am only in London when the House of Lords is in session and my presence is required. As for the upcoming York races and Newmarket races, I shall send my estate manager in my place to see about the horses I've entered. I doubt any are champions. Devil's Spawn will be, in time. He is not ready to run a race yet, and he is my best horse."

They had taken a turn around the streets near York Minster and the carriage now turned back toward the Shambles and Mr. Orsini's apothecary shop. The Shambles had been the butcher's row in medieval times, and it was said one could still see traces of blood from the freshly slaughtered animals within the crevices of the narrow road. Most of the stalls and ancient shops had been taken over by booksellers and artisans now, the apothecary shop among them.

"So, if I understand correctly," she said, wishing to be precise about this arrangement before he dropped her off at home, "I am to go with you to Cumbe Grange and do what I can for your sister. The terms of this arrangement will run from now through October when the final plants are harvested. You will provide me with all the supplies I require, feed and house me." She glanced down at her gown. "And purchase two gowns for me."

"As many as you wish."

"Two will do... perhaps three."

He nodded. "I'll have my aunt's modiste come to your home with fabrics and samples. We'll take it from there."

"Once we are at your estate, I will need a workroom, vials and jars for my lotions and potions."

"Yes, anything. You need only ask."

"Then come October, I am to quietly end our engagement, taking said lotions and potions with me to sell at Mr. Orsini's apothecary. You will receive ten percent of the profits."

"And you will receive a generous settlement of no less than

twenty-five thousand pounds. Do not argue with me, Josefina. I will not permit you to take less."

"It is a good thing we are not to marry," she said, tossing him a scowl.

"Why?"

"Because if I were your wife, I would feel compelled to take over the running of your finances. You are an incredibly bad negotiator."

He laughed heartily. "Only with you, I assure you. Otherwise, I am ruthless and always strike a bargain in my favor."

"Why are you being so generous with me?"

He leaned forward, his expression suddenly serious. "Because you are asking nothing of me. You did not even consider holding me to my promise of marriage."

"I knew you could not be serious. Who offers for someone they've only known for two hours? And despite your generosity toward me, I am fully aware you could crush me with very little effort. The rules of society are such that you could do almost anything to me and no one would care. You would come off blameless. Women would still worship and adore you."

He shook his head. "They would adore my wealth and title. They seek to marry the Duke of Bourne. Only my closest friends and family have any idea who I am as a man."

"You are obviously one devoted to your family." She sank back against the elegant squabs. "You are also one who knows what he wants and goes after it. But I have yet to decide whether you have any financial sense. That remains to be determined."

He smiled. "Josefina, I think I will enjoy being betrothed to you."

"Then you are the only man in York who feels this way. Oh, I know I have been referred to as one of the Seahaven Diamonds. But no one has given me a second look after I attempt to engage them in sensible conversation."

"They are fools."

She grinned. "I like you, Your Grace. You obviously have a discerning eye for quality."

"And you have an extraordinary ability to make me smile. I have not done so in months, ever since my sister was injured. In truth, I do not know what to make of you, for you are too impertinent, too independent for any man's liking, ridiculously passionate about your plants, and willing to take reckless risks in furtherance of your plans to build a medicinal herbs and potions empire. You are too frank in your opinions and lack all the qualities of a mercenary."

He studied her for a long moment. "Are you real, Josefina? Or am I dreaming you up in my head?"

"I was thinking the very same thing of you."

He nodded in understanding. "Is tomorrow too soon for us to leave for Cumbe Grange?"

"Yes. May we not wait until the end of the week? Each of us needs time to think this through."

"No, I do not need time."

She frowned at him. "You are being rash again. How can you know that I will not steal the silver when left to myself at your estate? What makes you think your sister will like me? And will you be introducing me as your betrothed? Not that I approve of the deception, but I think it will give me some leverage over her. I do not intend to be a tyrant toward her. But she will likely attempt to be a tyrant toward me if I am introduced as a mere companion for her. However, as your future wife? She will be more careful in her response and hopefully come to like me as time wears on."

"I haven't a doubt she will like you. But you are right in your assessment. She is willful and angry and will not hesitate to stomp all over you, at first."

Since they were now settled on the preliminary details, he asked for her direction. She gave it, sorry to see their time almost at an end. She did not even know what to tell her stepmother and sisters. Would he ever come around again after dropping her off? She expected he would come to his senses and declare their scene in the tearoom was merely a jest pulled on his friends.

"Shall I come in with you?" he asked, stirring her out of her musing.

She shook her head.

"Josefina," he said with a deep, rich laugh, "is that a yes or a no?"

"It is a yes and a no. I do not know. I am still overwhelmed."

He reached out and took her hand, but this confused her all the more. Her body tingled when he touched her.

"It is a lot for you take in. I shall come around tomorrow to see your family and take you out afterward for chocolates at Terry's. Or would you prefer ices? There is a quaint shop near the Guild Hall overlooking the Ouse. Do you know it?"

She nodded. "Yes, I've taken the little ones there a time or two."

"We should also discuss the more formal affairs going on here. Will you be attending Lady Fishton's soiree tomorrow evening by any chance?"

"No. I have not been invited." Dear heaven, she and her sisters had status because they were daughters of an earl. But impoverished circumstances put them on the fringes of acceptable society. They would be laughingstocks if anyone realized just how low in the pockets they were.

"You shall come as my guest. We are betrothed now. It will be expected."

"No… I…" Her face suffused with color. Were any of her sisters using their finer gowns tomorrow? Would there be one left over for her?

He rapped on the roof.

His driver peered in. "Yes, Your Grace?"

"To Stonegate," he said, and the driver immediately turned his team around and headed back in the direction from which they had just come. "Josefina, if you are to be believed as my betrothed, you will have to look the part. Do not fight me on this."

"Fight you on what? Where are you taking me?" Her gaze was on the passing buildings as the carriage clattered along the busy street.

"To my Aunt Philidia's modiste," he said, keeping hold of her hand as though they were romantically involved and he needed to touch her. "She needn't go to you. I am taking you to her right now and will set up an account for you, all bills to be sent to me. Do not even draw breath to protest. I will not hear of it."

"But–"

"You will need at a minimum three formal evening gowns. Silk, of course. Three suitably elegant gowns for afternoon events such as tea at the Castlegate tearoom, or an afternoon's promenade at the races, or social calls. What day are you home for visits? I suppose it doesn't matter since I am your betrothed and can call upon you any time. You will also require three sturdy gowns for working in the conservatory. Accessories for all of them. And what of nightclothes?"

She gasped. "Your Grace!"

"I am not going to see you in them, Josefina. But Clarissa might, and I will not have you looking shabby. Proper robes, nightgowns, and slippers. I had better come in with you or you will rescind my orders."

She cast him a guilty look, for this is exactly what she had intended to do.

"My aunt's modiste is discreet. You needn't worry there will be any gossip."

"Ha! Tongues will wag the moment we are seen entering her shop."

"So be it. You are my betrothed, and we have come to order your trousseau. We shall do our best not to make a fuss, but if word gets around, then there is nothing we can do about it."

"I cannot even pretend to repay you. I will never have the means."

"Did I ask you for so much as a farthing? Indeed, I will be quite insulted if you attempt to pay me back. This is my doing. I got you into this situation, and it is my responsibility to now protect your good name. My fault, Josefina, and I insist on making it right."

She sank back again as he released her hand. "Do I return the clothes to you when this... whatever this is... a sham betrothal, I suppose... do I return the clothes to you when it ends?"

He frowned. "What would I do with them? They are yours to keep."

The carriage drew up in front of a shop called Madame Yvonne's. The duke's tiger hopped down and lowered the steps for them, but the duke stepped out first and helped her himself.

He was a big man, and too handsome for words.

The now familiar tingles shot through her body as he held onto her for a moment longer than was necessary.

He smiled as he placed her hand on his arm and led her to the modiste's shop.

Everyone on the street noticed he was smiling at her.

The patrons inside Madame Yvonne's shop noticed, too.

Madame Yvonne and her seamstresses flitted around him like bees attracted to a honeycomb because the duke was not only irresistible, but undoubtedly one of their best customers and they were going to make some excellent sales.

"Your Grace," the petite Frenchwoman said, shooing away her assistants to attend their other patrons. "How may I help you?"

Josefina's cheeks turned hot when he introduced her as his betrothed and quietly listed his wishes for her. Five evening gowns. Five afternoon gowns. Five morning gowns.

*Five?* What happened to three? What would she do with morning gowns? She did not laze about in her boudoir sipping hot cocoa. She did not even have a boudoir, and her bedchamber was more of an army barracks since she shared it with several of her sisters.

The duke had the decency to keep his voice down as he proceeded to tell Madame Yvonne about the nightclothes she would require, which was humiliating in itself. Thankfully, the woman was as discreet as he had assured and did not so much as bat an eyelash when he mentioned them. "The nights are cool at the Grange because we are so close to the water. Make certain Lady Josefina's sleep attire is suitably warm."

"Your Grace, will she not be warmed by your arms?" she remarked in a suggestively knowing way all French ladies seemed to possess when it came to matters of the bedchamber. She had whispered the question, thinking Josefina would not hear it. But she had, and now her cheeks were in flames.

"Start taking her measurements. I shall wait."

Had he been here before?

Purchasing clothing for his paramours?

Dear heaven, what sort of scandalous attire would she find delivered to her?

She wanted to cry, but that would only draw more attention to herself. He was ordering nightclothes for her. Did he not realize what they all thought? That she would be sleeping with him. Is this what the modiste had meant? That they would be intimate before marriage?

She suddenly found herself struggling to calm her breaths.

Yes, she was appalled.

But not because everyone assumed the duke would sleep with her.

She was appalled because… she was not quite as horrified by the notion as she ought to have been.

She pinched her arm.

"Josefina, what are you doing?" he asked when they stood alone for a moment while the modiste and her seamstresses rushed into the back to bring out their most expensive fabrics.

"Trying to wake myself from this absurd dream."

He smiled again, his eyes crinkling slightly at the corners. "No dream."

"Are you sure, Your Grace?"

"You will make your arm black and blue if you keep doing that." His gaze turned surprisingly tender, and he lightly caressed her cheek. "Then again, perhaps you are right. Perhaps we are both under a sorcerer's spell."

She nodded. "You feel it, too? It is most odd."

"This feeling of enchantment? Yes, it happens to me every time I look at you. It is rather a nice feeling, is it not?"

## CHAPTER 4

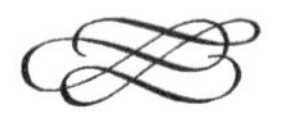

Gareth knew Josefina's family situation was an odd one, for she ran unsupervised around the streets of York as though she were an urchin. She had a stepmother not much older than herself, and sisters as old as her stepmother, as well as a host of younger siblings, and not a man around to watch over the lot of them.

Who was to stop him if he simply carried Josefina off to his estate? After all, they were betrothed.

Of course, it was a sham. But who was to question it?

They had met three days ago. He had since spoken to her eccentric family, made the appropriate assurances even to an overprotective butler, and was permitted to take her to Cumbe Grange. The consent had been given reluctantly, the elder sisters, Dorothea, Bess, Barbara, and Susana adding to stepmother Lady Seahaven's questions. In the course of his interrogation, he had heard Lady Seahaven referred to as Mama, Maman, Stepmama, and Patience, as well as by her title. He thought it unusual, but this was an unusual family. Also present were an aunt by the name of Honoria, and another female relation, Chloe. With all of them staring him down, he felt as though he was before the King's Bench being roasted alive by a panel of judges.

But he always knew he would win out because a connection to a duke was nothing to scoff at, especially under their strained circumstances. Whether or not any of them believed he and Josefina had fallen in love at first sight, the fact remained they were betrothed, and his aunt would be present at his home to lend respectability to the arrangement.

Also, the respected vicar of St. Catherine's Church in Scarborough happened to be in York and would serve as chaperon for their ride from here to his Scarborough estate. How could anyone find fault with this arrangement?

Was it such a terrible thing for him to invite Josefina to his home? How often did a duke come by and propose to a Biggleswoth? It could not have escaped their notice he was wealthy, titled, and would solve all their problems if Josefina were to marry him.

"How do you feel?" he asked her as his carriage rolled out of York the following day and his team picked up their pace upon reaching the open road to Scarborough.

She cast him a hesitant smile. "Excited to be on this new adventure."

"I should think so," Vicar Albright interjected with an emphatic nod. "There is no more fortunate girl in all of England than you, Lady Josefina."

Gareth cast her a smile meant to comfort her, for he knew she worried their deception would turn into disaster.

"It won't. I won't let it," he assured her the moment their carriage drew up to one of the better coaching inns and the vicar rushed off to tend to his necessaries and slake his thirst with a hearty ale.

After a quick meal the three of them shared in one of the private dining rooms, Gareth took Josefina for a walk in the inn's garden. He had meant his assurance sincerely, for he would never purposely hurt her. In truth, he had never felt more protective of anyone outside of his own family. The girl stirred his heart as no one else ever had in his twenty-eight years of existence.

He could not stop looking at her.

Discreetly, of course.

Nor had he been able to avoid it while they'd been seated across from each other on opposing benches in the carriage.

There was little excuse for his staring at her now, but he could not resist. The day was warm and beautiful, and so was she.

Tufts of white clouds dotted the deep blue sky, and a light breeze cooled them as they slowly strolled back to the carriage. He would send his tiger into the inn to fetch the vicar in a few moments.

He wasn't quite ready yet to end his time alone with Josefina.

Sunlight shone into the compartment as she climbed in, slanting across her auburn hair and bringing out the vibrant hints of red amid her dark curls.

Her eyes sparkled as they always seemed to do for any reason whatsoever and for no reason at all. It had nothing to do with the sunlight spilling into the carriage. That sparkle was her natural inner glow.

She had beautiful eyes, the rich green of a forest glade, and long, dark lashes to frame them. Those long lashes softened her appearance so that she reminded him of a gentle doe.

But there was no mistaking her vitality or her agile intelligence.

"Is that one of the new gowns you are wearing?" He knew it was, for she did not possess anything so fine as this forest green travel gown in her limited wardrobe. Madame Yvonne was a genius, he decided. Of course, Josefina was a perfect model. But it took a trained eye to design clothes to enhance a woman's best features and flatter her complexion. It was easily done where Josefina was concerned.

"Yes, it is one of your purchases." Josefina smiled wryly. "Can you not tell? I wanted to be angry with you for providing me with a new wardrobe, but these clothes are too beautiful, and I would be a fool to complain."

Her smile broadened with genuine sincerity. "So, I have resolved to say not a word about it and thank you graciously instead. Thank you, Your Grace."

"You are most welcome. The pleasure is all mine, I assure you. I am the one who benefits most since I get to look at you the entire ride to Cumbe Grange."

"My view is not so bad, either," she said with an impish smirk. "I am sure all the women of your acquaintance tell you how handsome you are."

He shrugged. "I don't believe most of what I am told. If I am flattered, it is because people want something out of me."

"Well, I have already won a conservatory and a betrothal from you, not to mention new clothes that must have cost you triple the already exorbitant price to have them made so quickly, and settlement of an obscenely large amount of money on me once we part ways. I don't think there is anything more for you to give me. So, you may believe my flattery, for there is nothing more behind it than the truth. However, we must discuss that absurd financial settlement."

"Is it not enough?"

She scowled at him. "It is too much, and you know it. Do not cast me that innocent smile. First of all, you are not innocent. Second of all, I do not want that much. It will make me a sought-after heiress, and then I will never know who wants me for my money and who wants me for myself. It is worse than your situation because, as a man, you hold onto your property. But a woman does not have that luxury. Once I marry, my property becomes my husband's. I will have no choice but to remain a spinster because I will never know whom to trust."

"Josefina, I will take it under consideration. We will come up with a solution for your dilemma. We must, for you are a rare person who will always tell me the truth, whether it is to your advantage or not, and this must somehow be rewarded."

"Good character is its own reward. Is it not enough to acknowledge honesty and know I can be a trusted friend?"

He turned serious a moment. "I think this is why I found myself betrothed to you. Believe me, it was not consciously planned. I have spent years avoiding the parson's trap and had become quite adept at eluding the marriage-minded schemers. And yet, I walked right into it with you."

"You did not merely walk, you leaped." She laughed. "We were both shocked, I think. Are we to keep up the pretense through October? It feels wrong to lie about it to your sister."

He nodded. "Let us see how she responds to you. We will tell her the truth once we feel the time is right."

"And what of your aunt?"

"No, Philidia cannot be in on it. Only you and I are to know. As far as anyone else is concerned, we are betrothed. My sister cannot be the only one left in the dark or she will feel as though we have all been plotting against her and hate us all."

"You are right." She began to nibble her lip, a quirk of hers when fretting.

He leaned forward and took her hand.

They were merely touching glove to glove, but it did not seem to matter. His body responded to her. "Do not be troubled, Josefina. We have told no lies. Our betrothal is real."

"Until it is undone."

"But it is not yet undone." Nor was he certain he would ever wish to undo it. He had until October to decide. He would do his best to get to know her. It would not be difficult since they would be seeing each other every day and in his family's company as well.

Her actions toward his loved ones would help guide his heart.

They spoke no more of their ruse as Vicar Albright climbed in and their conversation turned to other topics.

It was well after midnight by the time they reached Cumbe Grange. The sun had set several hours ago but they had kept going because the roads were familiar to Gareth and his trusted driver. They had made the journey so often between here and York, they knew each twist and curve by memory.

Josefina had fallen asleep a short while ago.

Gareth gently shook her out of her slumber as the carriage clattered into the manor's courtyard and halted beside the massive portico. "We are here, Josefina."

She stirred awake with a smile on her lips.

Ah, that would be a nice thing to wake up to every morning, he thought. "Let me help you down."

After unloading them and their belongings, the carriage continued to Scarborough to drop the old vicar off at the St. Catherine's vicarage house.

"My housekeeper and staff should have prepared your quarters for you," Gareth said as the conveyance rumbled off. "I sent word ahead. But I'll have them bring out some light refreshments while we wait for your bags to be brought up and your clothes put away. You will be next door to Clarissa, if that is all right."

She nodded. "Yes, more than all right. I hope she will feel comfortable enough to come into my room any time she wishes."

"Do not encourage her. She ought to have some respect for your privacy."

"None of my sisters ever did," she said with a light laugh. "I wouldn't know what to do with myself in a room of my own. It would be awfully lonely, I should think."

*I could visit you.*

He immediately banished the thought from his head. Exiled it. Squashed it. *Almost.* "Then I will encourage Clarissa to visit you often."

They handed hats and gloves to Timmons, his head butler, before settling in the summer parlor. Tea and plum cakes were brought in while the footmen brought up her bags and maids unpacked them in the room that was to be hers.

The summer parlor had a view to the sea, but it was dark now and Josefina would not see its magnificence. He would show her around tomorrow.

For now, he opened the doors that led onto the balcony and breathed in the sea breeze.

Josefina immediately joined him, no doubt intrigued by the sound of waves striking the rocky shore. "May we stand out here for a little while, Your Grace? The sea air is quite refreshing."

They remained on the balcony, staring into the starry night. Clouds and mist often obscured the stars, but not this evening.

The night felt enchanted.

Everything seemed to fall into perfect place when Josefina was beside him. "I will give you a tour of Cumbe Grange in the morning. I hope you will love it here as much as I do."

"So far, I have seen the entry hall and the summer parlor. If the rest of your home is as splendid, I have no doubt I will enjoy my time here immensely. Look, you can see the moon over the water. How beautiful it is."

*Not nearly as beautiful you.*

"Come inside now, Josefina. The wind off the water is cool and you are not dressed for it."

"All right."

She took his arm as he led her indoors. He could not shake this feeling of rightness as she walked by his side. But he once again squelched the unfamiliar quickening of his heart, this surprising yearning. It was too soon. They had yet to deal with Clarissa. He did not even know Josefina well enough to remember her family name.

*Big-something. Bigglesmith? Ah, Biggleswor th.*

Yes, that was it.

If only it would stay in his mind.

His dogs had liked her immediately, and he was beginning to understand why. There was no malice in this girl, only a vigorous optimism that he hoped would never be crushed. As for his dogs, he had brought them over from York, shipping them off along with gifts for his aunt and sister the day after he had met Josefina.

"Your Grace, the rooms are ready," his head butler said, entering just as they were finishing their refreshments.

"Thank you, Timmons. I'll escort Lady Josefina upstairs. Is my aunt awake by any chance? Or my sister?"

"I'll ask Mrs. Timmons," he said, for the housekeeper was his wife and would have been the one to supervise the maids as they prepared Josefina's bedchamber.

"No matter, we'll find out for ourselves soon enough."

He led Josefina upstairs.

"Ready?" he asked. They had reached the landing, and he could hear Clarissa and his aunt talking excitedly in the hall. Seems they were both awake, which answered his earlier question. No doubt his aunt was trying to calm his agitated sister.

Clarissa did not mince words as they approached. "Who is she?"

Gareth frowned to see her seated in her pushchair. The maid assigned to tend her looked as though she had just been awakened from a sound sleep, for her eyes were half open as she wheeled his sister toward Josefina's newly prepared room. "Nice to see you, too, Clarissa," he shot back, taking Josefina's hand in his. "We had an easy journey, thank you for asking. This is Lady Josefina…"

"Bigglesworth," Josefina chimed in since he simply could not keep that ridiculous name in his mind, especially while quietly seething over his sister's rudeness. "My father was the Earl of Seahaven."

"She is my betrothed," Gareth added, keeping firm hold of her hand, "in case you were wondering."

He saw the look of pain in Clarissa's eyes and almost felt sorry for simply dumping the news on her. But she had a way of getting under his skin with her constant anger. He was losing patience with her, try as he might to be understanding. "Aunt Philidia, may I introduce you to Josefina?"

"Oh, my dear. I am so happy for the both of you." Her smile was genuinely warm as she bussed his cheek and then did the same to Josefina's.

"Lady Philidia, it is a pleasure to meet you. His Grace has told me so many kind things about you."

Clarissa snorted. "I'm sure he's made me out to be the devil."

"No, Lady Clarissa. You are his angel. There is no one in the world he loves more than you, even when you go out of your way to kick him in the teeth. You may as well be kind to him, for there is nothing you can do to make him stop loving you."

Gareth stifled a laugh at the look of surprise on his sister's face.

He gave Josefina's hand a light squeeze to acknowledge her first victory. But he was well aware Clarissa would not be so easily conquered.

"But you are his betrothed," Clarissa said. "Should he not love you more than he does me? Or were you caught in a compromising position and he had to marry you? Is this why I've never heard of you before? Very clever of you. How did you pull it off? My brother is slippery as an eel. I did not think anyone could trick him into marriage."

"I was not compromised. Nor did I trick him. He caught me completely by surprise." She smiled up at him. "I think he was surprised, too. We were in the Castlegate Hotel's tearoom. He meant to order tea, and instead blurted 'will you marry me?'. I think he proposed to me because his dogs liked me."

His sister almost smiled, almost gave away that she was starting to like Josefina. "Wolf and Dragon? They are trained guard dogs. They don't like anyone outside of the family."

"Josefina will be family," Gareth said. "They adore her."

"They tolerate me. I am still not all that familiar to them." Josefina cast him a cautionary glance, for Clarissa would easily catch on if he overdid their supposed romance. "We haven't set a date yet or even begun to make our wedding plans. He wanted me to meet his family first."

"And end the betrothal if we did not like you?" The menacing glint in Clarissa's eyes returned.

He did not like that look at all.

When had she gotten so mean and angry?

Josefina gazed up at him with that look of starlight in her beautiful eyes. "He may end the betrothal for any reason he wishes. I would never force him to marry me if he did not love me."

*Blessed saints.*

He liked her more every time she opened her mouth.

Perhaps he had not lost his sanity in proposing to her. He was beginning to think ending their betrothal would be the insane thing to do. "It is late. We are all tired. Let us resume our conversation in the morning. Josefina, you have only to ring for Mrs. Timmons if you need anything."

She nodded. "I will. Thank you, Your Grace. Good night, Lady Clarissa. Lady Philidia. I look forward to seeing you in the morning."

Philidia smiled in response and retired to her room.

Clarissa said nothing as her maid wheeled her back into her quarters.

"Your bedchamber overlooks the sea," Gareth said, reluctant to part from her even though they had been riding in the carriage together all day, and he had already indicated it was time to part ways. "If you prefer a view to the rear garden, just let me know, and I will have your belongings moved to a room overlooking the flower beds."

"I shall be up to my elbows in your conservatory for much of the time. I think I will enjoy gazing out at the sea by the end of the day."

He nodded. "Goodnight, then. Sweet dreams, Josefina."

"And to you, Your Grace."

He made certain his sister had truly retired to her quarters and was not planning more mischief before he proceeded down to his own suite of rooms at the opposite end of the hall. His reliable valet, the elderly Calder, was waiting for him after having unpacked the last of his bags. "Go to bed, Calder. We shall have our work cut out for us in the morning."

"As you wish, Your Grace. May I take your travel garments to refresh them now? Your boots will need to be polished."

"Those chores will keep until tomorrow."

Once alone, he undressed, left his clothes draped over a chair, and quickly washed up. But he did not immediately retire to bed. His bedchamber was a corner room that overlooked the sea from one side and the garden from the other.

Being familiar with his room, he needed no light to get around. Besides, he did not wear nightclothes to bed, preferring to sleep unencumbered. He strode to the window overlooking the sea. From his vantage point, he also had a view of Josefina's room, although merely a corner of it. He would see her if she stood by her window to look out over the water.

To his surprise, this is where she was, standing in the glow of her lamp light.

She had changed into her nightgown, brushed out her hair so that it fell in a glorious tumble over her shoulders, and now stared out across the dark expanse. He could see the outline of her body under the thin garment.

She was full in the bosom, but otherwise slender.

He raked a hand through his hair, surprisingly rattled by his intense yearning. He ached to have her, to kiss her and touch her, to hold her in his arms.

He would do none of those things, of course.

As he watched, she suddenly turned with a start and emitted a yelp. In that same moment, he heard barking and realized it was coming from her room.

His heart leapt into his throat.

Blast his sister to Perdition!

He hurriedly donned his breeches and ran out of his room toward Josefina's without bothering to put on his shirt or boots. There wasn't time. He had to call off Wolf and Dragon before they harmed her. He would never forgive Clarissa if they did. "You have gone too far this time," he shouted and shoved his sister's pushchair out of Josefina's doorway to get at his hounds.

They were jumping on Josefina and… thank The Graces, they were licking her face. She was laughing and scratching them behind the ears in greeting.

"Wolf! Dragon! My chamber," he roared.

The massive beasts took off for his quarters. "Josefina, are you hurt?"

His heart was still caught in his throat, and his words came out raspy. Before he realized what he was doing, he had her in his arms and was hugging her to him.

Lord, she felt good.

What a body this girl had!

"I am fine, Your Grace. They were merely hoping I would give them shortbread. Alas, I had none on me."

She had nothing on but this skimpy nightgown that hid nothing of her curves. One sleeve had slipped off her shoulder, baring it to his view. He had seen more than his share of bare, feminine flesh. He had undressed plenty of women, bedded them, explored their bodies. All his experience had not prepared him for the intensity of his desire for Josefina.

He wanted to carry her off to his bed and never let her out of it.

"Look, Your Grace," she said softly, setting her hand on his chest to nudge him slightly away. "Your sister is now out of her pushchair."

"What?" His body was still raw with ache for her. "My sister?"

Her meaning finally penetrated his brain.

Clarissa was now clutching Josefina's door, the pushchair within arm's reach of her. She was wobbly on her feet… but she was on her feet and must have taken at least two or three steps on her own. Could she have walked downstairs to fetch the dogs and bring them up here? No, her maid must have done it on her orders.

But she was standing, and this was an accomplishment. She no longer looked smugly satisfied as she had been a moment ago while watching the unleashed dogs jump atop Josefina. Obviously, Clarissa had been hoping they would scare his supposed betrothed.

Only they hadn't scared her.

Or harmed her.

He turned on his sister in full fury. "For this bit of mischief, you shed your invalid ways? You won't do a thing to help yourself, not a single exercise. But you'll drag yourself to Josefina's door to see her brought to tears. Well, it did not work. Did it?"

She looked stricken, probably feeling terrible as her anger calmed and she realized how badly Josefina might have been hurt by Wolf and Dragon had they not considered her a friend.

But her remorse was short-lived. She tipped her chin up in defiance. "You said they adored her, that she had made friends of your dogs. I… I thought…"

"You weren't thinking." He took a step toward her, rage still coursing through him. "You were plotting. Scheming. You wanted to see her hurt."

Clarissa paled and began to back up as he slowly advanced on her. She fell awkwardly in her chair and began to wheel it back toward her room. "No, only… scare her a little. They are trained. They would not have attacked without my command."

"Were you going to give it?" He did not await her response. "Is it not enough to hurt me? Is it not enough to hurl your bitterness at me? Did you have to take your anger out on Josefina, too? What has she ever done to you? She is completely innocent, and the kindest soul you will ever meet, something you would realize if you took the time to know her instead of plotting to harm her."

Josefina stood beside him, holding onto his hand. "Your Grace, it is all right. A harmless prank."

He turned toward her. "No, Josefina. It is not all right. It was not harmless. She wanted to hurt you."

Josefina had a way of looking at him that softened his heart. He struggled to hold onto his anger and not let it simply dissolve as he gazed into her eyes. "Your Grace, do you not see? No one is hurting more than she is."

He snorted in disdain. "Hurting enough to get out of her pushchair and watch my dogs maul you?"

Clarissa was now in tears. "I am so sorry, Josefina. I would not blame you if you banished me from Cumbe Grange forever." She emitted a sob and wheeled herself back to her room, tossing herself onto her bed.

Josefina started to follow her, but he held her back. "Leave her to her tears. We will deal with her in the morning. It is remarkable, home less than an hour and you have her standing, even taking a few steps. If she can take one, why not two? What in blazes is going on with her? Do you think she even needs a pushchair?"

"I do not know. It is too soon to learn the truth. Obviously, she needs something."

He grunted. "Perhaps a good spanking."

She frowned at him. "Perhaps she just needs a friend."

He sighed and ran a hand through his hair. "You can talk to her about it in the morning. Are you sure you are all right?"

She had her lips pursed as she nodded.

Lord help him, he wanted to kiss her.

She cast him a thoughtful glance, unaware of his thoughts. "I am. But are you? Disaster was averted. You now know she can take steps, and this is a very good thing. There is nothing more to be done about it tonight, and in truth, I am tired from our journey. As you suggested, let us all turn in. I bid you sweet dreams, Your Grace."

He was going to pace in his room like a jungle beast on the prowl until his turmoil dissipated.

"Sweet dreams, Josefina." He ran his fingers lightly over her shoulder to straighten the sleeve that had slipped down, and then simply kept his hand upon her shoulder because he did not have the will to let her go.

"Your Grace?" Her eyes were big and filled with uncertainty.

"Good night." He kissed her cheek and returned to his room, almost stumbling over his dogs who were now stretched across the carpet in front of his bed in the darkened room. "Troublemakers," he grumbled, but gave each a pat on the head when they sensed he was angry with them and whimpered.

They were the size of small horses and yet behaved like children.

He scratched their bellies. "Do not ever harm Josefina."

They licked his hands, slobbering all over his fingers so that he had to wash up again. But he was calmer now as he stripped for bed and sank onto it with a soft growl.

Well, not quite calm when it came to Josefina.

How was he to keep his hands off her for the next six months?

# CHAPTER 5

Josefina's heart was madly thumping as she retired to the large bed that was all her own. She could not recall ever sleeping alone. It was an odd feeling indeed. A lonely feeling, for she had grown used to being elbowed or lightly kicked whenever a sister sharing her bed had tossed or turned in the night.

She probably did the same to them.

But this was not the only reason for her odd feeling.

The duke had held her in his arms after the incident with the dogs. Not only had he held her, but done it bare-chested so that she felt the warmth of his skin against her body and the light spray of hair against her cheek when she had rested her head upon his chest.

She was of average height but had felt small beside him, for he was big and muscled, and exuded strength.

Was there ever a more wonderful feeling?

If so, she had yet to experience it.

No wonder women fell over themselves to gain his attention. Wealthy, titled, handsome as sin.

What was he doing with her?

How soon would he tire of her and send her packing?

A tear slid down her cheek, but she quickly wiped it away. He had been clear as to the terms of their betrothal. He would settle a sum on her when the time came. There was nothing she could do to prolong their time together, so she may as well enjoy every moment spent in his company.

Life would go on afterward.

His settlement would enable her family to avoid poverty and live out their days in comfort. The amount he proposed to settle on her was too high, and she had told him so. Perhaps she ought to have said nothing about it and grabbed all he was willing to offer.

However, three of her sisters were now betrothed and several more had serious suitors. It was quite possible the family's financial circumstances would soon no longer be dire.

She would give their situation more thought. He did not have to deposit the entire settlement into an account for herself. Why could he not give her only part of it and spread the rest out among her sisters and Patience? Certainly, the twins, Iris and Ivy, could use this supplement in place of the proper dowry their feckless father had neglected to provide for any of them.

She fell asleep and awoke to the sun shining in her bedchamber and the caw of sea birds outside her window. She scrambled out of bed and hurried to the window, gasping as she took in the sun's magnificent amber light shining off the water.

She had never seen such natural splendor.

While the hour was still early, the sun barely above the horizon, it was still a vivid burst of color upon the waves. Even the clouds floating overhead were streaked in the lilacs and pinks of dawn, those colors reflecting off the water and blending with the wave crests and swirls of the tide.

A rainbow of colors all glistening against a backdrop of deep blue sea and pale blue sky.

She opened her window to listen to the sound of waves softly lapping the shore and their hollow roar as they struck the rocks and eroded caves hidden below.

"Good morning," she whispered, breathing in the sea air that was damp and salty. Cool as well, for at this hour the wind was surprisingly cold off the water.

She gave a light shiver but did not care. The view was new and marvelous to her. This estate and the duke were spectacular. She wanted to soak all of it in and all of him in, as much as her senses… and propriety… would allow.

A morning walk was the perfect thing to occupy her time until the others began to stir, she decided. Anyway, the day was too beautiful to miss a moment of it. She would return in plenty of time for breakfast.

Madame Yvonne had designed morning gowns that were easily slipped on and off without need of assistance, so she grabbed one of those gowns from her wardrobe, a russet muslin, and selected a pair of sturdy walking boots. These morning clothes were meant for sitting in the house, daintily embroidering, or mending, or writing letters to one's family. But walking was not a strenuous activity either, and in any event, she was not going to disturb the staff at this hour simply to don a more suitable gown.

This one would serve her just fine. Besides, she was not going to walk very far and would likely be back before Philidia or Clarissa awoke.

She washed and dressed, pinned up her hair in a simple twist at the nape of her neck, and then made her way downstairs. The head butler, Timmons, was just coming to his post. "Good morning, Lady Josefina. You are up early. How may I help?"

"I hoped to take a walk. Is it allowed?" She thought of the duke's dogs and wondered if he had more of them wandering about the grounds that she ought to be cautious of encountering.

"Oh, yes. His Grace just went out himself with his two ponies."

She laughed, knowing he referred to Wolf and Dragon. "Do you think he would mind if I joined him?"

The man cast her a kindly smile. "I think he would be delighted."

He escorted her to the door and pointed her in the right direction. She could hear the distant barks and followed the sound, quickening her pace to catch up to them. "Your Grace," she said, breathless from hurrying, "would you mind if I strolled with you?"

"Good morning, Josefina. I did not expect you up at this hour." But his smile revealed he was genuinely pleased to have her company.

"We are early risers in my family. May I?"

"Of course." He took her hand in his and gave a stern command to his dogs as they joyfully lumbered toward her. "Down!" he said with authority, knowing they meant to leap on her. "Their muddy paws will ruin your gown. They'll calm down in a moment and then walk alongside us. This is as good a time as any to show you the grounds. How do you like your view?"

"I am enraptured. Thank you for giving me that bedchamber. How fortunate you are to wake up to such a splendid sight every morning."

He nodded. "The sky is not usually so clear at this hour. Often, we wake to a mist upon the water. But you are here, and nature would not dare interfere with your enjoyment of all that Cumbe Grange has to offer."

She laughed. "Oh, yes. I am a daunting force, even more powerful than Mother Nature."

"You are daunting, but in a good way. You cast enchantment everywhere you go."

"What have you been drinking to spout this nonsense so early in the morning?" she teased.

"Just drinking in the sight of you, Josefina." He still had hold of her hand and did not seem in the least inclined to release it.

She glanced at their joined hands. "Do you think Clarissa is watching? Or Philidia? Are you trying to give them the impression we are lovebirds?"

He threw back his head and laughed. "No one would ever mistake me for a lovebird. I intimidate most people. I have no idea why you do not fear me when most people tense and paste false smiles on their faces whenever I approach."

"That is because you scowl at them. That is your natural facial expression, a furrowed brow and taut lips. But you smile at me, so it is easy for me to smile back at you. Anyway, cheerfulness is my natural expression when my face is at rest. You still haven't explained why you are holding my hand."

"I am holding onto you because the pathways are uneven and you are unfamiliar with them… and it does not hurt that you are young and beautiful."

"Nor do I mind because you are big and handsome. Is it possible for us to walk along the beach?"

"Later, when the water is calmer and the tide is out. The sea is beautiful on the surface, but dangerous. One must always respect its power. Can you swim?"

"No."

"A rogue wave can surround you in an instant and sweep you out to sea. Even a normal wave can drag you deeper into the water with the force of its pull."

She nodded. "I will be careful."

"Do you ride?"

"I have been on an old mare who moves at a creaky pace, if you call that riding. Our real home is in the village of Starbrook, about thirty miles from York, about the same distance as Cumbe Grange is from York, but in the opposite direction. It may as well be a lifetime away."

"But you also spend time in your town house not far from York Minster."

She snorted. "It was loaned to us for the Season by a kindly relation. My father was hardly a marvel when it came to business affairs. He rather enjoyed the privileges of being an earl, but did not really know what to do other than enjoy life and attempt to breed sons." She winced. "He wasn't successful at that either."

"You came out of it, Josefina. That is success enough for any man."

She laughed heartily. "Stop, Your Grace! It is too early in the morning for compliments. I would hardly call myself a successful product. Single-minded, determined, passionate, irritating."

"Never dull."

They came to a fork in the path, one trail leading to the sea and the other curving back toward the manor house. They took the manor house path. She studied his stately home as they approached it from the rear gardens, admiring its dark stone and imposing grandeur. She counted at least five chimney stacks, but her attention was drawn to the gardens and their abundance of hardy blooms. Off in the distance stood the conservatory, indeed twice the size of the one in his garden in York.

"Someone in your family was an herbalist, I am sure," she muttered, noting the willows and yew trees within this loosely walled expanse, and the beds of yarrow, lavender, comfrey, marigold, and mallow that dominated. Of course, there were roses. A must for any garden. And a pretty mix of daisies.

He shrugged. "Perhaps. Not in the recent generations, so far as I am aware. Cumbe Grange has been ours for about four hundred years."

"Ah, that is about the age of our cook in Starbrook," she jested. "May I see the conservatory now?"

"Yes, certainly. I am ashamed to say it is empty save for the gardeners' implements and potting soils. We do not grow anything in there in the winter since it is too costly to keep the place warm enough for plants to survive. But now that we have a purpose, I will gladly keep it going as the weather turns cold. Have at it, Josefina. As I've told you, make a list of your needs and I will supply them."

Could she add kisses to that list of needs?

Surely, any young woman ought to require at least one kiss supplied by this handsome duke.

But this was merely a naughty thought.

After touring the conservatory, they left Wolf and Dragon with his master of the kennels. Hunting was apparently one of the duke's favorite sports, and he kept dogs for it. But they were trackers and quite friendly, not ferocious as Wolf and Dragon were supposed to be.

They must have been out for well over two hours because Philidia and Clarissa were already seated in the summer dining room when they returned to the manor house. Josefina liked these smaller, cozier rooms because they brought families together with their smaller tables and more intimate seating arrangements.

The formal rooms, such as the main dining room she had peeked into earlier, were enormous and quite impressive, but not for her. It was much more fun to be practically atop each other and bumping elbows.

They joined Clarissa and Philidia for breakfast. One of the footmen had fetched cocoa for Clarissa and was reporting on the breakfast delights under each silver salver set out upon the sideboard.

She was back in her pushchair, feigning her inability to walk.

Perhaps they were being harsh on the girl, Josefina thought, for taking a few wobbly steps was a far cry from running through the meadows at full tilt. Still, cracked ribs and a broken leg should not have left her unable ever to walk again. Also, the easy way she bent and stretched to reach for objects proved her spine had not been damaged.

The duke was turning angry as he looked upon his sister. Josefina placed a hand lightly on his arm to keep him from growling at her. "Good morning," she said cheerfully, taking a seat beside Clarissa, since there were only the four of them around the table and the duke was obviously meant to take the head.

"Everyone help yourself," he said, coming around to escort Philidia and her to the sideboard.

He motioned to the footman not to serve his sister. "Lady Clarissa can do it herself."

The footman looked upon Clarissa with concern, for he had no choice but to obey the duke's command.

"Wheel yourself over," Josefina said, "and I will show you what your cook has prepared today."

"I am not hungry."

The girl was now sulking, and her brother was not making matters better by silently fuming.

"Too bad," Josefina said lightly, hoping to sound chirpy, but not as ridiculous as a twittering bird. "I am famished. I suppose the long walk and salt air does that to you. But you really ought to have something, Lady Clarissa. Your cook has obviously labored over these dishes, and it would be an insult not to even try them."

She waited for a response from Clarissa, and when she got none, she simply took it upon herself to wheel her over. "There now, isn't this much better? Lady Clarissa will have a poached egg. And those kippers. One of those honeyed buns. Honey is an excellent expectorant for the lungs. Shall we skip the ham? Is it too much for your delicate digestion? If there is a local apothecary in Scarborough, I shall purchase some burdock root and anise seed. Both can be brewed as a laxative tea, although I think anise seed will be milder. We usually reserve the burdock root for gout or leprosy, and–"

"Ham is my favorite. Pile it on, Rodgers."

The footman turned away a moment to hide his grin.

The duke was doing the same.

They all sat down to their hearty meals.

"Everything is delicious," Josefina remarked, knowing the duke was watching her, curious as to what she would say or do next. "I would like to personally convey my compliments to your cook. Is it permitted, Your Grace?"

"I shall take you to the kitchen after we finish. It will cause quite a stir, but Mrs. Timmons can warn Mrs. Beard and her scullery maids that you are on your way. I think I shall join you."

"Good," Josefina teased. "They will be too busy gawking at you to pay all that much attention to me."

"You are wrong," Clarissa said, joining in the conversation with obvious hesitation, for her words were shy rather than combative, "they will marvel at the woman who has captured the heart of the Duke of Bourne. None of us ever thought it would be someone like you."

"Nor did I," she said with a playful roll of her eyes. "Who knew his taste would be so execrable?"

"Josefina!" He almost spit out his coffee for laughing. "Kindly do not insult me. I have excellent taste, especially in the woman I chose to marry."

But they all had a laugh over it, mostly Clarissa who forgot she should be sulking. Josefina hoped she would forget that pushchair soon, too.

When breakfast ended, and after giving their compliments to Mrs.

Beard, the duke asked her if she would like to tour the rest of his home. "Yes, I would love it."

He placed her arm in his as he led her from one splendid room to another, pointing out portraits of his ancestors in particular. He was handsomer than all of them, Josefina thought. The rooms were opulent, but also durable and had a well lived-in look, which was not surprising if this place had been occupied by the Hollings family for the last four hundred years.

When the tour ended, she asked if they might return to the conservatory. "But I would like to invite Clarissa to join us. Do you mind?"

"No, even though I still want to throttle her. However, you have a way with her. In truth, with all of us. We have not laughed so much around our table ever."

Clarissa was in the ladies' parlor with Philidia, looking utterly bored as she sat with her embroidery.

"Lady Clarissa, may I ask for your assistance?"

The duke's sister looked up in surprise.

"You see, I would like to make use of the conservatory to grow herbs and medicinal flowers, and I could not help but notice that your summer garden already holds many of these plants. I am sure someone in your family must have been an herbalist in their day. Your brother does not have the time or patience for this undertaking, so I was hoping you might help."

"In what way?"

"Well, first to walk... or I shall push your chair... through the conservatory and decide on which plants to pot and where to place them. But I would also hope to go through your family records to find the herbalist's notes if they are anywhere to be found. We could more easily reconstruct that ancestor's knowledge."

She could tell the duke was holding his breath, hoping Clarissa would accept. In fact, he had walked to the window to look out upon the water, no doubt afraid that a mere glance on his part would have his sister instantly wary and refusing the request.

"Why do we not start in our library first? The records, if they exist, would be found in there."

Josefina took the seat beside Clarissa. "It is sensible, you are absolutely right. But I am worried this good weather will not last, so I would like to take advantage of it and do the outdoor surveying work first. Do you have a sketch pad and pencils? All young ladies do, I'm sure. We could look around the conservatory and decide what plants to put where. If your ancestor's records suggest better alternatives, we can always change our designs. What do you think?"

"All right."

The duke turned to her, his eyes revealing the smile kept hidden on his lips. "Will you require my assistance?"

"Only so long as you do not make a nuisance of yourself. But it is your property, and Lady Clarissa and I would be grateful for any sensible suggestions you offer."

"Sensible?" The smile now reached his lips. He looked so handsome when he smiled, his entire countenance turning lighter and more youthful. "I shall try my best."

The morning passed with surprising delight. Clarissa did not once attempt to rise from her chair, but she was no longer scowling or angry. In truth, she was quite excited to participate in the project and offered some helpful suggestions. "We ought to clear space off to the side of our kitchen for your workroom so that you can prepare your medicinal tinctures indoors. Even with the fires going in the conservatory, it would take forever for the plants to dry out and be too cold for us to work out there once the snows come."

Josefina did not have the heart to tell Clarissa she would not be here come winter. Well, they were far from bosom friends. She was probably being nice to her today because she felt remorse for her trick with the dogs and wanted to make it up to her.

In any event, she would teach Clarissa all she knew and turn her into another Hollings family herbalist. It might give the girl the confidence to stand on her own. Literally, to stand and walk again.

By the end of the first day, the color had returned to Clarissa's cheeks.

By the end of the second day, she and Josefina had sketched the basic beds to be laid out in the conservatory.

It rained on the third day, so Josefina and Clarissa spent the day in the library, pouring through the Hollings family records in search of the planting inventories, and giggling over the ones whose purpose was listed as enhancing male sexual prowess. "Garlic and fenugreek," Clarissa whispered. "My brother loves garlic in his food. No wonder. You can always slip some nettle juice in his tea if he gets too randy."

"Clarissa!"

But they both descended into snorts and laughter.

By the end of the week, they had fallen into the routine of taking tea in the library, and the duke made it a habit to join them. He was usually on his best behavior, to Josefina's delight. For days now, there had not been an angry word spoken between him and his sister. In truth, Clarissa hardly gave either of them a chance to talk since she was chatting so excitedly about the conservatory project she was embracing wholeheartedly.

After supper, the four of them established a further routine of playing whist in the parlor. They were now on their second week since Josefina's arrival. She tried to concentrate on her cards while rain pattered against the windows and the wind howled outside.

"It is quite a storm," she remarked, listening to the distant *whoosh* of the tide and pounding of waves against the rocks. It brought home the power of nature and how insignificant they all were in the scheme of life. But among themselves, they had become vitally important to each other, making up a happy family unit.

Only, her importance would come to an end by October.

Josefina knew she was the odd man out but did not mind. It mattered more that the duke was repairing his relation with his sister. He was less angry. Clarissa was more cheerful. Philidia simply adored them both.

The duke drew her aside once the card game ended and they were about to head upstairs to bed. Two footmen came in to carry Clarissa in her chair up the stairs, but Clarissa ordered them to stop when they reached the staircase. "Gareth, help me. Don't carry me. Just make sure to catch me if I fall."

He glanced at Josefina, as though seeking guidance on the proper response. Was there a doubt Clarissa had to be encouraged? It did not matter if she failed. It only mattered that she was ready to try. "All right," he said. "I am right beside you."

Josefina lagged behind with Philidia, taking the old woman's hand as they were both gleeful and anxious.

Clarissa's progress was achingly slow, but she made it up three steps before conceding defeat. "I'll never do it."

Josefina gasped. "You will! You have conquered three on your first attempt. I think that is amazing. I shall wager you can make it up these stairs to the very top without being carried."

She nodded. "Perhaps in time."

"No, I mean right now. Let me show you how. You haven't walked in so long, your muscles have weakened. I also think you must have fractured your hip bone, Clarissa. A tiny fracture, but enough to cause you too much pain to walk. I know you were not faking your difficulty walking."

Clarissa's eyes rounded in surprise and gratitude. "Thank you, Josefina. I was never faking, but no one would ever believe me."

"I believe you. That bone will heal in time. Indeed, I believe it is well on the way to healing already. Be patient and your strength will return. In the meanwhile, here is how you will conquer these stairs." She plunked herself on the third step beside her, placed her hands on the fourth step, and hauled herself up to it. She repeated the process on the fifth and sixth step. "You try it."

"I can't," she said, looking at the number of steps remaining and obviously feeling daunted.

"Why not? Your arms were not injured. If anything, they have grown stronger because you wheel yourself around the house."

"Someone usually does that for me."

Josefina wanted to shake her for giving up so easily. They had been having a perfectly lovely day until now. Clarissa was suddenly regressing, and she would not allow it. "But not always. Give it a try. Take your time. I will be next to you the entire way. And if you do make it all the way up, I think you must have a prize."

The girl smiled. "What sort of prize?"

"I think your brother must sing a silly song for you while he does a silly dance."

The duke looked horrified.

Clarissa squealed in delight. "Yes! It is perfect! My staid and sober brother dancing a jig? I would climb mountains for that. What do you say, Gareth?"

Josefina frowned at him. "Yes, you must. That would be a prize indeed."

He grumbled and groaned, cursed quietly, and glared at all of them, then relented with a sigh. "All right, but only if Josefina joins me in the song and dance. If I am to make an arse of myself, then so must she."

"I make a fool of myself daily," she blithely replied. "It is no skin off my nose."

Clarissa took almost ten minutes to make it up the remaining stairs, but she succeeded to everyone's delight and cheers, especially the footmen who had been watching and cheering loudest. "Well done, Lady Clarissa," Rodgers said, so obviously happy for her.

Once she was back in her chair and wheeled to her bedchamber, she laughingly demanded her reward.

"I shall start the song and dance since your brother is obviously a coward," Josefina said, breaking into a popular lilt and ridiculously hopping about. "Come on, Your Grace. Join me."

He regarded her, appalled. "Dukes do not hop."

"Then you may skip or jump. Do you not know any sea chanties? Clean up the words." She was still hopping and twirling as she spoke to him.

Clarissa rose from her chair and was laughing and clapping.

Philidia came to stand by her side, stomping and cheering.

"What about a Scottish dance?" Josefina persisted. "A highland reel. If the Scottish dukes dance them, then so can you."

"Josefina, I rue the day I ever met you," he said with a groaning laugh and placed his arms around her waist. "A highland reel it is. Do you know how to dance it?"

"Oh, yes. All part of my vaunted education. I earned top marks in the secret language of fan fluttering and how to swoon gracefully in the arms of a duke. I was also adept at floating like a butterfly as I twirled about a dance floor."

"Let's test it out, shall we? But I shall entomb all three of you if you breathe a word of this to anyone." He then twirled Josefina around the room as they both sang out of tune. Wolf and Dragon somehow escaped the confines of his bedchamber - perhaps that wily, old Calder had let them out - and lumbered into Clarissa's room, howling along with their out of tune song.

Timmons and several of his footmen came running up the stairs to see what all the commotion was about. The maids who attended Philidia, Clarissa, and her also came to see what was going on. Josefina thought the duke would immediately stop, but to her surprise, he continued to twirl her about the room and sing his silly song.

It was beautiful pandemonium, the dogs hopping and howling, the staff stomping and clapping, she and the duke performing the highland reel steps that neither of them really knew. Philidia and Clarissa were also singing at the top of their lungs.

Most important, Clarissa was beaming with happiness and standing, even stomping her foot a time or two.

Everyone cheered when their performance ended.

Josefina took a bow, then yelped and shot up as Wolf sniffed her backside. "You won't find any lemon biscuits there, you wicked thing!"

The duke could not contain his laughter.

His eyes were tearing with mirth and he clutched his side, complaining of a stitch. As his laughter subsided, he told Calder to take the dogs back to his quarters. He still had a grin on his face as he dismissed the rest of his staff.

Philidia was also dabbing her eyes and chuckling. "Oh, dear me. I can hardly catch my breath. I think we must make this the traditional Hollings dance to open every ball we hold here."

Clarissa, who was still standing, heartily agreed. "We must hold a ball in Josefina's honor."

Josefina blushed. "Nonsense, no one in society cares about me."

"My brother does, and he must love you dearly to make a giant jackass of himself as he has done tonight." She threw her arms around her brother as he approached. "Thank you, Gareth. This was the best prize ever."

He kissed his sister's cheek. "You were splendid, fighting your way up the stairs. I am so proud of you."

She hugged him fiercely. "I will try to do better. I promise you."

"That is all I ask, that you try your best. You are a Hollings, Clarissa. We can do anything we put our minds to."

Clarissa's maid came into the room to assist her in preparing for bed. Philidia retired to her quarters.

"Josefina," the duke said, walking her to her bedroom door. "What you did for us tonight was nothing short of a miracle."

"Nonsense. I crawled up your stairs on my backside. That is all."

He cast her an affectionate smile. "You have a lovely backside, by the way. My dogs were not the only ones to notice."

She giggled. "I must give Wolf a stern talking to."

"And I must give you a kiss goodnight. May I?"

"Is that my reward for getting Clarissa up those stairs?"

"No, that is *my* reward for that silly dance you made me do. But it worked. I haven't seen Clarissa this alive and happy since her fall off Devil's Spawn."

"She was quite splendid. And yes, you may kiss me."

She tilted her face so he could kiss her on the cheek, but he took her chin in his hand and turned her to face him directly. "Have you ever been kissed on the mouth before, Josefina?"

Her eyes widened and her heart began to pound. "No."

"Then mine will be your first romantic kiss?"

She nodded.

"Good. Close your eyes."

"Oh, my heavens," she whispered as she closed them.

Her stomach was aflutter.

Her lungs were squeezed so tight, she could hardly breathe.

He placed his arms around her.

She was going to swoon.

She was going to be an utter ninny and faint in his magnificent arms.

She felt the strength of him and wanted to run her hands up and down his finely honed body.

Who knew muscles on a man could affect a woman like this?

"Put your hands on my shoulders, Josefina."

Truly, this man was gloriously built. "Like this?"

"Perfect," he said and crushed his lips to hers.

# CHAPTER 6

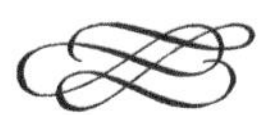

Gareth watched as Josefina frolicked by the edge of the sea in the late afternoon, her shoes and stockings off and her gown hiked up to her knees. "Join me, Your Grace," she called to him, looking marvelously unspoiled with her hair down and blowing in the wind, and her cheeks a lovely, sun-dappled pink.

Her eyes, as always, sparkled.

"I much prefer watching you." Three months had passed since Gareth brought Josefina to Cumbe Grange, and he could no longer imagine his life without her. Wolf and Dragon were playing at the water's edge along with her, cheerfully barking and running in and out of the waves on this hot, end of July day.

Josefina's laughter shot straight to his heart. He had kissed her only the once, that night of silly songs and dances, barely able to contain his desire as he tasted her sweet lips. He had known by the innocent confusion in Josefina's eyes that she desired him, too.

Why had he not acted upon it?

What was he waiting for? He had even purchased a necklace for her of Whitby jet and silver, the black gem carved into a cameo of her face and framed in a fine, silver mounting. He'd ordered it specially made a month ago and picked it up last week on an excursion to

Whitby. Josefina, Clarissa, and Philidia were on a day's outing with him, but he'd left them on their own to shop and take tea in a lovely tearoom overlooking the sea while he took care of some estate business and also stopped to pick up the necklace.

It had burned a hole in his breast pocket the entire ride home and was now stored in the top drawer of his bureau, waiting for the right time to present it to her. Indeed, what was he waiting for? It was time to make their betrothal real. Clarissa loved her. Philidia loved her. Hadn't he loved her from the moment she had burst into Mr. Orsini's apothecary full of fanciful ideas and talking so fast she was practically tripping over her own words?

"Josefina, we will be late for supper if we don't start back now."

She darted in and out of one last wave, laughingly shrieked as it washed up with more force than expected, and then hurried to his side. "Do you think Clarissa and Philidia are back yet from their trip to the shoemaker? I warned Clarissa to purchase sensible shoes since she isn't quite steady on her feet yet. But she is getting there. Can you believe the improvement?"

"It is all because of you."

"Nonsense. She is the one who has done all the work. I hope she managed all right without her pushchair. She took only a cane with her. Perhaps we ought to have gone with them."

"No," he said, "she needed to do this without either of us hovering over her. She has been managing well with just that cane for several weeks now."

She nodded. "And doing amazing work in the conservatory. It flourishes. And she absorbs everything I teach her about plant lore."

He took her hand as they made their way up the hill toward the manor house. The trail from the beach to the house was not an easy climb, even though Gareth had his workmen build steps into the hill wherever it was too steep.

"I think the sun and the sand will do Clarissa a world of good," Josefina remarked as she sat on a nearby rock at the summit and dusted the sand off her feet. "Do you think she is ready for us to bring her to the beach?"

He shrugged. "We can broach the topic at supper."

"Yes, let's." Josefina did not bother to don her stockings, merely tucked her feet into her shoes.

He took her hand once again as they made their way back to the house. The sun was starting its descent to mark approaching twilight. Of course, it would not be dark for several hours yet. But they had stayed later than usual on the beach, eager for relief from the oppressive heat. The sky was now particularly vibrant, streaked with the sunset pinks and golds Josefina adored.

He had never felt more at peace than standing beside her as they stared out over the water. But his peace was short-lived, for there were several carriages in the courtyard, and he recognized their unannounced visitors standing under the front portico.

"Oh, dear." Josefina glanced down at herself. "I am not presentable. I'll take the dogs in through the back. Were you expecting company? Do you know who they are?"

"Our cousins from York, and I did not invite them. I suppose their arrival is timely."

"Timely for what?"

"I will tell you later." He was going to propose to Josefina, this time in earnest, and it would save him the trouble of corresponding with the rest of his family if they were already here to learn of it. Of course, everyone already thought he had proposed.

Well, he had.

But ugly rumors were beginning to surface about him and Josefina in the York newspapers. It was time to address them and silence the malicious gossips who meant to stir up trouble.

Perhaps this would not be a proposal so much as an insistence they set a wedding date. No more sham arrangement.

He meant to marry Josefina.

He strode to the courtyard to greet his relations. Lord, they were a grim lot. His father had two sisters, his delightful Aunt Philidia and her sister, Ophelia, dubbed Awful Ophelia because this is what she was, simply a miserable person inside and out.

Incredibly, Ophelia had married well and was now the dowager

Countess of Chesmire since her husband's demise and her son's recent marriage.

Her son, Lawrence, an insufferable prig of a cousin, was now Earl of Chesmire, and had done his duty by marrying a suitably priggish wife with impeccable bloodlines. One would think they were made emperor and empress the way they lorded their status over everyone. The wife was with him, a thin, pinch-lipped young lady with overly styled ringlets in her orange hair. The color did not look natural, as though a henna rinse had been poorly applied to her curls.

Lawrence's two spinster sisters were among the unwelcome party, each as boorish as Lawrence. "To what do I owe the unexpected pleasure?" Gareth remarked with open sarcasm.

"We have come to save your wretched hide," said Ophelia, looking particularly prunish.

He arched an eyebrow. "I had no idea my hide was in any danger."

"Bourne," Chesmire intoned, "you shall make a laughingstock of us all if you insist on maintaining your betrothal to that Bigglesworth girl."

Lawrence's wife gave a haughty nod. "My mother knows Lady Seahaven, wife of the current earl, and she says their circumstances are horribly reduced. Why, the dowager makes bread to sell, and one of the older girls is a common seamstress."

He cast the lot of them a warning glower. "That Bigglesworth girl is properly addressed as Lady Josefina. I have no intention of breaking it off with her. I suggest you meet her before condemning her. And I further suggest you withhold from insulting her in my presence or I shall not hesitate to call you out, Lawrence."

"He is Chesmire now," Ophelia intoned. "Do give him the courtesy of addressing him by his title."

"I will grant him the courtesy when he shows proper respect to my betrothed."

"Come to your senses, man," Lawrence said. "That family is ridiculous. Everyone now knows they arrived in York impoverished. Is it any surprise they sent out the beauty of the family to entrap you?"

"I entrapped her, if you must know." He turned to Timmons.

"Open up the east wing. Have Mrs. Timmons air out rooms for them. Bring refreshments into the parlor."

He stormed back into the house to make himself presentable, for he was casually dressed in linen shirt and breeches. It was appropriate wear while on the beach with Josefina, but his elegant York family had obviously found it disdainful.

Since he had noticed his carriage in the carriage house, he knew Clarissa and Philidia were also home. He knocked at Clarissa's door. "May I come in? I need to talk to you."

Clarissa opened the door herself. "Yes, do come in. I've sent my maid to fetch me some warm milk. Did you want to hear about my day?"

He kissed his sister's cheek, loving the smile on her face and gleam of happiness in her eyes. It must have been a good day for her. "Yes, but can we save that discussion for later? Our cousins have arrived."

She grinned. "The Churlish Chesmires? I saw their carriages pull up shortly after Philidia and I returned from Scarborough. Why are they here?"

"To talk me out of marrying Josefina. To insult her and spread crude rumors."

Her eyes rounded in surprise. "You will not let them do it, will you?"

"Of course not. I love her. Is it not obvious?"

Clarissa threw her arms around him. "I knew it from the moment we were first introduced. The way you looked at each other, as though you were each other's sunshine. This is what I want for myself. This is why I am determined to walk again, and dance that silly dance right alongside you."

He laughed. "I shall never, ever, and I do mean never, dance that silly dance again. However, I shall happily open a ball by waltzing with you whenever you feel ready. Just let me know and we shall throw the party of the season."

"Josefina works with me every day. She's given me a comfrey poultice to rub on my leg and hip to strengthen the bones. And yarrow to ease the inflammation. Lavender to soothe my nerves. She knows so much about the healing arts. But I think it is her kindness that heals best of all, don't you think?"

"Yes, sweetling. I do. But there is something I must tell you about us because you will hear some horrible things from our cousins, and I want you to be prepared."

"I've seen those horrid reports in the York newspapers you have been trying to hide from us. Don't worry, Josefina has not read them. I, too, am trying to keep them hidden from her. One of those particularly vicious gossip rags claims you have made her your mistress and that you will never marry her now that you are aware of the impoverished state she and her family fell into once the Earl of Seahaven died. They also say that… that you've had her."

"It is a lie."

She crossed the room and sank onto her bed. "I know. I won't believe a word of what those horrid papers report or what the Churlish Chesmires say. I am sure they planted those false rumors themselves."

He snorted in disdain. "I would not put it past them. It is just the loathsome sort of thing they would do. Apparently, the current Earl of Seahaven is little better. I've written to Josefina's stepmother, Patience, assuring her those rumors are untrue, and I will address them personally. I hope you know there is nothing anyone can say to make me stop loving Josefina. But I was not honest with her or with you when I proposed to her. Most of all, I was not honest with myself."

"What are you talking about?"

He leaned his shoulder against her bedpost as they spoke. "I did propose to her in the tearoom at the Castlegate Hotel, that much is true. But I had not known her more than an hour or two when I did so."

"Very funny, Gareth. You would never do anything so foolish."

"But I did, incredible as it seems. What was she to say with a roomful of people watching us, me a duke and her wanting use of my conservatory? So, she accepted."

"Then it was not love at first sight?"

"No, Clarissa. It was stupid. She had a mastery of the healing arts, and I was so torn up about your situation, I was grasping for anything and anyone who might make you better. I never intended to marry her, and she knew it. She was a useful trinket I could discard when she was no longer of use to me. Being a duke, I knew I could terminate our betrothal at will and suffer none of the ill effects of my dastardly behavior."

"Gareth! You would never be so cruel, would you?"

"I bribed her, asking her to give me six months of her life. I told her that when those six months were up, I would settle a large sum on her and allow her to quietly break off this betrothal. I knew she had no choice but to agree. I had the power to destroy her reputation and leave her penniless if I chose. She fought me on the settlement, insisting on taking less even though her family was desperately in need of funds at the time."

Clarissa had a horrified look on her face. "How could you be such a beast to her?"

"Well, I am not going to be a beast to her now, am I? Perhaps I did fall in love with her at first sight, as you say. I cannot let her go, Clarissa. From the moment I met her, I do not think I could ever have let her go. She means everything to me."

"She means everything to me, too. I shall punch Lawrence in the nose if he dares speak ill of her. But Gareth, does she know you love her? You must tell her at once. It must weigh so heavily on her heart to think your time together will soon be over. It is so obvious she does not want your wealth or title. She wants you."

"I meant to tell her tonight. I even had a bride token specially made for her in Whitby, but I think I will put off giving it to her until the cousins are gone."

"No, you must give it to her in front of them. It isn't enough to just insist you love her. You must show it in every way possible. Pour your heart out to her and be prepared to make a monumental fool of yourself. That is so romantic."

He laughed. "I shall take it under consideration."

After leaving Clarissa's quarters, feeling deeply ashamed of himself for his highhanded manner, he knocked on Josefina's door. She had changed for supper, donning one of the elegant gowns Madame Yvonne had prepared for her. As always, she looked beautiful. "My cousins and Aunt Ophelia, she is Philidia's crab of a sister, will be joining us for supper. They are not nice people. Just be careful around them."

She nodded. "I can only be myself, Your Grace. But I will be on my guard. Thank you for the warning."

"There's more, Josefina."

"Oh?"

He sighed heavily. "I told Clarissa the truth about us."

Her smile faltered. "Yes… I see. Um, I thought we were going to talk to her together. But it is right that you should be the one to tell her of our situation. You are the brother she adores. How did she take it?"

"Surprisingly well. She claims I have been a heartless idiot toward you."

"No, you have a big, wonderful heart, caring for your family as you do."

He did not understand why her eyes were beginning to tear. "Josefina, what is wrong?"

"Nothing. It is done, and all has turned out just as you hoped. I had better finish doing up my hair. I shall see you all downstairs."

"No, I will escort you downstairs tonight. Wait for me. I shall come to your door."

"I see. All right. I will wait for you." She shut the door in his face.

He marched to his quarters and called for Calder to set out his formal attire. Of course, the old man was two steps ahead of him and already had it laid out on his bed.

Gareth took a moment to shave and wash up, then quickly dressed. Calder was aces at doing up his studs as well as fashioning his elegant cravat.

Not wishing to keep Josefina waiting, he strode to her room and rapped on the door. He heard muffled sounds and recognized them as sniffles and sobs. Why was she crying? The door opened a moment later. "You look so handsome, Your Grace."

"And you look miserable. What is the matter?"

"Perhaps too much sun," she said, the excuse obviously false and quite lame. "Will you give my apologies to your family? I–"

"You are no coward, Josefina. And I will be there to protect you. I will not let them eat you alive."

"Them? They cannot hurt me." She burst into tears. "I am so sorry. I thought I could do this, but I cannot. I am so sorry, I cannot."

"Do what? Josefina, please tell me what has you so overset." She tried to close the door in his face again, but this time he would not let her shut him out. "Talk to me."

"Go eat with your cousins. I have no appetite. I'll pack up my things… you did say they were mine to keep."

"Of course, they are. But why would you pack them?"

She dabbed at her wet cheeks with her handkerchief. "Are you not planning to send me away? Is this not what your discussion with your sister was about? And now your cousins have come to warn you about the evils of marrying a Bigglesworth. You and Clarissa thought to hide the newspaper reports from me, but I saw them. I am your mistress. You will never marry me. And now my time *serving* you is up, or should I say *servicing* you, as though I were some common… I cannot even say the word. All that is left is to pay me off and pack me up."

She burst into tears again.

"I'm a thickheaded arse," he muttered and led her into the hallway. "Stay right there."

He began to knock on doors. "Clarissa, are you ready to come downstairs?" He then moved to Philidia's room and pounded on her door. "Aunt Philidia, I need you in the hall."

They scrambled out of their rooms.

"Gareth, dear. Whatever is the matter?" his aunt asked.

"We are going downstairs as a family, and I have an important announcement to make." He strode to Josefina's side and took her hand before she could scurry back to her bedchamber. "I need you for this. Stop crying, Josefina. How can you think I would ever hurt you? Besides, you are strong. You are resilient. You are a…"

"Bigglesworth," she tearfully filled in.

"Right, that name. It is impossible to remember. We will have to change it as soon as possible." He kissed her on the forehead. "Trust me."

"Trust us all," Clarissa added, she and Philidia now leading the way downstairs.

Ophelia and her rabble were waiting for them in the parlor, having helped themselves to his finest brandy.

"Lawrence, do not pour yourself another just yet. I want you sober when you hear what I have to say."

"So, this is the girl they call the Seahaven Diamond?" He sneered as he looked at Josefina and her tear-swollen eyes and pink nose. She still looked achingly beautiful to Gareth. "She does not look like much, this fortune-hunting temptress of yours."

"This is *Lady* Josefina," he said, slipping his arm about her waist. "Not a fortune hunter, but most definitely a temptress. The woman I love. The only woman I shall ever have as my wife."

Josefina looked up at him, utterly confused.

"For real this time," he whispered, kissing her lightly on the lips and ignoring the gasps from the Chesmires as he bent on one knee before her. He was aware his entire family was watching, aware even his own valet had crept downstairs and was peering at him along with most of his staff.

"What are you doing, you fool?" Lawrence growled.

"What I should have done from the first… well, what I did do from the first. But this time, I intend to do it properly. Josefina, I love you with all my heart. I do not need another day or week or month to know how I feel about you. I love you. I adore you. I worship you."

She said nothing.

So, he continued. "I loved you when I proposed to you in the tearoom. I knew you had to be mine the moment I set eyes on you in the apothecary. I will always love you. Forgive me for leaving you all these months to worry about it. If it is any consolation, I was in utter agony all the while, doubting myself, not believing love at first sight was possible. Not trusting my heart to know the truth of it in an instant."

"You dared not," she said, her smile soft and sweeter than he deserved, "for a wrong choice would have put your dukedom at risk."

"But every day you proved my heart right. Every delay only proved what an arse I was… and still am… for not telling you how I feel about you, and setting a wedding date." He rose and ran his thumb along her cheek to wipe away a stray tear. "And now I've made you cry."

He released a ragged breath. "Never again, Josefina. I shall devote my life to making you happy, for you deserve only the best. As for me, I surely do not deserve someone as kind and beautiful as you. But I ask you anyway, because I want you and need you so badly. Make me the happiest man in all of England and marry me."

She cast him an impudent smirk.

So typical of the girl.

"Your Grace, I have already accepted to marry you. Would you kindly clarify the reasons for your second proposal?"

He grinned, for he had been babbling about it for the last five minutes. But he owed her quite a bit of groveling and did not mind at all. "Because the first time did not count. I forced you into it and held you hostage with my conservatory."

"And a lovely wardrobe," Josefina added. "I specifically agreed to *three* gowns and you gave me *five*. Although, to be precise about it, you gave me *five* times *three* to account for morning, afternoon, and evening. Most highhanded of you."

"What are you talking about?" Ophelia harrumphed.

"The only thing now held hostage is my heart," Gareth continued. "It is yours forevermore. Will you marry me, Josefina? This month. This week. Tomorrow. I will ride off to obtain the special license first thing in the morning."

She put a hand to his cheek. "I thought you meant to let me go."

"No, my love. It is the last thing I ever wish to do."

"Then you really do love me?"

"Yes, quite madly."

She laughed. "Indeed, you must be mad to fall in love with a Bigglesworth, as your cousins have so generously pointed out. But I think myself very clever to have fallen in love with you. I hope you know it is you I love, not your impressive title or the obscene piles of money you were trying to toss at me. It was quite crass of you."

He grinned again. "My apologies."

"You are forgiven." Tears welled in her eyes once more. "I love you so much. I have never been happier than my time spent here with all of you."

"Nor have we been happier since you arrived," Clarissa interjected.

"Does this mean you will marry me, Josefina?"

"Do I still have your promise of a conservatory?"

He laughed. "Yes, I dare not deprive you of it."

"I hope you know that you shall always be first in my heart."

"Even above your precious plants?"

She nodded.

"Is that a yes to my proposal?"

"It is a resounding yes, Your Grace. My heart is in desperate need of you."

"Do you hear that, Lawrence? I am to marry a Bigglesworth." He lifted Josefina in his arms and gave her a thoroughly improper kiss. "Thank you, my love. We shall have rooms made ready for all of your family so they may attend our wedding."

The next thing he knew, his dogs were leaping on them.

Then so was Clarissa.

Gareth had never been happier.

"Timmons, bring out the champagne," he said, laughing as Wolf dropped a big paw on his head and began to lick his cheek. "Glasses for the staff as well. This is a special day. Can you believe it? Lady Josefina Bigglesworth loves me and has agreed to marry me."

Josefina cast Gareth the softest smile.

Her body was still tingling after drinking the champagne, although she suspected it was his kisses more than those effervescent bubbles that were responsible for the effect.

Perhaps miracles did happen and wishes came true, for this was her father's dying wish for her. "I have made a muddle of my affairs, my dearest Josefina. But I have always loved my girls and wanted the best for all of you. Perhaps I was too absorbed in myself to properly attend to you… to any of you. So, I make this last wish in the hope it will come true. I wish a duke for you, my lovely girl."

She had laughed at the time, for her father always did think more of himself than any of his wives or daughters. That his dying remark was for her came as quite a surprise. "Really, Papa? Not an earl or a marquess?"

"No, child. Nothing less than a duke will do for you."

Those were her father's last words to her.

Gareth now stood beside her and placed his arm around her waist, the gesture casual but also quite protective. He was warning his cousins to behave themselves around her or face his anger. She hugged Gareth fiercely and then stared up at the ceiling. "Thank you, Papa," she whispered, hoping he was somewhere close and watching.

Her father had got his wish.

And she had gained her dream come true… this proud, loving, wonderful man. Gareth. Not only him but his Hollings family to now add to her own beloved sisters and assorted adored relations.

"I have something for you, Josefina."

She watched as he reached into the pocket of his waistcoat, then gasped when he presented her with a bride token and moved behind her to place it around her neck. "It is beautiful," she said, admiring the necklace of Whitby jet she appreciated more than any diamonds or sapphires he could have given her. She loved it because this black gemstone came from the earth, from trees crushed under the weight of ages.

She loved it because Gareth understood what it would mean to her. "I love you so much, Your Grace."

"The feeling is mutual, Josefina. I am so sorry I made you wait this long to reveal what was always in my heart."

"It does not matter. We needed the time to be sure. I hope you know it will always be you I will love and never your elegant title."

"I do, sweetheart. I have not a doubt."

She glanced up at the ceiling again.

*Look, Papa. You've got your wish.*

*A duke for Josefina.*

THE END

# SOCIAL MEDIA FOR MEARA PLATT

You can learn more about Meara Platt at these social media links:

**Facebook:** https://www.facebook.com/AuthorMearaPlatt/
**Amazon Author Link:** http://www.amazon.com/Meara-Platt/e/B00PO672QU
**Bookbub:** https://www.bookbub.com/authors/meara-platt
**Website:** www.mearaplatt.com
**Newsletter**: http://bit.ly/meara-platts-newsletter
**Free download** If You Kissed Me for free form signup link is this: http://bit.ly/free-novella-download

## ABOUT MEARA PLATT

Meara Platt is an award winning, USA TODAY bestselling author and an Amazon UK All-Star. Her favorite place in all the world is England's Lake District, which may not come as a surprise since many of her stories are set in that idyllic landscape, including her paranormal romance Dark Gardens series. Learn more about the Dark Gardens and Meara's lighthearted and humorous Regency romances in her Farthingale series and Book of Love series, or her warmhearted Regency romances in her Braydens series by visiting her website at www.mearaplatt.com

# A COUNTESS TO REMEMBER

SHERRY EWING

A Countess To Remember
By Sherry Ewing

*Sometimes love finds you when you least expect it...*

Patience, Dowager Countess of Seahaven, cares for a bevy of stepdaughters, and a Season for each to find husbands seems out of reach. There's been no chance for romance herself but fate intervenes in the form of Richard, Viscount Cranfield, in York for his sister's Season. Will Patience allow herself time for love?

# CHAPTER 1

*London, England, December, 1816*

Richard, Viscount Cranfield peered out the window to the neat row of brick town houses before his carriage came to a stop at one that was familiar to him. He briefly leaned his head back upon the soft leather of the seat, dreading the confrontation he knew awaited him inside. He had been putting this off for months but he knew he couldn't delay the inevitable any longer.

Mrs. Penelope Lenox has been his mistress for the past several years. Unfortunately, Richard had been preoccupied with business matters of late, and he justified this excuse to not visit her more often at her town house. But it was more than just business that kept him away. Penelope had become increasingly possessive of his time, and she had made it perfectly clear she wanted more from him than he was able to give. She never mentioned that she was in love with him. Richard had his doubts she was even capable of such sentiment, and he certainly wasn't in love with his mistress.

His closest friends had warned him of what he himself hadn't seen at the time they had come to an understanding. She was an ambitious woman who had her sights on finding a gentleman who was not only rich but could also bring her a title. He should have listened to the men instead of attempting to convince them that their worries on his behalf were unfounded. He shook his head with the realization his friends had been right all along, and he had been the fool. He was tired of feeling as if he was nothing more than a financial means in order for her to have a better life. He needed to end their arrangement without further delay, hence his arrival to finish this once and for all.

The footman opened the door, let down the step and Richard left the carriage with a determined stride. He had barely knocked upon the front door when Penelope's butler welcomed him inside.

"Good to see you, my lord," Branson said taking his hat. "My lady is still upstairs."

Even though it was almost noon, Richard wasn't surprised the woman was still in bed. "No need to announce me, Branson. I can see myself up."

"Very well, sir. Should I send up refreshments?" he asked.

"Perhaps for your mistress but nothing for me. I won't be here long," Richard answered, before taking the steps up to the second floor. When he entered her bedroom after a brief knock, his mistress was quickly folding down the sheet covering her naked form just enough to expose the tops of her full breasts.

"Richard, darling. I wasn't expecting you today. I hope you can stay for an early dinner. I can have cook fix anything you desire." Penelope flashed an encouraging smile, patting the mattress next to her. Seductive brown eyes held a promise of what was in store for him if he but accepted her invitation.

He made his way across the room to sit in a chair near the fireplace. Her eyes followed his every move. "Not today, Penelope. I'm only here for a short visit."

"You look far too serious, darling, for this hour of the morning," she whispered. A worried frown marred her face.

"It's noon, my dear," Richard reminded her before taking out his pocket watch to note the time. He was going to be late for his next appointment, and keeping his parents waiting would result in a set down as though he was just out of the nursery. But there was no help for it. He was going to be late, and they would just have to wait.

"All the more reason for you to join me in bed," she purred. "We can entertain one another before having that early dinner."

His dark brow rose when she lowered the sheet giving him a luscious glimpse of the bounty of her breasts before she once more covered herself with a laugh. The tease! She pushed her black hair away from her face. Those brown eyes twinkled in delight, thinking she had changed his mind. Her offer might have been tempting in the earlier years of their relationship, but she hadn't altered anything.

"We need to talk, Penelope," he replied seriously and watched when her face fell from her playful mood. "Perhaps you could put something on and join me here." Her eyes briefly flashed her disappointment when he motioned to the vacant chair across from him.

A nervous huff escaped her lips. Reluctantly, she left the bed naked, taking her time to stroll over to a nearby dressing screen in the corner of the room where a pink silk robe hung over the edge. She stretched as if to give Richard the extra opportunity to see her beautiful body and what he would be missing if he didn't take her up on his offer. She waited… as did he, knowing she wouldn't be changing his mind. With a heavy sigh, she pushed her arms into the garment and tied the sash around her waist. Her smile was seductive while her hips swayed when she gracefully walked toward him to sit in the chair. She crossed her legs, the robe opening to display her creamy skin. She positioned herself to show her body to its best advantage, a ploy she had used numerous times in their past.

But the action of her fingers drumming on the armrests of her chair gave away the true agitation she attempted to hide. She finally raised her brown eyes to his hazel ones. "Whatever do you wish to talk about, Richard?" She was nervous, and for good reason.

He raked his fingers through his brown hair with hints of blond highlights from the amount of time he spent outdoors. "I think you and I both know that our arrangement is no longer working for either of us," he began. She sputtered in anger.

"And whose fault is that?" she burst out, her fingers now gripping the arms of the chair, turning her knuckles white. "You barely come to see me anymore!"

"And we have had this conversation before. I cannot marry you. You knew this from the beginning yet still agreed you would be content to be only my mistress."

"I would be a good wife to you, Richard." Her comment only reaffirmed his decision to finally end their association.

She reached over to take a firm grip upon his arm. She was angry. He could see for himself the full effects of her displeasure, nor did he care for the look that crossed her features. "Don't be possessive, Penelope. It doesn't become you."

"But you promised me—"

"I promised you nothing other than to see that your financial needs were met in exchange for what you freely offered me," he replied. "But it's apparently long past the time that I settle our accounts, allowing you to find yourself another lover." His underlying tone conveyed he would not change his mind, yet still she pushed him further.

"You could dismiss me as easily as that?" she cried out in alarm.

"There is a reason I don't visit you as often as I used to, Penelope. If you stop to think about how our relationship has deteriorated over the past year, then you will realize you only have yourself to blame. You knew from the very beginning what would be between us was nothing more than a convenience. You agreed upon our terms. Yet you continue to ask more of me than I am able or willing to give. I will one day inherit my father's title of earl. For the last time, I cannot and will not ever be able to marry you."

His words were harsher than he intended. One look into her tormented brown eyes and he knew he had crushed whatever hopes she continued to have about becoming his wife.

"I just thought that perhaps with time..." her words dwindled away even as she blinked back the tears of the reality of what was never meant to be.

He reached out to brush one away with his thumb. "Unfortunately, nothing has changed from our original agreement, Penelope. I'm sorry if I have hurt you but you always knew the truth of the matter." Richard stood and headed toward the door.

"I wish I could change your mind," she whispered while she still held a margin of hope that they could remain together.

A previous conversation with his father echoed in his head when they had the never-ending talk about when Richard would finally wed. And his mother... if her son hadn't been their heir and they relied upon him to make a good match, she would have been throwing daggers in his direction. *Keep her as your mistress, if you must, but marry a title and a woman of worth,* his mother had all but ordered.

With thoughts of what his future held, Richard realized this would be the last time he would see Penelope. "It's well past time we went our separate ways, Penelope. I will settle your accounts and leave you enough to see you through the next six months."

A gasp escaped her before she composed herself into the strong woman he remembered when they first met. "That is more than generous. Thank you," she softly replied, nodding her head in agreement. She stood and made her way across the room. Standing on the tips of her toes, she kissed his cheek for the last time. "Goodbye, Richard."

He reached out to cup her cheek. "Goodbye, Penelope." He nodded, grateful she hadn't created a further scene.

Leaving her town house, he once more settled himself in his carriage, thankful Penelope took their parting relatively well. The driver put the horses into motion. Richard took another deep breath to prepare himself for his second conflict of the day, knowing a conversation with his parents seldom ended on a good note. Before long, the conveyance began to slow and he gazed out the window again to see another row of familiar town houses, one of them belonging to his parents. God only knew what awaited him inside, and he slowly walked up the steps to the brick structure in front of him. The door opened before he could even reach for the knob.

"Good afternoon, my lord," the butler said opening the portal wide.

"Good afternoon, Jenkins. How is Mrs. Jenkins?" Richard politely asked, as he handed over his hat and coat. The married couple had been in his parents' employ since Richard was a young man. How they remained loyal to their challenging employers was a mystery.

"Busy seeing to the household as always, my lord. The earl and countess are in the breakfast room, with Lady Josephine."

"No need to announce me, Jenkins. I know the way," Richard said repeating the words spoken to another butler earlier.

"As you wish, my lord," the butler nodded and left with his cloak and hat while Richard made his way through the town house.

He paid barely any attention to the opulent surroundings of one of several homes he had grown up in and would one day inherit. Luxury and wealth gleamed in abundance, a true testament to what his mother and father felt important in life. They cared for little else other than how others saw they lacked for nothing. Their summons had Richard guessing what could be so crucial, which is why he didn't care that he was running late. After all, they had been absent from most of his life and that of his sisters.

He made his way through the house to the breakfast room where the sun shone brightly through the floor to ceiling windows. He gave his parents a brief bow in greeting before smiling towards Josephine but her eyes portrayed her feelings all too well. What had they done to her now?

"You're late," his mother stated the obvious before taking a sip of her tea.

"You know how we hate to be kept waiting, son," his father said as he put down the newspaper he had been reading.

"But I am here now as you all but commanded." Richard took a seat next to Josephine who handed him a cup of tea. "How are you?"

"There is time later for the two of you to become reacquainted in this rare family reunion," his mother interrupted.

Richard nodded. "Very well, then. What exactly do you need from me this time?" he asked, not even making an attempt to hide his annoyance or remain polite.

His parents exchanged the briefest of glances before his father gave him his answer. "It's simple, Cranfield. You are headed to York for their Season to ensure Josephine finds herself a suitable husband."

"What?" Richard roared while Josephine's cup rattled in the saucer. He looked over to his sibling while she silently mouthed the words *I'm sorry*.

His mother set her own cup down before she proceeded. "You'll have the whole staff of the York town house available for your convenience or feel free to take your own. I really don't care who runs the household. You know enough people in the *ton* that introductions won't be necessary once you arrive in York. Make the rounds, get invited to any balls or outings that may be occurring, or be seen at the races. You breed horses and have enough of them stabled there. The only thing that matters is that you get your sister engaged to be married. Heaven only knows how hard I've tried to find her a suitable match with no success in London."

"To men old enough to be my father," Josephine burst out.

"Silence!" their mother warned. "Every one of our selections would have seen you living in the lap of luxury. What more could you possibly want out of life?"

"How about love?" Richard and Josephine said in unison, and they exchanged a knowing smile between them.

Their father held up his hand before his wife could reply. Her red face more than amplified exactly how upset she truly was. "The two of you were always close, and the way you reply in unison is exactly why we are counting on you, Cranfield, to see the matter done. Maybe you can have better luck finding her a husband. At twenty-five years old she's already on the shelf and a spinster."

"Better Richard than what you've put before me," Josephine replied lifting her chin, but her false bravado dimmed when her chin quivered.

Their mother pointed a finger at her daughter. "You will keep a civil tongue, young lady, and remember we are still your parents!"

Richard reached over to take his sister's hand. "Since you've obviously washed your hands of this situation, then by all means, I will see to Josephine's needs including a proper chaperon to accompany us to

York. Is there anything else you request of me?" he inquired, attempting to keep his voice calm when he was anything but. He wasn't angry at his sister since this was hardly her fault. But once again his parents proved they cared little for their well-being unless it elevated their social standings within the *ton*.

"Yes. Find your own lady to become your wife!" his mother exclaimed with a warning glare. "It's well past time you were also married."

*And there it was…* a grim reminder of his duties and the future that awaited him with some unknown woman.

Before Richard could reply, his father waved them off. "That will be enough. Your mother will see that the town house is open for your use in March. That should give you plenty enough time to settle whatever business you must attend to in London prior to your departure."

Richard stood, held out his hand to Josephine, and the two of them walked away from their parents. It wouldn't bother him in the least if he never laid eyes upon them again.

# CHAPTER 2

*Starbrook, England*

Patience, Dowager Countess of Seahaven looked out the kitchen window to see the sun about to crest the horizon. The sight of the sky turning shades of pink and orange gave her an idea of how far behind she was as she continued kneading the dough in front of her. She had been in the kitchen for hours working by candlelight in order to get enough bread made in time for the loaves to be sent to the market to be sold. Another day in an endless set of days, or years actually, in which her family depended on each other to try and make ends meet. How blessed they were that they'd kept from Society the fact they worked at various skills to bring income into the household. Some days, she was glad there was enough food to even feed her own large family.

Sectioning off the dough and forming it into multiple balls, she placed each one in a separate bowl, put a cloth over the top to let it rise, and cleaned off the countertop before she finally took a moment to sit down. Her tea had grown cold, but she was too tired to reheat it or make another cup. She took a sip, enjoying the rare bit of solitude that only this hour of the morning could bring.

Patience gave a weary sigh as the burden of her responsibility for all her stepdaughters, along with her own precious Jane, who was only three years of age, came crashing down upon her. She always tried to put on a brave front for everyone's sake, including her own, but she doubted she fooled her family, and she certainly didn't fool herself. They needed to scrape up enough money in order to see the oldest daughters wed but how could they ever afford a Season in London? It just couldn't be done.

She finished her tea and rose from her seat to head upstairs to her room to change since she had time before she would need to get the bread formed and into the oven. She tried to ignore the shabby cottage she lived in. Although neat and clean, the place was hardly befitting a countess. Most would expect to find her living in a lovely town house in London. But life was unfair, and Patience had come to realize that she had to depend on herself and those stepdaughters who were old enough to bring in whatever money they could from various trades.

Upon her husband's death, the new earl, who was a distant cousin, and his wife had given Patience a small amount due to her from her husband's will and turned her out. The will had appointed her as the custodial guardian of her husband's daughters from his previous marriages. Some of them were actually older than herself. The new earl had shared out a modest sum as a dowry, but it was a pittance once divided among all the daughters and wouldn't be available until after they wed.

Patience could dredge up the day when she had sat in the study once belonging to her husband while the new earl and his wife argued about the sum. She had a moment of pity for the man but it was short lived. His wife controlled him, and Patience could still remember the gleam of satisfaction in the woman's eyes when she had won the argument... the man was a spineless fool! Patience had left what once had been her home with her stepdaughters and Jane, and never looked back. She'd been given no other choice on the matter.

The last stair creaked despite her attempt to remain quiet so as not to awaken the household, and she made her way down the hallway to her room before soundlessly closing the door. Opening the drapes to let in the morning light, she went to sit at her vanity and stared at the reflection in the mirror. Her strawberry blonde hair had been swept up in a bun to keep the tresses off her face while in the kitchen, but it was the shadows beneath her blue-grey eyes that worried her. She was beyond exhausted, and it showed. She pinched her cheeks to bring color to them, hoping this would help, and quickly redid her hair for the day before heading to a wardrobe to pick out a gown. She was used to dressing herself; they all were. They could barely afford the housekeeper and nursemaid who followed her when they were turned out from Seahaven, let alone additional staff.

Who would have ever thought that, at the age of only twenty-two, she would not only be a widow but a dowager countess at that? *Dowager!* she thought in disgust. A frown formed on her brows while she dressed. She had always associated that word with a woman of older years, not someone who was yet so young.

Despite not wishing to relive unpleasantries, her thoughts still went to the day Henry Reginald Bigglesworth, Earl of Seahaven, had shown up at her parent's home... this very cottage, in fact. Although still a handsome man, he had been old enough to be her father, or grandfather for that matter. His proposal of marriage meant Patience would become a countess and would want for nothing, which was appealing, of course. Patience finally agreed to the marriage in order to help her parents.

Harold and Emily Egerton were far from the realm of high Society and had sold baked goods to a small bakery in Starbrook. Her mother had fallen out with her own family when she married beneath her station in life. They claimed she had disgraced the St. Aubyn name. Her mother had always told Patience that, when love found you, you needed to grasp hold of it and never let go. Not that love had anything to do with her decision to marry Henry. This had been a once in a lifetime opportunity to become elevated back into the *ton* that her mother had left behind, or so they had convinced their daughter.

She and the earl wed quietly in the village chapel in the spring of 1813 when Patience had barely turned eighteen. But her wedding was the first time she had glimpsed the faces of all his daughters sitting in the first two pews of the church. Nine girls ranging from older than her to two little girls. The reality that she would be his fifth wife hit her. She had quietly said her vows all the while thinking she was apparently his last chance at siring a son to carry on his name and title.

Eight months after their wedding, Henry passed away from some unknown ailment. Two months later, she gave birth to Jane. Henry would have been disappointed at siring yet another daughter. But fate, or perhaps God, wasn't done creating further catastrophe in Patience's young life. Her parents had come to Seahaven to support Patience through Jane's birth. They were returning home two weeks afterwards when a thunderstorm came up out of nowhere, and the driver lost control of the team on a narrow stretch of road. The carriage overturned and fell over into a steep ravine. No one survived. Tears threatened to well up in her eyes as she relived the memory. She had never felt more alone than she had from their loss. But God surely felt her shoulders were strong enough to bear the burden of this latest twist, including the responsibility of a household of step-daughters left in her care.

Patience inherited her family home, although, without her parents' presence, the cottage seemed to lack some of the warmth that used to fill each room. The place needed more repairs than she and her step-daughters could afford and was located outside of the small village of Starbrook. Their cottage was as different as it could be from her old home of Seahaven and thankfully was far enough away that the family never saw the new earl and his countess. Almost all of her stepdaughters also resided with her.

She shook off her sudden melancholy mood, lifted her chin and left her room to check on the youngest children in the bedroom next to her own. Quietly opening the door, she saw that Jane was still asleep in her crib. Emma who was twelve and Merrilyn age ten, from her husband's fourth marriage, also still slept in their separate beds. She closed the door and turned, almost running straight into the nursemaid, Hannah.

"M-my apologies, m-my l-lady," Hannah stammered softly as she righted herself along with the linens she balanced in her arms.

"The fault was mine, Hannah. You've done nothing wrong," Patience replied before grabbing one of the linens about to fall. She'd been so grateful Hannah continued to stay with them and accepted such a small amount for her services to the family. But Hannah had told Patience when they left Seahaven that she was committed to Emma and Merrilyn and would follow the girls wherever they may live. She had been more than happy when Jane was born, giving her another young child to care for.

Hannah nodded to the door. "The little misses are still asleep?" she asked, and Patience nodded. "I'll check on them later and change their bedding once they're up."

"Thank you, Hannah. I don't know what I'd do without you," Patience replied before heading toward the stairs. She met Barbara coming out of her own bedroom, and the two women descended and made their way to the kitchen. Barbara was from her husband's second marriage and was a music teacher.

Patience put a kettle of water on the stove before taking out several containers to put her bread in now that it had risen enough.

"You were up early, Patience," Barbara mentioned as she reached for a tin of loose-leaf tea and several cups. Patience smiled at the young woman, who was the second eldest of all the sisters and five years older than Patience.

"The bread won't bake itself," Patience replied as she lined up the pans. She was thankful she had been able to continue the same arrangement to sell her baked goods that her parents had had with the local bakery.

"You could have woken me to help." her stepdaughter said stifling a yawn.

"No, I couldn't, not when I know you have a full day teaching lessons in the village. You know I always manage."

Barbara sighed. "I know, but I still worry how we will continue to survive."

Patience gripped the edges of the counter, her knuckles turning white while she kept her head lowered. *I will not cry... I will not cry...* "As do I," she at last managed to whisper before going back to the task at hand. If she didn't get these loaves into the oven, they'd miss out on the extra money they so desperately needed.

The two women were silent as they began the chore of preparing breakfast for the family that had as yet come down to join them. A knock on the front door sounded in the distance, and Patience and Barbara exchanged a look between them.

"Who could that be at this hour?" Barbara asked causing Patience to shrug.

They didn't have long to wait before the housekeeper, Mrs. Crewe, came into the kitchen with a note held in her hands bringing it to Patience.

"This just arrived by special messenger, my lady," she said handing over the letter.

"Thank you, Mrs. Crewe." Patience exclaimed, once more thankful for another servant who refused to leave her employer. The woman left, and Patience went to sit at the kitchen table, breaking the wax seal. A shiny brass key fell onto the table.

She picked it up with a fair amount of curiosity. Patience began to read, her eyes widening at what the letter revealed. "We're saved," she exclaimed before handing the letter over to Barbara to read.

"Who is Rose?" Barbara asked after skimming the contents.

"Lady Rose St. Aubyn is a cousin on my mother's side of the family. She is the only child of a St. Aubyn earl, inherited his money when he passed away, and never married. While she is traveling in the East, she's invited us to live rent free in her town house in York. Can you believe it, Barbara? This can't come at a better time. We can be there when the York Season begins. We just might be able to find husbands for Josefina and the twins, Ivy and Iris!" These three step-daughters were from Henry's third marriage, Josefina being the oldest at nineteen and Ivy and Iris aged eighteen.

"Will we still be able to afford a Season for the girls, especially after how much we spent on presents for Christmas next week? With almost everyone coming home for the holiday, our expenses will certainly be higher than they normally are," Barbara asked, worry etched upon her brow.

Patience looked up from her excitement to briefly ponder the matter. "An opportunity like this won't come again but I see your point." She read the letter again. "The town house is available for the next six months. We might be able to manage six or seven weeks at the height of the Season. We'd have to swap dresses and trims, maybe even dyeing them and exchanging accessories. We need to have a meeting... all of us, say by Twelfth Night since Rose would like a reply as soon as possible. Perhaps you can see if Josefina is up and she can accompany me to Harrogate when I drop off the bread. I'd like her to go to confirm with Dorothea that she can make it home for Christmas. I won't have time to stop in the hotel where she's working beforehand to ask her myself, and I know how busy Doro's been with running the catering business."

"I'll check to see if Josefina is awake," Barbara said, before going to the stove, taking the kettle, and pouring two cups of tea. "Can you manage breakfast alone or should I send one of the other girls to help you?"

"I can manage but thank you," Patience said, waving her off. Barbara took her tea with her and hurried from the room.

Patience got to work on the bread and smiled. She could not even remember the last time that she had been so hopeful. She was excited for all the possibilities that awaited them in the months to come.

# CHAPTER 3

*Whites, London*

Richard entered his club for a much-needed respite from his parents, who continued to plague him even after two weeks of living under their roof. One would think that once he agreed to see Josephine settled in York for the Season, then that would have been the end of their harping. But, no. They continued their assault to ensure every detail for Josephine had been arranged and also argued he needed to wed within the year.

He had stayed through the holidays to ring in the new year so his sister would have moral support but he apologized when he couldn't stand being under the same roof any longer. He promised her he would see that they were settled into the York town house as soon as possible. As far as Josephine was concerned, the move couldn't happen soon enough.

Handing his hat and coat to the doorman, Richard entered the lounge and saw a far table already occupied by the close friends with whom he had attended Oxford. Frederick Maddox and Digby Osgood were the married men of the bunch, both busy with raising their families together with the lovely women they had wed. That left himself, Milton Sutton, and George Chadwick as the bachelors of the group. Digby raised a hand to a passing servant and, by the time Richard stopped at several tables to say hello to other acquaintances, a drink was ready for him when he arrived to greet his friends.

"Gentlemen," Richard said, taking a seat and reaching for the brandy. "It's been too long."

"Some of us have been enjoying wedded bliss," Frederick announced with a nod to Digby who smiled in agreement. "The three of you should try it."

"Good heavens, why?" George asked adjusting the cufflink at his wrist, not that anything was ever out of place with his wardrobe.

Digby chuckled. "You may find that you enjoy it."

Milton grimaced. "I'd rather pay for the upkeep on a mistress than have a wife harping at me every moment of my life." He gave Richard an odd sideways glance and cleared his throat. "I have yet to find a woman agreeable enough to marry."

Richard took a sip of his drink before setting it down on the table. "We can't all be so lucky as to find such lovely women as Margaret and Constance to spend our lives with." There was a round of agreements before Richard continued. "Speaking of mistresses… I let Penelope go last month. Should have done it sooner, but she's well taken care of until she can find another man to see to her needs."

Frederick's brow rose and a knowing smirk stretched across his lips. "I told you—"

"—don't you dare finish that thought," Richard warned.

Milton took up his drink with a knowing smirk. "From what you've told us, I'm surprised you didn't let her go sooner. You would think our mistresses would remember that if and when we marry we would need to find a suitable woman—"

"—and not someone of their ilk," George muttered.

"Don't be a snob, Georgie," Digby said with a warning glare. "They cannot help that they've fallen on hard times and must do what they can to survive. I highly doubt any woman just wakes up one morning and decides to ruin her reputation and have a man support her without marriage."

Richard remained silent for several minutes remembering how he had felt when he dashed Penelope's unfounded hopes. But that was now over, and he needed to move on with his life just as she did.

"In any case, I am traveling another road in life at the moment as I've been given the task of seeing to a Season to find Josephine a suitable husband," Richard said looking at the men before him.

Milton choked on his drink.

Frederick slapped him on the back. "She is still unwed?' he asked, his brow raised with his question.

"Apparently my parents think a man with one foot in the grave would make my sister a suitable husband. She thinks otherwise, and I agree. Josephine shouldn't have to marry some old codger just because he has plenty of money, and that's what's important in the eyes of my mother and father."

Frederick nodded in agreement. "Lady Josephine was always a lovely young woman. Margaret has told me a number of times any man would be lucky to call her his wife."

Digby sat back in his chair with a smirk. "Which reminds me that the three of you should be very careful."

Richard, Milton, and George all turned their attention to the two married men in their group.

"Should I ask why?" Richard murmured with a worried frown.

Frederick gave them a wicked grin. "Because my Margaret and Digby's Constance are ready to throw eligible ladies in your direction if you don't find yourself a lady of your choice to wed. They've made it their mission to end your days of being bachelors."

"Eh gads!" George groaned. "Tell them to leave me out of their plans.

Milton only took up his drink again, swirling the amber liquid in the crystal glass.

Richard shuddered before pinching the bridge of his nose at the thought of the two women throwing marriageable young ladies in his direction… no matter how well intended. "I cannot begin to tell you how much I do not need them meddling in my life."

Digby shrugged. "You know our wives. They just want you to be as happy as we are. They'd go to the end of the earth to make it happen."

"Then you and your wives will have to follow me to York, for that is my destination," Richard replied relaxing back in his chair.

"Why York?" Frederick inquired, before reaching for his glass. Finding it empty, he motioned to a passing servant to see the glass filled again.

"My family has a town house there. The earl and countess feel that Josephine has run her chances with any eligible men with a title here in London." Richard's low tone conveyed his underlying anger at the situation.

Frederick shook his head. "I could never understand your parents, Richard. You do yourself and your sister proud to remove her from their influence."

"York, you say?" Milton asked gazing at Richard who nodded. "I was thinking of attending the horse races they have there in May. Maybe I'll open my town house for the Season and join you."

Richard chuckled. "The more the merrier, and I could use the reinforcements. Not that Josephine is a problem. I'd do anything for my sister, and if it annoys my mother and father in the process, then that's a bonus."

The men laughed and clinked their glasses together as Richard began telling them more details of when he would depart. When he finally left White's, there was a new entry in the betting book about the estimated date on when Richard, Viscount Cranfield would get himself hitched and to whom.

# CHAPTER 4

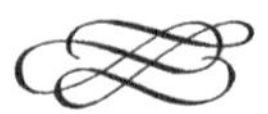

*Twelfth Night, January 6th, 1817*

Patience pulled the blanket over Jane, smoothed down her curly auburn hair and quietly left the nursery, knowing Hannah would check on her later before she, too, retired for the night. Her hand slid along the well-worn oak banister as she went half way up the second set of stairs to softly call out to Elizabeth, or Bess as she preferred, who was working in the attic.

"Bess... are you coming?" Patience asked, somewhat impatiently, knowing nearly everyone else was already in the sitting room.

"Yes. I'll be right there," Bess replied, but Patience knew her eldest stepdaughter, age thirty and the only daughter from her husband's first wife, would no doubt get lost while translating Egyptian hieroglyphics. If she didn't join them in the next few minutes then their meeting would have to go on without her.

As she was about to descend the stairs, Barbara and the twins, who giggled among themselves, joined her. She shared a knowing look at Barbara, who smiled at the possibilities for the girls if only they could scrape up enough money to make this work.

They made their way to the front sitting room where her stepdaughters went to sit in various places around the tidy but tattered room. Josefina was already seated near the hearth while Doro sat at a large desk that had seen better days, much like the rest of the room. Once again, Patience was reminded how different the cottage was to their past life at Seahaven where every luxury had been afforded them.

"Why are we all here?" Ivy and Iris asked at the same time, before they exchanged a look.

"Be patient, girls," Patience suggested, although it was hard to hide her own excitement.

Josefina looked around at her sisters. "Won't Bess be joining us?"

Patience looked toward the entrance to the room, but there was still no sign of her eldest stepdaughter. Doro stopped what she was doing but, at a short nod from Patience, continued her work. "We'll begin without her if she's not here by the time Doro finishes."

Patience made her way toward the desk to look over Doro's shoulder, although she tried not to hover. Doro drew a line at the bottom of the column of figures and began to add them up. Her nerves getting the better of her, Patience began to pace the silent room while her six stepdaughters watched Doro's movements with the quill. She continued moving up and down the page, jotting a figure down and then beginning again at the top. Gazing at all the women in the room, there was no mistaking the strong family resemblance identifying them all as sisters. Practically the same height, they each had that straight nose and determined Bigglesworth chin.

Doro finished adding up their expenses, wrote down the last figure and sat back in her chair. She looked around the room as all the women held their breath in anticipation of her news.

Barbara broke the silence of the room. "Well, Doro? Do we have enough?"

"Barely," she replied. "We'll have to make economies."

Barbara shrugged. "We've been making economies for the past four years. That won't change whether we remain here or are visiting York."

Ivy sat up straight in her chair. "York? We may be going to York?"

"To give Josefina, Iris and you a Season. If it can be done financially." Susana interrupted. She was the dressmaker in the family. At the age of twenty-five, she was also from Henry's second marriage and so Barbara and Doro's full sister.

Josefina, Iris and Ivy all gasped in startled surprise.

Doro turned her attention to her stepmother, who had yet to express an opinion. "What do you say, Patience? You are the one we will need to sponsor the girls. And it's your cousin Rose who owns the town house."

Barbara frowned. "I could stay here at Starbrook with the little ones, if that would help."

Patience raised her eyes in gratitude for Barbara's thoughtfulness. "Oh, no. I couldn't do this without you, dear one. Besides, the younger children may as well join us so we don't have the expense of running two households at the same time. I think we should proceed with taking my cousin up on her generous offer. I propose we move to the town house at the end of March, which will give us time between now and then to figure out any of the details I'm certain we're missing. I believe this is the best chance for your sisters, for all of us, really. Imagine if one of them makes a magnificent match."

Josefina, Iris and Ivy clapped their hands in glee, moved their chairs closer together, and began whispering among themselves.

Doro glanced among the women in the room. "The earl made it clear we can split the dowry trust as we see fit. Divided among all of us, it's a pittance. If we put the money all on Iris, Ivy, and Josefina—"

"—but Doro what about the rest of you," Ivy shouted out, in concern for her sisters.

"Don't interrupt, Ivy. Be sensible," Doro warned before continuing. "If we do this, we may just have enough for the three of you to snag a suitor. It benefits all of us to do so."

"If they find a husband who is kind and respectful, I shall be satisfied," Susana said. "If you think we can manage it, I believe we must try."

Patience came over to her and rested her hand upon her shoulder. "We would be relying on you to dye dresses and any other accessories so none of the girls would be wearing the same gown in the same week," she said thinking of the time and energy that would be needed to make this work.

Susana smiled before taking up the knitting she had left in her lap. "Don't worry. I can manage."

"Waiting does not make financial sense," Doro said, obviously still concerned with expenses. "Since Patience has been offered her cousin's town house for the Season, this will save us on expenses of running the cottage."

Patience nodded in agreement. "The only problem I foresee is we will still be without servants, as Rose stated she would be giving them a much-needed holiday. But I'm certain we can convince Mrs. Crewe to run the York town house and Hannah will be more than willing to look after the younger children. I have no idea, however, what we'll do for a butler. It might appear questionable for us to be answering our own door." Patience gave a heavy sigh as the logistics of a move began to overwhelm her. She finally quit her pacing and took a seat, picking up a garment with tiny rosebuds she had recently been working on.

"We can figure out the rest in the coming months," said Barbara. "I agree we should take the chance and go to York, including the little ones. With the cottage empty, we could rent it out, which will help us to fund the Season. Between us, we have earned enough to manage without working while we're there, though I suppose some of us could continue some of our enterprises in York."

Patience put down her embroidering. "Oh no, Barbara. We must never let anyone in Society know we work for our bread." She took a moment to look at each one of her stepdaughters. "This is very important, my dearest ones. We will be trading on your father's title, and must appear to be, if not wealthy, then at least solvent."

"We are solvent," Barbara replied, "because I teach piano, Doro has been managing a catering business, Susana makes the finest hats in fifty miles, you and Doro are wonderful bakers, Josefina sells her medical herbs, and Ivy and Iris are superb artists selling their trinkets."

"That is quite true, and I cannot express my gratitude to each and every one of you for what you've contributed to the household to keep this roof over our heads. I couldn't have done this without your help. But we must forget everything we've been doing to survive if we are to make a success of this enterprise." Patience picked up the letter from her cousin. "We can have the house until the Season is over in mid-May."

Barbara put down her own knitting and crossed to give Patience a kiss on her cheek. "We have a great deal to do, Patience." She went over to the desk, picked up a notepad and a pencil, and returned to her chair. "We had better start making lists."

Patience nodded her head in agreement and was momentarily lost in thought regarding Bess who remained upstairs. She would need to find some way to entice her bluestocking eldest to put aside her translations in favor of teas and receptions... no easy task. Returning to the present, Patience smiled in gratitude to her stepdaughters, who continued to all pull together to help one another out. She couldn't have survived without each of them. She was truly blessed.

# CHAPTER 5

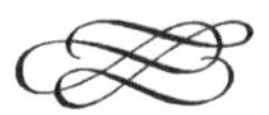

*York, England, March 28th, 1817*

Richard stared at his reflection in the mirror while he finished buttoning the beige waistcoat with embroidered flowers. His cravat was tied in an intricate knot and a ruby stick pin winked from the folds. Dark brown trousers hugged his muscular thighs while his boots gleamed from the sunlight reflecting through his bedroom window. His valet, Owen, held a matching coat ready for him that would complete his look for the day. The waistcoat had been a gift from his sister, and while the flowers were a bit much for his regular taste, he knew it would please her to see him wearing the garment.

Thus, when he pulled his arms through the sleeves of his coat and the garment settled on broad shoulders, he was ready for the onslaught of what his responsibilities entailed. Getting his sister engaged was his first priority. Finding a suitable wife was second on his agenda. He wasn't in the least bit hopeful he'd find someone whom he could one day call his wife in the short amount of time they would be in York. Better to focus on Josephine. She was all that mattered, so she wouldn't have to live under their parent's roof.

Owen smoothed the shoulder of the coat as though removing some unseen speck of lint.

"Will I do, Owen?" Richard inquired in amusement. He was well aware his valet would never allow his master to go out into the world looking anything but his very best.

"Yes, my lord. You will do very nicely, indeed," he said, before handing Richard his hat.

With a brief nod, Richard left the master bedroom in the town house he would now call home for the next couple of months. Josephine was waiting for him at the foot of the stairs, donning her gloves. She looked lovely in a light blue muslin gown with a darker blue ribbon tied in a fashionable bow at her back. The neckline and hem were embroidered in an intricate pattern and her bonnet with white lace at the rim framed her face. A few wisps of her blonde hair with darker highlights escaped her coiffure and curled pleasingly at her cheeks. She was like a breath of fresh air, and if the gentlemen in York didn't become smitten with her upon first sight, then they were all fools.

"Good afternoon, Richard," she said brightly, as she came over to kiss his cheek when he bent down. "It's a lovely day for a carriage ride."

"The sun will shine all the brighter to have my beautiful sister sitting beside me," he complimented her before placing her hand in the crook of his arm. "Are you ready to be *seen*, my dear?"

A groan escaped her when she halted their steps into the entrance hall. She playfully swatted his arm. "Please don't ruin the day with comments like that, brother. It's barely even noon! You make me feel as if I'm about to be auctioned off at the market."

"That wasn't my intention, Josephine. You know I only have your best interest at heart. Remember why we are here in York, and that's to find you a husband—"

"—and you a wife," she finished tossing him a smug look.

"Eh gads, don't start on that Josephine, or you'll start sounding like mother."

"Don't you dare compare me to her," she cried out in alarm, and

Richard felt horrible that such words had tumbled from his mouth.

He gave his sister a reassuring hug before leading her to the entrance door. "Please forgive me, dearest Josephine. Apparently I am doomed to allow my tongue to get the better of me today. You can remind me how obnoxious I become as the day progresses." Richard escorted her through the door.

Their open carriage waited for them in front of their residence, and as Josephine strode across the paved walk to the road, she shielded her eyes to peer down the street. "Oh look, Richard. It appears as though someone is moving in several doors down. Isn't that where Rose St Aubyn lives when she is not travelling around the world?" Josephine had been fascinated by the York housekeeper's stories of their enterprising neighbor.

"Perhaps she has let her house. Isn't that Lady Elizabeth Bigglesworth coming out of the door?" Richard asked, following his sister's gaze as a carriage left and another pulled up to the walkway. The lady at the door greeted several ladies heading toward the town house while the door to the next carriage opened. Another woman descended, followed by two younger girls.

"Yes, I think so. Remember, we met her years ago when you brought me up to York? You were here for the races, and so was their father, and he introduced you to her after church one day. I believe she likes to go by Lady Bess. Yes, it must be her, because that's her stepsister Lady Barbara getting out of the carriage. I met her when my governess took me to tea at the Seahaven town house. Those must be her younger stepsisters, though they have grown up since I met them five years ago. Have you met her, Richard?" She looked upon him as though she was about to play matchmaker.

"I haven't had the pleasure of being introduced to Lady Barbara but, whatever you are thinking, the answer is no," he warned, but Josephine was in a world of her own and wasn't listening to a word he was saying.

"Let me introduce you," she replied instead, tugging on his arm.

"This is hardly appropriate."

"Nonsense, Richard, don't be such a bore. They'll obviously be our neighbors, after all," she said brightly, and in order not to cause a scene on the street, Richard found himself escorting his sister to meet the lady.

Introductions were made while the two younger girls chatted about how excited they were to be here in York. Their elder sister made several attempts to calm them without much success before she turned her attention to the carriage, where a woman was attempting to hand a wiggling toddler to Lady Barbara.

"Let me take her," the lady exclaimed, as a nursemaid came from the household to usher the younger children inside.

The unseen woman was still in the carriage, as if she was still preparing to collect whatever had been left behind. A small dainty shoe poked out onto the edge of the step and Richard heard her heavy sigh that she made no attempt to mask.

Richard stepped forward, offering his hand. "May I be of assistance, my lady?"

"You are most kind," the lady inside said. She put her hand in his and Richard swore he felt a tingling sensation rush up his arm.

"Where are my manners?" Lady Barbara exclaimed. "May I introduce my stepmother, Patience, Lady Seahaven. Patience, this is Lord Cranfield and his sister Lady Josephine."

Richard was prepared for a matronly woman to reveal herself as she alit from the carriage. But when she lifted her head once upon solid ground to acknowledge their introductions, he was unprepared for the young beauty he faced. Blue-grey eyes that could rival the sky above met his. Wisps of strawberry blonde hair had escaped her bonnet while her porcelain skin was set in a lovely round face. But when her small bow mouth turned up into an enchanting smile, Richard became lost.

"Lord Cranfield," her voice reached into his soul. "It's a pleasure to meet you."

Richard bowed, completely bewildered in the spell she had captured him in with just one glance. At a loss for words, he could only stare at the woman before him, even while he continued to hold her hand in his. What had she done to him?

# CHAPTER 6

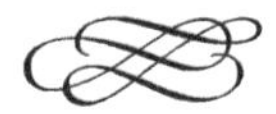

Patience continued to stare into the face of the handsome man before her. She couldn't do anything less, considering he still held her hand gently in his own. Hazel eyes had always been her downfall, and she swore specks of gold hidden in their depths sparkled like diamonds in the sunshine falling upon them. The lighter highlights in his dark brown hair gave Patience the impression this was a man of leisure who spent a considerable amount of time outside. His classical facial features reminded her of a marbled statue, since he sported that familiar roman nose, chiseled cheeks and a determined square jaw.

"Richard..." Lady Josephine whispered.

Patience cast a glance at Barbara, who only shrugged her shoulders. No help was forthcoming from her stepdaughter. She turned her attention back to the man who continued to keep a grasp on her hand. She estimated his age to be perhaps thirty, give or take a couple of years. Older than his sister, she assumed, and most certainly older than herself.

A moment of despair overwhelmed Patience at the sight of Lady Josephine. Would her own stepdaughter Josefina be confused with Lord Cranfield's sister since their names were so similar? Hopefully, this wouldn't become an issue, since they were so different in physical appearance. Inwardly she sighed in the knowledge that this changed nothing. Her priority was Josefina and not the lovely blonde before her.

"Richard," Lady Josephine said more forcibly, and her words at last broke the connection that had seemingly held them spellbound.

Lord Cranfield blinked before he raised her fingertips to kiss the air between his mouth and her gloved hand. "The pleasure is mine, Lady Seahaven," he replied, before he reluctantly let go of her hand.

Conversations continued between Barbara and Lady Josephine, but as far as Patience was concerned, she only had eyes for Lord Cranfield. A viscount, if she remembered her peerage correctly, and the heir to an earl. She finally remembered herself only when Merrilyn and Emma came racing out of the town house.

"Mama," Emma called out, a cross expression on her young face. "Why can't Merry and I have a room to ourselves? We're tired of sharing a nursery with Jane."

Merrilyn stomped her foot. "We're too old to be looked after by Hannah!"

Patience reluctantly turned away from Lord Cranfield, and once more the responsibilities of her position and the family she must see to took precedence over the brief moment of desire that had taken over her entire body. She stole another glance at the viscount, and heat flushed her face. The day had suddenly become overly warm. Another wail from one of her stepdaughters brought her back to the present.

"Girls, you forget yourselves," Patience softly scolded them. "Please return inside where we shall discuss this further. Conversations like this are not meant for the street."

"But, Mama..." Emma whined.

Barbara took a firm hand on the girls. "Inside... both of you. Please excuse me, Lord Cranfield... Lady Josephine," she said but waited at the door for Patience.

"My apologies for my girls. They are just excited to be staying at my cousin's," Patience explained, with a small smile.

Lady Josephine took hold of her brother's arm. "I fondly remember trips to town when I was their age. There is no need to apologize, is there, Richard?" she replied, with a kind smile.

Lord Cranfield appeared as though he were once more lost in his own thoughts before finally replying. "No apologies necessary, my lady. We shouldn't keep you any longer, as I'm certain you wish to get settled."

His sister continued to chatter on. "With the Season just beginning, I know we shall cross paths again, Lady Seahaven," she said happily.

Patience nodded her head. "I will look forward to our next meeting."

Lord Cranfield bowed, and Patience turned toward the front of the brick town house while Barbara entered with Jane. Patience hesitated at the door to cast one last look upon Lord Cranfield, who had just assisted his sister into their waiting carriage. He took his place next to her, but once he was settled, his eyes automatically sought out Patience. He tipped his hat to her as they drove by, and Patience watched until their carriage was lost from view.

Shaking her head at where her thoughts had momentarily gone, she entered the town house and breathed in a sigh of relief at the lovely entryway. It had been many years since Patience had visited her cousin. If the rest of Rose's home was as Patience remembered, she was going to be spoiled, and disappointed when they must return to the cottage in Starbrook.

Taking off her bonnet and gloves, she made her way to the master bedroom. The walls were painted a light baby blue while a four-poster bed dominated the room. Being head of the household would allow her the luxury of not having to share a bedroom.

A ruckus from the younger girls bellowing in a very unladylike manner from one of the upper floors caused Patience to roll her eyes. And so it began. Time to get an idea of where everyone would sleep and also where everything was located in the household.

Patience left her room and Josefina was just coming down the stairs. "You best hurry, Patience. Merry and Emma are about to have a go at it again, and they may just try to pull Hannah's hair out."

"I'm coming," Patience replied as Josefina walked up the stairs with her.

"Did you know we had a butler?" she asked quietly.

Her brow rose at her stepdaughter's words. "Rose never mentioned she was keeping any of the staff on," Patience answered, in confusion. *Good heavens, how will we pay him?* They hadn't planned or budgeted for additional staff!

"Well, he's here and down in the kitchen I think. His name is Mal… something. He's very handsome."

"Don't even consider it, Josefina. We're not doing all this so you can make a mesalliance with the household staff," Patience warned, pointing her finger accusingly at her daughter.

"I just said he was handsome. I didn't say I wanted to marry him," she scoffed before running ahead of Patience to find her own room.

Patience was going to have to dig down deep in order to calm her frayed nerves. First, a handsome viscount who couldn't take his eyes from her, reminding her how young she truly was. Second and more importantly, squabbling children who were going to try her patience. She almost laughed, thinking that her name befitted her station in life. Dropping her skirts as she reached the floor with the loudest noise, she lifted her chin to begin their life in York. May it be all she hoped for and more.

# CHAPTER 7

*Palm Sunday, March 30th, 1817*

Richard sat in a pew in York Minster, waiting for Morning Service to begin. They were neither late nor too early, since other parishioners continued to fill the church. Milton, who had arrived yesterday, sat to his left, while Josephine was to his right. They were also accompanied by a distant cousin on his father's side, Mrs. Juliet Elford, who was acting as chaperone for Josephine. She was a kind woman and so completely different than his father that Richard regretted not spending more time with her over the years.

A murmur of voices began to grow in volume from the back of the chapel, and Richard was one of several people who turned in curiosity in order to witness what was causing such a ruckus. And then he saw *her* again, and his heart flipped inside his chest as she came closer. He briefly closed his eyes, wondering if he was imaging this strange fascination with a lady he had only just met. But when he opened his eyes again, he had his answer. His heart stumbled before finding its rhythm again, with a thunderous hard beat loud enough for all the world to hear. She came ever closer, leading the way down the main aisle towards one of several front pews that had apparently been reserved for her and her family... the Dowager Countess of Seahaven.

She was the focus of the entire congregation and, as she strode past his pew, he witnessed her commanding presence despite her short frame. She was a countess, and he shouldn't be surprised she bore the title well. *My, what a beauty!* Yet he felt she was far out of his league. Richard wondered what the devil he was thinking to become mesmerized by a pair of striking blue-grey eyes.

The woman of his recent musings continued forward, holding onto her toddler with curly auburn hair while she nodded her head to several acquaintances. But what surprised Richard the most was the long line of taller young women who followed behind her. *Good heavens!* Was she guardian to all these ladies?

Josephine leaned over to whisper in his ear confirming his fears. "I learned Lady Seahaven was the earl's fifth wife. Those are all her stepdaughters from his previous marriages, the youngest being her own, or so I was told. Can you imagine it, Richard? I highly doubt she would ever wish to remarry. I mean...What man in his right mind would consider her as a potential wife when he would have to deal with an extremely large ready-made family?"

Richard's eyes narrowed when he turned to his sister. "Hush, Josephine, and do not gossip. You know I how loathe it."

She shrugged. "I'm only telling you what I've learned, since you appeared utterly stunned by her the other day. Honestly, you acted as though you were completely smitten, Richard," she teased with a knowing wink.

He gave her another warning look before she gave a short chuckle, snapped her mouth shut, and returned to her quiet conversation with Mrs. Elford.

Milton nudged him while attempting to keep the sly grin from his face. "Interesting to hear you've taken a fancy to a countess. Does she return your affection?"

"Shut up, Milton," Richard ordered only to hear his friend's quiet teasing.

Lady Seahaven began to settle her brood into the two pews while an older lady made her excuses to the women already seated. Josephine leaned over to whisper the woman was Lady Twisden, an aunt to Lady Seahaven and presumably her mother's sister. She made her way to sit next to the countess, who smiled in greeting. The two gave one another a brief hug, as much as the toddler would permit, as the little girl suddenly found the feather in the woman's bonnet an object for her little fingers to grab. Lady Twisden laughed before she cooed over the toddler, giving her chubby cheek a kiss.

Richard watched the countess as though he couldn't take his eyes off her. Josephine's comment had actually hit far too close to its mark, for Patience had been on his mind for the past two days. She turned in the pew, and their eyes met as if she had heard his thoughts. Their gazes held for more than a heartbeat or two, and Richard felt like there was no one else in the huge cathedral. Her smile was ever so slight, when she gave him a tiny nod of her head before she handed the toddler over the seat to what Richard assumed was the girl's nursemaid. With one more glance in his direction, she faced forward, disconnecting their shared moment, leaving Richard feeling the loss.

The service began and ended sooner than Richard realized since he had become completely lost in thought. Obviously he had gone through the motions of responding when needing to purely out of habit. The church began to empty, and Richard watched as the countess and her daughters left their pews. He was about to offer his arm to Josephine when Milton stepped forward.

"Allow me, Lady Josephine... with your permission, of course, Richard," Milton said while Josephine quickly took his arm.

"You're practically family, Milton. Of course, my brother won't object," Josephine said tossing a glance over her shoulder to Richard.

Mrs. Elford wagged a finger at her charge. "Be sure to stay where I can see you," she ordered, as the couple began to stride toward the entrance of the church. She obviously took her role as chaperon seriously. "Should I be worried?"

"He is a good friend, but that doesn't mean we allow Josephine any more freedom than what would normally be granted her," Richard replied while offering her his arm.

He watched Milton and his sister together. The two were speaking in hushed tones, and he wondered for the first time if perhaps his friend wanted more from Josephine than just being Richard's sister. Did he perhaps wish to court her? Or maybe he only considered her to be like his own sister? His friend was a good man, but perhaps too much like himself in that he knew Milton kept a mistress. That, of course, would never do in Richard's mind, and he would need to find time to speak about Milton's intentions.

Leaving the church, parishioners were gathering in various groups on the front lawn and, as Mrs. Elford went to stand near her charge who was speaking with several of Josephine's acquaintances, Richard took advantage of a rare opportunity that presented itself. The countess was standing alone under a tall oak tree.

He casually strode in her direction, even though the urge to run before someone in her family demanded her attention overwhelmed him. Instead, he took a deep breath and kept his stride steady. When he bowed before her, she offered her gloved hand, her fingertips gently sliding into his palm. Leaning down, he once more kissed the air between his mouth and her knuckles, all the while wondering how her skin would feel beneath his lips.

"Good morning, Lady Seahaven. It's a delight to see you again," Richard murmured, before he reluctantly released her hand.

"It's a beautiful day, isn't it, Lord Cranfield?" she asked in a breathy whisper.

He tried not to roll his eyes as their conversation was apparently going to be about the weather. Instead, his lips curved upward, and he swore he heard her breath hitch. "The day is as lovely as you are, my lady," he replied and watched the blush rise upon her face at his compliment.

"You are too kind, my lord," she said even as she peered around him, causing Richard to also look to see what drew her attention. "My apologies for becoming distracted with the antics of one of my younger daughter's. It's a bit trying to find a moment of privacy when you have a household of girls under your care. Sometimes they are a bit overwhelming."

Her confession startled him that she would reveal something so personal. Although he wished to stay with her, she obviously wanted to be alone. He hid his disappointment and instead tipped his hat. "Please forgive me for disturbing your solitude," Richard said bowing again before turning to leave.

She surprised him when she reached over and lightly placed her hand upon his arm. "Wait… don't go," she said before her eyes widened, "I mean… please stay if you would like to keep me company."

"You're certain? I do not wish to intrude," Richard said, all the while gazing into her incredible eyes.

Her hand trembled on his arm until she suddenly realized she still held onto him. She gazed down in apparent embarrassment before snatching her hand away. "Yes," she finally murmured before raising her eyes again to stare at him. "Please stay."

"I would be delighted," he replied with a grin. "What brings you to York? I know you are staying at Lady St. Aubyn's town house for she is well acquainted with my family."

"Rose is my cousin on my mother's side and graciously allowed myself and my girls to stay at her home while she is travelling abroad. We are hoping to give my younger stepdaughters a Season here."

"And I am here for the same reason, but for my sister."

She nodded her head. "I am certain Lady Josephine will have no issue finding enough eligible gentlemen to call upon her."

"Yes, it's my fondest hope," Richard agreed before continuing. "I would think, however, you would prefer to be taking London by storm."

She appeared uncomfortable for a moment before she regained her composure. "We preferred a smaller town. We also wish to attend the races planned in May before we return to Starbrook."

At least now he knew where she resided. "Such a loss for London but a gain for all the gentlemen residing here. Your daughters are lovely… as is their mother," he said while another smile turned up at the corners of his mouth.

"You will turn my head with such compliments, Lord Cranfield."

She blushed again, and Richard felt a sudden urge to kiss those perfect lips. Hardly the place or the time but still... how far down her exquisite neck did that blush truly go?

"A compliment that is well deserved, Lady Seahaven," he said while he watched her carefully.

"Patience," she whispered. "My name is Patience... at least when we converse alone, if you don't mind."

His eyes widened at such a bold request. He was about to respond when she gave a light laugh.

"I suppose being a countess does have its advantages, within reason, and as long as I am discreet of course." Her eyes twinkled in merriment while she waited for his answer.

"Then by all means, please call me Richard... when we are alone, that is."

"Richard." His name rolling off her lips sounded like heaven was shining down upon him.

"Patience... You do me a great honor," he replied and watched her whole face light up in delight.

A childish shriek filled the air, and Patience gave a heavy sigh when she realized it came from one of her girls.

"Duty calls, I'm afraid. I have enjoyed our stolen moment together, Richard. I won't soon forget our time here beneath this tree." She reached out her hand as though she were about to place it on his arm before she remembered herself. Clearly she would linger with him in the shade if she could.

"Nor will I, Patience," he murmured while taking in her features as if to memorize each one.

She tipped her head forward in a short nod. "Perhaps the next time we meet, my daughters will remember their manners and not put on such a public display disturbing an otherwise pleasant conversation. As usual, the responsibilities of my life take precedence over dallying the day away at my leisure."

He did his best to hide a smirk, as he could see for himself the younger girls were more than a handful. "I can only hope we can continue our conversation again at another time," he said taking her hand in his. He rubbed the back before raising it to his lips. She gasped when his mouth touched the fabric of her glove before her eyes then twinkled in delight… or was that desire? Richard hoped for the latter when he tucked her hand in the crook of his arm and escorted her to her family.

She gently held onto his arm, and shivers of desire traveled along his skin. Her nearness made him realize how right it felt to have her this close to his body. She was a countess to remember, and Richard could barely wait until their paths crossed again.

# CHAPTER 8

*York Assembly Rooms*

Patience was as excited as her daughters to be attending their first subscription ball. Barbara was also here chaperoning and had told Patience to enjoy herself. She had given her daughter a look of sheer gratitude. She wasn't sure she remembered how to just be young and carefree.

A miracle had been performed in order to get all the dresses and trim ready for the girls. Walking gowns, ball gowns, and accessories to match! Everyone had pitched in to help and now, studying Josefina, Ivy and Iris, Patience just knew they would find their match in York. They looked lovely, and their dresses could easily be changed so no one would be the wiser that the gown had been worn by one of the other sisters at a different function.

Patience continued to make her way through one room after another while she reminisced about the past several days. Patience knew none of this would have been possible without the thoughtfulness of her cousin Rose when she left letters of introductions for their arrival at her town house. And her girls… every one of them pitched in to ensure they were ready to take York by storm. In the few days they had been here, the women had taken turns in order to not overwhelm any one particular hostess. After all... the Bigglesworth women were a large group to have all in one room.

A ball! It was hard not to appear overly ecstatic about being here. Patience couldn't remember the last time she had attended a ball, but it was certainly before she became pregnant with Jane. Henry hadn't been much of a dancer and also wasn't one to spend his money on fripperies for his young wife. Considering they hadn't been married all that long, she wasn't given enough time to become acquainted with most of the *ton*.

She was perfectly well aware that she wasn't right out of the school room, but she was certainly still young enough at twenty-two to be able to have a bit of fun... within reason of course. She continued to remind herself why she was here. Her daughters came first, and Patience wasn't looking for a husband to call her own.

A pair of mesmerizing hazel eyes flashed inside her head causing her to look around the ballroom to see if Richard was in attendance. *Richard...* she had no idea she could be so bold as to ask him to call her by her given name, but there was just something about the viscount that drew her to him. She had never been one to believe in love at first sight. She had to be practical, didn't she? But when he took her hand that very first day upon their arrival in York, Patience had to admit, if only to herself, she had been stunned by their connection. She never felt with Henry the way that Richard made her feel. She could drown in his eyes and be perfectly happy to do so for the rest of her life.

*Good heavens! Where had such a thought come from?* And yet she continued to search through the faces in the crowd in every corner of each room she passed for the man who had charmed her with a gentle smile. Her heart ticked like an over wound clock when she caught a glimpse of him near the balcony doors. Broad shoulders fit perfectly in his dark jacket; his ivory waistcoat was in complete contrast to the rest of his attire that included black trousers encasing his long muscular legs. His cravat was tied in a sophisticated knot that must have had his valet fussing over it for hours. A lock of his dark brown hair fell over his forehead and Patience wanted to push those tresses back into place. He was the stuff dreams were made of and she inwardly gave a heavy sigh at the sight of such a dashing man.

Their eyes met across the room, and he gave her the briefest of nods before walking through the open doorway and out onto a terrace. It was a silent invitation and one she wanted to accept. Patience knew she shouldn't follow him, but all common sense seemed to leave where Richard was concerned. Besides, no harm could be done to meet him outside for only a few moments. Who would miss her?

Trying to keep her pace casual was harder than she thought. She skirted the outside of the dance floor making her way through the crush of people who watched on the sidelines or carried on their own conversations. She saw her girls being watched over by Barbara and she was again grateful that they were being looked after. With no further thoughts except her own personal agenda, she strode through the balcony doors and peered into the shadows to see Richard waiting for her. He held out his hand for her to take and she had a moment of hesitation, as prudence seemed the better course of action.

"Do you trust me?" His hushed baritone voice caused her to shiver in the moonlight and this had nothing to do with being cold.

"Richard… I—"

"Patience… I am asking for you to trust me," he calmly said. "Do you?"

"Yes," she answered him and she could barely make out his smile.

"Then come with me," he said before whisking her away into the night.

He seemed to know where he was going as he went down several steps and onto a garden path. She gazed back over her shoulder wondering where he was taking her.

"My girls—" she began before he interrupted her.

"We won't be gone long or go that far."

"Promise?" she whispered into the night.

"Yes. I promise. You are perfectly safe with me, my dear," he exclaimed and, true to his word, he halted near a gazebo awash in the moonlit sky. A romantic setting that caused Patience's heart to race.

"This is a lovely place, Richard, but—"

He turned her into his arms, and Patience couldn't object, not when she had been envisioning this in her dreams for the past several days. "I know this is sudden, Patience, but I've been dying to do this ever since we met," he said brushing a lock of her hair behind her ear before cupping her cheek.

She leaned into the palm of his hand. "What have you been wanting to do?" she asked hoping he wouldn't find her undesirable but also praying he would kiss her no matter that they had just met.

"This..."

She held her breath while his mouth slowly descended upon her own. At first, gentle, exploring to see just how much she might allow. A nip at her lower lip to tease her caused her gasp of surprise giving him the opening he had apparently been waiting for. His tongue dipped in to take hungry possession of her mouth, and she was more than willing to learn this new dance together.

She wasn't new to the intimacies between a couple but Richard's kiss flared into a burning flame in the pit of her stomach. Henry had never bothered with such affections, and yet, with Richard, she wanted to explore every aspect of what he could bring her. Did this make her one of those wanton women?

He deepened their kiss, and Patience wound her arms around his neck to play with the edges of his hair at his collar. His groan would have caused her to smile if she had been able to perform such a task. He brought her tight against his chest, and she could not mistake his arousal. She should have been shocked but this only made her want more of this man than he could obviously give her standing in a garden.

Whether he could read her thoughts or he just realized how entirely inappropriate their situation could become if they were found, he ended their kiss, leaving her wanting to return to his arms. He placed both hands on her cheeks, running his thumbs over them before giving her another quick kiss.

"Better than I could have ever imagined," he murmured before he bent down to place his forehead to her own.

"Was it?" she asked shaking from the experience of what almost felt like her first real kiss.

He jerked back before peering down upon her with a frown. "You didn't enjoy it?"

Her eyes widened at the thought. "Oh yes, Richard. It was wonderful!"

"I had hoped you felt something between us and I wasn't imagining our connection," he said before he scanned her features.

"I would be lying if I told you I didn't know what you were talking about, for I have felt it too," she admitted with a smile. "But, as lovely as this little interlude has been, I must return inside. I cannot risk being ostracized by Society, which would ruin the Season for my daughters."

"I understand, but I needed to have just a moment with you," he stated before holding out his arm. They began to walk side by side towards the building. "Will you save me a dance, Patience?"

"If I could, I would dance only with you for the entire evening," she replied giving his arm a gentle squeeze.

"I would be truly honored and cannot wait until we meet again. Will you be attending the al fresco party at Tyrell House?"

"Yes, the entire family plans to attend. If you are also attending, this will give me something extra special to look forward to."

"The night is still young, but I understand I will not be able to monopolize all your time. I, too, must see to my responsibilities with my sister, even though our cousin is chaperoning." He halted before leading her back up the stairs and gave her another kiss. It was far shorter than earlier, but she was happy to receive it all the same.

"I'll see you inside then," she said, reluctant to leave his side.

"And don't forget to save me a dance," he urged before raising her hand to his lips.

"I won't," she replied giving him a bright smile.

"I'll let you go in first so as not to cause suspicion."

She turned one last time to look at the man who had somehow stolen her heart. Who would have thought she would possibly find love in York? Miracles did happen.

# CHAPTER 9

Richard casually strode along the somewhat manicured lawn at the al fresco party. The owners of Tyrell House were in the process of bringing the estate back to life after years of apparent neglect. Those in attendance didn't seem to mind. But what really held Richard's interest was his conversation with the new Viscount Tyrell, John Bentley, and his cousin, Captain James Bentley, who were the driving force behind a proposed equestrian park. The two men had put on the entertainment today to gain interest in their horse training facility, along with a newly constructed practice race course. Richard was more than interested and looked forward to learning more at a future date.

Josephine was sitting with a group of friends on a blanket having luncheon, and he felt she was in good hands with Mrs. Elford sitting at a nearby table. Instead of intruding on gossiping women, he took the opportunity to wander among groups of various people, stopping on occasion to say hello to friends but, more importantly, looking for Patience and her family.

He continued forward in his quest to find one particular lady in a sea of women. Childish laughter finally caught his attention, drawing his gaze to a nearby lake. And there she was, giggling at the antics of her younger daughters who danced around the blanket she was sitting on with her toddler. What was odd, however, was seeing Milton chuckling along with them, including a few of the daughters Richard had yet to be introduced to. He lessened the distance to reach Patience, wondering if he had been wrong that Milton held some affection for his sister and instead was interested in the countess herself or one of her eligible daughters.

Milton had his back to him as Richard approached but what came next made him stop.

"I would not lie to you, Lady Seahaven," Milton confessed holding up his hands. "Richard and I were always trying to outdo one another when we were lads. One day when we were perhaps thirteen years of age, he swore he could swim to the other side of my father's lake faster than I. I tried to warn him that this particular section of the lake was shallower than the rest. With a dare for me to join him, he jumped in and slipped on the mud beneath his feet causing him to go under. He came up for air covered in mud, silt, tangled in the roots of water lilies, and dragging some of the flowers with him when he came out to the bank. To see a couple of lilies dangling from the top of his head as he emerged is a sight I have never forgotten."

Young Emma laughed, clapping her hands in delight. "He must have appeared like a rising sea monster only prettier with all those flowers!"

Richard groaned before placing a hand on Milton's shoulder. "You couldn't tell them something more flattering than that fiasco?" he inquired with a smirk.

"Can you blame me? It's one of our greatest memories from our youth," Milton exclaimed before leaning in to quietly whisper in his ear. "Besides… it was a tale more inclined for the amusement of ladies than some of our more daring escapades."

Richard cleared his throat hoping his friend's words hadn't been overheard. "And what brought this particular conversation on?" Richard asked good naturedly.

"It's my fault," Emma chimed in. "I wanted to go near the lake but

Mama said I might slip on the bank and ruin my dress. Lord Sutton said he'd share a funny story with us."

"I'd rather play in the lake. We never get to have any fun," Merrilynn chimed in.

Emma twirled around in a circle. "Not true, sister. We're here today, and I'm going to enjoy every minute of the party before Mama says we have to go home!"

Patience smiled at the girls while her toddler came and plopped herself on her lap. She gave brief introductions to the stepdaughters Richard had yet to meet before she continued. "As you can see, we can be a somewhat rambunctious group, and it was too nice a day to leave the younger children at home."

Richard nodded. "No reason why they shouldn't enjoy the outing. With the weather particularly warm for April, an al fresco party is just the thing." Were they chatting about the weather again, and this time initiated by him? He almost groaned aloud. Surely, he could think of another topic of witty conversation to amuse her besides the weather.

Milton excused himself to speak to the other young ladies on the next blanket giving Richard a small amount of privacy to have Patience all to himself.

"You look particularly lovely today, Lady Seahaven."

"Thank you, Lord Cranfield," she said bouncing the child on her lap.

Complementing her came as easily as taking his next breath, and her blush only enhanced her beauty. Dressed in a white gown, the square cut of her garment just rising above her breasts was decorated in tiny embroidered rosebuds, and he wondered if she had taken the time to sew them herself. Not that it mattered if she could sew or not… He was generally more interested in getting a woman out of her gown than into it. But the dress became her along with her matching bonnet. Was he becoming some sort of dandy? Thinking of the intricate detail of a gown would be more in line with something his friend George would consider and talk about. God forbid if Richard was becoming more like him!

As he continued to watch Patience with her daughter, Richard had a vision of his own child held in the arms of the countess. Given their kiss the other night, he knew his feelings were reciprocated no matter that they had only just met. Could this possibly be the start of something that could last a lifetime? Only time would tell. If anything, they had a friendship that was blooming right before his very eyes, and he had to admit he had missed her company since the ball. A smile came to his face as he remembered having the opportunity to have two dances with her. A waltz had kept her in his arms. A faster-paced dance kept their fingertips touching and laughter on their lips. At the time, he had wished he could have danced the night away with her. However, that would have caused a scandal.

He realized Patience was struggling to rise with a wiggly toddler balanced on her hip. Rushing over, Richard held onto her elbow until she finally stood on solid ground. She raised those glorious blue-grey eyes to him in obvious gratitude.

"My chivalrous knight coming to my rescue," she quietly said, beaming up at him with those glorious eyes before continuing, "Will you perhaps show up next on a white steed?" Her twinkling eyes told him much, and he couldn't resist the smile that turned up the corners of his mouth.

"If my lady so commands me, I will be more than happy to come to your rescue whenever you have need of me. I just so happen to have a white horse in my stables to await your pleasure."

Her laughter rang out, causing Richard's heart to swell. "I really think I'm going to have to be careful around you, my lord. You continue to turn my head with such flattery," she teased.

He leaned forward. "I would never tire of giving you the compliments you so deserve, my dearest lady," he murmured for her ears alone, before stepping back as protocol dictated.

Before she could comment, the squirming toddler made it known she no longer wished to be held by her mother. Patience put her down and before she could grab hold of her hands, the young girl wobbled over to Richard and grabbed him around his legs. His eyes widened in surprise until the little crumb crawler with curly auburn hair raised her blue eyes up to him and spoke.

"Papa up!" she demanded holding up her tiny hands for him to take.

"Jane!" Patience moaned in embarrassment, before some of her daughters all began speaking at once.

"Did she—"

"She did and—"

"Good heav—"

"We'll never live this down!"

Milton was doing everything in his power not to burst out in amusement while Richard could only stare at the little urchin who smacked his legs and repeated her demand only louder.

"Papa up!"

With one look at the horrified expression from her mother, Richard reached down to grab Jane who finally settled down once her demands had been met. Chubby hands patted him on his cheeks before a childish giggle escaped her.

"Hello, little moppet," Richard cooed to the girl, who stuck her thumb in her mouth and rested her head on his shoulder. It only took a few minutes with the Bigglesworth women whispering among themselves to realize Jane had fallen asleep in his arms.

"Lord Cranfield, I must apologize for—" Patience began but Richard quietly interrupted her.

"There is no need, Lady Seahaven. I am more than happy to become Jane's pillow for her nap."

"Perhaps, if you would be so kind, you could carry Jane to our carriage." If he had thought Patience's blush could become any deeper from his past experiences with her, then Richard was wrong. She snatched a fan attached to her wrist and began waving it before her face as though it was on fire.

"I'd be more than happy to carry her for you, my lady," Richard replied, trying to catch the woman's eyes. But she had other ideas and looked everywhere but in his direction.

Patience started to gather her belongings left on the blanket before instructing her younger daughters. "Come along, girls. You can return home with Jane and your nursemaid."

"We don't want to leave with Hannah," the girls complained in unison.

But a softly spoken warning from their mother quieted the pair down. "Do not wake your sister, girls. Now go with Hannah to our carriage."

The girls pouted, knowing their time at the party was over, and Richard did all in his power not to smirk at their attempts to change their mother's mind.

While the girls ran ahead, Richard reached over to offer his arm to Patience. Her hand trembled once she placed it into the crook of his arm. "There is no need to be embarrassed, my lady. Jane is young and the mistake is an honest one," he said quietly, although she continued to refuse to meet his eyes.

"I will never be able to face you again," she moaned causing Richard to stop his progress to her carriage.

He quickly looked to ensure they were for the most part alone. Since no one was within hearing distance, he felt no need for formalities. "Please don't say that, Patience. I would like us to continue to see one another to see if we might suit."

"I'm not sure this is a good idea, Richard," she said so calmly that he was afraid that what had started between them had already ended. "You make me forget my true purpose of being here in York. My daughters must come first before my own needs."

"Of course, you must think of your daughters, but that doesn't mean we cannot continue as before. Don't let the words of your youngest be the reason why you do not wish to see me."

"I-I need time," she choked out, and he could see she was trying not to cry.

"Then take all the time you need," Richard replied knowing he couldn't say anything more to change her mind… at least not now when her embarrassment over her daughter calling him papa was so fresh in her mind.

They reached her carriage and she turned to him. "Good day, Lord Cranfield."

"Good day, Lady Seahaven," he replied as he realized she was going to join her daughters and leave the party.

As he handed the small child into the arms of the nursemaid, he wondered if perhaps his heart was being won over not only by the countess herself but her bevy of daughters as well.

# CHAPTER 10

She was a coward. There were no other words for her to describe the past week of refusing Richard's notes so she might receive him. The bouquet of roses sitting in a crystal vase in the upper parlor taunted her as if questioning her sanity for not speaking to the man. He had done everything right in his attempts to put her at ease. But how could she ever forget the brief look that flashed in those hazel eyes when Jane had called him papa? She bit her lower lip as the memory rolled over and over again in her mind. Oh, the horror! She couldn't be with a man who didn't love her daughters.

He made up for it, of course. Watching him hold Jane protectively in his arms was one of the most beautiful things Patience had ever witnessed. Jane obviously felt comfortable enough to fall asleep on his shoulder, and who could blame her. Patience wouldn't mind being held in those magnificent strong arms again, and she had dreamed of him every night since the *incident*. She barely knew the man, and yet there was no way for her to get over the fact that, by having these unexpected feelings for Richard, she was not concentrating enough on the issue at hand. Seeing her daughters engaged to men worthy of them.

She turned her back on the blooms to gaze out the window facing the street while she tried not to chew at her fingernail. The object of her recent frustrations came out of his town house with his sister as they walked past her own house. She drew back from the window when he looked up as if to catch a glimpse of her. Was that disappointment that appeared to be briefly etched upon his brow? How handsome he appeared while he escorted Lady Josephine on their walk.

Patience knew she was being foolish, or was she? Stepping forward again, she moved back the sheer drapery in order to continue watching him until he was out of sight. Her mind wandered over the whisperings overheard during several events in York. They said he had the reputation of a renowned rake in London and currently kept a mistress. Patience was never one to base her judgement for a person because of gossip, but perhaps this was another reason why she hesitated on furthering her association with the man. Was he perhaps a bachelor only looking to take advantage of a widow? She wasn't sure her heart could take being hurt or easily dismissed if Richard's only thought was a brief carnal liaison.

She gave a heavy sigh. Nothing Richard had done had suggested the rumors were true and obviously she had let stupid tittle tattle rule her thinking where the viscount was concerned. He had been nothing but a gentleman while in her presence, and she should listen to her heart. Any concerns she may have briefly had about Richard's sincerity were unfounded, or so she hoped. Patience turned away from the image of Richard and from thoughts of their moonlit kiss.

Her eyes once more traveled to the roses that mocked her in her indecisiveness regarding the handsome gentleman. Could she honestly put aside the man for whom her heart called? Her mental struggle conflicted with her duties as head of the household. But it seemed a shame to give up on a chance at love while her own daughters searched for it themselves.

"Patience?"

Her name was called from across the room. She had been too lost in thought to keep up with the conversation going on around her. If she had bitten any harder on her lip, she would have drawn blood.

"I'm coming," she replied, as she made her way across the room to sit at the table with Doro and Chloe, who was the daughter of Henry's fourth wife by a previous marriage and so Doro's stepsister. This was the reality of her life—all three of them were twenty-two years of age, but Patience was head of this household. The two had their heads together looking at the figures Doro kept in neat columns.

"We can manage it, Patience," Doro exclaimed. "With the help of your aunt, Lady Twisden, and Chloe's brother Martin, Lord Tavistock, we'll have enough to purchase an entire garden of flowers and to pay the servers and musicians on the twenty-second of April."

Chloe smiled and reached over to take Patience's hand giving it a squeeze. "My brother was only too happy to contribute, especially since you graciously offered to allow me to be a co-hostess."

"We could never afford the hall without your brother's help along with your connections, Doro," Patience said, nodding while Mrs. Crewe carried in a tray holding a teapot and cups. Hannah followed behind with a plate of little cakes. Patience began to pour once the tray was set before her.

She took a sip of her tea, hoping the brew would calm her. "What about decorations?" she asked reaching for a sweet Doro had baked this morning. "I know between us, the kitchen will be taken care of. If you have these delightful desserts, we'll have all of Society calling at our door to find out who is baking for us."

Doro smiled. "We can have Iris and Ivy head into town to pick up what we'll need, and I'm certain they'll be more than happy to create anything to make the place our own. We'll have the day prior to the date of the ball to decorate plus the day afterwards to clean everything up."

Chloe nodded. "I'm sure we can make adjustments as needed if we forget anything."

Patience nodded. "I know I've said this more times than I can count, but honestly I could never have accomplished all this without everyone's help. You don't know how much it means to me that everyone has joined together to give Josefina, Iris, and Ivy a Season."

"They're our best chance of making a match," Doro answered

finishing her tea. "I'd best go take stock of the kitchen to see what other supplies we may need."

"I'll come with you. You can put me to work making lists." Chloe rose. She placed a hand on Patience's shoulder. "Everything will work out just fine so there's no need to worry."

"Was I worrying?" Patience asked, gazing up at the young woman before her.

Chloe gave a light giggle. "Well, the frown upon your brow tells me you're worrying about something. Honestly, Patience, everything that is meant to be will be..."

Patience smiled in response as she watched the two women leave. Of course she was worrying, but it had nothing to do with the ball and everything to do with a man whose hazel eyes haunted her every waking moment. There was something about Richard she couldn't easily dismiss, and in that exact moment she realized she didn't want to. For the first time in her entire adult life, Patience was going to think of herself and what may be with a man who made her heart sing.

Her decision made, she left the parlor to go downstairs to her bedroom. A desk sat against one of the walls and she pulled out the chair to take out paper in order to pen her note.

Forgive my foolishness.

Would you like to meet somewhere to talk?

Affectionately, P

Sealing the note with wax, Patience sent for Hannah to deliver her missive to Richard, knowing he currently wasn't at home. Hannah, bless her soul, didn't even blink but gave her a smile that looked as though she was on a mission of grave importance. Patience supposed she was, in many ways. It was a bold move on her part... asking a gentleman to meet with her, possibly alone. But there was no going back now, and all she had to do was wait for a reply upon his return home. She had the notion the waiting was going to drive her insane.

Keeping busy would restrain her from watching the clock slowly tick away. She went up to Jane's room. The little girl became excited when Patience entered. Jane was the light of Patience's life, and she picked her daughter up from her crib and tightly hugged the child to her. Placing a blanket on the floor, Patience put some wooden blocks down along with a cloth doll so they could play together.

The morning went by and faded away to early afternoon before Hannah appeared in the doorway, her eyes twinkling mischievously from the prospect of what she held in her hands. Patience was sitting in a rocking chair, Jane sleeping in her lap. Standing up, she gently placed her daughter back in her crib before turning to the nursemaid.

A smile escaped Patience when she took the note from Hannah, along with a bouquet of lilies in a lovely decorated vase. They weren't the water lilies Lord Sutton had spoken of but he had painted such a detailed picture of a young Richard that Patience suddenly relived the memory in her mind. A short snort, accompanied by a light laugh, caused a blush to rush to her face before she returned her attention to what she held in her hands. The colorful flower arrangement was a lovely reminder of an afternoon filled with promises if she had only stayed longer to enjoy his company.

Leaving her daughter's room knowing Hannah would take care of the child when she woke from her nap, Patience returned to her own bedroom to read Richard's reply in privacy. Setting the lilies on the desk so she could enjoy them, she went to sit on her bed, fluffing the pillows behind her before breaking the seal on his letter.

Dinner. My place. Tomorrow night at nine.

Yours, R

A startled gasp escaped her, but the fluttering in her chest more than spoke her feelings at what this evening might entail. There was only one reply she could give him, and she went to the desk to quickly pen her answer.

Yes!

# CHAPTER 11

Richard gazed around the drawing room wondering what he had forgotten in his attempt to create a romantic setting perfect for his countess. Candles were lit, illuminating the room in a soft glow. A small repast for two awaited only the occupants to seat themselves at the small intimate table. He thought of filling the room with flowers but realized that might be a bit much considering the number of bouquets he had been sending to the lady in the past week. He was certain the person that owned the flower shop had been more than pleased by his constant purchases.

Originally, he had planned for them to be seated in the dining room but the close proximity to the master bedroom would be even too much for him to handle. He had never wanted a woman more than he wanted Patience, but he had no intention of scaring her off. The fact she had accepted his invitation in the first place meant she had put her trust in him. He knew it was fragile, at best. He wouldn't ruin their night together or rush her into anything she wasn't ready for.

Seeing that everything was in place and only needed the lady of his musings to complete the perfect setting, he left the room to head downstairs to the ground floor. He had given the servants the night off. Josephine and their cousin were off to one of the many balls being hosted this evening. This left only Richard and his lady to enjoy the night alone together.

As he descended the last step into the inner hall, the grandfather clock chined nine. As the last bong resounded throughout his town house, the rap of the knocker on the front door could be heard. Opening the door, the light from the entryway shone upon a woman in a long blue cloak. A hood hid her face but Richard would have known this lady no matter what she was wearing. She quickly entered and Richard shut the door before the hood was removed from her head.

Patience… he took his time looking his fill while the lady unfastened the clasp at her throat. His manners kicked in when she handed him her cloak and he took the garment from her and placed it on a nearby table that of late had been filled with invitations. She took off her gloves and placed them on top of her coat before turning to gaze upon him.

He took her hands in his and for the first time felt her soft fingertips glide into his palms. He raised her hands to his lips, kissing each one before he held out his arm.

"Are you hungry?" he asked, watching her as they began to climb the stairs to the next floor.

Her look bore into his when she gazed upon him from the corner of her eyes. "For food?" she teased, causing Richard to almost trip on a step. Her eyes shined brightly while she suppressed a laugh.

"I suppose that's a good place to start," he replied when they reached the landing.

"That was probably a little too forward of me," she said softly with downcast eyes.

"I didn't mind," he replied before lifting her chin, so she had no choice but to look at him.

"Truly?"

"I want you to be yourself around me and feel comfortable enough to speak your mind. I don't mind your playful bantering. I actually find it quite refreshing."

"I would only dare to do so when we are alone."

He brushed back a lock of her hair that had fallen from her coiffure. "Then I am glad I've given the servants the night off."

He ushered her into the drawing room and her gasp of surprise made his heart rejoice, knowing she was pleased with his efforts. He had never been the romantic type, but for Patience he wanted to give her the moon if it would but make her happy.

"Richard! You shouldn't have gone to so much trouble," she whispered before stepping on the tips of her toes to place a gentle kiss on his cheek. The warmth of her breath was almost his undoing as heat radiated throughout his body.

"It was no trouble, my dear," he said holding out a chair for her.

"It's lovely."

He took the silver dome off their plates and their conversation was casual as they ate their meal. They spoke a little of their childhoods and families, of their dreams from their youths, and how their lives were far different than what they expected when they were young. She appeared somewhat reluctant to speak about her relationship with her late husband and Richard didn't push the issue. Nor did she mention her association with the new earl. He wanted the evening to go smoothly and not have any unpleasantries infringe on their time together.

With dinner over, he went to a sideboard and poured her a sherry and a brandy for himself while Patience made her way over to a couch. Arranging the skirt of her dress, she accepted the drink and took a sip. She appeared more relaxed than during dinner, and he was thankful she was letting her guard down around him. He sat down next to her, and he was pleasantly surprised when she took his hand. He raised her fingertips to his mouth giving them a brief kiss.

"You must be wondering about all my stepdaughters," she remarked after putting her glass down on the table in front of them.

"Only if you wish to speak of them. I am assuming your story has an ending that isn't exactly a pleasant one." He rubbed the back of her hand with his thumb and continued to hold her gaze.

She began giving a quick version of her husband's past marriages, ending with her own and her daughter Jane.

"I was apparently his last hope of gaining a son to inherit his title. One would have thought after all the daughters he had sired he would have known this was probably unlikely." Her attempt at a smile seared into his heart, but her tone had an edge to it, as though there was still more to her story. She took up her glass again, and he assumed she needed the liquor to continue her tale.

"Did you love him?" Where the bloody hell did that question come from?

She almost choked on the sherry. He patted her back before she set the glass down and nodded she was fine. "Love never played into my relationship with my husband. He was an end to a means. That must sound as if I was only after his money, which was not the case." She took a deep breath before turning to fully look upon him. "My father was a baker, my mother disowned from her family because they felt she married beneath her. I married Henry because I thought this would help my family. My parents convinced me this would be my way into Society."

"A dutiful daughter," Richard murmured before she continued her story.

"To be fair, Henry was indulgent with his daughters when he noticed them and was particularly fond of Josefina. He died before Jane was born, so he never knew he would sire another daughter. My parents passed away two days later from a carriage accident. In the end, there was little left of what was due me and the girls, or at least that was what I was told. Heaven only knows how Henry squandered the money before he died."

"You have had your share of misfortune for one so young." Richard frowned, wondering how this woman had been surviving. "Surely the new earl provided for you?"

"He gave me but a pittance, including what was left as a dowry for the girls once they wed." She placed her hand to her mouth as if to stop the words. He was about to tell her he didn't need to hear more when her voice burst out in embarrassment. "Good heavens! What you must think of me, baring my soul to you like this."

"I think you are incredible, Patience," he murmured giving hand a squeeze. "Please finish your story but only if you wish to do so."

She quickly composed herself, and with a nod of her head continued. "The new earl then basically threw us out of Seahaven with nothing more than the clothes we could carry. Fortunately, I inherited my parent's cottage in Starbrook after they passed. We've been living there ever since.

It was worse than he had imagined, but this only made him admire the woman before him even more. "I could make some inquires to see if the Earl has robbed you of monies to which you were entitled, or perhaps there was a hidden will. That is, if you wish it." Richard watched Patience who brought her eyes up to meet his own. He expected tears and instead he saw gratitude shining on her face.

"That is kind of you, Richard, but I want nothing from that man or his controlling wife. As far as I'm concerned, they don't exist. I look forward to the day when some situation occurs and they get their comeuppance. I won't have to do a thing to play any role in whatever fiasco comes their way, and I can just sit back and watch it happen."

A chuckle escaped him and her return smile warmed his heart. "You are truly a wonder, my lady. But how have you survived all this time since your husband's death?"

She raised her chin. "We've been capitalizing on whatever traits could earn us money, not that we've let anyone know in Society. All of my older stepdaughters have done their part to help the household. They have even sacrificed their own portion of their dowries to pool the funds together for the younger girls. Hence, our time here in York."

"And what of you? What part have you played other than being the stepmother to all these women?" he asked quietly.

"I've been baking, bread mostly, to sell in the local village," she replied honestly, before taking another sip of her sherry.

He had the vision of this lady rising from her slumber before the day had even begun and he was certain he wasn't wrong in his assumption. "What a brave woman you are, Patience." He ran the back of his fingers down her cheek.

"I've had to become a survivor, Richard. I would do anything for my girls."

"I applaud your devotion to your family, my dear. But still… what of yourself?"

Her brow rose at his question. "Whatever do you mean?"

"What do you desire for yourself, Patience?" He watched her eyes widen at his husky tone.

She watched him intently before a small smile graced her lips. "I suppose I want what every woman wants… to find someone to love. Someone who can help erase past memories that are unpleasant and build a bright future together in a loving household. However, not many men would like to marry a woman who has so many mouths to feed."

"Surely you do not think I am one of those men?"

She tilted her head while she studied him before her warm smile gave him her answer. "I wouldn't be here, Richard, if I thought you were."

His heart swelled at her words and there was only one thing he could do after she had confessed her deepest thoughts. He kissed her as she was meant to be kissed. Lovingly. Gently. And as she became folded into his arms, he had the notion of never letting her go.

Any thoughts of where the night might proceed left him, but he gave himself into this one moment together as he deepened their kiss. It was a beginning and a promise of what was to come. The start of building on a relationship he knew in his heart could last them a lifetime.

By the time he had thoroughly kissed the woman he was growing to love, the grandfather clock chimed in the downstairs entryway, telling him he needed to let her go home. His sister would be returning soon and he didn't want Patience to be found here alone. Her disappointment when he escorted her down to the floor below was written all over her face. She wanted more… as did he.

But he respected her enough that he would not take her to his bed this night even while a part of him warred with his mind. They would have plenty of time to grow their relationship, and Richard looked forward to the coming days where he could spend more time with his lovely countess.

## CHAPTER 12

For days, Patience felt as though she had been walking on air. Her step was lighter and she was happier than she ever remembered. There was only one person who was the cause for her sudden change from her every day normal and boring routine, and that was Richard. He brought her out of the gloom that had become her life and gave her hope for a future together.

But she had no time to contemplate the man who had filled her every waking hour, or dreams for that matter. Not with the ball she was hosting with her aunt, stepdaughters and Chloe about to begin. She was certain they had forgotten something, but for the life of her she couldn't think of any detail that had been left out from their efforts.

Everything appeared in place, and Patience was proud of the work her family had done to decorate Smithson's Assembly Room. The girls had created lovely favors in the form of tiny birds in a rainbow of colors that graced the round supper tables. The twins' trompe l'oeil on fabric stretched across the back wall, transforming it into a window on an Italianate garden. The ballroom floor gleamed from a recent polish of wax giving off the appearance of a golden glow. Boughs decorated with camellia blossoms had been brought in from the garden and were placed in various places adding to the beauty of the place. The musicians had arrived and were in the upper gallery tuning their instruments. White candles hung from the chandeliers as footmen came to light them. Yes… the place looked marvelous and only awaited their guests to fill the rooms for the evening.

Satisfied that all was ready, Patience went upstairs to a room reserved for her daughters to get dressed. Before she even came to the door, she could hear their laughter. It was an exciting time for all of them, and one they had been waiting on for several months. Patience could only pray that all their efforts would result in possible engagements.

Opening the door, Patience eyes began to water when she saw all her lovely daughters dressed in their finest. Susana had indeed performed a miracle with her sewing talents and no one would have guessed these dresses had previously been worn. Even Bess had taken a break from her translations in order to enjoy the evening. The Bigglesworth women were going to be the center of attention tonight, if the view before her was any indication.

Patience wiped a tear from her eye before she clapped her hands to get everyone's attention. "You all look lovely tonight and I couldn't be prouder of each and every one of you."

"Have the guests begun to arrive?" Barbara asked while putting on her gloves.

"The footmen are lighting the candles as we speak so we should be in our places downstairs when the first carriage arrives. The younger girls can head into the ballroom. Aunt Honoria, Bess, Susana, Lord Tavistock, and I will stand in the receiving line," Patience said, smiling in anticipation for the night to begin. She took another glance at her girls and they were all impeccably attired.

Ivy placed a fan around her wrist that would also act as a dance card. "I'm so excited. Just think, our first ball that we are actually hosting!"

Her twin looped her arm through her sisters as they headed out the door. "I can barely wait for a dance with a certain Captain," Iris was heard to say before disappearing down the hallway.

Patience noticed Josefina's eyes sparkled in delight but it was her smile that made her stepdaughter appear even more lovely than she usually did. She strode over to the girl and took her hand. "Is everything alright, dearest?" she asked wondering what secret the girl held to herself.

Josefina kissed her cheek. "Everything is… perfect."

The rest of the women began to leave the room leaving herself and Chloe alone. Patience went to a full-length mirror and checked her gown. The blue muslin gown brought out the color of her eyes and she pondered if a certain gentleman would agree with her.

Chloe picked up her fan. "Do you think it will work?" she asked waiting for Patience's reply.

With one last glance in the mirror, she took a deep breath before turning around. "Let's find out."

What followed was an interminable amount of time in a receiving line, greeting her guests. Invitations had been sent out to anyone in York of any importance and the faces became a blur as people continued to enter the Assembly Room. That was until *he* entered, and Patience was certain the world had stopped spinning on its axis.

It was hard for her to ignore the man who made her heart hammer in her chest with just one look from those brilliant hazel eyes. He took in her appearance while observing her from afar before the corner of his mouth lifted up into a small roguish grin. He was speaking with Lady Josephine but he continued to sneak peaks at Patience. Richard appeared impatient for his turn to be presented to her, and she shared the sentiment.

Were her emotions just as transparent as the feelings she detected flashing across Richard's face as he drew near? Adoration… happiness… and most of all, did she envision love reflected in his features? Or was it just desire to finish what they had started one night? She could no longer deny Richard awoke a passion in her that had been dormant her entire life. Was it truly possible she was in love with the man, although she had yet to speak the words aloud?

And then he was before her, bowing over her hand, his mouth respectfully hovering over her fingertips when all she wanted to do was throw herself into his arms. A few short pleasantries were murmured before he whisked his sister away, and Patience immediately felt his loss. She was certain she wouldn't recuperate until she was once more in his presence. Yes... this must be what the poets called love. It couldn't be anything less.

As one of the hostesses for the ball, Patience was kept busy for the majority of the evening. The dancing had begun, but she had yet to have the opportunity to enjoy the music. She had finally found a moment to sit down, and she wished she could take off her shoes to give them some relief. But all that changed when a certain gentleman made his way across the room in a determined stride.

Richard had sought her out, holding his hand out for her to take. His silent request to dance with her was answered when she lightly placed her fingertips into the palm of his hand. He led her to the ballroom. The music for a waltz began, and Richard put his hand at the back of her waist. She almost sighed aloud when tingling sensations rushed throughout her body. She was never going to make it through the dance let alone what was left of the evening with his continual perusal of her whenever they were in the same room.

"I couldn't wait any longer to have you in my embrace," Richard murmured in that seductive tone that would make any woman swoon. She stumbled at his words because they echoed her own sentiments. He quickly covered for her blunder and pulled her slightly closer into his arms. "Steady, my lady. I have you now."

"If you only knew how much I would like to have a private moment with you." Her hushed reply caused another wicked grin to spread across his mouth making Patience eager for his kiss.

"I feared if I didn't take the opportunity to dance with you now, your ball would be over, and I would lose my chance. Perhaps we can talk in a while when this crush begins to disperse for the evening," he said hopefully before he whirled her around causing her to become light headed.

"I would like that very much." She smiled into those mesmerizing hazel eyes and decided to enjoy this moment together while it lasted.

The dance continued, but Richard's features suddenly changed and not for the better. One moment he appeared completely at ease, and the next Patience swore his complexion paled before a muscle in his jaw started to tick. His eyes narrowed while peering across the room, and Patience attempted to see what had angered him.

"What's wrong, Richard," she asked nervously before he composed himself by looking into her eyes. But something had happened for he didn't appear as carefree as he had but moments before.

"It's nothing." His short sharp retort said otherwise, but she wasn't allowed to comment further. The dance ended. He bowed politely. She curtsied in return and, with a brief , he abruptly left her side without another word.

Patience was unsure if she should follow him or not, but she certainly was going to find out what in the world just happened to her perfect evening that suddenly was anything but!

# CHAPTER 13

Richard left the dance floor with barely a word to Patience. Nostrils flaring, he clenched his hands into fists at his side when he went from room to room searching for someone who shouldn't be here. How the devil was it possible *she* was here? He knew damn well she hadn't been invited.

A flash of her green muslin gown caught has attention as she rounded the stairs and he followed behind at a slower pace. His attempts to appear casual warred with his urge to rush up the steps to confront her. Peering into one room after another he finally found her as though she had posed specifically to gain his attention near a window, the backlight from the candles casting her in a soft glow. She was the complete opposite of the woman he had just left—darkness to the light that was all Patience. But none of that mattered at the moment. He crossed the space between them and grabbed her arm.

"What the hell are you doing here, Penelope?" he hissed. His cold glare should have been a warning, but her eyes glazed over with need and desire. He had seen that look before. She was in a temper and was out to prove whatever point she planned to make. Another reason he no longer kept her as his mistress.

"Richard, darling… I thought you would be happy to see me," she purred before rubbing her hand along the edges of his jacket. "How handsome you are this evening. I've never seen you look better."

He threw his hands up and backed away from her. Running his fingers along the back of his neck, he made another attempt to figure out what his ex-mistress wanted. "You didn't answer me. Why are you here in York… at this ball?"

She came over to him and, before he could stop her, she brushed her fingertips across his brow. "You really shouldn't frown, darling. You'll get wrinkles before your time."

"I won't ask you again, Penelope." He wanted her out of here before the situation got out of hand.

She went back toward the window to move the drapery as if there was something of importance she needed to see. But Richard knew this was just another ploy to keep him in her presence longer. "I would think you would know why I'm here, my love. I want to win you back. I knew if I could just see you again, I could convince you we belong together," she replied with a wave of her hand.

"I can't believe you actually think showing up at a Society ball would suddenly change my mind," he growled before pinching the bridge of his nose in frustration.

"Why not? Cannot I rival any woman who is below?" Her eyes narrowed before she once more came forward. "Unless…"

"Unless, what?"

She inspected her nails for a moment before she took hold of his jacket and pulled bringing them chest to chest. She yanked so hard, he steadied himself by grabbing hold of her waist. "Unless you think that young little miss you were dancing with could actually replace me? As if anyone could take my place in your heart." She wound her arm around his neck and gave him a coy smile.

"Richard?" A voice from the doorway broke them apart, but it was the stricken look in Patience's eyes that was Richard's undoing.

"Oh, there is the dear child now," Penelope sneered in contempt.

"Shut up, Penelope," Richard warned, but it was no use. Penelope was here for revenge, and she apparently wanted to take it out on the innocent woman with tears running down her cheeks.

"Who is this woman, Richard?" Patience asked with a trembling voice.

"No one," he replied before a shrill snigger left Penelope.

Penelope's eyes narrowed when she returned her attention to him. "Really, Richard? I've been *someone* for many years and you know it. Tell this lady who I am."

The color drained from Patience's face and he could not erase the betrayal that flashed in her eyes. "You may address me as Countess Seahaven," she said angrily. Her chin rose in defiance.

"Countess? Richard, you really are moving up in the world. What would a countess ever want with a mere viscount? It just isn't done, my dear."

"I told you to shut up, Penelope," he snapped, but that was when the woman drove her dagger home, aimed directly at Patience's tender heart.

"You have a lot to learn in the ways of men if you think he would ever propose to you, my lady. Richard is more of a rake than husband material. I should know, having been in his bed for the past several years."

A sob escaped Patience and she stumbled backwards in disbelief. Their eyes met briefly before she quickly turned and fled down the hall. With no further thoughts of Penelope, he ran to follow Patience, but he was too late when she ran into a room, slammed the door, and the lock clicked into place.

"Patience! Open the door," he demanded without success.

"Leave me alone, Richard," she cried out. "I never want to see you again."

"Please listen to reason," he attempted again resting his forehead on the wooden door that kept him from the woman who owned his heart.

"I have nothing to say to you."

He knew she had moved deeper into the room only because her crying sounded farther away. He swore, knowing there was nothing he could do to redeem himself if the lady wouldn't give him a minute to explain.

He returned downstairs to find Penelope waiting for him.

"Upset with you, is she? How will she feel when she sees me again and again around town? Do you think she will forgive you?"

"Why are you doing this, Penelope? You know it is over between us. What do you want from me? Because I will tell you now, if you hurt Lady Seahaven, I will make sure you live to regret it."

"Give me one thousand pounds, and I will go away," Penelope replied, without hesitation. "I have a chance in America, a man who will marry me, but we need a nest egg to make a fresh start." She tossed her head as though she knew she would get what she desired from him if it meant she would be out of his life for good.

"So, you decided to put on this little display to force my hand? You would have been better to ask me. I might have given you additional money for old time's sake. Have I ever treated you unfairly?" His voice rose when his anger got the better of him.

"That is hardly the point, Richard," she said. "I just need—"

"Go away, Penelope. I never want to see you again. If you've already gone through the settlement I left you, then that's your problem. You'll get nothing more from me." He left her in the entryway sputtering her displeasure.

Richard fumed at the gall of his ex-mistress, but he could not change the damage she had done. There was nothing to keep his interest in the ball now that Patience was no longer in attendance. His sister noticed him by the doorway to the ballroom and made her way to him.

"Can we go home?" she asked, a worried frown marred her brow. She appeared as if she was on the verge of tears.

"What's happened?" God forbid another catastrophe was in the making.

"I just want to leave. Is there anything wrong with that?"

"We're at a ball, and you were enjoying yourself, earlier. If I recall, you were happily dancing with Milton. Where is he?"

"Who cares! I want to go home, Richard. Now." Her raised voice caused several nearby couples to turn in their direction.

He watched her suspiciously wondering what happened. "Do I need to call Milton out?"

Her eyes widened before tears pooled in their depths. "No. We had a falling out. Now, can you please take me home?"

"Of course." He took her arm and escorted her from the Assembly room.

But as their carriage was brought around, he swore he caught the briefest glimpse of Patience staring at him from one of the upper windows. How was he ever going to make this up to her when Penelope had ruined an evening for Patience that should have been a happy memory?

# CHAPTER 14

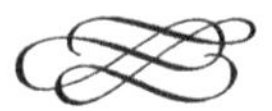

In all things that *really* mattered, her daughters, the ball had been a great success. For days, flowers and invitations had been sent to the town house until you couldn't enter any one particular room without the smell of one floral arrangement after another. Patience was happy for them, truly she was, and yet for her the ball had become a grim reminder that love would seemingly pass her by.

She could relive that horrid moment a thousand times, and everything would still be filled with the shock of it all. She had sworn time had stood still as she swayed on her feet at the audacity of the woman who apparently had been Richard's mistress. The fact the woman had showed up uninvited at *her* ball, only fueled her anger. Well... only after a lot of fallen tears.

But facts were facts, at least as far as Patience and her broken heart was concerned. Her world had turned upside down the moment she decided to follow Richard up those blasted stairs. A dark sickening grief had consumed her seeing another woman in his arms. Yet in many ways, perhaps this was for the best. She would be feeling more hurt than she was now if she had given herself to him that night at his town house. His betrayal would have then stung far worse than the bitterness now surrounding her heart leaving her feeling completely empty.

She had refused to see him even though Barbara and Doro told her to hear him out. They had been supportive when Patience confided in them and it had meant the world to her. But she still couldn't do it. She needed time to process what had happened and eventually she would most likely see for herself a vengeful woman who only meant to hurt a man by any means possible. Clearly the female wanted him back.

If she thought about it hard enough, she would forgive him instead of letting that woman unknowingly win by splitting them apart. So why couldn't she face Richard? Patience didn't have any answer. Consumed with self-pity and unable to take that first step toward reconciliation, she did the one thing to take her mind off her troubles. She baked.

Kneading the dough became a sort of therapy while she took out her frustrations by punching the ball over and over again before breaking it down into individual loaves to rise. She hadn't realized she had made so much until she ran out of tins to bake them in. They would never eat it all before it spoiled.

She decided to take the extra loaves to a local merchant who had been friends with her mother and father. Upon their arrival in York, this woman had recognized Patience, assured her that her secret was safe, but also said that if Patience inherited her parents' skill, the merchant would be willing to sell any baked items she could supply.

Which brought Patience back to the present, walking down a fourteenth-century cobblestone street in an area called The Shambles. The hood of her cape thrown over her head, she held her basket covered in a towel in front of her like a shield while making her way through this seedier side of town. She kept her head low in her attempt to not draw attention to herself until she looked up to get her bearings. A gasp escaped her when she immediately saw Richard riding a white horse.

Their eyes met, and a scowl crossed his features before he put his heel to the horse's side to pick up the pace to get to her quickly. She panicked and ran in the opposite direction, quickly ducking into an alleyway. Her back to the stone building, her chest heaved in an attempt to fill her lungs with much needed air. Her day had been bad enough, but it was about to get a whole lot worse.

" Eeup, look at this, lads. She's a fine un." A crude voice echoed between the buildings, and Patience gulped when several men stepped forward.

"A real lady, she be," another said.

"Naw! No lady would be showin' her face on this side of town." He smacked his lips before drawing closer inspecting her from head to toe. "How much for a tumble, girlie?"

She was trapped. Hands began to claw at her. "Get off me!" she hissed attempting to use the basket as some sort of useless weapon.

"Maybe she likes it rough," the first man grinned with her efforts to slap their hands away as the basket went flying.

"Who wants a go at her first?"

Her mind racing and eyes wide in fright, she screamed out for the only person who could save her. "*Richard!*"

"That's not me name, but thee can call me anything thee wish, doll." One came closer, reaching beneath her cloak to tear at the bodice of her gown. She let out another blood curdling scream while they all came at her at once. A gunshot exploded into the air, and the men stopped their attempts to ravage her.

Richard sat on his horse carefully reloading his pistol before he aimed it at her tormentors. "Put one more hand on the lady and the next bullet won't be in the air."

The men scattered like ants, leaving Patience mortified at what almost happened to her. Pulling her cloak around her to cover her ruined gown, she chanced a glance at the man who had come to her rescue like a knight in shining armor… white horse and all!

He dismounted, and yet his displeasure at seeing her in such condition only made things worse.

"What the bloody hell are you doing in this part of town, Patience?" he growled at her like some wounded animal.

She sucked in a sharp breath of disbelief at the nerve of him to chastise her after what almost happened to her. "I was almost attacked and you're going to berate me while going about an errand?"

"Yes!" he fumed. "That's what servants are for."

She straightened her posture to glare at him. "As you may, or may not be aware or perhaps forgot, I have limited staff to run my household. Not that it's any of your business." She looked around on the ground to see her basket, the loaves of bread now useless as they were strewn in every direction. She picked up the wicker hamper and made to whisk past him. He grabbed her arm, halting her progress to leave.

"Where do you think you're going?" he demanded while drawing in slow steady breaths as if to calm his unsuppressed anger.

"Where do you think? I'm going home!"

"Not without an escort."

"I don't need you to take me home, Richard." Her voice betrayed her as did her heart while he continued to hold her arm.

He guided her to his horse before cupping his hands to help her mount. She stood staring at him as if he had lost his mind. They couldn't be seen together on a horse!

She shook her head. "I don't think so."

His head cocked to one side before his eyes widened apparently in disbelief she would dare to disobey him. "Get on the damn horse, Patience."

Her chin rose defiantly. "No."

He swore before taking her about the waist and lifting her into the saddle. He put his foot in the stirrup and swung up behind her. The feel of the entire length of his firm muscular body against her back made her stiffen.

"What are you doing?" she barely managed to whisper when he reached around her to take up the leather reins.

"What does it look like? I'm taking you home and I don't want to hear another word of protest from those beautiful lips of yours," he warned, but the softer tone caused a moment of pleasure to rush through her. He could in no way conceal his concern for her welfare.

Before she could make any sort of protest, he kicked his heels into the horse's side and the steed took off in a trot. Every bump brought her into his hard chest reminding her of what she had almost had. Love… if only she had given it a further chance to bloom.

They rode in silence for several minutes before his gentle voice finally spoke. "Are you hurt?"

It took her a few minutes to decide on how to answer him, knowing if anything she needed to offer her gratitude from saving her from the worse possible situation a woman could find herself in. "From what those men did? Nothing that can't be repaired. Thank you for coming to my aid."

"You're welcome." He pulled on the reins bringing her closer when a dog ran in front of the horse. "And the other night? Will you let me explain?"

She nervously bit her lip before slightly turning her head, so she could glance into his face. She could see for herself the anguish he attempted to conceal, hidden just beneath the surface. She had asked this of him once… she would need to ask him for what she needed again. "I need time, Richard."

He nodded his head, and she returned her attention to what lay before them. "Take all the time you need, Patience. I'm not going anywhere."

He may not be going anywhere, but Patience knew her time in York was coming to an end. Still, his vow filled her heart with possibilities. Yet there was still some small bit inside her that wasn't sure if she could trust him. If he could give her time, then she would take what he offered in order for her heart to mend.

# CHAPTER 15

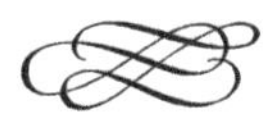

Richard's carriage made its way through the muddy streets of Starbrook. The rain continued to pour down from the skies and mirrored his mood of late. He knew he had told Patience he would give her all the time she needed to overcome the diabolical fiasco Penelope created, but how could he make amends if the woman he loved was no longer in York?

April had turned into May. Penelope must have taken him seriously, because he didn't see her again. Other than when he rescued the countess, he didn't see her, either, except for one day at the races. He wanted to run to her side, but when he happened to catch her glance, a simple shake of her head told him more than any words she could have spoken. She still wasn't ready.

With the Season over, even Josephine's chances of finding a match had dwindled to nothing giving Richard the impression she cared more for his friend Milton than she let on. He would need to talk to him and soon. In the meantime, he had made arrangements for his cousin to return to London with them and Josephine would now reside under his roof. There was no way he would allow his sister to remain in the toxic environment revolving around their parents.

Which brought him back to his mission to see Patience after

Josephine all but begged him to seek the lady out. It could be a mistake, but he was tired of waiting. He needed an answer as to her feelings for him. If she wished to no longer see him, then so be it. He would move on… as if he could.

The carriage left the village and the driver soon pulled up to a two-story cottage that had seen better days. Even with the rain pelting down, it was hard to imagine what didn't need to be repaired with the place Patience called home. He hated to think what the cottage appeared like on a sunny day. He let himself out before the footman could put the step down and quickly ran up the walkway to raise the knocker.

Lady Emma opened the door before he had the chance to knock a second time. Her bright smile welcomed him into her home. "I'm so pleased you are here, Lord Cranfield," she said waving him inside. A puddle formed beneath his feet confirming how hard it was raining before a woman he assumed was their housekeeper came and took his hat and coat.

"Is your mother available?" he asked. He raised his eyes as two of Patience's stepdaughters were poised on the stairs along with another who came from the front parlor with her gentleman caller. Shock at seeing him here was mirrored on their faces.

"Perhaps you can talk some sense into mama," Emma exclaimed with a heavy sigh.

"Emma!" Several of the sisters said her name at the same time before she gave them all a stern look and stomped her foot. For a twelve-year old it was something to behold.

"Someone needs to, and she refuses to listen to any of us," she argued tugging on his arm.

"Where is she?" he inquired as he followed her toward the back of the cottage.

"Standing in the middle of our garden. I suppose we should ask Mrs. Crewe to return your hat and coat before you go back out into the rain."

"Don't bother. How long has she been outside?" He shook his head sadly.

"Seems like hours," Emma sadly replied. "You will convince her to come inside, won't you, my lord?"

He looked down into the young girl's green eyes and gave her a convincing smile. "I will."

Satisfied, Emma nodded and pointed to the door. "You'll find her out there."

Richard didn't hesitate and opened the door Emma had pointed to. Patience's stepdaughter wasn't wrong. The countess stood in the middle of the garden soaking wet, and he could see her shivering from here. Eyes closed, her head was bent back as if the heavens held all her answers, but none were forthcoming. He took several steps forward before he stopped not knowing if he would be welcome or not.

"Patience." Her name escaped his lips with a yearning he had been holding inside for a month since he had last spoken to her. Her head came forward and she gave a heavy sigh before she opened her blue-grey eyes and turned slightly towards him.

"Richard." The sound of his name filled the missing void that had been barely holding him together. He took another step closer, pulled off his jacket, and placed the garment around her shoulders.

"What are you doing standing out here in the rain?" he asked quietly before extending his hand wondering if she would take it. When her cold fingertips traced his own, he took hold of them bringing them to his lips.

"Pondering life's mysteries?" she declared teasingly.

Her red-rimmed eyes couldn't mask the fact she was upset. "You've been crying."

She offered him a slight tilt of a smile before she lowered her eyes nodding towards the cottage. "They can't see my tears out here in the rain," she confessed. "I never expected to see you in Starbrook, Richard."

"I hope you're glad I'm here," he said waiting hopefully for her reply.

She turned to face him. "I am."

"Patience, I can't tell you how sorry I am about what happened at the ball," he began before she placed her fingertips on his lips to silence him.

"And I am sorry I didn't give you time to explain while I was still in York. I suppose it was silly of me. Here I am, a countess, and you would think I would be more worldly and handle things differently when a vengeful woman wants to claim she holds the heart of a man who clearly wants nothing to do with her." Her smile reached her eyes, and he was thankful she had come to her own conclusion.

"I never loved Penelope, and she never loved me, Patience. She pulled that stunt wanting more money than I had already given her when I ended our agreement before I ever came to York. There is only one woman who has ever held my heart, Patience, and that lady is you."

She nodded as the droplets of water continued to rain down upon them. "And you have owned mine from the very moment we touched. I never thought love at first sight could happen until it happened with you. I thought I had lost you through my foolishness in not letting you explain."

"You never lost me, Patience. You asked for time, and I could do nothing else but give you whatever time you needed to decide our fate. But I couldn't stay away any longer, and this is why I'm standing here with you now."

"You never gave up on me," she murmured looking at him with hopeful eyes.

"Never!" He brought her into his arms and leaned down to press his forehead onto hers. "Can you forgive me so we might start again?"

"Only if you can forgive me for not giving you a chance to explain the situation yourself."

"I never want anything to come between us again. Forgive me," he insisted taking her hand and placing a kiss on the inside of her wrist.

Her free hand cupped his cheek. "Richard… surely you know there is nothing to forgive. I love you, and I hope you can—

"I love you too, Patience," he finished before bending down to seal their love with a kiss. It was shorter than he would have liked, but he could feel Patience trembling from the cold. "Now, let's get you inside before you become ill."

He hugged her to him, and as they turned toward the cottage, the windows were filled with the smiling faces of her stepdaughters. Patience waved, and they returned her gesture. Laughter escaped her, and he chuckled as well to join in her merriment.

Patience would always be his countess to remember for the rest of his days. He had found the love of a good woman, and now he knew that love was returned. And as he walked toward his future with Patience at his side, he knew that she and her daughters would all become the family he had always wanted. Life with her was going to be heavenly, and Richard would do anything to ensure she never wanted for anything but the love they had found together.

# EPILOGUE

*London, England, One Year Later*

Her London house was filled to the brim with family and friends who had come to see the new baby held lovingly in Patience's arms and to witness the baptism. She only wished her parents yet lived to see their second grandchild. Richard, bless his heart, had seen to the much-needed repairs to the cottage, and it now appeared how Patience remembered it from her youth.

Her gaze travelled around the room, and a smile swept her face while she fondly looked upon her stepdaughters and the gentlemen they had fallen in love with. Happiness filled Patience's heart with joy with the knowledge that they, too, had found men who were worthy of them. York had certainly been a magnificent success, for they had all found their hearts desire and a love to last them a lifetime.

Richard's friends stood in a corner grouped together with a glass of brandy in their hands. Two were married and their wives, Lady Beacham and Lady Osgood gave winks of conspiracy to the remaining bachelors in the group. Patience had learned from Richard the women were on a mission to see them all wed. Patience had no doubt they would succeed.

Patience had taken on the title of Viscountess after a heated discussion with her at the time soon-to-be husband. He thought she should keep her original title, but the title of countess never meant as much to her as did taking on Richard's title. Love… it explained so much and could change everything. He had stopped arguing his point, but Patience knew he was happy with her decision. They had quietly married with their family and friends in attendance last year.

The whispering between Emma and Merry grew louder before Emma gave her sister a nudge. Merry got up off the floor and came over to her mother. Peering at the infant snuggled in a blue blanket fast asleep, she wrinkled her nose. "Whatever are we to do with a *boy*, Mama?"

The room became silent before everyone began to laugh. Patience put her free arm around her stepdaughter. "We will love him just as much as we love one another, sweetling."

"But he's a boy, Mama," she repeated, clearly not impressed at her new sibling. "He's not going to want to play dolls with us."

Richard, who sat in a chair on the other side of his wife, choked back his amusement and covered his mouth with his hand. Merry turned her face toward him. "I am certain we will think of something we can all do together when he gets older… as a family."

"If you say so, Papa," Merry replied with a shrug. She went back to sit on the floor with Emma and Jane to take up the dolls they had been playing with.

Patience gazed up at her husband. "Good answer."

He kissed her forehead before taking a finger to slightly pull the blanket to look more closely at his child. "Have I told you thank you for our son, my love?" he whispered in her ear causing Patience to shiver in delight.

"Many times, my lord," she returned with a brilliant smile. A yawn suddenly escaped her, and her eyes widened. "Oh dear, I guess I'm more tired than I thought."

Lady Osgood stepped forward. "Here… let me take him. It's been a while since I've held a little one."

Patience handed her son over. "Thank you, Lady Osgood."

"You must call me Constance. After all, our men are good friends, and I know we shall become the same," she replied before taking the baby over to Lady Beacham, who Patience knew would also ask her to call her by her given name, Margaret.

Richard helped her rise from the chair and gave their excuses so he could see Patience to their room for a much-needed nap. He waved off her maid, telling the girl he would see to his wife's needs before closing their bedroom door. With her gown removed, he pulled back the covers and tucked Patience inside. She gave a heavenly sigh, but as he turned to leave she tugged at his hand.

"Stay with me until I fall asleep," she urged.

He lay down beside her on top of the covers knowing he still had guests to see to. Still, he pulled her close to him. "I love you, my darling wife."

"As I love you, my dearest husband," she replied before she gave another yawn.

"Watch for me in your dreams," he whispered before kissing the back of her head.

"I always dream of you… my handsome knight who came to my rescue," Patience replied before closing her eyes.

His arms held her closely and happiness once again swelled around her heart and soul. Yes… Richard had rescued them all in more ways than Patience could ever imagine. Love had found her at first sight, and she was grateful to the man who fulfilled all of her wildest dreams. They had a bright future to look forward to, and she couldn't wait to see what their lives together could bring. She was dearly loved, along with her daughters, and life with Richard and her family had made her complete.

THE END

Richard Cranfield made his first appearance as a secondary character in my Regency novellas, *Under the Mistletoe* and *A Second Chance at*

*Love*. Now it was time for him to get his happily-ever-after story and Patience, Lady Seahaven was just the heroine he needed. I look forward to writing Milton and George's stories in the future. You can learn more about my other Regency, medieval, and time travel stories on my website at https://www.sherryewing.com/books.

# SOCIAL MEDIA FOR SHERRY EWING

You can learn more about Sherry Ewing at these social media links:

**Amazon Author Page:** http://amzn.to/1TrWtoy
**Bookbub:** www.bookbub.com/authors/sherry-ewing
**Facebook:** www.Facebook.com/SherryEwingAuthor
**Goodreads:** www.Goodreads.com/author/show/8382315.Sherry_Ewing
**Instagram:** https://instagram.com/sherry.ewing
**Pinterest:** www.Pinterest.com/SherryLEwing
**TikTok:** https://www.tiktok.com/@sherryewingauthor
**Twitter:** www.Twitter.com/Sherry_Ewing
**YouTube:** http://www.youtube.com/SherryEwingauthor
**Newsletter Sign Up:** http://bit.ly/2vGrqQM
**Facebook Street Team:** www.facebook.com/groups/799623313455472/
**Facebook Official Fan page:** https://www.facebook.com/groups/356905935241836/

# ABOUT SHERRY EWING

Sherry Ewing picked up her first historical romance when she was a teenager and has been hooked ever since. A bestselling author, she writes historical and time travel romances to awaken the soul one heart at a time. When not writing, she can be found in the San Francisco area at her day job as an Information Technology Specialist.

*Learn more about Sherry at:*
Website: www.SherryEwing.com
Email: Sherry@SherryEwing.com

# THE BELLES WOULD LIKE YOUR HELP!

Book reviews help readers to find books, and authors to find readers. Please consider writing a review for ***Desperate Daughters***, even a couple of sentences telling people what you liked (or didn't like) about the stories. Reviews can be posted on BookBub, Goodreads and on most eRetailers websites. For links to this book on those sites, see the *Desperate Daughters* page on the Belles' website: https://bluestockingbelles.net/belles-joint-projects/desperate-daughters/

**Malala Fund**

The Bluestocking Belles have chosen the Malala Fund as the charity they support, and to which they donate some of their royalties. Periodically, they take on projects intended to directly support this cause, which exemplifies their personal values and intentions: the right of girls and women to do whatever they choose with their lives.

**How can you help?**

Make a donation to our Team Page at https://www.classy.org/team/89502

# OTHER BOOKS BY THE BLUESTOCKING BELLES

Find buy links and story blurbs for all the following books on our website at https://bluestockingbelles.net/belles-joint-projects/

***The Bluestocking Belles donate a portion of the proceeds to benefit the Malala Fund.***

***Storm & Shelter (2021)***

When a storm blows off the North Sea and slams into the village of Fenwick on Sea, the villagers prepare for the inevitable: shipwreck, flood, land slips, and stranded travelers. The Queen's Barque Inn quickly fills with the injured, the devious, and the lonely—lords, ladies, and simple folk; spies, pirates, and smugglers all trapped together. Intrigue crackles through the village, and passion lights up the hotel.

One storm, eight authors, eight heartwarming novellas.

***Holiday Escapes (2020)***

Holidays, relatives, pressure to marry—sometimes it is all too much. Is it any wonder a woman may need to escape? The heroines in this collection of stories aren't afraid to take matters into their own hands when they've had enough.

These stories are republished here at 20% of the cost of collecting them all from each individual author.

Two bonus short stories round out the collection.

***Fire & Frost (2020)***

**In a winter so cold the Thames freezes over, five couples venture onto the ice in pursuit of love to warm their hearts.**

Love unexpected, rekindled, or brand new—even one that's a whack on the side of the head—heats up the frigid winter. After weeks of fog and cold, all five stories converge on the ice at the 1814 Frost Fair when the ladies' campaign to help the wounded and unemployed veterans of the Napoleonic wars culminates in a charity auction that shocks the high sticklers of the ton.

In their 2020 collection, join the Bluestocking Belles and their heroes and heroines as The Ladies' Society For The Care of the Widows and Orphans of Fallen Heroes and the Children of Wounded Veterans pursues justice, charity, and soul-searing romance.

***Valentine's From Bath (2019)***

The Master of Ceremonies announces a great ball to be held on Valentine's Day in the Upper Assembly Rooms of Bath.

Ladies of the highest rank—and some who wish they were—scheme, prepare, and compete to make best use of the opportunity.

Dukes, earls, tradesmen, and the occasional charlatan are alert to the possibilities as the event draws nigh.

But anything can happen in the magic of music and candlelight as couples dance, flirt, and open themselves to romantic possibilities. Problems and conflict may just fade away at a Valentine's Day Ball.

***Follow Your Star Home (2018)***

Forged for lovers, the Viking star ring is said to bring lovers together, no matter how far, no matter how hard.

In eight stories, covering more than half the world and a thousand years, our heroes and heroines put the legend to the test. Watch the star work its magic, as prodigals return home in the season of good will, uncertain of their welcome.

***Never Too Late (2017)***

Eight authors and eight different takes on four dramatic elements selected by our readers—an older heroine, a wise man, a Bible, and a compromising situation that isn't.

Set in a variety of locations around the world over eight centuries, welcome to the romance of the Bluestocking Belles' 2017 Holiday and More Anthology.

It's Never Too Late to find love.

***Holly and Hopeful Hearts (2016)***

When the Duchess of Haverford sends out invitations to a Yuletide house party and a New Year's Eve ball at her country estate, Hollystone Hall, those who respond know that Her Grace intends to raise money for her favorite cause and promote whatever love-matches she can. Seven assorted heroes and heroines set out with their pocketbooks firmly clutched and hearts in protective custody. Or are they?

Eight assorted heroes and heroines find more than they've bargained for when they set out for Hollystone Hall for a charity ball.

# MEET THE BLUESTOCKING BELLES

The Bluestocking Belles (the "BellesInBlue") are seven very different writers united by a love of history and a history of writing about love. From sweet to steamy, from light-hearted fun to dark tortured tales full of angst, from London ballrooms to country cottages to the sultan's seraglio, one or more of us will have a tale to suit your tastes and mood.

*Learn more about the Bluestocking Belles at:*
Website: www.BluestockingBelles.net/
Newsletter: http://eepurl.com/dAJU_9
*Teatime Tattler* twice-weekly gossip magazine: https://bluestockingbelles.net/category/teatime-tattler/
Free books: https://bluestockingbelles.net/teatime-tattler-free-books/

Printed in the USA
CPSIA information can be obtained
at www.ICGtesting.com
LVHW030331240224
772639LV00005B/447